The Hurdy (

C000294488

BY BOB G

Published by Spiffing Covers Ltd
6 Jolliffe's Court, 51-57 High Street, Wivenhoe, Colchester, Essex CO7 9AZ

Cover design by Spiffingcovers.com

More information on what inspired certain stories of "The Hurdy Gurdy Man" and the factual locations mentioned in this book can be found at:

www.bobgriffin.club

Acknowledgements

The author gratefully acknowledges the time and enthusiastic help given by Tommi Neilson of "T Neilson" - Shipbuilders and Riggers - Gloucester. Tommi's expert knowledge of the construction of historic wooden hulled sailing ships was pivotal to the authenticity of the loss of the schooner "Nicolette" and the extended story that concerned her.

~

The author gratefully acknowledges the invaluable review and critique of the "Hurdy Gurdy Man" by his friend of many years, Jules Fenton.

~

The author also wishes to thank Pat Bozworth for her painstaking proofing of the Hurdy Gurdy Man, and her subsequent role as the books historian. In this latter role, she unearthed many fascinating tales of village life in those times, and authentic photographs of the two Cotswold villages, including buildings that were central to the novel such as the blacksmiths shop. The story in pictures can be followed at *www.bobgriffin.club*.

~

Isaac's poem "Hours Fly" was inspired by, and is an adaption of, the 1904 poem, "Katrina's Sundial", by poet and author, Henry Van Dyke.

~

The quotation used in chapter 5 beginning: *"It was but the breath of a whisper overheard"* is believed to have been written circa 6th century BC by an unknown member of a religious order.

~

Those who know Exmore and beautiful Lynmouth in North Devon will recognise the retelling of the events of the 12th of January 1899 when lifeboat Louisa was hauled overland, to rescue the crew of the "Forest Hall", a feat of courage and tenacity led by their coxswain, Captain Jack Crocombe.

Because facts and fiction are so far removed from one another in The Hurdy Gurdy Man, the names of Louisa's crew and that of the stricken ship, have been changed, but what the author has tried to portray in his fictional version of events, is the remarkable bravery and courage of men who would willingly, and knowingly, put to sea in an open rowing boat, then sail into the maw of a ferocious storm to save the lives of strangers.

With Louisa's story, the author - once a seafarer himself - acknowledges the debt of gratitude all seafarers owe to the work of the RNLI and the remarkable men of the lifeboat, past and present.

To Naz
With Best Wishes

For Thomas

CONTENTS

The Prologue

~

Part One

~

Part Two

~

Part Three

The Prologue

Arthfael's Tale - (The Battle for Penmaenddu)
The Welsh Marches - 1279AD

THE PROLOGUE

The Welsh Marches 1279 AD

The old man looked up from his cooking pot at the beating of wings. Danger approached for the birds had told him so. The birds were his friends.

He scrambled to the cave mouth with a nimbleness that belied his years. There were fleeting shadows amid the trees on the far side of the gorge. He listened with dread to the sounds that disturbed the sleeping forest, the clatter of wings amid the leafy canopy, the thunder of hooves upon the brittle carpet.

Soon, soldiers appeared along the narrow path, their horses sweating beneath the weight of weapons and armour. The leader reared and whinnied beside the old man, fearful of the steep and leaf-strewn slope that tumbled hundreds of feet to the gorge below.

'Come old man,' said the soldier, trying to bring his steed under control, 'Make haste, make haste damn you. Lord Gwynfa is wishful of your council and I - to stay aback this stupid beast!'

He reached down with gauntleted hand and scooped up the frail and weightless hermit, then to gallop off in the direction from whence they came. Night was falling and they had no wish to tarry there, for was it not well known that the old man danced naked with the devil in this place? He it was, who could turn men to stone and drank the blood of children.

~

High above the black fortress of Penmeanddu flew the standard of King Edward whom they called Longshanks.

Edward was angry. Llewelyn - would be Prince of Wales - continued to harry his armies despite the bloody subjugation of all but the most desolate corners of that God forsaken land. He was angry too, at the shilly-shallying and hollow excuses of the Marcher Lords who seemed ill disposed to take up arms against the fierce mountain men. It was time to remind one and all of De Montfort's fate.

Such was the predicament in which the Marcher Lords found themselves, for Longshanks was not known for his patience. They had hoped in vain, that he might forget these wild mountains to the West, for was there not trouble enough with the Scots? Surely one war was enough for any King! For a lesser

1

man perhaps, but not for Edward Longshanks!

Llewelyn bothered his vanity like a fly about a dung pat, and he had sworn there would be no King of Wales save him; a vow that was to make him the most ruthless enemy Wales and Scotland had ever known.

Edward needed a general; a soldier in his own likeness who knew this bleak land and would close his "ring of steel" about it. If they would not bend, he would hack them to pieces, slaughter them in their beds and burn their homes and harvests. He would squeeze them tighter and tighter until they burst into the Irish Sea like pus from a boil.

Here before him was such a man as he sought. Gwynfa the son of Eldred - Marcher Lord of Penmeanddu.

Gwynfa had fought alongside Longshanks and if such a thing were possible would make an even deadlier enemy than Edward himself, for Gwynfa had no soul. Now his father, Eldred, lay ill, perhaps gravely so, and Gwynfa has seized the opportunity to rule the principality in all but name.

'Your father grows old Gwynfa,' remarked Edward across his porridge bowl.

'Forgive him, Lord, for he is gripped of the ague, but he is thy loyal servant nonetheless.'

'No doubt, no doubt, but what use a servant carried to his king on a cot? Your father dies Gwynfa, and I pray it will be merciful and soon, for he is as a brother to me... But who then will rule the far mountains in his place? This matter is of great concern to me.'

'My brother awaits his inheritance, Sire!'

'Ah, a fortuitous circumstance,' said Edward, watching the soldier carefully, 'Arthfael will govern wisely no doubt. But I see this does not please you, Gwynfa?'

Gwynfa snorted in disgust. 'I am a soldier Sire, and pray that it shall ever be so, but Arthfael prefers the cow-meadow to the battlefield. He has taken his hand from the sword and it is lost forever amongst his mistresses' petticoats.'

Edward smiled at these words. Secretly, he thought it would be an imprudent fellow indeed, who would put Gwynfa's words to the test, but they suited his purpose nonetheless. Arthfael - Eldred's eldest son - was a seasoned soldier and had fought with Edward against DeMontfort. He had so excelled with the sword that few men might come against him in equal combat and expect to live, yet there was something about Arthfael that Edward found... disquieting.

DeMontfort had paid heavily for his treason. Many knights and even Gwynfa

2

- then nought but a child - had taken their part in his castration and disembowelment. One by one, they stepped forward to hack and saw at the screaming man, stirring his bowels with their swords - all except Arthfael. Arthfael, so courageous in battle, sat upon his horse and watched in silence, his face expressionless as though carved of stone.

Edward returned his thoughts to the matter in hand.

'Would it be that I was blessed with Arthfael's good fortune Gwynfa, but alas I have many battles yet to fight!' He lowered his voice as though he were wary of eavesdroppers. 'Tell me my loyal knight, what would'st thou do if Penmeanddu were thine, and thine alone?'

'Sire, I would use the wealth and power it would bestow in thy service. To march against Llewellyn, if that is your pleasure.'

Edward smiled in satisfaction. He rose up to leave for his own quarters and as he did so he said, 'Indeed it would be my pleasure Gwynfa. Give me Wales and I shall give thee half thy conquest. Give me Llewelyn's eyes on this platter and I shall give thee my blessing and patronage.'

Edward donned the leather cap that lay beside him and made his way towards the door. There he turned and said, 'Wealth and power are the deserts of the strong, Gwynfa; tears and sorrow, the bounty of the weak. Let not small matters of family stand in your way!'

Gwynfa thought about the King's words. It was true his father lay ill, and if he died, as surely he must very soon, then Arthfael would claim Penmaenddu, its lands, its armies and its wealth. Gwynfa would be reduced to a lap dog, and he seethed at the very thought of it, but what if Eldred *and* Arthfael were to die!

~

The pigeon beat its wings upon the rising air. Higher and higher, it climbed, until it was higher than the mountains themselves. Then and only then, did it set its course for the north and the mighty fortress of Mynadd Banaug. About its leg there was a tiny piece of parchment, held firm by thread and tallow.

Gerald, the alchemist, entered the bedchamber where a soldier stood in the shadows. The light from iron sconces cast flickering fingers across the dull coldness of his armour. 'Go, leave this place,' said Gerald.

He crossed the room to a bed upon a stepped dais, high above the drafts. It was carved of oak, and was such a wondrous thing that only a King or a Lord might sleep upon it. He climbed the seven steps, and the creaking of its timber disturbed a rag bundle that lay at the foot of the bed. The bundle stood painfully. and shuffled across the dais to set his twisted body between the bed and the alchemist. His spine was cruelly bent and his limbs awry.

'Begone fool - get you from this place!'

The cripple clutched at his robe and made strange noises. 'Begone, begone! Can you not see I have a potion for your master? Within its power, lies the cure for this malaise. Begone, that I might do my work!'

However, Merek did not trust the alchemist. For twenty years, he had done his master's bidding, never leaving his side by day or night. Never did Eldred eat what Merek had not first eaten, nor drink what Merek had not first drunk. Never was a servant more loyal to his master; never was a master more trustful of his servant. Now, more than ever, he must protect his master from those who wished him harm.

Merek reached out for the cup to drink from it, but the alchemist pushed him away and he fell heavily to the stone floor, cracking his head on the steps as he did so. Gerald stooped across the bed and brought the cup to Eldred's lips.

'Drink Sire, drink, drink... yes it is well... drink deeply...drink.'

Eldred drank from the cup in tiny sips, as would a fledgling bird fallen from the nest. His skin was ashen grey and his cheeks sallow and lifeless, as though made of tallow.

His task complete, the alchemist hurried from the room, passing the rousing servant as he did so. Merek climbed the dais as his master turned his face toward him and reached out with a frail hand. The old man began to tremble and retch, and as he did so, he thrust out a tongue that was blackened and swollen, his breath smelling of bitter aloes. He tried to raise himself up, but the effort was too great and he sank back, eyes staring blankly. His hand fell limp and his body became still. The cripple began to sob in a high keening wail that was piteous in its anguish and sorrow. He clutched the frail body to his chest and began to rock slowly back and forth, crying as best he was able.

~

'Fool,' shouted Gwynfa, his rage knowing no bounds. His clenched fist struck the alchemist so hard that it threw him to the floor with the power of the blow.

'Mercy, Sire, mercy I beg you,' gasped the alchemist. Gwynfa's ring gashed his cheek badly, and he could taste his own blood on his lips. 'I tried to make him go, but he would not leave his master's side. He began to make a fuss - the noises he makes. I did not want to - to alert your father to our purpose, my

4

Lord!'

'Where is he now?'

'I do not know Sire, but Merek is a deaf mute, a simpleton, too crippled to walk more than a league. What danger can he bring us?'

'What danger, what danger? Art thou such a fool!' screamed Gwynfa. 'Does he not have eyes with which to see? The pigeon has been loosed. Soon Arthfael will come to Eldred's deathbed, but if - through your folly - he knows him to be murdered, it will be an army he brings, not a bible.'

'No, Lord, this shall not be. Arthfael will come and here he will die. Merek shall be found, fear not. He will be found and killed. Of this you have my word.'

The cart jolted to a halt at the huge outer gate of Penmaenddu, a little of its bloody cargo spilling over the barrels, to drip on the rutted mud of the gateway; its stench was everywhere.

'Halt friend, where bound and what is your cargo?' shouted the Captain above the hubbub.

'Bones, offal, rendering for the good monks of Llanthony,' replied the carter.

A soldier jumped upon the wagon, his boots slipping on the sticky wetness of the boards. He lifted one lid and prodded amongst the pink and purple intestines that filled the barrel almost to its brim. He nodded to the Captain and jumped down.

'Carry on then, friend, but beware lest you are robbed of your cargo. Surely everyone will know you are coming.' Those within earshot laughed aloud, but the carter said nothing. The cart rumbled on. The search for the cripple continued.

Some miles on, the carter drew the oxen from the road to a rutted track that took him alongside a rock pool fed by a waterfall. He looked about him, for these were dangerous parts. He brought the team to a halt, then took the lid from a cask and banged many times upon its side.

Slowly a head emerged from the bloody innards. The man in the cask held a water reed between his lips, and it was with this device that he had survived the ordeal of the barrel. The carter helped him down, for he was weakened with the cramp, and in this manner, they walked to the stream. The man stripped off his clothes and stepped naked into the pool. He stood beneath the falling water, and immediately the stream turned crimson, then pink, and began to foam like a jug of ale.

The carter looked with pity at the man's hideous deformity. His spine was bowed and protruding, his limbs were twisted and misshapen. He threw the cripples clothing into the water and again it turned to pink. Merek knelt and thrust the clothing beneath the surface again and again. He looked up at the carter and began to make strange guttural noises. He smiled a twisted smile and the carter smiled back. The carter went once more to the cart and returned with a loaf of bread, and then with a nodded farewell, he and the oxen were gone.

~

The guard came that night. Soldiers took the alchemist to the bowels of the keep and to a room he knew well. As they entered the room, his legs gave way beneath him. The soldiers lifted him to the wooden trestle, and a heavy iron shackle was hinged about his forehead and screwed tight until he cried out in agony. The gaoler drew a poker from the white heat of the brazier and plunged it into his eye. Cries of terror, turned to a shriek that never seemed to end, and filled every corner of that dark place with agony. With careful precision, the gaoler plunged the poker into the other eye, then loosed the iron clasps and set the screaming man back on his feet. He began to stumble about him, clutching his hands to his face. The soldiers laughed to see such comic confusion. 'Over here, over here,' they cried, 'here is the doorway.' He stumbled toward the voices, only to collide with the hard stone of the dungeon wall.

That same morning, he was taken to the main square, not fifteen feet from the well and there he waited amid jeering crowds. Soon, men brought a huge leather boot, and a hush fell over the crowd for they feared the boot more than the devil himself.

The boot was big enough to put a small pig inside. The alchemist's leg was placed inside it and then the gaoler looked up at the window to where Gwynfa stood watching. Above a pit of coals, was a huge smouldering cauldron with long iron handles at each side. They brought the cauldron from the fire and slowly tipped the boiling contents into the leather boot. The alchemist cried out in agony at this new, unseen horror. The molten lead rose slowly up the boot, cooking the poor man's leg as it did so, and boiling the blood within it. It would take many hours to solidify - it would take some days for the man to die. The pouring done, his misery was complete, for he was doomed to stand in this hideous device until that blessed release. He stretched out his hands like a beggar seeking alms and, in sobbing cries, pleaded for his torment to be ended, but no man dared step forward.

For three days, the gaoler struggled to keep Gerald conscious with the fumes of burning feathers, but no longer would this rouse him. The usually busy square had become strangely quiet, and trade had moved away to other streets. Only the ghoulish came to mock and throw faeces, and the womenfolk to collect water. They looked at their feet, never at the alchemist. His flesh had begun to rot and smell, and his leg was working loose from the hideous sock. That night, when the streets were deserted, a man stepped from the shadows, and, with one swift stroke of humanity, severed his throat.

The soldiers had journeyed far, but at last, they came to Penmeanddu. The old man looked up at the forbidding walls and his eyes were drawn to their wretchedness as a moth is drawn to the flame. Headless, rotting cadavers hung from huge iron hooks, the wall beneath them black with the blood and putrescence that no amount of purifying rain could expunge. Carrion crows fed upon them, unconcerned at the passage of soldiers below.

They took him through the stinking town with its seethed humanity, and through the main square where the corpse of a man lay slumped over a huge boot, his face blackened with blood, the stench of rotting flesh, overpowering. They passed on to a huge keep whose portal was carved with grotesque caricatures, then on through echoing passages, vaulted rooms and twisting staircases, until at last they came to a vast hall where there were many men gathered. One alone was seated. The hermit was afraid of this man whose dark brooding eyes watched him as a spider might watch a fly.

He looked about the high vaulted room amazed at its splendour. Vast tapestries hung from every wall. Silver plates and goblets stood upon carved tables, and high above them, the most wondrous thing; a window that was not a window at all, but a picture in the most beautiful colours. A mounted knight was slaying a dragon, and bright rays of light shone through the glass to cast its image across the room. Brightest of all was the redness of his sword, stained with the creature's blood. The bright ray of crimson crept relentlessly across the floor toward him.

'Tell me of yourself, magician, that I might know thee,' said the seated man at last.

'Lord, there is naught to tell. I am but a humble man of the forest.'

'Ah, a humble man of the forest,' repeated Gwynfa softly; 'yet is it not true,' he said, pointing a slender finger at the hermit, 'that thou art in league with the devil and through that dark union, can'st foretell the future?'

'No sire, I....'

'Think carefully of your words, old man of the forest,' said Gwynfa with brooding menace.

7

'I... I have visions, my Lord,' he admitted hesitantly.

'Then thou art a magician,' shouted Gwynfa angrily, crashing his fist to the table.

'No Sire, not a magician, I can work no magic, but sometimes...' The old man sighed as though a great weight had befallen him. 'If it pleases your lordship I...'

'What pleases me... is that thou foretell what will come to pass! That and that alone! Tell me of your gift, magician, for I have much need of your wisdom.'

With a sigh, the hermit told his tale, and a stranger story had rarely been told.

He spoke of a day when, as a boy, he had wandered deep into the forest. The deeper he went, the darker it became and silence fell over the forest like a heavy fog; no bird called from the trees, no fox scurried from its lair, no wind sighed in the branches. He was completely alone in that dark place - or so he thought!

'As I lay down to rest,' said he, 'I saw before me a woman dressed only in flowers and leaves. Never before have I seen such beauty. Her voice was sweet, her body soft and she beguiled me with her loveliness.'

'She took me to her and caressed me so that we made love, though not one word had passed between us; but as my seed was spent, so did her breath turn rancid in my nostrils, and her skin turn to icy scale's beneath my hands. Her face - once so beautiful - became hideously ugly and there began a howling throughout the forest like a mighty wind; yet not one blade of grass was turned, nor leaf plucked from its branch.'

'She pushed me from her, and her foul body swelled as though in childbirth. As I watched, ninety-nine goblins fell from her womb covered in the purple skein of birth and I knew then, I had copulated with the devil. She feasted upon them, but those she did not eat, suckled her breasts of which there were six, and these flowed with foul smelling milk. I feared that she would devour me also, but instead she beat the air with leathery wings and disappeared into the clouds above. I was never to see her again.'

Fear was written on the faces of all who heard this strange tale and even Gwynfa looked ill at ease. A low murmur passed about the room.

The hermit continued. 'Her spawn were all about me, and I could not rid myself of those foul creatures. They cavorted in my hair whilst I slept, in my pudding whilst I ate, and in my piss when I relieved myself. As often as I swept them away, so they would return to bite, and scratch, and torment me, until I prayed that my life would end, and I believe that it would have ended but for

8

'this.' He touched a rough pebble that hung about his neck.

'What is this wondrous thing that wards off such evil?' said Gwynfa.

'Lord, it is the gall stone of Saint Augustus who was purged at the stake. It was placed upon me by the good monks of Llanthony as I lay fettered to my cot in the grip of the madness.'

'You mock me magician!'

'No lord, upon my life I speak the truth. As it touched my flesh, so these foul creatures squealed and screeched and leapt from me, for they could not tolerate such goodness. Though I see them and hear the babble of their tongues, they no longer come close, for they are afraid.'

'Enough of this, said Gwynfa, anger in his voice. Tell me the future or I will have thee hanging from the walls within the hour!'

'Lord it is not so simple - it is the demons that have the gift, not I. It is they who speak, but beware, for they speak only of calamity and rejoice in its wickedness and misfortune!'

'When do they speak, these demons?'

'When I remove the stone... then and only then can they torment me.'

'How do you know they do not lie?'

'They never lie. What they foretell will come to pass, but my lord, beware! Know also that when I hear a lie upon another man's lips - so too do I see a demon dancing upon his tongue!'

Gwynfa was sorely troubled by the old man's words. He had no doubt that every word was true, for was it not well known that the devil's disciples were everywhere unseen? They hid in dark places, waiting for the opportunity to possess the body of another unwitting victim, therein to hatch their young. They would enter through the anus and rejoice in its warmth and comfort. He must be careful. When the hermit had served his purpose, he would kill him; but he dare not harm him himself, for upon his death the demons would seek another body: who better than the murderer of their host!

'Where... are these demons now?' he asked, his voice wary.

'Why sire they dance on the table before you!'

Gwynfa snatched his hands away and jumped up, stumbling over his chair, fear written on his face. He pointed a shaking finger at the hermit. 'Old man, if you lie to me I will cut out your heart!'

9

~

The small regiment made camp beside the river at Builth. 'It is as safe as we shall find my lord; we have the bluff to our backs and the river before us.'

'Then let us rest David, for I am weary of the saddle and more so of your tiresome good humour.'

They were sat eating when a horseman galloped into their midst with a hunchback cripple clinging to the horse as best he could. The cripple fell exhausted to the ground, uttering strange noises and beating himself in distress.

'God and the Saint's redeem us, it is the idiot Merek,' cried Arthfael.

'Take care Sire, the cripple is clearly mad!'

'Not mad I think, but a fool, I grant you. He is my father's servant David - a deaf mute and loyal above all others - this bodes not well!'

'He smells like chicken's innards on a hot summer's day! Let me throw him in the river Sire, and that may serve to calm him also.'

'No, sit you still. Something is wrong for the cripple to be here. Let us see what occurs with him.'

The sobbing man stood with great difficulty and in a great state of agitation. Taking Arthfael's hand, he kissed it many times sobbing and weeping as he did so, but each time he pressed his lips to the gauntlet, Arthfael felt a gentle tug in the direction of a small wooded hill.

Arthfael released himself from the cripple's grip and a look of understanding passed between the two men. Drawing his sword, he said to David, 'Watch for treachery about us David, but do not follow. I shall dispatch this fool on yonder hill if he has deserted his master.'

When they were well from sight and earshot, Arthfael holstered his sword and spoke to the cripple, 'Why do'st thou journey Merek, tell me in whatever way thou art able?'

To Arthfael's surprise the cripple spoke, though in a strange and stunted voice.

'What sorcery is this that thy tongue hath returned?' he said in astonishment.

'Not sorcery - not sorcery… masters command.'

'Command…! My father forbade you to speak?'

He nodded again grinning with pleasure. 'Enemies speak… Merek listen!' He

10

cocked his ear to imaginary voices, pressing his ear against first one tree then another in comic fashion.

'You listen to my father's enemies - to the court,' he added quickly, catching the cripple's meaning. They think you a deaf mute, but you listen to them plotting?'

Merek was beside himself with joy that Arthfael understood. He smiled a toothless smile and danced up and down in his excitement.

'You are a spy!' said Arthfael with a smile.

Too much for the cripple, he garbled incoherent, excited words. Arthfael was impressed with his father's duplicity that had held good for so many years.

Arthfael gripped the man's shoulders, 'Listen to me, loyal Merek, calm yourself that I may understand! What of my father?'

The man became agitated once more, beating himself about his head in his distress.

'He lies gravely ill; you have come to guide us home?'

The cripple shook his head.

'Then we are too late, he is already dead!'

The words were like a blade puncturing the cripple's heart. He stood stock still, looking at Arthfael, wretched in his misery, his eyes slowly filling with tears.

Strangely, Arthfael's thoughts were not for the father he had lost, but for the simpleton, Merek, who had been denied the usual fortune of the weak, to live on in a life of pain and torment. One such as Merek might expect to be murdered at birth, for men feared such burdens, possessed as they were by the devil; but his father's patronage had saved his life, and no one dared do Merek harm.

Arthfael understood his father's reason well enough. It would take very little to kill such a poor specimen. He was thus ideally suited to tasting all Eldred ate to test it for poison. But from that day onward, there grew a bond between Lord and crippled child, the latter devoted to his master, rarely leaving his side.

He would wash and dress his master and sleep at the foot of his bed lest Eldred need a candle's light by which to relieve himself. Now Eldred was gone, he had lost the only human kindness he had ever known, and his life would be in great danger unless Arthfael protect him too.

'Was it God's hand, Merek?' he asked, fearing the worst.

11

The cripple shook his head.

'Gwynfa then?'

Merek nodded.

Arthfael's anger knew no bounds. He vowed the killing of Gwynfa with his own hands. Placing those hands upon the cripple's shoulders he said, 'Faithful Merek! Thy bones are twisted and bent and thy countenance hideous, yet thine heart is as straight and true as any arrow. Go now and eat and sleep, for thou hast travelled far to bring me these sad tidings, but speak no more to any man! From now on thou shalt serve me as thou served my father - in loyalty, faith and silence!'

The cripple bowed to Arthfael through tears of joy and sorrow, and hobbled away as he was bid.

'I believe Eldred to be dead for the cripple to be here - murdered by Gwynfa, for Penmaenddu!' he said to those gathered about him. If we go on, we ride into danger - a certain trap to be rid of me and claim my birthright- but if we all go back, we will waste time and the winter cometh. There will be no food, and our wagons will be drowned in mud when we reach our mountains. We will camp here at Builth and David - thou shalt ride north to Mynadd Banaug to send back an army. Artisans, armourer's, cattle and wagons, they must be through the mountains as soon as possible.'

'Lord this is folly,' said David. 'We are travelling to a sickbed, not a war. We must expect danger now, and we have but thirty mounted knights and a small force of arms. We must all turn back.'

'You clack like a scold at her gate,' snapped Arthfael! 'Do not fret, David, for I have Cadwgawn!' He touched the huge broadsword that had slashed a bloody path through many an affray. 'Are we not worth fifty of Gwynfa's best?'

'Indeed sire,' agreed the soldier tactfully, 'but send another and let me stay.'

'No - enough of this fuss and nonsense! There is much for you to do at Mynadd Banaug. Thou art my trusted general and known to be so; no man will doubt your command nor slouch at his work. It is you who must go, you who must raise an army, and you who must lord Mynadd Banaug in my stead!'

'Then go I shall, but thou doth treat me cruel, sire! If thou would'st send me away when danger approaches, how many knights must thou think me worth… few surely?'

'I should say three!' said Arthfael, matter-of-factly.

David smiled a wry smile and bowed to his master. 'Thou art too gracious

12

Sire.'

With that, the matter was closed.

~

The old man removed the talisman and placed it on the table. Immediately, the room filled with a high-pitched babble like birds squabbling within the nest. The old man beat the air about him and clutched his face, raking his fingers through his hair, and when he caught an invisible demon, he would squeeze the life from the tiny harpy until the veins stood out upon his forehead. Slowly the old man tired of his exertions and resigned himself to his misery through sheer exhaustion. Gwynfa watched in awe as his body convulsed and tiny pinpricks of blood began to ooze through the flesh of his cheeks, as though tiny teeth were biting him. After a while, he became still as though the demons were sated with his blood.

'What did'st thou see?' hissed Gwynfa.

At first, the old man could not speak.

'What did'st thou see - what did'st thou hear?' said Gwynfa once more. 'Speak now or it will be the worse for thee.'

'War…terrible war and much bloodshed,' he sighed. 'They told of a man - an old man - a man of power and wealth, murdered and still, upon his cot. They told of a horseman- a giant with a mighty sword who journeys even now to avenge him.'

'Get out, bellowed Gwynfa turning to all who stood behind him. Get out and take all with you. Leave me with the magician!'

He drew a dagger and when all had gone, he spoke again.

'What else did you see, old man of the woods,' he said; sure now of the hermits skills, for no man save Gerald, the alchemist, knew of these things.

'I saw a barren land, riven with famine, plague and death!'

'Who's death?'

'Many deaths.'

'Does the horseman die?'

'Yes he dies.'

'Then the omen is good,' said Gwynfa, to himself. 'Thou hast served me well old man and soon thou shalt return to the forest - but not yet! Thou shalt tarry here a while methinks, lest I have need of thy council.'

The old man said nothing.

'Tell me one last thing magician,' said Gwynfa, his voice little more than a whisper. 'How then shall I die?'

The hermit looked up in surprise, for never before had any man asked him that question. He answered truthfully just as the demons had foretold. 'Here shalt thou die Sire - in Penmeanddu - in this fortress - and in thine own bed.' Gwynfa smiled at these words, for now he knew both his destiny and what he must do.

~

David turned in the saddle, to look at the camp for the last time before crossing the mountains beyond Builth. What met his eye was what he feared most. Perhaps a thousand foot and mounted soldiers were descending upon the ford from the other side of the river. 'Look there!' he cried to his companions and wheeled his horse about.

'Take up your arms, take up your arms, bowmen to the higher ground,' shouted Arthfael. A hail of arrows fell amongst them and many men fell. Gwynfa's army plunged into the river, leaving bowmen on the far bank to fire arrows above their heads. They crossed up to their chests in water; Arthfael's archers fired amongst them, but it was not enough - on they came.

The first horse fell heavily, pitching his mount into the water to drown beneath the weight of his armour; then another fell and another. Foot soldiers, too, were tripping and falling beneath the feet of their comrades. Then the deadly arrows fell among them. All was confusion.

'Well done, David, well done,' thought Arthfael, for the previous night they had laboured with their camps defences; tripping ropes and sharpened stakes having been concealed beneath the water. These provisions had brought down perhaps half of Gwynfa's mounted force, and a suited knight without a horse must expect to die. 'Be still my beauty,' whispered Arthfael to his own mount, for it knew well what awaited them.

Gwynfa's troops clambered up the slippery banks in disarray and were engaged by Arthfael's men, but slowly they pushed the defenders farther up the bank by sheer weight of numbers. The air was filled with the bloody chorus of war.

As Arthfael's defensive flank fell back, he made his charge. The mighty Cadwgawn - nearly six feet in length and twenty pounds in weight - came

14

slashing down his left flank, to rise high and then slash a path down the right flank to complete the deadly sweep. Screaming, shouting men, were trampled underfoot by the enormous horse, or their bodies were hacked open by the deadly two handed broadsword. Horse and rider were splattered crimson with blood by the time they were through and clear.

He galloped into open ground and then brought the stallion about for the next charge. One then two arrows hit him, knocking the wind from his lungs with the force of the blow, but the arrowheads could not penetrate the chain mail and only the tips had pierced his flesh. Once more, he rode into the enemy, his sword flashing through the air with deadly momentum. Men struggled to avoid the onslaught, but Cadwgawn laid open their backs and exposed their lungs, or decapitated them with the cracking of bone and sinew. Back and forth went the mighty horse, on and on went the bloody slaughter.

But to kill was tiring, even for such as Arthfael and so, with many men dead or dying, Cadwgawn lost its power. Exhausted, Arthfael let go the mighty broadsword and drew his stabbing sword from its sheath, at the same time, trying to push the horse through the throng. Though he fought like a demon, a soldier managed to climb on the horses back and his hands were about Arthfael's throat in an instant to drag Arthfael from his mount.

More hands tried to drag him down. Suddenly he was without his helmet or sword. He saw the blade of an axe rising above him and felt himself sliding backwards, but there was a terrible scream and the axe man fell; an arrow shot clean through his neck. Arthfael fell to the ground, and he knew the end was close. He was struck heavily and then all went dark.

David had loosed the arrow from his horse and he had been lucky, but he may yet be too late. He hit the body of men who had surged about his master at full gallop. He dragged the stallion about and fell upon the soldiers like a man possessed, hacking and slashing at their bodies and inflicting the most terrible wounds. Other soldiers came, and they stood and fought above the bloodied body whilst the fight raged on about then.

Arthfael looked up to see David kneeling over him and tried to rise.

'Be still, Sire, most of your blood is in your boots!'

'Tis naught, get me on my horse!' They stood him upright, but he had lost too much blood and fell back into David's arms. They carried him to safety and laid him beneath some trees on a soft carpet of moss, whereupon he fell unconscious. When he rallied, his head felt as though a thousand hammers were striking it. 'What of the battle, David,' he asked.

'Twas won whilst thou slept my Lord. Pity it was, you were unable to see me dispatch my three!' remarked David wryly.

'What of Gwynfa's army?'

'Scattered and in disarray.'

'Hunt them down! Hang every man who does not come over to us. Let no man return with news of our triumph to Penmaenddu, for I will have Gwynfa's heart on a platter for this bloody treachery.'

With these words, his eyes closed once more, and he slept the sleep of righteous exhaustion. Many hands carried him to his cot and there they stripped him naked and bathed and bound his wounds.

Three hours later, when David returned from the slaughter of the vanquished, he went first to the armourer to remove the light armour he had fought in, then to the river to swill the blood from his hair and ears. When dressed once more, he went to his master's tent and sat with him a while.

He peeled back the sheepskin blanket that covered him. There were four wounds to his back and legs, but he would live to boast another day. David smiled and left him, for there was much to do.

Arthfael slept for many hours before the alchemists powerful drug wore off. There were none of the usual tormented dreams the drug induced; instead, his "sleep thoughts" were of Mynadd Banaug, his wife, and the children he left behind.

All had been well before the pigeon keeper brought the tiny parchment to his bedchamber. It had been a night like every other. It was late, and the children were long abed. The first-born, his son and the heir to Mynadd Banaug, had been reluctant to leave his father's side so early. His second, a daughter as beautiful and graceful as her mother, was a rag doll, asleep and oblivious in her father's arms.

They had played chess as they often did, and, as usual, she had won, sparing him none of her chiding and mischievous scorn over the hapless way he had lost his Queen. Arthfael cared little, for it had not escaped his notice that with triumph on the chessboard, came wantonness on the bed-board. He looked at her then, bathed in the flickering light from the iron sconce - happy and content, flushed with the joy of beating the unbeatable warrior - of being his wife and mistress - of loving him.

She had been the most beautiful woman in the kingdom when he took her as his wife; her skin was the colour of buttermilk, her hair as black as the raven. She became even more beautiful with childbirth, and she was never more beautiful than through the deep sleep that drew his wounds together. His dream

16

ended with the knock upon the bedchamber door and the bowing pigeon keeper. He awoke from his slumber, aching in every sinew and muscle.

Six weeks later, they looked down upon the formidable castle of Penmaenddu. They had waited for the army from his northern lands, and the food with which to feed them. Now Mynadd Banaug lay vulnerable, but such was the nature of war.

'It is impregnable Sire.'

'Nothing is impregnable, David, but formidable, I grant you.'

Penmaenddu was indeed, formidable, for Eldred had built it well. But now he - Arthfael - would destroy it. Its massive walls of Welsh granite topped an outcrop of rock that fell away sheer on three sides. Its only approach was by a narrow rock causeway, which was itself hacked away to form a deep trench. Penmaenddu's only weakness was being overlooked by this tiny outcrop of rock on which they now stood. Arthfael had seen Penmaenddu just three times in his life, for, as Eldred built Penmaenddu, so Arthfael built Mynadd Banaug as reward for their services to Edward.

They discussed earthwork ramp's, siege engines, tunnels to weaken and collapse the walls, bonfires to crack and spall the stone, scaffolds across the chasm to the weaker side walls and all other means they could think of, but each had it faults. The surest was siege, but that would take time. Perhaps a year, perhaps more, for Gwynfa had taken every family, every grain of wheat and every animal inside the fortress. Winter approached and the land was bare.

'Let us try a firestorm, David,' said Arthfael finally. 'First, we will set the town ablaze and burn them out, then, Florin, the armourer, shall make ballistae with which we shall smash down the walls. All others will fashion shot and collect wood for faggots.' The decision was made and the work began.

Finally, two mighty siege engines were finished. They had been fashioned from the firs that clothed the hillside, and huge swathes were felled to feed the carpenter's axes. The ground shook as they rolled the heavy catapults into place.

Florin had built his weapons well. He pounded the inner fortress with huge shot, as round as a man's arm is long, each with a blazing faggot attached. Soon the town beyond the curtain wall was ablaze; the air was heavy with smoke and sparks and laden with the cries of men, women, and children. The town burnt for two long days and lit the night sky as though it were day. Only the massive inner keep remained unscathed.

That night Arthfael held a council of war with his Knights, Armourers, Priests and Carpenters. There was no doubt they had done much damage to the town, perhaps even to its stores of grain and fodder, but they were no closer to breaching its walls and that alone would bring victory.

Next day, David set about the mammoth task of filling the natural cleft between the hillside and the outer walls to the left of the causeway, the right being too open and too steep, ever to be filled.

David's plan was to sink holes into the earthen slopes, into which whole tree trunks would be socketed. In this way, he would prevent the backfill of earth and stone from sliding down the hillside into the valley below. It was difficult and dangerous work, for they were under constant bombardment from the fortress above; many men were bowled away by huge rocks, or scalded to death by boiling oil that cascaded down the slopes like a waterfall.

They laboured by day and night under constant fire from above, but despite these difficulties, the cleft slowly filled. Thousands of tons of rock and earth were tipped into it. More and more of the forest was cut down to build three mighty siege towers that would be trundled against the walls when David had compacted and levelled the ground.

Arthfael used this time to build these siege towers and even more ballistae. A smaller catapult had a different task. With it, Florin would hurl blazing faggots into the narrow causeway before the gate, which Arthfael's soldiers would fill with wood and bracken, and by this means, they would burn down the mighty gates.

After many weeks of labour the woodpile was ready, the scaling ladders were ready, the siege towers were ready, the ground was level and the soldiers had the lust for blood in their hearts. The moment had come.

Arthfael gave the command at dusk on a crisp November evening. Five thousand soldiers and archers set to their task. Men worked like soldier ants to carry the tons of wood that would be heaved into the trench beneath the drawbridge until it was level with the drawbridge itself.

Gwynfa's soldier's lit huge braziers about the battlements to illuminate the long expected assault, and the night air filled with the thrumming of arrows in flight. A huge battering ram - long enough to span the trench - was dragged into place before the drawbridge. Arthfael calculated that by the time he had burnt and battered the gateway to charcoal splinters, the mighty towers would be within scaling distance of the walls, for their progress over such difficult ground would be slow. He would then begin the two-pronged assault that would split Gwynfa's forces against the greater numbers of his own.

But when it seemed that nothing could stop the bloody battle, ropes were thrown over the battlements above the trench and scores of people began to descend. At first Arthfael thought that Gwynfa's soldiers were abandoning the fight and the battle was won, then he realised that these were not soldiers, but old men and women, children and the infirm.

Many fell screaming from the ropes, or were pushed to their death from the high walls - too terrified to make the climb. Those who made the descent huddled together upon the woodpile too terrified to move, for those who did were shot from the fortress embrasures by Gwynfa's archers.

When all was done, some four hundred souls stood upon the tar soaked bonfire, they were the old, the young and the infirm.

The fighting stopped of its own accord, and all eyes turned to the high hill from where Arthfael commanded his forces.

'He uses the innocents as a shield Sire,' said David, but Arthfael did not reply.

He turned to his master - 'If we go on it will be a slaughter!'

Arthfael was silent for many moments then without looking at his lieutenant he said, 'You see before you the damned, David, and I will pray for their souls.'

'Sire perhaps…'

'Perhaps nothing David,' said Arthfael, stopping his Lieutenant in mid speech. 'To Gwynfa they are worthless. Mere mouths to feed, yet in their very being they protect him. They are already lost, yet it is not I who condemned them.'

David, waited for his master to speak again, but he did not. Reluctantly he turned to Florin and made the sign. The armourer put the torch to the tar soaked faggot of sticks and it burst into crackling flames. The faggot hit the fortress wall high above the woodpile, then fell upon the huddled group in a hail of sparks and flame. The air filled with screams as the tar soaked wood burst into flames, and all those stood upon it were engulfed. The battle resumed as though a trumpet had sounded and the air was filled with the thrum of arrows and the shouts of men. Arthfael watched the battle and the innocents burning upon the woodpile, in grim silence.

Water poured down from the machicolations high above the gate, but nothing could stop the inferno. Soon the drawbridge was ablaze, then the portcullis, then the heavy doors beyond. Masonry exploded and huge shards flew in all directions. When the inferno was spent, all that remained were charred and blackened beams, glowing ash and scalding masonry.

The assault towers were within ten feet of the walls, and were filled with four hundred men on five platforms; each connected by ladders. At exactly the same time, hundreds of men made their assault on the fire-charred gate, the scaling ladders fell across the gap and men poured across the chasm. Many were speared or shot through by arrows, but some reached their goal and began the deadly combat on the outer wall.

Soldiers bridged the glowing trench with scaling ladders and clambered into the safety of the gate. They worked forwards throwing the heavy shards of fallen masonry and smouldering timber behind them. Soon, more than fifty men were toiling at the huge gateway, each eager to find sanctuary from the hail of arrows, rocks and boiling tar that fell outside. The gate was full to the roof with fallen debris, but slowly it was cleared.

Those at the work face thought that they must surely break through soon when shovels and spades hit solid stone. They scraped away the debris, to reveal not just spall, but tightly fitting block-work, for Gwynfa had bricked up the entrance.

Above their heads, they heard an odd sound like the sea lapping the shore. Soon, another horror cascaded upon them. Molten lead began to trickle then gush down tiny hidden boreholes in the roof. Screaming men fought for a way out, but there were too many for such a small place.

Above them, their comrades were gradually dominating the fight, for it was difficult to get reinforcements to the shattered battlements. Soon, Arthfael's men would have a foothold inside the walls and would drive Gwynfa's forces to the inner keep. What few had noticed, however, were tiny plumes of smoke that seeped through the soil of David's redoubt, like steam from a dung pile on a frosty morning. Gwynfa's masons had dug a tunnel through the base of the outer tower under David's redoubt. It had been dangerous work, but done with skill and stealth. Gwynfa's miners had lined their tunnel with stout timbers until finally they reached its furthest point. They broke through in the hours of darkness and concealed the mouth with bracken and other debris of the forest floor. That disguise was quickly consumed by fire that raced through the tunnel, engulfing it in howling flames and belching smoke.

Three hundred of Arthfael's soldiers had fought their way onto the wall of the outer keep when the first earth began to shift down the mountain. Men grabbed the tower and one another, as the huge structure shuddered, then toppled to one side. Those upon the scaling boards were thrown into the chasm, then the whole tower began to topple toward the valley. Earth and stone fell before it like an avalanche, and the tower slid in its path, bursting apart as it did so and spilling its human cargo into the churning landslide. Men on the other towers began to jump, as they too shook and tilted towards oblivion, but by then it was too late. Arthfael had lost nearly three thousand men in less than an hour and Gwynfa's losses could be counted on the hands of a thief.

Arthfael's defeat was total.

That night, Arthfael, David, and others of his council, ate a sombre meal. They could hold Penmeanddu to siege, but they could no longer attack it. Even retreat would be difficult for winter had set in and bitter winds, laden with rain and sleet, began to blow. Moving wagons and men over sodden ground and swollen rivers would be near impossible. Very soon the first snows of winter would fall.

Suddenly loud voices broke the silence. Guards with pikes and lanterns escorted six horsemen toward them. The horsemen carried Gwynfa's standard. They were cold, and wet, and had ridden far, for they were covered in the mud of the road. The leading horseman stepped down from his horse and addressed Arthfael.

'Sire, I am Sir Robert of Gloucester, Knight of the round table, loyal servant of your brother, Gwynfa ap Eldred, Lord of Penmeanddu and of His Gracious Majesty, King Edward of England.'

'What is your business sir, for I am at table,' came the curt reply.

'Sire thou art in defeat! My companions and I' - he waved a gauntleted hand in their direction - 'have ridden many days from Mynadd Banaug. Mynadd Banaug has fallen! Your land is seized, your castles taken, your forces vanquished... all is forfeit.'

'You lie - this is deception,' shouted David, rising up and drawing his sword in one motion.

'Hold your weapon sir - this is no lie - here is proof!' Robert of Gloucester hefted a leather bound chest from the rump of his horse to the ground. His companions drew their swords and rode forward to protect him, but a sea of pikestaffs held them back.

'Hold David,' shouted Arthfael, 'what use a dead messenger? Speak on, Sir Robert of Gloucester, and if thou should lie - prepare thy soul!'

'What I say is true - see here, your seal upon the lock.'

He lifted the rope loop for Arthfael to see and the mark on the lead seal was indeed his own; the chest could only have come from Mynadd Banaug. The knight continued his tale.

'After the battle at Builth, my lord Gwynfa dispatched those fighting men not needed at Penmeanddu, to Shrewsbury, where they gathered with the King's forces, thence to march on Mynadd Banaug...'

'Why should Longshanks concern himself with a matter of family honour?'

interrupted Arthfael angrily.

'Tis no longer a family matter, Sire. Edward has appointed Gwynfa Commander in Chief of his Welsh Battalions; your attempt upon his life is a matter of treason against the crown.'

'There is no treason here, only treachery. Have I not served Longshanks well? Was I not granted Mynadd Banaug for those services? Am I not the rightful heir to Penmeanddu, and your master nought but a murderer and usurper?'

The knight looked at Arthfael with a face that might have been carved of stone.

'How did Mynadd Banaug fall?' demanded Arthfael shaking with rage.

The man who stood before him was no coward, but only Arthfael's honour stood between him and a bloody death, for what he had to tell might serve to anger Arthfael more. He decided upon a half-truth.

'Sire, those defending Mynadd Banaug saw the standard of King Edward and that of the House of Grfydd at the head of the column and thought it to be your own triumphant return! Our forces rode in through open gates!'

It was not the truth, but it would suffice. In truth, Gwynfa's forces descended by night upon a small outpost of some fifty soldiers. Every man within the keep was slaughtered save the Captain of the Guard and his family. They were forced to watch in horror as the eldest son was tied to a post and shot through with arrows. To save his wife and younger children, the Captain rode to Mynadd Banaug before Gwynfa's column. The night was stormy, his cries barely heard as he shouted up at the mighty ramparts.

'Open up - open up, I say. Tis I, Hewell Williams, Captain of the guard. Arthfael returns victorious. Penmeanddu is fallen and Gwynfa slain, open up, open up I say!'

Arthfael was consumed with rage. With one sweep of the sword, he hacked through the chest of the nearest horse, which fell at his feet, great gouts of blood spurting from the open wound. The other horses became distressed, rearing up on their hind legs, dashing the air with their forelegs, their riders fighting to keep the animals under control.

'Sire... enough I beseech you!' said Sir Robert, his hand outstretched and eager to have done with his odious task. 'I have one last message before - in the name of honour - I beg you to give us leave from this place.'

Arthfael calmed himself enough to say 'Speak on, Robert of Gloucester; what is this further treachery that you bring?'

'My Lord Gwynfa has bid me say that in his grace, he does not forget that thou art his brother. In his love for you, he grants you alone, free passage from this land, providing thou surrender and leave this day and never return.'

Arthfael stood as though in a trance, unable it seemed, to absorb the enormity of his failure and the humiliation of his defeat.

'Your answer Sire?' asked the knight after a long silence.

Arthfael looked up at him and slowly lifted the mighty Cadwgawn until he was looking down its blade still red with the horse's blood. 'You see this sword, Robert of Gloucester? See how straight and true its fashion. It has passed from Arawn ap Grfydd, to Eldred ap Arawn to me - always to the first-born. It is our lineage and our line. It has defended that line with honour, justice, and faith, and so shall it be again - do not doubt it. I shall not leave this place until this blade is stained with Gwynfa's blood - that is my answer.'

'Then so be it,' replied the knight, mounting his horse once more. 'I bid you farewell Arthfael ap Eldred, and I salute you! Until we meet again!' He turned his mount and together with his companions, he made his way through the camp and onward to the fortress of Penmeanddu.

'What is this gift, so generously given,' said Arthfael looking at the chest that lay at their feet. David took an axe and hacked his way into the locked and iron braced chest. A hideous smell escaped, foul and rank, despite the cold of the night. Wrapped in coarse, blood soaked cloth were two severed heads.

'Uncover them,' said Arthfael in a whisper.

David took each in turn and laid them on the ground at his feet. Tugging on the blood soaked and matted rags, the heads fell out. One was Arthfael's beloved wife, the other his first-born child. Their hair was matted with blood, the flesh, shrunk and waxen, their eyes staring blindly from sunken, bloodied sockets. Tissue and tendons hung like tendrils of thread from what remained of the woman's neck. As if as one, a gasp of horror left the lips of all who stood near, and darkness fell across every heart.

Not even David dared approach his beloved master, for in his grief he would have no other human being near him. He sat in lonely solitude on the jutting rock, high above Penmeanddu, for all that night and all the following day. Now night approached once more and it grew chill.

Arthfael spent the long hours in grief and sorrow, rueing his errors, for he knew his poor judgement had cost him dearly. But now at least he understood. He had been out-soldiered and outwitted at every turn. He had been defeated

23

by strategy and wit and he had had no defence against it. Little wonder Longshanks had chosen Gwynfa to be his General. He had tricked Arthfael into throwing good men against the towering walls of this formidable place, whilst his own secret army marched into Mynadd Banaug unchallenged.

Now Arthfael had nothing. No family, no property, no title. His defeat was absolute. Come the spring Gwynfa's army at Mynadd Banaug would move south and he would be utterly destroyed.

The camp was lost to him amid the cold darkness of the night. Only the faint glow of the brightest fires pierced the gloom, for a chill drizzle had replaced the snow of the previous day, engulfing the bleak mountain like a fog. The flicker of a torch broke through the mist on the twisting path beneath him. Though darkness hid the bearer, he knew it was Merek for no other creature would climb so slowly. For the first time, he felt the wetness of the clothes that clung to his body and shivered with the cold.

Merek placed a woollen cloak about his shoulders and a steaming pot of porridge in his hands.

Arthfael smiled in unspoken thanks and ate the porridge gratefully.

When he was done, Merek tugged at his sleeve as though to draw him down the mountain. 'Sire - come - rest!'

'Rest Merek, what is rest? Tell me if thou knowest! Where now shall I find its charity? Not in sleep methinks, for sleep doth but stir the demons of my soul.'

The simple-minded Merek did not understand these words, but knew that his master was much troubled by them. Many moments passed before Arthfael continued.

'This day I have died, just as surely as if a sword had spitted my heart. I have fought many battles and faced many foes, and never have I feared any man for I knew that God and righteousness rode with me, but now God has forsaken me and I know not why. I know not why, for my cause is just, but I have failed and now I am called to answer for that failure.'

The cripple waited for his master to go on.

'Look yonder to the precipice Merek, do you not see him? He waits there patient in the shadows for God to discard my soul. He turned and looked at the cripple. Thou art a simple-minded fellow and know nought of these things, but I fear his terrible maleficence more than I fear death itself!'

Merek followed his master's eyes, but all was blackness. He could not see this terrible thing that frightened his master so much. Only the looming mass of the high mountains were blacker than the appointed spot. As he peered into the darkness, a freezing wind rustled the branches of the trees and forest creatures called out with urgent voices.

Arthfael looked at Merek in the flickering torch light but saw only concern in the man's eyes.

'Dost though not see him? Look there, not twenty paces from us. Could there be a more hideous creature to host eternity? See how he stands on hind legs, eyes as bright as watch fires. He watches my every moment and his eyes never leave me, but he is patient, oh so very patient. When my eyes close, then does he step closer - each time another pace. I am afraid to move or slumber, for I know that is when he will step from the gloom and pluck out my soul.'

Merek saw no devil - no cloven-hoofed demon of scales and horns - only the madness of cold, sorrow and misery. From his belt, he drew a slender dagger and grasping the burning torch, he shuffled towards the place where Beelzebub stood, thrusting forward with the torch and slashing the air with his dagger. He bid the devil gone in the strange noises he made.

As he neared the appointed place, so Arthfael saw the eyes flare with burning hatred and the hideous countenance contort with rage. A mighty wind, as cold as the grave, howled about them, dragging the blanket from Arthfael's shoulders and buffeting the forest until its boughs creaked and branches snapped before its fury.

The night air was driven into a cacophony of sound by shrill voices and the beating of leathery wings. A host of demons - their eyes small and bright - surrounded Arthfael, pecking and clawing at the air in their anger and rage. Thunder crashed among the mountains and in the flickering light, the hideous creature dropped down on all fours.

Merek fought on against his unseen foe, his steps taking him ever closer to the edge.

Arthfael shook himself from his stupor at the very last moment and leapt toward the devil and the cripple. Gripping Merek by the shoulder, he wrestled him from his step into the abyss. The demon that had crouched there, vanished and so too did all his disciples.

'Enough Merek - enough, enough, it is done!' he shouted, whilst holding back the cripple who continued to thrust with his tiny dagger. 'Beware, loyal friend, lest you drag us both into the precipice.'

He turned Merek about to lead him back to safety, and saw by the light of the burning brand that his eyes were filled with tears.

25

Arthfael gripped both shoulders in his huge hands and said, 'Weep not brave Merek, for through your bravery my demon is vanquished and my madness with it. Thy great courage and this tiny dagger hath prevailed. I thought I bore my burden alone, but I was wrong, for thou art by my side.'

They returned to the porridge pot where Arthfael took up the mighty Cadwgawn and heaved it to his shoulder to make their descent to the camp below. He shuddered to have been so close to insanity; he was not mad, nor was he yet dead. He had grieved as any man might grieve, but now he must act. Justice and revenge were his goal now and vengeance would be his saviour. If Merek could save him from madness, might he not also save him from defeat? Was he not his father's trusted servant, never leaving his side by day nor night? He must have heard every word his father had spoken for thirty years past. If there were a weakness at Penmaenddu, his father would have known of it, and therefore - perhaps unwittingly - Merek might know of it too. He started to quiz the cripple about the mighty fortress. Where were its underground excavations, how thick its walls, how full its storehouses, how many and how deep its wells. On the latter issue alone, there was hope, for Penmaenddu had but one well that drew from deep within the hard granite rock.

'Does it ever run dry?' he asked. In stilted tongue, Merek replied 'It never runs dry - save for the very deep of winter.'

'How can this be,' asked Arthfael, 'surely you are mistaken? How can it run dry if it springs from the very bowels of the earth and the earth is bloated with winter rain?'

'When the water is turned to stone!' came the reply.

Arthfael looked about him at the mountains shrouded in darkness, hope rising within him. There were no rivers nor streams close by - save for the dullest of trickles - yet many thousands drew water from the well each day. Somewhere above them - Arthfael knew not where - this underground watercourse must rise above the earth in order that it might freeze in winter. Where might there be such a place?

Merek's thoughts returned to the journey he had made in the barrel of offal, and the deep pool to which the carter had taken him.

~

26

Men laboured beneath the waterfall; hacking away at the slippery rock to cut a culvert from the pool into which the water endlessly flowed, but from which it never spilled.

After three days labour, the water had a new course and the work of damming the pool began. As the dam grew higher, so the level in the pool grew lower, until at last, they peered down the dark and water worn gullet.

'Bring me the fruit of your bowels,' said Arthfael in satisfaction. 'Bring me all that rots and putrefies. Bring me the bodies of the slain that they might be triumphant in death. Bring me the creatures of the forest and carrion of the air and bring me rats... most of all bring me rats!'

Arthfael turned a trickle back to Penmaenddu, but now it flowed over the putrefying remains of thousands of slaughtered corpses. A terrible plague befell those who drank from it, and no man, woman, nor child was safe.

The stench of death hung over the fortress like Satan's breath. Ever more bodies were thrown from the walls to lie rotting where they fell - one upon the other. The carrion picked them over until bones burst through flesh and a foul black liquor seeped from the rotting pile of humanity. Within the fortress each new victim had the tell tale blotches and swollen lolling tongues. Plague had come, just as the hermit foretold.

Gwynfa gathered his court. 'It is the magician who has brought this calamity upon us,' he raged. 'He has cast his spell upon us and now Beelzebub and all his hosts are amongst us. He must remove this incubus or we are lost. Bring him hither and prepare to cast out the demons, but first bring me the talisman.'

They brought the wretched man before Gwynfa, who now wore the talisman about his own neck.

'You, who have brought this plague upon us,' he said, pointing an accusing finger at the hermit, 'denounce thy master, Satan, and lift this cursed spell. Do this and thy death shall be merciful and swift and thy soul cleansed by it.'

The old man looked at Gwynfa with watery eyes, 'There is no spell,' he whispered, the words barely audible.

'Liar!' shouted Gwynfa. 'Where is the death of Arthfael of which you spoke? Does he not sit victorious upon the mountain as hale as any man? Lift this curse you have brought down upon us or thou shalt perish in agony.'

The old man smiled as though he were speaking to a foolish child. 'You cannot kill me, Gwynfa ap Eldred,' he said slowly, 'for I am already dead!' He drew back the long grey hair that hid his neck. Beneath the skin were large black rings.

27

A gasp went through the room. The mark of death was upon him and he stood among them. Those close drew back - fear written on every face. He was the first... the first within the keep!

The hermit raised his hand and pointed a finger at his accuser.

'Hear me Gwynfa ap Eldred, for thou art damned. Thy brother shall perish in glory, beneath the sword, just as foretold, but many years are yet to pass. It is you - Gwynfa ap Eldred who are about to die, and die you shall, in agony and wretchedness. But death is but part of thy penance,' continued the old man, his frail hand trembling with this final effort. 'Though thy body shall rot and fester in the cold ground, thy soul shall know no rest. Thou shalt become the damned and thou shalt walk for all eternity among the terrible shades of darkness. Misery and torment shall be thine handmaidens... misery and torment...'

'Stop him - stop him,' shouted Gwynfa. 'Cut out his tongue lest he damns us all!'

Guards dragged the hermit down, and a priest drew out his tongue with pliers and severed it through with a knife. Covered with his blood, they took him outside and there they crushed each bone in every limb. With each blow of the stone, they entreated him to make a sign that he had denounced the devil and lifted the curse from them, but the old man made no sound; no sign was made, nor was Beelzebub seen to leap from him. They placed him on a wheel and fed his shattered limbs through its spokes. They tied his shattered body in place and threw the wheel from the parapet.

The wheel rolled down the mountainside, reaching a great speed on the near precipitous slope. With every rock it struck, it leapt many feet into the air before striking the earth once more, eventually to burst into a hundred shattered pieces of wood and bloody flesh.

~

Arthfael and David walked through the echoing streets of Penmaenddu. A cart piled high with bodies clattered by; its driver slumped at the reins. Men stood watchful, silent and defeated. Corpses lay everywhere, in homes, gutters and doorways, rotting where they fell. There was no resistance and only the raven and carrion crow, disturbed from their feast, dared screech their displeasure. Everywhere was the stench of death, and Arthfael's soldiers walked among them, slaying all who showed the sign.

David pushed open the heavy doors of the keep and walked into the hall beyond. The now familiar stench was overpowering. On they went, guided by the cripple, pausing only to draw their swords outside a studded door. The room beyond was vast. There was a huge fireplace at either end, but the flames had long since gutted and died and the room was chill. More bodies lay there. Most were dead, but a few still clung to life. Arthfael walked about the room looking into each face in turn; sometimes turning a body to do so, but Gwynfa was not among them.

They found Sir Robert of Gloucester. At first, it seemed that he too was dead, but as they were about to move on, his eyes opened the merest fraction. Though the room was dark, even that amount of light was agonising and he cried out in pain. They turned him onto his back and his lips moved in whispers.

Arthfael knelt close so that he might hear him better and spoke to the stricken man. 'Do you see me Sir Robert of Gloucester?'

'I see thee, Arthfael ap Eldred.'

'Then hear me also! All is lost with thee - thy life is at its end. God shall take thee to task for thy treachery, so tell me now - that with the truth on thine lips - thy soul might know redemption. Where is thy master, Gwynfa ap Eldred?'

'In yonder bedchamber... He dies, as we all die... you are too late!'

Arthfael hissed in satisfaction for he did not want to find Gwynfa dead - not just yet!

'What of my family, my wife and child - was it your hand?'

The dying man gathered his remaining strength. 'I am a soldier, not a butcher,' he whispered. 'I did not know what lay within the chest, but if there is pity in thy soul, Arthfael ap Eldred, take thy revenge upon me!' He closed his eyes too exhausted to speak further.

Arthfael lifted the mighty Cadwgawn high above his shoulders and brought the heavy blade slicing through the soldier's upper arm then on into his lungs. Bubbles of blood gathered at the gaping wound but soon the chest faltered and was still. Arthfael wiped the blade on the knight's tunic, and the two soldiers and Merek moved on.

They walked along a corridor to a smaller room that was in near darkness. The last time Merek had seen the room it was to watch his beloved master die. Slowly, cautiously, they climbed the dais about the massive bed, wary of a final treachery from behind the heavy drapes. Arthfael parted them carefully with the tip of his sword.

Gwynfa lay upon the bed; he too, was close to death. He turned his head with difficulty to look at Arthfael.

29

'So brother… you have come!'

'Yes I have come - did you ever doubt it? I have come to seek revenge Gwynfa… for our father's life, for the needless slaughter on the battlefield, and for the lives of my wife and child, whose innocence meant naught to you. All these you slaughtered to your own ends.'

Gwynfa closed his eyes against the light, dim though it was.

'Then have done with it,' he muttered, 'but Arthfael; as thou art my brother… grant me this wish at least… Do not kill me here; take me from this place to do your work… this I beseech you as the brother whom once you loved.'

'Why should you care where you die,' said Arthfael. 'Is it not meet that it should be here, in the room that bears witness to your treachery?'

'No, this cannot be! If I die here, the magician's prophecy will come true. My soul will know no rest and I shall walk forever among the damned.'

Arthfael knew nothing of the magician or his prophecy and cared even less for it 'Then so be it,' he replied.

'Arthfael,' cried out Gwynfa; his voice shaking with fear. 'Wait, I beg you… I beseech you… Is it so much to ask? Take me from this place to slay me… would'st thou cast thine own brother into the pit?'

Arthfael lifted Cadwgawn as he replied, 'Brother - would'st thou spare a serpent?'

With these words, he pressed down on the hilt of the mighty sword. The blade pushed through the blackened flesh and sinew of Gwynfa's throat to plunge onward into the mattress beneath.

Gwynfa's body rose up the blade and his eyes opened wide in disbelief. He would have cried out if that were possible. Blood spilled from his mouth and his body slid down the sword to lie still on the mattress.

'It is done,' said David, 'our task complete. Let us hang out his carcass for the carrion.'

'No…! Bury him David… bury him deep,' said Arthfael. The world has known his stench for long enough.'

Arthfael passed to the window, took an arrow and loaded it to a bow. He shot the arrow high into the air and it flew far into the green, green valley before it tipped and began its descent. 'Bury him there where the arrow falls.'

He stood at the window for some time, Merek and David silent behind him.

'May the magician's prophecy come true,' he said to the green valley. 'May there be no solace in your beauty, no peace in your womb, no succour in your bosom! May he walk among the damned for all eternity!'

Part One

Llewelyn's Tale (The Curse)
Pencryn, South Wales -1964

CHAPTER 1

Rhodri Williams

Clouds, dark and menacing, gathered in the cooling air. Shadows like the fingers of some ghostly hand, crept down the mountainside with catlike stealth, engulfing the town below in a mantle of gloom.

Rain fell on the high peaks, gentle at first, then in earnest; seeking out every fissure and gully, gathering pace, leaping from rocky crags, cascading and tumbling, outwards and downwards; distant white threads against the dark mountain.

Where it was too steep for fir and too barren for bracken, the mountain gleamed dully, its facets reflecting the fading light like tiny fragments of a shattered mirror. Pencryn was a dark place; so high were the mountains and so deep the valley that twilight always came early to the grim mining town. Serried ranks of slate roofs clung to the hillside like the scales of a sleeping dragon, and beyond - towering heaps of spoil broke the skyline like the beast's blackened teeth.

Through both night and day, winding engines whispered, and steam - like hot spittle, crackled, hissed, and spat from piston rods, valve chests, and stuffing boxes. Wires sang and sorting sheds clattered. Trolleys rumbled and chimneys disgorged their sulphurous smoke. Beneath it all, miners, who rose in darkness and went home in darkness, burrowed ever deeper into the bowels of the earth for the precious coal, until they had all but turned the mountain inside out.

In the farthest corner of the steeply-sloped graveyard, Rhodri Williams glanced skyward as the first raindrops fell. The sky was black and it was raining heavily on the western mountain peaks. It was not the first rain they had had that week and the earth was saturated, but the grave could be left no longer, for Mary Llewellyn's burial was due the next morning.

The oncoming darkness overtook him with alarming speed. He cut a tiny cleft for his oil lamp, which he lit with cupped hands to protect the match from wind and rain. When he moved, its flickering light cast grotesque shadows about the pit in which he stood.

Stronger with every passing moment, the wind sighed through the trees; whilst above him, telegraph wires sang like a manic cellist sawing at his strings; back and forth, back and forth; on and on and on.

The rain became heavy, cold, and penetrating. Within moments, he was stood in a downpour, though Rhodri had little choice but to work on. The wind drew a higher note as it blew harder, whistling like a draft beneath a door. Sudden, booming gusts tore rotten boughs from straining trees and set a distant gate to creaking.

As he neared the grave's full depth, Rhodri's spade unearthed human remains; tiny fragments blackened with age and acid soil. Soon more appeared; ribs, backbone, a part of the pelvis. He cursed his ill luck and reached for a stout canvas bag, brought for the purpose. His discovery was far from uncommon for Pencryn was a very ancient burial ground, but remains could not be left for all to see. It was his practice to gather them up and return them to their resting place along with the new interment.

The clay quickly became a mud puddle. As his spade scraped the last of the soil, he heard the unmistakable sound of metal upon metal. Plastered in mud, the object he unearthed looked like a spider with many legs. Rhodri held the piece at arm's length so that the rain might wash away the worst of it. He rubbed with his fingers until in the dim light of the lantern, he uncovered a brooch in the fashion of the sun and its rays. At its centre was a huge stone, and about it, others of lesser size. The brooch was clearly handcrafted and almost crude in its fashion, though very beautiful. He removed the clasp pin and scraped it against the edge of his spade. Even there in that dark pit, there appeared the glint of gold.

The sound of the wind changed again, deeper, quieter, like a solitary monk in an echoing cloister, chanting a dark litany.

Rhodri could only speculate on the brooches age and worth. It was big; nearly five inches in diameter, and was probably a man's brooch, perhaps to gather a cloak or heavy robe. In all his years, he had never before uncovered the like of it. He placed it in the bag along with the remains.

For the first time, Rhodri noticed the odd, eerie sound of the wind. It must be the wind for by now the graveyard was in darkness and no soul - no human soul at least - would venture there without a light to guide them. But so human had the sound of the wind become, that Rhodri was compelled to stop and listen. It unnerved him that the wind could make such strange, compelling, word like, sounds.

'Who's there?' he shouted at the darkness.

There was no reply. Instead the litany continued; ancient words, barely understandable, yet spoken in his native tongue.

'Who art thou to move against me!'

'Who's there?'

34

'Destroy me, despoil me; cleave my bones without cause.'

'Don't think you're funny,' shouted Rhodri above the wind, 'come out and show yourself and stop this bloody nonsense.' But no good-humoured laugh came from the darkness; no telling light cast its glow among the graves.

'Beware the deep sleep that falleth upon man, for thine shall be the deepest.'

No tormentor appeared, laughing and jibing from between the monuments; nor in truth did Rhodri expect them to, for the voice was right beside him now - within the pit in which he stood.

'Skin for skin; yea, all that a man hath will he give for life; yet thine shall wither and perish and become but brittle bone and wasted flesh.'

Terrified by the unseen voice, Rhodri scrambled from the grave, leaving all behind him except the bag which hung from his arm. He ran as fast as he was able, not into the town and the sanctuary of other mortals, but the path that led to home. He'd lived all his life in a ramshackle hut among the ruins of the fortress that kept watch over Pencryn - the once mighty fortress of Penmaenddu. It was a lonely journey and without his lantern, a perilous one; but he knew every inch of the steep and winding path like the back of his hand.

CHAPTER 2

Autopsy

The pathologist ushered all assistance from the lab except his friend the doctor and closed the door firmly behind them.

'Are you ready Tremaine?' he enquired cheerfully, crossing the room to the autopsy table upon which lay a black rubber body bag.

'As I'll ever be,' Tremaine replied.

Both men were similarly dressed in rubber boots, tunic, apron, and gloves. They pulled on their masks before Mason drew down the zip and opened the bag from head to toe. The body within was totally naked. It was the body of a middle-aged man of average height and quite obviously of the working classes. His hands and face told of a hard life, his teeth of a poor diet. He had clearly been an active man for he was all sinew and muscle. There was dirt beneath his fingernails and similarly his toes; his hair too, was dirty, thinning, and unkempt. All suggested a poor lifestyle to Mason, who was well versed in observing the all-important small detail.

Large purple patches discoloured the skin, as is the nature of a body dead for that length of time, but Mason was more interested in the lesions. He inspected the groin where the greater majority of sores were gathered, taking unusual care not to damage the skin further. If Tremaine was right, he did not want to release any more body fluid than necessary.

'Hmm!' he grunted, lifting one arm then the other to inspect the soft tissue of the armpits. 'The sixth plague, Tremaine,' he remarked, before continuing his examination of the neck and tongue, drawing the latter from the mouth with pliers.

'I beg your pardon,' replied Tremaine.

'Cutaneous Anthrax, said to be the sixth plague of Genesis; you might know your diseases, but you don't know your bible old chap! Might go against you in the long run that! Tell me - where did you come across Anthrax of all things? Not so common these days!'

'Burma - Rangoon - just before the outbreak of war. People were dropping like flies; whole families, whole villages it seemed. It's something you never forget.'

'I can imagine,' replied the Pathologist as he lifted the corner of a lesion and twisted a swab beneath it. He took other samples from the surface, and extracted a small sample of blood before crossing to a table where he prepared his cultures.

'I'll be surprised if you're not right old chap, but we'll see! What were you doing in Rangoon?'

'I was a junior doctor attached to the Embassy. We were seconded to help, but had to leave them to it as war broke out. They were afraid we'd be caught up in it and got us out. It was carnage really - absolutely terrifying. Are you going to open the body?'

'No,' said the pathologist, shaking his head, 'the cause of death is quite clear and we don't have the facilities here for the containment of Anthrax. Now he's dead, his cadaver's become a bomb just waiting to go off; Pandora's Box, absolutely full of this dreadful disease. The sooner it's cremated, the better, frankly, but what am I telling you for; you were in Burma! We'll get these samples analysed, then have this poor chap cremated as soon as possible. Do you know the interesting thing about Anthrax, Tremaine?'

'Well, I know it's very long lived - outside the body.'

'Precisely! Decades - centuries sometimes! It's one of only a handful of microorganisms that have that ability, for most are very short lived, but Anthrax... that's a horse of a different colour! It can lie dormant in the soil for a very long time. Just needs the right host to come along and away it goes again, very impressive really.'

'Williams was a grave digger,' said Tremaine significantly.

'Was he, indeed,' exclaimed Mason with relish! 'There have been cases of people contracting Anthrax from plague graves, many hundreds of years old. They died in their hundreds and were buried in their hundreds in mass graves. It's not beyond the realms of possibility that that's how this poor chap met his end. It needs investigating anyway.'

'Do you know the local history as well as you know your bible, Mason?'

'How do you mean?'

'Well, as coincidence would have it; Williams lived in a hovel in the ruins of Penmaenddu where many died of the plague at the end of the 12th century. On the other hand, he's lived there since anyone can remember.'

'Seven hundred years is stretching it a bit, even for Anthrax,' replied Mason, 'shouldn't think that's the source; has he dug any graves lately?'

'A woman called Mary Llewellyn, a widow who recently died of cancer. I signed the death certificate myself. She certainly didn't die of Anthrax. When

Rhodri didn't turn up to close the grave, the undertaker went looking for him and found him lying on the floor of his hut. If he'd contacted it in Mary Llewellyn's grave, it took just one day to kill him.'

'It will be easy enough to find out with the soil turned over as it has been. The test is very simple, but Anthrax takes no prisoners, as you know, Tremaine. Cutaneous - this kind - is not so bad; perhaps twenty-five percent mortality, but with Pulmonary you might as well say your prayers. Everywhere he's been will need disinfecting; everyone he's had contact with before and after his death, will need decontaminating and watching very carefully... you too if you handled him.'

'Yes, I did - before I realised what might have killed him. I went straight home and had a good bath in carbolic and told the undertaker to do the same, but the fellow hadn't touched him fortunately.'

'Well, you're looking well enough to me! As for this poor fellow, it's the department's problem now! I'll inform them immediately and get them to sort it out.'

CHAPTER 3

The men from Public Health

The group of twelve men slowly picked their way up the steep and well-worn path. Each carried an identical suitcase; some carried tools like crowbars, saws, axes, billhooks and the like. One carried firearms, and another, a Jerry can of fuel. The group was led by Doctor Tremaine and the local bobby, PC Wibberley. Bringing up the rear was a man from the Ministry, a Mr Jenkins, who was sweating profusely in a dark suit and tie despite the crispness of the day. He frequently lifted his bowler hat to mop his brow.

As they reached what was once the curtain wall of the mighty castle of Penmaenddu, a small terrier dog ran from the ruins to greet them. It was excited, wagging its tail and barking all in the same accord.

As it neared the group - its tail still wagging at a furious rate - it fell to the ground and did not move nor make another sound, for the bullet passed clean through its brain. At the sound of the shot, other animals penned or tethered within the ruins, became agitated; the cow, lowering its head, mooed loudly.

The group removed protective clothing from their suitcases on the instructions of Mr Jenkins. Their kit included rubber boots, rubber gloves, and full-face masks. They dug a shallow hole, into which they put kindling wood soaked in diesel to burn the overall's they were about to use. Satisfied with the precautions, Jenkins and the main group continued on to the ruins - one of them dragging the body of the dog.

Within the ruins, were several ramshackle buildings of wood and corrugated iron, patched and repaired with whatever had come to hand. Most housed domestic animals including hens, a cow, and a sow with piglets. The largest hut, propped against the wall of what must once have been the inner keep, was Williams own dwelling. Its door was ajar just as Tremaine had last seen it.

Tremaine and the constable watched the men from the Ministry go about their carefully planned procedures. It was distressing to hear the continual mooing of the cow, the squawking of the poultry, and the terrified squealing of the pig. Shot after shot rang out, until only the pig was left. It squealed in terror to the end and then suddenly, it too fell silent.

'We call them dumb animals but they know more than we think,' remarked the policeman heavily.

'They have blood in their veins and a beating heart; of course they know,' replied Tremaine.

39

'What now?'

They'll gather the animals together and burn them with the buildings; then when the fires have done their work they will disinfect everything; the walls, the ground, everything!

'Will it be enough?'

'I think so! Anthrax is long lived but it's easy enough to kill; we just don't know where else is contaminated, nor how Rhodri contracted it, and that's the problem. Mary Llewellyn's grave was a possible source, but the soil sample proved negative.'

'But no one else in Pencryn has fallen ill; you are okay and so is the undertaker who found him, how long does it take.'

'It's usually very quick, and we are three days on now; I doubt there will be more.'

'Well, that's something to be grateful for.'

'Indeed!'

As the fire raged through the wooden hut, a small canvas bag burst into flames along with everything else. Human remains and a mud-encrusted brooch fell from it as it disintegrated. Soon the remains were turned to charcoal and the brooch to a tiny pool of yellow metal. Moments later, all was dashed into the earth by burning wood that fell from the roof above.

CHAPTER 4

Pencryn Library.

'Will this blessed rain never stop Mr Llewellyn?'

'I think we are paying for our summer, Miss Morgan.'

'Well, I think we've paid quite enough now Mr Llewellyn, just look at Etymology!'

Etymology had indeed paid a heavy price. The overnight bucket had overflowed and many books were water damaged; some would even need to be thrown away.

It was all the council's fault in the Head Librarian's opinion! They'd been told about the roof, weeks ago and now this had happened. True, it had never been quite so bad before, but then it had never rained quite as hard, either. However, that was no excuse! They had been told and this really wouldn't do!

Losing a library book was a little like losing a child so far as Emily Morgan was concerned - not that she had ever had a child to lose of course; she being a spinster - but other people's children were often left in the library whilst their mothers spent a penny or things of that nature, so she thought that qualified. Mr Llewellyn had been right about the summer, however!

Pencryn had enjoyed hot days and balmy evenings. There had been fetes and bazaars, charabanc trips to the Gower coast, and in the evenings; performances by the brass band and male voice choir of the Edward and Alice collieries. Men who worked together within the bowels of the earth, crawling on their stomachs and hacking coal on their backs, sang together of their lives, their country and their belief in God. Men and women, children and infants, miners and paymasters alike, would sit and listen to the music that touched the soul with its beauty. Many sat as though deep in thought; head bowed; eyes closed, the better to hear the wonderful harmonies that rose and fell like thunder through the mountains, or a whisper on the wind.

However, that was then and summer had passed. The days were cold now, and the nights, dark and long. Throughout the valleys, chimneys spewed out soot which rose through the cold, damp air, to fall back to earth upon walls, washing and windows.

With the colder days had come the rain, and it seemed that hardly a day had passed without a downpour. Rain fell upon rain, which cascaded down the black slate tiles like a waterfall, prising moss from sheltered roofs and flushing it into the gutters, filling them to overflowing. Sheets of rainwater cascading onto the streets below, until the steep cobbled streets became rushing torrents and the river that ran through the valley threatened to burst its banks.

It had fallen to Miss Morgan to mount the steps, carefully ladling out the bucket into another held by her companion. The higher bookshelves were all in her care for Llewellyn had suffered polio as a child. It had left him with a distinct limp.

Llewellyn was Head Librarian, she, his assistant. Despite working together for more than ten years, there relationship remained a very formal one. Llewellyn was not a good communicator, in fact, he would rarely speak at all, unless it concerned books; a subject upon which he too, was passionate.

'Perhaps you should call the council again, Mr Llewellyn.'

'I called them twice yesterday, as you are aware Miss Morgan.'

'Yes, I am aware, Mr Llewellyn, but we really cannot go on like this. We will have to close this section and clear the whole bookshelf until they do something.'

'Well, perhaps that will be the best course anyway, Miss Morgan. I was told the weather has caused so much damage that they are at full stretch and they doubted they could spare anyone just yet. I think it's a case of the Lord helps those who help themselves.'

'Frankly, I think the Lord has caused enough trouble already Mr Llewellyn. Better we get by on our own efforts.'

Llewellyn was surprised to see the man passing the isle between the ranks of bookcases, for the library door has a most distinctive creak. His glimpse had been brief, little more than a shadow, but Llewellyn was sure of what he saw. He was a stranger, heavily bearded with shoulder length hair and dark features, but it was his dress that caught Llewellyn's attention, for no one in Pencryn would ever dress in such clothing. It was as though he had just walked from the stage of Shakespeare's Macbeth.

Miss Morgan was astonished to see Llewellyn put down his bucket and leave her at the top of the steps - still clutching her bowl of rainwater - to dash off down the aisle as quickly as his leg would carry him. He looked right and left at the far end, then after a brief pause, disappeared from sight. She waited, but he did not return.

'Mr. Llewellyn,' she called, but Llewellyn did not reply.

'Mr. Llewellyn, is everything all right?'

'Did you put this here, Miss Morgan?' came the reply.

'Put what? she asked, pouring her bowl back into the bucket and clambering down the two steps to the floor. 'Is something amiss, Mr Llewellyn?'

She made her way between the bookcases to the reading area where she could see most of the library. Llewellyn stood by the booking desk. He was looking her way and it was clear from his expression that something was out of place.

'Do you know where this came from, Miss Morgan, I'm sure it wasn't here last night? There was a man... a stranger; I've not seen him before.'

'I hardly think so Mr Llewellyn, it's not yet ten to nine. The doors are still locked; no one could come in yet.'

'Then what about this book?'

A heavy leather bound book lay on the desk before him.

A glance was enough for her. 'This is not one of ours Mr Llewellyn.'

Llewellyn could see that for himself and did not reply; instead, he opened the book at the first page where he found many hand written entries with dates.

'It's a family bible... a family called Durcan... a military family judging by the salutations; Captains, Lieutenants, two Majors, Waterloo, The Crimea, India too; how very strange.'

'The last entry is 1932,' added Miss Morgan,

"Died tragically on the 21st of January 1932; my beloved husband, Major Richard Durcan of the Royal Gloucestershire Hussars and our beloved daughter, Polly. Rest in peace my darlings."

'How very sad,' she murmured; 'I wonder what befell them.'

There was a marker between two pages of the book of Job. Miss Morgan opened it there, and began to read, not from the scripture itself, but from a quotation, handwritten in the margin.

"It was but the breath of a whisper overheard,

It was the hour when night visions breed disquiet, as men lie chained in sleep.

Fear took hold of me; a fit of trembling that filled my whole frame and made my hair bristle.

All at once a spirit came beside me and stopped; there it stood no face I knew, yet I could see the form of it and catch its rustling breeze..."

Llewellyn closed the book with a snap. Miss Morgan was about to express her astonishment at his rudeness when Llewellyn turned and walked away from her. It simply was not possible for anyone to conceal themselves within the libraries two halls, but Llewellyn was in no doubt; he had seen the stranger and the stranger must have left the book. The only issue was - where was he?

His inspection of the library proving fruitless; he limped to the door and pulled on its handles but it was securely closed just as Miss Morgan had said it would be. Evermore confused, he glanced at the clock. It was two minutes past nine. He fumbled in his pocket for the key. As he did so, there began a sharp tapping on the door. Much agitated by the recent events, he finally got the key to enter the lock. The whole matter had upset him quite considerably.

Waiting beneath his porch was a short, squat woman with a heavy bosom and a face like a bulldog. She clutched an umbrella and a knitted shopping bag.

'I should think so too, Mr Llewellyn,' she began, 'fancy leaving folk outside in this weather.'

'Given the weather I'm surprised to see you at all, Mrs Davies.'

'The libraries is due and I know better than to expect any grace from you, Mr Llewellyn!'

'It's only tuppence, Mrs Davis...'

'Tuppence is tuppence in our house, Mr Llewellyn; that's what Mr Davis would say... besides, there's two of em.'

Llewellyn took the books and placed them on his desk, stamping each with its return date.

'On the matter of sympathy, Mr Llewellyn, I was very sorry to hear about your dear mother; she and I always partnered at the whist drives you know! We were very friendly in those days - very friendly.'

'I didn't notice you at the funeral,' he replied tersely.

'Mr. Davis was having one of his off days or I would have been there of course...! It must be a blessed relief for you though, Mr Llewellyn... things being as they were! I'm sure you're glad it's all over...'

Llewellyn passed Mrs Davis her card, mumbling something she didn't quite catch and left her to return the books to their shelves.

'What's got his goat?' she remarked to Miss Morgan, a little put out; 'he was downright funny with me... People shouldn't be funny with people if they want to be in public service.'

'He's just lost his mother, Mrs Davis and she was all he had; he's a little sensitive to the matter at the moment.'

'Well, all I said was, t'was a blessed relief! Mr Davis said the same only yesterday! I mean having to look after her with her being that way...! It's not as though he's even had a wife if you know what I mean, him being a bachelor and things...! I just don't think its decent is what I'm saying, Miss Morgan. It's one thing for a woman to tend for a man, but it's quite another for a man to tend for a woman, that's all I'm saying.'

Outside the library the rain fell unabated.

CHAPTER 5

Lodgings above the Bakery

Llewellyn turned the key in the lock before shaking down his umbrella. Before him were the stairs to his flat, and beyond the narrow hallway, a door to the backyard and the garden privy which he shared with the bakery staff.

Gripping the banister rail in one hand and the heavy bible in the other, he began the ascent of the steep and narrow stairs. So difficult were they to negotiate that he rarely left his rooms once he was home.

His apartment consisted of three rooms, the sitting room, his bedroom - and until recently - his mother's room. He could still smell her there for the smell of that kind of death can linger. She suffered multiple sclerosis for many years leaving her utterly dependent upon him, but it was cervical cancer that killed her. Those last few months... hearing her crying out in pain... "Oh God, oh God, please help me". The endless soiling, the hopelessness of it all, the pain and despair that no animal would be allowed to suffer, it was more than he could bear to think of.

Llewellyn placed the book on a table then crossed to the grimy window that looked down upon the street. The colliery shift had just changed and a few miners were dashing home through the rain, their hob nailed boots ringing hollow on the cobbles as they ran. Llewellyn struck a match, lit a gas mantle beside the fireplace and then pulled the heavy velvet curtains together to keep out the drafts. He revived the fire with his poker and threw on a precious log. The kettle squealed on its bracket as he pushed it above the flames. Exhausted with the day, he sank gratefully into a winged armchair, there to close his eyes for a while.

The rooms had once been very grand, not a miners terrace like most housing in Pencryn, but part of the town hall which had subsequently moved elsewhere with the advent of the railway. Part of the building was demolished to make way for the station, and what remained had become shops on the ground floor and living space above. Llewellyn had been fortunate. His job as librarian gave him the opportunity to rent the rooms above the bakery at a peppercorn rent, but thereafter, fortune had not been so kind. His mother, already unwell, became chair-bound and never left the apartment thereafter. That had been fifteen years ago. Since then, the rooms had begun their slow decay, mouldering with damp and grey with dust.

The room was very sparsely furnished; just his chair, a table, a writing desk and a cabinet in which he kept his food. He lived a very frugal life, partly because of his wages, which would support nothing better and partly because of his affliction which made it difficult to carry anything that was not utterly essential, up and down the steep stairs. His one exception to that rule was books. Books were everywhere; upon shelves, the table, the mantle shelf, in piles upon the floor; books were everywhere.

Books were more than mere knowledge or diversion to Llewellyn; they were his friends - perhaps his only friends. He could relate to books, escape within their pages, befriend the hero's, discuss their theory or philosophy; journey with them, adventure with them, share their joy and sorrows and tell them of his own. Books alone were steadfast, understanding and sympathetic. He never told them of his affliction however; they knew nothing of that. It did not exist if he was with them; instead, he was like them in every way. He too was a man of daring, of learning and achievement.

Llewellyn roused himself at the whistling of the kettle. He made a pot of tea; then settled down with pen and paper to investigate the handwritten entries within the bible. He began with "Who's Who" and "Debrett's Peerage", then military yearbooks and those of the church, for many of the male line of the Durcan family were soldiers, politicians, or men of God. He discovered that the family line went far beyond the first entry in the book, which was written in 1668, and there were many distinguished and gallant men among them, but after many hours of research, Llewellyn could unlock no clue as to why the bible might be so many miles from where it belonged. There were no links with Pencryn, no links with Wales or the valleys.

He read the handwritten passage once more and wondered why the marker had been at that page, whether it had any significance or not.

'It was but the breath of a whisper overheard,

It was the hour when night visions breed disquiet, as men lie chained in sleep.

Fear took hold of me, a fit of trembling that filled my whole frame and made my hair bristle.

All at once a spirit came beside me and stopped; there it stood no face I knew, yet I could see the form of it and catch its rustling breeze..."

Though the Durcans had often met with untimely deaths, only one entry in the bible stood out as unusual and that was the last one.

"Died tragically on the 21st of January, 1932 - Major Richard Durcan of the Gloucestershire Royal Hussars and our beloved daughter, Polly. Rest in peace my darlings."

Llewellyn determined to discover why they had died so tragically, but the hour was late. The log on the fire had burnt to ash, and very soon, it would be time to rise and get ready for the day ahead. Llewellyn closed the bible and reference books and made himself ready for bed.

CHAPTER 6

A Visitor Calls

Llewelyn had not been sleeping well these past weeks as one might expect. Perhaps, however, it was the words penned in the margin of the Durcan bible that troubled this particular night so badly; a night when his own night visions bred disquiet!

Before his mother's death, his nightmares were always the same. By some dreaded illness or through entanglement with some flailing, thrashing, unstoppable machinery, he too was destined to suffer the same agonising wretchedness of Mary Llewelyn's last few weeks on earth. In his nightmare, he spared her with a pillow, but in his wakefulness, he lacked the courage and merely stood by and watched as she died in agony. He had failed her in her hour of need. All his life was a failure.

When finally she'd died, Llewelyn prayed for the first time in his life. He prayed that when his own time came it should not be like that; he prayed that his death would be a painless one. He did not link the two at first - his prayers and his new, insidious, creeping nightmare that took over from the last - but as one night vision transcended another in its surreal horror, so too did the deaths of the players in his dreams become more vivid - more frightening.

Llewelyn could not remember which book had fed his subconscious imagination, or even who had written it. Perhaps it was Poe or M.R James, he couldn't recall, but as he had chosen a painless death for himself, then his dreams invited him to contemplate a death far more terrifying. In those dreams that followed his prayers, the poor innocent souls that inhabited his night visions were buried alive.

That most terrible end was far from uncommon in Victorian times when physicians had little better than a mirror to assist them in their proclamation of death. Many of their patients were not dead at all, but had merely slipped into a death like state, their consciousness and vital functions suspended. This dreadful condition that suspends all obvious brain, heart and lung activity of the human body, turning muscles rigid and flesh into a waxen, corpse-like state is called catalepsy.

There have been many well-documented cases, particularly in the terrible chaos of war, when those thought to be dead have been hurriedly buried, only to come alive from their deathlike state. Coffins exhumed from battlefields for the hero within to be buried at home have shown evidence of frantic scratching and clawing at the wooden lid, with flesh torn from fingers until only bony stubs

49

remained. Some known to have been at peace when buried, had the look of madness about them.

In 1806, Anne Carter Lee, the mother of Southern General, Robert E. Lee, suffered a cataleptic fit, and was buried in the family plot in Virginia. Hearing a noise some while later, a servant called attention to the sound and Anne Carter Lee was dug up alive, but most dreadfully traumatised.

In another rare case where a coffin was opened and the supposed corpse was still alive, the poor man was so deranged that he took a revolver and blew away his own brains, to be sure that he would never again relive his hell within that dark box, deep within the earth.

Perhaps most terrifying of all was a notable case from the Victorian records of Highgate Cemetery, of a woman of some wealth and social position who died in childbirth. She was buried with her stillborn infant in her arms, in the family vault. This - in common with the occasional fashion of the day - was notable for a glass skylight through which succeeding members of the family and the curious public, might espy the coffins interred within. Soon after the burial, it was noted that the coffin had moved upon its trestle, though the vault had been securely locked and sealed.

When the vault was opened and the contents of the coffin exposed, the priest in attendance was heard to say, "May God have mercy upon us," before collapsing to the ground.

Within the coffin, her lips smeared with blood, was the corpse of the once beautiful woman. Her face was contorted in fear and madness, and still in her arms, the part consumed body of her infant child - drained entirely of its blood. One might conclude, as Llewelyn did, that there are many things worse than a painful death.

When Llewellyn woke, it was to find that the nightmare that had troubled him so much those past few days had turned to reality, and he too had been buried alive. His terror caused his heart to stop, and he lay motionless in total darkness while he waited for his heart to beat again.

He felt the walls of the coffin all about him. Its silken lining had drooped across his mouth to smother and choke him; he gasped for breath, tearing at the suffocating silk, his heart pounding in his chest. His claustrophobia was overwhelming and panic seized him. He had woken from his cataleptic state and was alive again; but he knew it would not be for long. He knew he must die very soon, if not of suffocation, then of madness. Panic consumed him and he cried out for help. He was terrified - utterly terrified.

He thrust upwards in a desperate attempt to free himself from the suffocating, wooden tomb. He knew it would be futile, for many feet of earth pressed down upon the lid that incarcerated him. Already he was finding it hard to breathe, his breath coming in short frantic gasps; he could not get enough precious air, yet he tried once more, to move the lid.

Where he imagined the lid would be, there was nothing and his hands reached frantically into empty space. He tore the bed-sheet from his face and grasped for the coffin walls he had felt moments before. He sat bolt upright, his heart pounding; the faintest of hope returning. There was no silk lined coffin, no suffocating earth. He reasoned, therefore, that he must be in a vault, no less dark and no less silent. He reached out and grasped the box of matches beside his bed, but his hand trembled so much that he dropped the first and broke the second.

Eventually, a match erupted into flame. Even then, when the flickering match revealed that he was in his own room, and the silken lining was nothing more than bedclothes, he could barely believe it had been a nightmare, for as is the nature of nightmares - it had been so terrifyingly real.

He could not bear the thought of another moment of darkness. He lit the candle beside his bed and wept with relief, but his reprieve proved to be all too premature. He was still shaking from his experience when he heard the noise again; the noise he'd thought was his own nails, scratching and scraping at the lid.

Scrape, scrape, scrape came the sound - slow, methodical and determined. Afraid once more, Llewellyn held his breath, cocked his head, and listened. At first, he thought it to be a rat, for the yeast from the bakery and the carbolic soap in the washroom attracted them, but this was no rat. Rats are timid creatures, knowing well the fear and loathing they inspire. They are covert in their activities; gnaw a little, scratch a little, then listen. Listen for the ever-present danger; wait for it to pass; wait for the air to fall still; wait for silence!

This noise was not the furtive scratching of a rat for it was too purposeful, too single minded, too human. After his dreadful transition from nightmare to wakefulness, Llewellyn's nerves were at breaking point. They had no resistance to this new fear; the fear that he was not alone in that dark room.

Slipping from his bed, he held the candle high, searching every dark corner, but there was no one there. There was no fiend with axe held high, no scaly creature of the pit hanging from the ceiling with steely eyes unblinking.

Llewellyn tore open the door of his bedroom and stumbled into the room beyond. He opened the gas tap with a shaking hand and lit the mantle with the flame of his candle. The fragile dome glowed incandescent and cast its light into the dark corners. He stoked the embers of the fire and threw on a log. He needed light or he would go insane.

As the log began to crackle, he heard it again; scrape, scrape, scrape.

Llewellyn stopped and looked about him. He looked for the rat; for the murderer with the knife, and in the dark corners; not yet free of the horror of his nightmare; he looked for the fiend with the bright, tiny eyes. He heard the noise again, slow, patient, methodical, scratch, scratch, scratch.

Llewellyn crossed to his mother's room and with one swift movement he threw the door wide. He peered into every corner but the room was exactly as he'd left it; there was no one there.

As he turned back to the sitting room, he saw the handle of his apartment door move. It was just the tiniest movement, but he was sure his eyes had not deceived him. He heard the noise again - scratch, scratch, scratch. Then the knob moved once more as though someone was trying to get in.

'Who's there?' he cried, 'what do you want?'

The sound from the landing stopped and all was silent.

'Who are you; what do you want?'

For many minutes there was complete silence, then it started again; scrape, scrape, scrape.

Llewellyn watched in horror as the knob turned and the door he knew to be locked; slowly opened. In the gloom beyond the doorway stood a shadowy form dressed in a linen shroud. Long grey hair fell about the woman's shoulders and in her hand was a burning candle that cast no light save that which fell upon her face, and this had the ashen pallor of the grave. So gaunt had this hideous cadaver become, that it seemed the skull must soon burst through the parchment skin that covered it. So wasted was the flesh through the ravages of illness, death and the grave, that the lips were drawn back from the mouth in a hideous, mocking grin.

If I call the repulsive thing an apparition, do not imagine it to be a wisp of vapour or a fleeting contortion of light and shadow, for it didn't conveniently disappear within the blink of an eye. Instead, it stepped forward into the light of the gas mantle and only then did Llewellyn recognise his mother. She turned to look at him, staring at him for what seemed an eternity.

Horrified, Llewellyn, muttered, 'No, you are dead; I saw you die.' He stumbled backwards, knocking over piles of books, shrinking into the far corner of the room. 'I saw you die.'

Llewellyn closed his eyes tight, unable to look at her any longer, his hands covering his face. When he summoned the strength to open them again, she had gone, but within her room, the candle flickered.

Llewellyn, stood in the doorway, his own candle held high, trembling with shock and loathing for the hideous thing that lay upon the bed. Ravaged by disease, she had been little more than skin and bone in life, but death had taken an even more terrible toll. Her flesh was sunken, her skin ashen grey. The shroud was stained with the dark fluids of the grave and he could not bear to look at her.

Why had she come back? He was terrified that she might come from the room and reach out and touch him with her cold, withered hands. He slammed the door shut, locked it, and jammed a chair against it. A pointless precaution he knew; but he didn't want her to leave the room and take him with her; he did not want to be buried alive.

Llewellyn awoke next morning in his fireside chair. He couldn't recall how he came to be there, only the nightmare - just that terrible nightmare. It had been so real - so terrifying. Even now in the cold light of dawn, it was hard to accept it wasn't real. He threw open the door of her room, his heart thumping, but there was no one there; it had all been a dream, nothing but an awful, heart wrenching nightmare!

Or so he thought...!

The following night, Llewellyn awoke as before and at the same hour. Once more he'd been buried alive by unseen hands; once more the horror and panic; once more the scraping that jarred every nerve; once more the horrible, staring cadaver.

Every night she came and every night Llewellyn re-lived the same nightmare; each time she had rotted and festered some more.

The flesh had burst open on her neck and a foul putrescence seeped out; the rotting tissue writhed with tiny flecks of white. As each night of his living nightmare passed, the revolting creatures had consumed more. Her eyes, lips and tongue were all devoured. Her hideous grin grew ever wider.

With each successive day that passed, Emily Morgan grew more concerned for Llewellyn's health. He looked exhausted and at his wit's end, as though some terrible calamity had befallen him. Once, she heard him weeping and wanted to comfort him. She wanted to ask what ailed him, but she knew he would not want her interference and so she said nothing.

CHAPTER 7

Harry Evans

The cockerel screeched and squealed on rusty hinges, north, south, east, west - this way and that - back and forth - unable to decide which way to crow.

Rain, as heavy as any that month, swept through the graveyard in swirling, buffeting gusts. Great gouts of water spewed from gargoyle mouths like silvery vomit, then to be caught upon the wind and thrown to earth in a million shimmering droplets.

Also keeping watch, were stone grotesques with beaked heads and hooded eyes. Together they watched over the dead, their hideous forms, shining darkly in the light from distant street lamps. Within their mouths, the bodies of the vain, the wicked and the fallen, hung limp and broken; testaments if such were needed, to the perils of an ungodly life.

The yellow glow of a lamp passed through the side gate from the main street. Heavy boots rang out on the flagstone path that guided traveller's through the graveyard to the Bute Street exit, but it was unusual for anyone to pass that way at night, for it was a dark and lonely place.

Harry Evans was a miner, or had been so until the explosion in the Alice Colliery. A pocket of gas ignited deep within an abandoned spur; "Black Damp" they called it.

At first, it was no more than a whoosh of flame but it gathered speed with every millisecond, accelerating faster and faster, until it hurtled through the mine with the speed of a bullet. Wagons, ponies, men, pit props, all were plucked into the air like confetti. Winding machinery was torn from its footings and hurled down the shaft, crashing and groaning in metallic anguish, falling and falling, as though forever.

The ruptured bodies of men were ripped apart by thousands of feet of scything wire. The mighty flame consumed all in its path and sucked the oxygen from every corner of the pit until there was no more. Men who had survived the blast were plunged into darkness. They clawed at the air and their comrades, desperate for oxygen like fish drowning on a riverbank.

As wives and daughters gathered outside the mine, keeping their silent vigil, the off duty shift prepared for the hell that was to come. Grim-faced men lowered their comrades into the black abyss. Each man's heart pounded in his breast, but none held back - there was no question of what must be done.

55

Body after body was brought from the pit, and Harry Evans was one of the lucky ones. These days he was the battery man, collecting, checking, and charging. More than two thousand lamps were in his care and he maintained them with conscientious respect, but he could never face the pit shaft again.

He was making his way home from the working men's club, but the weather was so bad, he'd taken the shortcut through the graveyard. As he passed a huge monument adorned with a winged angel, he spotted what appeared to be a human form stood in the shadows. So unexpected was the encounter that he cried out in alarm, 'Jesus Christ Almighty!' he gasped.

Turning the flashlight full on Llewellyn, he said, 'Jesus Christ you gave us a fright!'

When Llewellyn did not reply, he tapped him on the shoulder; 'You all right boyo,' he asked; suspicious that something was wrong; wondering who in their right mind would stand in such a place on such a night.

'Do you need some help?' he asked.

'I'm waiting.'

'Waiting ...! Waiting for what?'

'For my mother,' replied Llewellyn simply.

'Waiting fer yer' mother!' Harry replied in astonishment. 'In this weather - in a bloody graveyard?'

'Where else might I wait,' said Llewellyn matter-of-factly.

Harry Evans swung his torch toward the grave on the opposite side of the path. It was very recent, a simple marker proclaimed, "Mary Llewellyn".

'She won't stay there. Every night she comes ...'

Evans shone his flashlight back to Llewellyn, expecting some sick joke, but the man had an odd look about him; his eyes vacant his skin pale; he looked ill - deranged almost.

'You're not right in the head mate! You need to see someone.'

Rain was running down Evans neck and he had to blink constantly to clear his vision. He stared in silence at Llewellyn, but Llewellyn looked straight through him. Evans decided to leave him to it. It was none of his concern. After a few paces, he stopped and shone the torch on Llewellyn once more, but Llewellyn continued to stare at the grave. Harry Evan continued on his way, it wasn't his problem; he'd enough of his own.

56

'A peasant and a fool!' said Gwynfa, 'Will he return?'

'No.'

Gwynfa laughed and the sound turned Llewellyn's blood cold.

'He couldn't see you - you are not real,' said Llewellyn with courage he didn't feel.

'It did not suit me that he should see me.'

'You can't harm me if you're not real.'

'Oh, can I not,' hissed Gwynfa. 'Who buries you alive each night, who drives her from the grave, tell me that? Who gives her the candle that sheds no light! Who sends her each night to scratch at your door - tell me that my fine friend? I can destroy you because you are a weakling - a milksop already in my grip. Disobey me and you will die in torment and madness!'

'Why is she helping you? Why does she torment me so? I did everything for her - she loved me - I was her son!'

Gwynfa laughed as though this was a splendid joke.

'What is so funny?'

'What a fool you are! You think she cared for you? She cared nothing for you, only for herself! You suckled at the breast of a whore and murderess. Not just one life did she snuff out but many - yes many! She is not whom you think my friend, oh no, no, no! Now she rots in my grave, and I must be rid of her and you will help me.'

'Liar - you are a liar,' screamed Llewellyn.

'Am I' he replied, 'am I indeed! Then ask her for yourself, Thomas Llewellyn!' As he spoke, the soil turned like boiling broth and Mary Llewellyn rose through the earth to stand before them; foul and ripened beyond description.

CHAPTER 8

Morning Call

PC Wibberley sat in shirtsleeves and braces, dipping a soldier in his breakfast egg when the phone rang. His wife picked it up and intoned, 'Pencryn 212, Pencryn Police Station, how can I help you?'

'Oh... Oh I see; well you'd best speak to Ken about that Idris; here he is.'

Wibberley took a quick sip of his tea before following her into the tiny room that served as Pencryn Police station. She passed the phone to her husband with a raised eyebrow. 'It's Idris Jones,' she said with a very odd look.

'Hello Idris, how can I help?' inquired the policeman.

'Good God,' he said when the caller had finished speaking, not expecting such a problem on a wet and windy Thursday morning. 'Who's grave?'

'And do you know who's responsible?'

'But you've searched nearby?'

'Well, hold the fort until I get there. Keep everyone away and please don't go near it yourself... yes, thanks... yes, I'll be there just as soon as I can.'

'Well, that's a new one,' said the policeman to his wife. 'Someone's taken Mary Llewellyn's body from her grave, left the coffin in the ground and the remains of the lid just a few feet away ...! Who'd believe it!'

'Why on earth would anyone do such a thing Ken, how awful...?'

'Well, I doubt its vandals; it takes a lot of work to dig up a body as I know well; it must be some bloody nutcase...! No doubt we'll find out in the fullness of time. I'd better...'

Just then the phone rang once more; 'Pencryn Police; PC Wibberley; how can I help?'

'I can't understand what you're saying Mrs Thomas,' he replied patiently; 'just take a deep breath and start again slowly... yes, I can hear you're upset, but just try to keep calm... that's better...yes, I see... okay...'

The conversation continued in this manner for some minutes until Wibberley was finally able to put the phone down. 'I think we've found Mary Llewellyn,' he said gravely; 'I'd best be off - I can see this is going to be one of those days.'

CHAPTER 9

Wibberley Calls

Wibberley knocked on the door. 'Mr. Llewellyn,' he called softly. There was no reply, so he squinted through the keyhole as Mrs Thomas suggested. He could see little of the dark room beyond, but the smell was enough.

No sooner had he put his bike on its stand than she'd rushed from the bakery to meet him; 'Oh, Mr Wibberley, whatever shall we do...?'

'Well, the first thing is not to upset yourself, Mrs Thomas. I'll look after Mr Llewellyn from now on, and in the mean time, Pencryn needs your wonderful bread, so you just carry on as normal. I'll look after things upstairs until Dr. Tremaine arrives.'

'Are you sure you'll be alright Mr Wibberley; you don't think he's...?'

'I think he's poorly at the moment, Mrs Thomas, and needs our help, but I doubt he's a danger to anyone.'

'Oh good, oh dear, I do hope so... I'm sure you're right, Mr Wibberley; he's such a quiet man and he's been through so much lately... I feel so much better now you're here - oh poor Mr Llewellyn! I just don't know what to say - I just don't know what to say...!'

'I think its best you don't say anything Mrs Thomas or people will gather around and that'll upset him won't it! We need to keep him calm if we can. You just carry on quietly, and we'll have things sorted out before you know it.'

She offered to put the kettle on and Wibberley thanked her before climbing the stairs to Llewellyn's apartment. The smell in the stairwell was appalling and he resisted the desire to retch. He was careful not to tread in the mud in the hall, nor the tiny scraps of cloth and flesh that clung to the stair treads - the gruesome discovery that had upset poor Mrs Thomas.

He reached the landing and knocked on the door of Llewellyn's apartment, 'Mr Llewellyn,' he called softly.

There was no reply.

He knocked again, 'Mr. Llewellyn, its PC Wibberley, you remember me don't you.'

Again, there was no reply.

'I've come to see if you're all right, sir.'

59

Again, silence.

'Would you open the door for me, Mr Llewellyn,' he continued patiently.

'There's nothing you can do Mr Wibberley,' said Llewellyn, finally.

'Well, perhaps there is, Mr Llewellyn; it may only be something small, but there's always something I can do to help... if people will let me.'

Llewellyn did not reply.

'I can't help you if you won't let me Mr Llewellyn, but if you will trust me, I promise you I will try; you know that don't you?'

Wibberley heard Llewellyn sobbing within.

'Open the door for me, Mr Llewellyn, there's a good gentleman.'

'Is anyone else there Mr Wibberley?'

'No, there's no one here, just me...!'

Wibberley heard the key turn in the lock, then the door opened slowly.

The room beyond was in semi darkness, lit only by the glow of the fire. Llewellyn stood before him, a broken and wretched man. Beyond him, sat bolt upright in an armchair, was a sight that even Wibberley's long service had ill prepared him for.

Staring ahead with unseeing eyes was the corpse of Llewellyn's mother. The stench within the room was foul beyond description.

A lesser man might well have shown his revulsion, but PC Wibberley would never allow his feeling to show. He'd been a police constable all his life and would probably stay so, for he had no ambition towards high office, but he was the kind of bobby every decent community needed. All knew him and trusted him; all looked to him for help when things went wrong as it had today. It was at times like this that PC Wibberley of the South Wales Constabulary, was at his very best.

He led Llewellyn to the chair opposite his mother and sat him down, he then locked the door once more. He drew the curtains on a grey dawn and opened the sash window as far as he could raise it; at just two inches, it was woefully inadequate.

'Mrs. Thomas is making us a nice cup of tea, Mr Llewellyn. I asked her to leave it outside and I'm sure she won't be long - you'll feel better for a cuppa I'm sure.'

Llewellyn began to shake and then his eyes filled with tears. The policeman drew up a chair beside him and gripped his arm firmly in his.

'Death is a part of life; Mr Llewellyn,' he said gently, 'and that's hard for us to understand I know, but there's a place for life and a place for death too. You must let her go there now; let her go with dignity...'

'You don't understand Mr Wibberley; he replied; I don't want her here.'

'Then why?'

'I had to... I had no choice... she will never leave me in peace as long as he's there. It's his you see; his place not hers.'

'I don't understand - do you mean the grave?'

Llewellyn nodded.

'It's just a grave Mr Llewellyn - just earth and soil, nothing more...'

'No; no you're wrong, it is a cursed place - a foul place. He's there and she can never go back - he'll never allow it.'

'Who Mr Llewellyn - who is this person you're so afraid of?'

'Gwynfa, he replied; Gwynfa ap Eldred... he's buried there - in that pit; in her grave.'

'There's no one else there Mr Llewellyn, if there had been... Wibberley stopped mid sentence. For the first time, he connected the unusual death of Rhodri Williams with these equally bizarre events.

'Who was Gwynfa ap Eldred,' he continued, 'this other occupant of her grave.'

'He was a Marcher Lord - the master of Penmeanddu - a wicked man - evil beyond belief. All these valleys and the mountains as far as the eye can see were his. He would have been king of Wales but for the curse.'

'The curse?'

Llewellyn told him the story of long ago; of the cripple who defeated him and the old man of the woods who laid a deadly curse upon him. He told him how Rhodri had awakened the curse by defiling the ancient grave, interring Mary Llewellyn's body where only Gwynfa's remains should be.

Now at last, after all these years, the curse had been stirred and Gwynfa would know no rest whilst she shared his grave. He told the policeman how Gwynfa had tormented him to the brink of insanity; forced him to exhume her body, forced him to bring her home, warned him that she must never return there.

For once PC Wibberley was at a loss for what to say.

'And where is he now, Mr Llewellyn' he asked finally, growing ever more concerned for Llewellyn's sanity. 'Is he safely back in the grave where he can do you no further harm?'

'No, not yet.'

'So where is he?'

'Stood beside you.'

Wibberley turned to where Llewellyn was pointing. He did so as casually as he could, but his heart was thumping nonetheless. The hairs were standing on the back of his neck and he felt a cold shiver run down his spine.

He glanced at his watch, but it was not yet seven. Where the hell was Tremaine when he was needed? He'd asked his wife to ring the surgery before he left and that was nearly an hour ago.

He turned once more to Llewellyn; 'Perhaps you should tell me everything this man Gwynfa told you, Mr Llewellyn... So I can understand what needs to be done - can you do that?' As the rain fell relentlessly upon their grey town, Llewellyn began his story in that dark and dreary room above the bakery; it was a story that Wibberley was destined never to forget.

Llewellyn spoke calmly, clearly and eloquently. He seemed to forget his anxieties over Gwynfa ap Eldred once he began, and for Wibberley it was a story so real and so moving that he forgot the foul cadaver sitting beside him, and listened instead to every word Llewelyn uttered.

Llewellyn told PC Wibberley the story exactly as Gwynfa had related it to him. It was the story of four generations of the Durcan family, beginning with Richard Durcan and ending with himself. But above all, it was his grandmother's story and a sadder, more beautiful, or more moving tale of love, there has rarely been. It was Polly Durcan's story, and I shall tell it to you now if you have a mind to read on.

Part Two

Polly and Isaac's Tale (The Promise)
The Cotswolds and North Devon - 1897 to 1932

CHAPTER 10

Polly Durcan

Parson Pimm felt the draw of the reins, but the nearby grass looked so unappetizing that he sauntered on to a greener patch. He heard the cry of exasperation and felt the dig of his mistress's heels, but chose to ignore both. He had looked after his mistress since she was a small child and saw no reason to pander to her now.

He'd noticed a change, however. She'd become a young lady just recently; as pretty as a picture and full of self-confidence. People - young men in particular - wanted to stop and talk with her, where once upon a time it was just the two of them - he'd liked that better.

She rode him far less now and sometimes days would pass. He'd wonder what kept her away, but when she did come, her touch was ever more gentle, her voice softer and her hugs longer. She would tell him all her cares and ask for his opinion on all manner of things and in truth, he understood none of them, but he would nuzzle her as he had always done and she would hold her cheek against his. He loved her very much.

Together, they would ride for miles among the beautiful Cotswold Hills; Uley Bury, Coaley Peak, Smallpox hill and the Long Down, to name but a few. They would go home tired and happy and she would clean him and brush him before passing him over to Ned whom he didn't care for greatly.

Ned thought him a waste of time because he was no longer a working horse and begrudged the time he needed to spend on him, but Parson Pimm had seen the likes of Ned Meadows come and go at the Home Farm. Ned dare not treat him badly for fear of the master; the horses were more valuable to the master than any stable boy, and he wouldn't tolerate any laxity or shoddy work at the Home Farm.

Major Durcan, or Lord Durcan as he'd become upon the death of his father; was fair to his staff, if not overly generous, but all had their board and lodge at the Home Farm; wood for the fire and cider aplenty.

The master would still spend time with him when he came to the stables, though it was many years since he'd ridden him. He'd check his teeth and lift his legs before patting his nose and passing on. Parson Pimm knew why. The mistress was the apple of the master's eye and he would never allow harm to come her way.

A thousand feet below them stretched the Severn Vale with its patchwork of woods and pastureland. To their right, hidden by the wooded hills lay Stroud, and to their left beyond Smallpox Hill, the market town of Dursley. Before them the Severn shone like a splash of Mercury, and beyond that, the Black Mountains of South Wales were a misty blue in the summer sunshine. It was a beautiful place, the air cloudy with the scent of summer grass and alive with the swoop and chatter of birds. It was like standing on the very edge of the world.

'Do you see it Parson Pimm?' she asked, patting his neck. She shielded her eyes from the glare of the sun as she sought the tiny red brick building that for some months had been the focus of many daydreams, some hardly befitting a young lady of good character. She knew they were wicked, but they were delicious too, and they set her whole body a-tingle.

'You can't really see it, I know that, but it's just a hundred yards from the church and you can see the smoke from the chimney.'

If Parson Pimm had any interest in smoking chimneys, he made precious little attempt to show it and carried on grazing.

'Oh, you're so boring,' she said in disgust; 'you're no fun at all. I shall have father sell you to the gypsies as soon as we get home, and that'll jolly well teach you a lesson.'

The escarpment from Uley Bury to Coaley Peak, was one of their favourite rides for once they had climbed the steep hill from the village, the path was level and the views breathtaking. On beautiful days such as this - with her duties done for the day - she and the Parson would ride for miles, coming home happy and tired in the early evening.

She was a competent horsewoman but could never match her father, or even her brother's skill in the saddle, for Parson Pimm wouldn't move fast if his life depended upon it. Whenever she rode another horse, he'd sulk terribly and simply refuse to look her way, so when she rode the estate with her father, she had to wait outside the stable until another horse was brought to her.

Her father was Major Richard Durcan of the Royal Gloucester Hussars. A distinguished cavalryman and soldier; he'd resigned his commission upon the death of his father to run the estate in general and the Home Farm in particular. His inheritance included the rambling 16th century Oxtalls Hall, some eighteen-thousand acres of farmland, many farms, thirty odd barns, innumerable cottages, three mills and a church. The Home Farm was about a quarter mile above and to the rear of the Hall which stood half way up the flank of a narrow valley, some two miles distant from the village of Uley. Besides Parson Pimm and the working animals, Richard Durcan kept many hunters that he used for the hunt and to transport him about the estate. Despite her mother's best efforts to turn her into a lady, Polly remained a tomboy, happier helping with the haymaking and the harvest than with the needlework and music that were Elizabeth Durcan's greatest joys.

She turned Parson Pimm downhill toward Frocester some two miles distant. She always walked him down the hill for it was steep in places, and anyway - the grassy banks were ablaze with the wild flowers she loved to collect and take home. Elizabeth Durcan took some small comfort from that.

Richard Durcan learnt to manage the estate the hard way as most men do. Unlike his father, who'd been a content and rather bumbling man, his son didn't suffer fools gladly and within a matter of two seasons had turned the estates fortunes upon its head, with no endeavour allowed to continue unless it showed a profit. Several tenants, deemed to have allowed their farms to run down, were sent packing and new tenants installed. Rent, the old man had either ignored or forgotten, fell immediately due.

Few of his tenants or domestic staff thought the change of pace was for the better and the new master was finding it difficult to gain the respect his father enjoyed, until a different side to his nature showed itself one day.

The village cooper was a man called Ted Rowland. One day, Rowland was hale and hearty, making and mending his barrels, and the next he was stone cold dead. With four children to raise and no way to feed them, it seemed the workhouse beckoned Mrs Rowland and her brood.

'That poor woman - she must be beside herself - can't you let her stay on in the cottage Richard,' asked his wife.

'Where will the new cooper work, Elizabeth; he needs the forge and the river nearby? I like it no more than you, but it has to be.'

'Well, you must do something! If those poor children go to the workhouse, I shall never forgive myself.'

'But what can I do? I can't bring the fellow back now can I, and therein lies the problem.'

'Well what would your father have done?' she said.

'My father was his own worst enemy.'

'Oh, do you think so Richard?' she replied with just a hint of sarcasm.

That afternoon he rode the hunter to Ted Rowland's tiny cottage and gave his condolences to Mrs Rowland, but confirmed she must move out as soon as possible after the funeral. However, there was a small cottage in the village she might like to take rent-free, if she had a mind to do so. Furthermore, she would receive a small pension of eight shillings weekly until such time as the children were working.

He left Mrs Rowland in floods of tears and was grateful to be on his way with his duty done, but by the time he reached the Hall, he felt very much at ease with the world. In the months that followed, he noticed village folk addressing him as "Mr. Richard" just as they had addressed his father as "Mr. William". Richard Durcan concluded that his father might not have been such a fool after all.

At Frocester, Polly rode to Coaley, along narrow lanes that twisted and turned through the patchwork landscape. It was a long and straggling road that would eventually take her home to Uley. The route climbed gently to the high saddle of land between the Bury and the Long Down. From there, she would descend once more into the Uley valley and home. They called the narrow saddle of rich green pastureland, "The Moors".

If they were lucky, they would spot one of the Great Western Railway Company's trains at Frocester for the road passed over the Gloucester - Bristol line near the station. She had been on a train several times, for she had an aunt in Northumberland whom they had occasion to visit from time to time, and she found it tremendously exciting to watch the countryside flash by at such speed.

She had been just six when she saw a train for the first time and watched open mouthed as the great thundering engine came into view. The engineer was leaning from his cab, his cap, black and shiny through years of grease and coal dust, his hand working the valves that throttled the steam and reversed the enormous cylinders. Polly stood enthralled, as the engine finally came to rest just feet from them with an ear-piercing squeal of brakes and the whistle and hiss of steam venting from cylinders and valves. The fireman, his face black with coal dust, stood on the footplate between the engine and tender, ready to jump down as they stopped. He smiled at Polly and nodded respectfully to her father, both equally amused to see her open-mouthed astonishment. The sharp tang of coal gas bit her tongue and she was wary of the jets of steam and dripping water that seemed to escape from every pore of the iron monster.

As she passed through the village, she became increasingly anxious about her plan. What could her excuse be this time? She decided to blame Parson Pimm - yet again - and practiced her speech until it sounded plausible. It would never do to let them think she was calling deliberately - that would be too embarrassing. She decided upon a hint of irritation in her tone, when explaining the unexpected delay to her journey. At last, she reached the tiny red brick smithy and could hear the clang, clang, clang of hammer upon anvil.

It was hot in the early afternoon sunshine and she told herself that that was why she felt so flustered. She slipped from the saddle and led Parson Pimm to a tether on the wall. With a deep breath, she opened the wooden gate and with the air of a busy young lady, much irritated by inconvenient events beyond her control, strode through.

'Eh up Isaac, it must be Saturday,' said John Smith with a smile. 'Here's Miss Polly come to see us again.'

CHAPTER 11

The Blacksmith Shop

'And to what do we owe this pleasure Miss Polly,' asked the blacksmith good-humouredly?

Polly stood framed in the doorway of the Smithy dressed in her summer frock though it was still only May. She had long fair hair, with a natural curl that toppled over her shoulders like a waterfall. She was small and petite, with a clear complexion, and if God had given her a fault, it was that her eyes were a little too big for such a delicate face. For all that, they were her best feature, for they were alive with warmth and mischief. It was impossible to take your eyes from them while she was speaking, for they spoke too. She wore a pretty bonnet to shield her eyes from the sun, and within its wide brim, she'd woven wild flowers in a tiny posy.

'I'm really sorry Mr Smith, but I'm sure Parson Pimm has a stone in his shoe, and as I was passing I thought... '

'What again!' replied the blacksmith in astonishment.

She gave him her deeply offended look. 'Well, it doesn't matter if you're too busy,' she replied, 'I'll just have to walk home that's all... even though it's four miles... And I'm sure Parson Pimm won't go lame, even though he's very, very old!' she added for good measure.

The Blacksmith chuckled and said, 'Perish the thought he'll end up in the knackers' yard on my account, Miss Polly! We don't want him turning up here in a pot of glue now do we?'

'I don't think that's very funny Mr Smith,' she said indignantly.

'No, nor I, Miss Polly, nor I,' he replied, still chuckling to himself... 'Now do you want me to take a look at the Parson, or would you rather it were Isaac?'

'I think it might be best if you went, Mr Smith,' she said, forgetting his unkindness now she seemed to be getting her way. 'Father says that no one in the whole county knows more about horses than you do! He said...'

John Smith smiled again; 'I'm sure your father said no such thing, Miss Polly and it ain't true anyway, but my respects to him nonetheless. Now then...! I'll take a look if you'd be good enough to keep your eye on young Isaac and make sure his jaw don't drop no further whilst I'm gone.'

She looked at Isaac and smiled and he smiled back - albeit a little self consciously - for he wasn't dressed to receive guests, especially not pretty ones.

There was an embarrassing moment of silence until she remarked. 'You're sweating an awful lot!'

Isaac returned his gate-pin to the forge. 'The fire's hot,' he replied.

She didn't mind the way he looked; in fact, she liked it. He was tall, better than six feet tall, and some eight inches taller than her, with dark brown hair tied behind his head in a ponytail. He was stripped to the waist, for the day was hot, as well as the hearth. Every muscle of his chest and arms glistened with sweat, whilst here and there it had formed tiny droplets that picked trails through the soot and grime.

'Perhaps you shouldn't use so much coke... I mean it's really, really hot today!'

'John don't buy it to keep me warm,' he replied with a smile, 'the forge is fer heating the metal... no other reason.'

He was embarrassed by her comments, for though a handsome young man, Isaac Smith was shy and awkward with people he didn't know well - particularly pretty ones.

'Is it always such dirty work - being a Blacksmith?'

'Not always, but if it's a big job like today and you've got to stir the fire a bit, you get a lot of fly ash. It's just the way of things; it'll wash off readily enough.'

'Well I'm sure you don't need as much heat as that,' she said confidently. 'John Long has a forge at the Home Farm and that hardly glows at all.'

'It needs to be hot to soften the metal,' said Isaac patiently, 'Its heavy going if the metals cold - hard going too - that's just the way of it.'

'Papa says mén are for hard work and horses are for heavy work. I think you should use less coke and get a horse, then all you'd have to do is keep an eye on him!'

'A black-smithing horse, now there's a thing,' said Isaac with a smile, 'And one who's going to finish this gate-pin for me too?' It's a nice idea, but I don't think I've met a horse that's quite that clever!'

'Oh yes you have!'

'Have I ...? Who?'

'Parson Pimm!'

Isaac laughed, clearly unconvinced. He was about to tell her what he thought of the notion, when she cut him off before he had spoken his first word on the subject.

'Don't you dare be unkind to Parson Pimm,' she said with mock indignation, whilst flirting with him in every way she knew how, 'He's very, very clever and much cleverer than you!'

'Oh, is he now,' replied Isaac with a smile, determined to challenge her on the matter. 'And how do you work that one out, may I ask?'

'That's easy,' she retorted, 'you're working on a Saturday afternoon, all sweaty and covered in soot, and he's enjoying a walk in the sunshine with me!'

He looked at her as pretty as a picture in her summer dress; its bodice cut low enough to reveal the swell of her breasts; her eyes shining with the pleasure of their nonsense. She stood closer to him than was truly necessary or comfortable, and suddenly he began to see her point.

'So in this Blacksmith's shop of yours,' he continued, 'which I would like to see very much...! Parson Pimm will be making his own shoes, then shoe himself into the bargain - is that right?'

'Well perhaps I might give him a little help with the back ones,' she replied with a giggle.

~

John Smith knew the Parson well and shod him regularly. He'd been her father's horse in his day, but Richard Durcan preferred a more headstrong animal and had passed him down to the children because of his excellent temperament. Both children had learnt to ride on him, but it was Polly who had fallen in love with him, and no one else had ridden him since to the best of John Smith's knowledge.

He lifted each shoe in turn, felt his joints for swelling and led him about in a circle, but there was nothing amiss. He was amused to see the small bunches of flowers tied in the Parsons mane.

From his pocket, he took a lump of sugar, beloved of blacksmiths and horses alike and laid it on the palm of his hand. Parson Pimm took it eagerly.

He heard the laughter from the Smithy and secretly applauded her guile, for it was not everyone who could reach young Isaac quite so quickly. He was a shy lad, despite his good looks.

71

'We're a pair of daft un's together you and I,' he said to Parson Pimm, stroking his neck gently. 'I think we've both got our work cut out with that young lady.'

~

'There you are Miss Polly.'

'Is he all right Mr Smith?' she asked with a look of concern as he walked through the Smithy door.

'Never better, Miss Polly - rock in his hoof as big as your fist; I can't imagine how you missed it! He'll gallop all the way home, an' thee'll need to hang on to that pretty bonnet of your'n, all the way.'

'Thank you, Mr Smith, you've been very kind. Do I owe you anything?'

'No, no, nothing to pay miss Polly, you just drop by anytime; were always pleased to see you, ain't we Isaac?'

Isaac smiled but said nothing. He didn't want to encourage John Smith in any way whatsoever.

'Well… I'll say goodbye… goodbye Mr Smith; goodbye Isaac,' She gave Isaac a particularly warm smile.

'Goodbye Miss Polly,' they replied in unison.

'Don't forget Isaac, will you?' she said over her shoulder.

'No, I won't,' he replied.

'Don't forget what?' asked John when he heard the clip clop of the Parson on the road.

'The Fair… she's hoping to be May Queen.'

'Is she now? Well if they pick the May Queen for 'er sauce, she'll win hands down!' he replied, whilst pumping the bellows with the treadle board.

'What's that supposed to mean?'

'The only lame thing about the Parson was that cock and bull story of hers,' he replied.

'Perhaps he was tired?'

'You've a lot to learn about women, Isaac,' replied the Blacksmith, taking his work to the anvil and picking up his hammer; 'horses too,' he added for good measure.

'She's supposed to be the prettiest,' Isaac continued.

'Who is?'

'The May Queen! The May Queen's supposed to be the prettiest girl in the village.'

'Well she'll win on that score an all,' said John Smith, confidently. 'She's prettier each time we see her! And that's quite often,' he added for good measure.

Isaac did not rise to the bait.

'No harm in her having a fancy fer thee lad, just don't get any foolish notions!'

'What's that supposed to mean?'

'You know exactly what it means,' he replied, choosing a pair of tongs from the row of hooks. 'Her father's got more change in his pocket than thee'll see in a lifetime, an' like it or not, his daughter's not for the likes of you!'

'I'm as good as any other man!'

'Better I should say,' said John looking up from his work and resting his hammer on the anvil. 'You know how to do an honest days' work Isaac, and that's more than I'd say for most of the gentry; but how old is she now, Fifteen... Sixteen... an' you're twenty-three...! Young girls get all kinds of silly notions at that age, its nature's way, but you mark my words... like it or not... one day some young Sir Jasper'll come along with a hanky in one pocket, an a bag of silver in the other and whisk her off to the altar before you can say "Jack Robinson," and that'll be the end of you lad!'

Isaac gave a snort of annoyance, 'I was just passing the time of day and so was she; you're making something out of nothing.'

'Aye, I'm sure I am... an you must think I'm as daft as you, if you can't see what's going on in that young lady's head! She's wine Isaac, and thee be vinegar, and the sooner you realise that, the sooner thee'll find a good woman of yer own kind, t' keep thee warm at night!

Isaac took up his pin once more and set about shaping its tang. He made a point of not looking John's way.

'And another thing!' continued John Smith with a chuckle.

'What now!' replied Isaac sharply, more than a little annoyed with the old man.

'Thee wants' to win the greasy pole this year, stead of coming a poor bloody third like last year!'

'Why?'

'So thee gets a kiss from the May Queen. That's one of her jobs if I'm not mistaken… kiss all the winners an' hand out the prizes! I can see that going down well with both of you.'

Isaac set about his gate-pin with totally unnecessary vigour. He chose to ignore John who was chuckling away to himself as he worked. He could be really irritating sometimes.

CHAPTER 12

Uley Fair

Polly couldn't believe how people could be so unkind! Everyone had said she would be May Queen that year - everyone - but they'd chosen Elle Newley instead. It was so unfair!

Elle wasn't even the second prettiest girl in the village, let alone the first, and she wasn't even pretty at all, unless you liked greasy hair.

To make things worse, Papa was presenting Elle with her bouquet and that silly crown. Why hadn't he insisted on Polly being May Queen, he knew she had her heart set on it and no one would have dared say no! She hated him and all the other judges too! What did those silly old fossils know about beauty anyway? All her best-laid plans were now in ruins thanks to them.

In her plan - once thought so foolproof - she would be crowned Queen of the May and the object of her secret affections, one Isaac Smith, blacksmith of the village of Coaley, would win the greasy pole, for no one else was anywhere near as handsome. The vagaries of balancing upon a slippery pole whilst being beaten senseless with a bag of straw, was a technicality she saw no need to concern herself with.

Her plan was based on the long tradition that when each prizewinner claimed their purse, they claimed a kiss from the Queen of the May. Usually it was little more than a peck on the cheek, but that was a matter entirely at the discretion of the May Queen, and in Isaac's case, she planned a far more lingering reward for his skill and courage. It would be a special kiss, a wonderful kiss, as tender a kiss, as there had ever been between a man and woman.

When their lips met, her touch would cast a spell, just like in the penny romances. Nana Dilly gave her the cheap periodicals - without mother's knowledge of course - and she read them eagerly by candlelight, imagining herself to be the heroine of each enthralling story. She would conceal them from prying eyes beneath the mattress of her bed and read them again and again. Though the characters changed each month, the plot was always the same. A beautiful young girl - not unlike herself - would, after many adventures - be saved from the clutches of a dastardly roué by her handsome champion, and in the final chapter they would kiss, as Polly and Isaac would kiss, then fall deeply in love.

Her plan - the plan that now lay in ruins - had been contrived because she had the most terrible crush on the young Blacksmith, whilst he didn't really seem to notice she existed. Perhaps he thought she was too young, even though she was nearly sixteen, or perhaps it was because of Papa, or perhaps the unthinkable... perhaps he thought her ugly!

Just recently, she'd had spots that Nana Dilly helped her conceal with zinc cream and she would never be very tall. She wished so much that she could be taller for Isaac's lips must be at least a foot above hers.

She tried so hard to be noticed but no matter how many times Parson Pimm picked up a stone, he never seemed to take the hint! The winners kiss was her best chance to make him notice her, but she had to wonder how anyone could be so slow to take a hint, and be quite such a numbskull!

Polly wanted so much to be in love. No, that was not true - she wanted so much to be loved and that is different. She didn't want to be loved as Mama and Papa, or dear Parson Pimm loved her, but as a man loves a woman - in that wonderful, beautiful, heart-stopping, frightening way.

They were not sexual, these thoughts, for in truth she had little knowledge of such matters beyond the knowledge that men and women were different; but she did have feelings that came to her in her dreams. In the morning, she would remember little except their delicious wickedness. The exploration of her body that followed made her feel wonderful but terribly guilty. She couldn't tell anyone about it of course, for she knew that only her own body did such things and others might not understand.

There was another worry too. Polly had never kissed anyone as they did in the penny romances, but she was sure she knew how. After all, she had practiced for hours, kissing her mirror, kissing her hand and even kissing Parson Pimm.

But now, alas, all those dreams lay in ruins. There would be no kiss, no touching hands, no falling in love.

She turned away in disappointment, pretending not to notice Elle Newley, who was looking her way with a triumphal smile. Instead, she made her way down the gently sloping meadow toward the stream where the river events were in full swing.

She found herself between the stalls of cakes and pickles, wines and jams, wheels of fortune, coconut shies' and hoopla's. There were stalls selling candyfloss and toffee apples and even a man selling ice cream. Everyone was enjoying themselves tremendously, and it was such a jolly time.

'Did you know Elle Newley is May Queen, Polly?' said the girl called Primrose Farmer.

'Oh, is she!' replied Polly with seeming indifference; 'I didn't notice.'

'Everyone was sure it was going to be you this year - everyone ...!'

'Oh, I'm so pleased it wasn't, Primrose; I'm sure I would have just died of embarrassment. I mean we are nearly sixteen now and it's so babyish to be May Queen don't you think? I expect you thought the same.'

'Yes, yes I did, it's very silly isn't it!'

Only two contestants remained in the greasy pole contest. Isaac Smith and a farm labourer called Jack Smart. All others had been eliminated by the two men who sat facing one another on a trestle above a bed of straw. Smart was a big chap, as tall as Isaac, but heavier, and Smart had been champion for five successive years.

Jack Smart could survive full body blows from an opponent's sack without losing his balance and that was difficult to do, for the pole was both round and slippery. On the other hand, when Smart swung his own bag of hay, he did so with such strength and speed that almost no one had managed to stay aloft and if Smart managed a second strike, following on the first, then there was little chance of surviving a tumble.

But Jack Smart was wary of Isaac. He had barely beaten him in last year's quarterfinals and Isaac had that look about him.

'You're going to be knocked into moon's orbit, Smithy!' he said menacingly. 'Best check you got no loose change in your pockets.'

Isaac smiled. 'I'll have two and six in me pocket when we're done Jack; I'll make such an ass of you, you'll wish you'd gone fer the jam making.'

'Yeah, yeah - prepare to meet your maker, Smithy!'

'Get on we' it!' came a chorus of cries from the expectant crowd.

'Aye get on we' it,' repeated the Master of Ceremonies, Tom Baldoodle, 'lest I call a draw and disqualify the pair of 'e fer windiness. Now then - when I drops this handkerchief... we wants t see some action!'

No sooner had the hanky left his hand than Jack's bag came Isaac's way with the speed of an express train and it would have all been over there and then, had not Isaac lain back horizontal along the pole as the bag flashed by overhead. Isaac parried the next onslaught with a swing of his own and so the battle began.

Isaac got in two good strikes, but it was as though he'd struck a brick wall. In the mean time, Smart's blows were unbalancing Isaac.

Isaac noticed, however, that John had been right about Jack Smart. When he saw a haymaker coming his way, he would tilt towards the blow with equal inertia. That was why his bag hit a brick wall every time.

Isaac gauged his chance and threw a mighty swing at Jack's shoulders, but at the very last moment, he drew the bag back sharply towards himself. Smart did just as Isaac had hoped and tilted towards the blow that wasn't there. Before he knew it, he was toppling sideways; holding on with nothing more than his legs, but Isaac's follow through was there in an instant. Jack Smart fell the six feet to the straw with a thud and a cheer from the crowd of onlookers. Backs were slapped and coins changed hands. Isaac punched the air with his hand and people clapped and cheered.

A bedraggled Jack Smart struggled to his knees and dragged Isaac from his perch. Isaac balled his fist ready to give Jack a thumping if that was how he wanted to play it, but instead, Smart raised Isaac arm in the air with great good humour.

'Tell you the truth, Smithy; I'm rather pleased you won! That was becoming hard work.'

'Well you'll be able to concentrate on your jam making next year like I said,' replied Isaac, and both men laughed as they clambered out of the straw.

The contest had been much enjoyed by everyone, with appreciative applause and cries of "Well-done lads". No one was more pleased with the outcome than John Smith, who leaned over and muttered; "He did well" in his wife's ear. She nodded and smiled in reply.

'That'll be thruppence you owe me, Ted,' he declared to a man in a check shirt. The thruppence was duly pressed into John Smith's palm.

'There's a dash of the gentleman about thee, Ted,' John continued with a mischievous smile, pocketing the coin as he did so; 'I'll ave' a beer on thee we' that!'

'Dash of the bloody fool more like,' his companion replied. 'Young Jack should ave' beaten your lad easy, don't know what 'e were thinking about!'

'Ah well there 'tis see! Thee might ave' the dash of a gentleman about thee Ted, but thee ain't never going t' be a clever one - an' that's a friend speaking! Young Jack's got the brawn right enough, but Isaac got the brains see! That's why Jack lost an' thee be thruppence the poorer. Brains Ted - 'tis all down to brains in the end!'

'Well I might not ave' many brains John, but I don't want what I've got addled by listening to any more of thy bloody nonsense, so I'll bid thee good day.' With that, he turned on his heel, whilst John Smith chuckled to himself and nudged his wife, 'I reckon that's upset un' - parting we' that thruppence!'

'It's your going on as upset un! You're all as bad as one another you men - just like overgrown kids, the lot of you!' John chuckled again but said no more.

He watched the two young men enjoying their moment; two strapping chaps as strong as oxen, through hard work and long hours. It seemed like only yesterday that Isaac had come into their lives - a shy young boy of seven years of age. He passed the Smithy every day on his way to school and took to stopping by on his way home, fascinated by the flying sparks and the sound of hammer on metal. He loved the rhythmic ding, ding, dunk; ding, ding, dunk; as John struck the hot metal, bending and twisting it at his will.

At first, he watched from the gate, peering between the slats, or swinging on the spar, but as time went on, he ventured closer, standing quietly in the doorway.

'Mind the sparks.' said John as he tried to answer the myriad of questions the small boy put to him. Soon 'Mr. Smith' became 'Uncle John' without either of them really noticing, and John began to look forward to the boy calling in with yet more questions about every subject under the sun. What John didn't know he made up, and so to Isaac, "Uncle John" became the font of all knowledge and wisdom.

John let him do small tasks in the forge like pumping the bellows, feeding the pony, and filling the quenching tank with water. He spent his Saturdays at the forge and John gave him a penny or two for his help. To the young boy, the blacksmith was a hero, and the smithy a place of wonderment. He would go home to his parents and say Uncle John said this, or Uncle John said that, and his parents would shake their heads in disbelief and try to tell him that John was pulling his leg as usual, and there were no Pelicans roosting in the church tower, and anyway you don't have herds of Pelicans; but Isaac would hear none of it for John Smith had told him about the Pelicans and so it must be true.

'All your nonsense'll get you into trouble one of these days; you wait and see,' said Amy. 'Filling that lads head full of such rubbish. No good'll come of it. He'll end up as addled as you,' she declared.

It was on one of those rare days when Isaac didn't call by, that the sad news came. Isaac's father, Jack Dimmery, died suddenly; a heart weakness of many years had suddenly given way.

John didn't see Isaac again until well after his father's funeral; then one afternoon, both he and his mother appeared in the smithy doorway. She looked old and tired and had clearly been crying.

79

'I'm sorry to trouble you, Mr Smith, but Isaac was insistent. There's something he wants to tell you - you be sure to thank Mr Smith for all his kindness Isaac.' and with that she walked back to the road, clearly upset.

'We got t' go to Tewksbury,' he blurted out.

'Tewksbury... What you got to go there for?' asked John. He led him to a seat outside the Smithy door where they often sat and talked.

'We got to move... t' my aunt's... my mum says she can't stay ere' no more 'cus of my dad.'

'Well Tewksbury's a fine town Isaac - or so I understand. You'll soon fit in and make new friends, and it'll be home afore you know it.'

Tears brimmed over the small boy's eyes as he sobbed, 'I don't want to go t' Tewksbury, I wants' t' stay yer.'

John put his arm about the boy's shoulders and gave him a hug. 'Now, now,' he said gently, as Isaac buried his face in his chest. His heart went out to the lonely little boy who had become his young friend.

'Look Isaac I got summat t' say to yer,' he said, when Isaac's sobbing stopped a little. 'An' I want you t' listen to yer Uncle John; 'cus 'tis important.'

Isaac wiped his tears with the backs of his hands.

'Things don't look good at the moment Isaac, I know that, an it'll be difficult fer thee to understand what I'm going t' say t' thee now, but The Lord has different job's fer us all t' do in this life, an' we don't never know what that job'll be till we d' get un... Now e's given thee thy first job and 'tis an important one fer one so young. Do you know what that job is?'

Isaac shook his head.

'Well, he knows thee be only eight; but 'e' want thee to look after thy mother now father's gone, an' be brave fer 'er sake. Twill upset 'er to see thee crying for this'll be difficult times fer 'er lad, very difficult times.'

Isaac did his best to wipe his eyes and nose on his sleeve. 'But why do we ave' to go to Tewksbury Uncle John, why can't I look after 'er yer?'

'Well sometimes when one thing changes, other things change too! You remember when we went down the hammer-mill fer the new shovel - you remember that don't you - an' we watched the swans on the millpond fer a while?'

Isaac nodded.

80

'Well they was a pair wasn't they — always together! Where one went, tother went too 'cus they cared fer one another. Trouble is Isaac - when summut bad appens' to one swan - tother ones lost and don't know what to do! That's like your mum, see Isaac, She's all alone now on that big pond an' she's missing yer father. We're all like swans when it comes down to!'

'But I can look after er yer, Uncle John, really I can; why can't I look after her yer?'

'Well twill be difficult fer you to make up fer yer pa, all on yer own Isaac, she needs her family about her see - I can understand that. It's sad for thee lad I know, but thee've got t' be brave fer mother's sake. Thee'll be brave for her won't thee?'

The small boy nodded and was quiet for a moment.

'Uncle John,' he said, trying his best to master his tears, 'Can I come an' see you… when I'm older?'

'Why course you can,' he replied, 'you come anytime you want! Look I got something for thee to take to Tewksbury.'

With a spike, he prized a rusty horseshoe from the lintel above the door.

'There that's a lucky one that is; that's the luckiest one I got, an' I'll tell thee something else too… When thee gets older - just thee come back an' be my prentice, how about that?'

'Oh, can I really… a real prentice?' said Isaac, with a joy that cut through his tears.

'Course you can lad, course you can. Now you take care of that horseshoe, and make sure the legs hang down or the luck don't work.'

With a smile and a heavy heart, John watched the little boy walk away clutching his rusty horseshoe and it was the hardest thing he'd done in his life. It was to be more than a year before John heard of Isaac again.

"Dear Mr and Mrs Smith", the letter began…

"I am very sad to tell you that my sister Lottie passed away three weeks ago. The doctor said it was pneumonia, but I don't think she ever really got over the loss of Jack. I'm sorry I haven't written sooner, but it has been a very difficult time for me.

Isaac is becoming very difficult. I just can't seem to get through to him and he won't do anything to help at all. I am very sorry about it for the boy's sake; he's lost his father and now his mother, but I simply can't cope with him with my own health being what it is. I've found him a place at the orphanage in Tewksbury and I feel sure he will be much happier there with children of his own age.

I know you were friendly with Lottie and Jack and I hope you will pass on the sad news of her passing to anyone who may have known her.

Yours, sincerely

Ivy Trollop."

They spoke very little that evening. John sat staring at the fire, the letter from Ivy Trollop in his lap. Amy sat opposite him, knitting by the light of a candle; the crackle of wood upon the fire and the rhythmic clicking of knitting needles, the only sounds to break the silence.

The fire burnt low and the room became cold.

'Shall I put another log on?' he asked his wife suddenly.

'Not for me dear - its past eight thirty! I'll be finished soon then I'll go on up… you stay if you want to.'

John shook his head, 'I'm ready fer bed.' He picked up the letter and folded it carefully, putting it back in the envelope in which it was delivered.

'It's such a shame,' she remarked, 'he was such a nice boy, always so polite!'

John nodded.

She glanced up at her husband, but he'd returned to staring at the fire.

'I know it's upset you, John,' she said quietly, 'but these things happen… Ivy was much older than Lottie as I recall, and must be well into her sixties… It's a lot to cope with if she's in poor health.'

'E' weren't no trouble Amy, not a bit.' John replied! 'E's just lost is mother an' father an' what 'e needs now is a bit of kindness - he'll find precious little of that in the workhouse.'

'She said it was an orphanage,'

'Same bloody thing!'

They fell silent again until Amy cast off. She put her knitting beside her chair and got to her feet,

'I'll go on up now, you won't forget the back door!'

He shook his head in reply. She rested her hand on her husband's shoulder and he put his hand on hers, squeezing it gently.

'I know it's sad for him John;' she said softly, 'but it's really not your problem. I'm sure Ivy's doing what she thinks is best!'

'It upsets me to think of him put away in a place like that Amy,' said John, looking up at her. 'Tis a terrible place... fer anyone - let alone an eight year old child! They'll beat un' black an' blue fer slightest thing and it just breaks my heart.'

The old lady sighed and gripped his hand the tighter.

'Then sometimes we have to do what's in our hearts John and let the ifs' and but's take care of themselves. If your heart is telling you to do something, then you must do it, for if you don't, you'll never forgive yourself!'

'What about you,' he replied, 'tis a lot to ask.'

'We'll manage dear, just as we always have.'

John reached out with his hand again and she squeezed it gently. No more words were necessary, not after forty years.

'You won't forget the back door!'

'No,' he replied, 'I shan't forget.'

He listened to the stairs creak beneath her weight, then the mantle clock striking a quarter to the hour. He closed his eyes and said the Lord's prayer, as he had done every day of his life, then he gave thanks for Amy and their life together, and asked that the Lord might guide his hand. With those jobs done, he locked the door and followed his wife to bed.

Next morning he walked the two miles to Coaley Junction, then caught the milk train to Gloucester where he changed for Tewksbury and Evesham.

The orphanage was a workhouse, just as he'd feared; a gloomy building three storey's high, of dark echoing corridors, barred windows, and the smell of carbolic soap. Within its walls lived the old, the poor, and the feeble minded. It was a grim place of harshness and brutality, for the poor were not to be encouraged to burden themselves upon the parish.

John stood, as bidden by the master, in the main hallway, which struck off to right and left, and seemed to have no end.

Inmates walked by, or stopped and stared. All were dressed in the same drab garb, some guiding the less able.

After some minutes, the master re-appeared at the very far end of the corridor, Isaac by his side. When Isaac saw him, he cried out 'Uncle John!'

83

John opened his arms and the boy began to run. 'Uncle John, Uncle John, Uncle John,' he cried, his feet echoing hollowly as he raced along the corridor.

He did not stop running until he ran into the blacksmith's arms and there he sobbed his heart out. It was all John Smith could do to hold back his own tears.

'They took my 'orseshoe, Uncle John,' he sobbed, 'they took my lucky 'orseshoe!'

'Did they now, well that's cus' they wanted the luck t'would bring lad, but a good lucky orseshoe like that one'll only work fer them's as rightful owns it, an' it don't stop working just cus' someone takes un away. It still kept working fer thee even though they took it, an' it told me to come an collect 'e and take thee back to the smithy so as thee can be my prentice.'

'A real prentice; can I really be a prentice - I don't I ave' ter' stay yer no more?'

'No lad, you won't never ave' to come yer no more, I promise thee that; now you shake the Masters hand an say thank you fer looking after thee, an we'll be on our way.'

They walked through the orphanage to the dormitory where Isaac had his bed for Isaac would not leave John Smith's side for a single moment.

As he gathered his few belongings, John said to the Master, 'Twas just a rusty horseshoe, Mr Peat, where was the harm in that?'

'Rules are rules Mr Smith. We have over three hundred of the destitute, the infirm, orphans like Isaac and the feeble minded. We have to have rules to keep order, for where would we be without them!'

'Oh, thee'd be completely buggered, I should reckon,' John replied.

'There is no need for vulgarity Mr Smith. We do the best we can on the parish purse; it is difficult enough I assure you. You'll need to sign for him before you leave; your full name and address, please - if such a rule is not too much to ask!'

The forms completed, John took the boy's hand.

'Let's go home son,' he said softly, 'let's go home!'

Polly reached the pole fighting just in time to see Isaac win and watched as he and Jack Smart made their way to the podium for the prize giving. Both were laughing and in high spirits; Polly tried to catch his eye, but he didn't notice her.

The prizes were presented by Major Durcan, Polly's father, who congratulated both men and made a silly joke about scarecrows, for both men had straw in their hair. They proudly collected their prizes; "two and six" and a flagon of cider for Isaac, and a shilling for Jack.

Polly looked on in dismay, as Elle Newley kissed Jack Smart, then Isaac, with far more enthusiasm than was either necessary or decent. Elle seemed to cling to Isaac forever, with very little resistance on his part. Polly was consumed with jealousy and vowed to hate Elle Newley for ever, and ever, and perhaps even longer than that.

'There you are child!' said a familiar voice. 'I quite thought the gypsies had carried you away!' Polly heart sank as her mother approached.

Elizabeth Durcan was a handsome and elegant woman of forty-two. She was as dark as her daughter was fair and was expensively and tastefully dressed in a buttoned frock that did full justice to her slender waist and full bosom. She wore a wide brimmed hat that perfectly complimented her dress.

'I was just watching the prize giving Mama,' she explained needlessly.

'So I see, but its nearly two-o-clock child and we're at luncheon with the Berkeley's at two… or did you forget?'

Polly's face said it all.

'That's quite unforgivable Polly, it really is! When friends - particularly important friends - are kind enough to seek your company, it is common courtesy to be on time. I shall have a word with Nana Dilly… I'm afraid she has left some woeful gaps in your education.'

'I'm sorry Mama!'

'Hmmph,' she replied; trying to remain stern for the purpose of pressing her point; 'Sorry butters no parsnips with me, young lady - turn about!'

Polly turned her back to her mother who ran her fingers through her hair to straighten those few strands that had fallen out of place. 'You really are a scatterbrain,' she added for good measure.

Unlike her mother whose hair had a natural curl - Polly's fell straight to her shoulders and then her waist, whilst that which would have fallen forward had been gathered back by a pretty bow of blue silk.

'There,' she said, pleased with the effect; 'if that doesn't make young Freddy's eyes pop out of his head, I don't know what will.'

Polly turned to her mother absolutely aghast.

'Mother…' she replied in disbelief, 'why on earth should I care what Freddy Berkeley thinks?'

'Because Freddy Berkeley is the most eligible bachelor in Gloucestershire, that's why!'

'Well I don't want to get married; especially not to Freddy Berkeley.'

'Not now perhaps;' replied her mother, studying her daughter and thinking how quickly she had blossomed from a duckling, into a very beautiful young lady; 'but soon... very soon, you will, and if you have an iota of sense, you will snap up Freddy Berkeley before someone else does!'

'I couldn't possibly marry him,' she replied, absolutely horror-struck; 'he lisps!'

'When you are about to inherit the Berkeley Estate child, you can have as many speech impediments as you like.'

She took her daughter's arm and they made their way to a small enclosure where the Berkeley's were already seated.

'Would you have married Papa if he lisped?'

'Absolutely!'

'And was starting to go bald?'

'I adore bald men!'

'What if he were a hunchback?'

'Well he'd never leave me child, would he!'

A tall slim man, immaculate in morning suit and top hat got up as they entered the enclosure. He was handsome in his way with a small, waxed moustache and bright smiling eyes. Beside him sat his wife, and to her left, looking a little uncomfortable, their son Freddy Berkeley.

The tall man smiled warmly at Polly and held out both hands.

'My look at you, how you've blossomed,' he said with obvious admiration and sincerity. 'Who would have thought it? She does you great credit Elizabeth.'

'Why thank-you Jonathan, say thank-you Polly!'

'Thank-you Mr Berkeley.'

'What say you, Freddy?' he continued.

'Yes, father,' said Freddy dutifully; looking up at Polly with a sheepish smile.

86

Polly thought Freddy terribly amusing, he seemed so petrified of her these days. They'd played together for hours as children; by the river and on their pony's; but now they had grown up she could barely prise a word from him, but she was flattered that he stared at her so much. He clearly couldn't take his eyes from her when he thought she wasn't looking.

She gave Freddy one of her most dazzling smiles and was delighted to see him go as crimson as his jacket. He was very sweet, but she could never think of Freddy in a romantic way, despite mother's attempts at matchmaking. However, she had to admit that he was passably good looking for such a soppy thing and his wonderful Hussar's uniform made him positively handsome.

Just then, her father appeared as if from nowhere saying hello to the Berkeleys and taking his seat near his wife. 'How's the army, Freddy?'

'Everything is going well Sir,' Freddy replied, 'I'm through Sandhurst now and awaiting my posting to Natal.'

'Good man, watch out for the sun,' he replied light-heartedly. 'Sun, Tigers and Boers in that order... all bloody dangerous!'

'We were just commenting on what a beautiful young lady Polly has turned out to be Richard,' said Mary Berkeley.

'Did you ever see prettier?' he replied proudly.

'But wasn't Polly to be Queen of the May this year; I'm sure you mentioned it?'

'Ah…yes... there were difficulties,' he replied carefully.

'Oh…?' replied Mary intrigued.

'I wouldn't allow it,' said Elizabeth Durcan, matter-of-factly.

'Mother!' said Polly in astonishment.

'Well, life isn't all about you, Polly,' replied Elizabeth rather tartly. 'Sometimes we need to take a back seat with these village issues. These people either work for your father or live in one of his cottages and they must have quite enough of the Durcan family by day's end. The least we can do is let them choose their own May Queen.'

'But everyone wanted me to be May Queen!' said Polly, quite hurt by her mother's interference.

'I think you will find "everyone" was mostly your father!'

Richard Durcan sneaked a glance at Jonathan Berkeley and raised his eyes to heaven before putting his arm about his daughter and giving her a hug. 'You'll always be my Queen of the May,' he said, 'and we won't take any notice of the wicked witch, not a jot!'

'Do you ever Richard,' replied Elizabeth Durcan in her most suffering tone.

'Well Polly,' said Mary Berkeley in an attempt to make light of the whole affair, 'that girl who's Queen in your stead... um...'

'Elle Newley...' interjected Freddy helpfully...'she's the Undertaker's daughter.'

'Yes Mr Newley's daughter,' continued Mary; 'she's a lovely girl as all can see, but frankly Polly, true beauty is about... and dare I say it? pedigree!'

'There you are Freddy,' said Richard Durcan with a chuckle; 'breeding's what it's all about! You've seen it on the home farm and now you've heard it from your mother.'

'Don't be so vulgar Richard,' replied Mary Berkeley.

'Now you see the flaw in your argument Mary,' added Elizabeth with a disapproving glance at her husband, 'and I'm afraid Polly's following in her father's footsteps. That's exactly why we're sending her to St Agnes.'

'Mother!' said Polly once more.

'Well don't pretend it comes as a shock Polly, we've spoken about it often enough! Poor Nana Dilly has done her best but quite frankly...'

'I want to stay here and help Papa with the farm...'

'Oh, don't be so ridiculous child - ladies don't do pigs! When you marry, a wife's job is to run the household and bring up a family - in that order! Mary and I have never done a day's work in our lives, yet the house would stop tomorrow without us, isn't that so Mary? One of these day's young lady, you'll have to run your own home and quite frankly; where will you start! The servants will run circles about you, you're so soft hearted; whilst your poor husband - God help him - will be so embarrassed by your lack of accomplishments that he'll have to keep you under lock and key like poor Mr Rochester, lest you shame the whole family.'

'Oh, that's not fair Elizabeth; Polly sings very sweetly; very sweetly indeed,' said Jonathan Berkeley, kindly.

'Well her voice is pretty enough I grant you, but tell me what else? Her spelling and grammar are atrocious, she cannot sew to save her life and if dear

Mr Sullivan heard her playing HMS Pinafore's overture on the pianoforte - as I have - I'm sure he'd rather go down with his ship, than suffer it ever again! No, I'm afraid that much though we shall miss you - and we shall miss you my darling,' she said, turning to Polly and placing a hand on her arm, 'I'm afraid three years at St Agnes is the very minimum you will require.'

'They are starting the tug 'o' war,' said Freddy; bored with so much talk about Polly, 'perhaps it would be fun to watch?'

'Oh yes,' said Polly enthusiastically.

A noisy crowd had gathered at the stream lower down in the meadow and most people were making their way in that direction.

'Why don't you young ones go,' said Mary Berkeley; 'I'm sure we would all prefer to stay here now we're settled.'

Freddy and Polly set off for the tug 'o' war, both heartily relieved to have found an excuse to leave. Polly insisted that Freddy take her arm and was delighted to see him flush once more.

'They make an attractive pair Elizabeth,' said Mary Berkeley.

'Yes they do Mary, but Polly is still just a child at heart. I don't think she's given any thought to such things...'

'There's plenty of time. Freddy has Natal anyway, best not to push these things!'

'Quite so,' said Elizabeth.

'Thank you for saving me Freddy,' said Polly when out of earshot.

'Humph! For saving us, you mean.'

'Yes they were awful weren't they; especially my mother, it must be awful to be so old and grumpy!'

'Ghastly!'

'Appalling!'

'No, worse... beastly!'

'Worse still... gruesome!'

'I don't think I would call your mother gruesome Polly, she's very beautiful!'

'How dare you say that about my mother when you've never, ever, said anything in the least bit complimentary about me!'

'I… I meant that… When I…'

'I know exactly what you meant! I shan't talk to you again or even think of forgiving you unless you buy me an ice-cream!'

A stuttering and flustered Freddy marched off in the direction of the ice cream cart with Polly in pursuit.

'Hello Freddy,' said the tallest young man of a group of other young gentlemen, all similarly dressed in Hussars' uniform; 'what's the rush?'

'Oh hello Charlie,' replied Freddy, not too pleased to have bumped into them at that precise moment, 'nothing really…'

'Introduce us to your companion then old chap,' he said, looking admiringly at Polly.

'Umm… this is Polly Durcan, Major Durcan's daughter; Polly this is Charlie and Archie Dickinson and Ernest; Ernie Tomlinson, they're um… friends…'

Polly smiled and shook hands with them all.

'You've been keeping her quiet Freddy… can't say I blame you,' continued the tall young man; 'didn't realise you were walking out with anyone, did we chaps?'

'I'm not; were just friends,' Freddy replied awkwardly.

'Well we're friends Freddy, but you never walk arm in arm with me now do you,' said Charlie to the amusement of the others?

Polly squeezed Freddy's arm even tighter. 'Freddy has been a dear friend ever since we were very small, and we will walk arm in arm whenever we please, so don't you dare be unkind to him!'

'Wouldn't dream of it,' replied Charlie with a smile.

'Perish the thought,' said Archie Dickenson with a mock frown. 'Freddy Berkeley! Best chap in the regiment; everyone says it - isn't that right Ernie?'

'Hear it all the time,' replied Ernie Tomlinson; 'we're off to see the tug 'o' war; why don't you join us Polly and bring that fine chap and absolute toff; Freddy Berkeley with you!'

They all laughed and Freddy glowered; 'Come on Freddy,' Tomlinson chided, 'don't be so bloody miserable; share Polly out a bit. Just think of it from her point of view old man! All afternoon spent with you! She'll be bored to tears in half an hour! Father owns this; father owns that! It'll all be mine when I bump him off!'

'I wish you'd all just buzz off, 'said Freddy in disgust.

'Not a chance old chap, lead on Freddy… to the ice cream cart!'

'Is Freddy buying?' said Ernie.

'Of course he is,' said Charlie.

'Best fellow in the regiment, just like I said!'

'Absolutely!'

'Definitely!'

They made their way to the ice cream cart, where several other friends joined them, many with young ladies on their arm. Inevitably, the conversation changed to military matters - the Boers in particular and the empire in general - subjects which Polly neither understood, nor had any interest in. It all sounded so pointless and so very far away. In the general chitchat, she slipped away among the throng of people, to the ford where two tug-o-war teams were taking their positions on either bank.

The water there was little more than eighteen inches deep and was a favourite bathing spot for village children and cattle alike. Close by the ford was an ancient clapper bridge and people were taking turns to cross over from one side to the other. It was such a jolly day - everyone smiling and dressed in their Sunday best.

The tug 'o' war teams were in high spirits; many men dressed like pantomime dames in their wife's old clothing; their elaborate ensembles completed with the most outrageous hats, wigs and make up.

The Coaley team were called the Crows, and the rivalry between the teams had its roots in years of skulduggery and tradition that helped make Uley Fair the best social event of the year.

One of those not in fancy dress was Isaac, for it was not his way to make a fool of himself, but for all that, he was fiercely competitive and through his success on the slippery pole had earnt his place at the front of the team. It was the place all young men sought, for no one in living memory had ever taken that position and survived five rounds without a ducking, and everyone wanted to be first.

The teams were settling in as Polly crossed the bridge; digging little ruts in the grassy banks to lodge their heels in. Isaac spotted Polly as she crossed over and smiled; she smiled back in turn. At least he had smiled.

She found a place on the far bank where there were less people. Nearby, a willow's leafy tendrils dipped into the gently flowing water to drift downstream like fishermen's lines. Most fairgoers watched from the nearside bank, for the stalls and other amusements were confined to the meadow where she had so recently escaped from Freddy and his chums.

The umpire stood in the centre of the bridge, and to Polly's disgust, Elly Newly stood by him, her posy at the ready.

'Now then gentlemen… and ladies;' he added diplomatically; 'let's get started! I want a fair contest; any of last year's shenanigans and I shall be giving out forfeits.' He said this to a roaring chorus of cheers, and boo's, and laughter, for the crowd knew well what he meant by that.

'I shall count to three then the Queen of the May - the lovely Miss Elle yer — will toss er posy in the water an off thee d' go. If I see that knot move, afore er posy hits the water, 'tis forfeit time. When someone ends up in the brook… that's a win! Tis best of five but any gentleman… or lady, as gets is feet wet is out, an' a reserve comes in fer next pull at the back of the team. Four reserves in total gentleman; that's the rules an' you make sure you stick by um'; Take the strain now… on the count of three, One… Two… Three!'

Elle threw her posy into the air and as it hit the water, the two teams began to pull, roaring like bulls as they did so.

The red marker that hovered above the river, barely moved for over a minute as both teams strained at the rope, pulling for all they were worth. Then at a pre agreed signal, the Uley team let go all so briefly. The sudden slackening of the rope was enough to upset the balance of the Coaley team and especially the third man back. He lost his footing and slithered forward into the next man taking the poor fellow's legs from under him.

Seizing their advantage, the Uley team gave a massive pull and the rope and everyone attached to it, shot forward by well over a yard. Isaac toppled helplessly on the very edge of the river and had no alternative but to let go the rope. Almost at the same moment the man behind Isaac, hit him fully in the back and catapulted him through the air to dive head first into the river, his arms and legs flailing. He hit the water with a mighty splash and a cheer of delight went up from the Uley supporters.

Isaac went into the water head first, his head hitting a stone the size of an ostrich egg. He hit it so hard that he blacked out and sank to the river bottom. Most people thought he was fooling, to stay so long beneath the water, but after many seconds had passed and he'd neither surfaced nor stirred, alarm set in. The chap behind Isaac, who'd pushed him forward, jumped into the water and waded to where Isaac lay submerged. He reached down and dragged him upright, getting his head out of the water. Isaac's eyes rolled upwards and his rescuer shouted for help. Several others jumped in and together the dragged Isaac to the bank. Coughing and spluttering, he brought up most of the water he'd swallowed and lay on the bank retching.

'You all right?' said one.

'What appened there then lad?' said another.

'He's all right,' said a third. 'Prop the bugger up agin' yonder tree.' Together they dragged him from the bank, beneath the willow tree's trailing branches.

'What happened?' asked Isaac, before relapsing into another fit of retching.

'Thee cost us the bloody pull, that's what appened!' said the man who'd dragged him from the water. 'Fat lot of use thee turned out t' be, Smithy! Anyway - are thee alright?' he added as an afterthought.

'No, I'm bloody not!' came the reply.

'Someone go find Nurse Priday.'

'I'm alright,' said Isaac, 'just leave us alone for a minute an' I'll be as right as rain.'

'You sure?'

'Yes!'

'Someone ought t' stay with thee just in case.'

'I'll stay,' said a small voice.

The man looked up, to see Polly standing behind them under the willow canopy.

'Right you are, Miss Polly, There's an offer we won't refuse. You keep an eye on this silly bugger, an' just holler if e turns funny or owt.'

She promised she would holler at the first sign of funniness and they left their fallen comrade in her care; pleased to go back to the tug o war.

Isaac sat against the bowl of the tree; his eyes shut, his head throbbing. Polly waited for him to say something, but he sat silently; head in hands.

'Are you alright?' she asked finally.

'No.' came the curt reply.

'Oh ...' she said concerned, but upset that he was being so offhand.

He heard it in her voice and instantly regretted being so rude.

'What I meant was … well, what I really meant to say is my head feels like someone's hitting it with a hammer, lots of em!'

'Oh dear,' she replied.

'I'm sorry I was rude…'

'That's okay. Would you like me to take a look?'

He nodded and turned his head toward her, 'But be careful…' he said anxiously.

She knelt close to him and very gently parted his hair to look at the scalp beneath. That alone was painful, but despite his discomfort, Isaac enjoyed her nearness. Her hair had fallen forward as she knelt over him, touching his face. It felt soft as silk and smelt of flowers and fresh air.

When she came to the injury, even the gentleness of her touch was too much and he winced with pain, sucking in his breath through clenched teeth.

'Oh, I'm so sorry,' she said with genuine concern.

'It's okay,' he replied stoically.

'It's difficult to see; perhaps I should be on your far side.'

Isaac leant his head toward her, 'Just come a little closer,' he suggested.

'You're awfully wet,' she remarked, 'Your hair is dripping on my dress!'

'It'll soon dry on a day like today. Think of this as an emergency.'

She knelt even closer and Isaac leant toward her supporting himself with his right arm. She wore a dress with a square bodice and he found himself looking at the swell of her breasts as the bodice fell forward. Her breasts were still quite small, but their softness and shape were beautiful and arousing, the dark edge of a nipple, just visible.

Once again, she touched the injury and pain shot through the broken flesh, but this time Isaac made no sound. He didn't want her to move; he wanted her to stay just as she was. Her closeness was more than any young man could resist and he wanted her to stay as she was forever.

'Well perhaps it is an emergency,' she replied, 'it's a very nasty bump.'

'Is it bleeding?'

'Yes a little… but I don't think it's a bad cut. Perhaps we should get Nurse Priday though - to put a stitch in it?'

94

'No, she'll shave a big patch of hair away and she's as blind as a bat. She'll probably sew my ears together.'

Polly giggled and sat back on her haunches.

'You're not a very brave blacksmith are you, Mr Smith!'

'Pain's not an issue Miss Durcan! I'm as brave as the bravest lion; braver probably, but lions don't like bald patches; they're absolutely known for that and neither do I!'

'Well, Papa says you should never ignore a bump on the head. He said more soldiers were killed falling off horses than were ever killed by the Boers, and all through bumps on the head.'

'Why were they falling off their horses?'

'He didn't actually say, but they must have done it an awful lot! One moment they were being terribly brave - just like you - the next they were as dead as a dodo!'

'So do you think Nurse Priday will prevent my death by stitching my ears together?'

Isaac had made a good point with this simple logic and Polly began to falter a little.

'Well perhaps… perhaps, she will do tests on you!'

'What sort of tests?'

'Well, I don't know - dying tests I suppose! Papa says there are lots of signs - if you know what to look for!'

'Such as?'

Polly racked her brain to recall her father's words.

'Umm… being sick!' she said, thrilled that she had remembered one of them, then said with alarm, 'Oh Isaac you were terribly sick when they dragged you out the river, I was so worried about you — you don't think…?'

'I'd swallowed half the brook; what else was I supposed to do?'

'Oh… yes… well perhaps it's okay when you've swallowed a lot of water - I really don't want you to die …!'

'Thank you,' he said, 'what else?'

She racked her brain once more; 'Seeing things,' she said at last, pleased she had recalled yet another of Papa's checklist. 'And going doolally!'

'Well I've not gone doolally,' he replied.

'You think you're a lion,' she said with a giggle.

'I didn't say I was a lion - I said I was like a lion - that's two different things. I have lion-like disregard for pain and danger - that's what I meant!'

Polly giggled again.

'Mother says all men are quite pathetic when it comes to a little pain; not lion-like at all in fact. She says child birth is definitely the most painful thing and men have no idea about any of that.'

'And how many times has your mother hit her head on a submerged rock?' he inquired.

'Well… none I suppose.'

'There you are then!'

'It's only a little bump Isaac; it's hardly a baby is it?'

'Not now perhaps! But who knows what it will look like in an hour's time. I might be giving birth to a seven pound bump on the head.'

Polly giggled once more; so pleased he'd overcome his shyness with her.

They had been totally forgotten where they sat beneath the willow canopy on the quiet side of the stream. The tug of war was still raging and was the focus of everyone's attention. Polly wanted everything to stay just as it was.

'Wonky sight,' she said at last. 'That's the last one.'

'Wonky sight…?'

'Yes, wonky sight. When you get a tap on the head and you're about to die, your sight goes wonky! Woo-oo, just like that. I'll have to test you; how many fingers can you see,' she said, holding one slender finger in the air.

'None!' he replied.

'Oh…!' she said with alarm, 'none at all?'

He shook his head.

'Well how many can you see now,' she asked with concern, holding up two this time.

'Still none,' he replied.

'Isaac, please don't tease me, it could be serious; I'm… I'm really worried about you - how many do you see now,' she asked, holding up five.

He shook his head, 'None at all.'

'Oh dear… well what do you see then; surely you can see something?'

He looked at her steadily and then spoke sincerely.

'I can only see one thing and everything else is a blur.'

'Oh Isaac, you're frightening me - please tell me what it is you can see?'

He spoke very softly, very earnestly, his eyes never leaving hers. 'You,' he said at last, 'your beautiful eyes, your pretty nose, your lovely face - you're beautiful and I can't stop looking at you!'

Polly gasped, hardly able to believe his words.

'I think you are the most beautiful creature I've ever seen… I expect you think I'm really doolally now?'

She shook her head, 'No… No of course not… I think what you've said is lovely.'

They looked at one another, both wondering if the moment was real, neither wanting to break the spell; both wanting to touch the other; even to kiss, but not daring to do so.

'I've always been such an ugly duckling,' she said at last. 'And I hate being so small! They didn't even want me as May Queen and I was so upset - and now you have said… You do mean it Isaac don't you; you're not just making fun of me?'

He shook his head, never taking his eyes from her.

'Well perhaps you are doolally,' she said, half laughing, half crying.

He smiled too, 'Mad as the Hatter!'

She wanted so much to kiss him; to tell him how much she wanted him to kiss her, but that would be a shameful thing for a young lady to do in such a public place. Whatever would he think of her?

Even in the penny romances… even when the hero and heroine fell deeply in love, they would never kiss until the very last page. Her heart was in turmoil; she couldn't understand why her body told her one thing, whilst her Christian upbringing told her something quite different. It was so very cruel. Her body put her through such agony of emotions and feelings; so wonderful, and yet so frightening all at once. She felt she must be very wicked inside to feel the way she did.

'I think you must be feeling better,' she said in a fluster.

'I am,' he replied.

'Then I am going to declare you cured! I... I think we should go back to the others.'

'Thank you Nurse Polly.'

'Did I save your life,' she said with a smile, her eyes not leaving his.

'Definitely; I was at death's door from the moment I went under the water; It was definitely you who saved me.'

'Goodness, what did I do, you must tell me?'

'I heard your voice!'

'Just my voice! Was that all I had to do?'

Isaac nodded, 'Absolutely.' I heard your voice even though I was under the water; you did call out when I fell in, didn't you?'

'Yes… yes I did; I was so frightened for you.'

'I could have slipped away so easily; I was definitely thinking about it, but I wanted to hear your voice again and that changed my mind.'

Polly was silent for many moments.

'Isaac,' she said at last, 'I know you're being silly, but you did mean some of what you said didn't you; you weren't just being cruel?'

He reached out and took her hand in his and their touch was like electricity. 'With all my heart,' he replied.

'Isaac... can we be friends?' she asked, her eyes moist with emotion.

'Of course!'

'I mean special friends?'

'I don't understand?'

'I want us to be special friends… when we can… sometimes! Perhaps we could go for walks with Parson Pimm. Could we do that - is there a day you don't work?'

'Sundays! We go to communion in the morning but after that…'

'Yes Sundays - after church. We could walk; you can tell me all about blacksmithing and I will tell you about the countryside, and we will watch for rabbits and squirrels.'

'I don't know much about creatures like that, you'll have to teach me.'

'They are fascinating - beautiful like all God's creatures, scurrying about, living busy lives just as we do. I talk to them and they talk to me.'

'What do they say?'

'They say "Hello Polly" and "How are you today Polly" and they tell me I'm welcome in their home and all they ask is that I do them no harm.'

They met that following Sunday after church, upon the Long Down. They held hands and walked, and talked about anything and everything, and time seemed to have wings.

When she could stay no longer, she left, turning to wave every fifty yards or so, but Isaac did not move from the high hill until he could see her and Parson Pimm no more. By some miracle, they didn't kiss that first time, but Isaac held her hand for many moments, their fingers entwined. They promised they would tell no living soul of their friendship, for if no one knew, then no one would try to stop them.

They called it their friendship in those early times, but it was love for all that. Innocent love, for Polly, would go no further than a kiss, but it was love and they both knew it was love and were frightened by it.

It was not a shallow feeling, nor just a wanting that is often confused with love, but a deep feeling within the soul that gave as much pain as it gave joy.

It was a love that grew stronger with every hour they spent together, a love that was treasured - by Polly at least - as a gift from God.

It was a love they would never betray, and a love that was never to betray them, even when death stole it from them like a thief in the night.

This book is the story of their love for one another. It was not always easy as you will discover, but it was a true and unselfish love. It never faltered and never could, for it was unbreakable.

CHAPTER 13

St Agnes

It was a wonderful summer - there had never been better. Every day seemed blessed with sunshine, whilst every Sunday was filled with the happiest of memories. It was the happiest time of Polly's life and she wished it would never end.

She counted the days, as a child divides a holiday into days past and days yet to come, for time ticked relentlessly on and the awful prospect of St Agnes loomed ever closer.

The time remaining for the two young lovers became less with every day that passed. It shrank like the space left in a suitcase; slowly filling with dirty laundry; waiting patiently for the journey home. Each new day was an unwelcome reminder that all happy times must one-day end.

St Agnes, the Northumberland convent and finishing school for young gentlewomen, hung like a dark and menacing cloud upon the horizon. Polly could not bear even the thought of it.

Within its towering, cheerless walls, the young ladies would be taught the essential skills of etiquette and deportment. They would read the classics, study Latin, lay table, sing, learn music, and attend worship three times daily.

Life at St Agnes was strict and simple, for the Nuns believed that to truly know God they must suffer in this world as Jesus had suffered. To want for comfort, however simple, was a weakness and a triumph of temptation over Godliness.

They asked for nothing and expected nothing, but without laughter or joy in their lives, their hearts slowly hardened. St Agnes; at best was to be endured.

Upon the station platform, her baggage already loaded, Polly's mother bid her a tearful farewell whilst father gave her a hug and said cheerily, 'Chin up Polly Pullet; Christmas will soon be upon us and you'll be home before you know it. We will have the most wonderful time with carols and charades, and we'll play "The Parsons Cat".'

Polly was trying to be brave about the whole affair though she felt thoroughly wretched, but she was sixteen now and a young lady. She wanted to prove that she was already a lady and that Mama had made a terrible mistake, but clearly, she had even failed with Papa whom she could usually wrap around her finger.

'That will be lovely Papa; you will look after the Parson for me won't you?'

'Of course I will.'

'He will wonder where I am; he will be terribly upset, I know he will; you must tell him it is all yours and mothers' fault! Ned will take him out and groom him properly won't he?'

'If he knows what's good for him!'

'He doesn't like soft or stony ground nowadays Papa; he feels unsteady; you will tell Ned won't you.'

'Yes I'll tell him; now on to the train, child. The Station Master is closing up and I know you won't want to be left behind.'

Polly leant out the window to kiss her mother.

'We shall miss you darling; she said.'

'I rather think that will be your own fault, Mama,' Polly replied tartly, before relenting and hugging her once more. 'I love you despite your cruelty.'

With a sudden jolt and a hiss of steam, the mighty engine gathered the carriages together and began its onward journey to Gloucester. Polly waved until they were out of sight and then took her seat in the first class carriage opposite a kindly looking gentleman with white whiskers.

He put down his newspaper and asked where she was bound and other polite enquiries one might expect from a friendly companion. She learnt that he was a Bank Manager travelling to Birmingham on business. He was sadly widowed but had a daughter of Polly's age. He promised to look after her when they changed trains in Gloucester, for she too would pass through Birmingham on her journey north.

Polly awoke to the sound of Anna whispering 'Shssh; Polly shssh... Sister Mary will hear you!'

Her head fuzzy with sleep, she opened her eyes, struggling to remember where she was in the darkness.

Anna was her newest and best friend. They shared a dormitory with eight other girls, but their cots were in a small annex off the main room.

'What's wrong; she asked in alarm?'

'Shssh...keep your voice down, who is Isaac?'

'What do you mean?'

'You were talking in your sleep; who is Isaac?'

'He's…he's my Papa,' she said unconvincingly.

'Isaac is NOT your Papa,' said Anna scornfully. 'No lady — no respectable lady anyway - would ever say their father's name in that way! Isaac is your lover and you must tell me all about him at once; this minute!'

Polly was uncertain.

'This very minute', Anna insisted. 'Or I will tell Sister Mary what you said.'

'You wouldn't dare!'

'Yes I would… jealousy makes you do terrible things!'

'If I do, you must never tell another soul!'

'I promise on my life,' she said and without further invitation, pulled back the covers of Polly's bed and slipped in beside her.

'What are you doing,' whispered Polly as Anna pulled the covers over both their heads like a cocoon.

'It's freezing and I must know every single thing about your lover, the mysterious Isaac.'

'We will be in terrible trouble if we're caught, they'll put us in the icebox!'

'Well, we won't be caught if you stop talking so loudly. Just whisper but tell me everything!'

'Well I can't promise everything; some things are very... well...private!'

'Those are the bits I especially want to hear,' said Anna with delicious excitement; 'Is he rich?'

'No.' Polly replied.

'But he will be one day?'

'Oh, I'm sure he will; he's very clever.'

'I didn't mean that silly; I meant does he have an inheritance?'

'No, I don't think so.'

'Then if he's a pauper with no family, he must be a struggling artist, a gentleman who has fallen on hard times. A poet like Shelly or Browning, wonderfully talented, but unable to work because of the beautiful and romantic thoughts that come into his head at almost any moment of the day — thoughts of you — and he must be able to write them down instantly, without delay.

Then he sends them to you in a letter and your heart stops because they are so beautiful.'

Polly giggled.

'Oh, you are making me so cross,' said Anna in an angry whisper, 'you must tell me about him this instant or I swear I shall go mad with jealousy.'

'Well...' began Polly, considering how much she should tell her friend; 'he's not a poet or anything like that; he's a blacksmith.'

Anna gasped in horror and disbelief. All the girls at St Agnes were of upper class families and it was little less than scandalous that they should be romantically involved with someone from the working classes. Anna was quite aghast, but could not deny that Polly's story was fast becoming even more exciting than even her fervent imagination could contrive. Here was a real live Juliet - Polly her dear, dear friend - now she must learn about her Romeo.

'Is he handsome?' she whispered.

'Oh yes; oh Anna I cannot tell you... When he looks at me... I cannot breath, my heart pounds and I feel... I feel that I am stood on nothing at all!'

'Have you kissed him?'

'Yes...'

Anna sucked in her breath in a great gasp; 'What was it like?' she whispered.

'It was wonderful... just wonderful... I always wanted someone of my very own to love, someone handsome, someone wonderful. All the love I have I gave to him when we kissed; I wanted so much to touch his lips, and for his lips to touch mine; I wanted to be in his arms and never ever leave.'

'Oh Polly,' gasped Anna... 'I am so jealous... Please tell me all about him... I must know everything now.'

'He is tall, over six foot tall and I am so tiny against him. I have to stand on tiptoe just to kiss him. He works, stripped to the waist in his smithy and he has the most wonderful body... like a gladiator or a God like Achilles, or Apollo. He is just the most handsome man you have ever seen but Anna... he has cruel, cruel eyes!'

Anna sucked in her breath, 'How cruel?'

'Well perhaps not cruel, but certainly resolute... yes resolute. I don't think you could ever change his mind, and I'm sure he's afraid of absolutely nothing. He ties his hair in a pony tail like a sailor, but when I am with him, I let it loose so I can run my fingers through it when we kiss and then he looks like your romantic poet.'

'Perhaps he really is cruel and wicked! Have you thought of that?'

'Oh no, Anna, it's quite the reverse! For all he's handsome, he's very shy, and it took me just ages to get him to talk to me at all, but now he's my Isaac and we have pledged our love for one another, and it's a true love, I know it is. If he ever stopped loving me, I would die. I am just sure I would die! He talks to me about everything and when he smiles it melts my heart, and oh Anna, when he tells me what is in his heart... when he tells me that he loves me... I want to cry.'

Anna too, felt her eyes begin to fill with tears and she dabbed them on her nightdress.

'Have you... you know; have you...?'

'No!' said Polly aghast, 'no, I could never...'

'But you've wondered?'

'Yes... how could I not?'

'Catherine Hardy says...'

'Shssh!'

'What's the matter?'

'Shssh!'

The two girls lay still as the grave as footsteps approached. They could see the thin light of a candle through the linen of the bed sheet and kept very, very still.

For some moments, there was complete silence as the candle hovered over them. Then the covers were whisked back and Sister Mary stood looking down upon them, her face etched with horror and disbelief.

'What is the meaning of this?' she hissed.

The girls said nothing.

'Anna Thompson, I might have known!'

'We were just talking, Sister Mary,' said Anna.

'Of what?'

'Of vespers,' said one, 'Of Easter,' said the other in unison.

104

'So… Not only do you behave in this most disgraceful fashion, but you are liars too!'

The two girls said nothing, fearing the worst.

'For this disgraceful behaviour, you will both go to the cloisters, just as you are, this very instant, and you, Anna… in the morning you will receive six strokes across your hands; perhaps it may teach you to think before you act; out, out both of you!'

'But Sister Mary,' began Polly, 'Anna… '

'And you will receive three strokes!' snapped Sister Mary. 'Off with you!'

Polly had never been so cold in all her life. The cell in the cloister was bare but for a stone writing tablet and stone seat upon which lay a thin rush mat. Here, in different cells, they would spend the next 24 hours clad only in their nightdresses. The day would be spent in prayer and written repentance under the watchful eye of Sister Mary. There were no doors to their cells, but there did not need to be. All St Agnes was their prison for two years to come. Their prayers — had Sister Mary, but known it — were that they might pass as quickly as possible.

CHAPTER 14

The Smallpox Hospital

Isaac sat astride the bole of a fallen tree, from where he could see for miles in every direction, for the Long Down was long, narrow, and fell steeply on either flank. An emerald saddle of wild bracken gave way to rugged grazing land on its lower slopes, which levelled to a patchwork of gentle pastures beyond.

It was impossible to approach the Long Down without being noticed. By this means, the young lovers had kept their romance a secret for more than a year without a single soul knowing of their friendship.

Since St Agnes, they had seen less of one another, but come the holidays, the train brought her back to him and they met at every possible opportunity. It was Easter and they were to meet on Sunday after the family had taken communion at the parish church, but she was late and Isaac began to worry.

He'd been waiting for two long hours when he saw her at last. He stood and waved and she waved back.

She jumped from Parson Pimm when the going became too steep for him, leaving him to follow at his own pace. She scrabbled up the steep slope made slippery by grass and fallen bracken; whilst Isaac scrambled down to meet her.

He held her in his arms and they kissed until they were breathless from kissing.

'I couldn't get away,' she gasped. 'Papa had guests for lunch and I was so worried, and I thought you would think I had forgotten, and it was just awful!'

They walked hand in hand along the spine of the hill, talking of everything that had happened since last they met. She told him of St Agnes and how much she hated its harshness and Sister Mary. She told him of Anna; of how precious their friendship had become in that cold and dreary place and how their friendship at least made it bearable. They were so engrossed in one another that they failed to notice the changing weather.

'It looks as though there's a storm brewing,' said Isaac eventually.

Polly looked west to the darkening sky; 'Do you think it will come to anything?'

'It's been unsettled these last few days; we must be due a storm.'

'It's turned cold now; I hadn't noticed; perhaps we should go.'

'You'll not get home in time; look where it's coming from.'

It was indeed heading their way from the direction Polly and the Parson would need to take.

'Let's shelter under those trees,' said Polly, pointing to a small copse, 'perhaps it will pass over.'

Instead the clouds grew ever darker, the air heavy and thunderous. What had been a blustery wind, quickly turned to a storm that buffeted the bracken, dashing it this way and that, carrying the first drops of rain upon its wings.

They took shelter beneath a huge oak, the soil beneath it bare, the ground uneven with the hooves of cattle.

Polly held her cheek against the horse's nose and stroked him gently, for he seemed fidgety and agitated.

The rain clouds drew ever closer, dark and menacing. The sky turned from ashen grey to black, and rain, heavy and cold, lashed down upon the moors, drenching the earth and all that stood upon it.

For some minutes, the leafy canopy held back the storm like a mighty umbrella, but the rain continued unabated, bearing down the outer branches with its ferocity until they all but touched the ground. Soon, heavy droplets began to fall through the lower branches and their fragile shelter was no more. Slowly their hair and clothes became wet, whilst water, cold and uncomfortable, trickled between their shoulder blades.

Suddenly, not a mile from them, the air was split apart by a thunderbolt that stabbed the earth, shaking the ground with its ferocity. The flash was followed by a clap of thunder that had the Parson snorting and stamping his feet. Isaac reached out for his halter to help Polly, for the old horse was clearly distressed.

'He hates thunder,' she shouted above the storm, 'he gets so frightened.'

'It'll pass soon; we'll just hold on to him, don't worry,' said Isaac, far from convinced by his own words.

Sheets of rain blew across the moor like spindrift on an angry sea. Suddenly, another thunderbolt struck the earth then another and another, each illuminating the granite sky with its eerie, flickering light.

Parson Pimm was terrified, shaking his head so hard that they could barely hold him; his eyes were wild with fear; he snorted the air and began to turn in circles.

'Whoa there boy, whoa there,' said Isaac. Polly stroked his ears and whispered reassurances.

A bolt of lightning hit a nearby tree and they watched in horror as a massive branch split away from the main trunk and fell crashing to the ground.

Parson Pimm reared up and nearly struck Polly with his hooves, 'We can't stay here,' said Isaac, 'it's too dangerous, it could be our turn next. We need to get into open ground; quickly, quickly, come on, Parson, come on boy ...'

They trotted the horse out into the open field and were instantly drenched to the skin, their clothes sticking to them wet and cold, their boots filling with water. The Parson was even more alarmed than he'd been beneath the oak and it was all they could do to hold him. Isaac took off his shirt and tied it about the Parsons eyes. Isaac could see that Polly too, had been shaken by the nearness of their escape.

'We must find shelter; let's go to the hospital,' said Isaac.

'Oh no Isaac - not there!'

'We can't stay here Polly,' he said, shouting to be heard above the storm. 'Look at the sky; this isn't going to let up. We need to find shelter or the Parson will hurt himself.'

They took him to the ruin as quickly as they could. It stood on top of a small hill, known as Smallpox Hill, for it had been an isolation hospital in years past, but a fire had ended its service and now it stood derelict and abandoned. Flames, forty feet high, had swept through the wards on that fateful day, reducing them to ashes. Only the administration block, the stables and a few blackened walls now remained. The stables were used by a local farmer as a fodder barn, but no one else ventured near, for the fear of Smallpox lived on in the minds of many, no matter how unreasonably.

They reached the courtyard where torrents of rain cascaded from roofs that had long since lost their gutters. The cobbles beneath their feet ran like a river; silver raindrops dancing from them like fairy ballerinas, leaping into the air from whence they came.

Isaac pushed against a door that had once been the grand entrance to the offices and nurses dormitory. It opened on creaking hinges, its padlock, long since wrenched away by some curious intruder.

Before him, was a long oak panelled hall, with a wide staircase leading to the floor above. There was little light in the vast hall, but what he could see was covered in the dust of time and the droppings of birds that nested in the vaulted ceiling. Rain spilled through a shattered window, by which the birds had made their entry.

He led the Parson through the door, as yet another thunderbolt crashed to earth nearby. Every muscle of the horse's body seemed to be a-tremble. Polly forced herself to enter the dark and gloomy place for his sake.

'At least we're out of this weather,' Isaac said lightly, trying his best to lift her spirits. He opened the first door he found, which opened onto a large and once splendid room, with a high, ornate ceiling. The windows were tall, with heavy stone mullions, but unlike the hall, the windows were unbroken.

It had clearly been the main office, for there were roll top desks, bookshelves, cupboards, a typewriter, and on the wall, a duty roster bearing the names of the doctors on duty that fateful day.

There were two swivel chairs; a long counter with a brass bell, and two long leather couches. Dominating the far wall was a huge stone fireplace, and about its hearth, a beautiful wrought iron surround, some ten feet wide by four deep, with a narrow leather seat about its top. Here and there, tufts of horsehair poked from cracks in the faded red leather.

The hearth was full of twigs and sticks that had fallen down the chimney, the work of industrious crows. The pile of twigs spilled across the grate, through the bars of the fire seat and into the main room.

The room was dark and dusty, but it was dry and largely untouched by time and the lesser fortunes of the hall.

'Do come into the waiting room madam,' said Isaac holding the door wide for Polly and Parson Pimm. 'The doctor will see you shortly... is this your husband?'

'Thank you kindly Sir,' she replied with a smile, pleased that this room was dry at least. 'Yes Parson Pimm is my husband and a man of the cloth, so no bad language please.'

'Excuse me for asking madam, but isn't he a horse?'

'Yes he is,' she said with a giggle, 'and would I be right in thinking that you are a drowned rat!'

Isaac laughed and said, 'Did you say a rat... in no manner whatsoever madam! I assure you — and your good husband — that you are in the presence of a gentleman!'

'I shall be the judge of that sir,' she replied reaching up on tiptoe and kissing his lips; 'but there is no denying you saved us from the storm. It was very frightening and you were... well you were so very gallant!'

'Thank you,' he replied, 'but surely this must prove beyond all doubt that I am the gentleman I claim to be,' He kissed her in return noticing how the cloth of her dress clung tightly to her breasts.

'Perhaps, but Mama says that no man can ever be trusted! All murderers are men and all men are murderers... she's always says that.'

'Your mother is very astute,' he said, in a sinister tone befitting the gloom of the room, 'who knows what fate will befall you here in my den.'

'Is this to be my fate then,' she said as she brushed rain droplets from his hair; her lips parted, wanting him to kiss her once more; 'Am I lost!'

'Perhaps... we shall see!'

'How can I save myself, what must I do? I am helpless against you; you are so strong, so powerful; should I scream?'

'Scream all you like,' said Isaac darkly, 'for no-one will hear you here! We are alone upon the moors and only your kisses can save you now.'

'Then that is what I must do, I must kiss you like this... and this... until you cannot bear the thought of murdering me.'

'I feel it working,' he replied, 'all thoughts of murder have completely gone!'

'The kisses are having an effect upon me too,' she cooed; 'I feel myself falling in love with you despite your cruel wickedness.'

They stood in each other's arms as a pool of water spread about them; their hair hanging in rat-tails, their sodden clothes clinging to them like dishcloths, but their discomfort meant nothing.

Another flash of lightning split the sky and illuminated the room with an eerie blue light. Parson Pimm began to tremble once more, nodding his head and snorting in alarm.

Polly rushed to him, putting her arms about him, speaking to him softly. 'Let's get him in the corner Isaac, away from the windows; maybe it will calm him.'

Isaac readjusted the shirt about his eyes, and dashed to the fodder barn for several sheaves of hay; the torrential rain soaked him once more. He spread the sheaves for the horse and Parson Pimm lay down gratefully, looking quite woebegone, his flanks trembling.

Polly knelt beside him, stroking him, talking to him, soothing him, concerned at how cold and frightened he was.

'Polly, look what I've found,' said Isaac excitedly. In his hand, he brandished a box of matches.

'Where on earth did you find them,' she replied in disbelief.

'In this drawer,' he said triumphantly. 'There's pencils, paper clips, rubber bands, all sorts.'

'Surely they won't be any good, not after all these years?'

'There's only one way to find out!'

He took a match and struck it on the edge of the box but only succeeded in scuffing the sandpaper. He tried another which fizzed a little before it petered out. The ninth match burst into flame and he immediately held it to a piece of paper, catching the corner. He whooped in excitement, 'Pass more paper Polly, I think this might work.'

Polly brought all she could find; faded menus, doctors reports, a notice about lights out.

Isaac gave her the burning paper. 'Keep it going whatever you do,' he exclaimed.

He dragged the twigs and straw from the grate, scraping out the ancient cinders and ash. He placed a burning page there, and placed some twigs upon it. They too, burst into flame and he added more and more and more. Soon he had a roaring fire, the flames bathing the room in an orange glow and leaping up the chimney in a crackling, sparking inferno. The warmth from their fire was wonderful, just wonderful.

Isaac lifted Polly across the surround and sat her with her feet among the twigs. He dragged one of the huge couches over to the fire, just behind the surround. 'It's a big room,' he explained, 'and we don't have that many twigs; it will throw the warmth back at us, I hope.'

She smiled at him gratefully, wringing the wetness from her hair and tipping the water from her sodden riding boots.

Outside the storm raged unabated; rain dashed itself against the leaded windows and bolts of lightning split the blackened sky. Somewhere above them, a loose window squealed on its hinges, occasionally crashing shut with a loud bang. A piece of rusty corrugated iron tore itself loose from the fodder barn and sailed across the courtyard cobbles; clattering and shrieking as it went. The sky was as black as night and the room would have been in darkness but for the fires glow.

Isaac clambered over the surround and sat gratefully with his palms to the fire. He was shivering from head to foot, having given up his shirt and endured a second drenching when collecting Parson Pimm's bedding.

Polly praised him for his gallantry, 'You always know what to do, she said, 'you are my knight in shining armour, my very own Sir Lancelot!'

'I couldn't possibly leave a beautiful maiden in distress,' he replied, 'even one who mistakes me for a rat and believes me to be a murderer!'

'Well, anyone can make a mistake,' she said unsympathetically, 'and murderers are masters of disguise — everyone knows that. For all I know, you've been waiting for just this moment to entice me into your lair and take advantage of me.'

'If this were my lair,' he said through chattering teeth, 'I'd have some dry clothes in the wardrobe.'

This thought seemed to make his mind up on some matter he'd been considering and standing up, he removed his boots, socks and breeches.

'Isaac, what are you doing,' said Polly in alarm.

'We can't stay in these wet clothes Polly; we'll both get a chill. We can dry our clothes in front of the fire and if I build it up, we'll be as warm as toast.'

Polly watched in disbelief as he unbuttoned his sodden underwear. 'Look away if you want to,' he said as he let his underpants fall to the floor. He picked them up and wrung the water from them before draping them over the surround with his socks and breeches.

She tried to look away as any lady should, but gave up on a lost cause. He stood in the firelight, bathed in light and shadow; his body bronzed by the blacksmiths hearth and muscled by the anvil. He pulled the gather from his hair, which fell to his shoulders, dark brown and sleek with the rain. He wrung it out as best he could, passing his fingers through his hair as he sat again upon the cushioned surround.

Polly looked at his body in fascination. She'd never seen a man naked before, except for marble statues and her brother Richard when they shared a bath as children, but that hardly counted. She decided his body was as ugly in its hidden places as it was beautiful elsewhere. She was frightened, curious, fascinated and shocked all at once.

'Your turn,' he said simply.

'Isaac I can't,' she replied, even though her own cloying, sodden clothes were chilling her to the marrow. Even though in her heart, she wanted him to see her, and wanted him to want her and touch her.

'What if someone were to come?'

'Who will come?'

'Papa may send men to find me, what if they find us here?'

'He doesn't know we meet on the moors; why should he look for you here? He'll think you've taken shelter in someone's cottage whilst the storm blows itself out. Why should he be concerned?'

There was truth in what he said and it would be a long, long journey home in wet clothing. She could not even think of taking poor Parson Pimm out into the storm once more, but to be here, alone and naked with him… It was the stuff of every fantasy, of every private touch, of every moral quandary. There were so many reasons to say no, so many reasons to say yes, so much to be afraid of, so very much to want.

Outside their ruined shelter, sheets of rain swept the moors; the loose window continued its squealing, crashing protest. The sky became darker than night and the thunderstorm continued unabated.

Steam began to rise from Isaac's clothing; he turned each over in turn. 'They'll be dry in an hour,' he said teasing her.

Wet, cold and uncomfortable; Polly made up her mind. After a deep breath, she said, 'Isaac, close your eyes!'

'What for,' he replied.

'Please close your eyes and don't you dare peep. If you peep, you'll have to go out in the hall and sit in bird poo!'

'It will be worth it!'

'Please Isaac!'

He groaned and shut his eyes.

'You must look away too, so you can't cheat,' she added!

Isaac sighed and turned his head to face the wall.

Satisfied Polly took off her clothes one by one, wringing each item out and hanging them over the surround with his. Satisfied, she arranged her hair to cover her breasts; her hands she placed carefully in her lap; 'You may open your eyes now,' she said primly.

Isaac opened his eyes and laughed. 'How long are you going to sit like that,' he asked, 'like a stuffed parrot?'

'Until my feathers are dry!'

'You look like lady Godiva!'

'And you look like Peeping Tom the Tailor, and you will go blind just as he did, and jolly well serves you right.'

Isaac laughed. He made a big thing of turning his clothes again, but he watched her secretly from the corner of his eye. She was as beautiful as he knew she would be. He wanted her so very much.

They talked of everything under the sun except their nakedness. They talked of St Agnes, where Polly must return in six precious days and it depressed them both.

'We will remember this time in years to come!' Isaac said, trying to lighten her mood.

'I'll remember all our times together, not just this one.'

'And what will you remember most?'

'How much I love you,' she replied, 'how frightened I am sometimes!'

'Frightened?'

'Of losing you,' she whispered. 'I shall go back there soon, to that awful place... It's so far... such a long time...'

'It only makes us stronger Polly, it cannot harm us. No amount of time can do that.'

'It can Isaac, I know it can... all this secrecy and hiding. It is like water wearing away a stone. One day we will be found out, or you will tire of me, then I don't know what I will do. I only know I will die if I lose you.'

'This is silly talk Polly, I think about you every day, every moment of every day; this is just silly talk. I could never forget you, never stop loving you.'

'Why...? Why should you love me when...?'

'Stop it Polly, stop tormenting yourself,' he said, moving next to her, wiping the tears from her cheeks.

'I love you,' he said softly; 'I love you with all my heart.' She looked up at him for a moment, reaching out for his hand, her eyes full of tears and the turmoil she felt inside. A great social divide separated them, one of which they

114

never spoke. It was a divide which history had so often proved was more powerful than love alone. He was a handsome man and could take any young woman for his bride except her. Her privilege had become their curse. She wanted his love, but as man and wife, honest and pure and with God's blessing. She knew that was impossible.

Another demon gnawed at her emotions. It was her other wanting, a physical wanting, her forbidden wanting. It took only his touch, or the nearness of him to wake the wanting from its slumber; it took only the sound of his voice.

'Polly;' he whispered softly, wiping her tears with his finger tips.

'I'm sorry,' she said, forcing a smile; 'I'm being very silly.'

Isaac smiled back; a reassuring smile he hoped.

'I want it to be forever,' she said, 'but I know it can't.'

He lifted her chin once more and bending over, kissed her tenderly on the lips.

'It will be,' he whispered, 'I promise you it will. There are problems I know, but none we cannot overcome.'

'You would never abandon me, would you?'

'Polly…' he began, taking a deep breath, 'I can only tell you how I feel. There have been others; you know that and I regret that now; but for a year, the only thing I have thought about, both night and day, is you. When you are at St Agnes, I'm like a clock, mindlessly ticking away the time until I can strike the hour and be with you again. You know when people wed and make a promise… a promise to love one another forever, no matter what… we can make that promise Polly; we don't need a church or a priest if that is truly in our hearts.'

'Then promise me and I will promise you!' she whispered through her tears.

He made his promise and she repeated it word for word. It was a simple promise to love one another and be true to one another forever.

'Love me…' she whispered.

'Polly …'

'Love me my darling; please love me, for I cannot last another moment without you.'

He lifted her in his arms and laid her on the huge couch, its leather now warmed by the fire and as comforting as the womb. He lay beside her, their bodies touching; he kissed her tenderly and she him. They kissed as they had never dared kiss before, and she felt her heart thumping within her bosom.

He put his hand upon her breast, cupping it in his palm, feeling its silken warmth, kissing it gently then more urgently. Her body trembled as though with an electric shock. They kissed and caressed one another, their wanting becoming ever more urgent, until Polly took him and guided him inside.

He heard her whimper and cry out as she gave herself to him. They made love for the first time, gently at first; then more urgently and there was nothing more precious in the entire universe than the love they shared. When the moment came, they lay together, still as one; she cried in his arms and he let her cry.

'You're trembling,' she said at last.

I know but I don't know why... I've never felt this way before.'

'Is it for me?'

'Yes it's for you; there is no one in the world but you, there never will be again.'

'Please tell me you love me,' she said through her tears.

'I love you with all my heart, Polly Durcan,' he said sincerely.

'And you will never forsake me?'

'Where would I go?' he said simply.

They lay there for a long time; their bodies close and warmed by the fire. Outside, the electric storm had passed over and the sky was brighter. The rain persisted but was less strident than before. Soon, reluctantly, they would leave the ruined hospital and each would make their way home as though nothing had happened; but something had happened and it was irreversible. A link had been forged, far stronger than steel and nothing earthly could break it, for it was precious, and pure, and belonged to them. They had found something very rare and their lives would never - could never - be the same again.

CHAPTER 15

Nana Dilly

Mrs. Hudson closed the wardrobe door with a heavy heart. Even after so many years, the air within was heady with the scent of the camphor wood from which it was so lovingly made. Behind the doors and below the hanging space were several drawers. She had checked the top drawer again today, as with every other day, but the linen towels were just as before. None had been used.

'Oh, Miss Polly,' she whispered softly, her voice a tremble, 'whatever has happened to you; whatever shall we do…?'

Mrs. Hudson; better known as Nana Dilly, had known Polly since she was a baby and had helped the doctor at her birth. Polly was as much a part of Nana's life, as her own children.

She had anguished for weeks about telling Mistress Elizabeth of her worries, but now there seemed little choice and her concern gave her the resolve she needed.

She made her way along the landing, descending the grand staircase to the hall below. Rufus and Satan watched her from where they lounged before the fire, sullen and unfriendly. She gave the two huge brutes a wide berth and carried on to the corridor that led to her mistress's day room. It was a cheerful, south facing room, flooded with light from dawn till dusk. Elizabeth Durcan sat as usual in her favourite spot near the window, a particularly fine piece of linen across her lap, a needle and thread in her hand.

'Is something wrong, Mrs Hudson,' she said, when she saw the housekeeper's concerned expression?

'I'm sorry, Ma'am, but it's about Miss Polly.'

Elizabeth Durcan had seen her daughter ride off on Parson Pimm not an hour before, as happy as a sand-boy and could only imagine that she might have fallen from the Parson, as unlikely as that sounded.

'Has she taken a tumble?'

'Oh no, Ma'am, nothing like that, I wish it were!'

'Perhaps you should tell me Nana!'

'It may be nothing Ma'am, but I couldn't keep it to myself any longer, it's about her monthly's…!'

'What about them,' said Elizabeth, concerned at the direction the conversation was taking?

'Well there hasn't been one recently Ma'am, not so far as I'm aware.'

Elizabeth paused for some moments... 'She's very young Nana, it's not unusual for that age, I'm sure you are worrying about nothing.'

'That's what I thought Ma'am, but it's been three months now,' she said significantly. 'There might have been a happening at St Agnes, but definitely not here.'

'Perhaps you're mistaken, Nana, perhaps you've missed...!'

'I would know Ma'am!'

'Yes, yes of course you would Nana!' said Elizabeth, reminding herself of how particular her housekeeper was, where affairs of the household were concerned.

Elizabeth Durcan was silent for a moment, considering the momentous implications of what her loyal housekeeper had just said.

'And she's been under par in the mornings, Ma'am...' she added.

Elizabeth Durcan could see Nana Dilly was very close to tears.

'She's just a child, Nana; she knows nothing of these matters; there must be a simple explanation. I will send for Dr. Wooton just as soon as Polly returns. I'm sure he will give her something to put matters right and all will be well once more. Please don't distress yourself.'

'Oh, I do hope so Ma'am, I really do hope so... Mr Hudson says...'

'Have you mentioned this to Mr Hudson?'

Oh no, Ma'am, we don't talk about such private matters! I would never even think of it, not afore I had spoken to you...'

'You must not tell him even now Nana, nor Mr Richard; he is not to know until I have spoken to Dr. Wooton. I dread to think what he will say...!'

Mrs. Hudson agreed that silence was the best course to take in the circumstances, being well aware of the master's feelings where his precious daughter was concerned.

'I'm sure all is well Nana, really I am. Polly is just a child, but she's a sensible, thoughtful child, and knows right from wrong. Mr Richard and I have brought her up with good Christian principles, as you know. I cannot believe for one moment that she would do anything foolish, and anyway, when would the opportunity arise? There would be no opportunity at St Agnes and there are no young gentlemen calling when she's home. If anything, I've been a little anxious about her lack of interest in such matters, and was even beginning to wonder if we might have a spinster on our hands. I don't believe this matter to be anything but adolescence, but I will have a word with Dr. Wooton just as soon as…'

'Begging your pardon Ma'am, but there is just one more thing… as I was saying about Mr Hudson! Mr Hudson mentioned something I thought was odd and I've worried myself about it ever since. John Hopkins, the cowman, told Harry Edwards he'd seen a lot of Miss Polly about the Long Down recently — three times this week alone! He thought nothing of it in itself, but each time there'd been a certain young man close by. Not with her, you understand, but the same young man, or so he thinks.'

'Did he say who this young man might be, Nana,' said Elizabeth, taken aback?

'He thinks he's the young blacksmith lad called Isaac Smith.'

For the first time, Elizabeth Durcan showed true concern and fell silent, deep in thought for many moments.

'You must not mention this to anyone Nana,' she said at last, 'least of all Mr Richard. These are women's matters and would upset him dreadfully.'

'Of course, Ma'am.'

Mrs. Hudson turned to leave her mistress, only to be confronted by Richard Durcan standing stock still in the doorway.

'And what might the matter be that would upset me so much Nana?' said her master in an ominous tone. 'Perhaps you might like to enlighten me?'

CHAPTER 16

Rufus and Satan

Ned Meadows jumped up at the sound of footsteps on the cobbles. It was the master for sure, for no one else had a stride quite like it. The faster the stride, the worse the botheration in his experience.

'Struts about like a bloody cockerel, 'e do!' was Ned's fond saying. 'Anding' out is orders to all an' bloody sundry! 'E' wants to try a day's work is'self, an' see what tis like, afore 'e goes telling other buggers what to do! Bloody bugger 'e is!'

'Be no good spending the day we thee then Ned,' would be the usual reply - Ned not being known for his grafting.

Ned scattered the hay where he'd been sat and grabbed a pail that lay close by.

'Have a care, damn you,' said Richard Durcan as Ned blundered into him in the doorway.

'Beggin' yer pardon, yer lordship, I never heard thee coming, I were just on...'

'Where's your mistress?'

'Mistress Polly?'

'Yes.'

'Ah,' said Ned... 'Now then... that's a good un' that is yer Lordship; thee've asked us a good un' thee ave! I'll ave to think about that un'! 'Er could be on't' Bury, or then again 'er could be ont' top pasture. 'Er could be along the Delkin, then again...'

'Didn't she tell you where she was going?'

'Er' don't tell I things like that yer Lordship; bless my soul no. I don't suppose 'er knows erself' till 'er gets going!'

'Where's Long?'

'John Long?'

'Of course John Long! How many other Longs do you know for God's sake,' said Richard Durcan, growing ever more exasperated with his idiot stable boy.

120

'I don't know no other Longs meself' yer lordship, but I thought thee might see… thas the thing! I thought I ought t' check we thee, cus' tis clearly important!'

'Yes it is important, so for the last time; where is John Long?'

'Right…! Now we've established tis John Long we're looking fer, that clears that up, but thee've asked another good un there, thee ave! That's another good un' that is! They'm replacing loose tiles ont' barn, but I can't see John Long climbing ont' roof cus' 'e d' suffer from verdigris. He's more likely t' be down the mill cus' they got a bit of bother we' the sluice an' thas another good un' that is! They got a job on there, they ave …! Course if 'e' ain't there, 'e might …'

Richard Durcan turned on his heel to find John Long for himself, his anger boiling over at Ned Meadows idiocy. He was almost at the door, when he noticed the Chestnut he'd ridden earlier, still sweating, and still caked in mud.

'Why has that animal not been groomed, he snapped?'

'I were onto that next yer Lordship; soon as I've fetched the water.'

'You're a malingerer Meadows,' he said in a blaze of anger, 'lazy, idle and deceitful like your father before you! Attend to that animal now and be bloody quick about it!'

'Right you are yer Lordship, just as soon as I've…'

'Now damn you, or by God I'll put this crop about your back and we'll see if that will wake your ideas up a bit.' With that, he strode across the yard toward the wagon shed in a mood the like of which the Home Farm had never seen before.

'Bloody bastard,' muttered Ned beneath his breath; 'bloody bastard 'e is.'

'Long…' snapped Richard Durcan as he entered the wagon shed; 'Where's Edwards?'

'Top pasture, Mr Richard,' said John Long looking up from his work, 'far as I'm aware! He's making good some fences - closing em off t' deer.'

John Long had worked for the Durcan family since he was thirteen, from farm hand to Estate Manager, but in all that time, he'd never seen the master so angry. Richard Durcan was shaking with rage.

'Then make your way there too and when you find Edwards, tell him Squire Exley has seen a fellow about the moors on our side. If you're quick, you may catch him red handed.'

121

Exley farmed the land to the far side of Cam Peak, the Long Down and Smallpox Hill. Like Durcan, he was bedevilled by poachers, stealing everything from pigs to fowl, and rabbit to deer. People were poor and times were hard. Poaching put food on the table, but it kept Edwards busy by day and night.

All too rarely did they catch the men whose stealing cost the estate so dear. Their nocturnal activities caused untold damage by breaking down fences and injuring livestock with crude traps that killed and maimed. Edwards spent much of his time destroying their handiwork but within days, it would re-appear.

However, the poacher did not have it all his own way. The law took a dim view of it, seeing poaching as no different to burglary. Magistrates handed down hefty prison sentences to those who were caught, whilst angry gamekeepers, eager to keep their jobs, were not above taking a shot at shadows, letting loose the dogs, or cracking open heads with the thick end of a stick.

'Does e know who t'wer,' asked Long?

'Exley thinks it's the blacksmiths boy.'

'John Smith's lad, said Long?'

'So I believe. Whilst you get over to the top pasture, I'm going to take the hunter up the Bury. I need to speak to Mistress Polly who might be that way with the Parson. If you see her, send her home. Don't listen to any of her nonsense. Take the dogs, and if by chance you find your man, keep him there. I'll see you well enough from the Bury.'

'Right you are sir.'

As Richard Durcan rode off on the hunter, John Long entered the stables.

'Masters got a job fer thee an' me Ned, so thee'd best finish what thee be doing.'

He's just told us to groom the chestnut or I'll get is crop across me back - right bloody mood 'e be in we' summat.'

'And I'm telling you t leave that, an' do as I say if you knows what's good for thee.'

'What ud' that be then... Me' aving' mor'n' enough work t' do round yer as tis?'

'He thinks there's a fellow setting traps on the Long Down.'

'Who's that then?'

'Isaac Smith... or so 'e thinks.'

'Smithy,' said Ned with a cackle of laughter; slapping his thighs and turning around in circles. 'That's a good un that is. I've erd' some good un's in me time, but that's a good un' that is.'

'What's so bloody good about it?'

'Don't say thee ain't erd?'

'Heard what?'

'Bout Smithy an' the young Mistress! John Collins as seen um twice now, billin' an' cooin' an' likewise.'

'Don't talk such bloody rubbish!'

'I'm telling e'!'

'Why would Mistress Polly talk to the likes of him?'

'Ah, there tis then! Now thee've asked the question… that's a good un that is!'

'I expect they were just passing the time of day… there's no crime in talking. Mistress Polly even talks to you fer God's sake; an' that's saying something. God only knows why!'

'Ah but er don't talk to I in't' middle of moors now do er! That's the difference! Twice now accordin' to Collins!'

John Long was at a loss for a reply.

'Oh, Mr Smith,' mimicked Ned in a high pitched voice, 'how nice t' see thee yet again… on these yer lonely moors… we no other bugger fer miles! 'Well bugger me if it ain't Miss Polly,' he continued in a lower voice, 'Fancy bumping into thee yet again…!' Ned relapsed into cackles of laughter whilst slapping his thigh with his hand.

'So summat's going on just cus' they've exchanged a few words on the moors? That's your theory is it Sherlock?'

'Course tis! They wouldn't be there, lest they was up to no good. Now our lord an' bloody master's found out about it, an' the shit's hit the fan! Serve um bloody right I say, ere'… you know what I think!'

'No - what do you think,' said Long.

'This poaching ole' Smithy's supposed ter' be doing! He's after summut furry right enough, but taint a bloody rabbit!'

John Long shook his head as Ned collapsed in a fresh bout of thigh slapping. Turning for the door Long said, 'You'd best not let the master hear you talk that way or you'll be out on yer bloody ear.'

'I don't give a shit!' Ned replied. 'Bloody bastard 'e is!'

Though against his better judgment, John Long needed Ned on this job. For all he was a simple-minded clod, he had a way with Satan and Rufus, and besides the master, no one else dared go near the brutes. The two dogs were bigger than a man when stood on their hind legs and dangerous with it. Satan would growl when approached; deep guttural and menacing, but Rufus would make no sound at all. Instead, he would slowly rise to his feet and watch whoever approached with unblinking eyes. It was impossible to know when the huge animal might attack, but few had the nerve to put him to the test.

Long didn't relish a scuffle with Isaac Smith and thought that with the dogs along there would be less chance of that. There was also less chance of Isaac Smith - if indeed he were the poacher - taking to his heels. Harry Edwards wouldn't flinch at a scrap, for he'd a reputation for dealing with poachers, but there was no guarantee he'd find Edwards.

Edwards had earnt his reputation many years before, over an incident with a poacher stealing swans. Edwards had lain in undergrowth into the early hours to catch him red handed with two birds under his arm. He brought the fellow down and then laid about him with his stick until he was no longer able to walk. Edwards tied him to a tree, bruised and bleeding, until the rest of the estate awoke, then they carted him off to gaol for four months for poaching and trespass.

'I'm going t see if I can't find Harry Edwards,' said John Long. 'You get the dogs together; an I'll see thee at the lower pastures.'

~

From his vantage point, Isaac watched her ride off on the Parson. From time to time, she turned and waved and he waved back. They had spent three wonderful hours together.

Eventually, he lost sight of her and began to descend the steeply sloping flank of the Long Down to the saddle of land between the Down and the Bury, from where he could pick up the lane for home.

Half way down, he noticed two men approaching from the direction of Smallpox hill. From further off, another man approached, half-running, half-walking, two massive dogs, dragging him along.

The two men looked as though they had some business with him, but Isaac had no intention of stopping.

He got to the end of the Long Down with the men still some way off. He turned away from them towards home, but one of the men hollered after him. 'Come here young fellah, I wants a word we thee.'

Isaac stopped and looked back. He recognized John Long for he brought the horses for shoeing occasionally, but the other man with the stick he only knew by sight.

'What about?' he replied.

'Thee be on private land lad; what's yer business?'

'Just walking. It's a good day to take the view.'

'Fer the view eh' said Edwards as they reached Isaac, 'well taint thy view to look at!' 'The master owns this particular view and 'e wants a word with thee young fellah!'

'What about?'

'That's his business!'

'I've no master save myself and I don't dance to another man's tune, yours included.'

'Don't you now,' said Harry Edwards taking an obvious dislike to Isaac, 'Well I'd like t know what's your business! This is private land an' thee be trespassin'... poachin' like as not.'

'Do I look like a poacher,' replied Isaac patting his empty pockets.

'You want to know what thee d' look like?' said Edwards. 'I'll tell thee what thee looks like! Thee looks like a cocky bugger t' me, an if the master wants t speak to thee, then speak to thee 'e will.' The last two words he spat out through clenched teeth as his stick came about in a vicious swipe that caught Isaac low down at the back of the legs. He cried out in pain, doubling to his knees. The stick rose to strike again.

Harry Edwards came in close, to deliver a crack across the shoulders to settle the matter, but instead; he got a punch in the groin that sent him reeling. Doubled in pain, he fell to the ground groaning in agony.

Isaac struggled to his feet, his legs barely taking his weight with the pain in his calf muscles. John Long made a move for him, but Isaac stepped back just in time, his fist clenched for a further attack. 'Come on then you bastard,' he said, 'let's see what you can do without yer friend.'

Thinking better of it, John Long went instead to the aid of Harry Edwards, who was still on his hands and knees clutching his groin. 'You're in a lot of trouble lad,' he said, as Isaac continued his journey to the road.

'Not from you buffoons I'm not,' he replied, as he set out for home once more. But no sooner had he finished speaking, than he heard a whooping and hollering from the man with the dogs.

'I'll sort un' came the distant cry, 'I'll bloody sort un...!'

All three men looked back in disbelief as Ned Meadows let loose Satan and Rufus. The two dogs raced towards them, baying and barking.

From his vantage point at the edge of the Bury escarpment, Major Richard Durcan watched events unfold through his army binoculars. He'd seen his daughter's passionate farewell to the young man who was clearly her beau, with a kiss that told its own story. He watched her ride home, turning every few yards to wave and smile.

Richard Durcan had never felt such anger and outrage in all his life. He felt utterly betrayed by the clandestine affair of a daughter he'd thought so innocent. Never had the family name been so humiliated and scandalized, and by the child he loved and adored.

The thought of his beautiful daughter laying down with a common blacksmith, rutting like animals, his hands pawing at her body, was more than he could bear. If the scoundrel were stood before him at that moment, he would take his pistol and shoot him where he stood.

He watched Edwards attempt to seize hold of the fellow, and then fall to his knees. He had seen John Long shy away, and the idiot stable boy letting slip Satan and Rufus.

The dogs were still some way off, but Satan was in full flight and would cover the ground in minutes. Rufus, being the bigger, older animal, loped along some hundred yards behind him.

Durcan had no doubt they would attack, for that was the very purpose of their existence, but with that distance to cover, and in their state of excitement, it was quite likely they would attack Harry Edwards unless he got himself up off the ground.

Richard Durcan turned the massive hunter towards the small group and began his gallop down the steep flank of the escarpment, clearing hedges and fallen trees at breakneck speed, but he doubted that even this splendid animal would get him there before the dogs.

126

Isaac looked at the dogs, then at John Long, at a loss what to do.

'Not so bloody cocky now then,' said John Long.

Isaac's only hope of escaping an attack was a gate that joined the field with an adjacent pasture. If he could reach it, perhaps he could close it. Taking to his heels, he ran as fast as his legs would carry him. He ran as he'd never run before, but Satan's baying grew ever closer. Reaching the gateway, he tried to wrest it shut but it was firmly entrenched in grass and mud.

Isaac had no choice but to face the massive brute and try to defend himself by making a stand before the gateway. Satan's jaw was open, his eyes wild with excitement, his black coat glistened and his jowls slavered with the exertion of the chase. Ten feet from Isaac he launched himself into the air, his forelegs outstretched like battering rams; intent upon driving his quarry to the ground beneath his superior weight and strength. Satan's instinct was to sink his teeth into Isaac's neck as they fell; ripping at the soft flesh and tearing open the windpipe.

Just at the moment of impact, Isaac stepped to the side and steeling himself for what was to come; thrust his hand deep into the animals open mouth, grabbing his lower jaw, dragging it open against the dogs bite.

Satan clamped his jaws together and Isaac cried out as the dogs teeth met through his flesh. But while the massive brute was still flying through the air, Isaac used all his strength and Satan's momentum to twist his adversary upside down and swing him in a wide sweeping arc, just as a hammer thrower might swing the hammer at the highland games.

The force and energy of Satan's attack drove Isaac forward and all but toppled him over, but his very life depended upon staying on his feet. With a gargantuan effort, he swung the biting jerking animal through a full circle at arm's length. At the last moment, Isaac took two steps backward. Satan gave one last savage bite as Isaac swung his body against the stone gatepost. The dog's eyes went wild; his grip loosened, his body convulsing as the impact broke his spinal cord. The splintering of bone and ripping of cartilage had been clear to hear as the creature's spine snapped in half.

The mortally wounded dog slid to the ground at the foot of the post, his forelegs trying to propel him into a further attack though his back legs dragging uselessly on the ground. As the agony of his shattered spine broke through, he convulsed and writhed, snapping at his own back, howling in pain in the most horrific and piteous manner.

Isaac had no time to worry about Satan for Rufus had reached the field and was loping towards him at high speed.

127

Rufus was an intelligent animal and seeing Satan writhing in his death throws veered away to his right to get beyond Isaac and drive him away from the gate.

With blood flowing freely from a hand that had lost all feeling, he knew he could not easily defend himself from Rufus's attack. Grabbing a stick from a nearby hedge, he dragged it from its entanglement then ran to open ground where he could swing it freely.

Having forced Isaac into open ground, Rufus ran straight at him, using his body as a bludgeon and closing his jaws about Isaac's wounded arm. But as he brought his teeth together, he howled in pain, for the end of Isaac's stick struck his temple, opening up a deep wound, then raking a large lump of flesh and fur from his back. The pain and smell of blood, from his open, flapping flesh enraged the animal to even greater savagery. Throwing the full force of his body-weight against Isaac, he tried once more to bite through the bleeding arm.

Isaac stumbled and fell under the onslaught. The stick had shattered and he was left holding a piece just two feet long. Rufus's teeth came together in Isaac's left cheek and he felt them jar against his own. He could taste the blood that flowed freely from the wounds.

Isaac knew the dog would kill him unless he could stop him in some way. With his good arm, he jabbed the stick up through the animal's heavy leather collar, twisting the stick like a Spanish windlass, drawing the collar into a garrotte that closed the dog's windpipe, starving him of precious air.

The massive brute went berserk, clawing at Isaac with forelegs, throwing his massive body in circles in the air, trying to free himself from the vice about his throat. He snorted through his nostrils, his jaw wide, eyes bulging, slaver and sputum, spraying Isaac's face.

Isaac held on for dear life, the dog dragging him about the field, trying his best to free himself of his assailant. At last he slowed, his strength ebbing. He could no longer bite, his clawing stopped, he stood still but for the occasional frenzy of effort, but Isaac hung on to him for dear life, twisting, choking and strangling the life from his enemy.

The huge dog fell to the ground, the tiny breaths he could take, coming in wheezing gasps. Isaac twisted the stick for all he was worth as the dogs face swam before him. He felt faint from his own injuries, but he dare not let go the grip he had upon the stick. The dog's legs were trembling now, kicking and scrabbling in their death throws, then falling still. Isaac felt himself fainting, his own body going limp; he must not faint whilst the dog still lived. There were others nearby; he could hear their shouting; why didn't they help him, he was drifting, falling...

A shot rang out and the brute gave one last jerk then fell still, the bullet that smashed through its brain, throwing splatters of blood and gore into Isaac's face.

Isaac's vision swam as waves of pain flooded his body and nausea burnt his throat with foul bile. He felt himself sinking and falling to the ground, exhaustion, pain, and loss of blood pushing him towards unconsciousness. Hands grabbed the dead animal, dragging it away, but he would not let go - could not let go - lest by some cruel miracle, the dog recover from his injuries and begin Isaac's nightmare all over again.

Then there came a gap in time of which he had no memory. The dog was no longer beneath him, the stick no longer in his hands. He was laid on his back, coughing up the blood that was slowly choking him. His breathing came in shuddering gasps. Wave after wave of nausea surged through him and his stomach rose, the bile bitter and stinging.

A man stood over him, peering down, prodding Isaac to wakefulness with a horsewhip. Isaac's vision was awash. He could not focus his eyes, nor clear the swimming veil of redness. The man prodded him again, making him cry out with pain. He knew instinctively who the man must be.

'Can you hear me, blacksmith?' said Richard Durcan angrily, but Isaac did not have the strength to reply.

'Can you hear me, damn you?' Durcan repeated, striking Isaac yet again with his whip. He shook him by the shoulders and then grasped a clump of hair, shaking Isaac by the head, forcing him to look his way. Isaac groaned at this new agony.

'Listen to me, blacksmith,' said Richard Durcan. 'You are trespassing on my land and poaching and stealing my property. You've caused the death of two valuable animals, and I could have you locked up for what you've done today; but I care nothing for that! I want you to listen to what I'm going to say.' He renewed his grip of Isaac's hair and lifted his face until it was inches from his own. In a venomous whisper, he said, 'Touch my daughter again… harm a hair of her head and, as God is my witness, I'll kill you with my bare hands!'

Isaac stared at him blankly, his strength gone, his mind in free-fall.

'Do you understand?'

Isaac continued to stare vacantly.

'Do you understand me, damn you?' he repeated, dashing Isaac to the ground and thrashing him with another stroke of the riding crop.

Isaac felt himself slipping into unconsciousness.

Richard Durcan stood up and Isaac could hear other voices nearby. Durcan spoke to them, shouting instructions, his voice shaking with anger and rage; then came blessed oblivion.

Isaac awoke in his bedroom at the smithy without any recollection of how he'd got there. Every tiny movement racked his body with pain. He heard John's voice and that of another, who looked at Isaac over pince-nez glasses. There was a syringe in the stranger's hand and moments later, only blackness.

From the windowsill of Isaac's room, bright green eyes watched the four humans within. There was the woman human who rarely came to the smithy and the man human who beat the glowing sticks on the anvil.

The young stick-beater was there too; but something was wrong with him, for he lay very still whilst the others watched to see if he would get up and go to the smithy, but he did not. Then the fourth human, whom the cat did not know, wrapped the young stick beater in white ribbon whilst the woman and the man looked on. They looked very sad and tiny droplets of water ran from the old stick beaters eyes.

Then the fourth human left - soon to reappear on the path outside. He passed below the windowsill upon which the cat perched. It was colder now, for a frosty wind had begun to blow and the stranger lifted his collar against the chill air before disappearing into the night. The woman and the old stick beater returned to the room and sat either beside the bed on which the young one lay. They watched him for a very long time. The cat returned to his home in the rafters of the Smithy from where he liked to watch the humans toil. He hoped they would come next morning to beat the yellow, glowing sticks, but they did not. It was the same the following day and the day after that. The smithy became colder than the cat had ever known.

CHAPTER 17

The lower Crown

As Daisy bent to scoop mugs from beneath the counter, Merridew took an opportunity that simply couldn't be missed. He prodded her dress between her buttocks, enjoying the warmth against his fingers, before giving her bottom a hefty pinch.

An incandescent Daisy cracked her head against the bar edge as she stood to confront her employer. Merridew smiled in satisfaction at her show of outrage.

'Keep yer' ands to yerself you dirty sod,' she snarled, her eyes flashing with anger.

'Come on now Daisy,' chided Merridew, 'don't pretend thee've become a lady all of a sudden; thee likes a bit of slap an' tickle, just like the rest of em.'

'Not with you I don't, you dirty bugger!' Her piece said, she moved to the other end of the bar and as far from Merridew as possible.

'That's told thee!' said a regular who was trying to order his first pint of the evening.

'Thee don't want to take no notice of that little show, Percy lad,' replied Merridew. 'That's just fer thy benefit that is. Tis a different matter when er ain't got an audience, I can tell e'. Er' be right up fer it then!'

Raucous laughter broke out from the drinkers in a corner of the public bar that was hidden from their vision by a large pine settle; its rough-hewn back, blackened and worn smooth by the brush of many hands, as customers made their way to the gents' latrine.

What's t' do in the snug,' said Percy.

'Just a bit of Ned baiting - he's the centre of attention at the moment, fer reasons as thee'll likely be aware.'

Percy Field was fully aware of the altercation on the moors, like everyone else in the village. He thanked Merridew for his pint and made his way to the snug.

A group of ten men sat upon chairs or the settle; the table they sat about was laden with empty glasses and overflowing ashtrays. The dominoes and cribbage boards that might usually be on the table were still in their place on the

131

windowsill. Among the gathering were such local characters as Blind Harry Atwell, Titus Farmer and Tom Baldoodle.

Blind Harry owned an ironmonger's where he sold everything from shovels to coal, and flypaper to candles. He was so named for his ability to turn a blind eye to where his stock came from; rather than any visual affliction. He was Ned's main protagonist, when Field joined the group of men who numbered farmers, cowmen, a carpenter, a farrier and a chimney sweep among their number.

'How come Harry Edwards is nursing a pair of swollen bollock's then Ned,' enquired Blind Harry, 'whilst thee managed t' keep thy good looks intact; thas what we'd all like to know?'

He spoke for the whole group in that matter, for there were few who believed that Ned Meadows, Long or even Harry Edwards would get the better of Isaac Smith in a fair scuffle.

'Ah, thas a good un' that is,' replied Ned, taking a swig from his fifth pint of rough cider, 'thee've asked us a good un' there thee ave!'

'Well what's the answer then?'

'Same as I told thee last time.'

'An' that's why we be askin' agin! Thy story d' change every time.'

'No it bloody don't! I d' just tell it from a different susspective thas all. One time I might tell it from Harry Edwards susspective as e's watching is bollock's go into orbit; then the next time I might tell it from Smithy's susspective when I lands a haymaker on un.'

Taking another swig of his cider, he continued, 'Next time I might tell it from Harry's wife's susspective an' thas a good un' that is.' His missus d' want un' to ave a scuffle more often, cus Arry's weddin' tackle be twice the size of normal.'

Laughter broke out again and Ned slapped himself on the thigh, pleased with his cutting wit.

'Here's a good un fer thee then Ned,' said Tom Baldoodle. 'I'll tell thee the story from Satan's susspective cus thee ain't covered that un yet. You tell us if this be somewhere near the truth! There's old Satan, loping across the field; slavering' an' slobberin', and baying an' a howlin', and carrying on like he's the hound of the bloody Baskervilles; an all the while e's thinking to is'self; "Bugger me... here's a good un then! This is a bloody good un this is! Now they've let us off the lead, I'll ave ter bite some bugger's arse in amongst all this bloody fracas, or I'll lose me bloody job! Then 'e says to is'self; "As I see's it: I can either bite young Smithy as is covered in Miss Polly's kisses; or, I can bite that silly bugger Ned Meadows as is covered in horse shit... ! I reckon I'll go fer young Smithy!'

The bar erupted into howls of laughter and no-one was more amused than Ned himself, who slapped his thigh again saying, 'Thas' a good un' that is, thee've come out we' a good un' there thee ave' Tom Baldoodle!'

'I thought you told us you laid one on him then Ned, an' that's what brought Smithy down. What's all this talk of the dogs?'

'It weren't bugger all t do we the dogs; I brought un down just like I told 'e an' that were the problem. After Smithy floors Harry Edwards, 'e starts getting proper mouthy, sayin' as 'e can do just as 'e pleases, an' what are we goin' ter do about it? Thas when I give the dogs to John Long an' says to Smithy, "Thee've asked us a good un there thee ave Smithy - thas a good un that is!" An' before 'e can get another word out, I gives un such a bloody haymaker as 'e thinks e's been knocked inter orbit, an' Harry's bollock's be a pair of shootin' stars.

'Aye - in thy bloody dreams!'

'I'm bloody tellin' thee. Thas when John Long d' get frit an' let the bloody dogs' loose.'

'Now then Tom,' said Blind Harry, 'don't thee be so quick t' cock a snoop at Ned's story just cus e's a bullshitter. I can vouch fer what 'e says cus I got the story from John Long is'self. He says Ned knocked old Smithy senseless right enough, but twern't the punch as did it; twer' is armpits!'

Amid more howls of laughter, Titus Farmer joined the fray. 'It were just as easy as that then, were it Ned? One smack from thee an' Smithy's out fer the count?'

'More or less,' said Ned.

'I'd give a lot t' see that appen' again,' said a clearly sceptical Farmer.

'An' what would thee be inclined t' give away then, Titus?' asked Baldoodle; 'thee being the tightest bugger I know!'

'I'd start out we' summat readily available, like a night's carousing we thy missus,' said Titus with a chuckle at Baldoodle's expense.

'I'll be appy' t' oblige Titus; appy t' oblige, cus that'll be the first thing thee've given away in all the years I've known thee. I don't know about Titus Farmer - Titus bloody Arsehole's more like!'

Amid much laughing and table slapping at Farmers expense, Blind Harry shouted out, 'Wos' think then Ned - here's thy chance t' show us this famous haymaker of thine. Here's ole Smithy, come to ave a word we thee.'

There were even more hoots of laughter at the look of abject terror on Ned's face, as all eyes swivelled to the empty entrance.

'I don't think thee got much t' worry about Ned,' said Percy Field, speaking quietly for the first time. 'From what I hear, Smithy ain't going to be calling by anytime soon! He's laid up we' the fever, so they say! Might not even make it, so I erd' tell!'

CHAPTER 18

Hotpot

'Here you are dear,' said Mrs Hudson, placing the tray of food near the window where there was light and cheer; 'here's a bit of Nana Dilly's hotpot! It'll cheer you up and things won't look so bad then, you'll see!' She returned to the door and closed it softly, locking it once more, for Mr Richard's instructions had been quite clear on that matter. Polly lay as she had left her; face down upon her bed.

Mrs. Hudson sat beside her on the edge of the bed; her concern for Polly growing with each hour that passed. She had grown into a beautiful, sensitive, trusting young woman, who had been hurt very deeply and even Mrs Hudson, who always knew just what to do when life went wrong, was struggling to reach her.

She touched her cheek, which even now - after two full days - was still damp with tears. She took the hair that had fallen across her face and smoothed it back.

'You must eat Polly,' she said softly, 'you will make yourself ill if you don't eat properly; then where will we be?'

'I can't Nana, I really can't. Please don't make me.'

'Humph...!' she grunted; 'When have I been able to make you do anything you didn't want to; but whether we like it or not, it is not just about you anymore is it? There's another little life to think of isn't there?'

Polly turned towards Mrs Hudson, her eyes dark with crying. It upset the old lady to see her so distraught. Mrs Hudson held out her arms and Polly came to her, hugging her tightly as new tears spilled over.

'There, there, there,' whispered Mrs Hudson softly, 'You have a good cry and let it all come out. It's the best way by far - Mr Hudson always says so!'

'Nana,' sobbed Polly, 'They will take my baby away, won't they?'

Mrs. Hudson had dreaded this moment, but she would have to deal with it herself, for Mistress Elizabeth was expressly forbidden to go to the room lest Polly use her to weaken Master Richard's resolve; such was his anger at the unhappy turn of events. Perhaps it was for the best, however. Mistress Elizabeth was a good wife to him, running the domestic staff as well as he ran the estate; she was intelligent, elegant, respected by one and all and loved her children dearly; but she was never a mother in the motherly sense of the word.

135

She preferred to pass her offspring to Nana Dilly as soon as they became the slightest bit grumpy, for Nana had endless patience and loved both children like her own.

Often accused of spoiling them by Master Richard, he could be every bit as soft - at least with Polly - but it was to Nana Dilly they ran if anything was amiss, or a tumble or fall needed kissing better. Never was there a more urgent need for her love than now.

She'd been with Polly when Dr. Wooton made his examination. He'd done so in his usual, silent, practiced manner, searching for the signs of new life that would confirm Mrs Hudson fears.

Polly lay still; her eyes closed tightly as he did those horrible, unforgettable things. There was a slight mustiness about him as he leant over her; she did not know whether it was his clothing or breath, but she could hear him breathing through his nostrils, slowly steadily. When it was over, he pulled her nightdress down and covered her over before washing his hands in the basin Mrs Hudson had provided. Picking up his bag, he smiled briefly and wished them both, good day. Though he said nothing, he didn't need to, for his face said it all.

Richard Durcan accepted the doctor's news with barely a flicker. Thanking him, he asked him for his discretion, which was duly assured. Equally calmly, he climbed the stairs to Polly's bedroom and there, in words shaped from ice, he told her that she had shamed and disgraced not only herself, but the good name of the Durcan family, and the latter was unforgivable. He forbade her ever to see or speak to her lover again, and as soon as the arrangements could be made, she would be sent north to Scotland to prepare for the birth and her subsequent convalescence. The story would be that she was at finishing school until the autumn. When the child arrived, it would go to a barren couple and she would never hear of it again. In the mean time, Polly would be confined to her room under lock and key, with only Mrs Hudson allowed to enter. She was forbidden to mention the incident to another living soul, ever again. With those words, he handed the key to Mrs Hudson and left. He didn't visit Polly thereafter; nor would he allow her mother to do so. For the first time in their marriage, Elizabeth Durcan was afraid to speak against him; for there was a boiling rage within him, the like of which she had never seen before. She prayed she would never see it again.

'Polly dear; your fathers plan is for the best, though it might not seem so now.'

'How can you say that Nana - I thought you would understand?

136

'I've said it because I want what's best for you, Polly! I know how you must feel for...'

'No, you don't!'

'Yes I do darling; yes I do! Nana has lost two of her own; you didn't know that did you, but I have? We had two beautiful babies' who died; one lived just three days whilst the other little mite never took a breath. That was thirty years ago now, but I don't think Mr Hudson has got over it yet, so Nana does know. But though your father's plan seems terrible, I know your father is only trying to do what's best for you and perhaps you'll understand one day.'

'No, he's not Nana! I'm sorry about your babies, I really am, but you lost them because ... well I don't know why, but losing them like that is different from having them taken away, isn't it? To have them stolen from you...! Papa doesn't care about me; he's just thinking of his precious family name.'

'Well. perhaps you're right Polly; but it would be a terrible scandal if folk got to know and there's no saying different. Perhaps that's why he thinks the way he does. You've got to remember that this family has been the village of Uley for centuries past and there would be no Uley without the Durcan family. Why, there's barely a family for five miles about that doesn't rely upon your father for their livelihood. He's much respected, just as you grandfather before him, and that's a good thing. Folk like to see families like the Durcan's setting an example, but if they knew you'd fallen pregnant to a common working lad, well...! The names they'd call you Polly and the things they'd say ... it doesn't bear thinking about. It upsets me just the thought of it and no one would ever forget it Polly. Believe you me - no one would ever forget it - not so long as you live!'

'Isaac's not common Nana, you don't even know him! He's kind and gentle and very clever, and he will own Mr Smith's business one day.'

'Well, that's as may be child, but if he was the gentleman you seem to think he is, he would have had more consideration for your reputation now wouldn't he?'

Polly fell silent for a moment, looking down at her hands. 'It wasn't his fault Nana; it was mine; it was my fault!'

Mrs. Hudson, looking just a little shocked and after a pause said, 'Well, that's a black mark for you too then, but it's still no excuse. He's older than you and he should have thought about things a little more.'

'It wasn't as Papa said, Nana. What he said was horrible...! We weren't like animals; it wasn't like that at all. We love one another, and it was the first time, the only time... It wouldn't have happened at all but for the storm.'

137

'What storm?'

'There was a terrible storm, and we were cold and soaked to the skin, and Parson Pimm was terrified. We took him to the hospital and waited for it to stop, but it rained and rained. We lit a fire and dried our clothes and... well it just happened Nana ...'

'Well, there's nothing we can do about what's finished and done Polly, but we need to do the right thing for the future and the little life inside you. I know you have this notion that maybe you and this young man should marry, but I wonder if you know what that means. Is he willing or able to support you, I wonder... he's hardly Freddy Berkeley is he? Turning your back on the family and marrying this lad would be hard Polly, harder than you could ever imagine possible. Endless damp washing, and a tiny house full of sickly children you'd likely share with another family. Your father would cut you off from everything and you'd be cooking and scrubbing from dawn till dusk!'

'Other women do it!'

'Only because they have to, child! Now tell me; does this young man know you're expecting?'

'No... said Polly, her voice faltering, I didn't know until Doctor Wooton...'

Well let's not upset ourselves by going back over what's done and finished; didn't you wonder about your monthly's?

Polly shook her head.

'You do know how babies come into the world, Polly?' asked Mrs Hudson, suspiciously.

'Of course I do, that's why I was careful.'

What do you mean - careful?

'I ... I jumped up and down...'

'You jumped up and down!' said Mrs Hudson in disbelief.

Polly nodded a little sheepishly. Letty told me it was okay if you jump up and down soon after; then it can't possibly happen. Letty's friend told her; and her father's a doctor.'

Mrs. Hudson shook her head. Giving Polly a rueful smile she said, 'I think Letty's friend should keep her advice to herself child. Nature has its own way Polly, as you now know! So we don't know what this young man is going to say should he ever find out?' she continued severely.

138

Polly shook her head once more.

'Well I can tell you Polly, that even the best of em have a habit of skedaddling when they do, and it's us women left carrying the baby, as they say!'

Mrs. Hudson fell silent for a few moments deep in her own thoughts. What she could not tell Polly, was that the young man was said to be so poorly, that he might not survive the mauling he'd received from those two brutes, Satan and Rufus. If there was one good thing to come from this whole, sad affair, it was that those two were no more.

Though Nana knew the truth, most believed he'd been caught poaching and that Ned had let the dogs loose to run him down. They'd near ripped him to pieces and he was lucky to survive. John Long and Edwards had carried him home in the cart on Mr Richard's instructions and Dr. Wooton had sewn him up as best he could, but he was in a pretty sorry way by all accounts. Mr Hudson had heard he was fighting for his life. He'd been told the young lads arm was terribly mauled, and the dogs had bitten him so badly about the cheek, that you could see his teeth through it. One thing Mrs Hudson did know was that he'd never look the same again, but she dared not tell Polly that.

'Polly,' she began, 'what's done is done and we can't turn the clock back, though God knows we'd all like to. We can't undo that little mite that's growing inside you, so you must stop feeling sorry for yourself and start thinking about bringing a healthy baby into the world. That... young lady... starts with eating properly. Mr Richard is going to send you off to Scotland in the next few days and there's nothing Nana can do about that, but he's asked Mr Hudson if I can go with you so you won't be there on your own. Now I don't know all the rights and wrongs of this Polly, and I can't say I agree with all the why's and wherefore's, but I can tell you this young lady; if you are only concerned about Miss Polly Durcan, you will lie back down on that bed and carry on feeling sorry for yourself; but if you care about the child that's growing inside you, you'll get up right away, dry your tears, and make the best of it! That's the only way to do things Polly, and if you do, then things have a habit of working out for the best in the end.'

She kissed Polly on the forehead. Getting up from the bed, she unlocked the door and left the room.

She waited quietly in the passage outside, and was pleased to hear the scrape of the chair before the window where she'd left the hotpot.

139

CHAPTER 19

Night Prowler

He crouched motionless in the shrubbery from where he'd watched the house since dusk.

One by one, the lights had gone out as the household made its way to bed, but the faintest glimmer could still be seen from the room he sought to enter; the room of the pretty girl. Too dim for a lamp or candle, it must be firelight that cast its pale glow, and for all he knew; the girl might be asleep already; but he dare not make his move for not everyone was abed.

Beneath the balcony was the masters study. Each time lightning struck, he could see Richard Durcan stood by the window, staring into the night, watching the storm that cast the valley and his hiding place in an eerie electric light.

The French windows of the girl's room opened onto a stone balcony and for all the night was wet and cold; the window was still ajar. When the time came, his task would be easy. The days had grown short and the nights long and cold. It had been another day of rain and sleet, the third without respite. It swept through the valley on swirling gusts of wind until the ground was sodden, the river and ditches, near to bursting.

He watched the man draw the study curtains, then make his way to bed. The candle he carried, flickering as he passed the windows on the first floor.

The prowler crossed the lawn to a huge oak tree that stood some yards from the house; its spreading branches almost touching the ivy covered walls. He climbed the sodden and slippery tree with ease.

Edging carefully onto a huge limb, he peered down into the room below. The girl was there; he could see her asleep in her bed, the covers drawn tight. It was not a sound sleep, for occasionally she would turn, and once or twice he thought he heard her mumble; but it was difficult to tell above the howl of the wind - even with his acute hearing.

Slowly, carefully, he inched his way along the heavy bough.

The bough became thinner and began to bend beneath his weight. He looked at the ground, some thirty feet below. If he fell, it would kill him; he had to judge his leap to perfection.

He moved along the branch as far as he dared and lowered himself to a crouch - tensing his muscles for the jump. When the moment came, he pushed hard on the branch to leap forward like a swimmer on a springboard, but as he did so, he heard the splintering of wood and the branch gave way beneath him. His momentum carried him forward, but it was not enough and he was falling. His muscles convulsed as the ivy covered wall shot past his eyes; he grasped and clawed at leaves, vines, and thin air.

Behind the ivy, crawling creatures scurried to crevices and cracks, or hid behind sturdy vines as stems split and leaves tumbled. Just as he thought all was lost, he caught a grip on the vine and arrested his descent to oblivion. His limbs felt as though they had been torn from their sockets; every muscle screamed and every sinew was stretched like a bowstring.

He held on to the vine not daring to move, his heart pounding in his chest, but he had survived and was safe; the pretty girls balcony was just four feet to his right. He rested for a while to catch his breath; waiting and listening. When he'd regained his strength, he moved across the ivy until he could reach the stone balcony. With one final effort, he leapt over the balustrade to land outside the open door.

Polly opened her eyes at the soft, unusual sound that woke her. She noticed a strange, sour smell in the room.

The fire had died to the dullest glow and the room was in darkness save for two luminous, green eyes, that watched her calmly, never moving their gaze from her.

Polly cried out in alarm, fearing some hideous creature from her nightmares had come to life in the darkness.

With trembling hands, she struck a match and held it high. It cast its brief light upon a black cat who sat impassively on the footboard of her bed.

'Oh goodness,' she gasped, breathless in her fright; 'you frightened me so! Oh goodness!'

The cat seemed pleased she had woken; it purred softly.

Striking another match, Polly lit a candle, and with her heart still racing, she raised it high to be sure the cat was the only creature who shared the room with her. An icy draft from the open window all but gutted the candle and she had to cup it with her hand to guard the tiny flame.

'Did you come to warm yourself? You must be frozen, poor thing.' She slipped from the bed to shut the window, but before she had taken two steps, the cat leapt forward to bar her way, crouching and hissing and baring its teeth in the most threatening way.

'I won't hurt you,' Polly whispered reassuringly, 'I won't close it if you're frightened.' She stirred the fire and put two logs on the glowing embers. Tiny sparks flew up the chimney like a firecracker and the fire sprang into life once more.

'There,' she said, 'that's better isn't it. I will call you Puss, and I'll sit here in my chair and you can sit with me too if you like. We can tell one another our stories. Mine is very sad and is making me very unhappy, but you must tell me yours first.'

The cat seemed reassured by her gentle voice. Crossing to the fire, it sat on its haunches, just out of Polly's reach.

'I'm going to close the window a little,' she said softly. 'It really is very cold and after all... it was you who pushed it open!' The cat raised its head, 'But I won't shut it,' she added reassuringly. The cat watched her carefully, but this time did not move. Polly returned to her chair and the cat curled up in a ball, enjoying the warmth from the fire.

Polly, talked to the cat, telling the creature everything, but if it understood, it gave no sign.

I've been very wicked,' she confided, 'and I tried; really I did; but I love him so, and it... it just happened one day.'

She began to sob and the cat looked at her curiously.

'I mustn't be silly,' she said, drying her tears. 'I have to be strong because they want to take my baby away and Papa is sending me to Scotland until it's all over. They will tell everyone I'm at St Agnes, and won't even let me see my baby, but I won't let them take it away... They have no right!'

The cat seemed to lose interest and turned its face to the fire.

'Are you hungry, Puss?' Polly asked; but the cat continued to stare at the fire.

Nana Dilly had brought Polly hot milk and biscuits at bedtime, but Polly had only sipped a little of the milk and eaten none of the biscuits. She tipped the milk into a saucer and put it on the floor between her and the cat who stared at the milk for some time.

'I'm not even allowed to see Mama before I go, lest she tries to persuade Papa to change his mind. Everyone is so very angry. Papa says I've shamed myself and the whole family, and I've behaved like a wanton trollop and other horrible things. I told him I loved Isaac, and he became very angry and said that I knew nothing about love, nor could I, until I was properly married.'

142

The cat rose to its haunches and moved cautiously to the saucer of milk. It ate hungrily until biscuits and milk were gone. Polly poured more milk into the saucer and the cat seemed unconcerned that her hand was so close.

'But I do understand what love is Puss; really I do. It's a feeling like no other and I cannot believe any feeling could be so precious or so wonderful. It is a wanting to be with someone and to hear their voice, to feel your heart skip a beat when they are near and to feel so alone when they are gone. It is a desperate longing to touch them and for them to touch you, but most of all it is to know they love you.'

When the cat had finished its milk, it sat near her legs, that being the nearest place to the fire. Polly continued to talk and the cat continued to sit.

'Are you warm enough now,' she asked, 'you must have been so cold out in that terrible weather, look it has started to snow.'

It had indeed begun to snow, but the cat seemed unconcerned; instead, it nuzzled against Polly's leg and she was pleased to have won its trust. She stroked the cat gently and it seemed quite content for her to do so.

However, when she took her hand away, she gasped in surprise. Her hand was black, as black as the cat itself. She rubbed her palm with a finger and the blackness wiped away. Polly raised her hand to her nose. The blackness was sharp and acrid, the unmistakable smell of soot.

Shocked at her discovery, she reached down and stroked the cat again, but there could be no mistake, the cat's fur was covered in soot.

Arthur' she whispered softly, 'You are Arthur aren't you?'

The cat looked up at the sound of its name; its interest renewed. It watched her with implacable green eyes.

'What are you doing here; why have you come so far?' asked Polly. She was convinced that it was the smithy cat, for she had seen it sat amongst the rafters and had laughed at Isaac's tales of its bad temper and independent ways. He told her how it appeared when he was sixteen and had made its home in the rafters where it was warm. It watched the two men by day and hunted mice amongst the feed bins by night.

John Smith let Arthur stay, as he was a good mouser; then he grew fond of the cat, ill tempered though it was. Neither man had ever got close enough to touch it; but Arthur was company in his own way.

'Why are you here,' she asked once more. 'Why have you travelled so far from home, and on such a night?'

It was a foolish thought. She knew it was a foolish thought, but she could not get it out of her mind that the cat had come to her because something awful; something terrible, had happened to Isaac. There could be no other explanation, irrational though it might seem.

She reached out to touch the cat once more, but this time it moved away. It moved towards the window, where it turned and stared at her for a moment, then, with a curl of its tail, it squeezed through the gap of the window and was gone.

CHAPTER 20

The Lane

With a pounding heart, Polly climbed down the ivy-covered wall outside her bedroom; her slender fingers and tiny boots, somehow finding purchase amongst the sodden foliage.

She dropped the last few feet to the ground, her boots sinking into the earth of the flower border. She found the coat she'd thrown on a nearby bush and slipped into it gratefully, for the wind was beginning to bite, and carried with it the first snow of winter.

She made her way to the stables as quietly as possible, and lifting the wooden latch; slipped inside. An oil lamp, with a glass chimney and huge copper reflector, hung from a staple on the wall. The stable was full, and many of the horses stirred to see who was calling so late at night.

Polly made straight for the Parson who nodded his head and whinnied at the sight of his beloved mistress. Polly put her arms about his neck and gave him a hug.

'Oh my darling Parson - have you missed me,' she whispered softly; 'I've missed you terribly, but something has happened to Isaac and now we must...'

Polly heard the rattle of a bolt and the creak of hinges from the loft above.

'Wos' going on,' cried a voice above her head.

'Ned!' She exclaimed, 'What are you doing here? You nearly frightened me to death.'

'I lives' ere' case thee forgot! Anyhow - I might ask thee the same question?'

She had forgotten Ned lived in the loft. A flight of stone steps led there from outside, but she had no idea there was a trap door. Ned was peering at her upside down through a square hole.

'I've come to see the Parson, if it's any concern of yours,' she said defensively.

'What at this time o' night! Tis gone eleven-o-clock!'

'I...I had a nightmare, I... I dreamt the Parson had been kidnapped by horse thieves and I had to come and make sure he was all right.'

'So thee've taken to sleeping we thy hat an' coat on then?' said Ned sceptically.

145

'It's none of your concern what I sleep in Ned Meadows, and I'll ask you not to be so familiar! I'm Papa's favourite and everything I want I get and you're just the stable boy and not a very good one at that, so don't you dare be rude to me!'

'You're running away, you are!'

'No I'm not!'

'I'm goin' ter tell the master,' said Ned, swinging through the trap door onto the straw strewn floor. He marched past Polly on his way to the door.

'No Ned, please! Please don't tell Papa,' she grabbed Ned's coat to hold him back.

'Why not?'

'He'd be terribly angry,' said Polly anxiously... 'With you!' she blurted out as an afterthought.

'With me? What ave' I done?'

'You're stopping me fetching Doctor Wooton!' she said, an inspiration coming to her. 'Mama's not well and Papa told me to get Doctor Wooton straight away; it's an emergency, now please put a saddle on the Parson.'

'Why don't e send Hudson or John Long or I?' said Ned, unsure if his young mistress was telling the truth or not. 'Why's 'e sending thee?'

'Because its ladies matters that why! It's very, very delicate and Mama is very ill, so if you don't mind, I'd like you to saddle the Parson straight away!'

'First tis 'orse thieves,' grumbled Ned; 'that were a good un that were! Then tis the mistress took poorly! Wos' it goin ter be next?'

'It's going to be you if you're not very careful! Papa doesn't like you much anyway! He says you are king of all the bumpkins and if you don't let me go, he will sack you for sure.'

'Ha...! There tis then - I thought as much! Runnin' away you are!'

'No I'm not!'

'Yes you are! You must think I've gone doolally or summat!'

'No I am not running away,' bristled Polly. 'And even if I was - it would be no concern of yours.'

'No, not until the morning when master wants to know where thee've gone. We'll all be fer the bloody high jump then, good an' proper. I'd be out on me

146

ear, we masters boot up me arse. I knows what's going on; yer supposed to be locked in yer room, you are. Everybody d' know that!'

'Ned, please help me,' pleaded Polly, thinking it best to use a softer approach with the truculent Ned. 'I have to see someone... it's most important.'

'I'm going ter tell master, I am,' said Ned turning for the door once more.

'Ned ...' said Polly with all the command she could muster; 'If you tell my father, I will tell Isaac Smith that I begged you for help and you ran to tell tales.' Ned faltered in his step and Polly knew that she had struck a chord. 'It will be the worse for you then Ned, and serve you right.'

Ned thought about the drubbing Isaac had given Harry Edwards. It looked painful even from a distance, and Edwards was still not right. As if that weren't bad enough, it was he himself who'd let the dogs loose, and Isaac might be a long time forgetting that. Ned was already having anxious moments, fretting about what might happen when he and Isaac next met.

'I don't know Miss Polly; you don't know what yer asking on us.'

'I'm not asking anything of you, Ned, except to go back to bed, and pretend you know nothing. I don't need the Parson, I'll walk; I'm just going to go to Isaac and deliver a message and come back. I'll be home by two and no one will be the wiser.'

'Well I don't know Miss Polly.'

'Please Ned'

'You can't walk Miss Polly, the roads is too bad. There be mud everywhere, and the Delkin's flooded deeper than anyone can remember it. Tis all across the dippy, as deep as yer shoulders where it crosses the moors' road, an' you'll never pass through on foot! Tis startin' t' snow an all.'

'Why don't you come with me Ned?' she exclaimed, 'we could ride the Parson to Coaley and no-one will ever know.'

She saw the stable boy falter and pressed home her advantage. 'I will tell Isaac you helped me. 'Please Ned' she cooed, as Ned swayed with indecision.

'Well... I suppose twill do no harm so long as we're back by two, but why don't we take the trap?'

'The trap will make too much noise. We'll walk the Parson down the orchard then no one will hear us leave.'

They set out a few minutes later, crossing the sodden orchard, then on to the lane which they followed until they came to the cross roads in the village. They turned left into Fop Street and the steep pitch that led across the moors to Coaley.

Flurries of snow blew through the open valley between the Bury and the Long Down. Ned lifted his collar against the chill wind as he walked ahead of the Parson. He held a lantern on a staff tucked beneath his arm; it rocked to and fro as he walked, casting an eerie glow and picking out each snowflake as it fell. He was often ankle deep in mud and puddles, whilst the Parson trudged on, head down against the bitter wind.

'You said we could both ride on the Parson,' grumbled Ned, as cold, muddy water seeped through his lace holes, 'That were a good un that were, bloody good un that was!'

'No I did not.'

'Yes you did.'

'Well even if I did, you can't, so you'll just have to put up with it!'

'Taint bloody fair,' mumbled Ned. 'Disturbing a body in is' own home!' Ned's voice rose in indignation at the injustice of it all. 'An' threatening on un!' he added for good measure.

'Oh do shut up Ned,' snapped Polly tired of his carping.

'An turnin' un' out in't middle of the bloody night - t' walk all over the bloody countryside! I ain't never erd' of nowt like it - tis bloody madness!'

'Look out Ned, cried Polly; but too late to stop Ned stepping in a flood that submerged the road ahead for a good forty yards. They had reached the dippy of the Delkin.

'Thas it,' shouted Ned; 'I'm off ome' - bugger this.' he said.

'Ned for goodness sake, it's only a little water! It won't do you any harm, and anyway, you promised to help me. If you don't, I shall tell Isaac you broke your promise and then you'll regret it.'

'Well, you promised, as I was to ride ont Parson, an' that never appen'd' did it! That were a good un that were! Now yer I am, we me boots full of water!'

'Well, I'm sorry Ned' said Polly unrepentantly, 'but when I said we'd ride to Coaley I didn't mean you'd actually "ride" on the Parson! Then for good measure, she added, 'And anyway, I'm Papa's daughter and you're just a stable boy - whatever would people think!

'They'd think I was bloody daft to listen to thy cock and bull stories, an' go gallivanting about the countryside on a night like this; thas what they'd think, but

148

they'd think I were even dafter if I was t' walk through that brook. I'd be up ter me bloody neck in it!'

Oh, all right then' said Polly in frustration and annoyance, 'you can ride with me through the brook, but you're to sit right back on his rump.'

Ned grumbled beneath his breath.

'And you're not to hold on to me either,' she added for good measure.

Polly guided the Parson to a fence where Ned clambered onto the Parsons back, grumbling all the while. The world and everyone in it was a "bloody bugger", though Ned was tactful enough not to mention any "buggers" by name.

Polly guided the horse back to the road and into the black waters of the Delkin.

The water became deeper and deeper, until it was higher than the Parsons belly. Ned swayed precariously upon the horses rump, with legs straight out before him, to keep them clear of the water. He held out one arm for balance, whilst the other held the oil lamp aloft so they could see where they were going.

Parson Pimm's shoe found a pothole and his stumble nearly threw Ned in the water. He saved himself by grabbing Polly about the waist, but it might have been wiser to fall.

'Ned I told you not to touch me; take your hands off me this instant.'

'Tis all right fer thee; thee've got bloody stirrups t' put thy feet in. Thee try staying on we thee...'

'I don't care,' said Polly, stopping Parson Pimm in the middle of the flood to glare at Ned. 'Don't you dare put your hands on me again!'

'Ow' am I supposed t' balance we' no ands' then - on the blind end of this panto horse,' replied Ned indignantly.

Oh don't be so stupid' said Polly, geeing the Parson on again. 'It's only a little water. And frankly Ned,' she added as an afterthought, 'If you did get a good soaking, it wouldn't be a moment too soon. You smell worse than any of the horses.'

Ned did not find this at all amusing.

'And don't you ever call the Parson a panto horse again - and while we're at it,' she added for good measure, 'I don't like you swearing!'

Ned wished with all his heart that he'd be struck by lightning, or fall in the brook and drown. Anything would be better than another hour of his mistress's company.

When they were through the flood, Ned jumped down from the Parsons back and they continued on as before. Very soon, they passed the dirt track that led to Spring Tyning and began their descent toward the village. The moors and the worst of the journey were behind them.

Polly would occasionally see the bright shining eyes of some wild animal as it watched them from the safety of the hedgerow. Life would be even more difficult for the wild creatures of the banks and burrows, now the winter snows had come; she hoped they had made their homes well. The lane was becoming quite deep with snow; it would all look so beautiful in the morning; perhaps it would be a white Christmas that year.

'Do you like Christmas Ned?'

'Tis all right I suppose.'

'And Christmas carols too?'

'Aye, they're all right,' replied Ned.

'My favourite is "In the deep mid winter"!'

'Thas a bit of a dreary un that is, Miss Polly.'

'Well perhaps it is a little bit Ned, but the words are so beautiful, would you like me to sing them for you?'

'You can if you like.'

Polly began to sing, at first a little faltering, for the cold night air caught her voice.

'In the deep midwinter,

Frosty winds made moan.

Earth stood hard as iron,

Water like a stone.

Snow was falling, snow on snow,

Snow on snow.

In the deep midwinter, long, long ago.'

Isn't that beautiful Ned?' she asked.

Ned had listened as she sung her song, and her voice sounded like icicles' being struck by tiny hammers, each note as clear and pure as the cold night air.

'Twas' beautiful the way thee sung it, Miss Polly. Thee could sing a little more if thee've a mind.'

'Doesn't it make you think of frosty mornings, and crisp new snow, and white Christmas's, and plum pudding?'

'I suppose so Miss Polly, but I'd rather summut a bit more cheerful meself.'

'Like what? Sing me something jolly then Ned!'

'I can't sing Miss Polly.'

'Of course you can; everyone can sing! Come on Ned, I sang for you!'

Reluctantly Ned began to sing.

When I wakes up one mornin' oh -

an I espies me darlin' oh,

er looks so sweet an charming oh -

in every single way.'

Polly took up the refrain.

'She looked so sweet an charming oh-

as I espied my darling oh.

Dashing away with the smoothing iron -

dashing away with the smoothing iron -

she stole my heart away.'

They laughed together as they sang their way down Ticks Hill to Far Green and beyond, and Ned began to think that perhaps the young mistress wasn't quite so bad after all.

Polly said to Ned with new found kindness, 'Is there a darling for you, Ned?'

'No, not for me Miss Polly,' said Ned, his voice serious once more. 'There ain't never bin' no-one fer I.'

'That's sad Ned,' said Polly with genuine warmth, for her thoughts were again of Isaac. 'Everyone should have someone for themselves.'

'I don't want no-one Miss Polly; I be better off on me own.'

'And so you'll stay, if you keep talking like that.'

'You don't know what you're talking about Miss Polly,' said Ned with sadness in his voice. 'You've always ad' everything, you av'; I ain't never ad' nothin'. No family, no home, no nothing.'

Polly began to speak, but before she could do so; Ned carried on.

'You're bloody daft you are, Miss Polly! Mucking about we the likes of Isaac Smith with all the fine things thee got, an upsetting the master an' mistress like thee ave.'

'Well I'm sorry Ned,' said Polly, hurt by his bluntness, 'it's not that I want to upset them; it's just that... What happened to your parents?' she asked, wanting to change the subject.

I don't know as I ever ad' any miss,' he replied. 'They both died long afore I can remember. I was brought up in the poor house, an' they told us as how I never ad' no parents, an' nobody wanted us, an' that were it an' all about it.'

Polly had never given any thought to the workhouse before, but she listened quietly to what Ned had to say.

'I didn't like it there, Miss Polly. They said as how I was lucky to be there, an ow' twas' thanks to good Christian folks charity an' kindness, but I never saw much kindness while I was there. They used t' beat us we a stick most days; cus they said it were the only way we'd learn. I ran off as soon as I was able, but they did allus' bring us back. They'd give us a beatin' we a stick, then lock us in a shed we' no clothes nor bedding so I'd learn. Twer' cold like tis now... they was buggers they was, Miss Polly.'

Ned paused a little before he continued, for memories - cruel and sadistic, under the guise of Christian charity - came flooding back.

'Then yer grandfather come an' got us fer a stable boy when I was nine. I was pleased about that, but then I just got a beating every day off Potter the groom, so twern't much different really.'

'I'm so sorry Ned,' said Polly with genuine sadness. 'You've helped me tonight in every way you can, and I've been horrible and selfish in return... just like everyone else.'

'Taint no matter Miss Polly,' said Ned matter of factly, 'everybody d' do it - taint just you. I'm used to it now. Everybody d' say, "there's old Ned; e's bloody daft 'e is." They don't know us, nor talk to us, they just kips on all the time.' Ned became lost in his own words as though she were no longer there.

'That's why I like the 'orses. When I'm with people I ain't nothin', but when I'm with the orses' tis different then. They don't worry if I ain't clever. It don't mean nothin' t' them. They just knows as I feeds um', an' mucks um' out an' that.'

Ned looked up at Polly expecting her to scoff at him; expecting her to tell him not to be so foolish, but she did none of those things. Instead, she sat silently in the saddle looking down at the unhappy, lonely man, who lived above the stable and who had never known a kind deed, or warm word in all his life.

'I love's the 'orses, Miss Polly.'

'I know you do Ned' she replied softly; 'and I'm sure they love you in return. We're very alike in many ways, you and I.'

Ned turned his head to look up at her and she could see his face clearly in the soft glow of the lantern. 'Why d' thee say that, Miss Polly.'

Her voice faltered just a little as she said, 'Because Parson Pimm has always been my best friend too... ever since I can remember. He can't talk, but that doesn't matter because I know he loves me. I'm sure the horses love you too Ned, just as much as you love them... I'm sure they do.'

These were the kindest words Ned had ever heard. 'Thank you, Miss Polly,' he said quietly.

They reached the centre of the village and their destination. Before them was the smithy and it alone, among so many dwellings, showed a light. They burned upstairs and down and Polly's heart sank, for why should the household be awake so late, if all was well? She had been right to follow her instinct about the cat. Something was most terribly wrong.

CHAPTER 21

Fever

'Ned, stay here with the Parson; I won't be long,' said Polly.

She opened the gate and walked the path to the shelter of the wooden porch; the wind had got up and was blowing the skirts of her coat in all directions. She lifted the doorknocker, only for her courage to desert her. What would they say at such an hour? How could she possibly explain the cat and her premonition for it would all sound so silly and foolish? Only the lights, burning so late in the night, steadied her resolve, for surely something must be wrong. She took a deep breath and struck the knocker against the door.

She heard curtain rings rattle along a rail and bolts being drawn. The door opened and a short heavyset woman with greying hair stood in the doorway; a candle held aloft.

'Who's there; what do you want?' she asked of the darkness.

'It's Polly Durcan, Mrs Smith.'

'Don't you know what time it is?' the woman asked in a hostile voice.

'I... I'm sorry Mrs Smith, I know it's late, it's just...'

'Don't you think you've caused enough trouble, young lady? You're not welcome here... we don't want you here again.' She began to close the door when another voice spoke from within. 'Who is it Amy?' asked John Smith.

'It's the Durcan girl,' came the curt reply.

The door opened once more and John Smith stood beside his wife. He looked weary and old, and there was none of the usual jolliness about him. He looked smaller than she remembered.

'It's past midnight, Miss Polly,' he said simply.

'I know Mr Smith; I am so sorry, but I have to speak to Isaac...'

'Does your father know you're out at this time of night... in this weather?'

She shook her head realising how foolish she must look to him. She was bespattered with mud, her coat and hat, white with snow; her hair was wet and bedraggled and her cheeks were blue from the cold. She must have looked a very sorry sight.

154

He exchanged glances with his wife and to her clear disapproval he said, 'Well you'd best come in for a while.'

Polly entered the tiny cottage, her coat dripping water on the flagstone floor. She was glad of the warmth from the fire that burnt so cheerfully in the grate.

'You'd better give me your coat, seeing as you're staying,' said Amy, clearly angry with her husband for bringing her into the house. 'I'll go and see to him while you explain to this young lady what kind of person her father is!'

They were in the parlour, for there were two easy chairs and a settle close to a cast iron grate. Polly recognised the room from Isaac's description of his home. The grate shone like a new pin and had a huge black kettle upon the hob. Wisps of steam curled upwards from its spout.

The room was drab, the walls clad with a high wooden wainscot, painted brown. Heavy curtains hung at both window and door to keep out the drafts, and a huge oak beam crossed the room from end to end. Horse brasses hung from it that shon brightly in the firelight. There was a smell about the room of wet clothes and Brasso.

To one side of the fireplace was a wooden step that protruded into the room, and above it, a door that led upstairs. Amy passed through the door and climbed the stairs to the rooms above.

John Smith motioned her to one of the armchairs, 'You'd best warm yourself up a bit,' he said.

'What did your wife mean, Mr Smith?' asked Polly.

'Don't you know?' he replied, 'I thought everyone knew! I'm surprised you're here, given what's happened.'

'Know what? What's happened... please tell me...?' Polly was becoming ever more anxious about the blacksmith's words.

'Your father set the dogs on Isaac with some cock and bull story about poaching. They damn near ripped him apart. Four men and two dogs against one defenceless lad.'

Polly's hand went to her mouth and she gasped in horror. She could only imagine what Rufus and Satan were capable of.

'There's wounds to his face and arms, his chest too. Dr. Wooton's sewn up what's left, but infection has set in and with it the fever. One moment he's burning hot; the next he's shivering with the cold. He's put up a gallant fight, but only the Lord knows which way it's going to go.'

155

Polly was stunned and shocked by what he'd said. Her mind ran wild with images of Satan and Rufus, slashing and tearing at Isaac's flesh, his hands dripping with blood as he fought off the two frenzied animals.

'And you'd no idea about all this?' asked John Smith again, seeing her shock and disbelief. She shook her head, her eyes bright with tears.

'Papa came home in a terrible rage and sent me to my room with no one but Mrs Hudson allowed to see me. I had no idea ...'

John Smith was unsure what to do for the best, to send her home or let her stay. Given what she'd just said, he chose the latter. 'You'd best come and take a look for yourself, Polly,' he said, 'but I'd prepare myself if I were you.'

He'd always liked the pretty girl and had been more amused than concerned by her infatuation with Isaac, but she'd suddenly stopped calling a year or so back, and Isaac had just as suddenly taken to walking the moors on his days off, something that was completely out of character. One thing John Smith was not was anybody's fool, and he'd wondered many times about them; but getting anything out of Isaac was like getting blood from a stone. Now it seemed, they had their answer, and things had come to this.

It was all very well to have romantic notions when you are young, but the reality of life was another thing altogether. If Isaac survived, as pray God he might, he'd have scars for life; and quite likely, a crippled arm into the bargain. It was as well she knew that now, while there was still time to go back to the life she knew and leave them to theirs.

They climbed the steep and winding stairs, to emerge on a tiny landing with nothing but a banister and a door at either side.

'To your left,' said John Smith from behind her.

She lifted the latch and opened the door on a tiny room, barely big enough for the bed, let alone the two chairs on either side. The room had the smell of sickness about it, of bitter medicine, sweat and stuffiness. A fire burned brightly in a tiny basket grate, but the room was chill from the open window.

'He's burning up again,' said Amy to her husband, wiping sweat from Isaac's face and chest. 'Five minutes ago, he was shivering with the cold; I can't keep up with it!' She cast a disapproving look at Polly and an equally cold glance at her husband.

'She's just come to see him before she makes her way home,' John said, in reply to the unspoken question.

156

Polly sat beside the bed and took Isaac's hand in hers; it was hot and sticky to the touch. He lay with his head facing her, his cheek and throat, swathed in blood stained bandages. His chest and arm were bandaged, and these too, were stained with blood and a foul looking discharge.

'Dr. Wooton says he'll be scarred for life,' said John, 'but at least they missed his eyes.'

Isaac's eyes were closed, and at first, she thought him asleep, but then she heard him mumbling. She put her head closer to him, but she couldn't understand the words, if they were words at all.

She leant over further and kissed him very gently on the forehead. John Smith and his wife exchanged glances.

'Isaac, it's Polly,' she whispered. 'I've come to be with you and everything will be alright now.' She kissed him once again.

Isaac continued to mumble, moving his head just tiny amounts.

'I think you should tell us what's going on, young lady,' said Amy.

Polly kissed him once more and sat up straight. She took a handkerchief from her sleeve and dried her eyes. She wanted to speak to them - had to speak to them - but she wanted to do so as a grown woman and not a foolish young girl.

'Mrs. Smith - Mr Smith,' she began; 'I know you love Isaac dearly, and I know he loves you too, because he has told me so many times; but what he couldn't tell you - because of all the things that are set against us - is that he loves me too - just as I love him. I love him with all my heart, and it might not be wise, or sensible, or what you or my parents want, but it has happened, and I cannot change it - nothing can change it. This terrible thing that has broken my heart, only makes me love him more.'

Amy opened her mouth to speak.

'Please let me stay,' Polly continued determinedly, before Amy could object. 'You are exhausted both of you - I can see you are - I could help, really I could; all you need do is show me how. I can't go home now I know what's happened, I just can't. If you let me stay, I will help you all I can and you will learn to trust me, then you can get some sleep. Please, please let me stay...'

John and Amy Smith were taken aback by the passion and sincerity of Polly's plea, for John Smith had expected the very opposite to happen.

It was Amy who spoke first and she was quick to come to the point.

157

'Are you expecting, young lady?' she asked severely.

It was the question Polly had feared most, but she looked at Amy without flinching.

'Yes,' she said simply.

Amy looked disdainfully at Polly then angrily at her husband.

'There! What did I tell you!' she snapped.

CHAPTER 22

Farewell

Ned and the Parson had taken shelter beneath a fir where they waited patiently in the falling snow. At last, the door opened and Polly emerged. John Smith stood at the porch; his lantern held high to light her way.

Ned knew she would be angry, for she must know about the dogs by now; she must know he'd let them loose. He wished it hadn't happened for she'd been kind to him and now she would hate him. He wanted so much to stay her friend.

'Miss Polly' began Ned, studying his feet, 'I'm very sorry fer tother day. Twer' the dogs what hurt un'; I never meant un' no harm. We was only doing the master's bidding; I didn't never mean un' no harm.' He looked up for her answer and could see she'd been crying, but when she spoke, her voice was steady and resolute.

'What you did was wicked and cowardly Ned, you know that don't you? There were four of you and he was on his own.'

'I know Miss Polly, but 'e hit Edwards first an' that's the God's honest truth. He caught un' right in the goolies, an' you can ask un' that yerself.'

'No I can't Ned, he's too ill to talk - he has the fever and he's very weak. He may die from what has happened.'

'Twer' the dogs' Miss Polly, honest to God,' sobbed Ned.

'Ned,' said Polly, calmly, 'I want you to take the Parson and go home.' She'd no emotion left that she could spare him, not even anger.

'Ain't you coming too, Miss Polly?'

'No Ned, there's no home there for me now.'

Polly went over to the Parson, who waited with eyes closed and head bowed against the swirling snow; waiting patiently as ever to do his mistress's bidding. He lifted his head as she reached out for him and his eyes turned towards her.

She put her arms about his neck and held him very close, her cheek against his. She sobbed quietly as she thought of all the adventures they had had together, all the miles they had ridden together and all the understanding and love they shared.

'Oh my darling Parson,' whispered Polly through her tears, 'I shall miss you so very, very much. I must go now for Isaac needs me, but I shall never forget you. You will always be my closest and dearest friend.'

As is the way with many creatures whom some believe to be just dumb animals, lesser in God's eyes than they, the Parson sensed the great sadness that came with her tears, and he too was sad. The child who'd been entrusted to him since before she could walk was the whole reason for his existence. He was happy when she was near and forlorn when she went away. He wanted only to serve her and be with her. Each time she'd shed tears like these, it had been he who was hurting. When his muscles were twisted or his flesh torn; when he was frightened or in pain; she had cried the tears he couldn't shed and she had comforted him. He wasn't hurting now, but still she cried and he was sad, for her tears must be for herself this time; they must be from deep inside. Now it was his turn to comfort her, and he pushed his nostrils gently against her neck; his breath warm upon her chest, his eyes closed. They stayed like that for many minutes, Polly's arms about him, her cheek against his, the snow falling about them.

CHAPTER 23

Vigil

Those who loved him looked on fearfully as he journeyed through that other world - the dark world of fever and delirium. It was a floating, swirling void, beyond consciousness and between life and death.

They knew nothing of his strange journey, but they knew he'd embarked upon it, for he mumbled incessantly, talking in riddles and crying out in fear. All the while, he trembled and convulsed whilst his heart raced. They feared for him; not knowing if he'd the strength to fight; fearing he'd not return from the dark place.

Polly had been beside his bed for two days and more. She was distressed to see him so ill, but she put her feelings to one side to do all she humanly could to help him.

She sat patiently, wiping the sour bile from his lips and the sweat that seeped from every pore. She fed him water from a spoon and from time to time, she would wring out the towel that cooled his brow in a bucket of water. When burning heat turned to shivering cold, she would cover his shoulders to warm him once more. All the while, she talked to him, and sang to him softly so he might hear her voice and know she was there.

Amy snored loudly in her chair; it was her first deep sleep since Polly came into their home and the first real sleep in days. She was exhausted, having barely left Isaac's room since they'd brought him home; but though still hostile towards Polly, she had become more accepting of her help as the endless hours ground on.

She'd been angry with John for allowing Polly to stay, 'She's naught but an over-privileged little hussy,' she'd said angrily and loudly enough for Polly to hear.

Amy fully expecting her to run home the minute sympathy turned to hard work, but to her surprise, the girl had rolled up her sleeves, dried her eyes and complained of none of the tasks that came her way. Polly would only leave the room when nature took its course with Isaac, and then only reluctantly; but there were limits to what Amy Smith would allow in a Christian household.

'That's the job of wives and mothers young lady, and you're neither of those, so out you go!'

As tiredness turned to exhaustion, Amy softened her heart towards Polly, addressing her by name, trusting her, and relying on her more and more.

She came to the conclusion that though she might disapprove of their alliance, there was no doubting her sincerity and love for Isaac. It was there for all to see, in her eyes and in the patience and gentleness with which she cared for him. She began to look on her with new respect, especially since speaking to Doctor Wooton on the matter, for there was little doubt she had sacrificed everything to be with him.

Doctor Wooton called every day to check his progress, and Nurse Priday called mornings and evenings to dress his wounds. He raised an eyebrow when he first saw Polly at the bedside, suggesting that she consider her position very carefully. However, the following day he confided in Amy that he'd tried to speak to her father on her behalf, but Richard Durcan had completely disowned his daughter for the disgrace she'd brought upon the family.

'Let us hope he pulls through,' he remarked, 'or I see two lives in ruins.'

'Is there nothing more you can do doctor?' asked Amy anxiously.

'His wounds are healing Mrs Smith we have no concerns there - it's the fever that's more to be feared.'

'But why a fever if he's healing so well?'

'He's picked up an infection from the dog bite. It's coursing through his body as we speak. The human body tries to kill an infection by raising its temperature, but it can go too far and the fight becomes too exhausting. We know the bacteria that cause the infection, but we've no cure as yet, save what we are doing.'

'Will he…?'

'He's young and strong,' he added, seeing the fear in her eyes, 'he'll fight all the way, but there's only so much the human body can cope with, so I just don't know the answer to your question.'

At Dr. Wooton's suggestion, Reverend Aubrey called that afternoon and gave Isaac the last rites.

John went to bed that night, to give them space in the room, and Amy succumbed to exhaustion at midnight. Polly begrudged neither of them a minute of it, for they had worked themselves to a standstill. As Amy snored in her chair, she leant over and kissed his brow and told him that she loved him. To her great pleasure, she heard him call her name.

'Polly,' he whispered.

'I'm here my darling, don't be afraid.'

'Polly,' he whispered once more.

Her eyes filled with tears as she leant over him and kissed him tenderly.

'Come back to me my darling,' she whispered. 'I love you so very much.'

'Only five Polly,' he muttered; 'only five more....'

~

The two slavering dogs kept up their relentless pursuit, never tiring of their baying. They chased Isaac across a desert of soft blue sand with seemingly effortless ease, whilst every step Isaac took seemed like a mile.

He saw the carnival ahead and made for it, hoping to find sanctuary amongst the flying boats, candyfloss stalls and roundabouts.

He called out to the revellers, time and time again, but no one turned their heads to look. They seemed not to hear his desperate cries, or the baying of the huge brutes above the toot and um-pah of the steam organ.

As he drew closer, he saw a river between him and the carnival which he'd have to cross, but the river was red, not blue - as red as blood.

Carnival floats were in full procession on the red river and Isaac couldn't understand why none sank below the surface.

Terrifying, finned creatures, leapt from the river into the jaws of larger, more hideous monsters, who then sank beneath the surface to devour their prey.

Men rode down the river on elephants and six legged rats that were bigger than the men themselves. Children with old men's faces rode upon their scaly tails, laughing and falling off as the tails whisked from side to side, scattering the children like water droplets; but the children jumped on once more with the next sweep of the shiny tail.

Naked, old women, with pendulous breasts, gross in their fatness, danced before the rats in red slippers sewn with sequins; each with an umbrella made of dark leathery material like bat's wings.

The procession passed by before he made the river; the laughter of the women and the squealing of the rats, growing less with every mile, until the odd procession was just a dot upon the horizon.

Just as he thought the dogs were upon him, the river flooded its banks and immersed him. It was soft, warm and cloying, but not wet, not wet at all.

163

He floated on its surface grateful to be rid of the ferocious dogs, when one of the huge swimming creatures rose up and swallowed him whole. Unable to grip its slippery gullet with hands or feet, he slithered into the warmth of its stomach.

The huge foul smelling gut pulsed with the beat of the creature's heart, but there was no sound save the tick tock, tick tock, of the town hall clock. It hung from a rib at the most alarming angle, but the other people seemed unconcerned. Some smiled and he smiled back, but mostly they ignored him and watched the man who stood beneath the clock.

The mayor was fat and wore a red cape, gold chain and black breeches. He counting each minute as it passed by; from time to time, taking a bright silver timepiece from his tunic pocket, then checking the clock against it.

At precisely seven minutes to each o' clock, he would summon one of Isaac's companions, who, with a final wave to them all, would clamber into the well.

'God bless you, and God save the King,' each would say before disappearing from sight.

Those that were left, Isaac included; moved closer to the well and when all was quiet once more, the mayor returned to counting the minutes. Isaac stood up to look into the well, but the mayor; greatly annoyed at his bad manners said, 'No queue jumping there! Sit down, sit down!'

'Sit down, sit down,' shouted Isaac's companions.

'No queue jumping and no shouting,' said the mayor angrily, 'I cannot hear the clock if you are shouting!'

'He cannot hear the clock,' mumbled his companions, 'the mayor cannot hear the clock, shssh, shssh...'

'No shssh-ing,' said the mayor. 'Definitely no shssh-ing!'

At this rate, it would be hours, days even, before Isaac would take his turn in the well and he was so tired, so very, very tired. He closed his eyes and listened to the hypnotic tick of the clock.

Someone jabbed him roughly in the ribs; it was the mayor, 'No sleeping, can't you read?' He pointed to the "No sleeping" sign with his pencil.

'No sleeping and no shssh-ing,' intoned his companions altogether.

When he thought he could stay awake no longer, he heard Polly's beautiful voice from the depths of the well. It echoed about the dark, warm stomach with its foul smelling bilge water, and his heart leapt to hear her voice.

He called out to her, hoping she could hear him, but the mayor shouted angrily and glared at Isaac, 'No helloing there, how can I hear the clock with people helloing, definitely no helloing.'

'No helloing and no sleeping,' shouted his companions, with equal hostility, 'no shssh-ing and no shouting.'

He wanted so much to jump into the well; to go to her, but the mayor would never allow it. There were five ahead of him on the wooden bench. Five hours and he would be with her; he wanted so much to be with her.

'Polly's in the well,' he said to himself over and over; 'Polly's in the well.'

'Ding Dong Dell, Polly's in the well,' mimicked his companions, Polly's in the well, Ding Dong Dell.'

'No chanting,' said the mayor, 'I said no chanting there, definitely no chanting.'

'Polly... Polly...' he whispered softly, so that the mayor could not hear him. To his joy, he heard her voice reply. 'Come back to me my darling; I love you so much.'

When he heard her beautiful voice, his eyes filled with tears.

'Only five, Polly,' he murmured; 'only five more.'

Five hours passed; minute by minute, tick by tock, and all the while he heard her sweet voice echoing up the well shaft, hollow but clear. She called for him and sang to him, and he whispered her name as loudly as he dared.

At last his turn came. 'Move along there, move along I say,' said the mayor, ushering Isaac impatiently to the well shaft.

Isaac clambered into the well, but it was not a well at all, but a chimney; a high chimney that rose higher and higher with every rung he climbed. All the while, he heard her voice calling him on. His body ached; he had never been so tired; 'Come back to me my darling,' he heard her whisper - somehow, he found the strength to climb on.

~

He opened his eyes to see her there by his side. He had no idea the chimney emerged in his bedroom or why she was there, but she was there, and that was all that mattered.

He felt her lips touch his, saw her smile through her tears, felt her fingers upon his forehead, the wonderful coolness of the towel she placed there.

165

'Water,' he whispered, with his remaining strength.

He heard Amy speak, 'The Lord be praised!' she said. She too was beside his bed exactly where the chimney had been.

'Not too much Polly or he'll be sick,' Isaac heard her say. Amy always fussed too much... John was there too, smiling yet upset, all at the same time. He'd never before seen John with tears in his eyes and wondered what had upset him so.

'Water,' he said once more, and gratefully sipped from the spoon that Polly held to his lips. He was glad she was there; he loved her and had missed her so. He'd been worried, for she didn't know about the dogs, or the red river, or the monster fish, or the unfriendly mayor. She must have realized something was wrong and he was glad she was there. He was tired - so very tired - and there was pain everywhere. He took another sip of the blessed water and closed his eyes.

'Sleep,' he said, as he drifted into the deep sleep that comes from total exhaustion.

'Yes, sleep my darling,' said Polly as she squeezed his hand.

'I love you,' he managed to add, and then he was gone.

Outside the window, Arthur watched the scene from his spot on the sill - his eyes unblinking. He was glad the pretty girl had come. The young stick beater liked her and the old stick beater too, but especially the young one. It was not right that the forge had grown so cold, the anvil fallen so silent, and the bellows so still.

She had come and the young stick beater had woken from his sleep, as Arthur knew he would. Soon the smithy would return to normal; his home among the rafters would be warm once more and that would be good, very good. It was time for him to leave for he was hungry and there were mice aplenty amongst the grain hoppers. He too had kept a vigil on the cold windowsill these days past; but the young stick beater had survived the dark place, and the pretty girl was there beside him, so all would be well.

He moved carefully, from sill to gutter and then to roof, his tail curling and uncurling along the way. He picked each step with caution for there was deadly ice beneath the snow.

CHAPTER 24

Rebecca

Isaac's wounds were dry and healing well, his strength, gradually returning. He sat out for most of the day but Amy refused to allow him downstairs until the doctor had called. Dr. Wooton inspected his stitches and concluded that though the new skin was fragile and taut, it was healing well and he was generally pleased with his handiwork.

'He can get up now,' he said to Amy, 'but no work just yet. I'll call again in a couple of days.' Turning to Isaac he said, 'You're a very lucky young man! I think you owe Mrs Smith and this young lady a big thank you. Goodness knows how they did it!'

'Will there be scars?' asked Polly anxiously.

'Of course...!' he replied candidly, 'nothing I can do about that! You've lost your good looks I'm afraid, but it'll get better with time. You've beaten the fever and that's the important thing - you'll get used to it.' Isaac cared little at that moment in time; he was just pleased to be leaving the tiny room.

Still weak and unsteady, he made his way downstairs with help from John and Polly. A meal of brown bread, chicken soup and beer awaited him in the scullery. No sooner had he sat down than the inevitable happened. Isaac braced himself for the onslaught. It lasted every moment of the time it took him to sup the broth and eat the two slices of bread, for Amy had waited long enough to give him this particular piece of her mind. Isaac ate steadily, dipping his bread in the soup or sipping from his beer, the bowl seemingly the most interesting artefact in the whole world. Polly too, listened in silence with head bowed; neither of them in any doubt as to what Amy thought of them. Shameful, disgraceful, scandalous, disgusting and other such words ricocheted about the room like stray bullets.

'You've ruined her reputation for evermore, and I don't dare think what the neighbours will say... and both of you of good family too! I'll never be able to hold my head up in this village again, so I hope you're both pleased with yourselves.'

Isaac tried to say something in their defence, but Amy cut straight across him. 'All I want to hear from you, young man, is "I'm going to put this matter right," and quickly too, before her shame becomes all too obvious.' With that final barb, she picked up the mug of tea she'd brewed for John, and with a last thunderous scowl for both of them; made her way to the smithy.

167

'Oh Isaac ...' said Polly, very upset at Amy's words.

'It's me she's got it in for, not you.'

'She's very upset... we've let them down so badly.'

'She's upset about the village, and I don't give a damn about the village!'

'It's about them too, Isaac. They're good people; respectable people, and we've let them down; that's what she's saying.'

Isaac grunted and wiped the remains of the crust about the bowl.

'Are you cross with me too?' she asked anxiously, for Isaac was uncharacteristically irritable and petulant after Amy's tongue-lashing. She was reminded of Nana Dilly's words concerning the fickleness of the male of the species.

'No...' he replied tetchily, 'but I'd like to meet your friend Letty! I'd help her improve her jumping with my boot up her backside.'

His words upset Polly terribly, for she'd never heard him speak so coarsely. It was clear who he blamed for their present situation. Things were all going wrong, just as Nana predicted.

Seeing her distress, Isaac regretted his words, 'I suppose this means I'll have to marry you?' he said, turning towards her with a wry smile that was a clumsy attempt at saying sorry.

'I suppose it does,' she replied, 'but only if you want to!' She wished he had put it differently. Long overdue tears fell to the table, bleached white by years of scrubbing.

When he saw her tears, he regretted his thoughtlessness for she must have been to hell and back these last few days. He cupped her chin and gently lifted her face toward him. He hated to see the dark rings about her eyes and her obvious exhaustion. Worst of all, he hated the hurt his selfish and silly words had caused.

She looked pale, worn and exhausted: her hair, usually so beautiful, looked lank and bedraggled. Her eyes were red with the worry and stress, but for all that, he was sure no creature on God's earth had ever looked as beautiful as she did to him that day.

He kissed her tenderly and with his thumb, he brushed away her tears. In a whisper, he said, 'Of course I want to marry you - I want that with all my heart. I love you Polly - you know that don't you?'

All the worry; all the exhaustion; all the wretchedness, lost sleep and fear of those last few terrible days, came to the surface at last, and she cried her heart out. He held her close and told himself what a thoughtless, stupid, selfish idiot, he had been.

'Polly,' he said tenderly, 'do you remember the promise we made in the hospital?' She nodded in reply.

'Would you like me to make that promise again?'

She nodded once more.

'Then I promise that I shall love you, and be true to you, and never part from you all the days of my life, because I love you with all my heart and this is my promise to you!'

'Yes, this is our promise,' she said huskily through her tears. He smiled and she smiled back, and they kissed one another tenderly, for everything that had been so wrong, was right once more.

'And as for the self-righteous folk of the parish of Coaley, they'll just have to get used to the idea that you are my wife and the mother of my children - who will be as beautiful as their mother of course - and they can put their heads in a bucket of water if they don't like it! What do you think?'

'I suppose so!' she replied with a smile, her heart lifting a little.

'Does this mean my bachelor days are over?'

'Oh most definitely; you must never look at another woman again,' said Polly, drying her tears with her handkerchief.

'And no doubt, I'll have to give you all my wages from now on!'

'Oh at least all of it, and possibly more, and I'll have to scrub your back every day... Isn't that what good wives do?'

'Not just my back Polly... everything gets dirty in the smithy!'

'Oh...!'

'And I suppose when I'm done with the day and I come home to you, I'll barely find a place to sit with all the children running about!'

'At least five... and that's only the girls...!'

'Five... I'll have to work my fingers to the bone...'

'It will help you sleep.'

'How on earth will I sleep with so many mouths to feed and so many things to worry about?'

'I'll make you forget your worries,' said Polly, her troubles forgotten now he was her Isaac again. 'I'll hold you very close and kiss you... I'll kiss you so much, you'll forget about the smithy, and the children, and your money, and you'll only have thoughts for me!'

'Hmmm! That's your master plan is it! As I recall, that's what got us in this pickle in the first place.' With his hand, he brushed her hair to one side and traced her lips with his fingertips.

'Yes it was,' she replied; closing her eyes and reaching for his lips with hers, 'but it was the most beautiful day of my life.'

'It's a vicious circle ...' he said softly, kissing her tenderly, 'is there no way out of this dilemma for a simple blacksmith!'

She returned his kiss, caressing him gently, taking great care not to hurt him. 'None whatsoever,' she cooed.

He touched her face once more, his palm against her cheek, his fingers, running through her hair. She sighed, her mouth open, their tongues exploring.

'I love you,' he said softly.

'I thought I would lose you,' she said hoarsely, looking at him as though he were the most precious thing in the world. 'I was so afraid - so frightened! I couldn't bear the thought of being without you...'

'And I thought I had lost you too!' he replied, his voice deadly serious. 'When I was in the grip of the fever, I was in a strange, strange land, full of fantastic, terrible creatures and the oddest people. I wanted to get home to you, but they always tried to stop me. I kept falling through holes into strange worlds, with other strange people and other terrible creatures. There were so many times I wanted to give up and slip away, but then I would hear your lovely voice; singing to me softly and telling me over and over... "Come back to me my darling, come back to me..."

'Oh Isaac I did, I truly did! I said those words to you again and again, and you did come back to me, didn't you... You fought all those terrible creatures and you did come back to me and I'll never let us be apart again.' She said this looking into his eyes, her own eyes sparkling with joy and relief.

'Then we'd best be man and wife as soon as we can — if you'd like that...'

'Oh yes... yes I would,' she replied happily, 'I'd like that very much!'

He was about to kiss her again when he spotted Amy's shadow passing the window on her way back from the smithy. She entered the room in every bit as black a mood as she'd left.

'And now you're down here - you'll be staying down here, young man!'

'What's that supposed to mean?' he asked in bewilderment.

'Just exactly what I said! You can't expect Polly to sleep in a chair in her condition! She'll be sleeping in your bed and you'll have to sleep down here in your father's chair.'

Isaac opened his mouth to protest, but she cut him short.

'There'll be no goings on under this roof, Isaac Smith! It's your arm that hurts, not your backside, so it'll do you no harm for the time being, but you mark my words my lad... If I hear a tread on the stair in the middle of the night, it'll be the worse for you!'

Isaac made a remarkable recovery from that day onward and though terribly disfigured, his arm healed far better than expected, slowly regaining the muscle he had lost. His face too - though scarred and frozen about the cheek - had healed sufficiently for them to be married some weeks later at Stroud registry office. All were in their Sunday best, with Polly wearing a new dress that Isaac had bought her.

It was a happy day, marred only by Polly's sorrow that her marriage could not be consecrated in a Christian church, but she did not allow her day to be spoilt by wishing for what could not be. Her letters too, asking her parents for their blessing, had been returned unopened, and this upset her very much.

The Reverend Aubrey did at least agree to a private blessing; his gesture to John and Amy for their many years of faithful worship, but given Polly's condition, he could not allow them to be married in St. Bartholomew's. Instead, he based his address on the teaching that heaven is full of repentant sinners.

There were few in the congregation beyond John, Amy and a young cowman called Jack Price, who was Isaac's friend of many years and his best man. It was to everyone's surprise, therefore, to see a handsome young soldier sat quietly at the back.

Polly was delighted, but Isaac less so. She put her arms about the soldier and kissed his cheek, guiding him from the church upon her arm.

'How are Mama and Papa,' she asked of her brother, as they exited the cool church into the warmth of the spring sunshine.

'They are well, but upset as you might guess. Mother has been in tears, and Father has upset her even more because he won't have your name mentioned in the house. It's all a bit difficult I'm afraid Poll.'

'Oh Will,' she replied sadly, 'I have hurt them so much haven't I?'

'Are you doing the right thing?' he asked, glancing sideways at Isaac.

She took his hand in hers and looked into his eyes, her own alight with happiness. 'Oh Will, my darling, darling Will; be happy for me... I have never wanted for anything in my life so much as this day.' She looked Isaac's way and continued; 'I love him with all my heart! He is my heart and I would change nothing about him. If you love me, be happy for me.'

'Then I suppose I should congratulate you,' he replied, holding his hand out to Isaac who shook it in silence.

'But if you ever ...'

'Don't you dare say anything horrible on my wedding day,' she snapped, pinching his arm.

'I had no intention of being unpleasant,' he replied, 'I merely wanted to let your husband know that if he should ever hurt you, I will kill him.'

'Well he won't hurt me, so you won't have to; and anyway, he would probably give you a jolly good hiding, so don't you dare even think about killing him.'

Her pregnancy went as well as they could expect and she began her labour in the tiny bedroom of the smithy, attended by Amy, Nurse Priday, and Doctor Wooton, whilst Isaac and John sat in the parlour listening to her screams, worried and helpless.

Eventually the stair door opened and Wooton stood there smiling, a towel in his hands. 'You can come and see your wife and daughter,' he said.

'Are they...?' Isaac began, his anxiety clear to hear.

'They're fine,' the doctor replied.

Isaac sat beside the bed, with the baby girl in his arms, kissing her forehead gently.

He looked at Polly, 'She's beautiful,' he said, his eyes glistening, 'I never thought... she's so beautiful!'

CHAPTER 25

Selworthy

The secret love affair between the daughter of one of the county's wealthiest landowners and a common blacksmith was the biggest scandal in years. Besides the workers who chose Lister's foundry in Dursley, or Winterbotham's cloth mill in Cam for their income, most able-bodied men were employed upon the land, either for Richard Durcan, or for other wealthy landowners like him. Most of John Smith's customers were those landowners, and he suffered a sizable loss of income from the work they sent elsewhere - claiming as they did, to be scandalised by Isaac's behaviour, and the disgrace Polly had brought upon her family.

'We'll survive without the likes of them,' was all John had to say on the matter.

He'd grown fond of the girl despite the circumstances, for she was trying to be a good wife and mother, despite Amy's hostility. It took the birth of Rebecca to soften Amy's heart towards the pair.

'Give the girl a chance,' he'd said on one occasion as they made ready for bed, 'she's more about her than you think, that girl; she'll get there in the end.'

'That's as maybe,' Amy replied uncharitably, 'but in the mean time, all that fancy schooling's taught her nowt that's useful to ordinary folk!' For good measure she added, 'And it might have been better if they'd spent more time teaching her Christian values at that monastery, rather than highfalutin airs and graces! Sin in haste, repent at leisure!'

'I haven't noticed much repentance where Isaac's concerned,' said John with a smile she couldn't see.

'If that's the start of some smuttiness, I'll thank you to keep it to yourself,' she muttered, drawing the covers to her chin. 'Husband and wife they may be, but all the village knows why!'

'You think it's all her fault then.'

'No I don't! It'll be a long time before I forgive that young man for such shameful goings on!'

Well at least she's even handed, thought John to himself. Pinching out the candle, he said philosophically, 'What's done is done! They weren't the first, and they won't be the last.'

'Hmmph!' she replied, but John Smith was already asleep.

Though Polly didn't complain, she found it hard to adjust to her new life. There was no Nana Dilly to make her bed, no maid to iron her clothes, wash her linen, or cook her meals. She had to do those things for herself and for Isaac and Rebecca too. Her life had changed from one of wealth and privilege, to one of endless toil, just as Nana Dilly had promised it would, but if Polly missed the privileges of her childhood, she said nothing. If she resented the unending toil, she never remarked upon it, and if the cold and damp of the tiny cottage chilled her to the bone, she never complained about it.

However, her change of circumstances took its toll in other ways. Except for Isaac's family, she knew very few people in the village, and those she did know were outspoken in their disapproval; but time, as they say, cures all ills, and slowly the wagging tongues turned to other matters and Polly and Isaac were - for the most part - forgotten.

Polly was a regular churchgoer at St. Bartholemew's to Amy's great approval, and joined the choir where the sweetness of her voice and the warmth of her spirit, eventually endeared her to even the less charitably minded of the parish. Amy softened her heart toward the couple as she saw her beautiful granddaughter emerge from the womb, and decided that Polly was now her family, and there was an end to the matter. The manner of her membership was never mentioned again.

Polly's belief became a bigger part of her life from then on, for there were many things within her heart she did not understand. After her daily prayer of thanks for Isaac and Rebecca, she prayed for forgiveness for what she saw as her own weakness and sin. Like Eve, she had been weak and given in to temptation, and like Eve, she had been cast out, albeit only by the village folk who were slowly beginning to forgive and forget. However, it hurt her deeply that her mother was unable to speak to her still, whilst the father she adored, had disowned her entirely.

When she lay in Isaac's arms, she knew Eve's true sin. It was not an apple they had taken against God's will but a far more precious gift. When they made love, her need of him took her to another place - a place of love, wanting and desire that needed to be honoured by marriage. She understood at last what her father had meant. Their stolen love had been her greatest joy, yet also her deepest sorrow and she wished - oh how she wished - that she had been stronger.

Isaac accompanied her to church each Sunday, sitting among the congregation with John and Amy, but there were too many questions for him to feel as she did about God. He said as much to John one day.

'Church's a comfort lad, and now she's got you and Becky she sees it as a way of protecting all that's precious! I've never known it do no harm, so don't you worry about it. Amy's always been one for the church herself,' he added for good measure.

'Now you know why I'm worried,' replied Isaac, to the amusement of John Smith.

One day when Isaac asked Polly if she was happy, she asked in return, 'Do you have a special dream, Isaac?'

'I don't like dreams anymore,' he replied.

'They are not all bad,' she said. 'I have a dream - a wonderful dream - I try to dream it each night.'

'Am I there,' he asked?

'Of course you are there, silly; it wouldn't be my special dream without you.'

'Tell me about it?' he said with a smile.

'It is very simple really; I dream that we have a home, just you, Rebecca and me... and the other children of course, but I don't know their names yet.'

'The others - how many others?'

'Ten!'

'Oh my goodness gracious me, it's gone up to ten has it!' he replied.

'We've chicken too,' she added, and Isaac smiled for he knew how much she wanted chickens.

'When you come in from the smithy, we sit in the parlour and eat our supper and talk about everything.'

'Don't we do that now; don't you like it here with John and Amy?'

'It's not the same Isaac, they are very kind, it's just ...'

'Where would we go Polly and what about the smithy ...?'

'It's just my dream,' she replied.

By the time Rebecca was one year old, Polly had become used to her new life. The old life was all but forgotten and Isaac was pleased to see she was much happier. She'd matured into a stunningly beautiful woman, and he was proud to take her out on his arm.

Soon Rebecca was three and their story may well have ended at this point, had it not been for the unexpected arrival of a letter. It was postmarked, Selworthy, near Minehead, and was addressed to John. John knew only one person in Selworthy and opened the letter expecting bad news, but it was not as he thought and he closed it with very mixed feelings. He mentioned it to Amy, but it was some weeks before he discussed it with Isaac.

The problem for him was a simple one. Since Rebecca's arrival, the smithy had never been so happy and the letter sought to change all that. His granddaughter was a happy child with her mother's beauty and her father's stubbornness. Loving, wilful and sometimes naughty, she was nothing less than an angel for her grandfather, whom she adored. Each night before bed; wrapped in her nightdress; she would cuddle against the old man; head on his chest with her thumb in her mouth as she listened in wonder to his bedtime stories. He smelt reassuringly of tobacco and comfortable clothes warmed by the fire.

He told her of fairies, goblins and far off places; of ice covered mountains, echoing halls, magic notes played on silver flutes, cackling witches, fire breathing dragons, mischievous elves and orphaned boy's who lived on silver clouds. Crystal streams that tinkled and sang, pied pipers with gaily-coloured hats, enchanted forests, dark and deep, and beautiful princesses who loved handsome princes. She especially liked the handsome princes.

'Like my Papa?' she said on one occasion.

'Yes, just like your Papa,' replied Polly with a smile.

Evenings were her favourite time for that was when they all sat together, John toasting bread upon the fire, her mother spreading it with beef dripping.

Whilst the grown-ups talked together, she would play with the spills that lived in a Toby jug upon the mantelpiece and were of many different colours. Becky would sort them, stack them, and arrange them into the castles and forests of her imagination.

All too often John's dog - a huge yellow Labrador called Bert - would roll across her efforts, as he lay sprawled upon the rug before the fire.

'Bad Bert' she would say, wagging her finger. He would look at her curiously before licking her face, then roll over once more as he closed his eyes.

As bedtime drew near - her eyes heavy and her body limp - Isaac would lift her gently from John's lap and take her to Amy and Polly for a goodnight kiss.

It only remained to turn Toby Jug to the wall, for his smile frightened her and she would not settle if she went to bed with him facing the room. Every morning though, Toby jug would be smiling anew from the mantle shelf.

'Who's Ira Grace,' asked Isaac, when John eventually brought the subject up.

'Bit of a character to say the least, but a good enough blacksmith. He worked for my father when I were a lad, but left fer more money in the shipyard at Watchet. From there he went to sea on a merchantman. He was in the Far East for years, till one day they salvaged a boat as had lost its rudder an' gone aground. They towed un' into Kowloon and a tidy sum of salvage between um'. Ira bought a smithy at Selworthy, an' married a local girl into the bargain, but lost her some years ago. His sister does fer un' now, if my memory is correct.'

'Well where does he live if he's renting out the smithy?'

'Perhaps he's got another place lined up. He were always canny with his money were Ira.'

'What do you think?'

''Tis up to you lad,' replied the Blacksmith in lighter tones than he felt. 'Stay or go, the smithy's your'n when my time comes; all I ask is you look after Amy when I'm gone.'

'Polly's always talking about a place of our own.'

'Course she is,' replied John; 'she wants to be a wife and mother in her own way, in her own home; tis only natural.'

'It would be wonderful,' said Polly, excitedly, as she lay in his arms that night; 'oh Isaac, just think about it; a home of our very own... It would be so wonderful.'

'It's right beneath a wood and you can see the sea from the hill above, so the letter says. The smithy's powered by a wheel and there's plenty of garden for Becky to play.'

'I'd have chickens, and a pig, and a cow too, if there was room. Oh Isaac, please let's do it!'

Next day when Isaac told John, the blacksmith grunted and took a spike down from the rack of tools. 'Come with me,' he said.

They went behind the house to what looked like the back of a stone oven. It was about a yard square, and capped with sloping copings.

John levered the copings off with the long handled spike whilst Isaac manhandled them to the ground, wondering what it was all about.

Soon John was into the stone blocks themselves, prizing them out one at a time.

Within the first layer of mortar he found what he was looking for. He rubbed the soft mortar away with his fingers and placed the golden sovereign in Isaac's palm.

'I don't trust banks an' neither should thee,' he said, breaking up more mortar and throwing the coins he found in a tin box.

They worked half way down the square before John said, 'There you are lad, that'll do thee.'

'I can't take this,' replied Isaac.

'Why not, thee helped earn it! Now give us a hand to build un' back up again afore anyone notices.'

One week later, they bid a tearful farewell to Amy at the smithy door, for with all their possessions loaded in the trap, there was barely enough room left for Rebecca.

Isaac, Polly and John, walked alongside the trap for the three-mile trip to the station and were travelling early to catch the milk train. The pony's feet clip-clopped a merry tune as they travelled, but Rebecca - wrapped in a blanket - slept on, oblivious to the bumps and jolts.

As they passed the Wheelwright's, they were wished good luck by Don Ellery as he opened up for the day's work. So too did the leading hand at the hammer mill as he opened a sluice and set the wheel in motion, amid a muffled clatter of gears and shafting.

The station was busy despite the hour, and carts loaded with milk churns and mail, stood waiting on the platform for the early services to Bristol and Gloucester.

They queued for their tickets and then sat in the second-class waiting room for the train to arrive. Isaac would not relax, preferring to stand at the window, occasionally going outside to pace the platform.

'Stop fretting,' said John.

'I'm just wondering if we're making the right decision.'

'The train that takes you there brings you back!' replied John sagely. 'You're a good Blacksmith; good as any, and it'll do thee the world of good - Polly and Rebecca too.'

'I suppose so.'

178

'Of course so!'

A few minutes later, a whistle blew in the distance.

It was the first time Rebecca had seen a train and she watched in awe as the engine came into view.

John lifted her into his arms, 'Are you coming too, Grampy?' she asked.

'Not this time princess, Grampy's got to look after Granny, but we'll come an' see thee come Christmas; now you give yer' granddad a kiss and make sure you look after your mum and dad down there in Somerset!'

'Are there fairies in Somerset?' she asked excitedly.

'Might very well be!'

'And goblins?' she enquired, with an equal measure of concern.

'I shouldn't think,' he replied, 'too near the sea; they're more fer mountains generally.'

Satisfied, she gave him one last kiss before he handed her to Isaac. With Rebecca in his arms, he stepped on to the train and went in search of an empty compartment.

'If she has nightmares, I will know just who to blame,' said Polly.

'Did Isaac no harm,' he replied.

'Oh no!' she said with a smile.

'You'd best get aboard; they're starting to close up and he don't have the gumption to find his way there without you.'

'Yes he does, he just wouldn't want to.' She took John's hand in hers and said sincerely, 'But he loves you and Amy too, you know that don't you. That's why he's unsure. We all love you, for you've been so kind.' She reached up and kissed him tenderly. 'Thank you,' she said, 'Thank you for everything you've done for us.'

She got on the train and almost immediately, it began to move out of the station.

Isaac stuck his head out of the window and waved, and the old man waved back.

He watched with a heavy heart as the train gathered speed and disappeared from sight, sweeping westward toward Berkeley Road and Bristol Temple Meads, steam and smoke marking its onward passage amid the far trees. The

179

early morning sun glinted from polished rails that reached into the distance like a shining scimitar.

By late afternoon, they had reached Minehead, passing through Bristol for Penzance, then changing to the branch line at Bishops Lydeard.

It was a journey of great adventure and excitement, particularly for Rebecca who caught her first glimpse of the sea as they approached the tiny port of Watchet.

There was the usual hustle and bustle about the station at Minehead but no sign of Ira Grace who had promised to meet them there.

They found a shady bench in full view of the station gates, certain that a pony and trap would appear at any moment, but after a half hour had elapsed they were still waiting.

A kindly man wearing the stationmaster's uniform asked if they were alright.

'We're waiting for a man called Ira Grace,' replied Polly, 'He's from Selworthy... He promised to meet us here, but he's very late and we think he may have forgotten us.'

'Is he a blacksmith?' replied the Stationmaster.

'Yes, do you know him?' asked Isaac optimistically.

'No, just a guess,' replied the Stationmaster, noting Isaac's tools on the platform beside them. 'But I do know Selworthy and it's a bit of a hike with your luggage, not to mention this young lady,' he added, pinching Becky's cheek and giving her a smile.

'What do you think we should do?' asked Polly.

'Well, you can wait for this chap to come, or wait fer the horse bus, however, that will be another three hours, for it only left fer Porlock fifteen minutes ago. Or you can borrow a hand cart for sixpence on the understanding 'tis back here tomorrow.'

'Oh could we? That would be so kind!' replied Polly gratefully.

'How far is Selworthy?' asked Isaac.

'Five mile or so, but it's all uphill and down dale, so it'll feel more like ten by the time you get there!'

'Thank you, we will take it,' said Polly, 'And Isaac will bring it back on time, we promise.'

The journey was as the Stationmaster predicted, but Isaac was fit and healthy and took the steep uphill pitches in his stride. The downhill pitches were much harder though, for the handcart had no brakes and Isaac's tools were heavy.

However, nothing the stationmaster said, prepared him for the lane to Selworthy. It branched off the Porlock Road and almost immediately began to climb the steep sided beacon, that hid them from the sea every inch of the way from Minehead.

Polly sat Rebecca in the cart and helped Isaac with the pushing. Very soon, they were both sweating profusely in the heat of the afternoon sun.

~

The heavy sack hit the trap doors with an almighty thud. Flour dust, filthy with age, and thick as a snowstorm, fell from the joists and floorboards, covering the man below.

'You stupid bastard,' he bellowed at the ceiling above, 'what the bloody hell are you thinking about?'

'Shut yer clack an' get yer' arse up here,' said an indifferent voice from above.

'You let the bloody thing go on purpose; you can clean this mess up yerself!'

'Like I said... come an ave' a look at this.'

Curiosity getting the better of him, Jack Ridler joined his brother at the window of the grinding room floor. Out in the lane, Isaac and Polly struggled on, pausing every fifty yards or so for breath.

'I thought thee was an ugly bugger Jack,' said Nance, 'but that were before I saw this un', he make's thee look right bloody 'andsome.'

'You got a big mouth, Nance,' said Jack peering through the tiny window and wondering nonetheless, how Isaac had come by such terrible scars to his cheek. 'Someone'll shut it for you, one of these days; I'm lookin' forward to that.'

'I could do a bit fer his lady friend,' continued Nance, 'take a look at them nice titties. What d' you think they're after in Selworthy, all loaded down we' the family silver?'

'How should I know? Maybe you should ask em.'

'Maybe I will at that!'

'Hot enough fer thee,' shouted Nance cheerfully from the open window, a smile upon his face.

181

'Plenty,' replied Isaac, 'are we right for Selworthy?'

'You are indeed, you are indeed, but we don't buy from tinkers here about's if that's yer' business.'

'We're not tinkers; we've come to see Ira Grace. We're going to rent the forge; I'd be obliged if you'd tell us where we'd find him.'

Nance chuckled to himself, 'Are you indeed, well good luck to you then - see the church?'

'Yes,' replied Isaac, who could just see the spire above the treetops.

'Opposite the church is Ira's cottage, but the forge is just two hundred yards on from here. Ira's place is number two; it's got a green door.'

'Thank you kindly.'

'My pleasure,' replied Nance, watching them continue on their way.

'Looks like we got a new blacksmith then,' he said to his brother.

'No bad thing if he's any good,' said Jack. 'Save a journey to Porlock.'

'No bad thing at all! I'll be the first to give um' me custom. 'I'll ave' a new maiden fer yonder shaker and a handful of thy wife's titties, if thee don't mind.'

'Remember what I said about someone giving thee a good hiding one of these days Nance? Instead of lookin' at her, thee'd ave done better to take a look at him - hard looking bugger! Thee keep thinking what thee be thinking, and I recon' 'e might be the one t' give us all a treat!'

Nance chuckled again but continued to watch them until they disappeared from sight. 'We'll see,' he mumbled to himself.

~

They looked at the forge in silent disappointment. Pretty though the cottage was, it was in a terrible state of disrepair, whilst the garden was chest high in weeds.

'He can't have worked it in years,' Isaac said with disappointment.

'Nor lived there in years - oh Isaac...'

They tried the door and peered through the windows, but they were so thick with grime that little could be seen within.

Around the back of the cottage the garden was every bit as overgrown, but a beautiful stream flowed through it, fast and crystal clear, tinkling over pebbles and slabs brought down from the hill above.

A little water gushed through a gap in a rotting sluice that held back the water in the leat. It was enough to make the water wheel creak forward a few inches at a time. Unlike the cottage, the forge door opened with a hefty push, enough for Isaac to squeeze through.

Once inside he could see daylight through most of the roof. The smithy was a shambles, with junk and rubbish piled everywhere - all of it covered in soot.

Along the gable wall though, were rows of tongs, swages, dolly's and punches of all kinds and sizes, whilst beneath some sheets of corrugated tin, he found two passable anvils.

Overhead, a line-shaft creaked as the waterwheel moved. Within the dark recesses, there was a drill, a drop hammer and even a lathe, all driven from the wheel.

'How does it look?' asked Polly as he emerged.

'It's a mess, but with a bit of work it could be a fine smithy. There's every tool you could want, just hanging there.'

'Well that's wonderful then Isaac,' Polly replied, with more enthusiasm than she felt. 'If the smithy's okay, that's all that matters. You can mend the smithy and I will make the cottage into a home; a wonderful home and we will be very happy you'll see.'

'I'm already happy,' he replied, giving her a kiss. 'Let's find this Ira Grace and see what the cottage is like before we get too excited.'

Isaac knocked on the door of number two. Like all the cottages thereabouts, it had tiny haphazard windows beneath an overhanging roof of blackened thatch, which made the windows look like doleful eyes, peering out beneath drooping lids.

Smoke curled from a tall chimney crowned with a terracotta pot, and built high above the ridge of the roof. The tree line of the beacon came down to meet the circle of tiny cottages, and the hill beyond was so steep that Isaac could no longer see its bracken covered top.

A woman came to the door and asked their business. She was heavyset, in her forties, and very plain looking - almost manly in the coarseness of her features. She wore a shift like dress, drab and shapeless; her greying hair was tied tightly in a bun, accentuating the prominence of her cheeks and forehead.

'We're looking for Ira Grace,' Polly said with a cheerful smile.

The woman disappeared without reply and was soon replaced by a much older man, as thin as she was fat. He wore loose breeches, collarless shirt and waistcoat, but it was his eyes that caught the attention. They were boy's eyes, full of mischief and artfulness.

'You're looking fer Ira Grace?' he said.

'Yes, are you Mr Grace?' Polly asked

'I am indeed, I am indeed, and who might this beautiful young lady be?' he asked, stooping to tip Rebecca's chin with his finger whilst the child gazed up at him open mouthed.

'I'm Isaac Smith, this is my wife Polly and our daughter Rebecca,' replied Isaac on their behalf.

'I thought you weren't here till next week,' replied Ira, straightening his back and clearly caught off guard, 'that's buggered things up a bit, pardon my French!'

'We agreed the 17th.'

'Did we now...! I was going t slip down the smithy next week an' tidy up a bit, put her all shipshape an Bristol fashion. Thee'll ave to take us as thee finds us now I'm afraid; haven't thee got no luggage?'

'We left it at the smithy.'

'Have thee now; good thinking; just thee wait on a minute while I get my hat.'

'How long since you've lived there?' asked Isaac, as they began their walk back down the hill.

'Eighteen month since I worked the smithy, twelve year since I moved up to the village! I lost me wife and parents, all about the same time, so it seemed sensible to move into the family home we me sister; her being a spinster fer reasons as might be apparent.'

'So Number two's your family home?'

'Right first time,' he replied. 'I was born and brought up there, but I wanted to be an engineer, not a farmer, and tis all farming hereabouts. I answered an advertisement fer apprentices to the Lister works at Dursley an' got the job, but I got the sack fer this and that. Next, I went t' work fer John Smith's father an' learnt the blacksmithing trade instead; there you have it.'

'So you know John well?'

184

'John and Amy both. I had a soft spot fer Amy meself, but that's another story!'

'She sent her best wishes, Mr Grace,' said Polly, thinking a little guile would come to no harm.

'Well, that's very kind I'm sure,' he replied with a smile. 'Here we are; Leathernbottle Cottage, pretty by name and pretty by nature. '

Taking a bunch of keys from his pocket, he asked, 'What's want to see first; cottage or smithy?'

'The cottage I think, Mr Grace,' replied Polly.

'Ain't it always the same, young Isaac, the women folk has always got an eye on the comforts of home, don't matter what earns the pennies.'

He removed the clasp lock from the door, which wouldn't budge until Isaac and Ira put their combined weight against it. They left wood scrapings on the flagstone floor.

'Swelled a bit we the weather, as you might expect,' said Ira. 'It'll fit like a glove once thee gets a fire going.'

The room they entered was in a state; every surface covered in dust and bird droppings with cobwebs hanging like grey curtains. The hearth was full of soot and twigs, two decomposed birds lying amongst them.

The scullery was no better for its walls were black with mildew, but at least the door to the garden swung freely on its hinges. There was a wooden sink lined with lead, and a larder, its shelves laden with bottled preserves just as Ira had abandoned it.

He turned a tap and water flowed into the sink.

'All the modern conveniences,' he said proudly, 'no more bucketing water fer thee, lass; fresh water straight off the Beacon and into the sink. I plumbed it in meself.'

Both rooms had bare flagstone floors and low timbered ceilings with high wainscoting about the walls. There was a dank and musty smell about the cottage that told a tale of damp and rot.

'And lookie here,' said Ira, swinging open the door of a baking oven and peering in. 'Neither brick nor fire bar out of place... good as new!'

'It's going to need a lot of work,' said Isaac.

'Not if you put yer back into it lad; tis all superficial, nothing a good fire and a stiff broom won't fix.'

Isaac tapping a patch of bulging plaster which promptly broke away.

'Come an 'ave a look at the bedrooms,' continued Ira, 'fully furnished so thee won't need a thing. They're a good size fer when thee wants to add to thy family and views to take thy breath away.'

They were indeed nicely sized rooms and had views across the valley to Dunkery and beyond. Both rooms were furnished with washstands, and the main bedroom, with an enormous mahogany wardrobe, but the ceiling had lost a patch of plaster and the floorboards were eaten through with woodworm. There was an iron bedstead with brass knobs and a sagging mattress.

'Finest mattress thee'll ever sleep on, this un,' he said, shaking the bedstead vigorously, 'an' no creaking joints neither; thas important when thee be thy age. Course it might need a bit of airing.' He prodded the mattress with a finger that passed cleanly through the striped material. 'On tother hand,' he remarked casually, moving himself between them and the damage, 'thee might prefer thine own,'

They looked at the smithy together and Isaac agreed that it was well equipped for work once the roof was repaired and the machinery made good.

'What's the rent,' asked Isaac finally.

'I thought fifteen shilling would be fair,' replied Ira.

'A month,' asked Isaac, thinking the rent at least, was good news.

Ira gave a little chuckle and said, 'I can see thee've got a business head about thee lad - no, twer' fifteen shilling a week I ad' in mind.'

Isaac's face fell, his disappointment clear to see; it was a staggering amount for buildings in such condition.

Isaac looked at Polly, obviously crestfallen at Ira Grace's outrageous demand. 'I don't know...' he began.

Isaac's sentence faded away and his confidence with it, as he wondered what to do next. John had always dealt with the money side, leaving Isaac to think no further than his ten-shilling wages. It seemed a lot to find before he started to buy iron and coke and pay himself a wage.

Not in the least put out, Ira took Isaac by the shoulder and led him from the smithy, Polly and Rebecca behind them.

'Tell me what you see, young Isaac?' he said.

186

'Woods, fields, farmland,' he replied, 'I'm not sure what you want me to see.'

'Tied land lad, that's what you see! Every building, and every blade of grass as far as Dunkery Beacon and beyond, belongs to the Holnicote estate. Every farm, every cow and every cottage. They d' all belong to the same man, except...' and there he paused for effect, 'except this smithy, fer that d' belong to me!'

'Don't think me rude Mr Grace, but I don't understand what difference that makes if I still can't afford it.'

'*Think* thee can't afford it,' replied Ira patiently, 'Thee've a lot to learn about business Isaac, take it from me. We a bit of work, this can be a fine and profitable smithy once more, and fifteen shilling a week'll seem like charity, you mark my words - but there's another thing! One of these days, I'll want to sell it and who better to buy it than the man as rents it! That's what I want thee to think on lad! It's a wise man as thinks of tomorrow as well as today!'

Isaac had no idea what to do. Now he had committed to their adventure he was looking forward to his independence as much as Polly, but fifteen shillings a week seemed like a King's ransom. He was, therefore, surprised and relieved when Polly came to his aid.

'Mr. Grace,' she began sweetly, giving him her warmest smile. 'It is such a beautiful cottage, really the prettiest cottage I have ever seen, with these wonderful views that just lift your heart. We would love to live here, wouldn't we Isaac; it's so sad we won't be able to.'

Ira's expression went from quiet confidence, to open astonishment in the blink of an eye. He hadn't given a second thought to the pretty young wife, for young ladies were not natural business people in his experience. However, Ira was wise enough to know that the prettier the smile and more comely the figure, the more that same young lady was likely to have her own way, and rarely for the good, some might say.

'Why's that?' he asked carefully.

'Because I wouldn't allow it, Mr Grace! Why, Isaac would need to work so hard, I would never see him,' She slipped her hand in his and giving him a tender smile said. 'And what would be the point of that?'

'A bit of hard work never did no one no harm,' observed Ira. 'We all have to work fer things.'

Polly gave Isaac's hand a 'leave this to me' kind of squeeze. If strength and courage were all that was required, her Isaac would have no equal, but when

187

craft and guile were handed out, her darling Isaac - honest and clever though he was - was well at the back of the queue.

'I'm sure Isaac would agree with you, Mr Grace, but that's not what Rebecca and I have in mind I'm afraid.'

She looked at Ira with such a steady gaze and charming smile that he felt quite lost for words.

'What do you have in mind then?' he asked, a little put out at having to talk business with Polly. 'I'm sure thee'll think fifteen shilling very reasonable in time, but what say we talk about twelve fer now.'

'I think nine would be much fairer,' she replied, 'we would accept that.'

'Nine bloody shilling,' replied an astounded Ira Grace, looking as though he would have a heart attack at any moment.

'From when the repairs are complete,' she added thrusting home her advantage whilst her opponent's guard was down.

'From when the bloody works done,' he continued in astonishment! 'How longs that going to take?'

'Just a week according to you,' she replied, 'Shipshape and Bristol fashion in a week - wasn't that what you said?'

'Well that were afore I saw what the crows ave bin up to. How long d' thee think this is going ter take thee then...?' asked Ira of Isaac. 'Assuming thee don't spend all thy time billing an' cooing!'

Isaac cast another glance about him, 'Six weeks, perhaps two months,' he suggested.

'Two bloody months,' exploded Ira Grace in disgust. 'You expect me to go without rent for two bloody months!'

'I do wish you wouldn't use such language in front of my daughter, Mr Grace,' said Polly, 'and I'm very surprised you expect us to repair your property - no doubt supplying the materials with which to do it - then pay you rent into the bargain! It hardly seems fair now does it?'

'Why not just fix it up as you go along,' he suggested.

'Because Rebecca has a weak chest and we couldn't possibly have her somewhere so damp and cold and filthy. I'm sure you wouldn't want a child's wellbeing on your conscience Mr Grace?'

'Ten shilling then,' he said in exasperation, 'that's my final offer!'

'From when the work is complete?' she asked.

'From when thee gets thy first paying customer!' he replied in disgust. 'Or after two months if that comes sooner,' he added for good measure.

The two men shook on the deal and Ira dropped the keys into Isaac's hand before setting out for No 2, muttering curses beneath his breath.

'You were wonderful,' he said, kissing her forehead, 'I would have given him the fifteen shillings. But what was all that about Becky's chest; I didn't know...?'

'There isn't anything wrong with her chest you silly noddle!'

'So you told that poor old man a pack of lies for your own gain and you supposedly a Christian!' he replied mischievously.

'For *our* gain, and anyway it was only a tiny lie. Whilst you men are being so self-important, and thinking yourselves so clever, and wanting to be in charge of absolutely everything, we women have to find more subtle ways of getting things done. Mama taught me that!'

'Perhaps that explains a few things about your father,' replied Isaac to a frosty look from Polly.

They stayed two nights in a tiny room at the Royal Oak in Porlock, whilst clearing up the smithy by day. Isaac worked like a titan, sweat pouring from every pore, for the days were hot and even the evenings provided little respite. Polly scrubbed her fingers to the bone and even Rebecca passed to and fro with tiny bags of twigs and rubbish to feed the fire that burnt so fiercely in the garden.

They managed to get the scullery and small bedroom habitable in that time, but the front bedroom was not safe to use, there being so much woodworm in the floorboards.

The mattress had long since gone up in smoke, but Mr Hoskins, of Hoskins Furniture Emporium in Minehead, was as good as his word and delivered a new mattress on the Wednesday night. Isaac had proudly walked into his store and purchased a mattress, a new spring and linen and blankets, the moment he had dropped the handcart back at the station.

He fitted the new spring, nailing the fine wire mesh to the stretchers, before tightening the heavy screws with a spanner from the smithy. They slept that night in their own bed, in their own home, all three cuddled close - sleepy, exhausted and happy, despite the warmth of the night.

Isaac arose at five and set to work immediately, for there was much to be done. They must clear the parlour of rubbish and bird droppings and then repair the roof so that rain would not ruin their hard work. That left the rotten floors, and one day - when the windows were repaired - he might even start on the smithy.

He hoped and prayed the joists beneath the bedrooms would be sound, but Ira assured him they were made of oak and therefore too hard for woodworm.

Ira stopped by each day to inspect progress and looked in despair at the height of the flames, the remnants of his mattress clearly visible on the outskirts of the ring of ash.

'Don't you burn the bloody furniture,' was his comment to Isaac, 'everything's got ter be new these days; young people don't value the old things.'

With Isaac's limited savings under siege, he could confidently assure Ira that his furniture was safe.

They were visited by many villagers who brought an assortment of gifts from a rabbit stew to a scrubbing board, in fact, anything and everything that might afford a reason to be nosy.

The consensus was that they were a lovely young couple and just what the village needed, for the smithy had been much missed.

Mr. Hazel, the vicar called to bid them welcome, and was pleased to receive Polly's assurance that their hard work would cease long enough to attend communion and evensong on Sunday.

By the following Monday, the parlour was useable, but the weather was so hot they favoured eating in the garden on a bench Isaac had fashioned from a few spare planks. When daylight finally deserted them and the work had to stop, they sat by the fire, tired but happy, their faces aglow in the firelight. Polly toasted bread at arm's length, whilst Isaac spread it with fresh butter they had been given by someone in the village. With a little cheese, no meal had ever tasted better.

They had bought a hen from a local farmer named McNab. It too looked content, its red feathers shining and resplendent in the firelight.

'One of my best layers that un,' declared McNab, 'worth twice what thee be paying fer un'! Double yolker every time an' just one egg'll be an off day.'

It had yet to lay so much as a single yolker, but Polly put that down to its strange surroundings.

'No one likes to leave their friends,' said Polly in the bird's defence, when Isaac enquired after the whereabouts of his breakfast egg.

'She's lonely; we must find her some company as quickly as we can, then you'll see.'

Whilst Isaac carried Rebecca to bed, the little girl already asleep in his arms, Polly set about shutting the bird up for the night. 'I shall call you Henrietta,' she said conversationally, 'and you will soon feel at home, you'll see. You'll be a member of our family and I promise we will never eat you... well providing you start laying eggs that is... I can't promise otherwise.'

The hen scurried into the coop happily enough and Polly turned the toggle on the door. She turned to look back at the cottage, its thatch seemingly on fire in the golden glow of the bonfire.

It was beautiful at Selworthy, not just the cottage but the village too. The beautiful views over Dunkery lifted the heart, whilst the majestic beacon above them, protected them from the stormy channel beyond. She looked up at the beacon's wooded flank, its outline discernible against the blackness of the night only by the line of stars that shone above it.

As she stood listening, the night seemed to come alive. The brook continued its unceasing babble, whilst within the woods she heard the shuffle and scrape of badgers, foxes, and who knew what else. Perhaps they too stood outside their homes, enjoying the evening calm, wondering what tomorrow would bring.

Suddenly, a movement down the steeply sloping lane caught her eye. A lantern shone briefly, and in that instant, she saw several men, perhaps three or four shadowy forms, gathered outside the Ridler mill.

Moments later, the sound of a cart descending the hill came to her on the still night air. It seemed an odd time to be delivering grain or collecting flour.

It was late and Isaac might well be wondering where she was, so reluctantly she decided to leave Henrietta and the stars for their rather stuffy bedroom, but at least it was their bedroom. She looked at Leathernbottle cottage, its thatch still aglow, and thought how beautiful it was.

'We will love you,' she said to the cottage, 'Even if Mr Grace didn't care about you. You'll be a happy place full of laughter and love.'

She had one last word for the wood, before entering the scullery and locking the door for the night. 'Stay away Mr Fox; there is no meal here for you tonight.'

She slipped quietly into the bedroom. Rebecca was fast asleep in her father's arms and Isaac was snoring softly. She knelt beside the bed and said her prayers. Tonight there were only thanks to be given, for nothing in the world was amiss and her heart was glad.

CHAPTER 26

Molly and Nance

The man and woman were both naked, she kneeling on all fours, with him behind her. In his hand, there was a slender cane with which he'd been beating her repeatedly.

They were at the height of their sexual arousal; his penis so engorged it stood near flat against his belly. Her breathing came in noisy, panting gasps as she fought for precious oxygen; the muscles of her legs trembled with the ecstasy of anticipation.

Nance strutted about the room with a cane that she had given him, for they performed this ritual often. When she had recovered enough, she dropped her head once more so she couldn't see him and then grunted as though she were a pig.

He walked behind her, the cane bent in his hands, then after two or three teasing, stinging pats, he struck her hard across her naked buttocks, causing yet more wheals to appear across the already swollen flesh. Tiny pinpricks of blood broke through the surface in crisscross lines.

The woman cried out in pain and excitement; panting frantically. He tapped her again, but she pleaded for time.

He walked in front of her; 'Up on your hind legs for farmer, Piggy,' he ordered. 'Up Piggy, up Piggy, Piggy.'

She did as she was bid. Immediately the cane cracked down across her large hanging breasts; she gasped again.

'What's your name,' he asked calmly; enjoying his control of her every thought and feeling.

'Piggy,' she replied.

'Farmer didn't hear you,' he said, whipping the cane down across her breasts once more, 'what's your fucking name?'

'Piggy,' she gasped... 'Piggy, my name's Piggy!'

'Grunt for farmer then,' he said softly, but it was not a request in which she had a choice. She made hog like noises whilst he gripped her hair; forcing her to look up. 'Be good to farmer,' he continued calmly; she took his penis as he asked.

192

Nance drew away from her and began to dress himself.

'Don't leave me like this Nance,' the woman sobbed; she was sat cross-legged on the bare boards.

'You can sort yerself out from here,' he replied, 'I ain't got all bloody night!'

'Please Nance,' she sobbed, 'look what you've done to me - please don't be so cruel!'

'Look what I've done,' replied Nance; 'who was it as came beggin'?'

The woman stood up and began to dress. 'You do love me don't you, Nance; it's not just...'

'What do you think?' he replied.

'Nance,' she sobbed, 'please be kind to me. I love you; I would do anything for you.'

Nance Ridler drew up the breeches he'd cast aside on the floor of the grain loft. 'Who're these folk who've moved into the smithy?' he asked, ignoring her nonsense. 'Is Ira selling up?'

'No, they're just renting it; they've got no money; I don't know what he's doing, he don't talk to me.'

'Hummph,' grunted Nance, unimpressed. 'What's a fancy bit of stuff like 'er doing with an ugly bugger like that if he's got no money?'

'I don't know; they're married and got a little girl, maybe he had an accident, I just don't know.'

'Perhaps her'd prefer a bloke as don't frighten the children, an' got a bit of money into the bargain,' he mused.

'Don't be cruel Nance; why are you always so cruel afterwards?'

Nance laughed, 'I'd still sort you out Moll don't you worry; I can't see a bit of fancy like that having your particular taste in things; I'd soon be back.'

The woman began to sob; 'Don't talk like that Nance, I don't want to share you with anyone; I'd die if I didn't have you.'

'No you wouldn't,' he replied matter-of-factly; 'you'd get used to it soon enough. You might even like a story or two; might set you up fer a session.'

The woman began to sob again, terrified that he was serious, 'I won't let anyone else have you; I'd tell the Revenue, honest I would; I'd ...'

Ridler's arm shot out so fast she didn't see it coming. His fingers gripped her throat like a vice, crushing her windpipe. He pushed her backwards, all in the same movement, until her body crashed into a wooden pier with a force that drove the breath from her. He continued to crush her throat in uncontrollable rage until her eyes began to bulge in their sockets.

He released his grip at the last moment and precious air filled her lungs; her throat rasping with every breath she drew. He did not let her go, instead he said slowly and with venom in every word. 'Don't you ever threaten me again you stupid, fat bitch!'

He brought the back of his hand smashing into her face. Her head was thrown back into the pier and she fell sobbing to the floor.

He left her there whilst he finished dressing; then helped her to her feet, passing her the remainder of her clothes.

'I'm sorry, Nance,' she said, still sobbing; the worst of her fears over, now he'd calmed a little.

'You shouldn't ave' mentioned the Revenue, Moll, now should you; that ain't none of your business, is it? When you're bad to the farmer, farmer's bad to Piggy, that's only fair ain't it?'

'Yes, I'm sorry.'

'You get off 'ome then.'

~

The woman lifted the latch on the door and slipped quietly into the parlour. She jumped when the man spoke, not expecting him to be up at that late hour.

Ira was sat in his armchair on the far side of the room, in darkness but for the dim light cast by the hearth. She was grateful for that at least; she did not want him to see her looking as she did.

'Where have you been?' he asked.

'It's none of your business,' she replied, making her way toward the stair.

'You've been with that bastard again; don't think I don't know.'

'I don't care what you know; it's none of your business,' she said defiantly.

'It's my business if you're disgracing yerself under my roof!'

'Who's roof?' said the woman, her anger rising; 'mother left half of it to me remember?'

'Aye, and what did you do to deserve it? Elsie and I nursed her to the end and where were you? The house should have bin' mine outright an' you know it.'

'Well it isn't is it, and if you don't like it, clear out!'

'I'm talking to you fer yer own good, Molly; no good will come of your getting involved with Nance Ridler. He's a rum un' as you well know. Just like his father before un.'

'At least he's not a miser! You could live in the smithy couldn't you, an' leave me in peace, but no! That would mean spending a bit of your precious money wouldn't it? You'd rather see other people fix it for yer wouldn't you, you bloody miserable old miser!'

With that, she went upstairs, slamming the stair door behind her.

Molly closed the door behind her and dropped the latch into place. Tears welled up in her eyes and spilled over to fall down her cheeks. She put the candle upon the dresser and collapsed onto the bed, sobbing.

It was a pretty room though it was small. It was her room and Ira never entered it. There was a cast iron grate with a brass fireguard, a brass bed with huge puffed pillows, and a hand knitted patchwork quilt. A washstand, chest of drawers and a tall wardrobe completed the furniture.

After some while, Molly raised herself from the bed and began to undress. She folded each garment neatly and placed them in a pile. It took some effort for she was very sore. Some of the garments were stuck to her by tiny beads of blood, which opened the wounds afresh when they were pulled away.

She crossed to the mirror and held the candle close. Heavy wheal's crossed her breasts and the skin was broken in many places.

It was always like this, never any different. It would be many days before she no longer felt the pain, but it would make no difference either. Sooner or later, she would go to him again and the same thing would happen. She sobbed quietly as she dabbed the blood away with a damp cloth. Her cheek was smarting from the slap that Nance had given her and she could taste the blood in her mouth from where her teeth had punctured the soft flesh.

'It's just his way, she sobbed to herself, he loves me; I know he loves me, it's just his way!'

CHAPTER 27

The Well

Ira was taking his daily walk along a bridle path between Selworthy and East Lynch. Despite the warm weather, he was not his usual sunny self, for there was still no sign of any rent.

He'd been calling at the smithy each day to see how the work was progressing. There was a lot of hammering and banging right enough, but precious little of it at the anvil. Ira couldn't understand the thinking one bit. 'Wasting all that time on the cottage,' he mumbled to himself. 'It don't make no bloody sense. The roof's sound and the place be dry - or summer-dry anyway. What more do em' want?'

It was throwing good earnings away in his opinion, and things had only come to this because of a pretty face. The fact that she was comely might keep Isaac happy, but it did nothing for Ira's pocket.

As he ambled along the lane that split the shallower arable land to his right, and steeply sloping sheep pastures to his left, he came to the very definite conclusion that womenfolk - especially the pretty variety - were the millstone about every good man's neck - yes, very definitely so. Only that morning he'd found Isaac sawing boards for a cart that had suddenly appeared.

'Morning young Isaac,' said Ira cheerfully. 'Thee've picked up a bit of work I see. Thee'll be wanting to pay I rent now, no doubt.'

'Morning Ira, I don't think this rightly constitutes our bargain as I recall it.'

'Well tis earning thee money ain't it?' said Ira huffily.

'Not as such! Tis a trade off for timber fer the cottage.'

'What's thee need timber for now?'

'Floorboards.'

'Bloody floorboards again! Thee don't need to replace every bloody floorboard just cus one or two got a hole in um! Thee could just as easy lay a bit of tin plate over the hole. There's tin plate aplenty in the smithy just crying out ter'' be used.'

Isaac put down his saw, straightened his back and looked Ira straight in the eye. 'I need the timber for the stairs,' he said patiently. 'My foot went through a tread the other day and I damn near broke my neck. Whether you like it or not, the cottage is falling down, and what kind of builder would you get for twelve shilling a week; materials and all!'

'Well times ticking on, fer all that; and tis time I got a bit of rent from e'.'

'And so you shall, but our bargain was fer a horse to be shod! Show me a horse with a wooden shoe and I'll call this blacksmithing.'

'Bloody twaddle,' said Ira in disgust, and without another word, resumed his constitutional, grumbling as he went.

It seemed to Ira, that young Isaac had picked up a few of his wife's bad ways, and now there was two of em doing him out of his pension. He concluded that he'd send them packing if anyone else thought they'd like to take it on, however, he'd not been able to make that happen over the last two years, despite his best efforts. The trouble was, now Porlock had grown so big, it was difficult to get folk to make the journey up the hill when other smithies were nearer; the very reason he'd packed it in - that and his leg.

Isaac went back to his work; a bit put out at Ira's ill humour. He was right of course, for it was time to be earning, and that was a worry in itself. Customers had not exactly beaten a track to his door for Ira's old customers had long since gone elsewhere, and there were smithies aplenty thereabouts; four in Porlock and one each in Bossington, Allerford and Luccombe.

Isaac decided upon a plan and it was a good plan. He'd fix the stairs today and the waterwheel tomorrow. Once that was running, the lathe would be running and then he'd be the only smithy that side of Minehead with a lathe, not to mention the drop hammer. Everywhere you looked these days; the fields were full of steam engines. They were the new workhorses and they wouldn't mind the steep pitch to Selworthy, but they needed looking after just like a horse. The fact he knew nothing about lathes or steam engines never entered his mind.

Ira was almost at East Lynch when he caught sight of McNab, wandering about a field with his eyes to the ground, totally absorbed in his task. Wherever McNab went, he was followed by an old dapple mare named Parsley.

'Morning McNab,' hollered Ira, lifting his stick in salute.

'Morning Ira,' replied McNab, 'how be thee then?' The two men met at the gate and began to pass the time of day.

'Fine just fine,' replied Ira. 'Thee d' look serious, as though thee've lost summut precious like a farthing, McNab.' He patting Parsley about the nose and blew gently into her nostrils.

'Exactly right,' said McNab. 'I should follow thy example Ira, an' keep a tighter grip on em.'

'Ira chuckled as he lifted Parsley's hoofs, one by one, out of professional interest. He and McNab had enjoyed the occasional leg-pull for many years past.

'I thought as how I might dig a well' said McNab.

'What's want a well for,' said Ira distractedly as he looked at Parsley's teeth.

'Cus there ain't no water fer the stock. What's think I wants' it fer, to brush me bloody teeth?'

'Parsley d need shoeing an all,' commented Ira.

McNab wasn't listening, being too engrossed in his water problem.

'Tis too bloody steep this paddock; that's the trouble. It d' just run off the beacon without stopping to wish this pasture so much as the time of day.'

'Where's thinking of diggin' un' then.'

'I thought over yonder where the slope do ease off a bit,' said McNab.

'Ah,' said Ira thoughtfully; 'thee might ave picked a good spot there! Course, on the other hand, thee might not! That's the trouble with guesswork,' he mused, 'there never nothing definite about it. Course thee could always do it scientific like.'

'How d' thee mean,' said McNab.

'Water divining' said Ira, 'it d' work a treat every time.'

'Well I don't know no bugger as knows nothing about water divining,' said McNab.

'Yes you do,' said Ira.

'No I bloody don't! Who do I know, as knows owt about water divining?'

'Me.'

'You...! What the bloody hell d' thee know about it?'

'That's the trouble we thee McNab; thee got a bad attitude; thee don't ave to know nothing about it, thee just has to have the gift that's all. There's some like I, as has it, an' there's some like thee, as don't!'

After much cynicism from McNab, and even more indignation from Ira, the two men went in search of nut sticks of a suitable size and shape. Ira stripped them of their bark and cut them to length, then both men set out to quarter the field - Ira with sticks lightly gripped between fingers and thumb. Back and forth, they went - farmer, horse and 'water diviner'.

The shallow sloping ground McNab was considering, yielded nothing; but as they climbed the slope to a flat grassy spur that jutted from the general slope, the sticks suddenly crossed and jerked downward. McNab looked at Ira, but Ira gave nothing away, for one swallow didn't make a summer.

Ira continued back and forth his expression inscrutable - an artisan forced to perform his art beneath the gaze of the common man. He crossed the spot repeatedly, every time he did so, the sticks crossed and pointed down.

'There thee be McNab! About eight foot down, an' lots of it if I'm not mistaken.'

McNab looked about him still a little unsure. Though flattish, it was one of the highest points of the field. 'Are you sure?' he said.

'Never was I surer McNab; never was I surer.'

'Well I don't know,' said McNab, 'eight foot down you reckon?'

'Thereabouts,' said Ira. 'Might even be a little less, twer' that strong a pull on them there sticks. I'll tell 'e what, I'll even put a wager on it.'

Three days later, whilst walking to East Lynch, Ira was not in the least bit surprised to bump into McNab.

'Yer, Ira,' said McNab, 'I've got a bone to pick with thee.'

Ira Grace, McNab and Parsley, stood side-by-side looking down into a large hole on the tump where Ira had divined the well. All about them was dirt, clay, and stone in untidy heaps.

'Took I all bloody day t' dig that,' said McNab, not in the best of humour.

'Can't understand it,' said Ira; 'twer' one of the best pulls I've ever ad.'

The hole before them was four feet across and about four deep, at the bottom of which, was bedrock, as dry as a bone.

'Thee an' thy bloody sticks,' said McNab,' I ought ter stick em where the sun don't shine.'

'Now then McNab,' said Ira indignantly, 'there's no need fer that sort of talk. I was only trying to do thee a favour. If that's thy attitude, I shan't bother next time an I'll bid thee good day.'

He started to make his way down the field once more but as an afterthought turned and said, 'Never let it be said I'm not a man of me word!'

He put his hand in his pocket. 'There's the shilling as wagered, and I'll trust thee t' keep thy side of the bargain.' With that, he took his leave of McNab and Parsley, and continued on his way to East Lynch.

The next day, Isaac walked about the horse, lifting each hoof in turn and letting it fall back to the ground. 'I'll shoe him if that's what you want,' said Isaac, 'but in truth he don't need doing for a month or so; it's up to you.'

'Thee carry on son,' said McNab, 'it ain't costing I nothing.'

'Oh,' said Isaac curiously, 'why's that?'

'Well tis a long story lad, but all to do with a wager.'

'A wager?' repeated Isaac.

'That's right,' said McNab, 'three pints of ale if I lost, or two shilling to get Parsley shod if I won, an' that were the eventual outcome.'

'Tell me,' said Isaac, 'this wager wasn't between you and Ira Grace by any chance?'

'As a matter of fact, it were,' said McNab, 'an' very pleased I am about it an' all, fer it ain't everyday thee'd get the better of Ira Grace as thee'll find out in the fullness of time!'

'I'm learning fast,' said Isaac.

CHAPTER 28

Glasgow docks

Lucy Skinner woke from a deep sleep, unsure of where, or even who, she was. She felt the warmth of the body beside her and it all came flooding back. The suffocating misery of a heavy cold had woken her from her slumber. She wiped her nose on the bed cover.

Lucy slipped silently from the bed and crossed the freezing room to a tiny-latticed window, there to look down upon the street below. The pallid glow of gas lamps cast their yellow light upon the nearest ships, and reflected dimly from iron bollards and wet, slippery cobbles.

She was in the attic room above the Blue Man; a squalid room of whistling drafts and loose, mildewed plaster. It was home to her and Nattie Gilkes, and a place to bring their clients.

She relieved herself into a chamber pot, then peeped around a heavy curtain that divided the tiny room.

There was no Nattie. She would be out working - on a ship most likely. Lucy dressed quickly, crossed to the bed and looked down at the sleeping man.

He was a pig, they were all pigs! John he'd said his name was - John the pig!

He'd been drunk when Lucy stopped him outside the Copper Pot. 'Want to do some business, Mr.?' she cooed sweetly. He staggered into the public house dragging her with him. He'd drunk till he could drink no more, then Lucy had taken him back to her room above the Blue Man tavern. He'd fallen asleep whilst he lay upon her.

She spoke to him quietly, careful not to touch him.

'Mr.!'

There was no answer.

'Mr.!' she said again, but with the same effect.

Satisfied, she went through his pockets. They were full of rubbish; string, tobacco, matches, a pocketknife and the like, but then she found his purse. She'd seen it many times the previous night as he paid for their ale; it looked heavy. She counted the coins quickly, took all but a crown and left the room quietly. At the bottom of the stairs stood Albert O'Hare, the landlord of the Blue Man. Without a word, she handed O'Hare the money and slipped out of the rear door of the tavern.

O'Hare took a heavy stick from behind a door and climbed the stair to the attic room. He prodded the sleeping man till he woke. 'Come on, get yerself up! Yer lady friend's gone an' there's a crown owing on the room.'

McInally found himself standing on the street outside the Blue Man, still in the grip of the drink. The cold night air hit him like a sledgehammer and he felt the vomit rising in his throat. He gripped the corner of the timber framed building and retched violently before walking on a few paces; there to collapse beneath the overhang of the rooms above. The tavern sign screeched with every gust of the wind that blew; a cold drizzle slowly soaked him through.

From the shelter of a doorway, Lucy watched him fall. She pulled her coat about her and shivered with the cold. Her nose was raw and what teeth remained, ached in the bitter wind. 'Go pig,' she murmured to herself, 'why don't you go?' She was tired and wanted her bed.

~

Abraham Pollard glanced at the brass clock hanging on his cabin bulkhead. 'Where the hell is the man,' he thought angrily. Though he didn't give a tuppenny damn if the bastard lived or died, he couldn't sail the ship without him and the Nicolette was due to leave Glasgow on the late morning tide.

Pollard slammed down the lid of the writing chest he used to complete the manifest. He was carrying 2000 empty whisky kegs for the wine trade at Bristol as well as Copra from the West Indies; they had already discharged the white lead, rum and molasses. His next port of call would be Newport for wool, then on to Bristol and the Ivory Coast with farm implements, medicines, machinery and furniture. His ship was the three masted sailing ship 'Nicolette', of which he was both master and owner. Within the hour, the steam crane would finish the last of the kegs and it was then up to McInally to make the ship ready for sea. That was a good three hours work and this was seven-o clock already, with not so much as a whiff of the drunken bastard's breath.

He climbed the companion stair to the deck above, and dispatched two sailors to search the waterfront taverns, and other pits of depravity that the wretched city had in such abundance.

'Drag the bastard back by his heels if necessary,' he shouted after them. As it transpired, it almost was, for McInally was still drunk, still sleeping, and still barely able to stand when found in the doorway of the Blue Man.

They walked him back through cobbled streets, trying to avoid the puddles of filth and garbage washed down by the night storms; but no amount of rain could cleanse the city of the dank, acrid smog that descended upon it as the good

202

citizens of Glasgow stoked the furnaces of trains, harbour steamers, mills and factories.

Pollard turned McInally to work without as much as a change of clothing. So it was that a very hung-over, and very wet John McInally, set about lowering the heavy king beam into its wrought iron crutches to span the gaping maw of the cargo hatch. How he didn't fall headlong into the hatch was beyond all comprehension, but he failed to do so with the good fortune that often smiles on Jolly Jack Tar.

They set about placing the heavy hatch boards into position on the starboard side. Each board spanned half the hatch between the side-coaming and the King beam. Each board had its place and was identified by numbers branded into the wood. At the end of one row, McInally realised he had made a mistake, for the last board wouldn't fit. It would take too long to find the problem and reposition all the boards, so he took one from another row and fitted it into the gap. It wasn't right, but it was near enough, and what did he care anyway! He carried on with the port side row, but ended up with a board that couldn't be fitted, no-matter what they tried.

'Sod Pollard, and sod the Nicolette,' thought McInally as he threw the board into the dock. He would be jumping ship in Newport and finding another berth anyway, for there was always a call for good hands like him. He muttered to the grumbling seamen to 'spread em out a bit,' to even up the gap.

The sailors rolled out the heavy canvas tarpaulins that covered the hatch, three in number; one upon the other. Disgruntled though they were, they knew better than to argue with the mate, especially this black-hearted bastard. It was a matter for Pollard; it was none of their business.

The tarps were held tight with loose beams wedged into channels about the coaming. Each wedge pointed aft so that the weather would drive it deeper. At last, the job was done and the ill-fated Nicolette put to sea on what was to be her last voyage.

CHAPTER 29

The Rock House

Charlie Parkin sat at the window of the Rock House Hotel, supping a pint of ale, as was his usual custom at that time of night. From this vantage point, he'd a perfect view of Lynmouth harbour and the Bristol Channel beyond.

The chair in which he sat was a sturdy thing of English oak with a high back, arms worn smooth by constant use, and gnarled legs, bruised and battered by years of dispute with other furniture. It was a very old chair, and everyone called it "Charlie's chair" for Parkin never sat anywhere else.

Parkin was a man of habit, as were all his kind, for fishermen don't like change. They like things to stay the same, reliable and solid like the chair itself. Here in their little town with its narrow cobbled streets, green and slippery harbour steps, and tiny thatched cottages clinging to the cleft cut by the tireless River Lynn, things changed slowly. Within each tiny parlour, damp clothing steamed, saucepans rattled, hearths glowed, and children played fiddlesticks as they had for centuries' past. Fisher-folk liked it that way and respected tradition and all that was familiar, for beyond the harbour wall was all the uncertainty they ever needed. The chair, like Charlie Parkin himself, was a part of that Lynmouth that was steady, solid and reliable.

Parkin was a quiet man, and though courteous enough, would rarely speak without purpose. It was true to say that there only a handful of men in Lynmouth, who truly knew him well.

Most evenings he would sit and drink three pints of Walt Tricket's ale and if Davis, Pulsford and Thomas were there, as was usually the case, they would play dominoes for a farthing a round.

Parkin had watched the weather worsen all day as high winds came in from the Southwest; yet despite its ferocity, the approaches to Lynmouth and the Bristol Channel itself had stayed fairly calm, for the wind was off the land. All the boats were home now, and that was just as well, for the wind had suddenly veered to the Northwest and huge swells were sweeping in from the North Atlantic. The white horses of the afternoon, had changed to vicious spray capped waves and deep troughs of foaming spindrift. Huge breakers crashed against the harbour wall, sending spray and tiny pebbles high into the air, there to be snatched up by the howling wind and thrown against the windows of the Rock House, like Romeo throwing stones at the window of his Juliet.

'Looks like Old Mother Leakey be whistling up the wind tonight Charlie,' said Walt.

'Aye,' said Parkin thoughtfully, not moving his gaze from the raging storm, 'an in a rare old mood an all, by look ont, Walt.'

'Let's hope tis a quiet night then, Charlie.'

Parkin nodded silently.

'Ready fer another?' inquired Walter Tricket.

'No thanks Walt, I'll bide me time if thee don't mind,' said Parkin.

'Most unusual,' thought Tricket, as he turned to welcome the bedraggled man who'd just entered the bar.

'Evening Walt - evening Charlie,' said Davis, rubbing his hands together to get the blood circulating. 'Tis some bloody night out there, I can tell e'.'

In the room above, Andrew Herrington stood before the mirror and made final adjustments to his dress. He drew a little more watch chain from his pocket, straightened his cravat, combed his moustache, then stood back to study the effect. Satisfied, he turned down the gas mantle, left the room, and closed the door behind him.

Herrington was in Lynmouth to "take the air". He told Tricket he was an accountant, but in reality, he earned a pittance as a clerk to a spice importer in Hatfield Lane. Even that job, humble though it was, had only been secured as a favour to his mother.

Always a sickly child, he had suffered lifelong, from a weak chest; but his present malaise had more to do with his penchant for the highlife, than the smog laden air of London as he would have her believe.

Usually, a bout of bronchitis was good for a society break in Bournemouth - at her expense, of course - but this time the silly old bat had insisted he try "Mr. Newnes" new resort of Lynmouth. "You will love it, I am sure my dear; it is so fashionable these days." It had turned out to be this horses' arse of a place. Herrington was a toff and London was his backyard, not this fishing village with its suffocating boredom.

In London, he enjoyed a social life well above his means and indulged his various "peccadilloes" at mother's expense. Street urchins came and went at discrete hours; some carried small parcels of brown paper bound with string, from the ships that docked from China or the Indies, whilst others brought only themselves.

Herrington had no love for his mother; in fact, he despised her. As she got older, she became ever meaner with the family loot. It was father who'd earned it for Christ's sake, and anyway, there was more than enough of the stuff to go around! There seemed to be no light at the end of the tunnel either, for she was in obscene good health.

To make matters worse, she read "Tit Bits" and Herrington blamed all his present discomfiture upon the ever-popular journal. Its publisher, Mr Newnes, never missed an opportunity to praise his adopted home for its breathtaking beauty and its health giving air, consequently - given that she held the philanthropist in the very highest regard - Herrington had been obliged to pass his time in that same horse's arse of a place.

~

Three hundred feet above the waves that threw themselves against Hurlston Point, Jack Eady, sat in his tiny shelter on the crenelated roof of the granite tower. He was coastguard at the remote station at Bossington near Porlock, which was some thirteen miles northeast of Lynmouth. He shared his shift with Andrew Marland, who was below in the warmth of the duty room. Hurlston Point was a wild place on such a night as this, and Eady was glad of the hot tea Marland brought to warm his hands.

As Eady sipped his tea, something caught his eye; it was the gleam of a far distant light. It had been little more than a flicker and Eady thought his eyes might be playing him tricks, but a minute or so later, it appeared again, a faint green light, almost certainly the starboard navigation light of a ship coming up the estuary.

Then another light appeared, but this time the light was red. The ship must be turning her head toward land for him to see her port light as well. If she kept her present course, she was heading for certain disaster upon the rocks that lay in wait beneath this most treacherous of coastlines. Eady shouted to Marland, then picked up his telescope to search the rain swept blackness.

~

Herrington wiped his mouth on his napkin and rose from the table after a most acceptable dinner of roast beef that had been cooked and served by Mrs Tricket. He made his way to the public bar, having no intention of ruining his clothing by venturing out on such a night. Where was there to go anyway?

By this time, the bar had become busy and the conversation had turned to animal husbandry.

206

'Made I bloody laugh I can tell thee,' continued a farmer called Jack Harding. As soon as 'er caught sight of Goliath, 'er turned 'er backside, an' stuck 'er fanny in't air... Reminded I of the missus on a Sunday morning.'

Laughter went about the bar and Tricket smiled to himself at the thought of the ample Mrs Harding on all fours.

'Now you correct me if I'm wrong Jack, but I'd say t'would be very difficult to tell um' apart from that angle,' said Bob Davis, with a chuckle.

'I shouldn't think so, Bob,' said Tricket solemnly; 'Jack's missus ain't got a tail!'

'Ow' the fuck would thee know?' said Harding, amid much laughter.

'Now then gentlemen, now then,' said Walt, 'just mind thy language. We've got Mr Errington ere', come all the way from London. He's an accounting gentleman and 'e ain't come all this way to hear you buggers a cussing an' a swearing, ain't that so Mr Errington?'

'Don't mind me gentlemen,' said Herrington, 'you just carry on milking or whatever it is your doing.'

'Don't suppose you as' a lot to do with cattle yerself, Mr Errington?' said Davis, 'you coming from London an all.'

'Absolutely right first time Mr Davis; you chaps seem to have cornered the cow market down here I'm afraid; barely a cow to be seen anywhere in London these days; one of the reasons I never drink milk! Have to make do with this stuff I'm afraid,' he continued, as he took a glass of brandy from Tricket's hand. He tipped his glass at Davis then raised it to his lips. On a later to be regretted impulse, he added, 'Perhaps you'd like to join me in a nightcap.'

A chorus of "Thank yer very much Mr Errington" and "Thas very gentlemanly of yer' Mr Errington," came from those who by their geographical location, could decently claim to be a recipient of Herrington's good will.

Herrington committed the round to his tab and commended Tricket on his tariff, which seemed very reasonable compared with London prices. Tricket thought it would be churlish to tell Herrington he was overcharging him outrageously, so he smiled graciously instead.

'There you are then Mr Errington; the more thee d' buy; the more thee'll save. Course thee'd know that, thee being an accounting gentleman!'

'Yes quite so, Mr Tricket!' Herrington was not sure if Tricket was the cleverest or stupidest man he'd ever met.

'You enjoying yer' stay down yer' then Mr Errington?'

'Um... a little quiet Mr Davis,' said Herrington.

'Well thee've picked the wrong time of year ter come, Mr Errington! Yes indeed, I think that's the trouble sir! Thee should ave' bin' ere' four weeks ago.'

'Oh, should I,' remarked Herrington, 'and what might I have missed Mr Davis, Morris dancing, cheese rolling, elver eating? Please don't say yes Mr Davis; I would never forgive myself!'

Davis took a long draught from his pint. 'No nothin' like that as I recall Mr Errington, but we weren't having all this weather, see, that were the thing! Thee could have taken a nice walk up an' down the harbour every day! Get a bit of fresh air in thee.'

Herrington wondered if he had been cast into an asylum.

'Tell me something Mr Davis? What on earth do you chaps find to do all winter long?'

Harding looked at him with some surprise. 'Oh, we as a lovely time Mr Errington. We sit yer an' we laughs, an' laughs, an' laughs.'

'Do you indeed Mr Harding - whatever at?'

'Why all you silly buggers as do come down yer from London of course,' said Harding.

Parkin sat quietly in his chair, pipe in mouth. He hardly noticed the baiting and noisy conversation that surrounded Harding and the gentleman from London, for his mind was elsewhere.

He had nothing against the ever-growing legion of well-to-do visitors who invaded their tiny village each summer. At worst, they irritated him as they promenaded the harbour with their pink parasols, fancy clothes and foolish questions hallooed down from the railings above. Whenever possible he ignored them, and got on with the task of mending his nets or whatever else engaged him. He wondered when Bob Davis would finish his nonsense and bring the pegboard to the table.

His pint was halfway to his mouth when the dull thud of the cannon sounded above the muffled howl of the wind; a thin arching tracer of sparks streaked skywards from the other side of the harbour, and seconds later the tiny town of Lynmouth was lit by an orange glow. A siren began its mournful wail.

For a split second, all conversation ceased. The flare picked out the features of each man in highlight and shadow as they turned to the windows.

Then, of a sudden, pandemonium broke. Parkin and three other men leapt to their feet and ran to the door, one of them turning over a table in his haste. They were swiftly followed by everyone else and in a matter of seconds, Herrington and Tricket were the only people left in the bar. Tricket set himself to righting the table and mopping up the spilt beer and ashtrays.

Herrington looked out across the harbour completely confused by the sudden events, 'What on earth is happening, Mr Tricket?'

Tricket looked up from his work and turned to his guest, 'They've called out the lifeboat Mr Errington; then to himself he added, 'God help um!'

Herrington crossed to the window and sat down in Charlie's chair for the excellent view it would afford him of events to come. This was more like it, a little excitement at last!

'I'll bet they get jolly well paid for that sort of thing Mr Tricket, I shouldn't fancy it myself?'

'They don't get paid at all, so far as I'm aware Mr Errington.'

'Not paid! Do they know these fellows or something?'

'I should 'ardly think so, Mr Errington.'

'Well why on earth do they do it then,' he replied in astonishment. 'It'll be their own fault if they get themselves drowned I should say!'

Tricket pushed the table back into place with a screech of wood, harsh enough to strip wallpaper. 'I'll thank you to sit somewhere else Mr Herrington,' he snapped... 'If you don't mind sir.'

'What on earth for Mr Tricket, we're the only people here?'

'Because you're sat in Charlie Parkin's chair, Mr Errington! He's the Coxswain of the lifeboat Louisa, as is about to take sixteen men of this parish out into that storm to save the lives of strangers, an' he'll be back to finish his pint afore long!'

209

CHAPTER 30

The Lifeboat

Pollard had been taken by surprise. Shrewd and skilful seaman though he was, he now regretted leaving the sanctuary of Glasgow docks for the boiling cauldron of the Irish Sea. The wind and swell had risen to gale force nine in no more than a few hours, now he and his crew of five had been obliged to work around the clock, as they beat down the West coast of Wales against a ferocious South Westerly.

With each tack, all hands manned the deck, to reset the sails of the three-masted topsail schooner. The slippery, spray washed, deck, was no place for the faint of heart as the stout booms swung violently from side to side. Not without good reason did they call these ships "the man-killer's".

As the wind strengthened, Pollard ordered less and less sail and the men worked aloft and about the deck, taking in sails with the roller reefing gear of the fore, main and mizzen booms, and heaving and hauling upon sheets and braces.

Pollard watched in barely controlled anger as McInally went about his work. There had been rows; several of them since he'd had the mate dragged back to the vessel; rows about his drinking, his work, and his bad influence upon the hands. Willing men had become sour and disgruntled; McInally himself had become sullen and truculent; his dignity ruffled by Pollard's criticism and the throwing of his gin into the Firth of Clyde.

Tired and exhausted from long hours and foul weather, Pollard decided that he must run to Swansea for shelter. The wind had slowly brought in long swells of alarming proportions from the vastness of the Atlantic Ocean. The brave little Nicolette climbed each crest and plummeted to the bowels of each trough like a child astride a rocking horse. Spray and seawater deluged the deck as the bows dug deep into each successive wave. A more foolish, more fearless man than Captain Pollard, would be exhilarated by this roller coaster ride, from the very top of the world to the howling vortex at the mouth of oblivion, but Pollard was not such a man. He saw its danger, and feared its fury, from a lifetime spent at sea.

He thought of his wife and daughter who were huddled together, frightened and distraught in the tiny saloon, and bitterly regretting bringing them on this journey. Earlier, he'd heard his wife scream and had passed the helm to McInally to investigate. When he entered the saloon it was in total darkness; his wife was shrieking in panic. No one had thought of replenishing the oil in the lamp and the flame had turned smoky, then gutted as it rocked drunkenly upon its hook. Pollard re-lit the lamp and comforted her with words of reassurance. He told her of the shipwrights and master craftsmen of Appledore, who had built the Nicolette, not yet forty years ago. Their skills were second to none and the Nicolette would see them all in their graves whilst she carried on sailing the oceans of the world. He assured her that the creaking and groaning of timbers were not to be feared. They were her way of fighting the storm, and she creaked, as the oak tree's from which she was made, would creak and bend in the wind.

What Abraham Pollard did not know, was that the boards on the starboard side of the hatch were moving with every pitch of the vessel. Slowly but relentlessly, they dragged upon the tarpaulin covers laid on them. Invisible rents began to appear in the lower canvas and the wedges began to loosen.

~

Heavy hobnails clashed against wet cobbles, as the stragglers of Parkin's crew ran through the streets of Lynmouth to the lifeboat station. The Louisa was a stout, sixteen man, clinker built rowing boat, with lockers fore and aft and a midships sail if needed. The brave little boat had been wheeled from the lifeboat station upon her heavy carriage and now she stood upon the slipway held back by ropes. Soon she would be ready for her short, steep, journey to the inner harbour.

Parkin stood in the stern of the boat, his hand resting lightly on the tiller as he supervised the preparations for launch; oilskin clad men were clambering up the wheels and tumbling into place on the athwartship boards. Occasionally, Parkin would hand out a brief instruction to his crew or the shore gang, which would leave his lips like the crack of a whip.

Despite the foul weather and the lateness of the hour, most of Lynmouth had come that night to the storm lashed harbour, drawn like a magnet by the enormity of the event. There had been launches before - bad ones - but never into a gale such as this.

Silent, anxious women, and stony-faced men, stood in the doorways of quayside houses, or wherever shelter was available. Some clutched the shoulders of excited children who waited impatiently for the spectacle to come.

The Reverend Ian Bacon crossed the open quay; the skirts of his cassock flapping about him in the howling wind. He spoke briefly to the men in the boat as they busied themselves arranging oars in rowlocks and donning the heavy canvas and cork life jackets.

'Godspeed, and come back safely,' cried Bacon above the howling wind.

211

"Thank 'e' kindly vicar," came the reply from those who heard.

Bacon moved aft to where Parkin stood in the stern. 'Take care Charlie and may God be with you to guide your hand.'

'Aye thanks Vicar,' replied Parkin. 'We'll need all the help we can get tonight. I'd take the devil himself, if I thought the bugger could row.'

Bacon gave Parkin a rueful smile but supposed that he should have expected little else. Parkin was not a religious man and only crossed the church's threshold for funerals and the like, but for all that, Parkin was the Lord's unwitting servant. Certainly, there was no man in the lifeboat, nor anxious wife, silent in the shadows, that didn't take comfort in the knowledge that Charlie Parkin was there. Only the crew of the lifeboat could elect their coxswain; there had been no doubting the man these twenty years past.

Parkin expected to give the order to release the carriage at any moment. All his men were in place, their oars held aloft in their rowlocks. Little more than six minutes had elapsed since the lifeboat had been called out; he was only waiting for information from the coast guard about the ship's position. He'd heard she was foundering near Porlock, and the Watchet lifeboat had been unable to launch due to the foul weather; it was up to them now. He understood that she was a three masted schooner and her name was "Nicolette".

Parkin watched the priest stand back from the carriage. He respected Bacon for he always came, be it day or night, even as now when it meant a good soaking for his troubles.

The weather, and the job they were about to do, took his thoughts back to 1871 when he'd been a deck hand on a wooden hulled steamer called "The Gallant". They had berthed in Buenos Aires in Argentina, the city of "good air".

Parkin had sat that night in the Stella Maris Mission to seaman drinking a beer. It was their last landfall before Punta Arenas, but first, they would need to round Cape Horn. Whilst his shipmates enjoyed their drink, Parkin sat and looked at a huge painting that hung high up on the wall of the gloomy room. It was dark and faded with age and was of a sailor in sou'wester and oilskins, stood at the helm of a ship. His hands gripped the wheel, his knuckles white, whilst a storm such as the one they now faced, raged all about him. Water ran in torrents from the brim of his hat and salt spray stung his eyes. His face was taught and strained with concentration and fear.

In the shadows behind the sailor, there stood another figure. He was very tall. A giant, perhaps three feet taller than the sailor, and he was dressed in a

212

course homespun cloak that hung loosely from his arms and shoulders. It seemed to Parkin that the sailor did not know the stranger was there.

There was a look of calm and serenity about this ghostly figure, who like the helmsman, stared straight ahead into the swirling maelstrom. His face was bearded, fine boned and handsome. His eyes were compassionate and yet there seemed to be a fathomless sorrow about them. It seemed to Parkin that they had known great pain. There was an aura that surrounded him and radiated from him - a ghostly ethereal light. One giant hand, resolute and strong, clutched the heavy wheel, holding it firm, whilst the other rested upon the sailor's shoulders so that he too might stand firm upon the heaving deck. About the stranger's head was a crown of thorns.

Never in all his life, had Parkin been so moved, as he was moved by the power of that painting, and in all the storms and tempests he was later to encounter, he would think of it - just as he was thinking of it now - and it would be a comfort to him.

The Gallant sailed the following day into stormy weather off Cape Horn. There she'd lost her rudder, and had drifted south to founder like so many before her, on the rocky shores of the Falkland Islands. Parkin and the crew of the Gallant had been lucky. They had survived a shipwreck where so many before them had perished, but he never forgot the painting in that dark and smoky mission, so many miles from home; now he resisted the overwhelming temptation to turn and look over his shoulder.

It was time! Parkin gave the order to free the carriage and it began its rumbling flight into the turbulent waters of the inner harbour. He lifted his hand in a brief salute as he passed the priest and Bacon nodded his head in reply. The tiny craft hit the water with a heavy thud that slowed her forward motion and immediately began to rock and pitch her violently. All that could be seen from shore was Parkin's glistening oilskins, as he stood as stiff as a poker before the aft locker. His lanyards held him upright as though he were carved from wax. A cloud of storm-whipped spray engulfed the boat, as bows and oars bit deep. The Louisa and her crew of sixteen lifeboatmen of Lynmouth, North Devon, were gone.

~

Pollard spun the wheel hard a port. He'd reefed as much sail as he dared, for he needed to turn across the wind with all that manoeuvres inherent dangers, but it was not enough. Just as the Nicolette came beam on to wind and sea, she began to slide down the side of an enormous forty-foot wave into the gaping trough beyond. The wind heeled her over until her port gunwales were awash.

213

As she hit the bottom of the trough, she went completely under. The whole main deck, back to the hatch and beyond, was submerged. Pollard and the seamen were stood at the wheel in two feet of swirling water. It sucked and pulled at their leggings and threatened to suck them from the deck as tons of water rushed through the freeing ports and over the side.

At first, Pollard thought that ducking apart, all was well, for she was coming about and had caught the wind once again. The bow of the Nicolette rose slowly from the water as she rode high on the crest of another wave, but as she slid down into the next trough, one of the sailors pointed for'ard and shouted 'The hatch; look at the hatch.' The suction of the first wave had ripped the torn tarpaulins off the hatch boards; its tattered remains floated away on the ebbing wave. Two of the heavy boards had been lifted from the hatch, one to be whipped overboard, the other to fall into the hatch itself. Seconds later, the Nicolette was into another trough, and once more, the little ship drove her bows deep beneath the waters of the Bristol Channel. This time she did not come back so quickly. Pollard and the crew watched in fascinated horror as hundreds of gallons poured into her hold. Once more, she plunged deep into a mighty wall of water. The giant wave engulfed the bow and swept all before it. Pollard watched in disbelief as the wave plucked up the tiny galley deckhouse that stood before the fore hatch, stove and all. It hurtled down the ship as light as a leaf in a storm, but to Pollard it appeared to be in slow motion. It hit the mainmast almost in one piece, there to explode into a thousand deadly splinters. They flew onwards, the length of the ship, like shards of shrapnel from a gun. Pollard was amazed that they could fly so far, it was as though they had wings.

He felt no pain - none at all. He could see the jagged wooden stake had passed through his chest, but only with his left eye. He lifted his fingers to his face, but it felt strange, as though a jellyfish clung to it. Pollard recognised the spar that protruded from his chest; it was black and had been the frame about the galley door. He would have looked longer at the wooden dagger that impaled him, but he needed to clear his lungs. It was as though he'd swallowed a lot of water. He coughed, and at last, pain broke through his shattered nerves. Great gouts of blood poured from his nose and mouth, so that he could neither breathe, nor speak. He sank to the deck, thinking not of the mortal wounds that had struck him down nor his wife or child below; instead, he thought of the galley; it would need to be rebuilt when they reached Plymouth; he must see to it that it was done. Dan Matthew would do it for him. Calm, such as he'd never known came over him and his heart stopped its beating.

~

214

Parkin stood in the stern of the Louisa with legs akimbo; the lanyard with which he'd lashed himself to the boat, as taught as a bowstring. Both hands clutched the tiller with which he fought a desperate battle to keep the boat into the wind. He watched his crew with eyes narrowed to slits against the ferocious stinging spindrift. They were at the end of their endurance and he knew that he must accept defeat and turn back or they too would be lost. Five times he'd tried to get the Louisa beyond the breakwater and into the open sea beyond, and five times, they had been beaten back by the ferocity of the wind, swell and rip tide.

Each man looked at Parkin as they leant backward on each pull of the oar, waiting for any new instruction he might give. They were exhausted and they were slowing down; they knew it and so did Parkin. If they did not have the strength to pull themselves clear, the wind and swell would dash them against the breakwater and the Louisa would be smashed to matchwood; there had already been two near misses. This had been Parkin's last attempt and it had failed. With lungs aching and heart pounding in their chests, they prayed that he would take them in.

Parkin had them marking time, neither going forward, nor back. He was watching the waves ahead as they crested each swell, counting them, timing them; looking for just the right moment to make his turn.

At last, Parkin saw his chance. Ahead of them, a huge wave was bearing down upon them, but the sea before it was confused; there was not the fearsome height in the waves. The lull before the storm thought Parkin. He would make his turn in the calmer water before this wave. He raised his hand in silent warning to his men. Hearts beat faster for they knew the dangers that lay ahead. Salvation or death awaited them and they watched Parkin for the slightest sign.

~

McInally and the crew knew they were fighting for their lives. Pollard's blood stained body lay forgotten in the gunwales. With each new flood, it washed across the deck, only to be dragged back to the bulwarks as the water rushed from the freeing ports.

McInally had to protect the hatch or they were doomed. Already the Nicolette was sinking for'ard and the rudder was out of the water, unusable. Pollard had got the boat about so that she was stern to the wind and he'd to keep it that way; if she came beam on again, they were lost. They made improvised sea anchors from sails and rigging which they threw into the water behind them to act as drogues. The sails that were still set, were heeling the boat

215

over at an alarming angle, and were pushing the Nicolette ever closer to the rocky coast of South Wales and certain shipwreck. With no rudder to guide them, they would be at the mercy of the sea; he had to cut the sails free.

McInally grabbed a fire axe from its hook and tied a rope about his waist. One by one, he hacked through the topping lifts and halyards at their lashings about the belaying pins and brought the sails crashing down. The sailors manned the bilge pump; its workings creaked noisily as the huge leather clad pistons sucked upon the hold bilge. On and on they cranked, but it was as futile as King Canute's attempt to hold back the sea.

McInally was all but swept away by the giant waves that crashed upon the deck, and only his lifeline saved him. Several times, he'd been swept from his feet and dashed against the bulwarks like a rag doll. Blood poured from a jagged gash across his forehead and it stung with the salt water. The sea poured into the hatch with each wave that broke across her deck, and with every minute that passed, the Nicolette sank deeper and deeper into the water.

He called to the sailors to lend a hand. They must somehow cover the hatch again, or they would surely perish. As they laboured, the wind slowly turned, and the South Westerly of the last two days veered about to the Northwest. The Nicolette changed direction and slowly began to drift back out into the Bristol Channel toward the Southeast and the beautiful, rugged, treacherous, coast of Exmoor.

~

The calm water before the huge breaker held its promise, and Parkin threw the tiller hard to starboard at the same time as he signalled to his men. Backs straightened and oars bent and bit deep. Slowly, slowly, the Louisa came about, but not fast enough for Parkin. The wave was bearing down upon them at breakneck speed and if it caught them broadside on, it would swamp them. Parkin bellowed to the lifeboat men as loud as he could above the howling wind.

'To the starboard... row! Row for your lives!'

Parkin could see the agony written across their faces as they bent to their oars. Veins stood out on temples and neck muscles tightened to breaking point. When the wave hit them they were only three-quarters about. It plucked them up and hurtled them forwards. Onwards they sped at breakneck speed, towards the inner breakwater and the Rhenish tower. The Louisa passed by the huge stone buttress with just feet to spare and was catapulted onward into the relative calm of the inner harbour.

When the lifeboat had been returned to the safety of its carriage, Parkin and his crew climbed the cobbled slipway and slowly walked up to the harbour road above. Wives came down to meet their husbands with warm rugs and steaming billycans. No one spoke for it was not necessary; they bore their failure in silence.

Bacon met Parkin on the slipway and they walked up together.

'Is everyone all right Charlie?'

'Aye Vicar, a few bruises, otherwise all's well; tis just their pride that's hurtin.'

'The Lord is the only one who can work miracles Charlie. It would be above your station to think otherwise!'

Parkin did not answer at once, but then he said - 'Men may be dying out there Vicar, and we have let em' down. That's the truth of it, and that's how we shall be obliged to remember this night, I'll warrant!'

Bacon put his hand on the Coxswain's arm and stopped him. 'Look at them Charlie,' he said calmly - 'just look at them! They are exhausted! They could not row another yard. Their wellbeing already lies heavy on your shoulders, and now you want to carry the Louisa, and all she represents, on your back as well. Only the Lord is invincible Charlie; you are not making sense my friend.'

Parkin turned sharply to look at the Vicar. 'What did you say?'

'I said you're not making sense Charlie!'

'No, before that - something about carrying the boat!'

'I was trying to say that you cannot do it alone Charlie. Your men are exhausted, and you must accept that you, and they, have done all that is humanly possible. They are done, and you cannot carry the boat to that shipwreck on your own.'

'No yer right Vicar, but what if we could get it overland to Porlock! We could launch n' from there I'll wager a pound!'

Parkin did not wait for Bacon's answer; he called to Tom Noakes who was Louisa's bowman. 'Gather up some horses Tom, well take the boat overland to Porlock an' launch un' there.'

'Av thee gone bloody mad Charlie,' said Noakes. 'Tis thirteen bloody mile to Porlock, we' that soddin' hill to go down at end ont. We'd never get the boat down un.'

'So what do thee propose we do then Tom,' said Parkin, 'go home to our beds whilst men are drowning. Thy mattress must be a bloody sight more

217

comfortable than mine, that's all I can say.' So it was that 10 tons of lifeboat, sixteen lifeboatmen, twenty horses and many more townsfolk, made their way up the twisting, rutted, Contisbury Hill, to the high coastal road beyond.

Half a dozen men went ahead with pick axes and shovels, to dig down the banks ahead of the thirty-four foot boat, using oil lamps and flares to light their way. A hundred or so men and women laboured behind them in the cold, pouring rain, to drag the huge load up the rutted and slippery Contisbury Hill.

Slowly, relentlessly, what had seemed impossible was made possible and despite a wheel coming off through continual knocking against the rocky banks, the lifeboat made it to the wind and rain lashed moors. Wet and exhausted by their exertions, most townsfolk returned to Lynmouth, but some twenty stalwarts remained to help Parkin pull Louisa across the high Moor's road. They were lashed by incessant rain and battered by the howling wind that blew relentlessly across the exposed moorlands. To their right was the beautiful valley of Lorna Doone. To their left, the sheer cliffs of Foreland Point and Contisbury Bay.

The road they travelled was the highest, most rugged, most remote, and some say the most beautiful coastline in all England, and it stretched out before them for thirteen tortuous miles. Ahead went a man with a lamp to steer them away from the worst of the ruts. All about them, they could see the eyes of hill sheep staring at them blankly, as they huddled together in small groups beneath the relative shelter of the banks. What strange and unpredictable creatures they were, these humans! When the boat passed by, they returned once more to their rest.

At Ashton Lane, they realised that the lifeboat carriage was too wide to pass through and it would be impossible to widen the road sufficiently for their purpose. It seemed that all was lost and despite their effort, they had failed, but they had forgotten their coxswain. Parkin was not a man to lose heart whilst there was strength in his body with which to fight on.

'We've come this far lad's and we're not going to turn back now,' he declared.

He had his men take the boat from its carriage and set it on skids, thereafter to be dragged by brute strength along the narrow lane. The wider carriage was taken onto the rutted moor, through gaps they made in the walls, and once past the narrow section, carriage and boat were re-united.

When the going became a little easier, the exhausted lifeboatmen climbed aboard the boat, some to sleep, others to yarn the journey away, for it was still a long way to Porlock. Besides the leading horse walked Bob Davis, for five of the horses were his. On the steeper gradients, Davis would turn them out to walk.

'Out you get you idle buggers; this ain't the bloody horse bus.'

'Did I hear a horse fart?' said one man to another.

'Aye you did Jack, and it sounded fer all the world like old Bob Davis was a talkin!'

And so it went on. All through the night they journeyed, hauling the huge load across the rugged moorland. Nothing so large had ever made such a journey before, for at journeys end there was the fearsome Porlock hill with its hairpin bends, one in four gradients, and rutted, rocky track. It was the steepest, most perilous hill in all England.

CHAPTER 31

Porlock Hill

It was dawn when the boat neared Porlock and word was already abroad in the tiny town. Curious men and excited children made their way up Porlock hill to greet it.

Isaac had risen early that morning to walk the 3 miles to Pierce's tannery at the back of the Methodist church. He wanted to buy leather off cuts to keep out the drafts beneath the parlour door and to make new hinges for Polly's chicken coop. She had six hens now and they could usually be sure of an egg for breakfast.

Business was still a bit slow on the conventional work, but he'd been right about the steam engine repairs and over the last few months he'd done well in that direction. It had begun with the repair of a stationary engine that drove a pump at the docks in Porlock Weir. With Ira's help, he'd made a good job of it, for Ira's experience as a marine engineer had been invaluable, and the unusual job had been a challenge that brought Ira to the smithy every day.

Isaac began to take a different view of Ira and they were getting along very nicely. Isaac looked forward to his visits and so too did Rebecca for despite Ira's legendary meanness, he always had a few sweets in his pocket for her. Of her own accord, she called him Uncle Ira and she had clearly won the old man's heart.

'What's supposed t' be the matter with it then?' he'd asked, when he saw the engine parked outside the Smithy for the first time.

'It keeps knocking out the big end; the shaft is as oval as an egg,' replied Isaac handing him the callipers; several people have had a go at it, so say.'

'So it's come to thee as a last resort!'

'Sort of!'

'You need to overhaul this safety valve an all lad; this lift levers rusted solid.'

He turning his attention from engine to boiler and a glimpse inside the inspection door produced much tut-tutting about necked stay tubes. 'Bomb , there's work a plenty here.'

al eye over the white metal bearing in question, which ndful of white nuggets.

220

'Crazed and broken away,' he remarked, 'poor bonding that! We can sort that out an all, but tis this oval journal that's started all the trouble.'

They spent many hours removing the shaft and chucking it in the lathe, which only had just enough clearance for the crank throw. They machined and polished the shaft, making it round and smooth once more; then with Ira's guidance, Isaac recast the bearing halves.

'Get the keeps up to temperature, afore thee d' pour; that's the secret. Throw a gob of spit at the keeps, and when the spit d' bubble, thee've got it right! Let the keeps cool down slow an even,' said Ira. 'Patience is the virtue we this kind of job - think of it like thee be courting a comely lass — slowly, slowly, catch a bloody monkey!'

After a little machining and scraping, the engine was re-assembled and worked perfectly thereafter. News soon spread about the handy young Blacksmith with the pretty wife. New work was slowly coming his way, and Isaac had found a mentor in Ira, who probably knew more about boilers and steam engines, than anyone that side of Watchet dockyard.

Isaac was grateful for his help and learned quickly. Ira would take neither thanks nor money, but could be relied upon to call by at lunchtime. 'Taint no hardship,' he declared, 'fer here's my choice! I can come down yer' an' jaw with thee over summat interesting, or stay at home an' watch our Molly turning the bloody milk sour! Er's only got t' look at it once.'

Isaac laughed.

'I'm bloody tellin' thee!' insisted Ira.

~

Isaac bent his head against the wind that pierced every stitch of his jacket like a needle, and pushed on for the tannery. Once in the town, he found himself amongst the throng of curious spectators who were climbing the twisting serpents' back of Porlock hill to watch or help with the lifeboat.

Porlock was no ordinary hill. Steep and twisting, it was just mud and stone for the most part, for no steamroller could ever climb it. Even a coach and four was obliged to double the horses.

'Gentlemen and ladies under forty step down, if you don't mind,' the coachman would announce as they approached the steepest part. Needless to say, this would all but empty the coach for the fair sex can be a little touchy on such matters.

221

Getting down was more hazardous, however, for the horses could not hold back the weight of the coach unaided. Instead, they would use a heavy, iron drug shoe, lashed to the underside of the carriage by chains and wedged beneath the wheels to lock them. The horses would then drag the carriage down the hill, leaving another groove behind them.

When Isaac arrived, the huge carriage was half way down and approaching the first hairpin. There was no drug shoe for the lifeboat carriage, so they had lashed the spokes of the rear wheels instead. Isaac stood silently by; fascinated at the sight of the huge boat and its crew of cursing, sweating men that looked so out of place amongst the trees and ferns.

There was no doubt who was in charge, for Parkin had that natural authority that other men accept without question. He had walked ahead of the boat to the first bend and Isaac could almost read his thoughts. How in blazes could they get the boat around the bend without losing boat and carriage over the side of the hill?

Parkin had Davis and the leader horses go as close to the edge as possible, before cutting the hairpin as tightly as they could. Even then, it was necessary to dig out some of the bank to let the carriage pass by. At Parkin's request, Isaac and others helped the boatmen hold the carriage steady as they rounded the bend. They made the first bend well enough, and the boat was dragged to the next bend. But Bob Davis had increasing difficulty keeping the huge horses quiet, for they didn't like the weight that was pushing them down the steep and slippery incline.

Whether it was a broken lashing or the lead horse stumbling, no one knew, but suddenly the carriage leapt forward without warning. The leading horse fell first; then two others lost their footing and all were dragged down the muddy rock strewn slope on their backs. Carriage and animals finally came to rest some fifteen yards on, in a deep storm ditch. Men ran shouting in all directions amid flailing hoofs and terrified horses.

Davis lay trapped beneath the leader horse, unconscious and with blood pouring from his mouth. The horse's legs were broken, but it tried desperately to stand. Each time it did so, it crushed Davis as it fell back. They could hear the breath being driven from his lungs and Parkin feared that if they couldn't get the horse off him, he'd be crushed to death. Another man was trapped between carriage and bank by the hub of the front wheel, but despite the pain written across his face, he seemed in good spirits.

'Lash the carriage, as fast as you can; take a bight about those trees and cut the horses loose,' shouted Parkin above the pandemonium that ensued. They tried to raise the leader horse to its feet, but it was hopeless. Its agonised cries filled the air, and could be heard in the village some half mile away. A shot rang out and the animal lay still at last, its brains blown clean away by the shotgun blast. The other horses were tethered to drag away the carcase, and at last, the rescuers could reach Bob Davis. Though he'd regained consciousness, he seemed strangely quiet as he lay in the ditch.

'You all right Bob?' asked Parkin.

The Farmer nodded but closed his eyes and slipped into unconsciousness once more.

Parkin was loath to move him until the doctor arrived, but had no choice as storm water had built up about him and was in danger of drowning him.

Parkin turned his attentions to the other man who was now shrieking in agony. Whilst Parkin had been trying to free Davis, the other lifeboatmen and onlookers had tried to pull the heavy carriage away from him, but they had only succeeded in shifting the carriage further into the ditch; crushing him all the more in the process.

Parkin had the horses coupled to the rear of the carriage, but horses and men still couldn't drag it from the rut. Every attempt saw it slip back at the end of their exertions, to crush the man still further. His name was Jeremiah Hoskins and he was one of Louisa's crew.

Again and again, they tried until Hoskins pleaded for them to stop, his agony, clear for all to hear.

Parkin sent for more horses, but until they could be found, there seemed little anyone could do. His mind was wrestling with the problem when Isaac spoke to him.

'Can I make a suggestion?'

'If it's sensible,' replied Parkin.

Isaac told him his idea and Parkin nodded and handed out his orders. 'Jack' he shouted, 'Take two men; go with this lad and do as he says. The rest of you get ready to pull with the horses when I say so.'

Isaac's gang took a manila rope from the boat and climbed the hill to take it about the trunk of a huge tree, then down the steeply wooded bank to a trestle of sawn logs. The trestle was supported on two heavy piles and Isaac and the men tied the rope about the logs, trestle and all. A horse was brought to pull away the piles so the falling log pile would pull heavily upon the lifeboat. The manila rope went as tight as a bowstring as the heavy bundle of logs began to fall. The weight of the carriage arrested them, but they had pulled the carriage back a foot in the process.

'Pull together now,' shouted Parkin as his whip came down hard across the flanks of the leading horse. With the additional help of the logs, the carriage bumped its way back onto the road. Hoskins began to slip, but hands reached out to hold him. He was in great pain, but he was alive, and there was no doubt whose quick thinking had saved his life.

People were saying, 'Well done lad,' and slapping Isaac on the back, but Parkin didn't stop to talk about it, for he had other matters to think about. He had the horses brought back to the traces, and the boat was on its way again. Isaac and most of the townsfolk followed the boat to Porlock Weir.

When they reached Porlock Weir, Parkin was well pleased. There was none of the vicious breakers they'd had at Lynmouth and though the weather was bad, it would not stop them from launching Louisa. Parkin's judgement as usual had been correct, and all their hard work had been worthwhile.

Whilst the lifeboatmen made ready for launch, Parkin shouted above the wind, 'I need a good man to row in Jeremiah's stead!'

Many volunteered, and so too - in a moment of foolhardiness - did Isaac.

'Can you row?' shouted Parkin above the wind.

'Yes,' lied Isaac.

'In you get then!'

The heavy carriage rattled down the ancient slipway and Louisa was launched and on her way.

Charlie Parkin watched Isaac three thwarts back on the port side and cursed himself for a fool. It was obvious that he couldn't row; the best that could be said was that he was getting the hang of it, but this was no time to learn how to row a bloody lifeboat.

The coastguard at Hurlston point was sending semaphore. WELL. DONE. LOUISA. STEER. WNW. FOR. GLENTHORN. GODSPEED.

Parkin brought the boat clear of the headland and far enough out to catch the ebb tide. They rigged as much sail as they dared and the boat began to fly. The lifeboatmen of Lynmouth and their trusty Louisa were on their way at last.

CHAPTER 32

The Stile

The gale that battered Exmore took its rage all the way to Gloucestershire and beyond, lifting tiles, rattling windows, and howling through gaps in doorframes.

John Smith had been awake for some time, suffering from a bout of indigestion and listening to the ferocity of the storm outside. It was almost as loud as Amy's snoring and between the two, there was little chance of him falling asleep once more.

At the first hint of dawn, he dressed quietly to avoid waking her. He heard Bert stir on the landing at the sound of his master rising. It was just like the old days all over again. No Isaac, Polly or Rebecca; just John, Amy and the dog. He'd always had a dog, but it wasn't like the old days really, not when he thought about it further, for they had been content enough then. They were lonely now, without the youngsters; it wasn't the same anymore.

He opened the bedroom door and passed through to the tiny landing, closing the door behind him. The dog was excited, but John shushed him quiet, patting his head and pulling his ears in a silent good morning. The dog contented himself with wagging his tail.

In the parlour, John got himself into his boots while the dog whined at the door.

'You won't be so keen when we get out there Bert,' said John, knowing the labradors dislike for windy weather, but the dog sat expectantly, nonetheless, his enthusiasm undimmed.

He went a long way towards filling the gap that Isaac and the girls had left, for he sensed the old man's sadness and was making an extra effort to keep him company in their absence. He'd taken to resting his muzzle on the blacksmiths knee as they sat before the fire of an evening, instead of sprawling on the carpet as before. John would stroke him, running the huge ears between his fingers. Bert was pretty much all fur and ears.

He'd had many a dog in his lifetime - all labradors - but Bert was his favourite. He was loyal as they had all been loyal, but this one had a bit of independence about him that tickled John's sense of humour.

John called it independence, but Amy took the view that it was idleness and was scathing where the dog was concerned. She'd wanted a collie, being concerned as she was about tramps, ner-do-well's and vagrants. John insisted he'd rise to the occasion.

'It'll only need a tinker to tickle the gate and he'll tear the bugger's throat out, don't you worry! That's part of his technique; the dozy look! He's like a sleeping volcano is our Bert.'

The dog had a habit of opening one eye and then the other - not unlike a crocodile - whenever he had reason to believe he was being discussed. In this manner, he was able to observe either Amy or John - depending upon who was talking - without the need to move his head. That stayed resolutely on the rug.

'Sleeping volcano,' Amy mocked, resigning herself to the fact that the two friends would never be parted, 'you've got half of it right!'

He lifted his hat and coat from the hook whilst the dog whined softly, eager to be off. Their habit was to cross the fields to Hall St. picking a few mushrooms if any were to be had, then home along The Ham, to meet the lane through the village. Each enjoyed the morning walk in their own way and for Bert; it was the scent of the creatures that had been abroad in the night. He recognised them all and would leave his scent for them too.

'Come on then you big furry buffoon, let's go'!

They walked across the pasture until they came to the ash path between the church and the old village at Garter Court. It was well trodden with several stiles along the way. At one of these, John felt giddy. A sharp agonising pain gripped his chest and he saw the ground rising up to meet him. The sky was above him, no longer grey, but streaked with red like a bloody veil. Soon he lay very still.

The dog could not understand this new game his master was playing but he was sure it was not right. He stood over him, licking his face, nudging him with his snout, willing him to get up so they could be on their way.

He sat by him for many minutes, crying and trying to stir him. He barked and barked, but no one came. Finally, he left him and ran back the way they'd come. He ran as fast as he could, for he didn't like to leave his friend and master. They were always together, always.

When he reached the Smithy, he sat at the door and barked. He barked and barked until Amy came, then together they rushed back to where Bert had left him. John lay just as Bert had left him; his leg's still entangled in the stile.

CHAPTER 33

Salvation

By some miracle, Parkin found the Nicolette amid the storm, which though abating, was still force 7 to 8. They followed the wreckage of rope, spars, sails and other detritus, back to where she'd foundered on a submerged reef, less than three cables from shore. They all but missed her, for visibility was poor amid the crashing waves and lashing spindrift. It stung their eyes like needles and drenched them to the skin despite their oilskins.

The ships bows and starboard beam were completely submerged and only her stern, the heads, and the companionway hatch, were above the water line. She was impaled upon jagged unseen rocks, which pierced her bowels and would not let her go despite the ferocity of the storm. She was lucky in a way, for had she been blown onto the jagged shore, she would surely have been ground to matchwood.

She'd long since lost her foremast; its shattered remains visible in the troughs, whilst the main mast was little more than a shattered stump. As the mainmast split and fell it sent gaffs and yards crashing down, bringing sails and rigging with them in a tumbled mess about the deck. Ropes and sails streamed from the stricken vessel with heavy pieces of wreckage still attached.

Through his glass, Parkin counted four men clinging to either the bulwarks or rigging, with one astride the Mizzenmast crosstrees. With every wave that struck the hull, Parkin expected them to be swept away, but as each receded they clung on resolutely. Clearly, they had lashed themselves to what was left of the doomed ship. Parkin estimated a full crew of six or seven, so perhaps they were already too late for some. No doubt, the sea would give up their bodies in time, but they would not be a pretty sight.

Parkin ordered in the sail and the lifeboatmen took to their oars once more. He brought the Louisa seaward of the stricken vessel and as close as he dared. She began to pitch and yaw alarmingly as Parkin brought the boat about; she started to take on water that had to be bailed from the bilges.

Noakes threw a cluster of cork floats over-side, and the line-reel sang, as the wind dragged them toward the Nicolette. Three of the four survivors fought their way to the Starboard bulwark, and with boat hooks, they snatched at the floats as they came close. Eventually, they caught the slender line and hauled the floats in for all they were worth. Louisa sent two more ropes across to them, one thin, one thick. 'Tom it off whilst we move into your lee,' shouted

227

Charlie Parkin through a copper megaphone, his words barely audible above the cacophony of wind and sea.

Parkin brought the Louisa over the submerged reef, and about the stern of the Nicolette, until she was in the lee of the bigger ship, with the ropes streaming out between them. The sea was much calmer there, for they were protected by both the headland of the little cove, and the stricken ship herself. They sent a breeches buoy to the Nicolette on the thicker rope, the thinner runner being used to tow the buoy back and forth. The men aboard the Nicolette hauled in the buoy over the fifty yards that separated them, whilst the lifeboatmen pulled steadily on their oars to keep the lines from snagging, and marking the distance they had to keep. Only Parkin at the stern, and Noakes at the bow, could see the first man slide down the hulk with the breeches buoy about him. Noakes pulled furiously upon the buoy as the sailors paid it out. Again and again, the man disappeared beneath the waves, only to re-appear moments later. He gripped the buoy for all he was worth and let Noakes and the sea speed him to the Louisa.

McInally the mate, and the second sailor, hauled furiously to retrieve the buoy when their comrade was safely aboard Louisa. The second sailor was next to face the ordeal, but he didn't hesitate, for it was a choice between life and death.

As he paid out the line for the second time, McInally looked at the fourth man, Amos Crick, who was lashed to the starboard bulwark some twenty feet from him. He made no effort to release himself that McInally had seen. His arms and legs jerked limply as each wave broke over the ship, sucking and clutched at his body with watery fingers. It didn't look well for him, not well at all.

'Should have followed us into the rigging, the stupid bastard,' thought McInally to himself. He calculated that with Crick, there were five lives lost; Pollard, the two sailors, Pollard's wife and their young brat. She and the girl must be dead by now, for no one could survive below those decks.

McInally watched the lifeboatmen struggling to get the second sailor aboard Louisa. The boat was pitching violently, and twice the Breeches buoy smashed against her as Louisa plunged from crest to trough.

Isaac glanced over his shoulder for a glimpse of the struggle being enacted so close to him. He'd never seen anything so dangerous, so thrilling, or so tense in all his life. He pulled steadily on his oar in time with the other lifeboatmen, skilled now, with its weight and rhythm.

McInally had time to think whilst he waited his turn. Pollard was dead and he was sure the others wouldn't talk, for why should they? They were with him in

228

Glasgow; they could have said something about the missing board, but they didn't. They were as guilty as he was and no one was ever going to speak out. He didn't give a damn about Pollards death, or his family for that matter; and why should he? Pollard was like all the rest of his kind, taking all the profit whilst the likes of him did all the work. He'd disliked Pollard more than most captains, for his bible bashing lectures. 'Self righteousness bastard,' breathed McInally to the wind.

The manifest had logged copra, white lead, tar, and two thousand empty barrels as the cargo, but McInally had done this run from Glasgow to Bristol and the Ivory Coast before, and he'd wager not all those barrels were empty. Some would be full of whisky, to be shipped out under the noses of the Revenue for a very handsome profit. The Ivory Coast, where they were bound was a living hell of malaria and disease, where there was nothing else to do but drink. A barrel of good Scotch whiskey was worth more than its weight in gold there. All the skippers were in on it and McInally guessed Pollard was as big a crook as any of them, for all his piety and praying.

With the second sailor safe aboard the lifeboat, McInally drew back the breeches buoy as fast as he was able. He tommed it off about a belaying pin and was about to climb over the bulwark when he thought again about Amos Crick. Amos had been a drinking man like himself and a good enough friend; just maybe he was still alive.

Charlie Parkin beckoned to him furiously, but McInally faltered, seemingly in a quandary about some matter. With his mind made up, he loosed his lanyard and lowered himself hand over hand down the bulwark until he was level with the companion hatch. It was in the centre of the poop deck and directly opposite Amos Crick.

The deck was awash with heavy waves that were trying to suck his feet from under him. In the lull between two surges, McInally re-tied his lanyard and swung himself across the deck like a pendulum. He made it to the companion hatch as the next wave hit him; smashing the wind from him and grasping him in its suction as it fell back down the steeply sloping deck. He clung to the companion hatch for dear life.

McInally reached Crick with the next swing and again was all but washed overboard by the force of the waves. He lifted the man's head by his hair. His eyes had rolled upward into what was left of his face. It had either been smashed to pulp by wreckage or ripped away by ropes and rigging. Either way, the poor bastard was dead.

McInally swung himself back to the companion hatch. Water poured into it as he clung to it like a limpet, gasping for breath. The level in the stairwell rose and fell with every surge of the sea.

He clung to the hatch coaming as he waited for his next chance. Pollard's wife and child were down there, but they surely wouldn't be alive; no way could they be alive! He waited his chance for the pendulum swing to the port bulwark when a thought struck him. The smaller forward cabins and lockers must be flooded right enough, as would the passageway from stairs to saloon, but given the steep angle of the deck there was just a chance there would be air in the saloon, just maybe! That was where they would be if they were anywhere; in the saloon that doubled as Pollard's cabin. He tried to dismiss the idea, for they weren't his problem; and even if they were alive, it was every man for himself. Then some primitive streak of humanity got the better of him and on an impulse, he gestured to Parkin that he was going below by pointing two fingers downwards. Seconds later, he disappeared.

'Two more below decks,' mouthed Noakes to Parkin, who nodded in acknowledgment. There was nothing they could do now, but wait and mark time. Without the sailor on deck to draw in the line, he couldn't put a man on the Nicolette even if he wanted to. The fellow must rescue whoever was left on his own, and in the mean time, they needed to stay out of danger, for floating spars and huge shattered timbers were everywhere.

Taking a deep breath, John McInally clambered down the companionway stairs with gallons of seawater pouring after him. It was hard to fight the violent surges in the narrow stairwell. He took one last deep breath, then plunged below the surface into the dark sump that was once the cabin passageway. His hand found the familiar handrail in the darkness, and he dragged himself upwards along the steeply canted passageway toward the saloon - passing his own cabin door to port, and the locker door to starboard. Suddenly, he was hit in the chest by the saloon door, which by some miracle was still on its hinges and swinging open and shut with every surge of the sea. Grasping at anything that came to hand, McInally dragged himself into the saloon - desperate to find air before his breath gave out. His head broke the surface at the very last moment, his lungs bursting.

There was little light by which to see in this watery tomb, except a dull greenish glow, low down on the starboard bulkhead where he could see a submerged and gaping hole. The hull rocked, as yet another massive wave hit her, and McInally was catapulted to the deckhead as the wave flooded the saloon once more. The cabin was a death trap and he'd been crazy to go there. He needed to find them and get out as soon as possible.

Clinging to a frame he shouted, 'Mrs. Pollard are you here? It's John McInally the mate; are you here?'

To his amazement, he heard a muffled sound, a sobbing that could only be a human voice.

Frantically he searched the tiny cabin, shouting at the top of his voice, Again and again, huge surges threw him against the deck head.

He heard the sobbing again, and the sound was to port - he was sure of it. He tore at a wardrobe door with all his might and there he found her clutching the child to her bosom. In the dull green light, he saw the stark terror in her eyes. She looked at him without recognition; it was a wretched face, lost and deathly, as though the soul had died and just the body lived on. She was clutching the child to her breast but the girl was clearly dead. Her head bobbed back and forth with every surge; her mouth hung open; her limbs were limp and lifeless.

He tried to drag Mrs Pollard from the locker, but she fought with him; screaming in her terror.

'We must go!' shouted McInally.

'Abraham, I must find Abraham,' she cried.

'He's dead! He's dead and the girls dead; we will be dead too, if we don't go!'

He tried again to pull her from the cupboard, but she began to scream hysterically, clawing at his face when he tried to take the child's body from her. He punched her again and again, until the child's body slipped from her mother's grasp into the black, swirling water, where it was lost from sight.

The woman screamed hysterically lashing out at the mate with all her strength, trying to get past him to the child.

'You stupid fucking bitch,' he shouted, 'we've got to go, or you'll kill us both! They're dead, can't you understand that! They're both fucking dead!'

He hit her again and dragged her from the cupboard, forcing her beneath the water. He dived for the hole in the stricken hull, dragging her with him by the hair. The water fell once more as the surge subsided and McInally and the woman were drawn to the splintered maw on the starboard side, by the sea's irresistible suction.

As their bodies passed through, a jagged splinter scythed his back so deeply, that he felt the wood scrape his backbone. Then the woman's dress became snagged on another jagged edge. He pulled and pulled at her arms, but the splinters only sank deeper into the cloth of her skirts. The air in his lungs was

231

running out and soon he would have to leave her there. With one last effort, he fumbled with the billowing cloth that trapped her in the gaping maw, and ripped away the skirt that held her. He swam to the surface with lungs bursting, Pollard's wife in his arms.

Parkin and Noakes watched in disbelief as they bobbed to the surface amid the boiling surf. 'Pull lads,' Parkin shouted to the oarsmen. 'Put your backs into it.' Parkin guided the boat towards the stricken hulk. He got as close as he could without snagging Louisa's oars on the rigging and ropes.

He brought the boat to where he thought the swell might take the swimmers. All they could do now was pray they could stay afloat for long enough. Many times, they disappeared beneath the mountainous waves, only to reappear again. McInally was a strong swimmer and would have made it, had the woman not regained consciousness and begun to fight him. She grabbed his hair, dragging him under in her frantic fight for survival or death - her objective not being immediately clear to those who looked on. He was too weak to fight her further, and they began to separate and sink beneath the waves.

The bodies passed within ten feet of the lifeboat; one moment they were high above Louisa; the next many feet below. Parkin dared not get closer for fear of crushing them. Noakes threw a line with customary skill that landed within a foot of the pair.

'Grab the line,' shouted Noakes 'grab the line.'

McInally reached out with what little strength was left and grabbed it. The woman slipped away from him as a huge wave tugged them apart. Pollard's wife was being swept ever farther away by the swell, as Noakes pulled hard on the line to draw the mate aboard.

Many hands reached out and grabbed McInally, but Pollard's wife seemed doomed as she drifted aft of Louisa. Parkin shouted his instructions to the crew and made to turn Louisa about in the heaving seas, but it would take time, perhaps more than she had. Isaac watched in horror as she disappeared again and again, beneath the surface of the foaming sea.

On an impulse, he let go of his oar, loosed his sou'wester, and before anyone could stop him, launched himself into the water.

'Jesus Christ almighty,' hissed Parkin beneath his breath, looking for his chance to bring the Louisa about.

Isaac struck out towards Pollards wife with powerful strokes, for he too was a good swimmer. In seconds, the current took him to her and he grabbed her head in the crook of his arm and swam for all he was worth. Parkin had got the boat about, and Noakes threw his line once more. The line fell across them, and Isaac tied the rope about her. He held on to it for all he was worth, as the men in the lifeboat pulled them in. Isaac had been in the water only seconds, but it seemed an eternity to Parkin and his crew.

Parkin shouted through the megaphone to McInally, 'Is that everyone; are there any more?'

McInally shook his head, 'The others are dead,' he shouted as loudly as he could, 'I got all that was alive.' He relapsed into another bout of retching and John Noakes had to hold him up, for he was done for.

Parkin nodded in acknowledgment, 'You're a brave man,' he said through the megaphone, then to his crew, 'There's no more we can do here; we can't save the dead. We'll clear the reef by oar, then set sail again for Porlock Weir.'

His survivors were cold and in shock, particularly the woman who stared continuously in the direction of the wreck though it was lost to their view behind the headland. Her hair hung in rattails, her face gaunt, her eyes distant and her skin chalk white. One of the lifeboatmen ran a lanyard about her waist, for she twice tried to clamber over the side.

Parkin had saved four souls from a crew of eight; better than he'd hoped, but perhaps there would only be three souls in the final reckoning, for he feared for the woman's sanity.

Noakes was doing all he could with brandy and blankets from the for'ard locker, but the blankets were soaked through in seconds in the spray and spindrift. Isaac sat again at the third thwart, but he was beyond rowing, his body shivering, his teeth chattering.

Noakes semaphored repeatedly in the hope their progress was being observed by one of the lookout stations high above the cliffs. How many survivors, what help they needed, how long they would be. Others bailed the boat to lighten their load.

Parkin sat on his narrow seat, the tiller in the crook of his arm. The wind was more or less before them, and he had to tack to take them back to Porlock, but she was happy enough, and cut through the waves at good speed when he gave Louisa her head.

What a beauty she was this living thing of wood and oakum and pitch. She'd taken the worst the storm could throw at her and she'd come through with nothing worse than paint scrapes. Thank God for her hardiness for she had taken them through hell and back these last twenty-four hours. He'd been on his feet for all that time, and now he was exhausted. He wanted to close his eyes

233

and sleep, but that would have to wait. His thoughts turned instead to the men with whom he'd shared those desperate hours.

It was nearly over and they'd done their job well as he knew they would. There had been times when he thought they might fail, but these were tough men, well used to hardship - they came no tougher.

What they'd done had taken all the strength that mortal men could summon and more besides; they too were tired, as he was tired. They sat with oars stowed, heads bowed, eyes closed and their oilskins drawn about them. Parkin knew them all, every one. He fished with them, drank with them, played dominoes with them, lived his life among them. They were ordinary men just like him, but he doubted they would ever be ordinary men again. They are heroes now and rightly so; he thought to himself. The Watchet lads would be growling with envy and stamping their feet at what they had achieved. Parkin allowed himself a smile about that small matter.

However, were they heroes in the usual way of things, or was their heroism that of a different kind? Hero's to Parkin were people like the young lad on the third thwart with the badly scarred face - men who would throw themselves into danger without a second thought. When they got away with it - as thank God, he had - then the world called them heroes, but that was not the kind of bravery that got Louisa through one of the worst storms in living memory. Theirs was a different kind of heroism.

When a place in the lifeboat became vacant, Parkin would look down the list of volunteers he kept pinned to the wall of the station house, and from it, he would choose a name. He'd talk to the man over a pint in the Rock House and tell him to go away home and think about it. 'Think quietly on what the lifeboats all about,' he would tell them. 'Talk to yer wife and talk to yer children; talk about coping if the worst were to happen,' he would say.

It's not easy talking to someone you love about your own death, but it needed to be done. Most would say yes when next they met, and some would say no, and there was no shame in that, but for those that did say yes, the clock began its endless, relentless ticking. Sooner or later the call would come. It might be next day, next month, or next year, but sooner or later, the call would come. Then they would dash pell-mell through the streets of their little town and put to sea when all other boats were running for shelter. They would sail steadfastly into the maul of a storm in nothing but their open rowboat, whilst all other vessels sought a lee.

They would have no choice when the call came for only Charlie Parkin the Coxswain, could make the decision to go or stay; it would never be anyone else. If the lifeboatman was afraid - as all right thinking men would be afraid - then duty would be his best friend, for duty would drive all other thoughts from his mind.

Lesser men could never understand why they did what they did, but forgot that the men of the lifeboat were men of the sea themselves. Those who crewed Louisa, worked the sea, fished the sea, and knew it dangers well. In risking their own lives for others, then maybe one day, when the cards fell against them, they would earn the right to call another man to do the same for them.

Theirs was no rash heroism like this young buck on the third thwart, thought Parkin - it was far more than that. It was a greater courage; a more unfathomable courage that each man carried with him every day of his life.

Parkin roused himself from his reverie to realise he had been staring at Isaac without really seeing him at all. Isaac looked back at Parkin, uncomfortable beneath the steady gaze of this formidable seaman who had just achieved the impossible with unerring judgement and sheer force of will.

He smiled at Parkin not knowing what else to do, and Parkin gave Isaac a nod and smile in return.

'Eh up, summat's buggered,' said one oarsman to his companion, 'Charlie Parkin's smiling,'

'That'll be a touch of wind,' came the reply.

Parkin heard it too and to everyone's amusement laughed aloud. He put his head back and laughed and laughed whilst rain and spray dripping from his eyebrows and sideburns.

It was not like Charlie Parkin to laugh, but this was no ordinary day. The burden of so many lives, the graft and superhuman effort of the last twenty-four hours; it had to come out somewhere and why not with laughter.

It was infectious, for if Parkin could laugh about God knew what, then it was high time for them all to relax. Lifeboatman shook hands with lifeboatman, and those that could reach, shook hands with Isaac, Parkin, John Noakes and John McInally.

Together they had done what couldn't be done and succeeded against all the odds. Perhaps that was why they did it, these men of Lynmouth and Penzance, Peterhead, Holyhead, Liverpool and Whitby. They and men just like them, who go down to the sea in boats to save the lives of others. They fear their mistress and her awful power, just as all men fear her, but they are not men to turn their backs and say, 'No - not me,' for they are the men of the lifeboat.

Ropes were grasped by willing hands and fishermen waded into the surf to drag the boat up the slipway at Porlock Weir. People were milling about, talking excitedly as they helped the crew and survivors to the warmth and welcome of the tiny cottages that edged the harbour.

Isaac thought for the first time of Polly and Rebecca, and guilt smothered the euphoria of the rescue. She would be worried about him, and if she knew he was in the lifeboat, she would be beside herself. What a fool he'd been. Here he was, five miles from home, soaking wet, his money gone, and lucky to be alive. In little more than an hour, it would be dark, and he should have been home hours ago.

Isaac slipped from the crowd and began to walk the long road home to Selworthy. Only one man saw him go in the general melee.

'Hallo there; what's your name friend?' shouted McInally.

'Isaac Smith,' replied Isaac.

'Where are you bound in such a hurry?'

'Home! My wife will be worried. I'm the blacksmith at Selworthy and I've a way to go yet.'

'Blacksmith eh,' said McInally; 'Where did you learn to swim so well?'

'In a mill race when we were kids, we'd have had a thrashing if anyone had caught us,' said Isaac with a smile.

'In a bloody pond,' laughed McInally! 'I'll take a beer with you one of these days then blacksmith,' he shouted after Isaac.

'Aye one of these days,' replied Isaac smiling.

Polly met him at the gate of the smithy as darkness fell. She held Rebecca in her arms and Isaac could see she was angry and upset.

'Isaac where have you been, I've been at my wits end with worry?'

'I'm sorry lass; something came up that's all. There's no need to fret about it.'

He reached out to put his arm about her and she began to sob in his arms. He knew her tears were for more than his lateness, for she was made of sterner stuff than that. Something else must have gone wrong.

'What's the matter, Polly?' he asked her.

'Oh Isaac,' she said through her tears. 'There's been a telegram... John's dead!'

236

CHAPTER 34

Amy's Homecoming

Polly heard the clip clop of Ira's pony long before it rounded the bend. Isaac was home at last and she was glad, for the past week had been the longest of her life.

Following the news of John's death, Isaac had returned to Coaley for the first time in over a year, to make the funeral arrangements and collect Amy and her belongings. It was agreed that she was to live with them at Selworthy, for Polly didn't want to leave their new home, and Amy didn't want to stay in a house with so many memories.

It was strange for Isaac to see the old Smithy cold and silent. Even Arthur had disappeared, but no one knew where. The cat hadn't been seen since the morning of John's death.

He ran his hand over the tools and treadled the bellows a couple of times. It creaked as it had always done. He heard the sound of the forge in his head; the rush of flame, the crackle of tiny sparks; the ring of hammer upon anvil. There were so many memories. He remembered the blacksmiths first words to him as a child, when Isaac had needed to clamber on the lower spar of the smithy gate to see over. "Clear off, you little bugger - go and swing on yer father's gate and don't you bugger mine!" What might have happened to his life if he'd taken any notice and gone on his way? He owed him so much. He had called him Uncle John, then dad, then Grampy when Becky was born. He'd loved and respected him so very much.

Isaac gave Amy the money he'd rescued from the mortar of John's "bank". He managed to sell the pony and trap to a farmer at Garter Court and the rest they left for the next man. John had always wanted him to take over at Coaley, but their home was in Selworthy now.

Taking Rebecca by the hand, Polly ran down the lane as fast as the child was able. She was better now, after the bout of chicken pox that kept them home in Selworthy. Ira had kindly offered to take the trap to Minehead to meet them from the 3.15 train, and seemed pleased that Amy was coming to live at Selworthy. Polly wondered what their friendship had truly meant, all those years ago.

When the trap came into sight, she waved excitedly, scooping Rebecca into her arms. 'Daddy, daddy!' shouted the little girl, every bit as excited as her mother.

Isaac walked beside the pony whilst Ira and Amy sat either side of the heavily laden trap; Amy dressed entirely in black. All three waved back and Isaac let go the pony's halter, quickening his step as much as the tortuous hill would allow.

He was overhauled at lightning speed by Bert, who had been investigating the hedgerows some fifty yards behind but who now raced ahead at the sound of Polly and Rebecca's cries. He got there first and Polly dropped to one knee to put her arms about him.

'Oh Bert, you've come to see us and look who you've brought.' The dog licked her face in his excitement and wagged his tail furiously.

Isaac scooped Rebecca into his arm and kissed her, then kissed Polly too. They embraced one another, whilst the dog ran back and forth between them and the trap, his tail wagging madly.

Polly kissed Isaac again, her eyes shining with joy of having him back.

'I'm going to be silly and cry. I know I will,' she said, wiping her eyes whilst Isaac laughed.

'We have missed you so much, haven't we Becky; you are not allowed to leave us ever again.' The little girl nodded her head and looked very serious, whilst Bert ran around in endless circles.

'Oh Amy, it is so good to see you,' Polly said. 'I am so sorry about John; he was such a lovely man, so very kind; I am so sorry.'

The two women put their arms about one another and Polly held her for many moments, sharing her sorrow.

'It's been a terrible shock, Polly,' Amy said. 'He was his usual daft self one minute, then suddenly...!' She did not finish her sentence but dabbed her eyes with her hanky.

'But I have my faith dear, and that has been a great comfort... We will see him again one day... in the Lord's good time.'

'Yes we will!' said Polly. 'Of course we will, and in the mean time we will look after you and it will be just like before.'

'I don't want to be a burden on you - you have your own lives.'

'Don't be so silly; you are a part of our lives... Things can never be the same again, I know that, but Selworthy is a lovely place and you will grow to love it here in time as we have; I'm sure you will.'

'Thank you dear, it's very pretty I must say.'

238

'Here you are Amy, what do you think?' asked Isaac as they reached the cottage at last.

'What is it called?'

'Leathernbottle Cottage,' supplied Ira proudly.

'Very pretty, yes very pretty,' she replied.

'It's got such lovely views,' said Polly.

'So I see,' replied Amy casting her gaze over the roofs on the smithy and cottage, 'most of em through the roof I shouldn't wonder!'

'That's my last job to do,' replied Isaac defensively.

'Doesn't it let the rain in?'

'A little - not a lot!'

'No wonder that walls bulging Isaac,' she said, looking at the bulge in the red brick wall of the Smithy, 'Once you get the water in...!'

'Yes that's the other job Amy...!'

'How much rent is this old skinflint charging you?' she continued.

'Ten shillings a week,' replied Isaac, sharing a wary glance with Ira.

Amy turned her attention to Ira Grace with a less than charitable expression.

'Disgraceful!' she said, and led the way into the house.

CHAPTER 35

Sergeant Robinson

Three weeks on from the wrecking of the Nicolette, it seemed the bad weather would never end. Ferocious gales lashed the coast, and the stormy sea had breached the barrier beach at Bossington for only the second time in living memory. Massive breakers beat down the huge pebble structure to let the sea burst through, flooding the low-lying pastureland beyond. Cattle and sheep were moved to higher ground, whilst folk watched the water creeping ever closer to their homes.

Though the weather still blew a storm, at least the furore in the papers had blown itself out. Reporters from the Daily Sketch, the Illustrated London News and The Strand magazine, had long since paid their bills at the Bath Hotel and left on the horse bus to Minehead. National pride in the Louisa's remarkable achievement had taken its course and Lynmouth had returned to peaceful tranquillity.

The same could not be said for its obscurity, however, for Mr Newnes - Lynmouth's wealthiest resident and generous benefactor - missed no opportunity to exalt its delights in his ever popular journal "Tit Bits", adding Louisa to its list of attractions, and heroism to its list of virtues.

Though the nation's interest had moved on, the tale of the rescue was still the main topic of conversation where there was any local gathering, and would probably remain so whilst the stormy weather lasted and the battered Nicolette clung resolutely to the reef.

Old sailors would sit jawing about the hearth in the Rising Sun, recounting tales of mountainous seas and vessels lost without trace. The ladies of the Women's Institute competed to bake the best "Louisa" fruitcake, complete with sugar icing oars and marzipan sou'westers, whilst the congregations of Lynmouth and Lynton churches gathered together beside the Lifeboat Station, to bless the boat, and give thanks for the safe return of her crew, and the four souls who might otherwise have been lost. The only person who did not go out of his way to talk about the events of that day was Isaac and for the very good reason, that any reference to it produced a very icy response from Polly.

It was not that she wasn't proud of him, far from it! It was the thought of the danger he'd placed himself in, and the risk of losing him to another reckless escapade that upset her so much. He had learnt better than to try to pass it off as 'nothing to make a fuss about' for it had twice reduced her to angry tears.

240

Even Ira - who had seemingly adopted the Smithy as his second home - and McNab, who liked to drop in for a chat most evenings, knew better than to mention Louisa - or lifeboat rescues - in front of Polly or Amy.

'Mum's the word I reckon,' remarked Ira, after Polly discovered the three of them discussing Isaac's escapade over a glass of cider. She gave them all a lecture on responsibility and consideration for others, then rounded on McNab for ignoring Parsley as he ate her borders.

'Aye; discretion's the better part of valour,' added McNab, tying Parsley's halter to the gate.

'It's only you two that keep talking about it,' replied Isaac. 'If you both kept quiet there'd be no problem.'

'Well there ain't no problem anyway,' replied McNab! 'Taint as though tis ever likely to happen like that again now is it! Trouble is - thee be living we' a gaggle of women Isaac and that's not healthy, not healthy at all!'

'What's not healthy about it?' enquired Isaac.

'Aye, and how would thee know anyway,' said Ira; 'thee being a lifelong bachelor - fer reason's as is obvious?'

'I've sin what it's done to others,' replied McNab tapping his nose knowingly. 'It d' addle the brain in't end.'

'And your brain's not addled then McNab,' said Isaac, smiling at his nonsense.

'Course taint!'

They broached the subject with far greater caution thereafter, avoiding all reference to Isaac's escapades, but the Nicolette remained a matter of general interest for the whole community. Despite the best efforts of wind and waves, she clung resolutely to the reef, like a loose button clinging to a shirtsleeve.

'The hole that sank her is the hole that's saving her,' remarked Isaac. 'It's big enough to let the sea in and out, so she sits there and wallows instead. It must be sizable, because the mate and the Captain's wife swam through it, side by side, by all accounts.'

'I'm not sure I believe that tale; why didn't they jump over-side like most drowning folk do,' remarked McNab?

Isaac shrugged his shoulders. 'All I can tell you McNab is what Parkin and Noakes told us. They could clearly see the deck and no one came up on it, but all of a sudden there they were, bobbing to the surface, not twenty feet from the boat.'

241

'Well either way, they're alive thanks to thee,' remarked Ira.

'Maybe,' replied Isaac modestly. 'Everyone thought the Nicolette would be smashed to pieces but she's still there large as life. I reckon they'd have been okay anyway.'

'Well, I shouldn't ave liked to take my chances! Who does the ship belong to I wonder, and who's taken the loss; they must be crying in their beer at the moment?' said Ira.

'The black rocks of Glenthorn; that's who 'er belongs to,' said McNab, darkly.

'The Captain they reckon,' said Isaac, ignoring McNab's irony, 'so I suppose it belongs to his wife now; but it'll be academic when she breaks up. She'll be worth bugger all then.'

'Loss of the treasure ship!' said McNab, cryptically.

'What's that supposed to mean,' said Ira?

'She's a treasure ship, I erd' it from the horse's mouth!'

Isaac smiled and sipped his cider.

'And what kind of treasure's she supposed to be carrying,' asked a highly sceptical Ira Grace, 'gold perhaps?'

'In a manner of speaking,' replied McNab. 'Liquid gold so I'm told, Scotch whisky by the barrel load!'

'They're all empty McNab,' said Isaac, pouring cold water on McNab's story. 'They lay down whisky in old sherry casks and vice versa or so I'm told. It's supposed to improve the flavour, so there's always been a traffic between Scotland and Harvey's of Bristol fer mature oak kegs, and it don't mean there's any whisky aboard her.'

'Not officially! Not so far as the revenue's aware... but unofficially...!'

'You're talking nonsense McNab!' said Isaac. 'Beyond some tar and white lead, her only cargo was empty barrels and bales of Copra; a lot of which is washing up and down the Bristol Channel as we speak. The cargo's worthless!'

'Right you are... If you say so...!' said McNab, returning to his cider in a huff.

'Well, am I wrong?'

'No, no, you know it all, same as all you young un's!'

Slowly they prized the full story from him. McNab had a small lobster boat he kept at Porlock Weir and he'd gone there a few days after the wreck to see if

242

the boat was still in one piece. That job done, he'd called into the Swan for a pint to find the publican, Alf Rudd, talking to a stranger, and it was obvious from the way the conversation suddenly stopped, that McNab had come at the wrong time. Rudd pulled his pint and passed some remark about the weather. McNab gave him fourpence ha'penny and went to warm himself by the fire.

McNab sat for many minutes thinking about nothing in particular; mesmerised by the sinuous smoke flutes that spiralled upwards to the chimney pot, like tiny ballerinas leaping and pirouetting about a floodlit stage.

Rudd and the man returned to their conversation, their voices low, but he heard Rudd say, "I don't want to get involved. The one to talk to is a man called Ridler, Nance Ridler.'

That was a name guaranteed to prick McNab's ears. Thereafter he strained to hear every word.

'Has he got a boat?'

'No, but he'll sort the rest out.'

'The fewer that know, the better!'

'Like I said; he's the man you want - he'll sort it out.'

Shortly afterwards, the stranger left, leaving McNab contemplating the fire, whilst Rudd tidied his bar.

'Are you sure it was the mate off the Nicolette,' asked Ira, his curiosity aroused by Nance Ridler's name.

'How many strangers do you know hereabouts we a Scots accent?' remarked McNab.

Suddenly McNab's "treasure" became a little more believable, for there had been some strange goings on with that most famed member of the crew.

Following his rescue and McNab's subsequent encounter with him in the Swan, John McInally, the mate of the stricken ship, had found work with a local farmer called Alf Hoskins, whose fields were among those affected by the flooding.

Hoskins, or "Oskins" as he was more often known, put McInally to work rescuing sheep pens, fodder, and whatever else was salvageable from the two feet of seawater that flooded his land, and as a consequence of which, McInally, found himself in the company of Hoskins daughter Dulcie.

Dulcie made up for any shortfall in intellect, with an ample bosom and very shapely rump. Her liking for the men was a positive bonus to McInally's employment that he took full advantage of. So it was, that a very angry Alf Hoskins found the mate having his way with his daughter in a shed where he kept his winter feed. The two were so engrossed in their rutting that neither heard the door open, or Alf Hoskins picking up a pitchfork.

He saw more of his daughter that afternoon than he'd seen since she was a babe in arms and with a bellow of rage, stabbed the tines of his fork as far into McInally's backside as he could get them. The unfortunate Romeo shrieked with pain and leapt to his feet, setting about the farmer with a length of timber that was conveniently ready to hand. He rained down blow upon blow until he'd beaten the farmer senseless. Dulcie fled naked from the barn, shrieking 'Murder, Murder!' whilst a panting McInally, looked down at the blood bespattered farmer who lay ominously still. When a hysterical Dulcie - now wearing a borrowed coat - returned with a neighbour, her lover had gone.

John Hall turned Alf Hoskins over and looked for signs of life, whilst the shed slowly filled with others who had seen or heard the commotion. Hoskins opened his eyes, to see an anxious looking Hall, and a sobbing Dulcie kneeling over him. 'Get Robinson,' he moaned, before losing consciousness once more.

With Hoskins injuries not as serious as first thought, the good folk of Porlock Weir thought the goings on at Hoskins barn the best sport they'd had in years. Everyone, except Sergeant Robinson of the North Somerset Constabulary that is, for he took a very dim view of attempted murder.

Dulcie's indiscretion was the one and only subject of conversation in the Swan that night.

'I 'ere Robinson's got a warrant out for is immediate arrest!' said one local fisherman as he lifted a pint to his lips, 'apparently e's looking fer a Scotsman we' three arseholes.'

Sergeant Robinson and two of his constables duly found their quarry at eleven o'clock that evening, drunk as a Lord and fast asleep in a fodder barn atop the beacon. He'd been tipped off by one Jack Ridler, the older of the two Ridler brothers of the flourmill at Selworthy and that was a tale in itself!

Isaac had been listening carefully to McNab's tale, which usually had a high degree of romance about them, so he rarely took much notice of Ira or McNab when they got going, but he'd clearly changed his mind about this particular story.

'Maybe you've answered a few questions, McNab,' he remarked!

'Such as,' replied the farmer.

'Such as how did Jack Ridler know where McInally was hiding? I'll bet he went straight there when he saw what he'd done to Alf Hoskins, hoping Nance would somehow save his neck - birds of a feather flocking together, and all that kind of thing!

'Maybe so, but I'm surprised Nance and Jack got themselves involved with Robinson,' said McNab; 'There's no love lost between the Ridler brothers and the law.'

'That's Isaac's point you silly bugger,' said Ira, 'There'd need to be a reason and a good un at that! Nance Ridler don't do nothing without a reason and tis always to his benefit!'

Just at that moment, Amy's footsteps were heard on the flagstone path that led from the front door. She appeared, clutching a bowl of grain with which to feed the chickens before locking them up for the night. All conversation stopped and even Parsley hung his head to avoid eye contact.

'What are you three up to?' she asked suspiciously.

'Nowt! We was just talking about the weather,' replied Ira innocently.

'Aye, and how it can turn chill all of a sudden,' added McNab.

Isaac topped up his glass and kept out of it, but with a wisp of a smile.

'If the devil should cast his net,' remarked Amy, scornfully, and went on her way. Isaac and Ira she knew of old, but she was still getting the measure of McNab. Early indications were that he was every bit as bad as the other two.

When Amy talked to Polly about the dubious trio, remarking that they were getting as thick as thieves, Polly described McNab as a "darling", and was clearly very fond of him. Equally surprising, was her fondness for Ira, whom she'd forgiven over the rent, because of the help he'd given Isaac over the workings of the lathe and the mending of the steam engines. The huge clanking monsters seemed to be as common about the smithy as ploughing horses, and both she and Rebecca loved them.

Isaac was gaining a reputation for a good job, at a fair price, and their little business was starting to do well. That was in no small way due to Ira Grace. Though his rheumatism kept him away from the anvil, his eyes and ears never let him down and never did a problem get by him.

Amy's conclusion was that Polly was entitled to her opinion, but she remained circumspect where cider-drinking men were concerned.

They went back to their conversation as soon as they heard the hens clucking and were not far adrift in their thinking. The Ridler's were - by most honest

245

men's judgement - out and out scoundrel's, and had no love for Robinson, or the law he represented. Nance, in particular, had fallen foul of the policeman on more than one occasion.

Robinson had long suspected Nance of being involved in the handling of stolen goods, even if he wasn't directly involved in the thieving and smuggling that abounded along their remote and rugged coastline; but there was no doubt in Robinson's mind, about his nature. Like his father before him, he'd shown himself to be a brutal and violent man, having put out the eye of a drinking partner during a drunken brawl, a matter for which Nance spent six months in Minehead gaol.

Nor did Robinson like the company he and Jack kept at the Talbot Inn, a rough house for all the ner' do wells and ruffians of Porlock and Porlock Weir. It was, therefore, to Robinson's considerable surprise that Jack Ridler handed over information that led to the apprehension of his quarry.

Barely able to walk after Hoskins attack with the pitchfork, McInally saw but one possibility for evading arrest on what he thought would be a charge of murder. He waited until darkness had fallen, before daring to knock on the door of the Selworthy Mill house.

'Are you Nance Ridler,' he asked as the door opened.

'I'm Jack Ridler,' came the reply from the man who stood before him; a lantern held high so that he could see the strangers face. 'What's your business with Nance?'

Jack and Nance listened to what McInally had to say. 'How do we know you're not the Old Bill up to some trickery,' said Nance.

McInally dropped his trousers, enough for them to see the bloodstained wounds. 'The crazy bastard came at me with a bloody pitchfork and I reckon I might have done for him with a length of wood. He looked in a bad way, anyway. Help me out, and half of its yours.'

'How many?' asked Nance.

'A hundred maybe, of barrels and hogsheads - that'd be usual. You'd be rich men! All I ask is you help me lay low for a while - what do you say?'

'How would we find em - among the thousands?' asked Jack.

'They'll float low, the empties will float high. You can't go wrong.'

After a few minutes, Nance made up his mind. 'You can't stay here,' he said to McInally, 'They might bring in the dogs from Minehead and come looking for thee. Take off yer clothes. Jack's your size, so he'll give you a change, so the dogs don't take no notice of thee. We'll burn these right now. There's a fodder barn, a mile or so yonder, through the woods near top of the beacon; no one never goes there. You'll be safe there fer tonight at least. Tomorrow we'll sort something out an' maybe get you a berth on a boat out of Watchet or Ilfracombe.'

Ridler showed him the door and put a cask of cider in his hand, before pointing out the path through the woods. As soon as he was safely away from the mill, Jack Ridler set off for Porlock in the trap.

Within the hour, Jack returned with Robinson and two constables and met Nance at the edge of the wood. They began their climb of the dark and leaf strewn path, to the fodder barn on the edge of the beacon. Time and again, they trod up to their ankles, in the tiny streams and muddy gullies that crisscrossed the steeply sloping woods.

Robinson, pistol in hand, opened the shroud on the carbide lamp and shone its light into the dark barn. They found their quarry asleep where he lay; the earthen jug by his side.

That's yer' man,' said Nance, kicking the sole of his boot.

There's no reward, if that's yer' game,' replied Robinson.

'I weren't looking fer none. I were only thinkin' of the reputations of the wives and daughters of the parish.'

'Yes I'm very well aware of your concern fer the wellbeing of others, Nance,' replied Robinson as he clapped his man in handcuffs.

CHAPTER 36

Bill of Sale

Nance brushed the flour dust from his Sunday best. The stuff seemed to get everywhere, even here in his wardrobe. Given the enterprise he was embarking upon, he went to the additional trouble of a collar, tie and bowler hat.

He reviewed his appearance in the mirror. 'Very smart' he remarked to the mirror, then set off for Doverhay and the home of Mrs Edwina Thomas - a widow of charitable disposition.

Mrs. Thomas was sixty-three years of age and became a devout Christian after losing her husband to a barmaid twelve years his junior; thereafter she'd devoted her life to God's work. However, in his wisdom, God had confined her efforts to Doverhay and Porlock, from where she'd not ventured in over sixteen years.

She was an excellent seamstress, did voluntary work at Porlock Cottage Hospital, played the harmonium rather badly at chapel, and took Sunday School lessons for the under sevens at the Union Workhouse. The wrecking of the Nicolette thrust a new and testing assignment upon the ever-willing Mrs Thomas.

The perpetually sobbing Mrs Pollard had been discharged from the Lynmouth Cottage Hospital into Mrs Thomas's compassionate care a week after the disaster, and had stayed with Mrs Thomas thereafter. She'd been joined by her sister, who had travelled from Liverpool to be with her in her darkest hour. Mrs Pollard did not want to leave Porlock for that city, until her daughter and her husband's bodies had been found and given a decent Christian burial; therefore, the three women prayed nightly for their souls in the parlour of Mrs Thomas's cottage.

The coastguard assured Mrs Pollard that the wreck could not survive much longer and was far too dangerous to board. Given the ferocity of the wind and waves, they assured her there was very little likelihood of recovering the bodies, but she had been adamant.

Mrs. Thomas answered the door to find Nance on her doorstep. He raised his hat, introduced himself as a believer, not unlike herself, and with much hand wringing and words of sympathy, explained the purpose of his visit. She ushered him in enthusiastically, welcoming him as a kindred spirit - albeit a rather common looking one - whose check suit reminded her of a door to door salesman who called occasionally, selling houseware.

In his politest tones, Nance began by offering Mrs Pollard his sincere condolence at her sad loss. He assured her that her tragic experience had so touched his heart, that he wished to offer her a personal act of charity, in this, her hour of need. He hoped that she would not be offended by a gift of fifteen guineas; however if - as he felt sure would be the case - she would not wish to receive charity, even in these exceptional and deserving circumstances, then he suggested it should be accepted in lieu of purchase of what remained of the worthless and mortally stricken "Nicolette". Though the vessel was breaking up as they spoke, and would soon be reduced to matchwood, his only concern was that the sum be adequate enough to cover her expenses, and the return journey to her loved ones in Liverpool. If she were to do him the honour of accepting his generous gesture, then he would be rewarded by the knowledge that he had in some small way, eased the tremendous and tragic burden that had befallen her.

The poor woman was overcome with gratitude at the kindness of yet another West Country benefactor and relapsed into tears once more.

Mrs. Thomas patted the weeping woman's hand, whilst smiling approvingly at Nance Ridler, who returned her smile with pious self-righteousness.

When the weeping abated, Ridler begged the lady's pardon for being presumptuous enough to have prepared a bill of sale, prior to calling. This was in order that he might additionally relieve her of the distressing formalities that must inevitably fall upon the owner of the stricken vessel, from His Majesty's Customs and Excise, The Board of Trade and the Coastguard, to name but a few interested authorities. The ladies had not given Mrs Pollard's legal liabilities the slightest thought or consideration, and with this revelation, Mrs Pollard burst into tears once more, overwhelmed that a gentleman she did not know, and had never met before, could be so kind to a lady in distress. Nance bowed and assured her it was nothing less than his Christian duty.

The document being duly signed and witnessed, he wished the weeping woman a speedy return to good health and took his leave of Mrs Thomas and her guests.

Ridler's next call was to Jack Prideaux at Porlock Weir where he agreed the hire of Prideaux's smack the "Ellen May" for salvage work of an unspecified nature. Prideaux was not that keen, for he guessed what the matter would be about, but eventually changed his mind on account of the fishing being so poor of late. He promised to do Nance's salvage job, as soon as the weather allowed.

CHAPTER 37

Blue and Gold

Salvaging the cargo was all very well in principle, but a different kettle of fish in practice as Nance was beginning to find out. Any thought of reaching her from shore was pointless, for she was wrecked beneath a five hundred foot cliff, with no way up or down. The only possible approach was from seaward, but that presented its own problems. The Nicolette was wrecked some 3 cables from shore, with jagged rocks all about her, some only visible at low tide.

Added to that, the bay she sat in was awash with debris, some floating dangerously low in the water because of the amount of iron stapled to it. It was a death trap to any boat with a reasonable draft, in anything other than a flat calm. It was only the Louisa's shallow draft, the high tide, and Charlie Parkin's skill, that had seen the lifeboat survive without incident.

Jack Prideaux reneged on his promise the minute the weather dropped to a six and the boats could get out once more. He knew Nance Ridler well enough to know that there was every chance he'd drag him into some shady deal, and no amount of money was worth losing his boat to the doomed wreck.

On the other hand, he knew that the weather keeping the debris in the cove would turn sooner or later, and it would all drift out into the channel where they could pick it up at their leisure. There was a lot of useful timber to be had and all that was needed was patience.

Isaac and Ira, on the other hand, were less concerned with timber than the malt whiskey they thought might warm their winter evenings. The tale they concocted for Polly was a lobster trip with McNab. He felt guilty about the small deceit, but it wasn't like the rescue; it would be safe enough.

'Aye up, yer's trouble' said Ira as McNab tied Parsley to the cottage gate. It was past seven in the evening and the light had all but gone.

'What's appened then,' said McNab, who'd promised he'd call in on his way home, 'I've got Parsley t' bed down, an' the pigs and poultry t' feed afore I'm done today. Tis all right fer you buggers we' nowt better t' do than sit around gassing all day.'

'Take the weight off yer feet McNab,' said Isaac, passing McNab a jug and the flagon of cider.

'You remember we were talking about this treasure of yours,' continued Isaac, when McNab was settled.

'Oh, ah - ere' we go!'

'Well I reckon there's something in what you say! Maybe it's worth a look before she disappears beneath the waves.'

'Oh, ah!'

'But we'll need a boat!'

'Right oh, I can see where this is going.'

'And trustworthy people.'

'What's Ira doing yer then,' said McNab caustically.

'Tis a job for someone we brains, and someone we a boat,' said Ira. 'As I understand it - thee've got the boat.'

'An' thee be supplying the brains then, professor...?' said McNab.

'Right first time,' said Ira. 'An' while we're on the subject of brains, who's the skipper of that boat of yourn, you or Parsley? I've never been able t' work out which one of you's the smartest!'

'Where are you off to McNab?' said Isaac, as McNab pushed his stool back.

'I'm off ome,' said McNab. 'I ain't got time ter listen to you two silly buggers.'

It took a good five minutes to calm him down and get McNab to listen to what they had to say; a disgruntled McNab supped his cider in silence.

They told him they were only going to try their luck, nothing more. If they found a cask, so well and good, if they didn't, well... they'd lost nothing! They would just take a look among the flotsam and jetsam floating about the wreck, nothing more.

'There's hundreds of barrels in that cove!' said McNab, 'thee can see em' from the cliffs by all account. Pointing his pint at Ira, he added, 'How's the professor, going to find a few whisky barrels amongst all that lot?'

'If it's full of whisky, it will float low!'

'And what if seawater's gotten in through the bunghole?'

'That's the whole point McNab,' said Isaac, 'they always bung the empties to keep em from drying out. That way they keep the flavour in the wood.'

'It'll have to be flat calm if we're going anywhere near that cove. It's a bloody death trap, with submerged rocks everywhere. That's why the fishing boats are leaving it alone fer now, but they'll ave their eye on all that wood, rope an' sail, don't you worry. They'll be in there just as soon as it calms down!'

'The early bird catches the worm McNab, said Ira. All the boats from Porlock Weir are out an' the glass is rising fast; some buggers got t be first.'

Next morning, a little after 5.30am, McNab reefed his sail and the little boat blew into the bay on the same wind that held the wreckage in the cove. It was still frisky in the channel and they had had a few scary moments on the way in, but it was much calmer near to shore, the rocks breaking up the swell as it surged against them.

McNab steered the little boat into calmer water and took to the oars to bring them closer to the wreck. She looked different to Isaac from when he'd seen her last; her deck more steeply canted and her stern further out of the water. He realised she must be giving up the fight below the waterline.

'I think we've wasted our time,' he said, 'there's staves aplenty, but no barrels that I can see; this cove is like a pulp-mill.'

'The boats still there though,' said Ira, the eternal optimist.

'Just about,' replied Isaac, 'I think she's on her last legs though.'

'We could always drop some lobster pot's now were 'ere,' said McNab; 'ideal spot fer lobsters this, not too deep, but deep enough; nice rocky bottom; I can taste the buggers now!'

'Get us alongside McNab, or as near as you can,' said Isaac slipping out of his breeches and shirt, 'I'll take a quick look afore we go.'

Isaac climbed aboard the wreck, dragging himself up the steep deck by the ropes that streamed from belaying pins and rigging. He reasoned that if there was anything of worth left now, it would be in the cabins, and anyway, he was curious!

He began to descend the companionway that led below decks, and found the same sump of water that McInally had encountered when he'd rescued Pollard's wife, but it was not as deep now; nor was there any surge to speak of. For all that, he paused before he entered the black water that he must pass through before he could reach the cabins. It lapped gently at the tread on which he stood and he felt its cold slipperiness beneath his feet. Green algae clung to the tread like treacle, the sea already making the wreck its own.

He looked at the black, murky depths, and began to have second thoughts. The alleyway was fully submerged, but only just, so he should get through the sump easily enough. On the other hand, the boat had moved since he'd first seen it. It would be a death trap if anything went wrong.

A mixture of pride and foolhardiness pushed him on, and taking a deep breath, he slipped beneath the water. He felt his way through the sump, panicking as he scrambled to find purchase on the slippery and steeply canted alleyway. When it seemed he'd have to turn back, his hand found the handrail.

He groped his way upwards, scrabbling up the steeply sloping alleyway beyond the sump. Almost immediately, he broke the surface and took in a deep breath of air. It had a foul, fetid stench about it that turned his stomach. He was all for turning back, when he saw a glimmer of light through the aft cabin door. It could only be coming from the hole through which they'd escaped. At least his own escape was assured and on that basis he carried on.

He found the small cabin and locker, but there was nothing of interest in either; both were so small he could almost search them without entering. He missed the cabin to starboard in the gloom and went on to the saloon instead.

He could see the huge hole - the source of the light. It was on the waterline and the sea constantly ebbed and flowed through it. He decided he would use it to get off the boat, in preference to the dark, foul sump he'd just passed through. The cabin was in ruins; every piece of furniture and every cupboard door was smashed to matchwood. Its air was every bit as rank as the stench in the alleyway, despite the hole in the side.

The light was poor, but Isaac picked out items among the debris; simple everyday things, like pages from a book, a tea cosy, cushions, a breadboard, clothing; candles and a hat. In one corner, a chair floated upside down; its legs splintered and jagged. Clinging to it was a piece of blue cloth - a tablecloth or some item of clothing perhaps.

Something bit his leg. It was little more than a nip, but then there came another bite, deeper, sharper and more aggressive than the one before. Isaac looked down to see the sleek shadow of a Conger eel, perhaps six feet in length, moving swiftly through the water, intent on striking again.

Suddenly another appeared as big as the first. They had clearly made the wreck their home and didn't want to share it with anyone else. Isaac had heard stories of Conger eels biting off fingers and hands with their powerful jaws and was alarmed to find himself trapped in the cabin with two of them.

He looked about for sanctuary, but there was none. One of the fish attacked again and Isaac jabbed the water with a timber splinter. He struck the Conger's head and it swam into the shadows, but the other attacked from behind. Isaac reached up to the deckhead and grabbing a brace that spanned the deckhead beams, pulled his legs clear of the water at the very last moment. He kicked out at the vile, snake like creatures, his heart pounding in his chest - all thoughts of whisky forgotten. The ship was a nightmare and he wanted to get out.

Hand over hand he used the brace to get nearer the hole in the hull, then with one deep breath he dropped into the foul water once more, striking out for the gaping hole in the ships side. He passed straight through and came out just feet from McNab's boat. He clung to the side, retching and gasping for breath.

'Find anything,' asked Ira.

'Conger eels - hundreds of em!'

'I quite like eels,' said McNab.

'Well you go and grab yerself one then McNab,' said Isaac with a shudder; 'I hate the bloody things, help me out you two, I've had enough.'

When he got his breath back, he told them what he'd seen. It seemed as if he'd been down there for hours, but it was just minutes.

'We're wasting our time,' he told them flatly, inspecting the bite to his leg. It was just a graze, but it could have been a different story.

'What about the hatch?' said Ira.

'What about the bloody hatch?'

'Well, that's where the whisky's likely to be ain't it! Can't think what thee bothered we the cabins for!'

Isaac was too exhausted to tell Ira what he thought of him; instead, he hung his head and got his breath back. They continued to cajole him about the whisky but he refused point blank to go aboard the wreck again. Ira assured him there would be no congers near the hatch coaming for it was in open water, 'They like nooks and crannies to hide in,' he said. McNab added that Congers could be a bit tough, but were fine eating if you cooked them slowly.

'And what do you know about congers!' said Isaac, ignoring McNab and concentrating his scorn on Ira.

'You ask me that... when I was born and bred on this coast and spent a lifetime at sea?'

'I'm not going near that bloody boat again, so you're both wasting your time!'

254

On and on, they went, like a pair of old women, until Isaac lost the will to argue with them, agreeing at last, to take one small look in the hatch before they went home. He told himself it was worth just one quick look.

Isaac clambered aboard the Nicolette once more. He lowered himself down the slippery deck with a length of rope, until he was under water and better able to see the submerged parts of the wreck. The water was clear enough, to see she'd lost the foc'sle and the for'ard hatch, but the aft hatch was intact, though its canvas covers were in tatters and waving in the water like sea anemones.

He surfaced and shouted to McNab that the aft hatch looked intact; he'd have just one go at opening it up. McNab gave him the thumbs up and rowed down the lee side.

Isaac took another deep breath and dived once more. He followed the deck for'ard and down to the aft hatch, dragging himself deeper all the while. After the scare in the cabin, he was wary of the dangers. He wondered why he'd listened to them - he must be mad - he didn't even like whisky that much. He began to bitterly regret the whole escapade and thought of Polly and his broken promise and vowed this would be his last adventure - most definitely his last. At least she had no idea what they were up to.

He reached the hatch and looked about for some way to open it. Several wedges were missing and he found another loose. He pried it free and used it to knock out another. He had to return to the surface for air many times, before he'd taken out sufficient wedges to loosen the side beam that held the tattered canvas covers in place.

The moment the beam came free, the wreck began to tremble. Heavy hatch boards erupted from the coaming and burst upward toward the surface, knocking Isaac senseless as they did so. As more and more came free, huge black creatures burst from the gloom of the hatch. There were hundreds of them, spewing from the bowels of the ship like a sturgeon laying its eggs. They passed him by, knocking him sideways with their hard shells, buffeting him, crashing into him, turning him over again and again in their pell-mell flight to the surface.

Isaac's head swam, for he'd been badly stunned by the onslaught and had swallowed a lot of water. Barely conscious, his sixth sense told him he must follow the creatures and swim to the surface. He broke surface near the boat which was rocking violently after the onslaught. Ira and McNab dragged him aboard and he slumped down between the thwarts, exhausted.

'What happened there,' shouted Ira, spotting the nasty bruise that was spreading across Isaac's chest and shoulder.

Isaac looked over the side of the boat and groaned with disbelief. The sea was black with hundreds of barrels.

'I thought they were turtles,' he said, 'or something worse!'

As Isaac finished his words, the Nicolette groaned and tilted sharply forward. She groaned again and they could hear her scraping across the rocks that gripped her hull. McNab picked up the oars and rowed for all he was worth. Before he'd rowed thirty feet from the wreck, she keeled over to starboard and slid beneath the waves with a creaking and splintering of wood.

The three men watched in disbelief whilst the tiny lobster boat, bucked and swayed in the wash from her sinking. Next moment they were floating in a sea of wreckage, rigging and barrels, but very little else for the Nicolette had disappeared completely.

McNab spotted the bundle first, 'Look over there he cried!' Amid the flotsam was the blue material Isaac had seen in the cabin, but there was another colour with it, gold this time. It spread out across the surface like a delicate fan.

McNab rowed towards the bundle. In silence, he turned the child over with a boat hook. Her hair was beautiful, almost as long as the body itself and was all that remained of the little girl's face, for the flesh and eyes were gone; eaten by the creatures that shared her watery grave. The tragic bundle smiled up at them with teeth and jaws picked clean of anything edible. Even McNab, who was well used to seeing slaughtered animals, was shocked by what they had found. Isaac leant over the side and was violently sick.

'Poor little mite,' said Ira, breaking the silence, as McNab drew the corpse closer to the boat.

'Keep her away from me McNab,' said Isaac; recognising the smell of the cabin.

'We have to take her home lad,' said McNab quietly, 'Give her a proper Christian burial, you shut yer eyes.'

He and Ira lifted the body into the boat by the pretty blue dress and lowered it gently into the bow, covering it with the boat tarp. There were still tiny feet in her boots, for the fish had been unable to feed on her in that small space. There was a smell about the corpse they would never forget.

'Let's get out of this cursed place,' said McNab.

He took up his oars and rowed them out into clear water, where they turned and set sail for Porlock Weir. It was eight a.m. and the sun was shining. It looked as though the long spell of stormy weather was over at last. The journey passed by in silence.

CHAPTER 38

Last Will and Testament

'Daddy's been very naughty and Mummy's very cross,' was Becky's view of things.

Out of the mouths of babes and children!' remarked Amy in response to Rebecca's remark, 'Pity you haven't got some of her common sense. Is there anything but air in that head of yours?'

The sinking of the Nicolette, and the finding of the corpse, rather spoke for themselves, so Isaac didn't bother flogging a dead horse where lobster-fishing tales was concerned, and decided to face the music instead. It was a trial he was forced to endure alone, for Ira and McNab had not been seen in days.

There had been angry words from Polly and even sharper words from Amy on the subject of brains and responsibility. Isaac went to bed that night, to find himself barred from the marital room by a chair beneath the doorknob.

He was obliged to sleep in the parlour, but Bert's snoring was so loud, he resorted to a catnap on a chair in the forge. At least it was warm in the smithy.

After two, angry, lonely nights, Polly - who'd barely slept herself - relented and let him back into her bed. She pretended to be asleep, but he knew she wasn't. He plucked up the courage to put his arm about her, but she pushed him away. He told her he loved her, and she said he clearly didn't love her, and she didn't care anyway. He said he was sorry and she said he was stupid and thoughtless. He promised never again, and she didn't believe him. He gave up and turned over, and she realised she had made her point. They lay in silence for a very long time.

He dropped off a couple of times, desperate to sleep, but he had to give it one last try. He said he was sorry and sounded as though he meant it, and she said nothing - progress of a sort.

She let him kiss her and he felt the tears on her cheek; he hated himself for hurting her so. He told himself it was time to grow up and realise what he had. What was whisky in comparison to his beautiful wife and daughter? They kissed again and the healing began.

They made love and she cried out softly when it came to that moment. He told her he loved her, and how stupid, and selfish, and cruel, he felt. She told him it was because she loved him so, that she was angry. He'd frightened her, and her greatest dread was that she'd lose him to some silly escapade. He

258

promised never to do such a thing again and meant it, and they fell asleep in one another's arms. It was the healing of one wound, but another, as yet unknown to them, became inflamed and infected over the next few days. It was a wound that would never be allowed to heal.

As though by magic, Ira, McNab and Parsley appeared the day after their reconciliation with a flagon of scrumpy.

The source of their seemingly inexhaustible supply was McNab's apple orchard, the press being driven more or less willingly, by Parsley. The fruit of their labours was enjoyed equally by the farmer and his horse, for Parsley was partial - not just to a pint of cider with his bran - but the apple pulp too.

Both men got a very frosty reception when they were discovered in their usual spot behind the gable wall, which had the twin advantages of catching the evening sunshine, and no direct line of sight from the cottage.

There was an uncomfortable moment while Polly gave them a piece of her mind, but at least they'd not been sent packing. Parsley went back to eating Polly's borders and within a very short space of time, life got back to normal at Leathernbottle.

Three days later, the child's coffin was locked in the Guards Van of the Bishops Lydeard train, on the start of its journey to Liverpool. Mrs Pollard and her sister travelled with it; all hope of recovering Captain Pollard's body now gone.

News of the breakup of the hulk, and the finding of the girl's body, spread like wildfire about North Somerset, and was not long in reaching Nance Ridler's ears. The trouble began soon after. Isaac was busy with the forge, when Nance and Jack Ridler, strode through the gate towards the smithy, their boots crunching on the ash path.

"Morning Nance, morning Jack,' Isaac said pleasantly.

'We want a word we thee, Gloucester,' said Nance, dispensing with the usual pleasantries.

'What about?' asked Isaac, sensing that all was not well with his neighbours.

'You know good an' well, what about!' replied Nance angrily.

'No, I don't Nance, and what's more, I've no mind to be swapping words with you, so you'd best come to the point.'

'We hear it was you as sunk the wreck!' said Jack.

'Have you now? Who told you that?'

'You was spotted clambering aboard her from the Foreland cliffs and an hour later the boat went down!'

'Why would I bother risking my neck on a death-trap like that?'

'Whisky!' said Nance bluntly.

Isaac said nothing as he drew his work from the fire.

'So we've come for what's ours.'

'I don't know what you're talking about Nance; we took nothing off the wreck, nothing but the child's body.'

'Do you think I'm bloody stupid? What were you doing there then; you and the other two clowns?'

'We were laying lobster pots, but what the hell's it got to do with you?' replied Isaac, angry himself now.

'That's what it's got to do we me!' said Nance, his eyes blazing as he thrust his bill of sale under Isaac's nose.

Isaac read through the document, a little taken aback by the unexpected development, but with the wit to say - 'So as I read it then Nance, you gave the Captains widow fifteen guineas for a wreck you thought was full of whisky, then come accusing me of stealing! How did Robinson know where to find McInally then, Nance? That was a queer business, wasn't it?'

Ridler looked venomously at Isaac. 'Don't come the smart Alec we me Gloucester, or you'll bloody well regret it. It don't matter what you think; the fact is, the wreck belongs to I, and you've stolen cargo from it, and I wants it back.'

'There's no whisky Nance. There never was any whisky; it was all hogwash! You've wasted your money and now you're wasting yer time.'

That was as good as a confession to Nance, who obviously intended to search the smithy, 'Stay out of my bloody way,' he said angrily, gesturing to Jack to start on the coke bunker.

Isaac's hammer came down upon the red-hot iron stay, with such force that a shower of sparks flew off the anvil in all directions. It startled the two brothers enough to stop them.

'If you've a problem with what I'm telling you - you call Robinson - but you'll not set foot on my property without my leave.' Isaac glanced quickly from one miller to the other, ready for the rough house that was on its way. They were fit for men of forty, but he wasn't concerned. At the first move, he would put Nance on the floor and Jack would back off thereafter, he was sure of that.

As he stood his ground with the hot stay still in his grasp, he looked a formidable opponent and that was not lost on Nance or Jack. Isaac was stripped to the waist as usual; his long black hair tied back. Sweat and fly ash glistened on the muscles that bound his chest. There was no fear in his eyes, as he watched the brothers for the slightest movement.

'We don't need no coppers round yer Gloucester,' said Nance slyly; taking a pair of tongs from a hook on the wall. 'We've got our own ways of dealing with thieving bastards like you - Porlock ways! You'll think twice about stealing from me next time, I'll warrant.'

Suddenly, the unexpected happened; there was a single crunching footstep behind Nance and a heavy iron pan hit him across the back of the head with a ring like a church bell.

'Clear off with you!' shouted Amy, as she raised the pan to strike again, 'Coming round yer' threatening decent folk with yer' filthy talk - pair of ruffians the both of you.' She turned her attentions upon Jack, but he was already making for the gate, for Polly had loosed the dog. To everyone's surprise, Bert set upon Jack, tearing savagely at his trouser legs. When Jack leapt over the fence, he turned his attention on Nance, who lashed out with his feet as he too ran for the road.

With the gate between them and the dog, Nance shouted above the barking. 'I'll sort you bastards out fer this, or my names not Nance Ridler; you wait and see if I don't!'

When Ira Grace heard the tale, he had a good chuckle; 'How did thee do it then Bert?' he said, stroking the dog's ears in admiration, 'Licked the buggers to death?'

'That's the strangest thing Ira,' replied Isaac; 'I never thought I'd see him turn like that; he damn near ate Jack alive, clothes an' all!'

'Dogs ain't stupid Isaac,' said Ira, seriously, 'they're loyal animals, always have been. He saw his master in danger and he weren't having none of it. It don't surprise me one little bit, not one little bit.'

'Well, that'll be the last we hear of it I hope.'

Ira looked up from fussing with the dog. After a pause he spoke, 'You've made a bad enemy there lad - you be careful!'

'I don't give a damn for either of em Ira.'

'Humph,' grunted Ira, pausing again to consider his words, 'Perhaps thee ought to then! I wasn't going to tell thee this lad, but Nance come to see I last night; offering to buy the forge.'

This brought Isaac up in his tracks. He put his work to the edge of the fire and sat the hammer on the anvil.

'How much did he offer?' he asked with concern.

'Two hundred and fifty guineas.'

Isaac stared at Ira in disbelief. 'It's not worth that!' he said; clearly anxious about such a good offer.

'Must be worth it to Nance' replied Ira, 'or he wouldn't ave made I the offer now would e?'

Isaac considered the unwelcome news for a moment, quite taken aback by the implications. Ira was right; he had indeed made a bad enemy. Nance's only reason for buying the forge would be to turn them out, and it seemed he would spend a lot of money to do it.

'What are you going to do?' he said anxiously.

Ira smiled; pleased he'd brought Isaac up a bit. He could be a little cocksure at times.

'I'd sooner ave' Beelzebub to supper afore I'd do business with that bastard!' said Ira.

'Thanks!' said Isaac simply.

'I told you it was yours should you want it, and I'm a man of me word - always providing thee keep paying I the ten shillin' that is!'

Isaac smiled and went back to his work, but after some thought he spoke again.

'I been doing a bit of thinking of late Ira; about the forge an' what you said about buying it one day... I can't afford two hundred and fifty guineas nor anything like it, but perhaps I could get a loan and put something down, perhaps we could become partners. The work's coming in now, particularly with the engine repairs, and between us, we're getting a reputation for a good job well done. It wouldn't take up much of your time; no more than you spend keeping me company.'

'I come fer the lunch lad,' added Ira with a smile, 'you're company's not that bloody scintillating.'

'Yes lunch too,' replied Isaac; 'what do you think?'

Ira knocked out his pipe on the side of the quenching tank. 'I'll think ont,' he said, 'time I went home; you be sure to thank Polly for supper as we're on that particular subject.' With that, he picked up his stick and made his way toward No 2 and home.

Ira said no more for some weeks, then finally spoke about the matter.

'I bin thinking about this partnership business of yours,' he said pausing to consider his words carefully. 'I can't be doing we' all that kind of thing at my age Isaac. If I were twenty years younger t'would be different, but my life's works done lad - it's you as is just beginning. You're a bright young chap and a first rate blacksmith, and you don't need an old fool like me getting in yer way, just cus of the smithy.'

Ira saw the disappointment so clear upon Isaac's face and continued.

'So I'll tell e what I'm going to do. I always said I wouldn't leave our Molly out, even though her's a fat lazy cow an' I don't like the company she keeps, but I wouldn't see her turned out fer all that, so I shall leave her my half of number two. That's fair an' proper and I suppose t'would be what mother would want, but that do still leave this place. It ain't much I grant you, but tis what I've earnt for my life's work. But what use is it to me when I'm gone? That's why I want you to have it - you, Polly, and little Rebecca, cus I know you'll value it and keep it nice. If I promise to leave it to you in my will, you can get on an' do what you want straight away, without no more worries!' He looked up at Isaac to see what he thought.

Isaac's pride was about to say no, when he thought of what it would mean - not just to him, but to Polly and Amy too.

'Are you sure?' he asked.

'Like I say; what use is it to me when I'm gone?'

Isaac took the old man's hand and shook it hard. 'Thank you Ira,' he said, his gratitude obvious, 'thank you very much, I just don't know what to say!'

'I ain't doing it fer thee,' said Ira, pleased with himself. 'I'm doing it fer the womenfolk... When thee can bake a cake like Amy, an' cook a stew like Polly, I might think of doing thee a favour an' all!'

Two days later, Isaac found himself in Ira's parlour at number two in the company of a man named Cripps. Cripps was a solicitor from the law firm, Francillon, Cripps and Cranway, of Porlock. He was a small man, balding and thin, with grey wispy hair and a superior air that made Isaac uncomfortable. He had dark sunken eyes in a face so thin, it was little more than grey skin stretched over bone. It occurred to Isaac that Cripps looked not unlike a vulture.

Cripps read through the will he had drawn up at Ira's request. It was exactly as Ira had promised, with his share of number two going to Molly and Leathernbottle Cottage going to Isaac in its entirety. Also to Isaac's surprise, Ira left the remainder of his estate to Rebecca, in trust.

'Taint a lot,' he said, 'just a few pounds - on account of the poor rent I d' get off the smithy!'

Isaac looked at the old man who had become his good friend and wondered how he - and so many others for that matter - could judge a man so wrongly.

Unbeknown to the men within the parlour, other ears listened to Cripps's words. It was difficult for Molly to catch everything through the cracks in the door, for Cripps spoke in a quiet monotone.

She had been listening so intently and in such an awkward position that she was suddenly gripped by cramp and had to move. The floorboards creaked beneath her tread as she retreated to the kitchen, her heart thumping furiously; surely, they must have heard her.

At that very moment, there came a heavy knock on the front door and Ira rose with obvious discomfort, his leg increasingly painful and arthritic. Molly was back in the kitchen, her knitting in her lap. As he went to let McNab in, she raised her eyes briefly as he passed through the hall.

McNab was in a high good humour that quickly got on everyone's nerves, particularly Cripps, who saw common folk like McNab, as an occupational hazard.

'Ave thee had a bump on the head then Ira,' asked McNab considerably amused by the turn of events; 'Mr. Cripps yer' says as thee be planning to give summat away!'

'Not to thee, I'm not!' replied Ira.

'That's a pity,' replied McNab, 'cus it don't look like I got long to change thy mind!' There was an embarrassing silence whilst McNab applauded his own joke with a bout of thigh slapping.

'I'm going to press my ear to thy coffin when the time comes Ira - see if I can hear thee weeping.'

Cripps could barely conceal his dislike for the farmer and intruded upon him by saying, 'Gentlemen...! I'm sure Mr McNab has much to attend to; perhaps we should press on with the matter in hand. As you are aware Mr McNab, you are here to witness that Mr Grace is signing this deed in your presence and of his own free will - the contents of which, being a matter for Mr Grace and Mr Grace alone.'

The will duly witnessed, Cripps made his farewells and set off down the hill in his trap. McNab went back to his fields, and Isaac the forge, after shaking Ira by the hand and thanking him again.

Molly made her way to the mill as soon as she could without rousing Ira's suspicions.

'What's up now?' shouted Nance from the bin loft, as Molly called up to him.

'Nance something's happened!'

'Like what; what're you talking about?'

'Ira's made a will; he's given the smithy away to Isaac Smith.'

Nance slid down the stair rails from the bin loft on his elbows, his feet not touching the treads until he reached the bottom.

'How'd you know that?'

'I was listening at the door as they read through the will; there was Ira, Isaac Smith, and a bloke called Cripps; then McNab come along to witness the signing.'

Nance knew Cripps to be one of the solicitors in Porlock; a strange looking character with the kind of face Nance would like to punch, not his cup of tea at all.

'You must have got that wrong,' he replied. 'Why would he give them the smithy? Why give it to newcomers when he's got family?'

I don't know,' she said, clearly upset by the whole matter. He's done it out of spite; he doesn't like me seeing you - you know what he's like.'

'I know what this Gloucester fellow's like!' replied Nance angrily. 'He's stolen from I - now he's stolen from thee! It's about time someone sorted that bastard out once and fer all!'

265

CHAPTER 39

Diphtheria

Isaac sat in his favourite spot, on a jutting rock, high above the cliffs at Hurlston Point. The sun would soon set on another warm and balmy summer's day. He often came here when he needed to be alone for it was a place of solitude and a place for quiet thought and reflection. There had been occasions in these last five years when he'd needed its peace and solitude.

He looked across the Channel to the far blue mistiness of the Welsh Mountains. "The Misty Mountains" he called them, for they seemed to float weightlessly on distant silvery clouds.

Far below, the grey blue water of the Severn lay calm and serene, but for the occasional plunging dive of a gull, or the strutting of a Sandpiper, as it sought its supper. The bird's labours would send ripples further than the eye could see, but the water would soon still once more, to glisten like satin in the thinning rays of the evening sun.

Beyond Porlock Weir, and below the headland cliffs, the water was pierced by rows of jagged rocks, like the open jaws of some terrible sea monster waiting to devour its prey. The Nicolette was still there beneath the waters of her hidden bay; just a few forlorn timbers like a rotting carcass, breaking the surface at low tide. So many things had happened, since he and the crew of the Louisa had done battle with her that stormy winter's day.

Since the signing of the will, Isaac had worked ceaselessly, spending every spare penny on the smithy and the cottage. Every bit of machinery worked perfectly, from the water driven forge fan, to the lathe, drill and drop hammer, and he had added a plate roller to help with boiler repairs. It was a joy to be at work and there seemed to be nothing that could not be made in the smithy, from new boilerplate to forged and turned crankshafts.

Polly was his occasional helper, at those times when he needed an extra pair of hands. He would tease her for closing her eyes when he hit the swage, even though she gripped it by its long wire handle. 'I can't help it,' she would cry, 'I would let go if I saw the hammer coming, and anyway... the sparks go everywhere!'

Amy would listen to their laughter and smile; it was good they had a common purpose, that was what marriage was all about, and it had worked out well despite her reservations. On such occasions when Isaac had a big job on, she would look at the clock in disbelief as it chimed eight p.m. and the forge was still

266

working. 'They've forgotten you again my little precious,' she'd whisper, as she kissed the sleepy child, 'but Nana Amy is always here, don't you worry.'

They were as happy in their home as it was possible for a family to be and there were few concerns beyond the usual to and fro of daily life. Their only worry was their inability to conceive another child.

'Are you doing things right,' asked Amy when Polly assured her that they had been trying very hard.

'I'm sure we are Amy, though I'm not quite sure what the wrong way might be, but I'm worried...' She didn't complete her sentence, not wanting to put her thoughts into words.

'Worried about what?'

'Do you think... would it be possible that the fever from the dog bite damaged Isaac in some way?'

'I don't know Polly,' replied Amy, thinking back on those frightening days, 'I suppose it might, who knows; but these things sometimes take time you know, so you might have to be patient.'

Ira too, was a concern, for he came less frequently now. His leg had become increasingly painful, making it difficult for him to walk to the smithy, and Isaac was increasingly busy repairing his engines, so it wasn't like the old days when they had time to sit and yarn for hours at a time. Nonetheless, Ira would take the short walk on his better days, and Isaac would drop him home in the trap if the hill was too much for him on the return journey.

Apart from those concerns, only the occasional unpleasantness from the Ridler brothers brought a cloud to their lives. Nance had a habit of telling his customers that Isaac had stolen from him, and inevitably, it got back to Isaac by and by; but if it annoyed him, he didn't show it. What no one dared mention to him, however, was Nance's stories about Polly and how she always gave him the glad eye.

'She acts the pretty little wife, all sugar an' sweet when there's someone else about, but tis a different matter when hers on her own I can tell e,' he would say cryptically.

Most took Nance's bitterness with a very large pinch of salt; some even seeing the funny side of it, for a couple of pints and a bit of bull about Isaac being partial to a glass of whisky, was sure to get Nance in a rage. However, some chose to believe there was no smoke without fire; there being many a man in Porlock who admired the blacksmith's wife and would be quite content to think such fancies, true. So it was that their life carried on relatively uneventfully, but it was to be shattered one sunny day in June when Polly received an unexpected letter.

It was from her brother Will, whom she had not seen in nearly eight years. It was clear from the confident handwriting that he was no longer the quiet, sometimes unhappy boy, she remembered so well. He was enjoying his commission in the Army and had become Captain William Durcan of His Majesty's Royal Gloucestershire Hussars. It was clear that he was thoroughly pleased with himself.

"So my darling Polly, now I must tell you how things are with me. I am well and happy, and very soon I am hoping to travel to the South Polar ice cap as part of an Antarctic expedition - studying whales would you believe! Of course, I know nothing about whales and have little interest in the creatures beyond wonderment at their size and beauty, but I acquitted myself very well during the rebellion in Peking, and again in Africa, so I believe the powers that be, think I'm a decent chap to have around in a tight spot.

Who knows, perhaps I shall do something daring and win a medal for endurance or adventure. Father will have to eat his words then wont he. I shall look him straight in the eye, shake his hand and say, Hello father, I trust you are well. I myself have recovered fully from my ordeal thank you! It would be great fun wouldn't it.

Polly - my darling Polly, I have missed you so. I am not ashamed to say that I cried my heart out when you went away. Father was angry beyond words and will not speak of you even now - except to mother. He says you are our shame and disgrace, but in truth, I think he is devastated at losing you. You were always his favourite; I never really had a chance. If I had one wish though, it would be for you and father to be reconciled with one another for I know that mother misses you so.

I am due leave before we sail for the icy wastes and I shall go to Northumberland to see Aunt Margaret and cousin Anne (who is sixteen this birthday and no longer a plain Jane apparently)! Aunt Margaret thinks that running off with your handsome blacksmith was the most romantic thing she has ever heard of and is the only one who dares to tease father about it. She would be so pleased to see you. Will you come Polly - to Northumberland? It would be so wonderful to see you before I go. You may bring your blacksmith with you if you please.

Do, do, come.

Yours affectionately,

Will."

And so it was that with a mixture of excitement and apprehension, Polly set out to see her Aunt and brother, leaving Rebecca at home with her father and Grandmother.

The porter bundled her trunk into the guard's van and Isaac lifted her portmanteau to the luggage rack above her seat. They bid one another goodbye on the platform. Isaac kissed her and held her very close, his cheek next to hers. The whistle blew and she drew away, but he pulled her to him again for just a few seconds more.

'Take care,' he said seriously, not pleased they would be parted, even for such a short time; Polly's heart was torn in two for it would be the first time they had been apart since John's death. She kissed Rebecca and Amy and knelt to place her arms about Bert's neck.

'Look after them for me darling Bert,' she whispered, 'I know you will, for you are the bravest, most fearless of all labradors and I know they will be safe with you.' As she hugged him, she remembered that winter's night so many years ago when she had said goodbye to her beloved Parson Pimm, the very thought of it, brought a pang to her heart. The dog sat impassively upon the platform, his tail still. Huge, unfathomable eyes watched her board the train and gently close the door.

Amy took the yellow dress from the bottom drawer of the chest of drawers she shared with Rebecca. She and the child slept together in the room above the scullery. It was small, but cosy, especially in the winter when the forge chimney made the wall warm to the touch; such a pretty dress, thought Amy to herself.

She slipped the dress over the girl's head and tied the ribbons in a bow behind her back. 'There! Don't you look as pretty as a picture,' she cooed to the child. 'Off you go and show your father - and don't get it dirty!'

Rebecca played that day with her best friend, Daisy Atwood, who lived in a tiny cottage just a few doors from Ira, and beneath the woods that girded Selworthy beacon. Amy collected her from Mrs Atwood at four p.m. and took the happy, exhausted child back down the hill to Leathernbottle. She put Rebecca to bed early, for the child could barely keep her eyes open.

Two days later, Amy awoke to the sound of the little girls breathing. It was harsh and rasping, as though she had a cold coming. She struggled from her bed and crossed the room to Rebecca who lay still in her cot. Amy expected her to be asleep, but Rebecca's eyes were open. They looked at her listlessly as she bent over to touch her forehead and throat; it seemed that all the life had gone out of her. Amy felt the heat of her forehead and the swelling of the glands in her neck.

She was concerned. 'I think you've got a bit of a fever about you, Becky, I think we'll just leave you where you are fer today and keep you still.' With that, she got herself dressed and made her way downstairs. It was six a.m. and she could hear Isaac in the scullery.

By the time they heard that Daisy had Diphtheria, Rebecca was much worse. Doctor McDonald left Daisy's bedside to come immediately to Leathernbottle pausing only to wash and sterilise his hands in a bowl of disinfectant. He left the distraught Mrs Atwood with a promise of return, and strict instructions on hygiene and the care of the little girl. Rebecca's breathing had become much worse and her strength was ebbing almost as they watched. McDonald opened the child's mouth with a polished ivory spatula. As though he needed any further proof, there was the telltale membrane growing across the throat and nostrils, making it difficult for the little girl to breathe. McDonald could smell her breath, foul with the virulent toxin. He looked at her throat again; mindful of any sign that the child might suddenly cough upon him.

'Where is her mother,' he asked of Amy.

'She's away,' replied Isaac, 'in Northumberland.'

'Your daughter is very ill,' said Dr. McDonald. 'We must get her to the hospital in Minehead as soon as possible; 'it might be as well if you fetch your wife home!'

The membrane grew rapidly across the little girl's throat sealing her nostrils and choking the breath from her. It was white and soft like a piece of wash-leather. By the time Polly returned from Northumberland, the little girl was too weak even to recognise her, her muscles were in paralysis and her weakened heart was barely able to flutter. The doctors did all they could, cutting away the membrane to ease her breathing, but just to touch it caused it to bleed and release more poison.

Rebecca died quietly in Polly's arms; her little heart, too weak to carry on - finally stopped its beating.

The sickness spread from Selworthy to Allerford, Bossington and Luccombe. By the time the outbreak had run its course, five children had succumbed to it. The tiny communities were in a sense of shock and grief at their loss. Only the wonderful new vaccine, and the ceaseless efforts of Doctor McDonald, averted a full-scale epidemic.

The happiness that Isaac and Polly had found in Selworthy was stolen from them that dark day. It was as though a pickpocket had robbed them whilst they were looking another way, and all that remained in the bottom of their pocket, was emptiness, grief and sorrow. The forge and Isaac's plans for their future had no meaning or purpose now. All were lost in that vortex of sorrow and disbelief.

270

They buried Rebecca in the tiny churchyard at Selworthy close to her friend Daisy. The church looked out over the pretty valley towards Luccombe and beyond, and the sun shone in a clear sky that day, the bright rays of sunlight reflecting from the many ponds and lakes in the valley below.

Reverend Peter Hazel gave a good address that he hoped would comfort and strengthen them at their time of sorrow. It had indeed been a comfort for Amy and Polly, to think that now she was with Jesus she was not so very far away; but for Isaac, Hazel's words were hollow and spoke of a God who was callous, cruel and uncaring.

'What use might God have, for an eight year old child then, Amy,' had been Isaac's reply when Amy had spoken of Rebecca and Hazel's words. He vowed that never again would he pass through the door of any church. 'If that is God's will; then I want no more to do with him,' he said angrily.

He left them at the graveside, too wretched with his own grief and anger, to think how they might need him at that time. Instead he walked the two miles to the rock above Hurlstone Point.

Isaac was not an educated man; his writing, when he troubled himself to write at all, was hard to read and childlike in its simplicity. Yet he wanted to write that day and had taken a crayon and paper from the prayer lectern with which to do so. These he carried with him to Hurlstone, and there, upon the rock that looked timelessly across the river, he wrote his own words to his beautiful, beloved Becky. They were not God's words, not Hazel's words, not anyone else's words who did not really know and love her; they were his words, and were the words he himself, wanted to say. That done and in the quiet solitude of that beautiful place, where nothing but the Misty Mountains could see him, he let the crayon slip from his hand as he wept for his beloved daughter.

CHAPTER 40

The Gallon Can

Nance looked up as Jack nudged his arm, for something had caught Jacks eye as they sat over a pint in the Gallon Can. It was four thirty on a Wednesday afternoon and the narrow thoroughfare on East India Lane - a cobbled tributary of the busy waterfront - was alive with people who had business in the port.

All manner of tradesmen plied their trade, or sold their wares in East India Lane or the nearby waterfront; the bar of the Gallon Can overlooked both, for the pub was on the corner at the town end. It was where the ships would lay by, before moving to the loading berths, higher up the river.

Bristol was still a thriving port and on every street corner, fishmongers rubbed shoulders with cobblers, tailors, chandlers, oil merchants, ironmongers, bakers, chart makers, instrument makers, cargo agents and sail-makers.

By night, East India Lane would become a quieter, less turbulent place, but business never slept. The alleys and doorways became the haunt of the "Waterfront wives" as they called themselves. It became a place of whispered conversations, the echoing clatter of female feet, the occasional clamour of revellers homeward bound; the incoherent babble of drunkards lying in their own vomit, and the shuffle of quick-eyed ner-do-wells, silent in the shadows.

East India Lane was a place the brothers knew well, and they'd come to Bristol to do business there, with two characters named Jeremiah Butts and Harry Tanner - warehousemen at the East India Docks.

Though the street was busy, Jack picked his man out immediately, even though he was walking away from the Gallon Can. Sometimes a man's walk, or set of the shoulders, can be every bit as recognisable as the face itself. Whatever singled him out, East India Lane was not the kind of place such a pillar of society might be expected to frequent, particularly in the company of the young man who walked beside him. Together they made a very unlikely pair.

Nance got to his feet and made for the door without a word. His two companions looked at Jack in confusion. 'He won't be long,' said Jack quietly; 'e's just spotted someone we know.'

As Nance tried to leave, other patrons were coming in, so by the time he made the street outside, the man and his companion had disappeared. Nance swore beneath his breath, looking in every direction. From the corner of his eye, he saw a door close at the far end of an alley that served the back of the

Gallon Can. Ridler opened the door to find himself in a dark hallway. To his left, was a cellar full of barrels, with a tin tray beneath each tap. To his right, was a passage leading to the public bar, and ahead of him, a wooden stair worn thin by the tread of many feet.

He heard floorboards creak on the landing above and climbed the stairs three at a time to see the two men at the end of the dimly lit corridor. There were numbered rooms on either side and the man Jack had recognised was turning a key in the lock of room 5. For a brief moment, Nance and the older man looked at one another and there was no longer any doubt in Nance's mind.

However, if the man recognised Nance, he gave no sign; instead, he followed his young companion into the room and quietly closed the door behind them.

Ridler returned to the public bar and his three companions. 'Something's come up; we'll see you next time,' said Nance to the two strangers.

'What about our bit of business?' asked Tanner.

'What about it?' said Nance.

'It all costs money Nance that's what. It ain't easy to get things out the docks no more; people has to be paid.'

'That's your problem, not mine. I pay you when the goods turn up at Selworthy, an' not before. If I start giving you two bloody characters credit, I'll never see you nor the money again.'

The two men grumbled about Nance's distrust but eventually went on their way.

'They must think I'm bloody stupid,' said Nance, dismissing the two from his mind. He was more interested in the other matter that had suddenly popped up and told Jack what he'd seen on the landing of the rooms above.

'What's he up to?' asked Jack.

'What do you think?' Nance replied. Without waiting for a reply, he took their jugs to the bar and ordered two more pints'.

'I might ave' a friend taking lodgings with thee today,' he said to the barman; 'I was just wondering if he might be here yet.' He described the older man in room 5.

'And what might your friend's name be then,' said the barman indifferently.

'He's a gentleman name of Talboys,' said Ridler without blinking an eye.

'Is he now,' came the reply, 'well your friend Mr Talboys must have made alternative arrangements, cus the only gentleman we've got staying with us at the moment is a Mr Jacobs of Bath.'

Ridler took a quarter sovereign from his watch pocket and placed it on the bar top between him and the barman, looking directly at the man as he did so. 'Tell me something? How often does your Mr Jacobs take lodgings at the Gallon Can and who might the young gentleman be as is with him?'

The barman slipped the coin into his pocket and began to pull two pints.' 'That's Mr Jacobs son,' he said without batting an eyelid. 'They often meet here on account of how young Mr Jacobs works in Cardiff but passes through Bristol on business.'

'How very nice!' said Nance.

'Family's important,' said the barman.

'Quite so!'

'Perhaps your friend might turn up later then,' said the barman, pushing Nance's drinks across the counter. 'In which case 'e can ave' Mr Jacobs room, on account of how Mr Jacobs only ever takes it fer the afternoon, anxious as he always is, to return to Bath before nightfall! You get a lot of unsavoury characters hereabouts, after dark,' said the barman looking Nance in the eye. 'Not the kind of place for a gentleman like Mr Jacobs.'

'Not the kind of place at all!' said Ridler gathering his drinks and taking them back to Jack.

~

The man looked down at the youth who lay naked before him on an iron bedstead. It sagged beneath his weight, slight though that was. The youth looked back at him with emotionless eyes. He fondled himself without shame, knowing the older man liked to watch.

The older man took off his clothing and laid them neatly upon a chair. He crossed to the bed and lay down beside the young man, his heart pounding.

His body began to tremble as he felt the young man's hand rest lightly upon the flatness of his belly. He pressed his lips against his neck.

~

As Nance predicted, the man and the youth left the Gallon Can and went their separate ways.

274

'Shall we follow him?' asked Jack.

'What's the point, we know where to find him; it's his young friend I want to meet; let's get moving before we lose him.'

'What you got in mind?'

'Nothing yet!' replied Nance.

CHAPTER 41

The Wedding

Nance watched the Porlock faithful leaving St. Dubricious from the window of the Tanner's Arms. Cripps was amongst them, his wife upon his arm. If he was like a vulture, then she resembled a rodent, thin faced and small eyed. Her's was a sour countenance of seemingly permanent displeasure. She wore a black dress that was as shapeless as the woman herself; but for lace about the bodice, the only relief was a pearl brooch she wore on the right lapel.

Nance tried to imagine Mrs Cripps having sex and couldn't do so. No wonder the respected Mr Cripps, solicitor of Porlock, North Devon became Mr Jacobs in the bustling anonymity of Bristol's East India docks.

Since Cripps had attracted Nance's attention, he seemed to be everywhere at once; at public meetings about the Minehead to Lynmouth railway and the opening of the newly metalled Porlock hill, to name but two occasions upon which he'd seen him recently.

Nance discovered that Cripps was not just Porlock's longest serving solicitor, but a lay preacher and Chairman of the Town Council as well. 'What a peach you are my friend,' thought Nance to himself, 'what a peach you are.'

'You knocking, Nance?' asked one of his companions.

Nance looked back to the table at which they were playing dominoes. Fours at each end and he'd no fours. He tapped the table and the play moved on. He glanced at Cripps once more and made up his mind about Molly. He'd plans where she was concerned.

Nance mused that Cripps had the kind of face he wanted to punch, just for the sheer joy of watching the man's face, as blood began to flow and teeth fell into his mouth. He wouldn't fight back; nothing was surer than that. Cripps was a weakling and Nance despised weaklings.

The round ended and the dominoes were turned over. All four men put a penny in the kitty and Nance took his empty glass to the bar for a pint.

Nance asked Molly to marry him two days later when she called at the mill. She could barely believe his words and began to cry, sobbing 'Nance, oh Nance.' She wanted to kiss him, but he wasn't in the mood for a fuss.

'I'll be a good wife Nance; I'll make you happy; really I will. It'll be nice when we're married; a man needs a wife don't 'e - where will we live?'

'You'll come an' live yer' of course.'

'What about Jack?' she asked, when she regained control of her emotions.

'What about un?'

'Will he live with us?'

'Course he'll bloody live with us; where else is 'e going ter live! He won't bother you none. Maybe you can tidy un' up a bit; sort is washin' out an' that kind of thing. We might even get un' married off.'

'What about Ira?' she asked, the first excitement giving way to the practical concerns; 'he's starting to have problems with his legs.'

Nance began to lose his temper. 'You've told me all these years you hated his bloody guts, an' now you got the chance t' be rid of un', yer worried about his bloody legs; what's the matter with you woman?'

'I want us to be together Nance, truly I do, but he's my brother fer all his ockard ways. Then there's the cottage - if I leave him on his own, he might get funny about it and give his half away, like he has the smithy.'

To Molly's surprise, Nance didn't seem concerned; instead, he said, 'You ain't his servant Molly. He can't expect you not to marry just cus his legs is playin' him up. Tell un' you're going to come an' live yer, but you'll come home every day and do for un; cook un' something an' sort his washing out an' the like; even that miserable bastard can't complain about that. Tell un' that, an' see what e says!'

And so she did.

Ira was surprised that Nance wanted the burden of a wife, but he was philosophical about it. 'You can do what you like Molly,' he said frankly. 'You know what I think of Ridler without me saying anything, so you'd best get on with it. He'll lead you a life of bloody misery though; on that, I'll wager a pound, and if you can't see that, then you deserve all you get. Don't say I never warned you!'

Ira's words upset her as always, but this time she said nothing; instead she asked, 'What about the cottage Ira?'

'We'll leave things just the way they are. When 'e starts knocking you about as we both know he will, you'll ave' somewhere to come back to, wont you! I've always said I'll leave you my half and so I will; you don't need to worry about that.'

'Will you wish us well Ira, it would mean a lot if you did.'

277

'I'll wish you good luck Molly,' he replied, 'let's leave it at that!'

They married ten weeks later in Selworthy church. Ira had to be helped the short distance from the cottage to the church door, his leg no longer able to climb the steeply sloping path. There were many people there for such a small village, for Nance was popular in his way and nothing if not well known. After the ceremony, the guests walked the half mile to Ridler's Mill for the wedding breakfast in the paddock.

Nance was in high spirits and a very good host. There was cider and beer and as much food as could be eaten. The celebrations became more raucous as time went on, with many womenfolk taking their leave of their drunken husbands as darkness fell, preferring to leave the men to it.

'Where's yer neighbour then Nance? I'd ave' thought e'd' be yer' to drink thy health,' asked one fellow mischievously. Another replied amid much laughter, 'If I had the choice of stuffin' me face we you lot; or stuffin' is missus up at the forge, then I wouldn't be yer neither!'

'I wouldn't ave' that thieving bastard yer' if 'e were the last bloke in the village, an I'll tell 'e this,' replied Nance; 'e' won't be sorting 'er out neither, cus I don't think 'e got it in un. You'd ave' thought er'd' ave' another babby after losing the first brat, but that ain't happened. Twill take a better man I reckon.'

'Well if one pops out all dusted in flour, we'll know who t' blame Nance!'

It continued well into the night until Nance was no longer able to stand. He was carried upstairs by the wedding guests and thrown unceremoniously on the bed.

'Thee'll still be a maiden come the morning Molly, lest thee can work a bloody miracle,' said one, laughing as he left.

Molly loosened his shirt and removed his boots and trousers. He was already snoring loudly. She drew a blanket over him, then settled herself down in a leather armchair that stood beside a marble washstand. The leather was cracked and brittle with age, but the chair was comfortable. She drew a blanket about her shoulders and closed her eyes. Soon she was asleep.

In the year that followed, Ira's health deteriorated rapidly. Molly kept her word, but Polly too had got into the habit of taking him a meal. Eventually, they worked out a rota of washing cleaning and cooking, but despite everyone's effort's his health continued to decline. Amy often baked a rabbit pie, or stew, for he would eat that, but many meals were left untouched.

He'd sit for hours in a high backed chair outside the door of No 2, where he could look out across the valley to Luccombe and beyond. He'd tell Polly stories of characters long dead and times long past to make her laugh; she would be pleased to glimpse the old Ira Grace for a few moments in time, but afterwards he would become quiet, thoughtful, and sometimes tearful, his hand reaching out for hers. 'You're a good girl Polly,' he would say quietly, 'a good girl!'

Isaac and McNab moved Ira's bedstead from the bedroom to the parlour for he could no longer manage the stairs. McNab was shocked to see how frail he'd become in the few months since he'd last seen him.

'What a poor old bugger e's become,' said McNab, clearly concerned; I don't think it'll be too long.'

'For what?' said Isaac, afraid of what McNab was getting at.

'What do you think!' said the farmer bluntly. 'You see it on the farm lad... that same look when the end's close - you can see it in their eyes. I've known Ira Grace for nigh on fifty year and I barely recognised him today. I'll lay a wager 'e don't see Christmas!'

It was the first time that anyone had mentioned death.

'Perhaps things aren't quite that bad McNab!'

'His minds going and 'e ain't eatin,' continued McNab, conscious that his words had stopped his friend in his tracks; 'and e's as thin as a bloody rake. His body is giving up on un' Isaac, tis as simple as that. Do you know what I think?'

'No tell me,' replied Isaac, upset with him.

'Humans is like 'orses! They be put on this earth to do a job of work, an' when they can't work no more, there ain't no point going on.'

Ira went into Minehead cottage hospital later that month and his left leg was removed above the knee.

He wanted to return home, but that was impossible; so he went to Leathernbottle where a bed was made up for him in the parlour. It was a great strain on them all, the cottage being so tiny, but Polly would have it no other way.

Isaac would get him up each morning and help him with the private matters with as much dignity as he could manage. Amy and Polly would wash and dress him and try to get him to eat a little porridge with Laudanum to ease his pain.

On fine weather days, they would take him out to the smithy for he enjoyed that very much. He would sit near the smithy door, with a blanket across his lap and a straw hat to protect him from the sun. Bert would sit beside him, his muzzle on his lap. The old man would fondle his ears and watch the world pass by.

One day, he called Isaac from the forge and insisted he sit down. He spoke in a voice so frail that Isaac struggled to hear him clearly.

'When I'm gone, you go and see Cripps. He'll sort it out - you won't ave' to worry about nothing, I've sin to all of that.'

'I know you have Ira, and I'm very grateful.'

'She's a good girl, Isaac; I couldn't 'ave asked fer better.'

'Who is Ira?' asked Isaac gently, confused about what Ira was trying to say.

'Our Polly - she's a good girl.'

'Yes she is - she's wonderful,' replied Isaac.

'You too lad, you've been a good un' too.'

Isaac smiled.

'When you come an asked fer her hand we both said yes right away, there weren't no discussion. We knew you'd take proper care of er.'

'Who's we, Ira?' asked Isaac, upset to see Ira so befuddled, 'do you mean you and Amy?'

'Of course me an' Amy - who else? You asked us fer our Polly's hand, don't you remember?'

'Yes - yes of course I do,' replied Isaac, not knowing what else to say.

'She's a good girl Isaac; the best daughter a man could want fer.'

Isaac held the old man's hand; too sad to know what to say.

'I want you to promise you'll look after um' - both on em?'

'Yes I will Ira, I promise you I will.'

'I ain't no good now they've taken me legs away.'

'I know Ira, but it was for the best.'

'They've got to do it all fer I now, Isaac; I can't do it fer meself no more.'

'They don't mind Ira - not a bit; they both love you dearly, you know that don't you,' said Isaac, holding Ira's hand tighter, for the old man's eyes had filled with tears.

'I'll take you in now for its getting cold, I think you need to rest.' The old man nodded his head and Isaac carried him into the parlour and laid him gently on his bed.

Ira Grace passed away peacefully that same night.

CHAPTER 42

The Night Watch

Next morning, the undertaker removed Ira's body from Leathernbottle to number two, where he was laid out for viewing and put in a coffin on the front room table.

Molly wanted to stay with the body until the funeral, but Nance would not hear of it; nor would he have him at the mill either. Molly was so distressed at the thought of leaving him in the empty house that Isaac volunteered to keep vigil through the night in her stead.

The day before the funeral, Polly and Isaac received a letter from Porlock Solicitors, Francillon, Cripps and Cranway, and quite correctly guessed that it concerned Ira's will, however, the letter was not what they expected.

Polly began to read aloud, but her words petered out as she read ahead in disbelief.

'What is it?' said Isaac, wondering what was wrong.

'I can't believe it - oh, Isaac!' She read the letter again, this time more slowly.

Dear Mr Smith.

I write on behalf of my client Mrs M. Ridler of Selworthy Mill, Selworthy, Porlock, from whom I have received instructions in matters related to disposal of the estate of the late Mr Ira Grace of Number 2, Selworthy, whom I was privileged to represent in law over many years past.

I understand from my client that the testator was in your care following surgery upon his leg in June of this year and thereafter until his recent death. Mrs Ridler has particularly asked me to express her gratitude to both you and your wife, for your kindness and attendance to her brother at that difficult time.

You will recall that upon the sixteenth of May 1900 and in the presence of myself and Mr Hamish McNab, the testator made provision for you to benefit under the terms of his will, to whit, the bequest of the property known as Leathernbottle Cottage, Selworthy, inclusive of all adjoining land and outbuildings thereof and also water rights to the stream known as Eddow's brook, between the properties' boundaries wherein the latter crosses the said property.

I regret to inform you that the testator subsequently made amendment to the aforementioned will by appending a latter codicil, effectively revoking all such provisions to which you were beneficiary, this instrument being duly signed, witnessed and attested in accordance with the law on eighteenth of August 1908.

Subject to probate, the aforementioned property, together with all land and outbuilding will now succeed to the testator's sole surviving relative, Mrs Molly Ridler, as per the provision of the codicil so dated.

Probate is set for 30 November 1909 and my client has instructed me to notify you of her intention to dispose of the said property as of 1st December 1909. This letter serves to give you formal notice of termination of tenancy and you are hereby required to vacate the premises on or before that date in pursuance of her wishes.

Rental of ten shillings weekly will be payable to the deceased estate for the interim period. Payment is to be made in advance at this office no later than 3pm Friday; a pro-rata sum being payable for any part week thereof.

You are further instructed that no furnishings, nor loose tools other than those wholly owned by yourself, nor fittings nor fixed items of machinery, nor any part of the construction or fabric of the house or its outbuildings, shall be removed from the property other than by prior arrangement with the beneficiary who may be contacted through this office.

My client trusts that the generous notice now served will ensure that you may comfortably locate suitable alternative premises.

Yours sincerely,

Reginald Cripps,

Francillon, Cripps and Cranway.

Solicitors at Law.

Amy was first to speak, 'I, I don't understand Isaac, Ira left Leathernbottle to you; he made a will; surely it's all a mistake!'

'The mistake was believing a scoundrel like Ira Grace in the first bloody place... that was the mistake!' said Isaac angrily.

'What does it mean Isaac,' asked Polly in disbelief; 'what will happen to us now?'

'It means we've lost our home love,' he said. 'It means we've just six weeks to get out.'

'But you've done so much work here Isaac,' said Amy, 'all the money we have, all John's savings, it's all gone into the house; it can't be right. There must be a mistake; how could he do this to us.' Tears welled up in her eyes, and Polly led her to a chair for she seemed near to collapse.

'What are we going to do Isaac?' said Polly, kneeling beside Amy, holding her hand.

'I don't know love,' he said, 'I just don't know'! He crossed to the door and took down his heavy leather jerkin from its hook. 'I know who's behind it all though,' he said, as he snapped his fingers at Bert.

'Isaac, don't do anything silly,' said Polly anxiously; but he was already through the door. She left the old lady and rushed to the door, relieved to see him turn left for the village and the beacon, away from the mill and Nance Ridler. Why did he always walk the beacon when there was trouble?

The dog ran ahead along the steep, familiar path above the village. They passed through the darkened woods, with its muddy tracks and amber carpet of leaves that occasionally rustled with the movement of some woodland creature.

The dog disappeared from sight. Isaac halted, scanning the edge of the ground above him. Sure enough, the dog re-appeared ears pricked, eyes bright, looking this way and that for his master. As soon as he saw him, he wagged his tail and was off once more. Bert didn't like to lose sight of Isaac for too long. Isaac smiled despite his woes for he knew exactly what Bert would do, if only all things in life were as predictable as his faithful dog.

Soon they made the beacon. He felt the wind and sun on his face once more, as he walked from the tree line, out onto open ground. The dog was a long way off now, nose down, tail high. Isaac reached his favourite rock where he'd written his poem for Becky, and there he took out his pipe. He lit it with hands cupped against the gentle breeze from the river. He was angry with himself for leaving them as he had, but he needed time to think.

It was worse than they realised - much worse. He'd borrowed money against Ira's goodwill, to rebuild the smithy and buy tools - one hundred pounds worth of it - and it still wasn't fully repaid. What they were going to do he didn't know, but there was no point talking to Molly, for he was sure Nance was behind all this and she wouldn't dare go against Nance.

Nor did there seem to be any point speaking to Cripps for he was just the messenger. If Ira decided to change his will in favour of his sister, that was his choice, why should Cripps think that unreasonable? He wouldn't question it for a moment. They'd have to accept the fact that they were going to lose their home and that with Molly's help and Ira's confusion, Nance had won. He said he'd get even one day and by God, he had. What hurt most was the betrayal. He'd never thought about owning Leathernbottle until Ira promised it to him, and now he wished he'd said nothing at all.

The dog reappeared from the bracken to sit beside him, panting heavily, trying to sniff the breeze that blew up the hillside. Isaac put his arm around the dog's neck. You can't lose something you never had Bert, but I've still got you and Polly, so bugger the lot of em. We'll get by - let's go home.

When he returned, Polly came out to meet him, clearly distressed and upset.

'Something's wrong Isaac, I am sure of it; I can't believe Ira would do such a thing to you; he thought the world of you, you know he did. I think you should speak to Cripps.'

'To squabble over a man's belongings when he's barely cold? I might have very little Polly, but I've got my pride and what d' you think life would be like if we did get that will revoked? Ridler would make our lives a bloody misery! I'm a good blacksmith and people always need blacksmiths. I'll find another job and we'll start again, don't you worry.'

He kissed her tenderly on the lips. 'We'll be alright lass, I promise you.'

Amy did not want Isaac to go to No 2 that night; 'He don't deserve it!' she said.

'I'm going so the Ridler's know that I'm a man of my word, even if Ira's not!'

He lit the lantern in the chilly parlour and shivered with the cold of the room. He got a fire going and the room quickly filled with the smell of wood smoke and lamp oil.

'Get out the bloody way,' he said to Bert, in rare bad humour, as he pushed a chair in front of the fire. No sooner was any fire lit, than Bert was sprawled in front of it. The dog moved a couple of feet then lay down again, laying his muzzle on the carpet and looking at Isaac with disgust.

Isaac sat staring at the flames for more than an hour, then on an impulse; he took down the lamp and walked through into the dark hallway with its brown wainscot and flagstone floor, then into the front room where Ira had made his will, and where he now lay in his coffin. The coffin was on the very table where they'd signed the will, and Isaac could see Ira and the scrawny solicitor in his mind's eye, the will spread out before them.

Isaac put his lamp beside the coffin and lifted the lid, placing it carefully against the wall. Holding his lamp high, he looked down at the corpse within the coffin.

Isaac hardly recognised Ira in death. There was no colour, only a deathly grey pallor; his eyes were closed and sunken into his skull, his skin waxen. He was dressed in his Sunday best suit; his hands crossed on his chest. Isaac touched the old man's hand. Though he was fully expecting it, he was still shocked at how cold the body felt.

Although he'd stayed every night as promised, this was the first time he'd wanted to view the body. He'd decided to do so on this last night, because of the events of the day.

He thought of the last time he'd seen Ira alive, when he'd held Isaac's hand, his words full of urgency, his eyes filled with tears. He thought too of the words Ira had spoken, "When I go Isaac - go and see Cripps, he'll sort it all out - you won't ave' to worry about nothin' no more." Was it really in the power of a frail old man so close to death, to trick and deceive in that way?

'You were my friend Ira,' he said softly; 'I thought I was your friend too! I'm going to believe we parted as friends, and that Molly and Nance are behind all this. I don't suppose you really knew what was going on toward the end, and that's what I'm going to carry on believing.' Isaac picked up the coffin lid and lifted it carefully over the coffin. 'Because I don't hold out much hope for your soul if I'm wrong!' he added quietly, as he lowered the lid into place.

Isaac picked up his lamp and went back to the parlour and his chair by the fire. Bert lay fast asleep in its orange glow, his muzzle upon his paws.

CHAPTER 43

Robinson visits Cripps

Ira was buried the following day in the tiny churchyard at Selworthy. Many came to pay their last respects including the Ridler's; however, only Jack spoke.

'Where's Amy,' asked McNab, who was looking most uncomfortable in his collar and tie.

'She's very upset about the will,' said Polly.

'I don't blame her, the miserable old bastard,' said McNab in disgust. 'Who'd a bloody thought it after all his talk? I always said he were a bloody scoundrel. I'll bet Old Nick's come to collect him in person. They'll be shakin' ands' and doing a jig as we speak - what are you going to do now?'

'Find a job as soon as I can,' said Isaac joining the conversation. 'We've got to be out by the 1st of December, come what may, so I'll need to be quick about it, or we'll be on the parish.'

'No you won't, don't you worry about that,' said McNab, 'you come an' live we me an' Parsley if things don't work out,' he said, holding Polly's hand reassuringly. 'The house d' need a bit of a clean up anyway!'

Polly looked at McNab with his tight collar, creased suit, and hair awry. McNab's farm was worse than the smithy had ever been, if such a thing was possible, and it would need more than a little cleaning; but the offer had come from the heart, as did everything from this funny, gentle little man. She held his hand in hers and kissed him on his cheek. 'Thank you, McNab,' she said softly, 'thank you for being a lovely, dear friend.'

A few days later, McNab sat in his usual corner of The Swan at Porlock Weir supping a pint. As chance would have it, Sergeant Robinson had also called in for a drink and took his beer to McNab's table to pass the time of day.

'Hello Hamish, could you stand some company?' asked Robinson.

'Afternoon Harry,' replied McNab, pointing the policeman to the chair opposite.

'Well, I've found the Captain, where's the rest of his motley crew,' asked the policeman cheerfully?

'Tied up outside the last time I saw un.'

287

I'm not talking about Parsley; I'm talking about yer fellow pirates; the whisky gang.'

'You won't be seeing them no more,' replied McNab; 'ones just died and tother'll soon be sailing different seas.'

'Who's died then?'

'Ira Grace; they buried un' last Friday.'

'Did they now; I didn't know that. I knew he'd lost a leg, but I'd no idea he'd passed away.'

'That's a turn up fer the books then,' said McNab. 'I regularly walk to Wiliton fer a fart, so as thee don't get to know about it.'

Robinson chuckled; McNab was always good for a bit of earthy humour.

'What got Ira then?'

'Old age... old age and weariness I'd say. All the life went out of un' an 'e just faded away. Young Isaac - who rented the smithy off un' - took un' in after e lost is leg, but he weren't never the same again.'

'He's moving on too, if I understand you correctly; what went wrong there?'

'Well might you ask!' replied McNab. 'Tis all a rum do if you ask me, and with Ridler involved I shouldn't be surprised if there weren't some shenanigans.'

Sergeant Robinson's ears pricked up at the sound of Ridler's name.

'What have the Ridler's got to do with it?' he asked.

'Nance married Molly Grace about a year ago, that's what.'

'So?'

'So Ira left her the smithy in his will and Nance being Nance, wants em out cus of the bad blood over the wreck.'

'That's what happens when you've a mind to break the law McNab! It's bad luck on the lad, but that's life I'm afraid and why should there be shenanigans; there's nothing rum about leaving yer worldly wealth to yer sister!'

'Except when you can't stand the bloody sight of 'er and you like 'er husband even less!'

'Maybe so, but who else is he going to leave it to?'

'That's my point,' said McNab, tapping the table. 'He left the smithy to Isaac Smith, lock stock and barrel fer they got on very well, them both being

288

blacksmiths and whatever. Not only that but his young wife did just about everything fer un' toward the end. I signed the will in Ira's own parlour, so I know that to be a fact. Then soon as 'e dies, up pops Nance we this other bit of paper as says that's all bollocks and e's suddenly leaving the lot to Molly!'

Robinson raised an eyebrow, 'Was that through a solicitor or just something they found?'

'Proper job through Francillon's as I understand it; Cripps looked after both.'

'Cripps is straight enough, McNab; he'd make sure everything was in order.'

McNab snorted in disgust and took another sip of his beer.

'All I'm saying is, Ira thought the world of em, and funny old bugger though he was, the more I d' think ont; the less I think 'e ad it in mind to do em down; that's all I'm saying.'

The policeman took a draft of his pint and the conversation moved on.

The following day Robinson leant his bicycle against the wrought iron railings of a little house in Doverhay. He scraped his boots on the scraper beside the door; knocked, and let himself in.

'Is that you, Jack?' inquired a woman's voice from the parlour.

'It's Harry, love,' replied Robinson!

'Oh Harry; hello dear,' came the woman's voice, clearly pleased; 'I thought you were Jack coming home. I'm just about to put his tea on the table. Go on in the front room and we won't disturb him there; you know what he's like about his tea, would you like a cuppa yourself and a rock cake?'

'Thanks Edie, a rock cake will be splendid,' he made his way into the tiny front room his sister kept for best.

'What a stranger you are,' said Edith Edwards as she entered the room, tray in hand. 'We'd quite given you up for dead.'

'Things have bin' a bit busy lately Edie - what with one thing and another!'

'Well, you're here now and that's all that matters.'

Robinson talked to his sister for some while about this and that before asking, 'How're things at Francillon's then Edith; how's old Cripps these days?'

'Well how strange you should ask dear,' she replied, 'I'd normally say he doesn't change a bit, but he's been most peculiar of late; I just don't know what's got into him.'

Robinson's sister was Cripps secretary and had been so for years.

'Perhaps he's a bit under the weather!'

'Well perhaps...! He was taken ill at the office a little while ago and had to go home. I've never known that before, but he's been acting so strange of late; I think something else has upset him.'

'Such as?'

'Well, I can only think it's to do with a gentleman who called the day he was taken poorly, because he was quite his usual self until then. He came along on Wednesday afternoon, about a fortnight ago. He just barged in without so much as a "by your leave" and insisted on seeing Mr Cripps. I told him Mr Cripps was already with someone; but he wouldn't take no for an answer and just walked straight into his office. I can't imagine what Mr Cripps must have thought. I tried to explain what had happened, but he said it was okay and he would deal with it, but he looked very upset as you can imagine. The first gentleman left straight away and who could blame him. The gentleman was with him for about five minutes and after he'd left, I went into Mr Cripps office because he wasn't answering the phone. There he was, sat at his desk looking terribly upset. Shortly after, he said he was poorly and had to go home and I wasn't surprised, for I've never seen him quite so put out in all the time I've worked for him.'

'This chaps name wasn't Ridler by any chance Edith?'

'Yes it was Harry, how on earth did you know that?'

'Just a hunch! I know a fellow called Nance Ridler's become a client recently and what you've told me's about right for Nance; he's a very nasty piece of work. He's a petty criminal with a violent temper and known to handle stolen goods, though we've only caught him once. He did six months for assault about eight years ago for blinding a drinking partner and beating him within an inch of his life - all over a hand of cards.'

Edith Edwards put her hand to her mouth, clearly shocked at this revelation.

'Oh, I do worry about you sometimes,' she said.

'Trouble is love; he may have a perfectly legitimate reason for wanting to see Reg Cripps, so would you do me a favour ...? Would you ask Cripps if I can call in and see him tomorrow, just for a chat?'

'Yes of course I will Harry: I do know he's free between one and three, perhaps you could come then; oh I do hope this man hasn't been causing trouble.'

290

Robinson and his sister chatted on until her husband arrived home, whereupon she left the two men talking to make a cup of tea for her husband. With a final peck on the cheek for his sister, he left the little cottage and began to push his bicycle in the general direction of Porlock and home.

Robinson arrived the following day and took a seat in Cripps outer office where his sister had her desk. Cripps came to welcome Robinson almost immediately and he could see what Edie meant about him looking unwell. Gaunt at the best of times, Cripps looked as though he had all the troubles of the world on his shoulders.

'Good afternoon Sergeant, Mrs Edwards tells me you'd like to speak to me?'

'Only if you can spare the time Mr Cripps; I daresay you're busy as usual.'

'Well, yes, but please do come through.'

Robinson removed his helmet and followed the solicitor into a small high ceiling room with an arched window that looked out over the graveyard of St. Dubricious, notable for its unusual truncated spire. Its walls were oak panelled and lined with shelves of books and manuscripts which seemed to have no order or form to their storage. Robinson had known Cripps for many years, but this was the first time he'd seen his office. Cripps sat at his desk before the window whilst Robinson sat in one of the two other chairs in the room.

Cripps looked painfully thin and ill at ease. His skin was a pallid grey, with dark rings encircling tired, haunted eyes, that never looked directly at him. To the astute Sergeant Robinson, he looked a worried man.

'What can I do for you, Sergeant?'

'Oh, it's a routine matter Mr Cripps, nothing important, but you don't look very well if you don't mind my saying so!'

'I, yes I haven't been sleeping too well just recently Mr Robinson and a dose of flu hasn't helped; I'm beginning to get over it now though.'

Robinson gave a knowing smile, 'Well, you need to look after yourself Mr Cripps, I don't suppose a man like you stops fer a dose of flu! If it's not business, it'll be your civic duties and that can be a mistake I often think!'

'I daresay Mr Robinson, I daresay, but there's much to be done when people are relying on you as I'm sure you know yourself.'

'Indeed, I do Mr Cripps; indeed I do.'

Cripps waited for Robinson to end this polite exchange, anxious to hear the purpose of the policeman's visit, but Robinson seemed to be in no hurry whatsoever.

He just sat across the table looking out of the window, seemingly miles away.

'What was it you wanted to speak to me about Sergeant Robinson?' said Cripps finally.

Robinson looked up at the sound of Cripps voice. 'Oh, I'm very sorry Mr Cripps, how rude of me; I was miles away! I was just looking at the church spire and wondering how you can look at something every day of your life and not give it a second thought; then one day you see it through completely different eyes. I was just trying to decide how it lost its top; fire do you think, or dry rot, what do you think happened?'

'I really have no idea,' replied Cripps, seemingly ever more on edge, 'if you don't mind I...'

'No, no of course,' continued Robinson, 'I'm taking up your valuable time; no; it was just a small matter I wanted to discuss regarding a will.'

'Your own?'

'No, a client of yours, a fellow called Ira Grace!'

Robinson watched his man carefully to see what effect the words might have. Cripps seemed taken aback and stumbled over his reply.

'I... I'm not sure what you mean Sergeant.'

'Well, I understand he's just passed away and folk being folk, there's always someone who thinks they should be getting more than they have; I'm sure there's nothing for me to be concerned about, but these matters do pop up.'

'There's an issue of client confidentiality here Sergeant Robinson.'

'I understand that Mr Cripps, that's why I think it will be so much better if we have a quiet chat and put the matter to bed between you and me, rather than Minehead getting involved.'

Cripps tried hard to control his voice, but Robinson noted that his hands were shaking. 'Mr. Grace's will was quite normal and straightforward Sergeant; I can't think why - I mean - what concern might it be of the police?'

'Well as I say Mr Cripps, probably none at all, but unexpected changes were made quite late on as I understand it?'

'A man may change his will Sergeant; there is no law against that!'

292

'No that's right Mr Cripps, I quite understand that, but that's providing he does so of his own free will, is it not? My concern would be if anyone caused him to change it against his free will - if you see what I mean! That would be a criminal offence, as I'm sure you appreciate.'

'Mr. Robinson, I hope you are not suggesting that Francillon Cripps and Cranway are in any way involved in...'

'I am not suggesting anything of the kind, Mr Cripps,' said Robinson, butting in; 'I've known you and Mr Cranway for far too many years to think that; no I had something else in mind. Can I ask you - have you ever heard of a man called Nance Ridler?'

Cripps became increasingly agitated; ill at ease and defensive in his replies, 'Well I know *of* him Mr Robinson, I wouldn't say I know him!'

'You've met him though?'

'Yes.'

'You know he stands to benefit from the late changes.'

'Well in as much as he will benefit through marriage; he is not a direct beneficiary.'

'Amounts to the same thing Mr Cripps - amounts to the same thing! Did you also know that Nance Ridler is a convicted criminal, a man who has served six months in gaol for grievous bodily harm?'

'I - I don't quite understand what you're saying Sergeant.'

'What I'm saying is that Nance Ridler is a nasty piece of work Mr Cripps; a very nasty piece of work indeed. He wouldn't think twice about swindling you, me, or anyone else fer that matter, and certainly not an old man who's lost his marbles. fer my money it's not so much a question of would he, as did he? That's why I want to establish that the gentleman who died, and yourself, and the law I represent, have not been deceived!'

Robinson waited for Cripps reply, but Cripps just looked at the policeman in stunned silence.

'I understand it was you that drew up the new will; all done here in your office I take it?'

'No - no I went to see him, he was not well at the time - his leg I think.' The trap had been a subtle one, but Cripps had not fallen into it.

'Ah yes of course, I'd forgotten; so you visited him in the home of the original beneficiary where he was resident?'

'No Mr Robinson, Mr Grace was at No 2 Selworthy when we met. It would hardly have been appropriate for it to be at Leathernbottle Smithy, given the nature of the visit.'

'I can understand that Mr Cripps; who was there, as a matter of interest?'

'Myself, Mr Grace, Mrs Ridler, Mr Nance Ridler and Mr Jack Ridler - they acted as witnesses.'

Robinson looked up at Cripps with a look of surprise. 'So all those who were there were to benefit, either directly or indirectly, is that lawful Mr Cripps?'

'Yes that is lawful Mr Robinson, only Mrs Ridler would benefit and she was not a witness. Also in my opinion Mr Grace was fully aware of the changes he was about to make and was doing so of his own free will. He very definitely instructed me that he'd had a disagreement with the previous beneficiary and that was why he wanted it changed. I've honestly lost count of the number of wills I've seen changed on an exactly similar basis and I have to say I find the inference of your questions most offensive, Sergeant!'

'Cripps rang the bell on his desk as he spoke and Mrs Edwards came into the room; 'Would you be good enough to fetch Mr Grace's will, Mrs Edwards,' he asked, regaining some of his composure.

'Well, I do apologise if I've given you the wrong impression Mr Cripps; as I said you would be the last person I'd suspect of impropriety, but suggestions have been made and given the reputation of some of the parties concerned, I wouldn't be doing my job if I didn't look into the matter.'

At that point, Mrs Edwards returned with the manuscripts which Cripps laid out before the policeman. Robinson looked briefly at them but could make out very little without his glasses.

'Well, I've taken up enough of your time Mr Cripps, he said, rising to his feet. I'll thank you for your help and leave you in peace.' He pushed his chair beneath Cripps desk and walked to the door. Just as Cripps thought his ordeal was over, Robinson turned and said, 'Should you by any chance speak to Mr Ridler at any time Mr Cripps, it would help the police no end if you didn't mention our conversation. I'm sure you understand!'

'Of course Sergeant; do you intend to take the matter further?' he asked as casually as he could manage.

'Let's just say I shall keep an open mind! By the way - there's just one more thing. I took the opportunity in the outer office to have a few words with Edith on the same matter and I understand that there was another gentleman with you when Ridler so rudely interrupted your consultation; I wonder if you can recall the other gentleman's name?'

Cripps looked as though he had received an electric shock. His mouth moved, but the words were barely audible.

'No... I... he was not a client as such, just a gentleman wanting to ascertain his position regarding a land boundary; we are often asked to give advice in that way; I can't remember his name; Reynolds was it; I really can't remember.'

'Oh I can help you there Mr Cripps,' said Mrs Edwards. 'His name was Mr Charles Chesney, I remember it most clearly.' She smiled at her brother, 'I always make a note of such things Harry. He was from Bristol I think!'

Bless you Edie, thought Robinson to himself. 'How do you know that?' he asked.

'Well his accent dear. You can always tell a Bristolian now, can't you!'

It took little more than a ten-minute wait beneath the coach arch of The Royal Oak, for Sergeant Robinson and PC Arthur Baker, to see Cripps' trap making its way through Porlock at almost reckless pace, and in the direction of Selworthy.

'Off you go Arthur,' said Robinson to his assistant. The constable swung his leg across Robinson's Hercules and started to pedal off after the fast disappearing trap, the bicycle creaking with every turn of the pedals. Robinson rarely rode it, except to coast downhill, and was distressed at the noise it made through Baker's efforts. 'Needs a bit of oil on that chain,' he thought to himself.

Baker was sweating profusely beneath the heavy uniform, his helmet hanging from the handlebars as he pushed Robinson's bike the last few hundred yards. Had it been any other bicycle, he'd have left it at the bottom of Selworthy hill without any qualms, but everyone hereabouts would recognise Harry Robinson's bike. The kids would have it away for devilment, and then there'd be hell to pay!

He saw the trap outside Ridler's Mill just as Robinson had said he would. His job done, he swung his leg over the crossbar and rode the heavy bike back down the hill with brakes squealing.

Robinson listened silently to Baker's report. It was some moments before he spoke. 'That's a pity; I hoped I might be wrong. I think it's time to take this matter seriously, so I'll write you out a telegram and you can take it down the Post Office.'

Baker read the message upside down as it lay on the post office counter; it read:-

DS WOODS BRISTOL CONSTABULARY STOP DO YOU HAVE A CUSTOMER CHARLES CHESNEY STOP ROBINSON PORLOCK STOP

~

Cripps knocked on Ridler's door in a high state of agitation. Molly let him in and they entered a dark room that smelt of old carpet and damp. Nance came into the room from a passage that led to the rear of the house. He was dressed in his shirtsleeves; his trousers held up with heavy leather braces. 'What do you want?' he asked, clearly annoyed to be troubled by the solicitor.

'Robinson's been to see me,' blurted Cripps. 'He was asking all sorts of questions, I told you this was madness!'

'What did you tell him?'

'Nothing; I told him what we agreed; but he's suspicious and he knows about Charlie. He'll find out about Charlie and I'll be ruined. You've got to do something Nance, send Charlie away; get rid of him. I'll pay whatever it costs.'

'Why should I do anything? What's Robinson going to find out, Cripps - that you're a faggot! That's your business, nothing to do with me!'

'But you told Charlie who I am, where I live! You're blackmailing me, both of you! He knows you were there together - Robinson...'

Nance pushed Cripps against the wall with a heave that knocked the breath from him.

'Who's blackmailing you,' said Nance menacingly, shoving Cripps once more, cracking his head against the wall. 'Chesney's blackmailing you my friend; I just happened to be there on legitimate business when your faggot friend calls by!'

'They'll find out about the will; they'll know it's a forgery; the signatures nothing like...'

'He was an old man Cripps, a few months from death; of course his signature will look different. You'll swear he signed it of his own free will and no one will be able to say different.'

'They'll send me to prison,' gasped Cripps frantically, 'it would kill me; I'd tell them everything Nance, everything! They'd understand; they'd ...'

Ridler head butted the solicitor so hard that Molly heard his teeth crack. His glasses flew from his face and smashed to pieces on the flagstones of the parlour

296

floor. Cripps eyes rolled upwards into his head and blood spurted from his nose as he sagged to the floor in a crumpled heap. Ridler's boot hit him full in the chest and the solicitor's body jerked like a puppet on a string.

'Stop Nance stop, you'll kill him,' shouted Molly, grabbing her husband and trying to pull him away, but she wasn't strong enough for Nance in such a rage. Jack came from nowhere and dragged his brother off.

'You crazy bastard,' said Jack Ridler, standing between Nance and Cripps. His hands were pressed against Nance's chest, which heaved with the adrenaline pouring through him. Jack looked into his brother's eyes, bright with blood lust and the thrill of violence done against the helpless man who lay in a crumpled heap on the flagstone floor. 'You'll swing one of these days Nance; I'm telling yuh,' said Jack, his hands shaking. 'You're a fuckin' maniac!'

He pushed Nance to one side and knelt over the solicitor. Blood was pouring from his face and there were bloodstains on his shirt. He opened Cripps collar to find two huge wheal's where Ridler's boot had hit him.

Cripps regained consciousness when Molly poured water over his face. She wiped away the blood and dabbed as gently as she could at the bruised flesh. Cripps slowly opened his eyes and looked up into the woman's face. His eyes filled with tears; his words came in shuddering sobs, 'Why is he doing this to me. Why is he killing me?'

Cripps returned to Porlock in such a state of shock that he could not remember an inch of the journey. One eye had closed and breathing was an agony. The bruises on his chest had turned purple; he told his wife the pony had kicked him.

That night he lay in considerable pain from his injuries, but his thoughts were only for the recent events that were destroying his life. His career and reputation would soon be dragged through the gutter, and he would spend the rest of his life in prison - all because of this monster of a man. The very thought of him sent shudders of fear and dread down Cripps spine. He was mad, quite mad, and Cripps was sure he was a killer - a killer who would enjoy killing. Why him - why not this Isaac Smith he hated so much? Why did he not kill Isaac Smith and leave him alone? 'Oh God,' thought Cripps to himself, 'oh God, please help me!'

He curled himself up into a ball beneath the covers and wept. With time, he fell asleep, but not before he had decided what must be done.

The following day Cripps told Edith Edwards that he was not to be disturbed on any account. He sat at his desk writing letters that he placed in a neat pile.

When five-o-clock came, Cripps heard Edith knocking gently, speaking to him through the door.

'Mr. Cripps, I'm leaving now!'

Cripps did not reply.

'Are you all right Mr Cripps?'

'Yes I'm all right Mrs Edwards, goodnight.'

'Goodnight Mr Cripps,' said Edith reluctantly.

Cripps was about to let her go, then on an impulse he said, 'Mrs. Edwards!'

'Yes Mr Cripps?'

'Will you do something for me?'

Edith Edwards slowly opened the door. Her employer stood before her looking close to collapse.

'Would you be good enough to post these for me?'

'Of course Mr Cripps, is that all?'

He nodded silently.

'You look so unwell. I have been so concerned about you of late!'

'Goodnight Mrs Edwards!'

'Goodnight then Mr Cripps.' She took the pile of twenty or so letters and placed them in her bag. With a last look of concern, she bade him goodnight once more and gently closed the door behind her.

Cripps slept in his chair for several hours, at peace with his conscience at last, for it was done now; there was no turning back. He woke at eleven-o-clock to the peal of St. Dubricious. He rose from his chair to turn down the gas mantle on the wall beside him. The fragile mantle changed from incandescent white to pale yellow and deep shadows cast their fingers into the dark recesses of the room.

Cripps walked to the window and looked out upon the churchyard below. He could see the main street from his vantage point. Men were turning out of the White Horse to wend their way home, mostly on foot, but occasionally he heard the clatter of a horse and trap along the cobbles. It was time for decent folk to be abed; it was time for what he had to do.

Cripps had made up his mind to go away, to leave his old life forever, before this maniac murdered him. There was nothing left to stay for now; his loveless marriage was a sham and his reputation would soon be in tatters, but he had money to see him through. He would slip away as soon as the town was asleep. He would start again, build a new life and forget the misery of these last few days. He'd put everything right now and he was pleased about that. He had even left a note - soon it would all be forgotten.

Cripps knelt beside the heavy safe that was built into the wall of his office. "Seddon's and Son, Locksmiths of London by royal appointment to her gracious Majesty, Queen Victoria 1874" declared the heavy cast brass escutcheon.

Cripps opened the safe door and instantly heard the tread upon the stair. Before he could close and lock the safe, the door of his office opened and a figure stood framed in the doorway.

'Hello Reg,' said the soft voice, the face still hidden in shadow.

'Charlie!' said Cripps, his voice a mixture of surprise and alarm, 'what are you doing here?'

'I came to see you Reg.'

'Why have you come, I can't see you anymore; I've given you the money; why don't you leave me alone?'

'I need more Reg! I can't stay in Bristol any longer; the coppers are asking after me. That's your fault isn't it; you must have told them!'

'No - no I said nothing; honest to God I said nothing,' said Cripps, the pitch of his voice rising as he sensed the danger in Chesney's words.

Chesney entered the room, and made for the safe Cripps was trying to conceal with his body. It was then he noticed a portmanteau and a small intricately carved chest beside Cripps desk. Chesney reached down, picked up the chest and placed it on the desk. Three elephants with Howdah's on their backs walked majestically across the lid in single file, each carrying the tail of their companion. Chesney lifted the lid, and the pungent, aromatic smell of camphor, immediately filled the room. He lifted a tiny bottle from its silk pocket and sniffed the Gentleman's toilet water within. There were other fine things within the chest, each in its own pocket.

'These are lovely things Reg,' said Chesney. He opened a shaving razor with an ivory and gold handle, its blade sharp and polished from daily use. 'Lovely things,' repeated Chesney more to himself than to Cripps. He opened the Portmanteau, which was full of clothing.

'Going somewhere Reg?'

'Please Charlie - I can't...'

Chesney saw the note on Cripps blotter; he picked it up and read it in the light from the mantle. His lips parted briefly in a thin smile as he read the few words it contained.

'So you are leaving Reg - just like me. We're on the run together, why didn't you tell me, aren't we friends anymore?'

'I'm afraid of you Charlie, you've helped Ridler. You've helped him and he's an animal; look what he's done to me.'

Cripps pulled his shirt to one side, his chest a mass of purple bruising.

'I had no choice or he'd have done for me too, you know what he's like. Let's go away, I'll look after you.'

'No Charlie you'll have to go now, please leave me alone,' sobbed Cripps.

'I thought you loved me,' whispered Chesney.

'I do love you but it's over now. Please leave me alone; I'll give you more money, but please leave me alone.'

Chesney drew Cripps towards him and placed his lip against his. He kissed him as they had kissed many times before, but he heard Cripps whimper with the pain in his chest. Chesney did not let go; instead, he kissed deeper until the solicitor began to relax.

Chesney lowered his hands to Cripps genitals, caressing them. Cripps drew in a sudden breath and Chesney felt him respond. Chesney smiled and began to squeeze. He squeezed harder and harder. He watched with pleasure as Cripps expression changed from joy, to agony, and then to fear.

Cripps opened his mouth to scream, but Chesney pushed a kerchief deep within his mouth. Cripps tried to scream again, but no noise came out. Chesney pushed the cloth deeper and deeper with his fingers. Cripps tried to lash out but felt the edge of the shaving razor across his Adams apple. Cripps froze to the spot, barely able to breathe; it was then they heard the landing floorboards creak once more.

'Where the hell have you been,' asked Chesney, clearly taken by surprise.

'I've bin' busy,' said Nance.

Chesney was about to swear at Ridler when he felt Cripps move. He thought he was going to struggle, but realised Cripps was fainting. He let him fall.

300

Nance looked at the razor in Chesney's hand, 'Thought you'd start without me then?'

'They threw me out at closing time, what else was I supposed to do; I couldn't hang about in the street!'

'Did anyone see you in the pub?'

'Of course they saw me. I told um' I was staying overnight at the Royal Oak, to catch the Lynmouth horse bus in the morning, like you said.'

If the mantle had been burning a little brighter, Chesney may have seen Ridler smile.

'Let's get on with it then,' said Ridler, 'take that handkerchief out of his mouth before he chokes. We'll see what's in the safe then we'll have a chat with our mutual friend.'

Ridler bent to the safe and pulled out its contents. He counted almost two thousand pounds from a steel box.

'A thousand pounds each Charlie, that's not bad for one nights work! I told you he'd have money, solicitors always do; let's see if there's more in the bag.'

Chesney opened the Portmanteau and tipped its contents on the floor but he found only clothing. Among them, there was a silk dressing gown with a braided and tasselled cord. Chesney tied the end of the cord into a noose and placed it around the solicitor's neck. He kicked him several times but Cripps did not stir. 'You've killed him,' said Nance. Chesney shook his head; 'I can see him breathing; we're wasting time keeping on looking, let's bring him round and he'll sing like a canary.'

Chesney took a bottle of smelling salts from the camphor box and passed it beneath the solicitor's nose.

'Get up Reg, get up,' shouted Chesney. Cripps rose groggily to his knees his nostrils aching from the flame of the salts.

'Up you get Reg,' continued Chesney, throwing the cord over a beam in the ceiling as he did so.

Cripps rose unsteadily to his feet, dragged up by the pull of the cord on his neck. 'Are you going to kill me?' he whimpered.

'Lord no!' replied Chesney, 'We're only here to rob you, I wouldn't hurt you Reg, you know that! But you must get on the chair; get up now; get up now Reg.' He held the razor to Cripps throat and the solicitor clambered on the chair. As quick as a flash Chesney pulled the cord tight and tried to tie it back to the beam, but Cripps fought with him in panic and terror at what was happening. Nance picked up the razor and held it to Cripps throat, 'Keep quiet and stop struggling, or I'll give you a great big smile.' Chesney pulled the cord tight, tying it back upon itself in a double knot.

'There Reg, that wasn't so bad was it, but you'd better stay still now or you might fall. If you fall it will be your fault wont it Reg.'

Cripps only sobbed in reply. Chesney gripped Cripps testicles once more and squeezed for all he was worth, 'Wont it Reg?' he asked once more. Cripps nodded his head barely able to speak or even breathe for the tightness of the cord.

'You should have told me who you were, Reg. You didn't tell me who you were and now look what's happened; is there any more money Reg?'

'No,' gasped the solicitor!

'You're lying to me again Reg; solicitors have got lots of money, everyone knows that! What about at home, I expect you've lot's more at home?'

'No, there's nothing more Charlie, please; please don't hurt me, I...'

Ridler prodded Cripps belly with the blunt end of the razor, 'Charlie asked you a question Cripps,' he said quietly.

'I've told you; I've told you!' screamed the terrified man, 'It's all there in the safe, everything I have; I was going to leave tonight; Oh God help me.'

'Where's the will,' asked Nance, believing him about the money.

'In the outer office, in the filing cupboards... GR it's under GR.'

They left him teetering on the chair whilst they searched the cupboard outside. The forged will was there but not the genuine one. Nance took the forgery and stuffed it in his pocket, replacing all the other manuscripts carefully so they did not appear disturbed.

Ridler and Chesney returned to Cripps office where Nance picked up the razor and went over to the terrified solicitor.

'Where's the real will?' he asked venomously.

'It's... it's in the cupboard, please I...'

'It's not in the cupboard so where is it; I need to get rid of it so I'm going to ask you just once more...?'

'I, I don't know, it should be there, I...'

'It don't matter one way or the other,' said Nance, 'I've got the forgery, so I must be on my way and so must you!' With one swift movement, he turned the solicitor's wrist over and slashed it down to the bone.

Ridler stepped away smartly, pulling the chair from under Cripps as he did so. Cripps dropped almost to the floor, the noose drawing tight about his throat. It choked away the air to Cripps lungs as he thrashed about on the end of the dressing-gown cord. Blood flew everywhere about the room. Cripps lifted his arms in a futile attempt to pull the choking cord from around his neck, but he could only grip with his right hand; his left slapped at the side of his face like a drowning fish.

The solicitor was red with his own blood; his hair matted with it. It bubbled about his nose and mouth and dripped from his fingertips. Ridler watched the slowly spinning body in fascination, the blood spurting from it like a Catherine wheel. Soon Cripps stopped struggling, the flow of blood beginning to ease, his heart faltering, his legs jerking spasmodically, the spinning slowly coming to a halt. It was the first time Nance had seen a man die, and he enjoyed it very much.

'Like a puppet on a string!' muttered Ridler to himself.

Chesney stood looking at the body, his mouth open in disbelief. 'Jesus Christ Almighty,' he muttered.

'Suicide!' said Nance. 'Faced with shame and disgrace he took his own life; a great loss to the community; he's even left a note and in his own hand - how very thoughtful.'

He picked up the note Cripps had left and read it aloud.

To Earnest Cranway.

When you read this, I will be gone. There is much I regret about my life, but I leave with great affection for our long partnership and as an honest man.

Your colleague and friend

Reginald Cripps.

'What could be better?' said Nance.

He wiped his own prints from the razor; squeezing it in the solicitor's lifeless hand before letting it fall to the blood soaked floor.

Chesney backed slowly away from Nance, barely believing what he had just witnessed. Cripps was right; Ridler wasn't quite right in the head; he'd just murdered a man in cold blood and couldn't care less, if anything he was pleased with himself. Charlie Chesney was suddenly a very frightened man indeed.

'Jesus Christ Nance,' said Chesney once more.

'Don't step in any blood, or they'll know he weren't alone!' replied Nance.

'What did you do it for; you said we'd just soak him for the money?'

'Dead men don't talk!' Nance replied matter-of-factly.

'But its murder Nance, you'll swing if they catch you!'

'Who'll swing?' said Nance, looking up from his handiwork. 'Who was it spent the evening waiting for someone in the Royal Oak, who was the "son" he visited at the Gallon Can? Who was it as blackmailed and robbed him? I don't think they'll be looking fer me, Charlie boy!'

'You set me up!' said Chesney, panic setting in.

'I needed an alibi Charlie; you don't mind do you?'

Chesney eyed the door, afraid for his own life, but Nance had moved between him and the door, cutting off his escape. 'What are you going to do now,' Chesney asked warily.

'What I said I'd do, I'll get you on a boat for Dublin and you'll have a thousand pound in yer top pocket, No one in Dublin's going to help the British police Charlie, they'd sooner boil their babies in oil.'

'Give me the money then,' said Chesney.

Nance sat at Cripps desk and counted out nine hundred and fifty pounds; 'I've got expenses,' he said, looking up at Chesney.

The two men left the solicitors office, and slipped through the churchyard along a darkened path to where Ridler had left a horse tethered. They both mounted the animal and Ridler rode off along the narrow lane to Bossington beach. It was late and there was little light from either stars or moon. The lane petered out into little more than a mud path and Ridler rode carefully for there were steep ditches to either side. Eventually, they came to the long pebble beach that stretched from Hurlston point in the East, to Porlock Weir in the West. Ridler and Chesney picked up a small rowing boat from beside the derelict limekilns and dragged it down the steeply sloping pebble breakwater to the water's edge. Chesney got in first and Ridler pushed the tiny boat out into the gently breaking waves. At first, progress was slow, then Ridler managed to get the boat past the ebb and flow of the beach.

Chesney talked constantly, nervously making plans for what he would do. Ridler said nothing.

After Nance had rowed for some minutes, Chesney realised that he could see neither the coast of Somerset nor Wales. 'How long will it take Nance,' asked Chesney, not sure how wide the channel must be at this point, for Ridler's Dublin boat was supposedly berthed at Barry Docks.

'To get where you're going? No more than a few minutes I shouldn't think!'

Chesney did not see the quick movement; instead, he felt the boat sway and heard the oars rattle loose in the rowlocks. Next moment, a searing agony filled his bowels. He reached out instinctively to grasp his stomach and as he did so, Nance's knife cut deep into his hand as he withdrew the blade from Chesney's gut. He drove the blade home again. It plunged into Chesney's belly to the hilt.

Chesney felt his blood pouring from the wounds - wounds so large, his intestines pushed through the breech as he tried to hold them back with his hands.

As though in slow motion, he felt Ridler lashing his feet together with rope and felt something hard touch his legs; he felt Ridler snatching the envelope of money from his inside pocket. Next moment there was a splash and his legs were drawn to the side of the boat by some invisible force. Chesney fought for his life as Ridler struggled in the rocking, pitching boat, to lift Chesney's body over the side. Chesney grabbed Ridler's hair between his fingers and pulled for all he was worth until a heavy fist hit him hard in the face. Again and again, Ridler punched him until Chesney had to let go. With one final heave, Ridler pushed him over the side.

Chesney drew a deep breath, but in an instant his nose and mouth filled with water and he felt his body falling through the depths. His lungs filled with water and it was no longer possible to contract them. Chesney didn't want to drown; he tried to find air to breathe, but there was none to be had in this cold, black world, through which he slid inexorably downward.

The pain in his belly was agonising. He felt his feet come to rest upon the silt of the Bristol Channel and tried desperately to draw himself upward to the surface, but his body would not rise against the pull of the anchor tied to his feet.

CHAPTER 44

The Copper

Molly drew back the curtain, at the sound of a horse in the yard. She strained her eyes to see who it might be, but the night was dark and the yard too full of shadows.

For some reason, Nance departed on foot that morning, without a word about where he was going, or what he was doing. He'd left the pony and trap in the stable and it had worried her all day. As the clock ticked into the small hours, she'd gone to bed, but couldn't sleep. Jack was no help, for when she'd asked him about Nance, he said it wasn't a woman's place to be mindful of her husband's business.

Molly thought of the weeping solicitor, so brutally beaten in the parlour only the day before and knew it was in some way related to Nance's disappearance; she'd been expecting Robinson to call at any time. This new development only added to her worry, for if it wasn't Nance, who could it be so late at night?

She thought it might be one of his "business associates" as he liked to call them, rough, unpleasant looking men, who spoke little and called late. They would disappear into the parlour with the brothers to drink and talk. Their business done, they would leave as silently as they came.

Molly had always known of their business interests, but told herself there was no sin in it; it was only stealing from the excise after all. When all was said and done, what had the government ever done for anyone on Exmoor save send them off to war? All she worried about was that one day it might land Nance in trouble. For all he was wild and unpredictable, she loved him; she feared him it was true, but still she loved him.

Nance opened the washhouse door as quietly as he could and slipped inside. It was in darkness, but for a dull glow about the cast iron door of the boiler. He lifted the latch with the toe of his boot, to find the fire had died to its last embers. He poked them back to life and threw more logs upon them; then he lifted the bleach-white wooden lid of the copper and bailed out a bucket of hot water. He stripped naked and plunging his hands into the bucket to wash Chesney's blood from his face and arms; that done, he picked up his breeches and stuffed them into the tiny grate. A stale, musty smell like burning hair filled the room. Nance reached down for the blood soaked shirt when the door opened without warning; Molly stood before him a candle held high.

'Jesus, Moll,' said Nance, 'what are you doing creeping about at this time of night?'

'I'm sorry Nance, I was worried about you. I thought something had happened - it's so late, I, I...' Her voice petered out as the breeches burst into flame and filled the outhouse with a flickering yellow glow that illuminated his nakedness and the blood soaked shirt in his hands.

For a moment neither spoke.

'It's not what you think, Moll,' said Ridler as he thrust the shirt into the grate; 'nowt's happened!'

Molly wanted to speak, but fear at what was happening to their lives churned her stomach and she felt sick.

'Moll' said Nance his voice softening, 'go an' get us a shirt an' breeches there's a good lass; there's bin' a bit of a scuffle; you know how it is sometimes; it's nowt to fret about.'

'Are you all right Nance?'

'Of course I'm all right! Some bugger said I owed un money, that was all. It was all 'is own doing; I bloodied his nose fer un, an' that was that. He'll be right as rain come the morning.'

Molly looked down at the blood soaked shirt on the flagstone floor. 'There's so much of it Nance,' she said, the tremble in her voice giving her disbelief away.

'What's this,' said Nance, his temper flaring, 'Are you calling us a liar? Me own bloody wife checkin' up on us; snooping about the house; calling us a liar!'

'No Nance, I wasn't, I was worried that was all. I've been worried all day; I thought...'

'Well don't think! Don't fuckin' think Molly! If I wanted someone as could think, I'd ave married the fuckin' horse! Now get an' do as I say; an' get me my bloody clobber.'

A tearful Molly climbed the stairs to their bedroom. She picked up a pair of breeches from the footboard, and a shirt from a drawer - her mind in turmoil. There had been so much blood on the shirt, far too much for nosebleed. She recalled how vicious Nance had been with Cripps, and couldn't stop her hands from trembling.

Nance knelt before the fire, his face a twisted caricature in the glow cast by the burning clothing. With the rushing flames, went the last real evidence to link

307

him with Cripps' death. Soon he'd leave for Minehead and return the horse to the Kings Head from whence it came. Sykes would say nothing for Nance knew far too much about Harry Sykes! Tomorrow, he'd walk the five miles home from the King's Head for all to see and no one could prove a thing; they'd all be looking for Chesney anyway.

He smiled at how easy it had been to dupe them, the spineless solicitor and the gullible Chesney.

'Bloody Faggots,' whispered Nance beneath his breath.

The warmth of the burning clothes was soothing; he felt the tension of the last few hours melting away and just the exhilaration was left. Molly returned and gave the clean clothing to him.

I've got to go out again" said Ridler; 'I'll be back in the mornin. If anyone asks you where I was today, you tell um drinkin' in the King's Head in Minehead - you got that?'

'Yes Nance.'

'Good!'

Ridler looked at his wife as she stood in just her nightgown. 'You're a good wife Molly,' he said, 'loyal, like a wife ought t' be.'

'Nance I...'

'Come over ere.'

'Please Nance I...'

'Do as I tell yuh, come over ere.'

Molly hesitated then did as she was bid. She could hardly see Nance now; he was hidden in the shadows at the far end of the washhouse.

'Stop there.' said Nance.

He could see her body, silhouetted in the fire's glow. Through the thinness of her nightie, he saw the heaviness of her breasts and the spread of her backside. She was a big woman, but he liked that - a man had to keep himself warm at night. He could see the swell of her thighs, near touching one another across the feminine mound between. He felt himself harden and unbuttoned his flies.

'Lift your nightdress Moll,' he said urgently.

'Please Nance, not here,' pleaded Molly.

'Do as I bloody say - why are you always arguing with us?'

Slowly, reluctantly, she lifted her nightdress above her breasts.

'Get back where I can see you!'

She walked backwards until the glow of the fire fell fully across her body.

'Go on then Moll,' gasped Ridler, his excitement rising.

Slowly she put her fingers between her legs. Nance could only see her breasts and sagging belly, not the tears that filled her eyes. She heard him moan softly in the darkness.

CHAPTER 45

D.S Woods

Woods and Robinson stepped carefully from stone to stone. Although the brook was only inches deep, neither wanted a boot full of water. The heavy iron wheel turned with patient indifference, spewing its liquid power into the shallow stream that separated Ridler's Mill from Selworthy lane; each crystal bucketful the same as the last.

They entered the open sack room, and everywhere they looked, there was flour dust. It covered ledges and sills, ceilings and stairs alike. Only the handrails and centre of the heavily worn treads were free of it. Dusty cobwebs, long abandoned, hung heavy in the darkened recesses of the room. It looked like a Christmas snow-scene, long forgotten in a dusty attic.

Above them, the steady rumble of millstones all but drowned the busy chatter of hazelwood teeth, as wooden gears meshed relentlessly.

'What'd you want,' said a hostile voice from above.

'Just a word Nance,' replied Robinson.

'What about?'

'This is D.S. Woods from Minehead. He's come to pay us a visit,' said Robinson, not prepared to be rushed.

'I couldn't give a shit if e's Father Christmas,' said Nance descending the stairs, 'what d' you want,'

'Firstly we'd like you to be mindful of your language Mr Ridler, and secondly we'd like to know where you were last night,' said Woods coming straight to the point. He'd no time for Robinsons famous cat and mouse tactics today, and anyway; that was unlikely to get them anywhere with this fellow.

'I weren't in bloody Porlock, if that's what you're thinkin,' said Nance.

'Why should we think you were in Porlock?'

'Don't come the clever bugger we me,' replied Nance. 'The whole bloody county knows what's 'appened to Cripps. You want's to tell your sister to keep 'er bloody mouth shut if you wants' to keep secrets around 'ere, Robinson! You're all too busy mindin' other people's business in your family,'

Woods gave Robinson a none too appreciative glance, then returned his attention to Ridler.

'So if you weren't in Porlock, where were you?'

'At the King's Head in Minehead playing cards. I never left there all night an' I've got witnesses to prove it,'

'And who might those witnesses be?

'Ginny Roberts, David Grimes and Harry Sykes,'

Woods gave a wry smile. 'Pillars of Minehead society and paragons all,' he said.

'I ain't got time fer all this bloody rubbish,' snapped Nance. 'If you got summut to say, say it now an' be on yer way - I got work to do!'

'Keep a civil tongue in your head, Nance,' cautioned Robinson.

'I don't have to. If you two ain't got no more to say, get off my bloody property.' With that, he turned on his heel and climbed the stair.

Woods and Robinson stood outside the Mill once more. 'So that's your man then?' said Woods.

'It is fer my money.'

'You might be right.'

'Why do you say that?' said Robinson, turning to look at his superior.

'His boots,' said Woods.

'What about them?'

'How many pairs of boots have you got, Harry?'

'Just the one,' came Robinson's reply.

'Precisely,' continued Woods, 'and so, I suspect, does Nance Ridler. Whoever murdered Cripps - if murder it was - would be covered in blood. He could wash his clothes or get rid of em, but he'd need to clean his boots.'

Robinson looked at Woods with new respect. 'And Ridler had clean boots?'

'They were the only things in that mill not covered in dust,'

'Do you want to bring him in?'

'Let's not show him our hand just yet. Anyway, we can't hang the bastard for having clean boots, much though I'd like to.'

'What about his alibi?'

311

'I'll get it checked out, but it won't change my opinion of things; especially with Roberts, Grimes and Sykes providing the alibi; they've all been customers in their time.'

After a moment, Woods spoke again. 'Cripps was left handed, but it was his left wrist that was slashed and that says murder to me. Question is, how many were involved, one, two, more perhaps? For my money your man's one of em, but then there's this other character supping ale in the Royal Oak! Let's see if his description fits Edie's description of this Chesney fellow and in the mean time, we'll let our friend sweat about things for a while!'

CHAPTER 46

Dragnet

It is curious how the finger of fortune, can tilt the hand of destiny. It takes but a split second for the hunters shot to reach its target, yet their paths must still cross together. Life lies on one side of time - death and oblivion upon the other. So it was that just five minutes were enough to separate a lifetime's happiness from a lifetime's sorrow.

Robinson had risen earlier than usual, for Woods had chosen to stay at the police house rather than return to Minehead, and no doubt he'd be expecting hot water in the washstand and porridge on the table. All this extra work was bad enough, but to have Woods into the bargain was an upset he could do without!

Woods was looking the worse for a late night, when Arthur Baker knocked on Robinson's door.

'What's up,' asked Robinson of his perspiring constable.

'They've found a boat up Bossington beach; it's all covered in blood!' replied a breathless Baker.

The three policemen left the police house at a run, all thoughts of porridge behind them. Just five minutes later, the postman delivered Cripps' letter.

Woods looked carefully over every inch of the boat. There were bloodstains on the thwartships seat and the starboard bulwark. The water in the bilge was dark brown and had an odd, fetid smell about it.

'Is this where it was found?' asked Woods.

'Yes,' replied Baker.

'Who does it belong to?'

Woods was introduced to Jack Norris, who owned the tiny boat. Norris had left the boat a mile away near the limekilns and had no idea how long it had been missing from its usual place.

Within hours the discovery of a bloodstained boat was common knowledge, and it didn't take much imagination to link this sinister discovery with the untimely death of Reg Cripps. Stories abounded, some wildly inaccurate, other not a million miles from the truth, but all growing more elaborate and fanciful with each passing hour.

313

Woods had the scent in his nostrils now. He walked a brisk two miles to Porlock Weir with the portly Robinson puffing behind him. He wanted to speak to Jack Prideaux, whom Robinson assured him, was the man to talk to about tides in the channel.

He put a tricky problem to Prideaux that Prideaux didn't want to answer. Woods, however, was insistent. Prideaux umm'd and ahh'd over the impossible question, for there were too many if's and but's for his liking. Woods tried flattery and persuasion to no avail, then finally settled on threats of obstruction and having "something to hide."

This had the desired effect, and Prideaux finally gave Woods an answer to his question of... "How far out might a fit man row Norris's boat - at midnight on the night Cripps died - for it to drift one mile along Bossington beach in the process.

The good folk of Bossington, Selworthy and Porlock, stood patiently on Hurlston Point, where they had a perfect view of the police operation off the beach below. Woods had brought in the steam launch Pandora and now sat upon its polished deck in his overcoat and bowler hat. He smoked his pipe and watched the men with nets and grapples go about their work.

The atmosphere on Hurlstone Point was almost carnival. There was a mixture of excitement and awe at the goings on. Curious men and women came and went throughout the day, each speculating on what the police might be looking for. At times, there might have been thirty to forty folk on The Point or about the Coastguard Station; some saying they sought the weapon that murdered Cripps, others that they sought the murderers clothing weighed down by stones. All was speculation, except for the thoughts of one man who alone knew their true quest. Nance said nothing, barely acknowledging anyone else; his lips were set in a thin, grim line for it was not going at all as planned. He watched and wondered how much Robinson and Woods already knew.

The men in the boat heaved and hauled on the net for the seventeenth time that day. So far, they'd been rewarded with nothing. This time, however, there was something wrapped about the shiny metal hooks of the grappling net. It was bluish pink, bulbous and swollen, like the intestines of an animal; the tails of the impaled loop stretched over the side of the police launch, and back into the Bristol Channel from where they had so recently emerged. Woods leapt to his feet and called for the Police Doctor. The stricken man emerged from the tiny cabin where he had been suffering from seasickness brought on by the relentless rocking of the tiny police launch.

'What is it?' said the detective.

314

'Part of the gut; the large intestine by the look of it,' came the doctors reply.

'Human?'

'Maybe; it's hard to say!'

'Get those divers booted and spurred whilst there's still some light!' snapped Woods.

The two police divers donned the heavy brass helmets. Other men screwed home the turnbuckles and placed the heavy diving weights about their waists. Two more men turned the heavy wheels of the air pump that croaked and wheezed like a bullfrog. The leather accumulators rose and fell as they tried to match their speed to the breathing of the men.

They followed their gruesome discovery down into the depths of the Bristol Channel until they found what they were looking for. Chesney floated as though on tiptoe, some six feet above the seabed - his arms outstretched like Christ crucified. His feet were together; tethered to a heavy anchor that held him down. His bloated intestines emerged from the gaping wound like an umbilical cord.

Chesney looked straight at the divers with sightless eyes. 'You're too late,' they seemed to say. He swayed slightly as they trod water with their flippers. Tiny crabs and other scavengers swam or crawled from his mouth and gut, the movement having disturbed their feeding.

Ridler watched in silence as the body was lifted aboard the tiny steam packet. He'd not expected this and couldn't understand how it had gone so wrong, so quickly. Soon Woods and Robinson would call again, with questions ever more difficult to answer. Now they'd found Chesney; they'd know there were two men involved and he was already on their list of suspects. Ridler felt danger closing in. It had all seemed so foolproof and now it was falling apart. He turned and began to run along the beacon to Selworthy and home.

When Woods and Robinson finally returned to the police house, it was late and they were exhausted. Robinson would have left the mail unopened, but the franking on the envelope caught his eye. It was from Francillon, Cripps and Cranway.

Inside the envelope was a will in the name of Ira Grace, leaving Leathernbottle Cottage and adjoining smithy to one Isaac Smith, and this was accompanied by a handwritten letter. Robinson read the letter grim faced and passed it to his superior. Woods read Cripps damning admission in disbelieve at his good fortune, for it confessed his complicity in a fraudulent will, and his fear of Nance Ridler who had blackmailed him into writing it. It confirmed that the

315

will enclosed, was the true last will and testament of Ira Grace, and that he committed it to Robinson's safekeeping so that he could see justice done.

Woods slapped the letter on the table and rose to his feet saying to Robinson; 'You were right Harry; let's go get the bastard!'

Woods, Robinson, and five deputies harnessed the Black Maria to the dapple mare. Within a quarter of an hour, they were on their way to arrest Nance Ridler for blackmail, theft and murder, but when they arrived at the mill, the bird had already flown the coop.

CHAPTER 47

On the Run

When Nance realised the game was up, he raced along the Beacon and through the woods until he reached the mill, stumbling often, on the steep and leaf-strewn path.

He rushed into the parlour, brushing Molly aside in his haste. From beneath a loose board in their bedroom, he took a revolver and a large brown parcel. A distraught Molly pleaded with him to tell her what was going on, shocked at the sight of the revolver in his hand.

'They're after me, Moll. Some buggers murdered Cripps and they want to pin it on me. I've got to get away or tis all over for us. You stay put an' don't tell um nothing d' you hear me; don't tell um nothin'. I'll come back for you when it's all died down - don't you fret.'

Molly was in tears, pleading with Nance to tell her more, but he wasn't listening. He grabbed a few small items and seconds later he was making for the door. 'Tell Jack to get rid of the stuff,' he shouted over his shoulder, and the door slammed shut behind him. He retraced his steps back up the wooded path to the Beacon.

He guessed rightly, that Woods would bring in the dogs when he found him gone. He half walked, half ran, the five miles from Selworthy to Minehead, along the lonely Beacon path; then when he reached Minehead, he took a chance, and walked openly through the town to the station, where he bought a single ticket to Bristol. Twenty minutes later he was on the six-fifteen service to Bristol via Bishops Lydeard. With luck that would mean the end of the trail for the dogs.

Nance made his way to the rear of the train. He waited for it to slow for the Dunster halt, some two miles from Minehead. He leapt into the darkness, landing heavily and twisting his ankle, but at least he'd broken no bones and was able to walk on. He climbed the fence that separated the track from the pastureland surrounding the medieval castle of Dunster, its craggy, weather-beaten walls, looking down on the tiny market town that bore its name, from the summit of a wooded tor.

Nance walked to the east of Dunster; then on a further ten miles toward Tiverton, until his ankle would take him no further. His efforts had taken him as far as Timberscombe, but his ankle told him that he'd be unable to move the following day.

317

He'd neither plan nor place to run to, and it was only the peculiarities of the landscape that drove him south down the valley. He slept that night in a cattle byre, some half mile to the east of the Dunster to Tiverton road, and cursed his ill fortune as he bathed his swollen ankle in a cattle trough.

The night grew cold and Nance realised how poorly equipped he was for this desperate game of survival. He drew a bed of stinking straw about him, and slept a fitful sleep. The next morning, almost as soon as it grew light, he was awakened by the sound of traffic on the road below; not the usual cattle and farm carts, but a horse drawn police van. As Nance watched, it drew to a halt and two policemen in helmets and black tunics stepped down. One had a dog with him and both had guns. Almost immediately, the van moved on.

The cattle byre was high up on the open field overlooking the road. If he moved, he would be seen in an instant and that would be the end for him, but his ankle was so badly swollen he could no longer put his weight on it, so he was obliged to stay where he was. Whatever was about to happen, would happen there in the cattle byre.

He opened the breach of the revolver and counted the bullets. One for the dog, two for the coppers, and one for himself seemed to be the way of it, for he'd rather a bullet than the gallows.

Hours went by where nothing happening. The two policemen and the dog stayed exactly where they were, whilst Nance lay within the cattle byre - gun in hand. He couldn't understand what was going on for the coppers were content to stand and talk and seemed almost bored. Occasionally they would sweep the hillside through binoculars, but mostly they stood and talked.

As mid morning approached, all became clear, for over the brow of the opposite hill, men appeared - walking slowly, fifty feet apart. Some were police, some were soldiers, and most were armed. The unarmed men had dogs and it was clear that Woods was sweeping Dunkery Beacon in his manhunt.

The line of men disappeared into a belt of trees, whilst the two policemen on the road trained their rifles on the open pastureland between the road and the tree line, waiting for their quarry to be flushed into open ground.

The man hunters emerged from the trees to join their colleagues on the road where they gathered in a large group. Nance's ankle was too painful for him to run, so he resigned himself to waiting until they discovered his hiding place. He'd take as many of them with him as he could, before blowing his own brains out.

Others joined them from the direction of Tiverton, but instead of beginning their sweep on Nance's side as he expected, they waited on the road for the police van, which appeared some minutes later. A man stepped down wearing an overcoat and a bowler hat. Nance recognised Woods immediately. He spoke to his men then got back into the van once more. Soon they all moved off in the direction of Dunster, leaving Nance to count his blessings. He'd chosen shelter to the left of the road, but had he chosen the right, he'd be in police custody or more likely, lying dead in a pool of his own blood by now. Either way amounted to the same thing and even if they took him alive, they'd only fix him up good enough for the hangman to do his work. Nance had cheated the rope twice now and he wondered how long his luck could last. He closed his eyes and sank back into the filthy straw; exhausted and bathed in sweat despite the cold.

He began to consider his next move. He couldn't walk; therefore this place would have to do for the time being. Now the police had gone, it was as quiet and lonely as he could wish for, but he couldn't stay there forever; sooner or later, a cowman would come. After two days and nights, Nance was stinking and desperately hungry. Even the water in the trough was filthy, and alive with tiny creatures.

Woods had been obliged to end his manhunt somewhere, and he'd chosen the Tiverton Road as his South East boundary. He'd swept Exmoor, some twenty mile inland of the coast without avail, using all the resources he could muster, for he couldn't ignore the possibility that Nance was still on his home turf, but he personally believed Nance had made good his escape on the train.

The ticket clerk was adamant that Nance had boarded the 6.15 at much the same time that Woods and Robinson had knocked on his door. What Woods didn't believe, however, was that Nance had travelled all the way to Bristol, for not one witness could be found that had seen him on the Bristol train, or saw him changing trains at the Bishops Lydeard junction.

He favoured the busy port of Watchet for Nance's debunk, for there were fishing boats and cargo ships in and out with every tide, but Woods' hunch was to lead him many miles off course. As he searched the railway line and villages to the east of Dunster, so Nance set out west to cross the remote moorland that would take him back to Exmoor and the only place he thought he might be able to escape the law.

He travelled by night and only by night. He let the moon guide him west until he found himself in familiar country once more. He stood on the summit of Dunkery Beacon on a cold, wet, winter's evening, and looked down across the valley to Selworthy Beacon and the scattered lights of Selworthy and East Lynch.

Hatred and anger rose in him, like bile in the throat. Selworthy was his home; he'd never lived anywhere else, now he could never go back there. His twisted, embittered mind, reasoned that his predicament was Isaac Smith's fault, for if he'd not come to Selworthy, none of this would have happened. He'd robbed him over the Nicolette and robbed Molly over Leathernbottle. As the night grew older and all honest men were abed, he made a vow. If he were to live long enough, he would come back, then they would see.

Nance had known all along that he couldn't stay on the run forever, for sooner or later he'd be seen and caught. His only real chance was a boat out of England, but that would be difficult, for Woods would surely be watching the docks. Instead he made alternative plans that would take him west of Porlock and Lynmouth and on toward Ilfracombe.

Once beyond Culbone, the going became much harder as he crossed the desolate, wind-swept moors and precipitous wooded valleys of Lorna Doone fame. Because he could only travel by night, one false step in the darkness could see him slip and tumble hundreds of feet to his death.

Ridler was in desperate danger with every moment that passed, but the lonely moors and steep wooded hills of Exmoor were now his best friends. But for a few shepherds, very few people lived in that lonely, bleak place.

His only food had been turnips from a clamp and a chicken he'd killed and eaten raw. Progress by night was hard and slow, for the hills were agonisingly steep to climb and dangerously slippery to descend. However, on a cold, wet night in late December, six miles on from Lynmouth in North Devon, and after two full weeks on the run, Nance looked down upon his goal from the shelter of a fir tree.

Below him at the bottom of a railway embankment, were the smoking chimney pots, haphazard caravans and ramshackle, corrugated iron sheds, of a navvy encampment, all standing in a quagmire of mud and timber duckboards like some Wild West mining town.

Nance could smell wood fires and food, and could hear a fiddler playing an Irish reel in the hut below. A dull light could be seen through curtains made of sacking, nailed tight to the window frames to keep out drafts and prying eyes.

He watched the camp for some time as he weighed up the risks of going further, but his situation was desperate either way. If he stayed on the run then sooner or later he'd be caught; but if he walked into the camp and the navvies realised who he was, then the chances were they'd turn him in to the law, for there might well be a price on his head by now.

Nance thought of Cripps, and how he'd danced a jig as the rope grew tighter, his blood pumping from his wrist like a slaughtered pig. Once he'd enjoyed that memory, now it sent a shiver down his spine.

There was little shelter to be had beneath the fir, for, like him, the branches were sodden through with days of cold, relentless rain. It ran sour smelling, down the dense needles, dripping on him from the very deepest branches.

Since dusk, the temperature had fallen fast, and there was sleet amongst the rain. Bleak at the best of times, the lonely moors of Exmore would kill him just as surely as the hangman if snow came, for many a hardy sheep or pony had been lost to exposure, or tumbled to their death over a steep drop.

He made his decision and touched the revolver in his pocket for reassurance. If needs be, he had Cripps money with which to bargain for his life. At that moment, he heard a faint sound like the cracking of a twig.

'Make a move friend and I'll slit your throat,' whispered a voice behind him. The sharp blade of a knife drew Nance's neck firmly backwards against the trunk of the tree.

CHAPTER 48

Home

Dawn drew back the mantle of night, as, with a flourish, an artist draws the covers from his masterpiece, his work of art complete. With a cloak of virgin snow, nature transformed Selworthy Beacon from the ashen grey of December, to the beauty and crispness of deep mid winter.

Selworthy huddled beneath the apron of trees like a bird with its head beneath its wing. Each branch and bough, sighed with the weight of snow that bore it down and many cracked and fell amid powdery showers, their wooden arms frail and brittle like the bones of old men.

Fingertips rubbed at frosted glass and eyes squinted through icy smears. Farmers cursed beneath their breath, children shrieked with excitement, old folk watched the falling snowflakes with silent dread, whilst sheep and cattle called to their masters, frightened and forlorn.

Gritting his teeth, Isaac slid from the sheets as naked as the day he was born, and snatched up his clothing from the footboard, whilst drawing his breath in short shuddering gasps. Polly slept on beneath the huge feather eiderdown she'd drawn about her like a womb.

He heard Amy stir in the room beyond. She too would soon be up and about, and the day would start anew.

Isaac was looking forward to his day's work, for the smithy would be warmer than the house, and quite probably the warmest place in Selworthy. McNab would likely appear once he'd seen to his livestock, and others had been calling recently to congratulate him on getting the better of Nance Ridler. Isaac thought it would be time enough to celebrate when Nance was hung for his crimes.

When he drew back the bedroom curtain, the world outside looked as though some unseen hand had snatched the view from their window and replaced it with another, for every familiar feature was lost beneath a thick blanket of snow. The garden, the hawthorn hedge, the jumble of machinery outside the smithy and even the lane itself, had entirely disappeared.

Perhaps it would be a quiet day after all. If anyone ventured by, it was likely to be McNab, begging help with his livestock as he'd done the previous year, for many of his sheep had been caught in drifts, or snagged on unseen wire.

He took one last glance at Polly as she lay sleeping, each slow breath freezing with the coldness of the room. He thought of how warm and how near her body had been; how tender their words as they fell asleep, how much he loved her.

The two weeks since Cripps' murder were the happiest since Rebecca's death. Thanks to Cripps' letter to Sergeant Robinson, they were assured of the smithy and all they had worked so hard for, for Cripps had laid bare Nance's plans for blackmail and fraud. A mantle of darkness had been lifted from their lives and it had purpose and direction once more.

When first they knew the will would stand, Isaac danced a jig with a bewildered Bert, who nonetheless wagged his tail in the spirit of things. Isaac let go the dog's paws and threw his arms about Polly until she cried for breath, tears of joy in her eyes.

'There you are,' he said; 'what did I tell you!'

'I don't recall you telling me anything, except that Ira was a crooked old b'...!

'I'll tell you what I'm going to do love,' he said. 'I'm going to find McNab and take him for a couple of pints - to celebrate!'

Polly glanced at Amy and raised her eyes to heaven. It was not like Isaac to show his emotions and even less to think of drinking during the day, but this was no ordinary day and she wouldn't deny him a little celebration after he'd worked so hard for it.

Slipping her hand through his arm, she said 'Come along then, Mr Nothing Better To Do! Let's give him the good news together.'

As Isaac turned into the rutted lane for East Lynch, Polly said, 'Isaac, there's something we must do before you go drinking with McNab, something more important!' She turned him into the lower graveyard and walked him to Ira's grave.

The soil was beginning to settle and someone had already begun to tidy the topsoil and plant some winter flowers. Isaac wondered who on earth that person could possibly be; quite sure it would not be Molly. He realised there could be but one person and she stood at the foot of Ira's grave whispering a silent prayer.

Polly looked up at Isaac and smiled, her eyes bright with happiness. She came to him and threaded her hand through his arm.

'I just couldn't believe he could be so unkind,' she said, 'your friendship meant so much to him.'

323

'What did you say to him?'

'Just then?'

'Yes.'

'I just said thank you from both of us.'

He smiled and thought how beautiful she was, not just her physical beauty, but deep down within her soul.

'Come on lass,' he said quietly, 'let's take ourselves home.'

'I thought you wanted to go drinking with McNab,' she said, surprised at the sudden change of heart.

'I can do that another day; this is our day - let's spend it together.'

She looked up at him and smiled, gripping his arm even harder. 'Then let's walk the Beacon,' she said.

They walked high above the Bristol Channel, a chill wind - the forerunner of the snow to come - making the grass shimmer like silk. They walked for hours yet it seemed like minutes. They talked of everything, yet it seemed they'd talked of nothing, for there were so many things left to say.

That night, amid the click and clack of Amy's needles, there was a conspiracy of smile and glance to be together as soon as they could. Later they lay naked in one another's arms, Isaac's fingers caressing her; kissing her eyes, kissing her lips, gently at first, then with increasing urgency and passion.

She felt him pressing against the softness of her belly and reached down for him; drawing in her breath at the thrill of touching him. He moaned softly and she kissed him tenderly, just as the floorboards creaked in the room beyond their own. She took her hand away, but Isaac put it back once more.

'No Isaac, she whispered softly, Amy's still awake.'

He tried once more, but she pulled away from him, half pleased; half annoyed with his persistence, 'No Isaac- not yet! We will make too much noise; she will hear us!'

'It might bring back some happy memories!'

'Don't be so smutty, she chided; 'you know I don't like you talking like that.'

'You're getting too alike, you two,' he remarked.

It seemed that Amy's floorboards would never stop creaking. 'What on earth is she doing?' he whispered, for usually she'd be asleep within moments. He tried to touch her again.

'Will you stop it Isaac,' she hissed angrily.

'You were happy enough just now!'

'Well I'm not anymore!'

'I won't understand women so long as I live and that's a fact,' he replied in exasperation.

'No, I don't suppose you will, and that's because you're a man, and I don't think men are very bright if truth be told.'

'He grunted in disgust.

'Lay still my darling,' she whispered softly, drawing his face to her bosom, stroking and kissing his hair. 'She will be asleep soon,' she added. 'I'm loud Isaac, you know I'm loud.'

And so they talked. They talked of the many things that had happened in their lives; their joys and their sorrows, and as usual, they talked of Rebecca.

'I pray for her each day,' she whispered, 'and I ask that He blesses us with another child and that He will look after Becky until we see her again.'

'Why take her in the first place,' said Isaac cynically, 'what use has He for a child of eight? What use has He for any child? What use has He for our Becky?'

His words cut her soul like a knife. She turned away from him and immediately he regretted his cruel stupidity.

He touched her shoulder, 'I'm sorry, he said, I shouldn't have said that.'

It was a while before she spoke. When she did, her voice was just a whisper.

'I can't turn my back on what I believe Isaac - even through all this. I know you think I'm foolish; I know you don't believe in God, but don't you see it is all I have. The thought that my darling lies cold, and frightened, and alone in her grave, and that I might never see her again, is more than my heart can bear. I have to believe that He is watching over us and cares about us, or my heart will break in two.'

Isaac heard the tremor in her voice and hated himself for having hurt her so.

'Do you think we've been punished for our wickedness?' she continued.

'What wickedness?'

'That we did what we did, and had to wed for her sake?'

'There was nothing wicked about my love for you Polly, nor your love for me. There was no shame in our love that I could see. And if I loved you in that way, it was because He made me love you in that way, I just didn't have a choice. I think if you love someone enough, the rules don't apply, because you are how He's made you, and I shall tell him so when we meet at the pearly gates.'

'Well don't argue with him, or he won't let you in and then where will we be!'

'We will always be together Polly, I promise you that, for there would be no point to heaven without you. If I go first, I will come to you in your dreams and if you go first, then you must come to me! Perhaps you won't see me there when you dream of me, but I will always be there beside you. If God can love you; and always be beside you, then so can I.'

'Do you really mean that?'

'Of course I do!'

She kissed him tenderly; 'That is why I love you so very much,' she whispered.

He kissed her in return.

'I think it's gone quiet next door,' she said softly.

'And what about you know who? Is He still watching us?'

'Of course He is.'

'Hmmph!' said Isaac, reaching out to the bedside table. 'Best I put this candle out then!'

CHAPTER 49

The Navigators

The man with the gutting knife at Ridler's throat gave a low call like a night creature, and almost instantly, others appeared from the darkness.

They forced Nance to clamber down the steep, slippery embankment, the sharp edge of the knife pressed hard against his windpipe, one slip spelling the end of his life.

Other joined them as they reached the duckboard, and he felt the cold steel of a revolver press against his neck.

The knife man rapped the door of the large hut, and a voice spoke from within. 'Who's there,' asked the voice? 'Jacko,' came the reply. The door swung open and Nance was pushed into the room. It was stuffy with the heat from a pot bellied stove and the stale sweat of many people. The fiddler stopped fiddling and the room fell deathly silent. All eyes turned to the stranger in their midst.

There were perhaps a hundred men, women, and children there; most sat in a broad fan about the stove which glowed a dull red in the dim light. In the centre of the group was a large cauldron from which came wisps of steam and the rich smell of stew. Hanging from a rafter was a single Tilley Lamp, which cast a dim yellow glow over the gathering.

Though low, the hut was very long. At its end was a bunk with heavy curtains that could be drawn closed; upon the bed sat a solemn faced woman, suckling a child at her breast.

Sat at the furthest point of the circle from Nance was a giant of a man. He was striking in appearance, with blond, shoulder length hair. His face was fine-boned and handsome, with a moustache and goatee beard that reminded Ridler of a print he'd seen of Guy Fawkes and his ill-fated companions conspiring over supper. However, it was his eyes that truly caught the attention; piercing blue, they watched Nance with a steady, unblinking gaze.

Although he was big, he was tall with it; maybe six feet eight inches in height, but he was made to look even bigger by a heavy fur coat which he wore despite the heat of the room. Nance felt more than saw the eyes that watched him, for a wide brimmed hat cast the man's face in shadow. They watched Ridler as a cat might watch a mouse.

He motioned Nance to sit near the cauldron and within the circle, which closed in behind him, hampering his escape route.

'You look hungry friend; help yourself to some food!'

The same man who'd held the knife to his throat passed him a plate. He was a thin, lank haired fellow, with the sharp, pinched features of a rat. Ridler took the plate and helped himself to a generous amount from the cauldron. He sat cross-legged and ate, grateful for the warmth and nourishment it gave him.

Ridler was surprised at the big man's voice. He expected a deep powerful voice for such a giant of a man, but it was quiet with a soft Irish lilt. Ridler took a second, and then a third helping, and while he did so, the fiddler took up his tune once more.

Ridler handed the plate back to the rat faced man and wiped his mouth on his sleeve. 'Thanks,' he said.

'You ate well,' said the big man.

'I was hungry.'

'Sure you'd need to be hungry to eat three bowls of Brendan's stew,' remarked someone close by. Others laughed at the expense of the unidentified Brendan.

'Ah, tis wonderful stuff Brendan' said another; don't be mindful of O'Riorden's talk. Afore I met you, I'd be five days between shite's, and now I'm shitting all the time.'

Laughter rippled about the gathering and they began talking amongst themselves once more, their interest in the stranger waning.

'Tis a recipe thee'll take to the grave Brendan,' said another above the hubbub; for I can't see anyone stealing it!'

'Jesus, don't say that,' replied O'Riorden; 'I'll be having the shits in heaven as well!'

'St Peter don't take murderers, O'Riorden,' said Brendan quietly. His comment revealed him to be a small man with a withered arm.

'You shut your big mouth Brendan, or I'll shut it for you,' replied O'Riorden, rising to his feet.

'I'm trying to talk...!' said the big man angrily raising his voice above the clatter. It subsided almost immediately. O'Riorden sat down, glowering at Brendan.

'What's your name friend?' said the big man when peace was restored.

'Edward Gibson.'

Pretty nodded, 'Welcome to you then Edward Gibson; my names Daniel Pretty, I'm the ganger here; you've already met my cousin Jacko,' he said, nodding towards the rat faced man who smiled briefly through a row of rotten teeth.

'Why the reception party?' he asked, turning his head in Jacko's direction, deciding to one day wipe the smile from the rat-man's face.

Pretty shrugged, 'There are fifty horses tethered in the cut, and tools and machinery in the store. These are hard times friend, and we can't be too careful. You were lucky Jacko didn't cut your throat.'

Nance turned again to Jacko whose smile became even broader at Pretty's words. He looked as though a bowl of stew would do him no harm, for there was no meat on his bones, but something told Nance to beware the rat faced man who moved through the night so stealthily.

'What's your business friend?' asked Pretty.

'Work if you've a mind! You'll find me a grafter and no complaining.'

'You picked a strange time to look for work!'

'Is there a better time when you're cold and wet?'

'Maybe not, but you took a risk my friend. We don't like strangers creeping about at this time of night.'

'I weren't creeping about,' said Nance; 'I've come straight up from Ilfracombe an' just appened to get 'ere now, that's all. What the problem we that?'

Pretty took a pipe from his pocket and began to draw tobacco from a leather pouch.

'Ilfracombe's a long way off; you must have fallen on hard times?'

Ridler shrugged his shoulders; 'You know how it is.'

'No, I don't.'

'I broke a fellow's head fer robbing us at cards. I took me money an' legged it fast. I don't suppose 'e's any the worse for the scuffle, but I never stopped to ask. There weren't no work there anyway, an' the talk hereabouts is that the navvies is always looking fer good hands.'

'Maybe, but not if they bring the law behind them, we don't need more trouble than we've got.'

'Like I said, 'e probably got now't worse'n a headache. If that's a problem, I'll move on.'

Pretty pressed tobacco deep into the bowl and lit it with a match, which he threw on the floor before him.

'I don't think that would be a good idea,' he said casually, drawing gently on the pipe to get the tobacco burning evenly.

'Why not?' replied Nance, becoming increasingly edgy about so many questions.

Pretty exhaled the tobacco smoke and Ridler could smell the unusual sweetness wafting across the room. Pretty said nothing for quite some time, whilst he considered what he would do with the man who called himself Edward Gibson.

He ran more than three-hundred navvies at this particular work camp, where they were cutting the new Lynton and Lynmouth railway through a pine-wooded hill, to join with a viaduct on the other side. They had blasting gelignite and steam shovels to load the wagons, but most of the work was done by hand and that meant men.

Most were his own family like cousin Jacko, or were other families from their homeland in County Clare, but not all. Others were the riff-raff and flotsam and jetsam of England's underworld. Muggers, bludger's wife beaters, swindlers, abortionists, forgers, even murderers; all were there, lying low amongst the Navigators, trying to stay out of sight of the law.

Their past didn't bother Pretty so long as they worked hard and gave no trouble. The problem was, Pretty didn't believe what Ridler was saying.

'Because you might not be the only one wandering the moor, Mr Edward Gibson of Ilfracombe!' continued Pretty, pushing him a little more. 'Chances are you've been sharing it with the most wanted man in England - a nasty piece of work, or so I'm told! A man called Nance Ridler, perhaps you've heard about him?'

Nance shook his head.

'There's three hundred guineas on his head and I'd say that might go up. It will be a wealthy man that turns him in, wouldn't you say Edward Gibson?'

330

Ridler didn't like the direction the conversation was taking. He felt for the revolver through the material of his coat and moved his hand to his pocket. He curled his fingers slowly about the butt.

'They say he's killed twice.' continued Pretty.

Nance began to draw the revolver from his pocket, bit by tiny bit.

'They say he gutted one man and threw him into the Bristol Channel still alive an' screaming; the other he hung from a rafter, all cut an' slashed to ribbons. Word is he watched him bleed to death like a pig with its throat cut.'

Nance looked about him like a rat in a trap; all conversation had ceased; all eyes were upon him and Pretty. The rat-faced man had a knife in his hand once more.

'He's wanted dead or alive, but I'd say a man like that was as good as dead, wouldn't you, Edward Gibson?'

Ridler drew the gun hoping that if he shot Pretty, the rest would scatter and he could make his escape; but before he'd drawn the revolver from his pocket, Pretty's foot shot out and an instant later he was engulfed in searing, agonising pain. The stew burnt into his eyes, his face, his hands and chest. He felt his body being snatched into the air by an invisible force that threw him bodily backwards. More pain came and Nance screamed in agony. A voice shouted close by; there was a gunshot, then he blacked out.

The moment Nance drew his gun, Pretty had lashed out with his foot, sending the heavy cauldron spinning towards him. It struck Nance as he sat cross-legged on the floor, throwing its boiling contents over him. Before he could even scream, Pretty leapt forwards with the agility of a cat and grabbed him about the neck. Pretty dragged Nance upward and backward and as he did so, the momentum of his enormous twenty-two stone, cut a swath through the navvies like a raging bear through long grass. Pretty kept going until Ridler hit the glowing coke stove. There was a crash as the cast iron chimney smashed to pieces amid a shower of smoke and sparks. Pretty held Ridler over the searing heat of the stove; pressing him down with the full weight of his body; holding his gun arm in a giant fist. The stench of burning flesh and filthy, damp clothing filled the air. Nance's screams were deafening in Pretty's ears, but he didn't relax the iron grasp on his throat until Nance was unconscious. Nance managed to pull the trigger once before the weapon fell to the floor, the stray bullet winging one of the young women in the gathering.

The men in the room surged forward to lend a hand. 'Stand back,' shouted Pretty lashing out with his foot at those who came closest. One man snatched up the revolver and the room relapsed into relative quiet, but for the shrieking of the unfortunate girl, and those doused in the steaming hot stew.

Pretty rifled Nance's pockets until he found the waterproof pouch. He slipped it in a pocket of his own coat, then let Nance's body fall to the floor. In less than ten seconds, Daniel Pretty had all but killed his would-be assassin with his bare hands, and it might yet be that Nance would die from the affray. He was badly scalded by the cloying stew, but his back was deeply burnt and open to the bone in places. The searing heat of the stove had ripped open the flesh the full length of his back, pulling the skin away in broad patches and leaving him bleeding and blackened. Pretty shouted to his wife who sat upon the bed, still feeding the child.

'Oona! Is that babby going to keep your tit in its mouth all bloody night, or are you going to sort this bastard out!'

CHAPTER 50

Painful Recovery

For three weeks, Ridler's life hung by a thread, and he would surely have died but for the skill of Oona Pretty. She tended his wounds with care and gentleness, for every touch was agony. Slowly the wounds began to close, thanks to a poultice she applied morning, afternoon, evening, and night.

Oona was well known for her remedies that healed faster than any apothecary bought medicines could do. Passed down from mother to daughter, there was no formula written in pen and ink, for none who knew their secrets were able to read or write. They learnt instead by folklore passed down through the ages, or by the gift of healing that is given to some but not others. Oona Pretty possessed that gift. She made her medicines from what she gathered from the forests and hedgerows, or what she caught in traps and cages. The poultice she used for burns smelt of sulphur and earth.

For days, Nance lay in agonising pain in a tiny lean-to shed off the main hut, the door of which was locked from the outside. Only a draft of a brown medicine gave him any relief, for it turned the unending pain from unbelievable agony, to blessed sleep and the tolerable numbness of nettle rash. Soon after swallowing the draft, he would slip away to another world, a world that spun endlessly above Exmore. From this funnel of spinning air, he could see the police and soldiers hunting him with sticks, dogs and guns, but they never found him, for they never thought of looking up. When his mind returned to the cold shed, so too did the pain; it was then he would cry out for Oona and the brown medicine.

One night, as Nance spun weightlessly in his drug induced stupor, hands snatching him from the cold shed and half carried, half dragged him into the freezing wetness of the cut. The wind was chilling and cut through his bandages to press with icy fingers on fragile wounds. His abductors skated, slipped and staggered like drunken men, for there had been more snow in the night and the cut was wet and slippery; the duck-boards icy and treacherous.

He heard men shouting, feet running, women screaming and angry cries, but he could see nothing of their reckless flight, for Oona had bandaged linen pads over his eyes to cleanse and protect the scalded lids.

He was dragged along by arms, legs and clothing; anywhere the men could find a purchase. The pain was agonising as the fragile wounds burst open once more. Through it all, he heard the urgent shrill of police whistles.

Suddenly, a numbing, freezing coldness engulfed him, and water filled his mouth and lungs. He fought for his life with what little strength he had, but the men were too powerful for him. They pushed him deep down into a trough of freezing, rushing water. He was dragged by his hair into a long tunnel, his wounds pounded by slime-covered walls only inches away on either side. He felt his body pulled along against the flow, his head ducking beneath the water time and time again.

He gasped for air, but there was none to be had in the watery tomb. Just when he thought he would surely drown, a hand raised his head to the roof of the tunnel where there was cold fresh air. After several precious gasps, he lost consciousness.

When he awoke, he was back in the blackness of the wooden shack, but he was warm now, and could feel the heat of a nearby stove, though he couldn't see it for the bandages that covered his eyes. He felt blood oozing from the wounds as it had in the first days, and only the side on which he lay was not wracked with pain. He drifted to sleep once more, then slept for a further two days. When he awoke, the room was cold. He cried out for Oona Pretty, but she wasn't there. He sensed another presence in the room instead.

'Who's there?' he cried.

Nance heard the unmistakable sound of a match being struck. Soon there was the smell of tobacco, sweet and unmistakable; Pretty's tobacco.

'Where's Oona,' he asked.

'Sleeping.'

'I need the medicine, my backs on fire.'

'I said she's sleeping.'

'Where's my money,' said Ridler angrily, instinct telling him that Pretty had relieved him of the oilskin pouch.

'Safe,' replied Pretty.

'It's not yours to keep safe fer me; I want it back!'

'Why? It's no use to you here, and outside this camp the gallows wait for you my friend!'

'If you steal from me, I'll kill you,' said, Nance venomously; trying to raise his head from the pillow, but the effort was too much and he fell back exhausted.

Pretty stood up from the chair and crossed to where Nance lay. A giant hand gripped his face and twisted it; pressing finger and thumb into his scalded cheeks until Nance cried out in agony.

'Listen to me, you murderous piece of shit,' hissed the Irishman in the soft voice that seemed so strangely misplaced. 'You couldn't kill me when you had a gun and I had nothing but my bare hands! Do you think you frighten me now?'

He threw Ridler's head back to the pillow and added, 'You have your life my friend; be content with that! If you trouble me more, I'll bury you beneath Mr Newnes railway for the trains to rattle your bones.'

Some hours later Oona Pretty came. He began shouting obscenities, cursing Pretty, dragging at the bandages that covered his eyes.

'Hush, you must lay still; you'll open the wounds again.'

'I need my money!' he shouted angrily.

'Forget the money; it's no use to you here.'

'Without that money, I'm a dead man.'

'Why don't you listen to me!' she cut in angrily. 'Don't you realise where you are? These men are not your friends! If you make trouble they will kill you. If some knew you had that money, they'd kill you anyway. Forget the money and do as Daniel says. If you fight him, you'll never walk out of here alive.'

'We'll see!'

'You are the stupidest man I have ever met,' she said in exasperation.

'Then why help me?'

'Because he told me to!'

'Why should he care?'

'Why indeed! You mean nothing to him, but he's just saved your life - you didn't know that did you? So why should he bother doing that either? Who knows why Daniel Pretty does anything!'

'What do you mean, he saved my life?'

'The police came three days ago, perhaps fifty of them! They had guns and dogs.'

'How did they know I was here?'

'I don't think they did know, they are just looking everywhere. The men had just minutes to hide you. They dragged you to a culvert beneath the railway and

Daniel hid you there while the police searched. There was so much water; the tunnel was almost full and Daniel had to kneel for a quarter of an hour to keep your head above the water. It was freezing with all the snow we've had, and he was all but dead himself when they dragged you both out.'

Ridler was shocked to discover his nightmare had been a reality. 'Why not turn me in? Why not claim the reward?'

'We don't do business with the police - not for any reason! That's why you're here isn't it - to hide from the pigs! Well now you know the price!'

'Maybe it weren't just me as was hiding from um - maybe he'd have questions to answer himself!'

'You think everyone is like you, don't you?'

'I know all I need to know about that bastard!'

'No you don't,' she snapped angrily; 'you don't know him at all! Daniel's a good man, a kind man, ten times the man you'll ever be. I know that sounds foolish after what's happened, but you don't know anything about him!'

She packed up her things, angry and upset. She'd finished dressing his back and was pleased with what she'd seen, for there was no sign of infection and he was recovering well from the setback in the culvert. She'd left the bandages off his eyes for the very first time, for the scalds had healed nicely too.

'You'll need to learn some things if you're going to survive here,' she said angrily, clearly thinking little for his chances. 'Have you heard of the potato famine?'

'No,' replied Nance.

'No, why should you,' she snapped. 'What are two million Irish deaths to an Englishman? I'll tell you anyway, then perhaps you'll understand why Daniel might bother himself with scum like you.'

'Fifty years ago,' she continued, 'most of Daniel's family starved to death in the famine. He's from County Clare - most of us are from Clare. Jacko - the man who caught you - he is my uncle and Daniel's cousin. Most here are our family, or families we know. All of them lost someone to the famine. Ireland was our home, yet our land was owned by you British. You taxed every man so high, for such tiny pieces of worthless land, that only potatoes bore enough to feed a family and then only poorly. You took everything Ireland would give and you left us nothing! When the potato crop rotted in the ground, you did nothing. You made us live like animals, in hovels not fit for pigs, and if a man could not work or pay his rent, you burnt his hovel down and left him to starve.

336

Oona Pretty spat on the ground beside Ridler's cot. 'Two million men, women and children starved, whilst you sat at your tables covered in fine Irish linen, stuffing your faces like the pigs you are, on good Irish beef, and still you did nothing! There is nothing on God's earth we hate more than you British... nothing! You asked me why Daniel would keep you here when you've killed two men; well that's two murderers less, so far as he's concerned. Now the tables are turned and it is your turn to work like a dog and live like a pig for him. If you work hard, you may survive; if you don't, you'll starve or hang. Either way, no-one here will give a damn!'

Nance stayed silent in the face of the hatred within Oona Pretty; the one person he thought might be his friend among the navvies. He knew they were a law unto themselves; a race apart, who dug the canals and railway tunnels; travelling the country as they did so, in brightly painted caravans with clanking pans, bedraggled ponies and smoking chimney pots. They had a reputation for thieving and violence, and the police would only go among them in great force. That was why he'd sought them out; he just hadn't understood who, or what, they were.

'Your only hope is to work hard and give no trouble, for there is no law here but my Daniel. There's no police, no judges, no courts, just Daniel Pretty! He's the master here and what he says goes. If you go against him, you'll find yourself chained to the parish-pump somewhere hereabouts, your name about your neck so the hangman will know who you are. If you hurt one of us, you'll find your throat cut and your body buried beneath the railway. No one will know and no one will care!'

She went on to tell him how Daniel Pretty kept order in the camp among men who were the hardest, most drunken and most violent men to be found outside prison. She told him of the night, many years before, when Pretty had been ganger on a bridge across a tidal river. He was young for such a job, but he had already proved his worth as a tough and shrewd manager of men; a man who could drive the worst of jobs by the sheer power of his will. His gang became the toughest, hardest of them all, and the men who worked for him were loyal, for he cared nothing for a man's past; only how hard he could work.

Pretty would hire and fire the men and sell them their tools, candles, fuel, food and drink through the company shop. He paid them better than most, but even so, they were usually so much in debt through drinking and gambling that they worked more as slaves than free men. Most would receive their wages on a Saturday evening and be penniless five hours later.

Black John MacKensie was just such a man. Monday to Saturday, he would graft without stopping for up to sixteen hours a day, but on Saturday night, he would drink himself to oblivion. When Black John had the drink in him, he would go home to the squalid hut he shared with his wife and children, and there he would beat her senseless. Others would hear her screams, but no one interfered for what a man did in his own home, with his own wife, was his business.

On one such occasion, Black John came home ranting and raving, calling her a whore and worse and set about her with his fists and the leather belt about his waist. He beat the helpless woman until she fell sobbing to the floor; then he beat her some more with the folded belt, kicking her with his boots if she reached out her arms to ward off the blows.

The children cowered beneath their bunk; sobbing at the violence raining down upon their mother by the man they feared above all things on earth; but this time was like no other, for the rage was on him. He swung his fists into her face again and again, calling her the filthiest obscenities. Her eyes glazed over; her nose bled and her lips swelled. Her tongue - half-bitten through - poured blood from her mouth and nose.

Distressed at his mother's plight, the youngest child ran towards Black John screaming 'Leave her alone, leave my mummy alone,' bravely beating at Black John's legs with tiny fists.

Anger surged through the navvy at what he saw as disrespect by his own child, and in his own home. He turned his anger upon the boy, kicking, stamping and punching until the tiny body was nothing but a lifeless and bloodied bundle upon the floor, his eyes staring sightlessly toward oblivion. The chest lay still and only the tiny fingers twitched involuntarily. The woman clutched the lifeless infant to her breast and screamed and screamed. Not for help for he was beyond that, but in a mother's anguish and misery.

'Shut up you stupid bitch,' he cried, 'folk'l hear you. You'll have every bastard down here.' Anger turned to fear as he realised how dangerous the situation had become. Even here, even amongst the navvies, murdering a child would not do.

He began to reason with her. It was all the child's fault; he shouldn't have criticised; shouldn't have got in the way; but the woman was not listening anymore; she continued to scream, and scream, and scream.

Then her cries changed to just one word. This word she repeated over and over again. 'Murderer, Murderer!' she cried, over and over, at the top of her voice. No amount of punches would stop her, for pain had ceased to register.

Black John's thumbs press deeply into the softness of her throat. He choked off her cries but kept pressing, for her fingers clawed at his face. He shook her and shook her, his hands about her throat, until he heard her neck snap and felt her go limp in his arms.

A sobbing, weeping Black John MacKensie carried the corpse to their bed and laid her there. He lay down beside her, calling her name and telling the lifeless body that he meant her no harm. Tears filled his eyes as he cried and cried; mumbling incoherently, and calling her name repeatedly until he fell asleep in a drunken stupor. Only when they heard his snoring, did the other children dare to leave their sanctuary beneath the bunk, and run sobbing into the blackness of the night.

Pretty walked into the shack, a lamp held high. Men and women gathered in silence at the door, for the news that murder had been done had spread through the camp in minutes. Pretty found Black John and his wife upon the bed. He was snoring loudly and no amount of shaking would wake him. Pretty dragged the woman from beneath the navvy's embrace and her body fell to the floor. It was then he saw the child. Its face was bruised and bloody and the rags it wore were stiffening with congealed blood. A gasp came from those at the doorway as the pale yellow light from Pretty's lantern fell on the tragic bundle. Soon there were angry shouts and calls for Black John to be taken out and lynched.

Pretty pushed them back saying, 'There will be no hanging; I'll take care of this, go back to your huts.' He detailed a man to guard over the hut whilst he harangued the angry mob into dispersing. Angry though they were, they were not yet prepared to stand face to face against Daniel Pretty. A grave was dug amid a small copse, and mother and child were laid to rest within the hour.

When Black John awoke in the early hours, it was to find John Cobb watching over him. Cobb had a revolver cradled on his lap and this he cocked as Black John stirred. MacKensie began to sob and plead with Cobb for forgiveness. It wasn't he who'd done them to death but the drink! It was the drink! 'He loved um; God knew he loved um; everybody knew that. He wouldn't harm none of um, not ever, for he loved um as any honest man would bear witness. It was the drink and just the drink; no man would deny another man a drink - not in this God forsaken life!'

He begged to see Pretty. 'Dan'l will understand,' he said, 'he's a drinking man himself; he knows a man needs a drink; Dan'l's a good man; a fair man.'

'Dan'l's sleeping; best you sleep too,' was all Cobb would say!

At dawn break, Cobb took him to the base of the mighty tower that thrust hundreds of feet into the sky. He helped the incoherent man onto the first ladder of the scaffolding that clung to the tower like a spider's web. At first, Black John refused to climb, but Cobb told him that this was Pretty's instructions. He must work alone that day at the top of the north tower; for it was the only place he would be safe from those who wanted to hang him.

A still sobbing MacKensie began to climb. Upwards he went, rung by rung, until Cobb was little more than a tiny dot against the grey blue mud of the river. From time to time, he would turn upon the ladder, holding on precariously with just one arm, whilst he waved with the other and shouted obscenities and protestations. So careless was he that Cobb moved back for fear he would fall, but finally he reached the top. He placed his hand over the edge of the parapet and still mumbling, hauled himself onto the wind-swept tower.

Black John did not expect to see the man who crouched there, sheltering from the wind beneath the parapet. The man's hair blew wildly beneath the wide brimmed hat; a briar pipe; clenched between his teeth, threw wisps of smoke to the wind.

At first, MacKensie did not recognise him, but then he cried out in surprise, ' Dan'l! What are you doing here?'

No one saw what happened that day; no one save God that is, for it was out of sight to all but The Almighty and the birds of the air. Daniel Pretty would never be drawn on the matter and Cobb alone saw Black John fall. Over and over, he spun and down and down he fell, until his body hit the soft mud of the riverbank. Cobb heard the bone's snap and the lungs cry out in a death moan like a wounded bagpipe. Cobb was splattered with foul smelling mud. For a few moments, Black John lay face down in a deep hollow of his own making, but slowly, the soft mud seeped back and swallowed up the body of Black John MacKensie. When he had disappeared from sight, Cobb turned and walked away.

From that moment on, Nance never mentioned the money again. Six weeks later, he was able to work without the wounds breaking open and Pretty put him to work with pick and shovel at the face of the limestone cut. He was as good as his word and worked hard without complaint. He kept the beard and whiskers grown on the run and let his hair grow long until it was hard to recognise the Nance of old.

He took a wife, and they were married by Brendan, who did such things in the absence of a priest. She was fourteen and the eldest of seven children. They slept together in a one-room shack with her parents and six other offspring. Almost immediately, she became pregnant and gave birth to a healthy baby girl.

Soon the navvies forgot Nance's past and he became just another navvy, no better nor worse than any other man. He was careful to stay in the camp, though he was known to very few people that side of Porlock. Soon, the whole camp would move to Kent to build a sewer and there would be an end to the matter. The three hundred-guinea bounty and Wood's efforts had all failed. Nance Ridler had disappeared as if from the face of the earth.

CHAPTER 51

The Waterfall

Eleven months later on a cold, wet, stormy winters night - the navigators made ready for their journey to Kent. It had been a difficult job but in less than two weeks, the first scheduled train would make the historic journey from Barnstaple to Lynton.

The road wagons were loaded with every useful item, the horses shod and the caravan axles greased for the long journey ahead. The night was to be their last night in the cluster of sheds that would become the maintenance yard, sitting as they did, near the Barnstaple road. The night before decamp was traditionally one of revelry and celebration, but this occasion was turning out differently, for a child had been lost and couldn't be found.

'Have you searched everywhere?' asked Pretty, when he was told.

'Twice Dan'l, inside and out, every caravan, every hut, underneath um too, she's not in the camp.'

'And down by the line? What about the pond where they play?'

'Everywhere she knows, Dan'l.'

'Then turn out the wagons, maybe she's been playing in them and fallen asleep.'

'But we've only just packed um.'

'Then unpack them; we can't set out without her - who saw her last?'

'No one's seen her since morning. She was out playing with her dog near the cutting and the dog got back just before dark.'

'Have you asked the rest of the kids?'

'They've not seen her either.'

It wasn't like the girl; she was sensible for all she was only six. She knew to be home by dark, and she knew the camp was on the move first thing in the morning. Those matters aside - why did the dog come home without her, why hadn't she returned home when the rain began?

Pretty stood deep in thought, the mud he stood in quickly turning to a quagmire, whilst cold rain ran in rivulets from the brim of his hat. It would be difficult to search beyond the railway in this weather but he seemed to have no choice, for the search of the equipment wagons had revealed nothing.

'We'll search the woods and the line in both directions.' continued Pretty. 'Jacko, break out the lamps and set twenty men to search the cutting, everyone else to search the woods. I want everyone out looking except mothers with babes in arms. Get yourselves organised into four gangs, north, south, east and west, and work out from the camp in a fan.'

There was a hubbub of voices as they sorted themselves into groups led by their working ganger's and foremen. They armed themselves with oil lamps, firebrands and carbide lamps to light their way. The child's mother was hysterical; sobbing that someone had stolen her child away, conjuring up the fears in her mind that all mothers dread.

Pretty was hoping she had fallen and hurt herself, or was fast asleep somewhere, or was up to one of the other pranks that children were capable of, but secretly he was beginning to fear the worst. It wouldn't be the first time a child had been taken from the navvies, for there was a ready market for those who traded in such goods, and no one would care if a navvy child went missing.

Pretty went to the hut where Oona sat with their children. He took down a carbide lamp and, having primed it, lit it with a spill from the potbellied stove.

'Do you think she's okay Daniel?' asked Oona Pretty.

'I don't know!' he said, taking a revolver from a box beside the bed, 'let's hope so,' but doubt was clear to hear in his voice. 'When I'm gone - lock the door!'

Outside, he fitted his lamp to its bayonet on the front of the pump trolley. 'I'll run up the line as far as Lynton with Jacko, two more of you take the other trolley as far as Blackmoor Gate.'

Pretty and Jacko pumped the handle and the heavy trolley squealed into motion until the slope took over. Very soon, Jacko had to apply the brake, for the trolley had gathered a frightening speed - its handles thrashed the air like a flightless bird. Pretty swept the carbide lamp across the track from side to side, the smell of the lamp, acrid in his nostrils. Steam spat from its corrugated roof as raindrops fell upon it. Occasionally, they saw the lights of other searchers amongst the trees; then when they were a half mile out of camp, Jacko suddenly cursed himself.

'What's up?' shouted Pretty, above the clatter of the handles.

'Dan'l there's something I'd best tell you,' Jacko shouted back. 'There were strangers about just recently - fly-looking characters.'

'You've not mentioned them before Jacko!'

'I never gave it a thought before! They were walking the Barnstaple road innocent enough; the only reason I mention it was they were talking to Gibson!'

Pretty grabbed the brake and slowed the trolley so he could better hear Jacko's words. 'Gibson,' he snapped, clearly astonished at Jacko's revelation; 'What were they talking to him about?'

'Who's to say; he reckoned they were just asking directions.'

'What did they look like?'

'I only caught a glimpse of the one but he was a rum looking bastard. About five feet four, grey whiskers, black felt topper, greatcoat and breeches - scruffy like.'

'Did they look as if they knew him?'

Jacko shrugged. 'Maybe! As soon as I came along, they were on their way.'

Pretty let the brake off. 'Keep looking Jacko' he said, 'give me chance to think.' The heavy trolley gathered speed again. Pretty brushed aside the rain that flew into his eyes and made it difficult to see the track ahead.

Pretty was surprised that Gibson - or Ridler as others had once known him - would take the child, for the only place in England he was safe, was among the navvies. He was capable of anything, murder included, there was no doubt about that, but he knew that to hurt one of the navvy children was to sign his own death warrant. Word would go out, and every dockside bar, every travelling fair, every tinker, tramp and horse trader would be watching out for him. Wherever there were men building sewers, or railways, or canals, or bridges, men would be on the lookout for him. No road, no wayside tavern, no bridge arch, nor penny lodgings would be safe. The law might give up looking for him, but the navvies never would; sooner or later, he would feel the stab of a knife in his gut, or the blow from a cudgel that smashed his brains to jelly.

'I'd stake my life he knew them Jacko, or he'd never have spoken to them in case he was recognised. Was he among the searchers; I didn't see him anywhere?'

Jacko shook his head, 'Not that I remember.'

'I think we might have our answer Jacko; find that bastard and we'll find the girl.'

Pretty hung the lamp back on its hook and without another word leapt from the trolley dragging Jacko with him; they landed together in a ditch of sodden bracken at the side of the track.

344

'Jesus Christ, Dan'l,' began Jacko, 'what did...'

'Shut up and listen,' hissed Pretty. 'I think Oona's in danger as well as the girl. We've got to get back to the camp and quick!'

'Why? We've searched the camp and she's not there!'

'No, but I think Gibson's there! He was a petty crook before he turned his hand to murder - smuggling an' thieving cargo from the docks was his bag, so he'll know people. Perhaps he's been waiting all this time for a ship out of England, and those coves you saw are old friends who are going to get him on a boat. I think the girl was a way to get everyone out of the camp.'

'But why, Dan'l, why not just walk out. No one'd stop him?'

'Because he wants his money back!'

'What money?'

'The two thousand guineas I took off him the night you found him in the woods; the money he murdered the solicitor for. It's in the hut along with Oona and the children! He wanted us out on a wild goose chase so he could get his money back.'

'Jesus Christ,' said Jacko, 'Why didn't you do for the bastard there and then an' save us all this bother.'

'Why indeed! I want you to go back alone. At the top of the cut is the road back to camp. At the side of the hut is the tool shed and it'll be open, but the door into the hut will be locked. Call to Oona and stay with her and the kids. Hide yourself under the bed and tell her to give him the money then let him go. Shoot the bastard dead if there's any trouble or if he tries anything - otherwise let him go.'

'What're you going to do?'

'I'm going to watch the hut, and if I'm right, he may lead us to the girl when he's got the money. If she's not already dead, she might be his hostage for a safe passage. Get going Jacko there's no time to spare. With any luck, he'll think we're still on that trolley that's on its way to Lynton.'

Jacko slipped back to the camp as swiftly as he was able. He squatted in the trees for a few moments, before crossing the open ground to the hut. He opened the tool-shed door and entered as quietly as he could. He felt his way across the earthen floor, toward the sliver of light about the inner door.

Just as he was about to knock, he heard voices from inside. He listened carefully and could hear Oona Pretty sobbing and the children crying. There was another voice too, Gibson's voice. Jacko cursed beneath his breath.

It had all gone according to plan for Nance. He'd waited amongst the trees until he saw Pretty and Jacko leaving camp on the pump trolley and the other setting out to search the woods. He smiled to himself in satisfaction, for they'd left the camp virtually deserted.

He knocked urgently on the door of Pretty's shack.

'Who is it' Oona Pretty asked?

'It's Gibson, Oona, I've found the girl, but she's hurt real bad! She's bleeding all over the bloody place! You've got to do something or she's a goner fer sure.'

Bolts rattled through hasps and the door opened. Nance pushed his way through in an instant and slammed the door behind him. He grabbed Oona Pretty and pressed the blade of a knife to her throat.

'You scream just once and the kids are orphans, you got that you Paddy bitch - now where's my money?'

'I don't know,' she said bravely, her heart thumping in her breast.

Ridler punched her so hard that she fell to the floor, blood streaming from her nose and mouth. The children started sobbing. She tried to get up, but Nance kicked her to the floor once more, his boot landing full in her face.

'Don't lie to me Oona,' said Nance calmly; 'you were good to me once so don't piss me off! Where's my money.'

'Where's the girl,' she sobbed, blowing bubbles of blood from her nose; 'you said you had the girl.'

Nance grabbed the nearest child; the boy she'd been suckling the night they met. Holding him at arm's length, he pressed the knife to the screaming child's throat.

'Listen to me you stupid Irish bitch,' he growled. 'Give me my money or, so help me, I'll do for this brat here and now!'

Oona dragged herself to the double bunk and pulled back the mattress. Lifting a board from its base, she produced a box and handed it to Nance Ridler. She grabbed the child and clutched it to her breast as Nance stooped down to empty the box on the floor.

Still in its oilskin pouch was Cripps' money, and a little more besides.

'Well that's it then,' he said in satisfaction, smiling at the woman whose eyes were closing and whose lips were swollen and broken. 'I'll be saying goodbye!'

'Nance,' said Oona Pretty bravely, 'Why don't you let the girl go; she's only a child!'

'We'll see!'

'If you harm her Daniel will hunt you down - you know that don't you! Everyone will be looking for you and when they find you, they'll kill you. Let her go and I'll talk to Daniel; please Nance, I don't want more bloodshed; it's your only chance!'

'So he's going to do for me is he? Well he's got to find us first, hasn't he? You know the trouble with that husband of yours, Oona? He thinks he's the only hard case - that's his trouble! He wants to remember that I might come lookin fer him! Yeh, you tell him that Oona! You tell him Nance Ridler might just come looking fer him!'

Nance stuffed the money into his pocket and drew a revolver, cocking its hammer.

'You see this, Oona,' he said pointing it at her blood-spattered chest. 'This is what's going to get me out of here!' He pushed the gun in her face. 'If you start shouting when I've gone, someone's going to get hurt an' you wouldn't want that would you? Maybe I ought to take one of your brats; that'd keep your big mouth shut wouldn't it? Yeh, I'll just take one of your brat's fer a moonlight walk!'

'No Nance,' she cried, her eyes wild with fright, 'please don't take my babies! I won't scream! I promise on my life I won't scream; just take the money and go!'

'All right then,' he said, 'that's better! Just so long as we understand one another!' He took one last glance at her and then left the hut quietly, pulling the door to, behind him.

Just moments later Jacko slipped through the door of the hut, Pretty's pistol in his hand. Oona Pretty sat on the floor, her arms about her children; she looked up at Jacko her face bloodied and beaten; 'He's gone,' she said simply!

Once clear of the hut, Nance picked up a lamp he'd hidden amongst some sleepers and put a match to the wick. He walked off along the cutting as though nothing had happened.

347

Pretty had made his way along the ridge of the cutting just in time to see Ridler lighting the lamp and walking off. He'd heard no gunshot so assumed all had gone to plan with Jacko.

'He's a cool customer, I'll say that for him,' thought Pretty to himself, as he watched Ridler's lamp swinging from side to side about two hundred yards ahead, the light reflecting dimly from the rails.

Pretty made up his mind to kill Ridler the minute he'd found the girl. He'd kill him, not because of the money, or the girl, or revenge, but because the world would be better off without him. He rated Nance as one of the most dangerous men he'd ever known and if he got on the run, he'd surely kill again. If he found him first and killed him, no one on the face of the planet would give a tuppenny damn. He followed Nance from the lip of the cutting, as silent and stealthy as a cat.

He could see the lamp swinging gently in the darkness some hundred yards ahead. The moon was up at last and gave just enough light to move by, but the rain clouds were skittering across the night sky, making it difficult to follow the path. Pretty prayed they would steer their course in his favour, for he was sure the girl's life was in his hands.

Ridler walked along the track for perhaps a mile. At one time, he bumped into a small group of searchers. 'Any sign' he enquired, 'No not yet.' came the reply, 'What about you?'

'No, nothing yet!'

He carried on another mile; then left the track and climbed down a steep bank to a broad stream that flowed along a rock-strewn gully. Pretty heard him splashing through the water and let him get further ahead. He knew the gully well for they had built one of the many bridges across it. It was deep and sheer for most of its onward path and thickly wooded along its banks. He would have no alternative but to follow Nance along the course of the stream, and it would be dangerous without light.

The moonlight - such as it was - was no longer enough, because the gully was deep and overhung with trees. He progressed in almost total darkness, just keeping Nance's light in view. The slippery stream held many treacherous potholes, and loose rocks with which to trip him. Each time he fell, he skagged his shins or bruised his legs, which soon became torn and bleeding. The stream was becoming ever steeper, with quite alarming drops as the rushing water cascaded from one rocky level to another.

Suddenly, Ridler's lamp stopped. Pretty waited for many minutes, crouched low in the cold, fast flowing water, but he could hear nothing above the low rumble of the river. Was the lamp a trap? Was Ridler stood by it, gun in hand? Had he left it knowing anyone following must surely wait for it to move? Ridler had been clever coming this way. It was proving almost impossible to follow him undetected. The rocky banks had turned to a deep gorge and no one would be able to see his lamp unless they were stood on the very edge of it. Ridler was surely walking to freedom, and it looked very bad for the girl.

After five minutes of inaction, Pretty decided he had no choice but to move on. He reasoned that as he couldn't see Nance, Nance couldn't see him, and the river was far too noisy to hear his approach. He moved forward slowly, the stream becoming easier and not so rocky, but deeper and faster flowing. The rumble became louder and he realised he was nearing a waterfall. 'Jesus Christ,' he whispered beneath his breath. He needed to be careful.

The lamp was more than five yards ahead, when Daniel Pretty stepped into nothingness. At that horrifying moment, he knew he had stepped over the edge of the falls.

Nance had placed the lamp, well beyond the waterfall on some unseen ledge, like a siren calling unwary sailors to their deaths. Pretty tried to regain his balance on the other foot, but the flow of water was too strong and he began to fall.

In panic, he twisted himself about until he was facing the cascade. His flailing hands — by some miracle of good fortune - found a prominent jag of rock beneath the rushing torrent of water. He clung to it desperately, his body hanging over the edge, his feet dangling in oblivion. His arms were near torn from their sockets by his fall and by the relentless pressure of water trying to drag him down.

He clung there in limbo, the crook of his arm about the jag of rock, not daring to move, and barely able to breathe - his chest pressed against the very edge of the fall. He tried to drag himself onto the lip once more, but it was impossible against the flow of water. He realised that sooner or later he would have to let go and he'd fall into the darkness, most probably to his death. For the first time in his life, Daniel Pretty was truly afraid.

He kicked out with his legs as much as he dared, but there was no foothold he could find. He tried repeatedly, to drag himself upwards against the flow, but his strength was failing fast in the freezing torrent. It was becoming impossible to breathe and he was slowly drowning.

Just as Pretty thought he could cling on no longer, something hit him in the face; it hit him again, and this time he felt its rough surface scrape his cheek. It felt like a rope rather than a vine or branch; pray God it was a rope. It must be the way Ridler had beaten the falls.

Pretty snatched at the rope with his free hand. After several attempts, he got a grip on it, and let go the rock with his other arm, to grip the rope with that hand too. He slipped six feet before he arrested his fall, taking the skin off the palms of his hands as he did so. He spun slowly in the ceaseless flow of water, whilst he took some precious breaths.

One thing Pretty could be sure of, was that if the girl was still alive; she wasn't with Ridler, for she could never have negotiated the waterfall. It looked increasingly likely that Nance had accomplices, or that the girl was already dead. Pretty vowed that if he survived the nightmare, he would kill him as soon as he knew her fate, and kill him with his bare hands for preference.

With precious air in his lungs, Pretty lowered himself, hand over hand, his feet scrabbling against the rock face whenever he could find a purchase. After dropping some fifty feet, the rope ran out. He hung in space, in total darkness, wondering what next to do.

With no other choice, he reasoned that Ridler must have thought it through and it must be safe to let go; surely there could not be far to fall. With one last breath, he let go of the rope and plummeted twenty feet into a deep rock pool of swirling water. He struck out for the bank as soon as he resurfaced and found himself in shallow water, little deeper than his waist. He looked about him, surprised to be alive.

The moon was visible again, for no longer was he in the narrow gorge. The rain too had passed over and the night sky was far clearer than before. The fall had emerged into a shallow valley with slippery rocks and velvety grass banks to either side. There was no sign of a light, nor Nance Ridler.

Pretty clambered from the river and began a stumbling run along its bank. When the bank petered out, he picked his way through trees and bushes and when that became too difficult, he jumped back into the river again. Many times he fell, but he carried on, ignoring the painful cuts and bruises, for he had to catch up with Ridler as quickly as he could. The ordeal of the waterfall must have set him back by five or ten minutes and there was no time to lose. He begrudgingly admired the planning that had gone into Nance's escape route; it was all but foolproof and might yet succeed.

After a mile, the banks widened and the river became broader and shallower, the going quite easy. The moon dipped in and out from behind whispery clouds, alternately bathing the water in silvery light, or plunging the world into deep shadows.

350

It was on such an occasion, when the moon broke free from a period of blackness, that Pretty caught sight of Ridler again. With the moon shining on the water, he could clearly see Ridler up to his neck in a deep part of the river, abreast of him, but on the other side.

Nance's progress had been slowed by a tributary that joined the river on that side. It was the first real mistake Nance had made, for it had badly impeded his progress and allowed Pretty to catch him up.

Pretty dropped to his knees and crawled into the trees, hoping Ridler had not seen him. He moved on quickly, never letting Ridler out of sight. Ridler climbed the bank once he'd crossed the tributary and walked quickly on. After a mile or more, Pretty saw the silhouette of a hump back bridge spanning the river. Atop the bridge, there was a carriage of some kind, for he could see the dark shape of the horses.

This could only be Ridler's men. Why should honest men wait on top of a bridge, in the middle of nowhere, at such a time? Although Pretty half expected it, this complicated things and he swore beneath his breath.

He'd hoped that Ridler would lead him to the girl, but that seemed unlikely now. If Ridler once got to the carriage, they'd be away, and the girl lost forever.

'Jesus Christ, Nance, about time too,' said a voice from the carriage! 'We been waiting ere 'alf the bloody night. I thought you was never going to turn up.'

A sodden Nance Ridler looked up at the man with ill-concealed contempt.

'What the fuck are you talking about?'

'Well, like I said, we thought summat 'ad gone wrong!'

'So what was I supposed t' do then - beg the gypo's pardon? Sorry fer robbing you so early in the evening, but I've got two gentlemen as wants ter be on their way!'

At that moment, Ridler caught sight of the driver for the first time.

'Who's this cove?' he said angrily.

'Don't take a fit Nance; it's a lad of mine - Billy Baggs.'

'Where's Tanner?'

'I couldn't rouse him; he'd found a bottle of whisky somewhere, an' that, was that, so I got Billy instead. You don't want ter fret about Billy; he's okay.'

'As long as I gets me money,' said Billy Baggs speaking for the first time.

'You'll get yer money,' came Nance's reply. 'What about Molly?'

'She's waiting, just like you said; stop frettin!'

'I ain't frettin, I just know you and Tanner that's all. Give us the dry clothes an' let's be on our way.'

'They're in the cart,' said Butts, with an anxious glance at Baggs.

Ridler swung himself onto the bed of the cart to find not just his dry clothes, but a small child who was looking up at him in terror, a rope pinning her arms and legs; a gag about her mouth.

'What she doing here?' exploded Ridler.

'Nance we ain't…!'

'I told you to get rid of er!'

'Nance we don't want nothin' to do with murder; kidnapping's bad enough! None of this is worth the drop.'

'You think you won't hang fer kidnapping then?'

'Let's leave her here by the side of the road, Nance. You'll be long gone by the time they find her.'

'You never did have a backbone Buttsy,' he said, dragging the bundle to the edge of the cart. 'I'll tell you this though! Fifty quid don't come your way fer nothing, and if I take the drop - you take the drop, an if you ever stitch me up, a backbone ain't the only thing you're going t' be missing!'

He dragged the girl from the cart then over the bridge until he was able to roll her into a ditch. He reached into his pocket and withdrew the revolver. He aimed at her head and pulled the trigger.

It misfired - perhaps because of its soaking - so Nance pulled the trigger again. It misfired again; but in that instant, Nance caught sight of Daniel Pretty leaping from his hiding place and charging towards him like a bull.

Ridler turned the gun on Pretty, who was almost upon him when he pulled the trigger. This time the barrel exploded with a bolt of flame that lit the scene for a brief moment. Pretty cried out and dropped to the ground at Ridler's feet.

'Jesus Christ, lets go - let's go!' shouted Butts to Billy Baggs, who whipped up the horses without any further encouragement. The cart began to gather speed as it clattered down the other side of the bridge. An angry Nance Ridler was forced to leave the two in the ditch and run for the coach or he'd never see Butts again. He would have liked to finish the girl and be sure of Pretty too, but he needed Butts if he was ever going to get away. He took to his heels and chased after the two Bristol warehousemen.

Nance had planned his revenge and his seemingly foolproof escape over the long months he'd lived with the navigators. He'd sent a letter to Molly, who passed it to Jack. Jack took a trip to Bristol where he told Butts and Tanner what he wanted them to do. It wasn't the fifty quid that bought their assistance, though that was a fortune in itself, it was the thought that Nance Ridler was still alive and still on the loose, and might come looking for them if they didn't do as he said. That thought alone made Jeremiah Butts a very frightened man indeed.

CHAPTER 52

Westward Ho

'Can you keep a secret, McNab?' asked Isaac.

'Can I kip a secret?' he replied indignantly. 'Can I kip a bloody secret! Let me tell thee summut Isaac lad! When it comes to secret keeping - talking to Hamish Malachi McNab is like being in a confessional! It's just like talking to the Pope, 'cept thee don't have to put up we all that praying malarkey.'

'Malachi,' said Isaac with a smile.

'What's wrong we Malachi!'

'Nothing at all - it's a very nice name!'

'That's what my mother thought and thee ain't so bloody perfect thyself - case thee ain't noticed!'

Isaac, ignoring McNab's reference to his scars and said, 'So talking to you is like being in a confessional is it?'

'No different!'

'I don't think I'd confess what I had fer breakfast to you, McNab. The whole world would know about it within the hour.'

'Well don't bloody tell us then,' said McNab getting in a huff, 'I won't bloody care.'

'I don't have a lot of choice if I want you to do us a favour!'

'Ah, now we're getting down to it ain't we! Be as rude as you like one minute; ask a bloke a favour the next... What's this favour then.'

'I want you to take Polly and me to Porlock, so we can catch the Horse Bus to Lynton.'

'What's thee want to go to Lynton fer?'

'That's the secret McNab - I want to take her to Westward Ho.'

'Westward Ho - where's Westward bloody Ho?'

'It's in Cornwall; they've got a sandy beach and sunshine all year round; it says so on a poster I saw in Minehead station.'

354

McNab looked at Isaac as though he had taken leave of his senses. 'What's wrong we Blue Anchor then? They got sand at Blue Anchor and tis only ten mile away. Why spend a fortune going all the way to Westward Ho?'

'Because they ain't got the sunshine at Blue Anchor, and that's why Westward Ho's called the Cornish Riviera; so will you take us or not?'

'Waste o' bloody money,' said McNab, who couldn't understand this new fad for going on holiday, never having gone farther than Exford in his entire life.

'I'll take that as a yes then!'

'Why start from Porlock? Why not Minehead if they've got all the posters?'

'Because Mr Newnes railway is about to open at Lynton, and I thought she'd like a trip on the Horse Bus to Lynmouth then a trip on the new train to Barnstaple. That way we'd keep sight of the coast near all the way.'

'Waste o' bloody money!' repeated McNab.

'You know something, McNab! I've just realised why I'm taking Polly and not you!'

'Suit yerself; some folks got work to do anyway!'

'In fact, I'd rather it were Parsley than you!'

''E's got work to do an all! 'E ain't got time t' go gallivanting off down to Cornwall with you two silly buggers!'

'So are we going to have the pleasure of your company at the barn dance tonight, or are you and Parsley going to be too busy chewing turds!'

'There you are, see!' said McNab, 'That's just what I was saying! Why go gallivanting off to Westward Ho when thee can go dancing on thine own doorstep, an' drink we thine own kind, an 'ave a bit of a frolic fer next t' nowt! Bloody Cornwall indeed!'

'What a misery you are McNab,' said Isaac with a chuckle, pouring himself and the farmer another glass of McNab's excellent cider.

Later that evening, the food had been cleared away and the trestle tables pushed to the side to make room for the dancing. The tithe barn soon thrummed to the sound of accordion and violin, and being the last village event of the year, almost everyone had turned out.

Isaac and McNab found a quiet corner to sit talking, and before long, the far end was taken up with the pair, and others who preferred a quiet drink to making an exhibition of themselves.

Occasionally someone would be dragged away to "join in like all the other husbands," but in the main, McNab's corner was viewed as a lost cause.

Polly was quite content to leave Isaac to it, for she was having the most wonderful time. Most of the women of the village had been cooking, or decorating the tithe barn throughout that day and Polly had volunteered to give out drinks as the guests arrived. It was a job she thoroughly enjoyed for it entailed chatting to all and sundry, whilst ladling hot punch from a huge pottery bowl.

When the meal was over, the dancing began, and she was immediately asked for her hand, for she looked breathtaking in a blue dress with an open bodice and trim waist, her long golden hair curled and cascading in ringlets.

By ten 'o clock, she had been dancing for two hours, for there was no shortage of men willing to be her partner. Finally, she was exhausted and sought a seat on which to rest and catch her breath. She found Amy and squeezed herself in beside her.

'I don't know where you young folk get your energy from. I'd like some of it, that's fer sure!'

'I've none left to give you Amy, I'm afraid; I haven't another step left in me. She began to fan herself with her hand, her face flushed but happy and her skin glistening. Where is Isaac?'

'So you've remembered you have a husband then!'

'How could I forget when he's so boring! He won't dance and when he does, he tramples all over you as though he's treading grapes with his boots on backwards. But did you see Mr Harry Balfour dance with me! He's a wonderful dancer and just a farmer himself so there is no excuse for Isaac. He's such a gentleman and very handsome too!'

'Yes I saw both of you and I can't say I approve. These dances are all too free and easy if you ask me. They give the men the wrong idea and that don't take much! It wouldn't do in my day that's for sure.'

'Well, I don't believe Isaac even noticed Mr Balfour, even though I danced with him several times. Just look at him now!'

She pointed to Isaac, who was slouched across the table he shared with McNab and several others - all clearly drunk. 'If he really loved me Amy, he would take Harry Balfour outside and give him a jolly good thrashing!'

'Don't' talk such silly nonsense!'

Polly giggled.

'Have you been drinking?'

'Just one small glass of punch!'

'Aye and six big ones!'

Polly giggled once more, 'Of course, I wouldn't dream of him hurting poor Mr Balfour, but he really should pay me more attention, Amy. I think he'd far rather McNab's company than mine, just look at them.'

'Well, that's typical of men. They want their dinner on the table and their bed warmed at night an' that's it. You can't get a word out on um' the rest of the time. Get um' off with their mates though, an' you can't get a word in edgeways. Tis all rubbish talk what's more... hello, his lordships stirring.'

Isaac rose unsteadily to his feet and wandered through the centre of the dance, the dancers being obliged to let him through lest he knock them over. 'Pardon me,' he mumbled repeatedly to all in his path, until he'd made it to the open door and staggered off in the direction of the hedge that adjoined the churchyard - his intent quite obvious for all to see. Polly watched his progress in total embarrassment, hoping a hole would appear to swallow her.

'Oh dear...! Amy, I think it is time we took him home!'

'You should have done that an hour ago.'

'Well we mustn't be too hard on him; he works so hard and it's nice to see him relax for once, but maybe he's had enough now!'

They gathered their belongings and weaved their way through the throng, bidding everyone goodnight, and agreeing with all that it had been a wonderful evening.

Isaac returned to the barn, his head swimming from the chill air. A young lady called Primrose, who was a parlour maid at the big house in Allerford, grabbed his arm and dragged him amongst the dancers, pumping his arms up and down and trying to turn him about in time to the music. He heard her laughing and the music playing, but all he was otherwise aware of was a milky white cleavage.

'How do you promenade, Isaac?' he heard Primrose ask gaily.

'Very badly,' he replied.

She thought this was just the funniest thing she had ever heard and tried to spin him again.

The ground rose up to meet him and he grabbed out for her, but it was too late. Both of them fell to the floor at the feet of the other dancers and there Isaac passed out.

'Just wait until I get him home,' hissed Polly to Amy; 'I've never been so embarrassed in all my life.'

Several hands helped him to his feet and Polly put his arm across her shoulder to steady him, Amy taking his arm on the other side.

'Hello sweetheart!' he said smiling.

'Isaac how could you… in front of all these people!'

Isaac looked about him, his eyes struggling to focus, 'Bugger um,' he managed to mumble, 'Hey, Polly… Polly… where's my bestest and friendest… my oldest and… my dearest oldest friend… Hamish, Malachi, McNab! And also Polly; also… Where is his furry fetlocked friend… who is also my bestest friend… Parsley!'

'Right that's it,' said Amy, 'home you go!'

Just as they thought matters could get no worse, there appeared the man himself.

''Ere' we are then,' said McNab, his voice slurred, his breath reeking of cider and a grin on his face like a Cheshire cat, 'ere's the holiday makers then! Ere' Amy… wos' think of this…?'

He began to sing, both very badly and off key; his eyes locked to Amy's eyes, his hand on her arm. She looked back at him in disgust; wearing a scowl that would grind glass.

'I belong t' Westward Ho…

Dear old Westward Ho town…

There's summat about old Westward Ho,

er's going round an' round…

I'm only a…'

'You belong in the Porlock lock up, is where you belong McNab, not Westward Ho for this is all your fault! Just you wait till you turn up at the smithy next time; I'll give you Westward Ho! Now get out of our way.'

As an unrepentant McNab began to sing *"The northern lights of old Westward Ho,"* an understanding voice said, 'Would you like a hand with your husband Mrs Smith?'

'No thank you Mr Balfour, that's very kind of you, but we'll manage him thank you,' said Polly.

Together the two women guided the drunken Isaac down the lane toward Leathernbottle Cottage, 'What on earth was all that nonsense about Westward Ho,' said Amy?

'I have no idea,' replied Polly.

Neither of them saw the three shadowy figures that sat on top of a cart, in rutted tracks that led to the woods and beyond.

'This is bloody madness,' said one of the men when the women were out of earshot. 'Hawkins won't wait, an' the tide turns at two!'

'Shut yer clack Buttsy,' replied the shadowy form of Nance Ridler. 'There's time enough an' more fer what I've got to do!'

CHAPTER 53

Revenge

By the time they reached Leathernbottle cottage, the cold evening air had gotten to Isaac and he was violently sick in the garden - much to Amy's disgust, and Polly's consternation.

'Well we know who to blame for all of this,' said Amy.

'I think they're both as bad as one another Amy, how we'll walk into church tomorrow without dying of shame, I do not know - are you all right Isaac?'

Isaac nodded feeling anything but all right.

Once inside, Isaac slumped into his armchair and closed his eyes, whilst Amy lit two candles to give them light. Minutes later, he was prodded into wakefulness by Amy who was holding a cup out to him. 'Here you are - drink this,' she said testily, 'not that you deserve it!'

Somewhere in the lost minutes, they had tucked a blanket about him, and as Amy held the water for him, Polly shoo'd an indignant Bert away from his favourite spot before the fire. She prodded the dying embers back to life and threw a log on the glowing remnants.

'What's going on then Poll,' asked Isaac, his head lolling this way and that as his befuddled brain, pondered the purpose of the blanket.

'It's quite simple Isaac,' replied Polly, 'you can sleep with your dearest friend McNab, or you can sleep with your other dearest friend Parsley, but you are most definitely not sleeping with me!' With that, the women took a candle each, and followed one another up the stairs, leaving Isaac in darkness but for the glow of the fire.

His protests were met with the slam of the stair's door, so he opted for sleep once more.

Isaac awoke to find the grate and its crackling log, spinning slowly and relentlessly in space. His chair was spinning and Bert was spinning with it, making him feel sick all over again. He found his way to the front door by the light from the fire, where he somehow managed to turn the lock and slide the bolt. Out in the garden he threw up repeatedly, vowing never to drink cider again.

The waves of nausea passed in time and he was able to stand up straight once more. It was then he heard the sound. There were many night sounds to be heard at Leathernbottle, it being so close to the woods, but this was not a wind-made sound, nor the sound of woodland creatures, this was the sound of metal scraping metal.

He walked about the end of the cottage, to discover the smithy door slightly ajar, even though he was sure he had closed it before they left for the Barn Dance.

Isaac cautiously pushed the door with his foot. The smithy was in darkness but for the faintest glow from the forge.

'Who's there?' he asked.

There was no reply, so he entered far enough to be able to reach above the doorframe for the matches he kept there.

Holding the match high, he looked about the forge for signs of disturbance but there were none.

He wondered if a fox has got in, for they abounded about Leathernbottle. Dropping the dying match, he lit another, then touched it to the wick of a lamp that hung from a rafter. As the wick caught, a voice behind the door said, 'Hello, Gloucester!'

Isaac turned at the chilling sound of the familiar voice, just in time to see the heavy tongs swinging toward him. They struck him a vicious blow to the side of his head. Isaac fell to his knees then slumped across the coke pile; knocked unconscious by the blow.

'There you go, Gloucester,' said Nance venomously, 'I said I'd get even... don't ever say I 'ain't a man of me word!' Nance kicked him in the chest to assure himself that Isaac was no threat. 'I can't stay and chat,' he continued; 'cus I don't live round yer no more - thanks to thee!'

Nance looked about the smithy for anything flammable but there was nothing ready to hand. He'd decided to throw the oil from the lamp over the coke stack when he heard a low growl behind him. He picked up the tongs as the dog leapt at him, smashing them down across the animal's neck. Bert fell to the floor at his feet, his body trembling, his paws scrabbling at the earthen floor.

He heard a cry from the doorway and looked up to see Polly looking at the scene before her in disbelief, her mouth open in shock. Nance was on her in a second, dragging her into the smithy by her hair. She tried to scream; 'Shut your fucking mouth,' he snapped, slapping her hard across the face.

361

He dragged her further into the room, drawing a knife from his pocket as he did so. 'Give me any trouble,' he hissed, pressing the blade of the knife to her throat, 'and you'll get the same as him.'

Polly looked in horror at Isaac's body, lying in a heap on the coke pile. She tried to run to him, but Ridler was too strong. Holding her back with one hand, he slipped the knife under the cord of her dressing gown and cut it through. The garment fell open to reveal her naked body in the glow of the lantern.

'Well there's a pretty sight!' said Nance, looking her up and down admiringly. 'We don't want none of that to go to waste now do we?'

She screamed and he punched her viciously, forcing her to her knees and yanking the severed cord from her dressing gown. He tied it about her mouth as she fought with him and then used the other end to tie her arm to the leg of a bench. Ridler dropped his breeches to his knees and forced her legs apart so he could kneel between them. He pulled her gown apart once more, whilst she fought with her free hand to cover her nakedness.

Ridler grabbed her wrist and pinned it to the ground, then with his free hand; he caressed her body, thrilled by its warmth and softness, thrusting his fingers deep inside her.

'I've thanked yer husband, now I got something for you,' he said, before raping her violently. Nance thrust himself into her, again and again, until he reached a shuddering, gasping climax. Finished, he rose to his feet and hitched up his breeches.

'I'd like ter stay,' he said casually, 'but I gotta' go now. But I might come back one day and parlez with thee again,' he added smiling. Nance knelt beside her to fetter her other hand to the bench with the spare cord. 'Yes I might just come back very soon to finish what I started and burn this place to the ground. That'll put us quits then, Mrs fancy bloody Smith; won't it!'

Moments later Nance was gone.

Isaac woke to see a weeping Polly, scrabbling to free her bonds, her body filthy from the soot and dirt of the floor. She was still tethered by the cords that bound her to the bench and he could see the horror of what had happened in her eyes. Somehow he managed to crawl to her and untie her bonds, holding her close as she wept in his arms. 'Did he hurt you,' he said, holding her to him. 'No,' she lied, not wanting him to know what Nance had done, 'What has he done to you my darling!'

Suddenly, Isaac toppled to the ground, his whole body in a tremor.

Polly pulled him to her; begging him to talk to her, screaming for Amy at the top of her voice; panicking when she found his blood on her hands. 'Oh my darling,' she sobbed; 'oh what has he done to us?'

When Isaac did not stir, she ran to the house to wake Amy, then stayed with Isaac whilst Amy knocked up their nearest neighbour, Frank Giddings.

Giddings got himself dressed and roused his two boys. One he sent to Porlock to alert Sergeant Robinson, whilst the other ran back to the Barn Dance to find Doctor McDonald, who'd still been there when they left.

'Take care,' he said to both boys, as they parted company, 'that bastard's a killer!'

Giddings took Amy back to Leathernbottle, his shotgun under his arm, to find Polly and Isaac in the Parlour. Polly had washed his wound and bandaged it as best she could, but Isaac was clearly groggy, the few words he was able to speak, slurred and incoherent.

Giddings helped Polly get him upstairs and put him to bed.

Giddings assured them they were safe after their ordeal and his two boy's would soon return with the Doctor and Robinson. With that, he sat downstairs with the door bolted and his shotgun across his lap.

Two hours later, Nance Ridler and his two accomplices turned the cart into the harbour at Watchet. They were late, for their progress had been slower than they had hoped, the horses already wearied by their journey from Lynton to Selworthy. It was three-o-clock, rather than the appointed hour of two when they arrived. As the three men jumped down from the carriage, Billy Baggs said, 'Look!'

He pointed beyond the harbour wall, where the stern light of the Miranda glowed faintly in the distance. Sparks flew from her funnel as she made her way out into the channel and on to Ireland.

.

CHAPTER 54

Peter Holly

Doctor McDonald was concerned. Though there was little blood, the gash was deep and Isaac had clearly suffered a heavy blow. The problem for McDonald was that he had witnessed Isaac's performance at the dance and knew well there may be other reasons for the slurred speech and vomiting. With the wound dressed and his patient comfortable, he saw the best option as rest.

'Keep him in bed and let him sleep the drink off, but call me if anything changes. I'll call again first thing in the morning.'

He met Robinson on the road outside, the policeman having just arrived in the police van.

The two men exchanged a few words about Isaac's injuries. 'It's very difficult, given that he's drunk,' McDonald remarked. 'Booze and a bang on the head have much the same affect on the brain; however, the immediate cure for both is sleep and he's sleeping now. I'll leave the rest to you, but it seems the hunt is on again, Sergeant!'

'So it would seem, Doctor, so it would seem... I'll have one of the constables escort you home - given the circumstances.'

Robinson spoke to Polly and Amy at some length about the goings on that evening. Satisfied that he could glean no more, he returned to Porlock and the police station, where he phoned Woods to alert him that Ridler was still in North Somerset, and still as dangerous as ever. The other constable he left to guard the household in Frank Giddings stead, a revolver resting in his lap.

'Don't think - just shoot the bastard on sight,' said Robinson matter-of-factly. 'We'll call it resisting arrest!'

Amy went to look in the scullery, for a distraught Polly had gone there as soon as Robinson left, and for no good reason she could think of. She found Polly at the sink; her frock held high above her waist; washing herself between the legs with frantic urgency, the gushing tap spilled cold water onto the floor.

'Polly, whatever is the matter dear,' Amy asked with alarm?

Polly turned toward Amy, wretchedness and shame written on her face, the sopping towel in her hand. 'He must never know,' she said through her sobbing, 'promise me he will never know!'

Shortly after daybreak, Isaac got up despite Polly's entreaties to rest. He washed and had a little porridge, then declared that he was going to work. He got as far as lighting the forge and setting the wheel in motion, before he fell unconscious to the ground.

With the constable's help, they managed to get him back into bed once more. He seemed distant and confused, drifting in and out of consciousness.

With Polly beside herself with worry, the policeman said, 'I'll go and fetch McDonald. I'll be as quick as I can.'

A grim faced Doctor McDonald put his instruments back in his bag and snapped the catch together. There was little doubt in his mind that Isaac had haemorrhaged. His eyes were dilated and unresponsive, his heart rate slow, and his verbal responses - when he made any - slurred and irrational. There were other signs to suggest Uncal Haematoma, but McDonald was no expert, and decided to leave the final diagnosis to better men. One thing he did know was that his patient was gravely ill, and time and their location were against him.

'It's not good news I'm afraid,' he said, explaining the bleed as simply as he could.

'Will he be all right doctor,' Polly asked anxiously, barely able to believe what McDonald was telling her.

'If it's as I think, he'll need surgery to release the pressure on his brain and that's always a dangerous operation, but I don't think we have a choice. I'll try and get him to Minehead as soon as I can, but in the meantime keep him calm and keep him in bed. The journey will be our greatest risk, but it has to be done, so you might like to ask Reverend Holly to give him communion before he sets out.'

His meaning was not lost on either of them.

'He's young and strong Polly,' said McDonald as kindly as he could. 'That's on his side, so try to stay calm for his sake. I'm going to phone Mr Nightingale, the Neurologist at Bridgewater and ask him to come to Minehead. He's the best man I know for this kind of work, so he'll be in good hands once we get him there.'

When they descended the stairs, McNab was in the parlour with Amy, the look on his face saying everything. As soon as McDonald departed, he set out for the church to find Holly.

~

Reverend Holly looked up from his task at the creak of ancient hinges. He was treating woodworm in the tiny private gallery above the porch, where the Acland family had worshipped for centuries' past. The family owned almost every acre of land as far as the eye could see, thus they enjoyed "the best seat in the house" as Holly always chose to describe it.

When the door opened, a million specks of dust that were floating listlessly in bright shafts of sunlight, suddenly tumbled and turned in the gentle draft of air. Holly waited to see who had entered his tiny church through the door below. He gripped the time worn balcony to help himself up, for he'd knelt too long at his task, the straightening of his spine, a sharp reminder of his advancing years. To Holly's surprise, it was McNab who stood in the chancel beneath him.

'Thee here vicar?' he shouted to the apparently empty church.

'I'm up here Hamish,' he said to the farmer, 'what can I do for you?'

'I got the saddest of jobs fer thee, vicar!'

They gathered in the tiny room, Holly with the instruments of their faith on a tiny makeshift altar in the windowsill. He read the service of communion and put a tiny piece of wafer, dipped in the communion wine between Isaac's lips, gently pressing them together. He said prayers, asking that God in his mercy, spare their blacksmith. With McNab close to tears, they sang Isaac's favourite hymn,"The King of Love my Shepherd is", but before they had finished Isaac had drifted to sleep again.

Amy and McNab sat with Isaac, whilst Holly spoke to Polly in the parlour. Holly asked her if she would like them to say a prayer together and they knelt whilst Holly prayed for Isaac's safe deliverance at the hands of Mr Nightingale, the Neurosurgeon.

'Mr. Holly why is there so much wickedness in the world?' she asked tearfully.

'Ah, Polly, if only I knew the answer to that question - what a wise man I would be! We humans think we are superior to other animals because of the skills we possess, yet we alone kill for greed or spite. I don't know the answer to your question Polly, but I do know that flawed as we are, for every evil man like Nance Ridler, there are a thousand more who will look upon what he has done these past two years and hang their head in shame for all mankind. We should feel pity for him, Polly, not hatred, for he will carry a heavy burden in the life after this one.'

'Will there truly be a life after this one, Mr Holly?'

Holly watched her carefully, concerned about the direction of her questions. 'Are you asking because you are afraid for him, Polly?'

366

She nodded, her eyes filling with tears. Holly took her hand in his and let her weep for he knew well the value of tears.

'Where there is life there is hope Polly, and we must be steadfast in that hope, for I am sure our prayers will prevail, but if you would like me to, I will try to answer your question with a story. It is a beautiful story; perhaps the most beautiful story I know, and if you can believe in it, then I think it will give you the answer you are looking for. It's about a little boy of four, whose name was Peter Holly!'

She looked up at the sound of his name and he smiled at her warmly.

'People think I've always been a parson, but no, I was once a child like every other child, and every bit as mischievous I might add!'

She smiled at him in return.

'My earliest memory is of being taken from my bed to a tiny room in a strange house. It was very late and the room was very dark. There were people about a bed where an old man - my grandfather as I now know him to be - lay sleeping peacefully. I wanted to go elsewhere and play, but something told me I must be quiet and so I sat silently on a little stool.'

'All of a sudden, he sighed and my mother and aunt began to weep. The others then spoke in whispers, and one by one, they kissed him and stood back, silent once more. Then my mother took me to the bedside and told me to kiss him too. I recall his skin was grey and felt like paper. Very shortly, we went home and mother put me to bed, telling me he that my grandfather had gone to live with people she called angels, and I was never to see him again.'

'Years later I went to my aunt on holiday and had the most wonderful time with my cousins. We played most days about a derelict mill, splashing in the water, clambering up steep banks and swinging across the stream on thick furry vines. It was cool beneath the trees, and there were butterflies and other insects sheltering from the heat of the sun just as we were. I recall the whole world smelt of wild garlic. We dammed the stream to make a waterfall, and dared one another to poke sticks into holes in the bank, to brave the wrath of the creatures that lived there, but none ever appeared.'

'Then one day it rained and we had to play in a tiny room at the back of the house. It had French windows looking out over a valley whose slopes were so steep that even the grass was in danger of tumbling down it.'

'When my aunt called me for lunch, she found me sitting alone in the rocking chair near the window, fascinated by the storm that swept by outside. I recall it was full of gusto that storm! The wind blew in violent, swirling fury, whilst heavy raindrops - full to bursting - danced upon the windowsill, catching the light like sparkling diamonds.'

'Your Grandfather liked this room, Peter, my aunt said. 'He'd sit for hours, watching the comings and goings; just as you are now!'

'What was he looking for Auntie?' I asked.'

Memories I think,' she replied. 'You are too young to remember your grandfather, Peter, but if he was here now, he would be sitting where you are sitting, telling you stories of this valley and days gone by.'

'I loved stories and asked if she could remember them still. She smiled and said she could remember them all, for many were about her and my mother when they were children. I wanted so much to hear them and she promised me she would tell me when there was no dinner to serve, but I pressed her for just one story nonetheless, so she told me the one I am about to tell you now.'

'Your grandfather was a cobbler,' she said, 'and our home was in that tiny house between the trees.' I followed her finger to the head of the rain swept valley where several cottages marked the horseshoe road that climbed ever upwards to the village beyond. 'We were very poor like most folk in those times, but we had everything that mattered to us children. Most of all we had love, for it was a happy home and I do believe that happiness was in its very walls, along with the smell of leather - his workshop always smelt of polish and leather.'

'There were two of us children, myself the eldest, and your mother Kate, but there was also a third child who died at birth and never had a name as I recall. She was never spoken of, but every Sunday mother and father would visit her grave and lay flowers there.'

'They were church folk and never missed communion or evensong. We had to go too of course, but your mother thought it terribly boring and picked the biggest hole you ever saw in the plaster at the end of our pew. This made me laugh, for there is something quite delicious about your parent's own naughtiness.'

'As we grew older we left home to have children of our own, but that little shop with its strange tools and funny smells will always be my most precious memory.'

'What happened to them?' I asked, 'grandfather and grandmother?'

'They grew old,' she replied with a sigh. 'It was mother who died first. She became very forgetful, then very confused. Firstly she didn't know us children; then she didn't know your grandfather and that made him very sad; but every now and then, when she knew who he was, she would tell him that she loved him and he would be content with that.'

'One day she slipped away, and father came to live with us, but he was never the same again, for he loved her dearly and was lost without her.'

'Did he die of a broken heart, Aunty?' I asked, having heard people use that expression.

'Yes I believe he did Peter, for I have no other explanation, except to tell you what happened in this very room, just a few weeks after she died. I came to call him for dinner, just as I am calling you now, but instead of turning to answer me, he continued to stare out of the window. 'Are you all right father,' I asked? Without turning his head he said, 'Violet, when will it be my turn?'

'Your turn for what,' said I.

'For the Lord to take me too?'

'Father you mustn't talk like that,' said I, going to him to see what was amiss, 'The Lord will take you in his own good time and it's a wickedness to wish your life away, so don't you talk so.'

"I knelt beside him and took his hand in mine for I knew instinctively that he was deeply upset. When he spoke, he turned toward me and I saw his eyes were brimming with tears. 'I have had a good life, Violet,' he said quietly, 'a wonderful life, but I miss your mother so... I want to be with her again.'

'I didn't make him come to the table for dinner that day; instead I gave him a tray and let him sit here in this chair, with the valley and his memories. He died just a few days later.'

'By this time there were tears in my eyes too, and I told her it was a very sad story.'

'She smiled at me and said, 'No my darling, you are wrong, you must think of it as a happy story, not a sad one. It was sad for us of course, for we loved him dearly, but for your grandfather it was not sad at all for he wanted to take that journey to be with someone he loved very deeply. Because of his faith, he set out on that journey without any doubt or fear, for he believed with all his heart, that she would be waiting for him on the other side; not old and frail and confused anymore, but young and beautiful as he remembered her in their youth.'

'Did he find her Auntie?' I asked in my innocence; tears running down my cheeks and with sadness in my eyes.'

369

'She dried my eyes with her hanky and kissed my forehead. 'I'm sure he did darling, now let's see what's for lunch; I believe there is blancmange.'

Polly looked up at Holly and smiled gratefully, 'Thank you, Mr Holly,' she said, 'that was a lovely story.'

'I hope you can take comfort from it Polly, but for now we must not think of such things. You must be brave for Isaac and we must put our faith in Mr Nightingale, and pray that Isaac's strength, and Mr Nightingale's great skill will prevail, as I'm sure it will.'

'I will, Mr Holly, and I must go to him now if you don't mind, but I want to ask you - do you think he found her again at journeys end?'

'Yes I do Polly,' he replied, 'I believe that with all my heart! I have no doubt that it is just the body that dies, whilst the soul itself lives on. Do not ever fear for those who have to leave us behind Polly, for we will be reunited one day; of that I am certain.'

'That will be wonderful Mr Holly, won't it?'

'Yes Polly - it will be wonderful indeed.'

~

The horse ambulance arrived at midday and they carried Isaac to it, as gently as they were able.

Polly rode in the van with the nurse whilst Amy sat with the driver. The horses struggled to hold the ambulance on such a steep hill, but the going became easier once they reached the Minehead to Porlock Road.

Despite the driver's best efforts, it was an uncomfortable journey, for the road, though metalled, was not in good condition. Even so Isaac seemed in good spirits, albeit, tired.

Polly held his hand and with the help of the nurse tried to steady him as much as they were able.

Isaac smiled and said, 'I was thinking about us going on a trip, but I didn't have Minehead hospital in mind; I was thinking of Westward Ho.'

'So that is what you two were hatching up,' she replied with a smile, 'I should have guessed.'

'They call it the Cornish Riviera because it's sunny all the time Poll; it said so on the poster.'

She kissed him and said, 'We will go there as soon as you are better and we will have a wonderful time.'

'Where are we now Polly,' he asked.

'We are in an ambulance darling; we are taking you to hospital to see a doctor.'

'But it's so dark, why are we travelling so late at night?'

Polly did not answer for his words cut through her like a knife. Doctor McDonald had told her one of the bad signs would be loss of sight. She kissed him tenderly her eyes brimming with tears.

'I love you,' he said softly, gripping her hand tightly, 'I have always loved you and I always will.'

'And I love you too my darling,' she whispered, kissing him once more, 'I love you with all my heart.'

Amy knew what had happened the instant she heard the scream. Heart thumping in her bosom, she jumped down from the carriage before the wheels had stopped turning. The nurse was trying to revive him, but he lay with eyes staring blankly into space, all life gone - his body jerking to the rhythm of the nurse's compressions.

Amy climbed into the van and put her arms about her daughter-in-law and they wept together. Polly was beside herself with grief, saying 'No, no, no,' over, and over, and over again.

CHAPTER 55

The Roland

The telegraph clanged Dead Slow Ahead. The engineer followed the command with the engine telegraph and throttled the steam valve until he had settled the revs at forty-five. The triple expansion engine slowed to near silence bar for the crackle of spittle of steam escaping from a leaky gland on the low-pressure cylinder.

He felt a gentle bump as the port bow contacted the harbour wall, then came the anticipated clang of the telegraph, first stop, then standby. He wrote, "Bump felt" and noted the time in the engine-room log; he then shut the throttle and the steam stop valve, before taking advantage of the opportunity to fill the oil boxes. A few moments later he heard the familiar sound of the steam capstan above his head and wrongly assumed they were tied up in the lock. He shut the dampers and blew the boiler gauge, more out of habit than necessity, and happy that all was well with his engine room, took a peek on deck.

To his surprise, it was pitch black on deck, for instead of being in the lock, they were tied up beneath the outer harbour wall; but he could clearly see the glow of the harbour taverns beyond the lock gates that towered some twenty feet above the Roland's deck.

He heard the rush of water and felt the bows pushed off the wall as thousands of gallons gushed through the sluice and out into the river not yards from them. It would take a good fifteen minutes to empty the lock, then another ten to clear whatever craft were leaving the harbour. There was time enough for a smoke.

He sat in his favourite spot; an aft bollard above the steering gear. From there he could hear the telegraph should it ring, but with ropes fore and aft that was unlikely. Once or twice he'd heard the Weirs pump clank into action, but with no draw of steam now the capstans were still, it too had fallen silent. Next thing would be the safety valve's feathering, for there was still a lot of heat in the furnace despite the dampers. He cast his eye toward the funnel for the tell tale plume.

It showed nine-o-clock by the engine room clock when they tied up. He calculated another hour to be through the locks, then ashore for a pint by eleven. It would be many hours yet before the waterfront closed its doors to business, and it had been standby all the way from their last port of call at Watchet, so a beer would be well deserved.

The Roland left Watchet at four-thirty a.m. that morning and he'd been in the engine-room every minute since, for the old man had a bee in his bonnet about the Bristol Channel. "As treacherous as the serpent himself," was his usual comment.

With his eyes adjusted to the darkness, there was just enough light to make out two characters on the bridge wing. One was the skipper, for he could see the outline of his cap; the other he assumed was the mate.

They spoke briefly, then the skipper went back to the wheelhouse whilst the other man disappeared altogether, presumably down the ladder onto deck but no one subsequently appeared. Shortly afterwards, someone climbed out of a deep recess that protected the iron ladders along the harbour wall. He saw him briefly, silhouetted against the glow of light beyond the lock, and concluded that it was not the mate for this fellow was too heavy set. Strangely, he didn't recognise him as any of the crew either, and the agent was too old to be clambering up wet and slippery dock wall ladders; he would most definitely wait for the gangway. The fellow looked about him for the briefest of moments then disappeared into the shadows.

The telegraph rang and the engineer returned to his post at the engine controls. He asked the stoker to open the dampers and blew the steam drains while he waited for the first engine movement. Some quarter of an hour later they were in the lock. He was about to take another peek on deck when two armed policemen clambered awkwardly down the ladder.

'Are you the Chief Engineer?' they asked.

He nodded.

'Who else works down here?'

'Just the stoker on this watch,' he replied.

'Have you seen any strangers on board this trip?'

He shook his head.

'What's in here,' one said, pointing to the heavy bunker doors?

'Coal!' he replied.

'Seen anything unusual happening?'

He shook his head once more.

'Don't say much do you?' said the older policeman, yanking on the lever that raised the hopper door. A broad shoe of coal slid out onto the boiler flat in front of the ships' two Scotch boilers. Satisfied, he swept his lamp into the darker recesses of the bilges before leaving the pair to it. They were checking every boat in and out of the dock for the murderer Nathaniel Ridler; especially ships like the Roland that had recently docked in a Bristol Channel port. The Roland was the seventh ship that evening, but they'd found nothing so far. That was okay, for given the bastard's reputation they'd rather someone else find him, anyway.

CHAPTER 56

The Silver Mountains

'Polly?' he whispered softly, wondering where she'd gone.

'Polly?' he whispered once more.

He couldn't understand why she didn't answer; he'd only closed his eyes for a moment; they'd been talking about Westward Ho.

'Polly?'

'Polly?'

There was something strange about his surroundings. The jolting carriage had stopped and was still. He became anxious for the darkness was total. His voice echoed her name over and over again in some vast cavernous space and the echo seemed to go on forever and ever and ever.

He reached out with his hands, but they touched nothing at all.

He was afraid to move, for there was an edge to where he stood - an edge in every direction. Or was it that there was nothing there at all. For the first time in his life, he was afraid. He feared that he would fall into endless nothingness, there to fall and fall forever more. To the emptiness, he said, 'Someone please help me. My name is Isaac Smith; I cannot see; please help me.'

He heard distant voices; 'Please help me,' he cried again, 'My name is Isaac Smith; I'm blind; I cannot see...'

'Isaac' said a kindly voice, 'don't be afraid, no harm will come to you.'

'I don't know this place,' he replied, 'I'd like to go home now, Polly's waiting for me; she'll wonder where I am; we were going to the hospital!'

There was a murmur among the people then the kindly voice said, 'Polly knows you are with us Isaac; she knows we will care for you.'

It was at that moment he understood.

'I'm blind,' he said, his voice trembling, 'I can't see.'

'Then we shall be your eyes Isaac, don't be afraid.'

'Why are you helping me?'

'Because you are alone and there is far to go.'

375

'Where... where are you taking me?'

'To anywhere you wish to go, to Becky perhaps; will you come with us?'

'My Becky is dead, she died of diphtheria; she was just eight years old.'

The voices spoke among themselves then another voice said, 'All things die Isaac; you know that don't you. Don't be afraid of death, for in its way, it too is a beautiful thing.'

The first voice spoke once more. 'Death is not to be feared Isaac, nor must it be sought, but accepted as a part of life itself. Death gives way to new life and within that new life is both the wisdom of the old and the beauty and hope of the new. One is not possible without the other Isaac. You were sad when Becky died for you loved her with all your heart and we were sad for you too, but soon you will understand and you will no longer be afraid.'

'Is it a good place - where you are taking me?'

'Yes,' whispered the kindly voices together, and in a way that Isaac knew must be true; 'it is a wonderful place!'

'Is it beyond the Silver Mountains?'

'The Silver Mountains?' asked the voices, unsure of his meaning.

'When Becky died, I walked to Hurlstone point, high above the village. I had never been so sad and I wept for her there. It was so high it seemed I was above the world. The water below was calm like quicksilver and in the distance there were the mountain's. They were turquoise and grey and capped with silver. I called them the Silver Mountains and I told myself that she was there for they were so beautiful but so far.'

'The Silver Mountains - that's a good name,' said the voices; 'take our hand Isaac and don't be afraid, for though it is far - to the land beyond the Silver Mountains - it is just as you saw it!'

'I can't follow you; there is nothing there; I will fall.'

'No Isaac, you must take the first step; we will not let you fall, but you must step into the nothingness to pass through it. Be strong and trust in us.'

So he stepped into the void and they travelled together. They held his hand in theirs and they travelled far. Though he couldn't see the way, he thought they must be near the mountains for it became very cold, and he felt the chill of the land in the air that rose about him. When they passed over the mountains, so it became lighter, then lighter still, until he could see once more, and what he saw made him weep, for it was beautiful just as they had promised. Nowhere could have been more beautiful.

'I don't understand,' he said, 'we travelled so far. I expected somewhere - somewhere unknown.'

'We brought you to where your heart lie's Isaac, just as we said we would. It was your soul that made the great journey, not you body, for that is lying at rest now and soon it will return to the earth from whence it came.'

'Is Becky here?'

'Yes, she's here.'

'Is Polly here?'

'No not yet!'

Before them was the tiny green, and above them towered the beacon. To either side were tiny cottages of stone and thatch and beyond them the smithy. He could see smoke curling skywards from its chimney; sunlight glinting from the chains and hooks arrayed along its walls; the wheel spilled its power into the race with the familiar creak of every revolution and splash of every bucket. All was just as he had left it.

From a path between the cottages that led from the wooded hill, two small children walked hand in hand onto the green. Isaac ran towards them, and as he came close, he fell to his knees and held out his arms to the nearest child.

She ran to him; her arms outstretched and with tears in her eyes. She put her arms about his neck and pressed her cheek against his, and to him she cried over and over, 'My daddy, oh my daddy.'

Isaac held her in his arms and could not let her go; tears filled his own eyes and he wept for joy.

High above them, in the woods above the village, a heavy mist gathered in the trees. It began to descend - slowly at first - then with greater speed. It engulfed the trees so that only the very tops were visible above the silver mist. The mist spilled from between the trees and the gaps between the houses, until the village, Leathernbottle Smithy, Isaac and the children, were gone.

CHAPTER 57

Burial

Slanting rain that seemed to defy both gravity and umbrellas, swept across the Beacon on a chill North Westerly wind.

It buffeted the mourners assembled about the grave, tearing at Holly's cassock and the pages of his prayer book. He struggled to be heard above the buffeting gale that snatched his words away as soon as they left his lips.

The pallbearers struggled on the wet and slippery boards; keen to lay Isaac to rest as soon as was decently possible. All in all, the weather well befitted the occasion.

During the service, Holly spoke movingly of Isaac and his achievements. Of the many hasps, horseshoes, ploughshares and pitchforks he'd forged in the furnace heat of the workshop and to the benefit of the whole community.

He spoke too, of his selfless bravery in saving a drowning woman in the worst storm in many years and reminded them that in a very short time, Isaac had endeared himself to the whole village, gaining the respect of all for his skill and gallantry.

He told of a shy man who was also a kind man, with a gentle humour and a deep love for the devoted wife he had left behind. He spoke of the evil men do, and the calling to account that would confront Nance Ridler in the next world. He spoke too, of his sureness in the better life beyond the veil of darkness. Death, he assured them, had taken the body they recognised as Isaac Smith, but it could not take the soul they loved, for its energy was indestructible.

As he spoke these words, he looked Polly's way, smiling with kindness and reassurance. He was pleased to see she was coping with strength and dignity.

The weather was such that few mourners, noticed a tall stranger, sheltering beneath a tree on the boundary of the graveyard, his weight resting against the flint stone wall. He was unusually dressed, in a heavy coat, a wide brimmed hat, and leather boots - certainly not attire that befitted a funeral.

He watched the ceremony with interest, studying each of the mourners carefully. He had intelligent eyes, set in a strong, handsome face and he took particular interest in the pretty widow dressed in black. His hair was blond and unusually long for the convention of the day. His appearance suggested a gypsy, or a man well used to the road.

When all had paid their last respects, the mourners walked or ran the few hundred yards to the tithe barn, glad to be out of the wind and rain. There they gave their condolences to Polly and partook of a cup of tea and slice of cake.

The sexton had set about his task when the stranger walked over to the foot of the grave. He stood there peering down at the coffin of polished oak.

'Sad day,' remarked the sexton.

The stranger nodded.

'Know him well?' asked the Sexton as he worked.

'No,' the man replied.

The sexton looked at him curiously; it was not the weather to attend the funeral of a man you didn't know.

Where was his smithy?' asked the tall stranger.

'Down the hill, just after the village; you'll see a couple of traction engines outside, but this ain't the time to be bothering his family,' said the sexton, straightening his back to take a better look at the stranger.

'Just curious!' was the reply.

The stranger walked off and the sexton noted he limped quite badly and was clearly in some pain. He bent to his task once more, for he was already soaked to the skin. The sooner he was done, the better.

When the last of the mourners had left the barn, Polly, Amy and McNab returned to Leathernbottle. McNab did his best to brew them a cup of tea, professing himself to be more of a cider man than a tea man, an observation that made Polly smile despite the gravity of the occasion.

'Dear McNab,' she said, taking the tea from him gratefully; 'where would we be without you?'

He had been a very kind friend those last few days, sleeping at the Smithy each night in place of the Porlock policeman - an arrangement that was much to the liking of the hard-pressed Sergeant Robinson. They made a bed for him in Amy's room, whilst Amy slept with Polly. He promised to stay with them every night until Ridler was caught and hanged.

Soon after their return, there was a knock at the door. McNab answered it and was surprised to find a stranger stood there.

'What d' thee want?' asked McNab unceremoniously, not liking the look of the fellow.

379

'I'd like to speak to Mrs Smith,' the stranger replied in an Irish accent that was far too soft for such a huge frame.

'There's been a bereavement; her can't speak to thee now,' said McNab, closing the door as he did so.

Pretty shifted his weight to his good leg and jammed his stick in the door. Ignoring McNab's protests, he stooped to get his head under the doorframe and spoke over McNab's shoulder into the darkness of the room beyond.

'Forgive me for troubling you at such a time, Mrs Smith... my name is Daniel Pretty. I'm looking for a man named Edward Gibson. You know him better as Nance Ridler!'

CHAPTER 58

Leather Apron

The Gallon Can was busy, for over two hundred merchantmen were berthed two and three deep along the busy wharves, and there was a brisk trade in beer, gin and the ladies. A fiddler fought to be heard above the general hubbub, whilst in the dark recesses, busy hands worked beneath petticoats and bodices.

A woman entered the tavern and passed from table to table. She was not the usual strumpet to be found in the Gallon Can, for she was pretty and spoke well, a woman who'd fallen on hard times perhaps.

The landlord, a man named Slack Harry Jacobs, made his way around the bar and grabbed her, throwing her back into the street without ceremony. 'Don't come round yer again,' he snarled.

Returning to his companion, he cursed angrily, 'Bloody hay-bag!'

'What's up we' thee?' said his thin faced friend, a slaughterman called Leather Apron.

'She's a nose!'

'Right,' said Leather Apron, no lover of spies and informers himself.

'Asking after Billy Bagg's she is, going round every bar on the waterfront so the story goes!'

'What's she want with Baggsy?'

'Same as everyone else I spect'... turn un' in fer a few quid. The laws after the bugger fer murder an' so are the navvies by all account; fifty guineas to the man as fingers him.'

'What d' the navvies want un' fer?'

'Recon 'e kidnapped one of their young uns.'

Leather Apron raised an eyebrow. 'Best 'e stay low then, or he'll find is throat cut! Anyhow... what about that bit of Mary - 'er don't look like no Gypsy moll. Maybe er's nowt t' do we the murder, an' Baggs's just put 'er up the duff or summat?'

'Baggsy,' said Slack Harry with a sneer, 'don't make me laugh. He ain't got a good shag in him! Anyway... if they don't want ter get caught, they should kip their bloody legs shut. A bloke don't want ter be bothered we that kind of thing, now do e'? He's paid is money an' that's that. I reckon they does it deliberate, half the time. It's bred in um' see…! Like when you've ad' a few beers an' you're bustin' fer a piss… Nothin's going ter stop yer is it! Well it's the same we women an' babbies; they ain't never happy unless they're avin' bloody babbies. The street's is full of em' - thieving little bastards; running round like bloody rats they are.'

Leather Apron rose from his seat and made his way to the door.

'Where you going?' asked Slack Harry.

'Well… If er's already up the duff 'er can't blame it on I now can 'er,' said Leather Apron with a sneer. 'Besides; she looks like the only bit of fancy round yer as won't give 'e the glim.'

As the tavern door swung closed, a heavily built stranger who sat drinking close by, made his way to the street.

All was quiet outside; neither the woman nor Leather Apron were anywhere to be seen. The stranger was about to turn toward the docks, when he heard low voices along an alley that struck off from the narrow street. He moved as fast as his leg would allow.

At the head of the alley was a small yard, overhung by high buildings that blotted out all but a glimpse of stars, hanging in an indigo sky. A block and tackle creaking on a jib and the hubbub of the nearby taverns could be heard in the background. The stranger sank into the depths of a doorway and listened.

'That sort of information'l cost yer,' said Leather Apron.

'I've only got two shillings.'

'Give us that then.' There was a pause whilst the woman handed over the money, then the man carried on. 'What do you want Baggsy for?'

'I… I need to speak to him.'

'So do a lot of people!'

'Please… you have your two shillings; please tell me where he is?'

'You never said, "Where he is" you said "did I know him!" If I knew that I'd be worth fifty guineas now, wouldn't I? Why should I tell you for two shilling, what might earn us fifty Guineas eh?'

'Please…' begged the woman once more.

'Besides… this is Bristol case thee ain't noticed! Being a nark around these parts can earn 'e a swim in the dock an' being a nose ain't healthy neither!

That's the talk see,' said Leather Apron menacingly. 'They reckon you're a nose!'

'I don't know what you mean; I just need to talk to Billy. The two shillings are all I have, please I...'

'Oh no it ain't,' he said slyly. 'Your worth much more than that my pretty miss. I'd say you're worth another shilling fer those nice titties and another two fer that nice little Mary of yourn.'

He pushed her roughly against the wall, fumbling for the warmth of her body. She tried to move her face from him, recoiling at the smell of rotten breath. She felt him swelling against her belly, pressing hard against her as he panted in short gasps, his fingers tearing at her undergarments.

She screamed and bit the hand pressed against her mouth, just as Pretty came through the passage and into the tiny courtyard like a bull. Before Leather Apron had time to move, Pretty brought his stick across his calves with such force that both shaft and bone snapped like matchsticks. Leather Apron fell screaming to the cobbles, but Pretty caught him as though he was a child and twisted the neck of his shirt until the scream was choked from his lips.

'Where's Billy Baggs?' he hissed.

Leather Apron shook his head gasping for breath, 'I don't know no Billy Baggs,' he said, fighting for breath. Who the hell are you, I...?'

Pretty twisted Leather Aprons arm behind him, then drove him full force against the wall. He felt the flesh flayed from his cheekbone with the force of impact and howled with pain, his eyes wild with shock and fear; the grip on his collar closed his windpipe and strangled the air from his lungs.

'I'll ask you again -where is Billy Baggs?' said Pretty, calmly.

'I don't know fer Christ sake... I were just aving' a bit of fun that's all.'

Pretty spun him about and punched him so hard in the gut that he vomited.

'For Christ's sake... you're killing me,' he cried.

Grabbing him by his lank hair, Pretty lifted his face and smashed his fist into it, once, twice, and then again, breaking what teeth were left and closing both eyes.

Pretty brought his face very close to Leather Aprons. 'Do you want to die, Mr Leather Apron?' he hissed.

'Jamaica Street,' blurted Leather Apron. 'He's a warehouseman at Catesby's yard on Jamaica Street - 'e ad a pad there an all... in the rookeries... in a tenement

383

off Calico alley. That's all I knows; I ain't seen him in days, as God is my witness.'

'Where's he gone?'

'I don't know; no-one knows; he's gone to ground cus every bugger's after un; he's as good as dead. I don't know nothing else, an' that's the God's honest truth!'

'The God's honest truth!' said Pretty. 'Now there's a precious commodity to find at the Gallon Can. I hope it is the truth you tell, Mr Leather Apron, I really do, for I shall know where to find you!' He let the weeping man slump to the cobbles and grabbing Polly by the arm, took her back to old Bristol town.

CHAPTER 59

The Rookeries

From an attic window, Polly watched the comings and goings about the Rookeries of Bristol town. She'd neither candle by which to see, nor fire for warmth. She was tired, cold and afraid, both of Daniel Pretty, and of that awful city.

Polly watched the flotsam and jetsam of Jamaica Street ebb and flow in the street below. Sailors and their jennies embraced in doorways, drunks and revellers staggering from one tavern to another, and beyond the lamplight - patient in the shadows - sharp-eyed ne'er-do-wells were on the lookout for any chance to profit. It was business as usual in the Rookeries of old Bristol town.

Pretty lay on a cot, seemingly asleep but she knew he wasn't. The room smelt of unwashed bodies, stuck together in the hurried, carnal union of panting, groaning strangers. She wished she'd never listened to him - never left Amy, Leathernbottle and Selworthy. He was no different from Ridler, and she'd been a fool to listen to him. They were violent, ruthless and brutal men, and she was afraid of them both.

She could feel his presence though he lay silent in the darkness. It filled the room like heavy air before a storm; a dark, brooding presence that terrified her for he was the most awesome man she had ever met. She had been keeping her vigil for several hours; long enough to rue the moment of madness that brought her there.

Daniel Pretty had forced his way into her life within an hour of Isaac's burial; at a time of hopelessness, wretchedness and despair; but he'd been plausible and so very believable. Most of all, he had offered them safety at a time when she and Amy lived in constant fear of their lives.

He said they were kindred spirits, victims together. He told her how Ridler had kidnapped and almost murdered an innocent child; how that child had not spoken, such was the trauma she'd undergone. He asked her in the name of humanity, to help him find Nance Ridler and bring him to justice.

He told her he was a gang-master; a leader amongst the navvies, gypsies and tinkers, and his soft Irish accent did indeed remind her of the funny little scissors' grinder whom she'd watched in fascination as he sharpened knifes outside the kitchen of Oxtalls Hall.

385

He told her he'd spies everywhere his countrymen lived or toiled. On the roads, the railways, the canals, the wharves and ports, and on the barges, boats and ships that used them. The word was everywhere, and all were on the lookout for Nance Ridler.

What they knew so far was that he'd missed a boat called the Miranda on which he'd hoped to escape to Ireland with Molly, but he'd stowed away on the Bristol-bound Roland instead, leaving her to travel on by road with his two accomplices. They had returned the cart to Catesby's yard; drawn their wages and promptly disappeared, but they'd not shipped out of Bristol by road, rail or ship, of that he was sure. He believed they were still hiding in the city so familiar to Jeremiah Butts and Billy Baggs.

He asked her to help him bring Ridler to book, for Polly alone could recognise Molly, and Molly alone would be able to walk the streets of Bristol unnoticed. Pretty was convinced that Molly would lead them to their quarry and when he was in the arms of the law, then the good folk of Selworthy could feel safe once more.

She protested that she could never leave Amy, but he took her through the scullery and whistled at the woods beyond. Two men appeared on the other side of the brook and raised their hands in acknowledgment. 'They've been there for three days,' he said, 'watching the mill and your cottage, just in case he returns. Amy will be safe, you have no need to fear for her.'

So despite Amy and McNab's entreaties to stay where she belonged, they left within the hour. She had done what she thought was right, at a time when her mind was beyond all reason and it had brought her to this terrible place.

She heard a groan from the cot and wondered if he was hurt, for he'd groaned often on their way to the shilling lodgings. He lay down as soon as the landlord left, with instructions to call him if she caught a glimpse of Molly. She hadn't liked the landlord who was a weasel of a man with leering eyes and a toothless sneer. He'd looked at her knowingly as he showed them the room, his eyes rarely leaving her bosom.

The pain in Pretty's leg was so bad that rest had been impossible. The fight with Leather Apron had opened the wound again and he could feel it seeping blood. He lay as still as he was able and watched the girl to take his mind off the pain. She was silhouetted before the window like a tiny miniature; a thing of grace and beauty, so out of place in that grim city.

He regretted bringing her with him for she'd become a liability - another thing to worry about. He also regretted the ordeal she'd suffered at Leather Apron's hands; he'd not planned it that way.

386

'Get some sleep,' he said, rising painfully from the bed, 'I'll keep watch now.'

'You don't know what she looks like.'

'I will watch out for a fat, ugly woman. If I spot one, I will call you.'

'I'm not sleepy.'

'Suit yourself,' he said indifferently. He sat opposite her squinting through the filthy windowpanes at the street below.

'Are you sure he's here, Mr Pretty?' she asked.

'Ridler? He's here all right,' he replied.

They fell silent for a while. Her eyelids kept drooping; he could see she was exhausted.

'You're tired; lie down.'

She wanted so much to sleep but couldn't face the filthy bed. 'I'd rather sit if you don't mind.'

'I won't harm you if that's what you're thinking.'

She looked away from him at the street below. 'What could I do if you did? You just take what you want, don't you! People like you, and Nance Ridler, and Leather Apron!'

'I don't hurt women or children, or those who've done me no harm if that's what you mean.'

'I'm sorry,' she said, recalling how he'd rescued her from Leather Apron, 'that was unfair...'

'I shouldn't have brought you here; I should have left you at home to mourn your husband!'

'Then why ask me?'

'You know why.'

'Yes but how do you know he's here; he could be anywhere?'

'He's here,' he said simply.

'But how can you know these things, how can you be sure?'

'I'm of the common classes, Mrs Smith, and we inhabit places like this!' He pointed a finger at the street below. 'We look out for one another and see justice done our own way - in our own time. We never forgive, nor do we forget. Word has passed from mouth to mouth, town to town, city to city, that

Daniel Pretty is looking for Nance Ridler - also known as Edward Gibson - so nowhere is safe for him anymore and he knows that! Every road, every canal, every bar, wharf and railway arch, every face that doesn't fit is being watched. We are like rats living beneath your feet. You may not see us in the sewers below, but we are there nonetheless, all looking out for Molly, or Butts, or Baggs or our friend. They're here and we will find them, never fear.'

'I can't stay in this awful place Mr Pretty, I'm afraid of these people, afraid of you ...! I shouldn't have come here, I must go home, I must take Amy away from Selworthy.'

'And how will you get home?'

'I - I'll manage; I just know I can't stay here. You can't make me stay.'

'You'll not last five minutes on Jamaica Street.'

'I don't care; I just need to go home.'

Pretty was silent for a moment, then put his hand in his pocket and took out a key. He dropped it into Polly's hand with a shrug.

She got up and went to the door expecting him to change his mind, but he seemed to have lost interest in her. He turned his attention to the comings and goings on Jamaica Street instead.

Polly put the key in the lock. It turned easily. She slipped out onto the gloomy landing and four flights below, in the dimly lit hall, the landlord stood talking to a man in a top hat. The man had a woman on his arm; she was very drunk and holding on to the stair banister for support. She wore a wide brimmed hat trimmed with ostrich feathers and Polly could smell her cheap perfume wafting up the stairwell. Money changed hands between the topper and the weasel before he showed them to a room on the first landing.

A voice from the landing below said, 'Doing any business yourself love?' Polly saw a man step from the shadows. He started to climb the stair.

She ran back into the room as quickly as she was able, slamming the door and turning the key with trembling fingers.

Her heart was thumping in her chest, 'Why didn't you stop me?' she said, her voice shaking.

Pretty looked up from the window, 'I thought you didn't like it here?'

'There's a man on the stairs.'

'It's a brothel, what do you expect.'

'I hate you,' she said, sinking back into the chair and sobbing with fright and anger; 'I hate you and I hate this awful city.'

'All the world's not Selworthy, Mrs Smith,' said Pretty, turning his attention back to the street. 'Most of it's a dung pile like Jamaica Street - nothing I can do about that, but I promised you you'd come to no harm and I meant it.'

They fell silent for a very long time.

'What will you do if you catch him?' she asked, breaking the silence at last.

Pretty loaded his pipe, its pungent sweetness filling the room. 'We'll see,' he replied.

'You're going to kill him, aren't you?'

Pretty didn't answer.

'I don't want more violence Mr Pretty; I don't want murder in Isaac's name.'

'I don't know your husband from Adam, Mrs Smith and I don't need his name for an excuse. I'm looking for Ridler because of the girl. Besides, why should you care what happens to scum like that.'

'Because more violence won't help your little girl or bring my husband back...! You think it's the answer to everything don't you... just as you did with Leather Apron.'

'Shed no tears for the likes of him, he'll shed none for you.'

There was no further conversation for some while, but as the clock crept into the small hours of the morning, the pain in Pretty's leg became unbearable. He groaned with every movement, unable to get comfortable, the pain hitting him in waves.

'You're hurt,' she said, hearing how he was suffering, 'why don't you let me look at it?'

'I'm all right, it's nothing.'

'Don't be stupid, I can tell it's hurting you; let me look.'

Reluctantly he lit a candle.

Blood, black as wet tar, saturated the cloth of the breeches that stuck to his thigh. Polly gasped when she saw the spreading patch, fearing the worst for the wound beneath.

'You're bleeding badly,' she said, 'you must let me dress it.'

'It's nothing,' he replied.

'Of course it's something! Don't be so stupid; why are men always so stupid! Take off your breeches and let me look at it.'

'I'm not sure I can,' he replied.

'Then I'll help you…'

'Pretty kicked off his boots, loosed his belt, and lowered his breeches as far as the wound. She drew the cloth from it as gently as she could.

Pretty sucked in his breath for the pain was as bad as he feared. His leg was purple and badly swollen; a black sticky mess oozed from a wound she could have pushed her finger into.

There was a bowl and jug on a dressing table. Polly pulled down her petticoat and tore it into strips. As gently as she could, she bathed the wound and cleaned his thigh.

'It's very bad. You need an antiseptic… you could lose this leg so easily,' she said.

Pretty reached in his coat and took out a tiny bottle of brown liquid. 'Use this,' he said.

'What is it?'

'Gypsy medicine - better than any of your fancy potions!'

It had a sour, earthy smell; she poured a little into the wound.

Pretty drew in his breath, 'Jesus Christ Almighty!' he gasped.

'Please don't swear Mr Pretty!'

'I didn't swear!'

'Yes you did!'

'Well what did I say then?'

'You took the Lord's name in vain.'

'That's not swearing!'

'Yes it is swearing, it's swearing and its vulgar - vulgar words from a vulgar man. You're so used to your common ways, you just don't notice them.'

Pretty groaned, 'Well be a bit more careful then!'

'I'll be as careful as I can, but please don't use language like that again. I'm not one of your Gypsy wives.'

390

'Well, I'm sure we're all very grateful for that!' he replied.

She was as careful as she could be from then on, washing the wound and the blood from his leg, applying the ointment as deep in the wound as Pretty would tolerate.

'It's a very nasty wound, Mr Pretty, but I don't think it's infected. With care, it should heal.'

He grunted.

'Your medicines very strange smelling; how did you come by it?'

I have a wife - Oona. She's got a knack with healing. Where we come from in County Clare, there are no doctors; what medicines we have come from the land - remedies passed down over centuries. She gathers what she needs from the woods and hedgerows, and she's a cure for most everything except death.

'Is the bullet still in there?' she asked.

He shook his head.

'How did it happen, please tell me... was it him?'

He nodded and told her how Ridler had come amongst them; how he'd married a gypsy wife, how he'd kidnapped the girl for ransom and had ordered Butts and Baggs to kill her. How he'd then tried to kill her himself, and how he'd shot Pretty instead. He told her about the waiting cart, about Butts and Billy Baggs and the words "Catesby's Yard"; clear to see in the flash of the pistol.

'Is she yours, Mr Pretty - the little girl?'

'She's a Gypsy girl' 'he replied, as though further explanation was unnecessary.

'Do you have children of your own?'

'Five including the newborn, but three more were stillborn or died soon after! What about yourself?'

'I had a daughter' she said with great sadness. 'A little girl… Rebecca. We loved her so deeply, but we lost her to diphtheria. She was just eight.'

'I'm sorry,' said Pretty with genuine sincerity. 'It's nature's way sometimes - best to have several just in case.'

'We couldn't have more,' said Polly, though we tried. 'Isaac was bitten by a dog and nearly died. I… I think what with the infection and the sickness…'

'And now he's gone too!'

'Yes...'

'I'm sorry,' he said kindly.

'Thank you,' she replied, looking at him with new eyes... 'Thank you for saying that.'

'Mrs. Smith, don't take me wrong; I mean no disrespect, but you're young and if I may say so - a handsome woman...'

'I know what you are trying to say Mr Pretty, but I don't want anyone else, if that is your meaning.'

'Not now perhaps, but in time? It will be a lonely life on your own...!'

'I'm not alone Mr Pretty,' she said, looking up at him as though he had made the strangest remark. 'You're wrong to think that. I can't see him, nor touch him, nor talk to him it's true, but he's here with me for all that.'

She touched her breast and with a tremor in her voice said, 'He's with me every moment of every day!'

Pretty said nothing.

'You think I'm foolish, don't you?'

'I think you've lost someone you loved very much.'

'Yes I have ...' she said sadly. 'I loved him with all my heart.'

They did not speak for many minutes.

'Are you a spiritual man Mr Pretty?'

'Not really.'

'I didn't think you would be - neither was my Isaac. I think you are a lot like him in many ways - not that he was given to physical violence of course,' she added quickly. 'What I meant was - he was quiet in his ways, but stubborn as a mule and very determined. He was afraid of nothing that I knew of. I'm sure he would have respected you - had he known you!'

Pretty smiled and took his pipe from his pocket. Her care and Oona Pretty's poultice had started to do its work and he was happy to let her talk. She told him of his fight for life after the dog attack, and his bravery over the Nicolette.

'I loved to watch him working for he was such a good blacksmith,' she continued. 'As clever and as good as any... I was so proud of him. He was a kind man too, and would help anyone that needed it. I think that if I scratched the surface I would find a kind man within you Mr Pretty! You risked your life for that little girl, didn't you - and for me also - perhaps you're not quite all you seem.'

Pretty lit his pipe and let the sweet, aromatic smoke fill the tiny room. He drew on it steadily, encouraging it to burn evenly across the bowl and with each draw; she saw his face lit in highlight and shadow. His eyes were the deepest blue she had ever seen.

Satisfied his pipe was alight, Pretty looked her way again. 'Tell me what happened,' he said finally, 'the night Ridler came back?'

She told him everything and it took great courage, but she thought he should know.

'I think Isaac knew he was dying for he kept telling me he loved me, over and over, as though I didn't know, but of course I did know.'

Pretty drew steadily upon his pipe and let her continue.

'We talked of death sometimes, never really believing it would happen of course, but he told me that if anything should happen to him, I should remarry. I told him I couldn't do that, because I could never love another man as I loved him; and even if death did separate us for a short time, I knew one day we would be together again, but that wouldn't be possible if I loved another man, so I told him I would wait. It wouldn't be possible Mr Pretty, would it?'

'No, I suppose it wouldn't,' said Pretty.

'So I made him a promise that I would wait until we were together again, in a better place, with our darling Becky and he made the same promise to me. That way we would be a family once more and nothing could ever separate us after that. It was then he told me he would always be by my side and always love me and that is why I know he's here with me now.'

'Do you really believe that?' said Pretty.

'Yes I do,' she said softly, 'I really do! And when I am able to see him again, it will be wonderful won't it?'

'Yes it will,' Pretty said sincerely, 'it will be a truly wonderful thing and I hope you are so blessed.'

'Thank you Mr Pretty.'

Pretty smiled and they fell silent once more, but he concluded that though his life had been cut short, Isaac Smith had been a very lucky man indeed.

He'd been listening so intently that his pipe went out. He knocked the spent tobacco on the windowsill and then pressed a new wad into the bowl. He lit it, and drew on it, until it was alight once more.

He could see she was exhausted, falling asleep as she sat, only to be woken seconds later by the bitter cold.

'Why don't you rest,' he said.

'I can't,' she replied glancing toward the filthy bed, 'not there!'

'Then if we must sit here in the cold, let us at least keep one another warm.'

He opened the buttons of his greatcoat for her to lean against him and she did so without a second thought. He brought the coat about them and she was grateful of the warmth from his body, and he of hers. Within moments, she was fast asleep.

Pretty smoked his pipe and returned his thought to the matter in hand. Word had gone out, and every navvy, tinker and tramp was looking for Ridler - not to mention the law. Surely, he must break cover soon. The pretty young woman sleeping against him might be the one to change their fortune, for there was just a chance she'd spot Molly on the street below. Pretty guessed they'd be hiding not too far away, for Ridler would feel quite at home in the Rookeries.

Polly was becoming heavy and he needed to move. He slipped his arm, free of the coat, then laid her gently beside him; drawing his enormous coat about her as he did so. He was cold without it, but he'd been cold before.

He lit a candle and passed it across the window. A bundle stirred in a doorway opposite.

Pretty held the candle above her and studied her face as she slept. Her eyes were dark with recent tears, but nothing could completely dull her beauty. She was perhaps the most beautiful woman he'd ever met.

'Dream your dreams, pretty lady,' he said in a whisper, 'I hope they all come true.'

Moments later, there were footfalls on the stairs and Pretty slipped from the room to the landing beyond. Jacko and the lurker from the landing below stood on the threshold.

'What news,' he asked in a whisper.

'He's here Dan'l, nothing surer.'

'Where?'

'I don't know where, but they've found Butts floating face down in the basin with his throat cut. He's lying in state on a mortuary slab in Whitelady's.'

'So the thieves are falling out!' remarked Pretty.

'That's not all Dan'l. A Mrs Parsons took Billy Baggs lodgings the very day Baggsy shipped out. She's alone and so say - waiting for her husband who's due in on a ship from Santos.'

'Have you seen her?'

Jacko shook his head, 'She's keeping low, but it'll be her.'

'Yes, it'll be her,' repeated Pretty with quiet satisfaction.

CHAPTER 60

The Pier

It was past midnight of their third night in the squalid brothel room above Jamaica Street, and Pretty's leg was getting better thanks to Polly and Oona Pretty's poultice. The news from Jacko had pleased him too, for the appearance of Butt's body in the basin meant he was right about Ridler's whereabouts. The simultaneous arrival of "Mrs. Parsons," lying low in Billy Baggs lodgings dispelled any last doubts. Sooner or later, she'd make a move and then they would find their quarry.

Polly insisted he take his rest whilst she kept the night watch, for she was too afraid of Jamaica Street to sleep during the night hours. She'd been terrified of Daniel Pretty at first, not just for the opportunity their situation provided to take advantage of her, but fear of what might follow. After watching his cold, methodical beating of Leather Apron, she had no doubt he was capable of killing, however, as the hours passed, her fear of him subsided; he'd promised to do her no harm and he'd kept to his word.

Daniel Pretty was the most awesomely terrifying man she'd ever met; a man with an iron resolve that horrified her, yet he had shown her only kindness and she began to feel that while he was close, she would be safe.

They talked to while away the long hours and for no particular reason, she told him of her upbringing in Gloucestershire and her cherished childhood at Oxtalls Hall. She told him of her family, of her beloved Parson Pimm, and with great pride, she told him of her grandfather who had sat in the House of Lords. It was a story of happy memories, wealth, rank and privilege. To her disappointment, Pretty fell silent, an atmosphere like heavy fog, permeated the room.

'Won't you tell me of your own childhood Daniel,' she coaxed quietly.

'If you wish,' he replied.

So began a story of grinding poverty in County Clare and a childhood that was no childhood at all. He was the eldest child of a family of nine and they lived in a tiny cottage in the village of Ballycara. Theirs was one of a cluster of such cottages, built beside a rutted road on a rock-strewn hillside; the road, little more than a stony track littered with filth and garbage. The children were taught to beg from travellers by their mother who begged with them; an infant invariably clamped to her breast. She would offer travellers the worthless, in exchange for a few coppers, a shiny stone or a sprig of heather.

The windowless cottage was built of stone and manure, its roof of turf, rotting, fermenting, and infested by vermin. They slept on straw, on a dirt floor, their precious animals beside them in winter. He told her how he watched his mother die during the birth of her thirteenth child, a woman of thirty-five who looked sixty. The cottage also took the lives of her weaker children; their tender lungs, unable cope with the foul air and smoke from the fire.

His father was a tenant farmer who eked out a living growing potatoes on a tiny square of hillside. Almost every penny he earned was taken in rent and taxes. From the time they could walk, the children were set to digging stones from the field, or sent to scour the beach and rock-pools for shellfish and any other living creatures by which they might make a broth; but no matter how many hours they laboured in the field of stones, did it ever make a difference to the number that remained. It was as though the devil himself, pushed more to the surface from the depths of hell below. Their only escape was school, to which they walked seven miles each day, but at all other times they worked; hungry, cold, barefoot, and dressed in rags. No hour of the day was lost to the fight for survival, not from dawn of day, till fall of night.

He told her of the great famine of 1848 to 1852 which reshaped Ireland's history forever - An Gorta Mor as he called it - the great hunger. Though before his own time, those desolate years were a bitter memory for those, who - like his father - survived the ravages. From the pulpit, about the hearth, and wherever men gathered, they engraved the memory of their suffering on all who came after them, so that they in their turn, might never forgive or forget. As the family huddled about the peat fire through long winter nights, he would tell them tales of terrible suffering and injustice, whilst the children sat silent, their grimy faces streaked with tears; their sleep that night, troubled with nightmares that the blight might return one day, to starve and murder them also.

After fear, he taught them hatred; hatred for those he deemed responsible through their greed and indifference. He taught them a hatred and distrust of all things Protestant and British, which warped and twisted every sinew of their soul until it was no longer recognisable as belonging to a human being.

'But why, Daniel,' said Polly, upset and distressed by his story, 'why should you hate others for what was surely an act of God.'

'Aye, an act of God you might well call it,' he replied, 'but just as God brought the blight, so did our masters in Westminster bring the famine.'

Polly knew he meant her grandfather; she asked him to tell her more, and for once Daniel Pretty was content to talk freely. She could barely believe the poverty he described, or the harsh injustice of the laws that for centuries had kept them so poor. There were poor people in Uley, but no one slept on filthy straw, or died of starvation and disease. No child had sticks for legs, ate grass, or had a belly bloated by hunger and ripened for the grave.

He told her a little history she did not know, of how Oliver Cromwell and Henry VIII had given his homeland to their Protestant cronies. Rich families like her own, who rarely troubled themselves to visit Ireland and cared for nothing bar the rent and what the land would produce; the absentee landlords as they were known. They kept the good land for farming and pushed the likes of the Pretty's to the worthless margins like Ballycara, where thuggish middlemen subdivided the land so many times that only potatoes would crop heavily enough to pay the rent and feed a family. Upon potatoes, they dined and upon potatoes, they lived and died.

'Then one day; in 1848; the blight came,' continued Pretty, 'and within two days the potatoes were rotting in the fields - so began An Gorta Mor, the great hunger. Those who couldn't afford their rent were turned out of their cottages in what became known as the clearances, with constables at hand to see the law enforced. As Father Riley and the village looked on in angry silence, bailiffs with burning torches and battering rams razed their hovels to the ground. A million Irishmen emigrated and a million more died of starvation on British soil - not three hundred miles from your grandfather's parliament at Westminster.'

'Yet there was no shortage of food in Ireland,' continued Pretty, 'nor ever was! Cattle, sheep, butter, cheese, wheat and corn, all were there in abundance; enough to feed the starving four times over; yet without money it could not be bought and all was loaded onto ships for the tables of our British masters. Men like your grandfather and Prime Minister Russell, who mopped up gravy made of Irish beef, with bread made of Irish flour, then told the world the famine was God's retribution upon an idle nation.'

Polly was shocked to hear the hatred and loathing in Pretty's voice and sat in silence as he continued.

'Russell closed down the soup kitchens then watched a nation starve. He could have stopped ships leaving Ireland and given their food to the poor. He could have done everything, but he did nothing!'

Polly listened in disbelief that her grandfather's government could let such a thing happen.

'Do you hate me also,' she asked, 'just for who I am?'

'I have no cause to love you,' he replied, as he drew on his pipe, the squalid room the better for its sweetness.

'Then perhaps you should carry on and tell me all that I have done!'

398

His told her how, after his mother's death, his father married his cousin. Her husband had been hanged for the murder of a middleman and she brought her own brood to their tiny cottage, including his cousin Jacko, to save them from starvation. The two boy's became friends and spoke of running away to London Town where the streets were paved with gold.

'Fool's gold,' declared Father Riley, when they told him of what they would do one day. 'Fool's gold for foolish boy's and such thoughts will get you nought but a strapping from your father.'

'But when you didn't know what real gold looked like, then fool's gold was as good as any, and at the age of thirteen, Jacko and I walked out of the valley that was all we'd ever known, to find our fortune. At the fork that would take us to Dublin, we looked back at Ballycara and I said to Jacko, "No man shall ever be my master again!" With that, we set out on our way, with all that we possessed tied in a bundle. We never saw the streets of London, or its pavements of gold, or the field of stones, or Father Riley, or our family ever again.'

Pretty's story moved Polly to tears. She could not understand how such a tragedy could happen, nor how her grandfather - who was the kindest, gentlest man she had ever known - could have played a part in it - however small.

'I am so sorry, Daniel,' she said at last, to which Pretty merely grunted.

'We are all human and fallible, Daniel, and it was not your generation. We all make mistakes; can't you find it in your heart to forgive?'

'You can't forgive murder for greed and hatred,' he replied. 'Ireland was left to starve because we were poor, and Catholic, and there were too many of us for our masters liking.'

'One day you must try,' she said with feeling. 'You must try, or that terrible blight will rot your heart as it did the potatoes, and live on there forever. You've been so cruelly wronged, but worse than that, it has filled your heart with bitterness and hatred, and I feel so very sorry for you.'

Pretty turned his gaze back to the street. All was much as usual with the odd passer-by caught in the glow of the street lamp, the narrow alley that led to Billy Baggs tenement, dark and empty. He regretted telling her his story for it had served no purpose, and he cared little for what she thought one way or the other; but she was there, and he could do little to change that for now. At least she had tended his wound, which was so very much better for her nursing. He liked the girl for she had pluck. It had taken great courage to leave her home and join his crusade. Perhaps she was not like the others of her kind.

'Parson Pimm's an odd name for a horse,' he remarked to break the mood.

'He wasn't a real parson,' she'd replied, 'but he was named after one. Papa thought he looked just like Parson Pimm because he had doleful eyes. He thought the name amusing, but I'm not sure if the real Parson Pimm was quite so pleased! He was our village priest you see, and we knew him very well - oh Daniel - look!' Polly spotted a woman emerging from the dark shadows of Calico alley.

It's her - it's Molly,' she declared excitedly.

'Are you sure?' he asked, pressing his nose to the window, following her gaze.

'Yes, there's no doubt; I'd recognise her anywhere!'

Pretty watched her turn onto Jamaica Street in the direction of the docks. She was walking hurriedly for someone so stocky, but as she passed beneath a street lamp, he caught a brief glimpse of her face. She had small features in an over-round face and at his most charitable, he'd describe her as being of plain countenance. She wore a pork pie hat and a dark coloured coat against the cold of the night. Pretty passed a candle by the window and moments later, they saw Jacko emerge from Calico alley. Other men appeared as if from nowhere and followed her on the opposite side of the street.

'Who were those men?' Polly asked.

'The scrawny one's my cousin Jacko - the others are his sons. They'll follow her and see where she goes; they'll nab Ridler if they get the chance, but either way we'll soon know where he is.'

Seeing Molly running to meet her husband was like a knife in Polly's soul. How could a woman love a man like him so much? Why should they have life and happiness - or a kind of happiness - whilst her own life had been destroyed?

She felt pity for Molly rather than hatred but she wanted Pretty to find Nance and bring him to justice. It would not bring her darling back, but at least it would bring her ordeal to an end, and she and Amy could live the rest of their lives without fear.

Thirty minutes later, there was movement on the stairs, followed by a tap on the door. Pretty opened it and two men entered the room. The first was a thin, rat faced man who smiled constantly, whilst the other was notable for his bulging eyes. He was the same man Polly had encountered on the landing.

'Meet Jacko,' said Pretty, pointing to the older man who smiled even more, revealing a mouth full of rotten teeth; 'and I believe you already know Skate Face Moffat.'

Polly looked at the second man in astonishment, realising she'd been duped, 'I hate you,' she said to Pretty, her anger clear to see. Skate Face Moffat smiled and tipped his cap towards her.

'So?' asked Pretty of Jacko.

'He's a sly one Dan'l and no mistake. He's on what's left of a timber jetty in the old harbour, difficult to get to without being seen. Most of it is falling in the water, but there's a derelict warehouse on what's left.'

'Can we get to it along the pier?'

'No chance Dan'l, it's a boat job.'

'How did she manage then?'

'A fellow met her at the wharf and rowed her out. She called him Mr Baggs!' said Jacko with a triumphant smile. 'They talked about a boat called the Pandora that sails for Portugal on the morning tide. I sent my boy to stake out the Pandora then I came back here.'

'Five more hours till the tide,' said Pretty, reaching into the folds of his coat and drawing out a revolver, 'and with all the birds together on a derelict pier. Let's go before he gives us the slip again - we won't get the bastard stood here.'

Polly grabbed Pretty by the arm, 'You promised you'd go to the police,' she said in horror, 'you promised there would be no more violence.'

'Stay here and lock the door,' he said ignoring her.

'You promised me,' she shouted, 'how could you be so deceitful?'

Pretty pulled on his wide brimmed Fedora hat and followed Jacko to the door.

She grabbed his sleeve again. 'Please don't do this Daniel; please call the police; hasn't there been enough killing?'

'We don't do business with the Old Bill,' he said, matter-of-factly. 'Anyway, this isn't a game anymore - he knows the score!'

'Daniel, please… he's shot you once and your leg is still not healed. You'll be a sitting duck in a boat I… I don't want you to be hurt again!'

'You just said you hate me.'

I do,' she said, holding him back by his coat sleeve, 'but I... I still don't want to see you hurt again!'

He took her hand from his coat.

'I've got to finish this myself Polly,' he said gently, 'for me, for the girl, and for you. We are all in danger whilst he's at large. I promise you I'll take him alive if I can; the hangman will do the job just as well as I can; I just need to be sure it's done this time and no mistakes - that's all.'

On an impulse, he put his hand beneath her chin and lifted her face towards him. Very gently, he bent over and kissed her lips. He could taste the saltiness of her tears.

'Lock the door behind me and open it to no-one. In an hour, I'll take you home and you can live the rest of your life in peace.'

Moments later, they were on the street and Polly was left in the room alone. They moved through the dark streets as quickly as Pretty's leg would allow.

'What's been going on in that room Dan'l?' said Jacko.

Pretty said nothing.

'Not like you to go soft over a pretty face.'

'Shut your mouth, Jacko!' replied Pretty.

'You ain't really going to hand him over are yuh? Let's be rid of the bastard once an' fer all!'

'Let's get the money first - then I don't much care.'

The tiny boat they'd purloined from the many tied beneath the wharf struck the pier with only the slightest bump. Jacko stepped onto the crumbling landing and lashed the painter whilst Pretty watched the pier for any sign of danger, his pistol cocked and ready. The two men signalled to one another, then climbed the rotten steps as quietly and carefully as they could. Before them was the warehouse, bigger than it looked now they were up close. They could just make out a door in the gable end, by the feint sliver of light that escaped through the joints of time-weathered boards.

There was a walkway about the warehouse, but it was in such bad condition, with planks rotten and missing, that it would surely have tipped them into the harbour had they tried to walk along it. The only possible way was through the door before them. It would be dangerous and they would need to rely on the element of surprise.

All about them was the debris of obsolescence and decay; rotting rope, disused sacks, timber beams, iron hooks and the like. Pretty thrust his pistol into the belt of his trousers and took up a heavy spar with a steel-ferruled end, that might once have held a rope and tackle. He signalled to Jacko that he'd use it as a battering ram. Jacko stood close to the door, revolver in hand, ready to leap into the room the moment Pretty smashed it open.

The door burst inwards the instant the spar hit it and Jacko rushed into a small anteroom. It was lit by an oil lamp hanging from a rafter, and by its light, he could see decaying rubbish, a sailor's trunk, a portmanteau, and an open jawed gin trap. At such a rush, Jacko had no time to stop, or leap over the deadly mantrap; instead, he trod straight on it. He heard the howl of metal upon metal and felt the blinding agony of its grip. The pain and its weight dragged him screaming to the floor.

Pretty charged past him at a run, his finger about the trigger, but there was nothing to shoot at and he looked with despair at the unexpected inner door of the room beyond - their element of surprise completely gone.

Pretty's heart was racing and adrenaline was pumping, every nerve in his body screamed danger - beware! Jacko's agony was ignored.

'For Christ sake help me Dan'l,' screamed Jacko before passing out in shock, the iron teeth of the gin trap, red with his blood.

Pretty expected the door to burst open at any moment and a pistol fight to ensue, but a voice above his head said calmly... 'Hello Dan'l; looking fer me?'

Pretty looked above him to see a smiling Nance Ridler, crouched on a rafter, his pistol pointing straight at Pretty's head.

'Put the gun down, or I'll blow your fucking brains out,' he snapped.

The door at the far end of the room opened and a smirking Billy Baggs stood there, another gun pointing straight at him. There was nothing for Pretty to do but throw his gun to the floor.

'Meet a couple of my old friend's Baggsy,' said Ridler pleasantly.

'Let me get the trap off Jacko,' said Pretty.

'You leave the bastard be,' replied Nance with a snarl. 'I put it there especially for him.'

'Molly,' he shouted to the door at the other end of the room. Molly emerged in a state of panic and hysteria. 'Get some rope an' be quick about it! Shake yerself up a bit, you useless cow! You know where Baggsy got that gin trap from Dan'l?' said Ridler conversationally; 'a pall of his called Leather Apron!

403

There's a thing,' he said smiling! 'E's a bit tasty is that Leather Apron, but they don't reckon he's going to walk no more an' that's your doing that is... He don't like you one little bit!'

~

Alone in the brothel room, Polly wished she'd never listened to him and couldn't believe she'd been persuaded to leave Amy and Selworthy to help him. She wiped her eyes, ashamed to have been so stupid. He was just a common thug, little better than Ridler himself; she didn't care what happened to him anymore.

She went to the window to see if she could see him or Jacko on Jamaica Street. It was so late that even Jamaica Street had fallen quiet, but it wasn't completely deserted. What she saw on the street below shook her to her very core.

A man stood beneath the gas lamps glow, his features cast in shadow, but she knew the man better than she knew herself. She called out his name - not a cry, but a whisper of disbelief. He looked up at her and smiled - she was sure he smiled. She called his name once more - over and over - her eyes filling with tears. He beckoned for her to come, then walked off in the direction of the docks. His image swam before her eyes as he walked away; 'Oh no,' she cried in alarm, 'oh my darling, please don't go!'

She fumbled in her pocket for the key. She had to catch him, touch him, and hear his voice one more time. The key turned in the lock and she was running down the stairs as fast as she was able, all thoughts of her safety abandoned. When she reached the street, she saw him in the distance, still walking toward the docks; she called to him but he neither answered nor looked back.

Her shoes rang out on the cobbles - a hand reached out and grabbed her coat. 'What's yer hurry love' said the man in the doorway, but her momentum dragged the coat from his grip and she was gone. She ran so fast, she all but ran into the dock at the end of Jamaica Street; sobbing frantically, she called his name, again, and again, and again.

'Here Polly; I'm here.'

The voice came from the black and oily water of the harbour. She ran down the slippery steps, until she was knee-deep in water for the night was as dark as pitch, and the shadows were deep beneath the quay wall. He spoke again as she heard the slap, slap, slap, of water against the hull of a tiny boat; she stepped into it and her arm was steadied by an unseen hand.

'Isaac - oh my darling is it you?' she cried.

'Hush Polly, don't make a sound. No one must hear you for there is great danger ahead - but no harm will come to you my darling, I promise you. You must row now - row the boat to the pier.'

It was Isaac's voice, there was no doubt about it, but cruelly, she could neither see him, nor reach out for him, for fear of capsizing the tiny boat. She pulled on the oars in the pitch black of the night.

'I love you!' she whispered.

'I love you too,' he replied, 'more than words can say.'

'I've missed you so much.'

'I've missed you too Polly, but you must row now my darling, you must row or it is all over with them.'

'Please come back to me Isaac, for I don't think I can live without you.'

'Then close your eyes and think of me when you need me most and I will come - I promise I will come.'

The tiny boat bumped against the jetty and she climbed the rotting steps in a trance, thereafter to walk across the debris-strewn landing. She walked through the shattered doorway and took the oil lamp from its hook just as Isaac told her to.

No one saw her, nor heard her pass through the anti-room and into the room beyond. She moved silently as though gliding on ice.

She saw them all, Molly, Nance, Daniel and Jacko and the stranger who must be Billy Baggs. They moved in slow motion, like figures on a canvas who'd come to life with oily stiffness. They seemed unreal - nothing was real.

Pretty and Jacko lay on the floor at the back of the room, Jacko in a spreading pool of blood, a bloody gin trap discarded nearby. Slowly they turned to look at her, but neither spoke. Molly stood with her back to Polly, pointing a gun at them with trembling hands. Nance and Billy also faced away from her as they poured paraffin over anything and everything. It was obvious they meant to burn the pier down with Daniel and Jacko still inside.

The floors, walls and piles of sacks were all soaked with paraffin that Nance and Billy tipped from the can, but to Polly's eyes, it was red blood that poured from the spout.

They did not see her, did not hear her, it was as though she were invisible. She walked over to Nance and stood behind him. For the first time in her life, hatred for another human being rose up in her breast and consumed her with loathing. She could see the smithy as it was that night, her darling slumped and unconscious upon the floor. She could feel Nance's body against her, feel his hands upon her - feel him within her. She could hear him grunting, calling her foul names, feel him thrusting and spilling inside her with her darling just feet away as she endured her shame.

Overwhelming hatred for what he was and what he'd done to them engulfed her and she wanted to see him suffer as he had made them suffer. She threw the lamp on the floor beside him and it smashed on the instant, splashing hot burning oil over Nance as he stood in the centre of the paraffin-soaked sacks.

'Murderer!' she whispered softly.

Ridler turned as burning paraffin engulfed his breeches, the paraffin can in his hands bursting into flames.

Billy Baggs clothing was on fire too, for he was stood in the rapidly spreading pool of flame. He shouted in alarm as his breeches caught the flames and beat at them with his bare hands. He ran screaming onto the pier and they heard a never-ending shriek of agony as he fell among the stiletto splinters of the shattered wooden piles.

Molly ran to Nance and tried to beat out the flames with her bare hands and dropping the gun as she did so, but she too was alight in seconds - her dress engulfed in flames.

Polly watched transfixed as Ridler beat at his clothing, screaming for help, writhing in agony, throwing himself to the floor to escape the terror that clung to his limbs. His clothing fell from him in blazing strips, his hair and beard a burning torch, his fingers leaving skin and flesh wherever they touched. He thrashed about wildly, no longer able to see. He was dying and dying in agony.

Pretty leapt to his feet and dragged the crippled Jacko to the anti-room, calling to Polly to run as he did so but she wouldn't leave.

'Murderer', she kept repeating as she watched Nance burn, 'murderer... murderer...'

Pretty dragged Jacko onto the pier to the head of the steps and then went back for Polly. She fought with him, not wanting to leave the room whilst Ridler still lived. He picked her up and carried her to Jacko and safety.

'Jesus Christ Almighty' he hissed, above the noise of the flames; 'Can you row, Jacko,' he shouted.

'I could row, but I can't get down to the boat Dan'l!'

'Ok, put your arms around my neck. I'll get you in the boat. Get her away from here as fast as you can; I'll go back for the woman.'

He ran up the stairs to the warehouse, past the still burning Billy Baggs who hung impaled through his stomach on a rotten pile, his body twitching in its death throes.

'Get in the boat - go with Jacko,' shouted Pretty as he passed her on the pier, but she stood stock still, watching the flames as though in a trance.

Pretty ran through the anti-room to the inferno that was the inner room. The heavy sacking curtains were ablaze, flames bursting through the barred window into the cold night air. All the room was ablaze now; the roof was already open to the night with sparks flying skywards like a Guy Fawkes bonfire. Heavy smoke choked his lungs and his ears were filled with the howling of air that fed the flames, but nothing on earth could drown Molly's cries.

He stood at the door; his face seared by the heat within. He could see her, but he could not reach her. She knelt over Nance's body, every inch of her ablaze. Heavy timbers began to crash down and the burning floor opened up about her. He knew she too was lost and that was a good thing for it would be better to die of such terrible injuries than to survive. He closed the inner door and after a moment's hesitation, slid the bolt home. He grabbed the portmanteau before escaping to the pier once more.

He swept Polly up in his arms and ran down the rickety steps to the landing, throwing Polly into the tiny boat and casting it off. He threw the portmanteau after her and shouted, 'Go Jacko; there's no room for me, take care of Polly first.'

He thrust them away from the pier and Jacko pulled hard for the inky blackness of the basin as he'd been bid. Pretty fumbled with the painter of another boat, but the knot was too tight.

A crowd had gathered on the nearest quayside. 'Look!' they cried, 'a woman at the window… a man on the pier… she shouted murder; I heard her shout murder!'

Molly stood at the window shrieking, trying to wrench the iron bars from her prison; her hair, long since burnt off, her flesh blackened and raw, her cheeks open to the bone, her body engulfed in flames.

Unable to loosen the painter, Pretty jumped from the pier and swam toward the boats that were setting out from the quay.

Jacko had rowed them beyond the ring of light cast by the blaze and away from the wharf where the crowd had gathered. He'd waited for a while outside

407

the ring of light, but Pretty was swimming towards the onlookers and the launching boats. There was nothing he could do to save his friend and so he began to row once more.

'Stop Jacko, please stop,' she cried. 'Why is he swimming away from us; why are you going the wrong way?'

Jacko thought back to Daniel's words. "Get her away as fast as you can" was what he'd said. He pulled steadily on the oars, rowing them ever further into the darkness of the basin but he answered her in a whisper as he rowed, 'He wants you to escape Miss Polly.'

'But he's swimming into danger; they will say it was him.'

'He's trying to give us a chance, Miss Polly. Sound travels far on water so be quiet now, there's a good mistress.'

'Please forgive me,' said Polly to the darkness. 'Please forgive me for what I've done!'

As the tiny boat slipped deeper into the darkness of the basin, she wept for him. Though he was a violent man, he'd always been kind to her. He'd tried his best to take her away from danger, to comfort her and protect her, and she'd felt safe whilst he was near. Now he swam into terrible danger for her sake.

CHAPTER 61

Bodmin Gaol

Abraham Malachi Cato, stepped to the platform from the second-class carriage of the 15.07 train from Bristol Temple Meads, on the last leg of his journey from Harrogate. Oblivious to the howl of steam, the shrill of whistles and the clatter of luggage carts, Cato stood - bag at his feet - in the path of the human flood that swirled and eddied about him.

He checked the time by the station clock; it was eleven minutes past the hour. Cato pulled a gold watch from his waistcoat and confirmed that it, and the station clock concurred, before snapping the lid shut and replacing the timepiece in his breast pocket with one deft movement.

Cato was dressed in an old, but immaculately pressed suit, with matching waistcoat, white shirt and starched, rounded collar. His features were unremarkable but for a slight laziness of his left eye. He wore a bowler hat over thinning hair, which he compensated for by a very generous moustache in the fashion of the day. To the casual observer, Mr Abraham Cato was a gentleman of the middle classes, a clerk or bank manager perhaps; In fact, Cato's profession was that of gentleman's hairdresser.

Cato raised his hand to engage a hansom cab, 'Where to guv?' asked the cabby, humping Cato's well-travelled case into the carriage.

'Bodmin Gaol, cabby.'

'Bodmin Gaol... right you are guv, Bodmin Gaol it is, an' the second gentleman fer the gaol today! There's a thing,' he said, looking pointedly at Cato! When his fare did not respond, he continued, 'You'll ave' come fer Thursdays do then?'

'I beg your pardon,' said Cato, in a tone that discouraged conversation.

'Thursday's do... they're hanging a Gypo on Thursday. You'll 'ave come fer that I suppose?'

'Then you would suppose wrongly,' said Cato. 'For what it is worth to you sir, I am His Majesty's Inspector of Kitchens and Utilities and as such, I have nothing to do with the penal administration at Bodmin Gaol - or any other gaol for that matter!'

'Well beggin' yer pardon, my mistake I'm sure; no offence meant guv! Surprised thee ain't erd' of this un' though, fer all that. Bin in all the papers - can't bloody miss it! Some saying he should ang' - some saying e shouldn't -

appeals afore parliament - all sorts! Me; I recon they should ang' the bloody lot! Ang' every last bloody one on um! Save us all a load of trouble. Why I know's folk as do go round makin' trouble just ter get in there - ave' you ever erd' of such a thing! Three square meals a day and a warm bed — tis a bloody scandal! Course...!' added the cabby hastily - his tip in mind, 'taint your fault, thee being on the grub side of things! I expect you got your orders just like the rest of us.'

Cato did not trouble himself to reply.

'An them as they don't ang' they ought to deport! Deport um all like the frogs do! They deports shiploads they do - shiploads an' shiploads! Now I don't like the frogs no more than the next man, but one thing you ave' ter admire um' for - they know's ow' ter treat criminals! Why you've only got ter fart in France an' they've got yer on a boat fer the South Americas. We ought ter do the same but send um t' France instead... Ere you are governor, Bodmin Gaol and very nice to ave' bin of service to a gentleman such as yerself.'

Cato took the bag from the smiling man and placed the exact fare of thru-pence three farthings in his hand, before bidding him good day. Abraham Cato did not approve of tipping.

'Mr. Cato, do come in, please take a seat, I hope you had a pleasant journey,' said the governor.

'I do not consider travel a pleasurable experience Mr Reynolds, furthermore; the train was a full four minutes late!'

'Oh... oh, yes,' said the governor, 'very inconvenient I'm sure.'

'Punctuality is the cornerstone of good order, Mr Reynolds. Where would we be without it?'

'Where indeed, Mr Cato, where indeed!'

'Unfortunately, one's own standards are not always reflected in that of other public services,' continued Cato.

'Quite so, quite so! I imagine you will wish to take some refreshment and see your quarters and I am sure I need not remind you that you are required to remain within the prison until your...ahem... work has been concluded.'

'Quite aware Mr Reynolds, thank you. With regard to your kind offer, I would prefer to see the prisoner and inspect the apparatus before taking my supper if you don't mind. I would also mention that, under the terms of my contract, half of my fee is due upon arrival, with the remainder due upon conclusion.'

'Oh, I do beg your pardon, Mr Cato, yes, how remiss of me; I have it here; signed and dated of course - seven guineas.' He offered the cheque to Cato, who checked its details before filing it in his wallet. He then stood up and both men made their way across the yard to the doorway of the administration block. They passed along a shining corridor with doors to left and right before descending five steps into the cellblock for the condemned. There were two cells, each with a spy hole in the door and a hatch in the wall for food. Cato slid back the spy-hole as quietly as he was able and peered within. Two warders sat about a table with the condemned man. They were playing what appeared to be whist.

'How tall and what weight, Mr Reynolds.'

'Six feet eight inches and twenty-two stone.'

'Exactly?'

'Exactly. He was weighed this morning.'

'Good! He is a man of unusual stature, would you be good enough to have him stand for me.'

The governor nodded to the head warder who in turn spoke to a warder through the spy-hole. The prisoner pushed back his chair and rose to his full height, looking unwaveringly at the cell door.

Cato examined him for a full two minutes at one point asking for the man to turn about so that he might see his neck from behind. 'Thank you Mr Reynolds,' said Cato finally. 'Perhaps we could see the apparatus now.'

As they retraced their steps Reynolds said, 'If he gives trouble I am not sure how we will contain him. He is as strong as an ox and known for his violent nature though he has been quiet enough so far admittedly, but containing him in such a confined space might be very difficult. I have to say I am most concerned Mr Cato - most concerned!'

'Then I urge you not to alarm yourself Mr Reynolds for I'm sure your fears are unfounded. In my experience, the condemned man is usually resigned to his fate and when the time comes, wishes to meet his maker with dignity and a firm step. There are exceptions of course,' he added for good measure. 'I would advise the administration of my universal panacea… a good stiff brandy. I trust he's been well prepared in other ways.'

'The priest calls daily if that is what you mean, but he won't see him.'

'Then you can do no more, Mr Reynolds.'

411

They passed across the yard once more; this time turning left toward the execution shed. It was an open fronted canopy adjacent the outer wall that could not be overlooked from inside, or outside the prison. Normally used for the storage of hay, it had been swept clean and the scaffold prepared.

Cato cast an experienced eye over its construction. It had been well made and appeared to comply with Home Office regulations though Cato would check its dimensions in the morning. Satisfied with his preliminary inspection, he took his leave of the governor and retired to his quarters where he was served a meal of roast pork and vegetables, with a fruit and pastry pudding. Having consumed this with a pint of beer - his last whilst at the prison - he settled down to read the Illustrated London News which carried a serialised story by the celebrated author, Mr Conan Doyle; a gentleman whose work Mr Cato had a particular admiration for.

At 9.30 p.m precisely, Cato extinguished his lamp and took to his bed. He did not sleep well as was usually the case in such circumstances. Though a servant of The Crown, Abraham Cato did not take his duty in ending another person's life lightly — far from it. If one day he were not so affected, then he would retire, for to be untouched by such an act of finality would be to render him as inhuman as some of the unfortunate creatures it had been his duty to dispatch.

Worst of all was the execution of women. This was particularly distressing and he was pleased that this onerous duty had befallen him only thrice. This execution too, was not to his liking. The man was undoubtedly guilty of taking another man's life and the punishment for that crime was death by hanging, yet Cato was troubled by the circumstances of this particular case.

He has deliberately sought out and killed a vicious and brutal murderer, who - if apprehended by the forces of law and order - would undoubtedly have met with a fate similar to his own. Perhaps it would have fallen to Cato to dispatch the man for his crimes, and if so, where might the line be drawn between Pretty's actions and his own duties? In the eyes of the law no doubt, it would have been the judicial process of that law, but in Gods eyes... Cato was not so sure!

There had been great debate in parliament and the papers, and there could be no doubt that popular opinion held for the man, but popular opinion would never be allowed to dictate the path of justice. Cato deliberated that he would leave the ultimate judgement to God Almighty, and avowed to dispatch Daniel Pretty into his care with the least distress and greatest speed and dignity that lay within his power.

412

His day began at 5 a.m by introducing himself to his assistant, Mr Seth Adams, who had travelled the previous evening from Manchester. Together with Adams, Cato prepared for the work that lay ahead. He began with an inspection of the rope that was purpose made to home office specification. It was about the thickness of a man's finger and made of silk hemp. Over the following day and night, it would be stretched on the scaffold by bags of sand to remove all springiness and ensure Pretty's neck snapped instantly.

Cato inspected the eyelet and the rubber ring that would prevent it from slipping, then he and Adams secured the rope to the scaffold and attached sand bags roughly equal to Pretty's considerable weight. Thereafter they checked the trap door by launching the sacks into the darkness of the pit. On each occasion, the crack of the doors swinging open and the dull thud of the arrested sacks reverberated about the prison. Clerks looked up from their work and prisoners fell silent in their cells.

Governor Reynolds crossed the courtyard to the shed in a state of clear agitation. 'Mr. Cato,' he began, 'that is four times now! I understand your need to check these things, but is it necessary to do it quite so many times?'

'I have been testing the apparatus and, at the same time, adjusting the drop, Mr Reynolds; everything is correct now.'

'It is having a very unsettling effect upon the whole prison, Mr Cato.'

'As I mentioned, Mr Reynolds; the work is now complete.'

'Thank you Mr Cato, I am very relieved to hear it. May I inquire what the drop is to be?'

'Three feet six inches.'

The governor looked astonished at Cato's words. 'Three foot six! Surely that is not enough, Mr Cato?'

'It will be sufficient Mr Reynolds.'

'But... but he won't even pass through the doors! You will choke the man to death surely! It has been my unfortunate duty to attend two hangings by your colleague Mr Ellis - who is very experienced in these matters - and on each occasion the condemned man has passed fully through the doors.'

The atmosphere within the shed dropped like a stone. 'Mr. Reynolds,' said Cato, with more than a tinge of irritation that his professional judgement had been brought into doubt, 'You will be interested to know that I was assistant to Mr Ellis for fully three years, and were Mr Ellis here now, he would judge the drop to be three feet six inches!'

413

'May I inquire why sir?'

'For the very good reason sir, that it will take thirty hundredweight's of striking force to break the condemned man's neck. His body mass will effect such a force by falling the distance I have mentioned. A man of eight stones might require a drop of ten feet to achieve the same effect. If we do as you suggest, we will execute him by decapitation and not by choking as you fear, however... I am very conscious of your ultimate responsibility for the proceedings... Should you care to provide me with written instructions...!'

The colour drained from Reynolds face. 'I am sure that will not be necessary Mr Cato; please conclude your work as quickly as you can and I'm sure we will all be most grateful to you.' With that, he turned on his heel and made his way back to the administration block.

'He sounds a bit miffed, Mr Cato?'

'A reluctant host I'm afraid, Seth.'

'Why bring this fellow all the way down here anyway, what was wrong with Bristol.'

'He has many friends among the common classes' - ruffians, tinkers, navvies and the like. I think they were afraid of trouble - a riot or an attempt to spring him perhaps.'

Within the admin block, Reynolds spoke to the waiting man in a pinstriped suit. 'You may see him now Mr Foley, my apologies for the delay.'

'Thank you, Mr Reynolds.'

They led the solicitor into Pretty's cell and he caught his breath on the wreaths of sweet smoke that rose slowly from Pretty's pipe to permeate the whole atmosphere of the cell. He began to speak excitedly without bothering with the usual niceties.

'I have what might be very important news Daniel. I have received word from the asylum for the insane at Bristol, that a woman who claims to have been with you that evening, says it was she, not you, who was responsible for Ridler's death.'

This clearly took Pretty by surprise, 'What's been said?' he asked.

'She claims to have been the one who started the fire - she says your intention was to arrest him, not burn him to death.'

'You say she's in an asylum?'

'Yes, yes I'm afraid she is - a fact that does not help our case I'm afraid... She is the wife of one of his victims and there is now some question over her sanity. However, during her more lucid moments she clearly believes herself to be guilty of your crime.'

'And when she's not lucid?'

'Then she has to be sedated for her own wellbeing.'

'If she's mad - why are you bothering with her?'

'Because I don't believe your story, Daniel! Because I cannot believe you do not know this woman, nor that she could so accurately describe you and the events of that night without having been there.'

'She wasn't there.'

'Then why would she claim she was?'

'I have no idea!'

'Mr. Pretty, please think about the implications of what she is saying. If there is any truth in this - even if we could only prove her presence - we could get a stay of execution and ultimately we may yet save you from the gallows!'

'And hang her instead? I am beginning to believe you, Mr Foley, the woman must indeed be mad! It sounds as though she's in the right place to me!'

'Be that as it may, my duty is to you, not her. If there is any truth in what she says, you would be very foolish to keep it from me.'

Pretty did not reply for some time, then he looked Foley in the eye, 'I don't know who she is, or what she is talking about.'

'Then how does she know of your bullet wound? How can she describe the man you crippled, the slaughterman they call Leather Apron?'

'I've no idea.'

'I don't believe you!'

Pretty shrugged.

'I'm your council Mr Pretty. I can only help you if you tell me the truth.'

'Mr. Foley,' said Pretty, with rising anger, 'please listen to what I am saying! I do not give a tinker's damn for your opinion, nor do I want to rot for the rest of my life in your English goal! Bring Ridler back from the dead and I will kill the bastard again if that is what it takes to convince you! Stop interfering in things you do not understand, Mr Foley. England wants to hang a murderer... keep your nose out and England will not be disappointed!'

'That is your final word?'

'Yes.'

Foley rose angrily and, gathering his papers, almost threw them in his briefcase. He nodded to the warder and made his way to the door.

'Mr. Foley!'

'Yes Mr Pretty?'

'One last thing if you would be so good?'

'What is it?'

'Would you come back this evening?'

'For what purpose Mr Pretty, I really see no point?'

'To collect a letter.'

'Might I ask whom it is for?'

'For my priest, Mr Foley,' said Pretty with seeming astonishment, 'who else?'

The following morning, Cato and Adams rose early to remove the sacks from the rope, check the scaffold, and practice the pinioning of arms and legs for the last time, until Cato was satisfied that it could be done no quicker.

Those persons who had been invited to witness the hanging, Foley, the press, the Mayor, magistrates and the police, gathered in a silent group in the courtyard. Reynolds, the High Sheriff, a Catholic priest, warders, Cato and Adams, assembled in the corridor outside the administration office. Reynolds checked his watch continually until at 07.55 hours he said to Cato, 'Are you ready Mr Cato?'

Cato nodded in reply and the solemn procession made its way along the corridor and down the five steps to the condemned cell. The warder unlocked the cell door as another inside said, 'The prisoner will stand.' Reynolds entered, followed by Cato, Adams, and the others, and as though by instinct, Pretty picked out Cato and bid him good morning. Cato nodded in reply.

'A last request Mr Cato,' said Pretty, as Adams made his way behind him to pinion his wrists.

'What is it?' enquired Cato, outwardly calm, but inwardly alarmed at this diversion.

416

'I'll take my pipe with me if you don't mind.'

Reynolds shot an angry glance at the warders for not taking Pretty's pipe from him earlier. It was still gripped firmly between his lips, blue smoke rising steadily from it, the now familiar, sweet aroma, accentuated in everyone's nostrils by the tension of the event.

'Quite impossible!' said Reynolds. 'Totally out of the question! Home Office regulations clearly forbid any...'

Cato and Pretty ignored the Governor as each man looked at the other. Pretty stood a full thirteen inches taller than Cato, and Cato believed his reputation that he could kill him with bare hands before anyone could stop him, but Cato was not afraid. This was not a desperate man who would grasp at straws; there was neither fear nor anger in his eyes, only dignity and self-respect. Cato took Pretty's hands and passed them behind his back to Adams who waited with the leather straps; then to Pretty he said, 'When we reach the scaffold, stand inside the chalk square. You're a tall man Mr Pretty; you would oblige me greatly if you would then lean forward.'

Daniel Pretty nodded and Cato loosened the clothing about his neck. 'Please follow me,' said Cato and with hands tied behind his back, Pretty, Adams and the various officials filed out through the doorway where two warders positioned themselves either side of Pretty as he began his walk.

Cato walked at a rapid yet dignified pace, up the stairs, along the corridor, and out into the chill of the courtyard. They climbed the gallows and Pretty stood within the square as Cato had bid him and bowed his head. Cato took the pipe from Pretty's lips letting it fall to the boards. He quickly passed the noose over his head and pulled the eyelet tight as Adams trussed his ankles. Cato pulled down the rubber ring and pulled the white cap over Pretty's head in one practiced movement.

He darted to the lever and, as Adams moved off the drop, he pulled it hard. Only then did the priest's litany of prayer break through Cato's subconscious. As he recited the twenty-third psalm, the doors opened with a resounding thud, hitting the walls of the twelve-foot pit as Pretty's huge frame plummeted into the dark maul of the drop. The rope snatched bar tight without the slightest quiver, and Cato breathed a sigh of relief, for he knew that Pretty died instantly and painlessly at his hands.

A mere forty-five seconds had elapsed from the time they had left the cell. From the confines of their cells, prisoners shouted incoherent oaths, whilst cups clattered against bars in a cacophony of sound.

The warders stood down from heavy beams which spanned the drop and upon which they had been positioned to support Pretty, had that been necessary. A trickle of urine began to drip from Pretty's trousers, though this was not visible to the witnesses, but they saw the body twitch and convulse as his muscles relaxed. The doctor examined the body and nodded to Reynolds. 'Thank you Mr Cato,' he said quietly, 'very cleanly done. Snapped between the third and fourth!'

The assembly started to break up, some clearly distressed at what they had witnessed. Cato and Adams screened off the gallows with a black drape; then Cato dismissed Adams for a cup of tea. He examined Pretty with a professional interest and noted that there was little abrasion of the skin, with the neck appearing to have stretched about two inches. It was now his duty to stay with the body as it hung for the sixty minutes prescribed by the Home Office. Cato used that time to strip the body of its clothing, leaving a cloth about his loins as a mark of simple human decency. That done, he climbed into the pit and retrieved the pipe that was still alight when he found it.

With the drape erected, the body was in semi darkness, and light and shadow highlighted the dead man's muscles and sinews. What hung there like meat on a butchers' hook - its feet becoming ever more purple by the minute - was one of the finest human bodies Cato had ever seen. Everything about it was massive yet in perfect proportion. It was a highly intelligent machine of near perfection and Cato had destroyed it. He wondered what such a man would be, had he been born several centuries earlier - Surely such a man would be a King.

Adams returned when the hour was done. He and Cato hoisted the body and passed it to the care of the warders, who put it in a rough wooden coffin for the journey to the yard, where a grave had been dug and back-filled with quicklime. That done, Cato shook hands with Adams and the two executioners wished one another a pleasant journey home.

Cato was shown into the Governor's office where Reynolds sat behind his desk, clearly upset by the morning's events. 'Very distressing, Mr Cato, very distressing indeed, but these things have to be done I suppose. I would like to thank you, however, for the efficient way in which you conducted this sorry task. Thank goodness it all went so well. You may be sure I will write to the Home Secretary and commend you to him.' That said he pulled open a drawer and took out a cheque which he offered to Cato. 'Seven guineas Mr Cato - on completion!'

'Thank you Mr Reynolds.'

'I will have you taken back to the railway station as soon as you are ready, but there is just one other small matter before you return to Harrogate - the pipe! I need to include it in his possessions.'

'Yes, of course,' said Cato. He put his hand in his pocket and withdrew the pipe, placing it on the desk before the Governor. 'Thank you very much Mr Cato!'

Cato watched the fields flit by as he sat in the second-class compartment of the 11.15 train to Bristol, Temple Meads. There he would change for Birmingham Central. He expected to make Harrogate by 9.30 p.m.

It would be a long journey with plenty of time to ruminate the events of the day. He looked at his companion in the carriage; a middle-aged man who sat opposite. They exchanged pleasantries on entering the carriage, but had fallen silent thereafter by unspoken mutual agreement.

Cato reached into his pocket and withdrew a pipe. It was a fine briar with an ivory stem, not a cheap item at all, but then Pretty was reputed to be a wealthy man. It had cost him his own pipe to obtain it, but that was a small matter. No doubt, Reynolds would dine out for many months to come, on tales of Pretty smoking his pipe all the way to the gallows and proudly showing off Cato's old pipe into the bargain.

Cato took out a penknife and selected the pipe cleaner. He scraped the bowl, knocking out the scrapings on the edge of the open window, before filling it with his own tobacco and pressing it firm. He took a silver lighter from his pocket and lit the pipe, drawing successively upon it until it burnt evenly across the bowl. It tasted quite different; Pretty's tobacco clearly changing the flavour of his own to one of unfamiliar sweetness. Cato concluded that it was, however, not unpleasant for all that. He looked up at his companion who smiled back in tacit approval.

Cato drew deeply on the pipe closing his eyes as he did so. He thought of the man to whom it once belonged and wondered if justice had truly been done. He thought, also, of the priest whose litany had been completely blanked out by Cato's mind, as he concentrated on his own tasks. With eyes shut, he began to repeat the verses softly.

Yeah though I walk through the valley of the shadow of death,

I shall fear no evil.

For thou art with me!

Thy rod and thy staff, they comfort me!'

419

The other gentleman looked up at Cato's softly spoken incantation. He raised an eyebrow, then returned once more to his paper, preferring to ignore the rather bizarre behaviour of his chance companion. One could never be sure whom one might share a carriage with these days!

CHAPTER 62

Bristol Asylum for the insane

Forks of ice blue lightning split the sky, and for an instant, the lawns were bathed in its eerie light.

Movement near the gates caught Richard Durcan's eye and he strained to see who approached through the rain lashed gloom. Two carriage lamps - bobbing like fireflies - danced this way and that as the pony and trap sped up the gravel drive. He turned from the study window where he'd been watching the electric storm, to feel in the darkness for the bell cord.

'The parson's about to pay us a visit Jeffries!'

'Tonight Sir?' said the incredulous butler as he lit the lamp.

'It's his trap unless I'm much mistaken. I can only assume something's amiss.'

'So it would seem sir, but let us hope not!'

Umbrella held high, Jeffries dashed out into the rain to steady the pony as the Parson climbed down. As if by magic, a groom appeared and took the trap away, whilst Jeffries escorted Pimm into the hall, closing the door against the night.

Richard Durcan greeted his friend of many years and helped him remove his carriage cape.

'What a sorry sight you are Pimm. See if you can find the vicar a change of clothes Jeffries - come into the study Pimm and dry yourself by the fire.'

'Shall I prepare a room sir?'

'No, no, I must get back!' said the parson hurriedly. 'Mrs. Pimm doesn't like thunderstorm's one little bit - not one little bit - but thank you all the same Jeffries.'

'So Pimm... let me pour you a brandy whilst you tell me what sends you abroad on such a night.'

'Well there you've said it Richard - what a night indeed - but I really had no choice. I have the most distressing news I'm afraid, and come by in the most bizarre manner! Not an hour ago - just as night was falling - I spotted a tinker walking up my drive as bold as brass, you'd have thought he owned the place. He was a tall, thin fellow with an eternal grin, a narrow face and small eyes -

quite a distinctive looking chap, and to my eternal discredit I couldn't help thinking he bore an uncanny resemblance to a rat. Anyway - he had the look of the common man about him and I can't say I cared for the fellow at all.'

'Mrs. Thomas has instructions to give these unfortunate people the leftover's and a night's shelter above the stable in exchange for doing some small tasks about the garden, so we get them regularly. I thought little of it at that time, but when I opened the door he was sheltering beneath the porch, soaked to the skin, and seemingly, not the least bit put out about it. In fact, he had a most insolent and cocky manner about him. "Parson Pimm?" he enquired of me and when I answered in the affirmative, he took down a shoulder box that was tightly wrapped in oilskins against the weather. It was a Hurdy Gurdy box of all things, and from somewhere within its innards he took out an oilskin pouch. Without another word, he covered his music box, hefted it onto his shoulder, doffed his hat, and walked back into the rain! I was so astonished I'm afraid I let him go!'

He handed Richard Durcan a letter, which Durcan took to the lamp to read.

"Sir," it began.

I enclose and entrust to you, the sum of one thousand guineas.

You may recall a young woman who became known to me as Mrs Isaac Smith, of Selworthy in Somerset and whom I understand knew you as a child. She spoke of you several times and clearly held you in high esteem.

I regret to inform you that she has recently been widowed, the tragic circumstances of which have so afflicted her mind, that she has been committed to the asylum at Bristol.

I ask you as a man of God to do what I cannot; namely all that is within your power to secure her release from that dark place, in the hope that with your benefaction and the sum enclosed, she may be speedily recovered to good health."

'It is signed D.P?' said Durcan, with a questioning glance at the priest.

'I have no idea!' Pimm replied.

'This is all very unfortunate; Pimm, but frankly it could be anyone. It may even be an elaborate hoax!'

'A hoaxer who gives away a thousand guineas?' said Pimm, placing the contents of the oilskin on the desk.

An astonished Richard Durcan spread the tattered notes across the table. There must indeed, have been something approaching a thousand guineas on the table before him.

422

'Richard I know this is opening up old wounds, but the young man Polly ran away with was called Isaac Smith as you will recall, and there is a very real possibility that this letter is about your daughter.'

'I don't accept that Pimm!'

'But surely you will inquire?'

'It is all a very sorry state of affairs, but she made her choice! Her fortunes are no longer my concern.'

'Richard, for goodness sake!' said the parson in astonishment, 'We are talking about your own flesh and blood!'

Durcan crashed his fist on the table, his legendary temper more thunderous than the weather.

'I'll thank you to mind your own damned business!'

'Richard... my dear friend...' said the parson, searched for words to redeem the argument he saw so resolutely slipping from him; 'Surely you don't intend to abandon her - she is your daughter!'

'My daughter you say! Let me tell you about my daughter Pimm! My daughter was brought up in a Christian home, with every freedom and privilege I could give her, and she repaid me by behaving like a common trollop! She ran away at the dead of night - unwed and pregnant with the bastard child of an illiterate blacksmith - conceived, as I understand it - amid the filth and braying of a cattle barn. She has brought shame and disgrace to the family name, and that Pimm - daughter or no daughter - is unforgivable. Now I think you should leave!'

'Very well, if that is what you wish,' replied the parson equally angrily! 'I cannot demand you take action over this issue Richard, but if you are of a mind that this unfortunate woman is not your daughter, then you can hardly have any objection if I use this money for the purpose intended and I shall trouble you no more with the matter.' He began to gather the notes together.

Neither man noticed Elizabeth Durcan enter the room, drawn there by familiar voices raised in anger. She took the letter from her husband's hand, the colour draining from her face as she read the words.

'Parson Pimm,' she said calmly, 'would you be kind enough to take me to the station?'

'Well I... Of course I will, but there are no trains until the morning Elizabeth.'

423

'I will wait,' she replied.

'Elizabeth I forbid you to…'

'Forbid all you like Richard,' she said, interrupting him mid sentence. 'Forbid daylight if you will, but I am not leaving my daughter in a lunatic asylum! I have lived with your anger for too long and I am going to take my child away from that hellhole as soon as I possibly can! And if there is no place for her at Oxtalls when I return,' she added for good measure, 'then there is no place for me either!'

~

Their footfalls echoed like a clarion call along endless corridors of distempered walls and polished floors. Shuffling, pyjama clad men and women gathered to stand and stare; most silent and watchful, some reaching out to touch and grab like traders at an Arab bazaar.

A man stood in a doorway masturbating slowly, without joy or shame, mumbling an incoherent litany as they passed by. The smell of disinfectant and soiled clothing filled their nostrils and drove up bile to the throat. On and on they went, past vacant faces and solid doors until the nurse stopped at ward 26.

Elizabeth Durcan barely recognised her daughter.

'Polly,' she said softly, touching her shoulder.

Polly looked up at her mother but did not recognise her, for the drugs had numbed her senses and dulled her wits. Her face was gaunt and ashen, her eyes dark ringed, her once beautiful hair, thin and almost grey. Elizabeth Durcan drew in her breath, 'Oh my God,' she gasped in disbelief.

Polly thought the lady was very beautiful. Her face was kind and she was smiling though she looked very sad. Polly looked at Amy and Amy smiled in return.

'Polly, your father and I have come to take you home.'

They seemed familiar - the handsome man and the beautiful woman.

'Do you want to come home with us Polly?'

'To Selworthy?'

'No, not to Selworthy darling, to Uley - you remember Uley? Uley and Parson Pimm - faithful, gentle, Parson Pimm - you rode him everywhere, do you remember? He's very, very old now, but he wants you home so much!'

'Please don't cry,' said Polly, for the lady had begun to weep.

'I'm sorry,' she said, wiping her eyes and trying to regain control.

'He loved me,' said Polly.

'Yes he loved you, we all love you darling.'

'I loved him too!'

'Yes you did darling; that's why we want to take you home where you belong.'

'Isaac doesn't like this place, Mama!'

Elizabeth's heart skipped a beat for she had called her "Mama," just as she did as a child.

'It's a horrible place Polly; that's why we want to take you home.'

'But Amy must come too.'

'That's not possible Polly, this lady works here.' She looked at the woman for the first time. She was old and dressed in black. She had a severe, rather unfriendly face.

'She must come too,' Polly said, becoming agitated, reaching out for Amy's hand. She repeated the words over and over, her voice slowly trailed away to nothing; 'She must come - must come - must come...'

'I'm not her nurse, Mrs Durcan,' said Amy, taking the slender hand that reached out for hers. 'I'm Amy Smith, her mother-in-law.'

Elizabeth looked as though she had been struck across the face. She looked toward her husband, but he stood stunned and silent; too shocked at what had become of his daughter to speak.

'Mrs. Smith,' she began, 'If I could turn back the clock...'

'Yes I daresay we'd all like to do that Mrs Durcan!'

'I can understand how you feel,' Elizabeth replied, 'And I don't expect you to forgive or forget. All I can say is that I am truly sorry from the very bottom of my heart. I cannot change what has happened, nor bring back your son - though God knows if it were in my power I would do so - but I can take Polly away from this place - if you will help me.'

She took the old lady's hand, tears welling in her eyes and spilling down her cheeks, 'Mrs. Smith, if you love my daughter, please, please, help me! We will pay you well and you will lack for nothing I promise you.'

'I don't want anything from you, Mrs Durcan,' replied Amy. 'I don't expect to be paid for looking after my own.' She looked to Richard Durcan and added,

'We may be common folk, your lordship, but we don't abandon our children the minute a problem comes along.'

It was then that Elizabeth noticed Polly's swollen belly.

'Are you pregnant, child?' she asked with concern.

'She's six and a half months,' said Amy.

'It will be a girl,' said Polly matter-of-factly. 'She'll be four pounds two ounces and she'll be born on August the seventeenth - in the morning when it's still dark, and her name will be Nancy.'

'You can't possibly know that Polly,' said Elizabeth Durcan; 'No-one knows these things.'

'I know!'

'But how can you know darling?'

'Isaac told me.'

'But he's...' Elizabeth Durcan looked at her husband, her sentence unfinished, utter desolation written in the lines of her face.

Richard Durcan made arrangements to take Polly home that very hour. It took a generous cheque in favour of the hospital, and yet another in favour of the governor's personal account to achieve it.

'This is a very delicate matter Lord Durcan, and requires considerable intervention - personal intervention if you understand my meaning. There are records and processes to deal with as I'm sure you understand.'

In return, Durcan saw all record of her confinement under the mental health act, removed from the records and burnt before his eyes.

They travelled to the station at Bristol Temple Meads, in two separate carriages for their onward rail journey home. Polly, Pimm and Elizabeth Durcan rode in one, with Amy Smith and Richard Durcan in the other.

At his request, Amy told him of the fateful night when Ridler beat Isaac near to death and ravaged Polly. She told him what little she knew of Daniel Pretty and the inferno on the pier.

She entreated Richard Durcan to provide for the unborn child if Polly survived until its birth, for it was innocent of its father's crimes, terrible though they were. Finally, she entreated him to engage the best physician possible, to arrest Polly's failing health before it was too late.

426

'I shall do all these things,' he promised her, 'you have my word on it, but what is the physician to treat? The hospital tells me there is nothing physically wrong, yet I am shocked beyond belief at what has become of her.'

'There's nothing I can give a name to and I know this will sound foolish to an educated gentleman such as yourself Lord Durcan, but it is my belief - my earnest and heartfelt belief - that Polly is dying of a broken heart.'

Durcan listened grim faced to Amy's words. 'Mrs. Smith!' he said finally, 'We sit here as strangers and possibly even enemies in your eyes, for I acknowledge that I have done your family a grave injustice in the past, but I believe we are united in one cause at least - the wellbeing of my daughter whom you clearly care deeply for. I am going to ask you for your help. Will you give it to me, for without it, I fear for what will become of her?'

Amy nodded her ascent.

'But I entreat you also,' he continued, 'that no-one must ever know about this man Pretty - not even Elizabeth. The money he provided I shall give to Pimm to benefit the poor of the parish and that, I hope, will see the end of that sorry affair. In return for your care - if care for her you will - I will make you as comfortable as I possibly can; will you agree to that?' Amy nodded again and he thanked her for it.

Polly did survive until the birth though she had become very weak and there were grave fears for her as she went into labour. However, Dr. Wooton delivered a healthy baby girl at three o' clock in the morning, on August the seventeenth. Amy whisked the newborn from the room, still covered in the skein of birth, so that Polly should not hear it cry nor see the child's face.

The baby was given into the care of a wet-nurse with whom it began a journey to Northumberland and the home of Richard Durcan's sister - all before the household had stirred. Later that day, Richard Durcan gathered the house staff and the men of the Home Farm together and informed them of a stillbirth, giving them instructions that the matter was never to be mentioned again.

Polly received the news of the stillbirth without emotion. Holding Amy's hand, she closed her eyes and fell into a deep, exhausted sleep.

Some months later, and against Richard Durcan's better judgement, the baby girl came back to Oxtalls Hall under the guise of Mrs Jeffries orphaned niece. It was at Amy's insistence that the child be returned to where she at least could watch over it, albeit from a distance. They called the girl Clara and Mrs Jeffries duly brought her up with Christian charity, if not with actual love.

427

To the concern of all involved in the conspiracy, Polly insisted on calling the girl Nancy, not Clara.

'Why do you call her by that name, Polly,' said Elizabeth Durcan with concern. 'Her name is Clara, why do you call her Nancy?'

Polly looked at her mother and said matter-of-factly, 'So that I can never love her, Mama!'

Deeply shocked, Elizabeth Durcan exchanged glances with Amy, who looked similarly upset. From that moment on, Elizabeth gave instructions to the household, that the child was never to be allowed upstairs nor on the lawn before Mistress Polly's room.

For the rest of her life, Polly rarely left the room and it became a prison of her own making. She spent her days at the French windows waiting for Isaac to come for her. She did so with unswerving patience, as though waiting for a dear, dear, friend who was a little late for dinner.

The windows were never fully closed, no matter how harsh the weather, for she was terrified that Isaac might come whilst she slept and find the door barred against him. It was hard on Amy's poor old bones for she slept in Polly's room too, but there was wood aplenty for the fire.

For months after her ordeal on the pier, the nights were a trying time for Amy, for Polly had a recurring nightmare that woke her each night. She would see Daniel Pretty hanging by the neck in the execution shed of Bodmin Goal, his body slowly turning on the rope's end for what she saw as her crime. She saw Molly too, screaming in agony at the window of the blazing warehouse; her clothes and hair burnt to ash, her eyes and the flesh of her face, melting in the heat as she cried out for the help that would never come. Amy would wake to find her sat bolt upright and crying out in the darkness; awake, yet still living the nightmare that was so vivid and so real.

Then one evening in late March, on the anniversary of Daniel Pretty's death, there came a strange occurrence which, in Amy's opinion, saved Polly's life. Night had fallen and the meadow beyond the garden was bathed in moonlight, fully back to the trees that marked the edge of the wood. As they made ready for bed, they heard a haunting melody drifting across the meadow. It was the unmistakable sound of a hurdy gurdy organ, and the melody it played was the Londonderry Air.

It came from the very edge of the wood, yet despite the distance, they could hear it clearly on the still night air. Polly stepped onto the balcony, searching the darkness to see who might be playing the instrument.

428

After some moments, lamplight appeared beneath the wooded canopy and in its glow there stood a thin, wiry man, dressed in common working clothing made dirty and dishevelled by the road. He watched her with a steady gaze as he turned the handle of the hurdy gurdy, its long wooden leg taking the weight of the instrument.

The sonorous sound of the pipes were crystal clear on the cold night air and very beautiful in their melancholy simplicity. Polly's hand went to her mouth and her eyes brimmed with tears. She sang the familiar words in a faltering whisper, missing many through her sobbing.

And if you come, when all the flowers are dying,

And I am dead, as dead I well may be.

You'll come and find, the place where I am lying,

And kneel and say an "Ave" there for me.

And I shall hear, tho' soft you tread above me.

And all my dreams, will warm and sweeter be.

If you'll not fail to tell me that you love me.

I'll simply sleep in peace until you come to me.

'What is it Polly, said Amy anxiously, who is that man?'

'His name is Jacko,' she said simply, her tears spilling over and tricking down her cheeks.

The Hurdy Gurdy man hefted the organ to his shoulder and hung his lamp upon it. Taking his hat from his head, he bowed deeply in Polly's direction for some moments, before replacing the hat on his head once more. At that moment, John Long and two other men from the home farm appeared in the meadow, John Long armed with a shotgun, and hollering to the man to stay just where he was. The lantern was snuffed out in an instant, and the wood was plunged into darkness once more.

Amy led a sobbing Polly back into the room and sat her down on her bed, her arm about Polly's shoulder.

'Who is this Jacko person Polly; is he someone who wants to hurt you? What does he want with us, why has he upset you so?'

It took some while for Polly to collect herself, enough to speak.

'He means us no harm Amy, don't be afraid, but they won't catch him - he's far too clever for them.'

'But why is he here Polly; what does he want with you so late at night?'

'He wants to tell me that Daniel forgives me. He knows how much it hurts me and he wants me to know that Daniel forgives me - I know it in my heart.'

Polly explained how Daniel Pretty and Jacko rescued her from the burning warehouse. It was he who had slipped the note beneath the door at Leathernbottle; telling Amy of Polly's plight in the hospital.

'Then let us be glad this Daniel has forgiven you and his friend is watching over us, and let's say no more about it,' said Amy, secretly alarmed that an Irish tinker should be watching them by night from the nearby woods, but pleased that Polly had found solace in his strange appearance and the beautiful melody he played for her.

That night Polly slept peacefully, free of her nightmare for the very first time and as a consequence, Amy slept soundly too.

Amy didn't hear Polly stir in the small hours, disturbed from her slumber by a soft sound on the pillow beside her. She opened her eyes but all was in darkness; the fire reduced to ash. She felt the gentle touch of breath upon her shoulder, then the familiar, tender warmth of another human being laid beside her.

'Isaac is that you?' she whispered to the darkness; wanting, yet not daring to hope that it was him. She had asked God to send him so many times - she so wanted him to come - so wanted her prayers to be answered.

'I'm sorry I woke you,' he whispered, 'you were sleeping so peacefully.' He put his arm about her waist and she took his hand in her own.

'I was dreaming of you,' she said softly. You told me that if I dream of you, you will come.'

'And I do my darling; I am always here - always beside you - you are never alone.'

She began to sob softly at the sound of his voice. She turned towards him and he held her very close whilst she cried in his arms. He whispered that he loved her and she whispered that she loved him in return. She rested her head upon his shoulder and he felt the wetness of her tears upon his chest.

They wept, and kissed, and held one another close; then Isaac took her by the hand and together they rose up from the bed and went to the balcony. They climbed onto the balustrade above her father's study, the lawns far below them, the woods lost in darkness beyond the meadow.

'I'm frightened, Isaac,' she said, the alarm clear to hear in her voice, but he told her not to worry for he'd let no harm befall her if only she'd put her trust in him. Hand in hand, they stepped from the balcony, but instead of falling, they flew like Peter Pan and Wendy, just like the wonderful story by Mr J.M. Barrie. They flew and flew, hand in hand across the Silver Mountains, until Polly saw their beloved Leathernbottle Cottage appear beneath them. Everything was just as it they had left it and her heart filled with a joy she thought she would never know again.

Isaac had so much to do in the forge and she in the cottage. Becky helped let out the chickens and collect the eggs, whilst Amy was busy making up the fire and dusting down the mantelpiece. All was just as it should be.

Come the afternoon, Ira and McNab called by and it was a joy to hear them pulling one another's leg by the smithy door. That evening, with the day's work done, she and Isaac walked the Beacon, hand in hand in the late evening sunshine, the river still and shining like a silver mirror.

That night, when Becky and Amy had fallen asleep, they lay in one another's arms in their tiny bedroom, and Isaac told her that he loved her once more. He told her how he had loved her from the moment he bumped his head at the Tug 'O' War, and she had saved him from certain death and doolallyness beneath the willow tree. She told him she loved him too - with all her heart - and parted her lips so they could kiss. He made love to her then; passionately and tenderly, and when they were done with their lovemaking, she wept in his arms.

It was then as they lay together in that wonderful tender moment, that Isaac and their tiny room began to shimmer and mist and fade. She cried out for them not to go, but did go, and instead there was just the chill room at Oxtalls Hall and Amy sat beside her, calling her name softly and rocking her gently in her arms.

'Why did it have to end?' she sobbed, 'oh why did it have to end?'

Amy knew instinctively, without words, what had happened.

'Be patient, my darling,' she whispered softly; 'for I promise you will see them again one day.'

CHAPTER 63

Jonah Tull

The Daimler Motor car spluttered several times before coming to an undignified halt. The chauffeur lifted the engine cover to look within, but the hot and oily workings were as much a mystery that day, as on any other.

'What's the problem, Jefferies?' said his mistress.

'Nothing obvious I'm afraid Ma'am.'

'Well, we can't stay here all day while you scratch your head - perhaps someone at the public house can help?'

Jeffries entered the noisy hubbub of the Trouble House Inn, whereupon most conversation ceased. Curious eyes turned to the uniformed intruder.

'Does anyone here know anything about motor car engines?' he asked.

'Eh up, Jonah! Yer's thy chance to shine, lad!'

'I'm yer to drink, not work.' replied the sullen young man playing dominoes.

'There's a shilling in it, if you can get us on our way,' said Jeffries.

Jonah Tull put down a four and three and said, 'Peg us five,' before following the chauffeur outside.

The Daimler was beautiful, and polished so you could see your face in it. A woman sat patiently in the cab - a handsome woman for her age. He doffed his cap and she gave him a curt nod.

A glance was enough, but he made a big show of fiddling, and twiddling, and screwing up his face.

'I need a wet rag,' he announced finally.

Jeffries brought the requisite items from the luggage compartment and tried to watch what the young man was doing, but a withering stare from Tull sent him two steps backward. Shielded by his back, Jonah reconnected the loose magneto lead, then pressed the soaking rag against the exhaust pipe, thereafter to disappear in clouds of steam.

Jonah closed the engine cover and tossed the filthy cloth to Jeffries, who caught it instinctively in immaculately gloved hands. Jonah swung himself into the cab and made a few adjustments to throttle and ignition before ordering the

432

hapless Jeffries to crank the engine. The engine burst into life at the first swing, then settled down to a steady popping rhythm.

'Well done,' said Elizabeth Durcan, 'how clever!'

'Each to his own Ma'am,' replied Jonah.

'What was wrong?'

'Well, begging your pardon Ma'am,' he said glancing at Jeffries, 'but t'was more to do with the driving than the engine! Too much advance. That makes un' hot and boils the carburettor. That's what I was cooling down; yer petrol was all gassed up. A Daimler's as good an engine as money can buy, but too much of that kind of thing and you end up knockin' the bearings out, or you might even have a fire! I've seen that a few times.'

'Oh goodness...' she replied, giving Jeffries a scathing look. 'What's your name?'

'Jonah Tull, Ma'am.'

'And what do you do for a living, Jonah Tull?'

'Millwright at Winterbotham's at the moment Ma'am...' till something better comes along!'

'Well, perhaps something might! My husband is Lord Durcan - I am sure you will have heard of him. He's much taken with all this newfangled technology; we don't understand it ourselves, do we Jeffries? I imagine there is a lot a clever young man like you could do about the estate, not to mention driving the car. I'll tell my husband how helpful you've been and I'm sure he would like to speak to you.'

'Thank you Ma'am, very grateful I'm sure.'

'With a shave and a smart uniform, I'm sure you'd make a very presentable young man, Jonah Tull!' Tull grinned and doffed his hat once more. A scowling Jeffries pressed the promised shilling in his hand and the Daimler ground off in a haze of blue smoke.

On consideration, Jonah Tull decided that he'd landed in clover.

He'd a brand new uniform, a room to himself above the garage, a fair wage, and after little more than eight weeks, a pretty kitchen maid more than willing to show him her favours.

For somewhat different reasons, the master and mistress both thought Jonah could do no wrong. The mistress would never use the Daimler unless he was

433

driving, whilst the master fancied himself as a bit of an Armstrong and thus needed a mechanic for the mucky bits.

His "newfangled" projects, included water pumped directly to the house, with piped hot water for Elizabeth's bath, and electric light in every reception room, all powered by large glass batteries, in a newly installed generator room. It had become Tull's job to ensure they were kept fully charged and the Ruston generator fully maintained. There was also a telephone in the study and two steam-ploughing engines had recently appeared at the Home farm.

As soon as he told the master he could save money mending the machinery, a ratchet drill turned up and a treadle lathe was on its way. By all accounts, it was equipped with back-gear, a screw cutting lead screw and an American tool-post! The rest of the staff saw Jonah Tull as sullen and arrogant and eagerly awaited his comeuppance, but Jonah cared little for their jealousy!

Life was good, very good, and unlike most previous employments, there'd only been one problem since he'd been there. Even that hadn't been his fault, and for that reason, he couldn't make head nor tail of it. It was very strange goings on indeed.

He'd been sent to look at the drive chain on a thresher John Long had wheeled into the Meadow. Jonah had tied his hair back, for the weather was hot and the thresher oily. He'd walked from the yard about the side of the house, then out into the meadow. As he passed by the house front, he heard a voice cry out. Curtains at a first floor window were hastily drawn, but not before he saw a grey-haired woman at the window, her hand held to her mouth.

Moments later the mistress came from the house in a rare old temper. She forbade him to wear his hair tied back again; in fact, she insisted he cut it short immediately. Not only that, she forbade him ever to pass in view of that side of the house unless he was expressly told to do so. Jonah was left open mouthed and wondering what he'd done wrong, especially as the next time he saw the mistress, he could have been forgiven for thinking that nothing had ever happened.

Jonah became curious about the woman at the window. He asked about her at the Home Farm and below stairs, but no one would talk about it. They were either too busy or would avoid the question altogether. 'Best you speak to Mr Jeffries,' they would say. Even John Long - the man he was friendliest with - told him he'd do better to get on with his work.

Jonah let the matter lie, until he and Long sat drinking cider together one evening.

'If thee keeps askin' the wrong bloody questions, thee'll find thyself taking a long walk down the drive; chauffeur or no bloody chauffeur,' said Long.

'Come now John, I'm only asking what every other bugger seems to know!'

'Oh, do they!' he replied.

Long packed his pipe and thought about it. 'What everyone else knows,' he said finally, 'is probably only half the story, but I'll tell thee what I know, so thee don't find thyself disadvantaged. Thereafter's an end to the matter though!'

Jonah agreed.

'Master and mistress had two children - a boy and a girl,' he began. 'The boy was a Captain in the Royal Gloucester Hussars - a fine lad too. He went missing on an expedition to the Antarctic in 1907 or thereabouts. The great age of polar exploration they called it, every bugger trying to be the first to reach the South Pole. Anyway, summat went wrong an' the ship an every bugger in it were never seen nor heard of again; they was all adventurers like the young master or Clever Dick scientists, by all account.'

'What was an army officer doing on a scientific ship? That don't make no sense.'

'Like I said - twer' the great age of polar exploration and Antarctica was the last great wilderness to be conquered. Young Master William were a fine soldier decorated fer bravery during the trouble with the Boxers, an' a crack shot to boot! An all anyone knew of Antarctica in them days, were that it were a bloody dangerous place t' be, an' that would attract young master William like a magnet, brave as a lion 'e were.

'So what's that got to do with the woman at the window?'

Nothing, I were just telling thee about young Master William that's all. Then there were his sister, Mistress Polly. She were two year younger than Master William and it was her you saw at the window.'

'Couldn't ave been,' said Jonah; 'The woman I saw were much older.'

'Nonetheless, that's who you saw! Madness and sorrow have turned her old before her time, and to the best of my knowledge her's only left that room a handful of times in eighteen years.'

Jonah whistled, 'Is she a prisoner or something?'

'In a manner of speaking - but tis not chains or locks that bind her Jonah, but a broken heart!'

John Long had Tull's undivided attention.

'I come yer when she was a young girl - running about the estate like a mad thing an' into everything. Climb anything - ride anything - talk to anyone - absolute apple of her father's eye she were! She was as pretty as a picture even then, but she grew into a great beauty - as beautiful as any young woman you've ever seen! She broke many a heart just looking at her - mine included! One day she's just a slip of a girl, the next …'

'Tis no exaggeration to say er could have had taken her choice from any young gentleman as took er fancy. Lawyers, doctors, landed gentry like the master. There was even a mention of young Freddy Berkeley would you believe! Legend has it that the Berkeley's can ride on their own land, all the way from Berkeley Castle here in Gloucestershire, right through to Berkeley Square in London Town if they've a mind to, an she could ave' married into all of that, but she weren't interested in none of em. Instead she had 'er heart set on a blacksmith's boy - a young fellow called Isaac Smith.'

Long drew heavily on his pipe. 'Tis not as though they were even much alike, now I think back! She was a tomboy an' a chatterbox and into everything; he was quiet an' shy - purposeful like! Well she falls pregnant by un', an' tis the biggest scandal in years. When master finds out, e's in a temper the like of which thee've never seen and never wants ter see what's more! Straight away 'e sends meself an' Edwards the Gamekeeper an' a bloody idiot called Ned Meadows t' find er lover boy an' sort un' out, once an fer all. As bad luck should have it we did, an Edwards got a bloody good hiding fer is troubles.'

'Anyway, Ned's so frit he damn near shits himself an' sets the dogs on young Isaac. They were two vicious buggers called Rufus an' Satan and they damn near ripped un' to pieces. The Master always kept dogs to discourage burglars, but never were there any before or since, as vicious as those two black-hearted bastards. 'Anyway, to cut a long story short, he survives his injuries by some bloody miracle and the two of em runs off and gets wed. She gives birth to a daughter who they lost to tuberculosis some eight year later, then just when she falls pregnant again, he's beaten to death in his own forge by a bloke on the run fer murder. Tis all too much for Mistress Polly, and master and mistress find her in the looney bin down Bristol way.'

'They bring her home an' she's looked after by Amy Smith, her mother-in-law, cus old Mrs Hudson, as was the nurse here fer many years, retired through ill health an' at the same time, Mr an' Mrs Jeffries takes over as Butler an Housekeeper. Then Amy Smith, 'er mother in law, dies of old age some five years ago, an' tis all bin on Mrs Jefferies shoulders since then.'

'What happened about the other babby you mentioned,' asked Jonah?

'I were coming to that,' continued John Long, 'Her has the babby here at Oxtalls and in that very room, and tis supposedly a stillbirth, but as the poor little mite is taken away in a basket, one of the parlour maids swears she hears a baby cry. Er got the sharp side of Jeffries tongue fer saying that, let me tell you, so being early morning, twas all put down to tomcats scrapping on the roof. Everyone thought that was an end to the matter, but a few month later we hear Mrs Jeffries' sister - who no bugger's ever erd tell of afore - has died suddenly, an Mrs Jefferies is to look after her babby. Well, that set tongues to wag I can tell e!'

'Well, I got a brother, but I ain't told thee nothin' about un,' returned Jonah in defence of Longs tale.

'Perhaps thee ave,' said Long, 'but as your brother got a young un' as is the spitting image of a Durcan! What's more, there weren't never no funeral, as I recall.'

'What happened to the babby then?'

'Nothing much! The Jeffries brought her up and when she was old enough she went into service in the kitchen, but Mistress Polly never took to her, so she's never allowed to set foot on the stairs, a little like you an' the meadow!'

'Which one is she?' asked Tull.

'The little plump one as is ready fer plucking,' said Long, 'the one they call Clara!'

Jonah pondered these matters for some time before saying, 'Thing I don't understand is why there should be such a fuss over tying my hair back; that don't make no sense.'

'Not to you,' replied Long, 'But that's what the whole business is all about! Mistress Polly sits at that window all day long, re-living her memories an' waiting fer her lover to come back from the dead. Tis as though she can't accept he's gone. What's more - nothing she can see from that window is allowed to change - not so much as a blade of grass.'

'I still don't see …'

'Anytime I ever saw Isaac Smith,' said Long, interrupting him, 'he had his hair tied back in a cue; I never saw it no other way. You're a handsome lad, Jonah, an' you comes striding across the lawn we yer shirt open an' yer hair tied back, an' she thinks you're him come back from the dead. I shouldn't be surprised if thee didn't break her heart all over again. I can see thee thinks this all a bit strange, but I'll tell 'e' something now as is even stranger! One night, some months after the Mistress come home, we hear's music coming from under the

437

wood though the night's as black as a bloody coalscuttle. I takes up me shotgun an I'm heading across the meadow thinking there's some prank afoot, when I sees the Mistress on the balcony, dressed in her nightgown, looking as thin as a rake, an terrible distraught; singing and crying and Lord knows what else. All the while er's looking at a tinker with a hurdy gurdy organ stood under a Tilly lamp, winding away at the edge of the wood. I shouts out to un, thinkin' he's up to no bloody good; but the moment I do, the lamp goes out an he's gone - sharp as a bloody jack rabbit. I gathered a few fellows together an' we searched the wood, but we never found un.'

'When we get's back there's all hell on, with Mistress Polly in floods of tears. Amy's trying ter calm her down - not cus the tinkers upset her - but because we saw the bugger off, would you believe! Master's right fer sacking the lot on us fer upsetting her so, till Mistress Elizabeth tells him we was only doing our job, an 'e calms down a bit then. Next day, 'e says if the tinker ever comes again, we're to mind our own business; but not one word of an apology of course.'

'Why so much fuss about a tinker?' asked Jonah.

'How the hell should I know?' replied Long, 'all I know is tis like treading on eggshells where Mistress Polly's concerned, an' that's why folk are wary of all thy questions!'

The tinker seemed like a tale too far to Jonah and he didn't know whether to believe John Long or not. 'What song were 'e playing then,' he asked out of curiosity.

'An Irish folk song, name of "Danny boy",' replied John Long.

'I thought you said 'er fellows name were Isaac?'

'So it was.'

'Well that don't make no sense neither then,' said Jonah.

'Well if thee can't make no sense of it, you're in the same boat as the rest on us - right; now you know! Let that be an end to the matter!'

The bell clanged and woke Jonah from his sleep. With typical ingenuity, he'd made a crude water clock that struck a bell when a counterbalance tipped sideways. It was surprisingly accurate providing he filled the can with water on the stroke of eight. Tull needed to be woken at four thirty before Jefferies and Long roused their respective staff, for it would never do for anyone to see the pretty parlour maid leaving his room above the garage so early.

'Come on Clara, tis time to be gone,' he said sleepily.

438

CHAPTER 64

The Dursley Gazette

Clara had been brought up by Mrs Jeffries, who explained at the earliest point of comprehension, that she was an orphan, and as such, her fate would have been the workhouse but for the patronage of Mr Richard and the charitable benefaction of Mr Jeffries. It was expected that this should be repaid in the short term, by good manners such as speaking only when spoken to. From her fourth birthday, she rose at 5.30 a.m to do simple tasks about the house, and from her fifth, she attended the village school for her education. At six, she adopted certain daily tasks such as collecting milk from the home farm and churning it into butter.

She was taught to curtsy to the master and mistress and was forbidden - on pain of boxed ears - to ever go near Mistress Polly. Mistress Polly, she was told, was unwell and unable to tolerate children.

Her strict routine only changed on the Sabbath, when Clara would attend morning communion followed by Sunday school. To drive the message home, she attended evensong too, for Mrs Jeffries believed that hard work and a good Christian upbringing were the making of any child.

It was not until puberty that Clara had some control of her own life. Her breasts began to bud and her body changed in many ways. boy's were keen to see and touch and Clara enjoyed their attention; sometimes pleasing them, sometimes not, but it was not until the handsome and persuasive Jonah Tull came along, that she gave away her virginity.

Despite everything, Clara might have lived an uneventful life, had it not been for Jonah, but a sinuous bond grew between the scullery maid and chauffeur, for they were like two peas in a pod. Perhaps, however, that is unfair to that sweet vegetable, and the unwholesome widow's cap that thrives amid the dark decay of the forest floor, might describe their alliance better.

After Long's revelations, Tull courted Clara more attentively, for if rumour and tittle-tattle had any foundation in truth, she was the rightful heir to a fortune. How that might be proved was quite another matter of course, but Jonah quizzed Clara about the big house and its occupants as casually, and as often, as he could.

'John Long told me an odd tale about Mistress Polly tother day,' said he, the next time they were free to talk.

'She's mad' said Clara, 'mad as mad can be. I'm frightened of her - especially after what happened to Millie.'

'Who was Millie?' asked Jonah; intrigued by what promised to be another bizarre twist to Long's story.

'She was the chambermaid about the time of Amy Smith's death. They called her Mistress Polly's companion, but she was really her mother-in-law and she cared for her right till she died of a stroke some five years past. When she died, Mistress Polly went to the funeral and to the best of my knowledge, she's not left her room since. Mrs Jeffries took over her daily care, taking her meals and that kind of thing, but one day she sent Millie into the room for the linen. Mistress Polly takes Millie's hand and won't let go. "You must tell them," she said! "You must tell them it was me - it was all my fault!" She said it over and over until Millie begins to scream and Mistress Elizabeth came rushing in to take her out. Millie would never go near her room again and left service shortly after.'

'What was she supposed to have done then?'

'I don't know - nobody knows! Mrs Jeffries told Millie the mistress just says such things and there ain't no meaning to em.'

'John Long told me a tale about a tinker, and that sounded a bit fanciful an all.'

'No it's not - I've seen him.'

'Have you now! What's he all about?'

'I don't know; he just plays a tune and goes. He comes every year on exactly the same day - or did until three years ago! No one's seen him since, so the talk is he's dead too. He used to stand in the meadow, just under the wood. It was always the same tune - I'll sing it for you, it's beautiful.'

Clara began to sing "Danny Boy", a song that Jonah had never heard before. She had a lovely voice and sang the haunting melody beautifully, rising to the high notes, clearly and with ease.

'You sang that well Clara,' he said with genuine sincerity.

'Thank you,' she said, glad to have pleased her lover.

'How do you know it was always the same day?'

'Because it always fell on Mr Jeffries' birthday, March the 25th, Mrs Jeffries said so.'

'And is it true the tinker plays just for Mistress Polly?'

'Yes,' she replied, 'she waits for him on the balcony, no matter what the weather. Master Richard has instructed all the staff that they are not to go near the wood nor show themselves beneath Mistress Polly's window, nor even be that side of the house on pain of dismissal. It'll be the same for you come March.'

'That don't make no sense!'

'It's so no one frightens him off and upsets Mistress Polly.'

'I thought you said he don't come no more?'

'It doesn't make any difference; she waits on the balcony just the same!'

Jonah said no more to Clara that evening, but part of what made him a good mechanic was his disbelief in chance, and the high regard he gave to logic and reason. To his logical mind, every problem must have a reason, and all you need do is identify the reason to find the solution.

Jonah believed his philosophy worked every bit as well for humans, and on the strength of that belief, made the four mile walk to Dursley on his next day off. There he visited the offices of the Dursley Gazette, with a cock and bull story about his father being killed in India on the 25th of March 1912, and wanting to find out if it was reported. The archivist enthusiastically searched for the issue covering that week and left Jonah with a plea not to tear out any pages.

One issue dominated the news that week; the execution at Bodmin gaol of an itinerant Irish navvy gang-master by the name of Daniel Pretty; the date of the hanging was the 25th of March 1912.

The story portrayed Pretty as a kind of folk hero, hunting down a violent murderer and administering the people's justice. There were vigorous representations to the Home Secretary for a pardon; not least because Pretty was alleged to have an accomplice, but in the absence of any hard evidence to that effect and a flat denial by Pretty himself, the execution went ahead at 7a.m in the morning; conducted by the Crown's Chief Executioner, Mr Abraham Cato of Harrogate and his assistant, Mr Seth Adams.

'Well, well, well!' said Jonah Tull to himself.

He recalled what Mistress Polly had supposedly said to Millie the chambermaid. "You must tell them it was me - it was all my fault!"

What was her fault, he wondered, and who was the tinker who played an Irish folk song on the edge of a wood - in darkness - on the anniversary of an execution for murder?

441

The newspaper mentioned an accomplice; Jonah Tull began to wonder if perhaps there might have been two!

CHAPTER 65

The Milly Dory

A few nights later in his room above the garage, Jonah told Clara his suspicions that she might be Polly's daughter and thus the rightful heir to the family wealth. Clara listened open mouthed for though the likes of John Long had their suspicions, no one would dream of risking their position by mentioning it publicly, let alone to Clara.

Astonishment turned to tears, then anger at the news she should be above stairs wearing fine clothes, instead of skivvying in the kitchen.

'I hate them,' she said through her tears, 'how could they be so cruel!'

'They must all know, Clara, Mistress Polly, Master Richard, Mistress Elizabeth, Mr and Mrs Jeffries... they're all in it together.'

'They told me I was an orphan; I've believed that all my life - how could they be so unkind?'

'I don't know,' said Jonah, 'but in the meantime, they've had you washing the dishes an skivvying fer em... skivvying fer yer own flesh an' blood - skivvying fer yer own mother!'

She frightens me,' said Clara deeply upset by Jonah's revelation. 'She watches me from the gallery - she thinks I can't see her, but I can! She watches me from behind a Chinese screen. Mostly she just looks and stares, but once she began to cry and called me Nancy. Amy Smith took her away in tears and I wasn't allowed into the main house for weeks.'

'Why did she call you Nancy?'

'I don't know.'

'This is the rummest do I've ever heard of - I ain't never heard the likes of nothin' like it!'

'Let's run away Jonah; we could be married, have a family, we could be happy.'

'On what!' said Jonah, family life not being top of his agenda at that particular moment? 'I ain't got no money and neither have you, though God knows you've a right to it.'

'What are we going to do?'

Jonah told her of his plan and she listened to every word. Eventually, they fell asleep in one another's arms.

Tull bided his time, waiting for Harry the Horse to appear before setting his plan in motion. Harry turned up in early January, and pitched his caravan in Dursley on the banks of a stream known as the Yellow Hundred, and at a spot where the sprawling Lister's factory, gave way to open farmland and the Uley Road beyond.

It was deep mid winter and cold - very cold. The Yellow Hundred was frozen over, gravel crunched underfoot and grass stood sharp as knifes.

Jonah found Harry sat over a blazing fire, tending his breakfast. Ten or so horses and ponies were tethered nearby. Harry was an itinerant horse trader who travelled the farms and villages by winter, and the shows and markets by summer - buying and selling as he went. There was little he didn't know about fixing up an old nag long enough to sell it, then be on his way.

'One spoonful, no more,' said Harry as he passed Tull a tiny bag of white powder. 'Anymore and you'll kill the bugger there and then.'

Three nights later whilst the big house slept, Tull climbed through the scullery window and was helped down by an anxious Clara. She had done well, for the Doberman was sleeping soundly, its eyes open, its mouth slack. There would be no trouble from him.

Jonah closed the study door behind him, leaving Clara to keep watch in the hall. He switched on the electric lamp that stood on Master Richard's desk; a huge, time worn bible lay on the desk beside it.

He searched everywhere, in cupboards and drawers, through ledgers and files and photographs, but not one mention of Clara's name did he find in any of them. On the verge of giving up, he had an inspiration. He dragged the heavy bible toward him and opened the cover. It was a large and heavy tome whose pages were dark from the touch of many hands, its leather binding, cracked and split with age. There inside the cover, was exactly what he sought.

Hand written on the first few pages was two hundred and twenty seven years of the Durcan family history. Every birth, marriage and death was recorded there.

The last two entries were especially interesting.

Of Elizabeth and Richard, their beloved son, William, lost in service to his country in 1907 on a date and at a time unknown. Though his body lies in the Antarctica's icy wastes, his heart lies forever in England.

444

To Polly, daughter of Elizabeth and Richard, wife of Isaac (Smith) - blacksmith - a daughter, Clara, born August 17th, 1912.

Tull smiled in satisfaction. They could live a lie it seemed, but not write one in the Holy Bible. Like it or not, Clara was their granddaughter, and Tull intended to benefit from it.

As he began to tear the page from the book, there was a thunderous crash from the hall. Moments later, he heard Clara's frantic tap on the door, followed by movement about the house.

Too late, Jonah realised the room had but one exit. He slammed the bible shut and ran into the hall where he saw the brute had fallen among the fire irons; it was howling from contact with the burning embers and struggling to get up.

Someone was moving in an upstairs room. Mistress Polly's room was directly above the study, the master's bedchamber much further along the corridor with Mr and Mrs Jeffries in the servant quarters toward the rear of the house. Tull heard a door closing and footsteps upon the landing.

There was no time to escape. He hid behind heavy curtains at one of the hall's french windows, his heart pounding, his hands trembling. Seconds later Richard Durcan came down the stairs, revolver in hand.

He took in the scene immediately, the dog, the fire irons and the light that escaped from the study.

He slowed at the foot of the stairs. 'I have a gun,' he announced with a steady voice; 'stay where you are, or I'll shoot.' He entered his study and saw the disturbance there. He reappeared immediately, casting his eyes about the hall. Something about a window caught his eye, perhaps the unevenness of the drapes.

'Come out you damned scoundrel, or I'll shoot you out,' he said angrily. The drapes parted and a terrified Jonah Tull found himself looking down the barrel of a British Army Remington revolver.

'You!' said Richard Durcan in surprise. It was to be the last word he ever spoke.

The clawed foot of a bronze lamp sent shards of bone into his brain. He fell to the floor, dragging the lamp from Clara's hand, the clawed foot reluctant to let go the hole in his skull.

'Clara, what have you done?' said a stunned Jonah as he looked from Richard Durcan to the girl.

'He was going to shoot you,' said Clara, sobbing, 'I couldn't let him hurt you Jonah - I love you.'

'This is murder, Clara, they'll hang us!'

'No,' she replied, 'they'll never know; they'll think it was burglars, we'll make it look like... oh Jonah look!' She pointed to the gallery above.

Polly stood at the banisters in her nightgown, shock and disbelief written on her face.

'Do something Jonah,' said Clara in a voice close to hysteria.

Jonah picked up the revolver in a daze; perhaps Clara was right; perhaps he had to do something to make it look like burglars, but the mad woman had seen them... perhaps this was the only way. Halfway up the stairs - stunned and shocked at the sight of Durcan's brains spilling from his skull - Jonah had a vision. The five treads before him melted from sight, and in the gap that remained, there was a deep glowing pit with blood red sides, like the incandescent gullet of a furnace. So deep was the fire pit that there was no visible bottom to it. He cried out in terror for he'd all but toppled into its maw.

In shock - the revolver shaking in his hand - Jonah looked once more to the balcony where the woman had been, but he could no longer see her for there were others milling there. They were sad people, with sorrowful faces - grey ashen faces - the faces of the dead.

Jonah turned in panic and, grabbing Clara, together they ran to the yard.

'What are you doing Jonah - she saw us?' said Clara in alarm.

'Get in the car!'

'But she saw us...'

'Get in the bloody car,' he screamed.

Within moments, he had the engine running and the heavy motorcar churned the gravel of the drive.

Tull drove at reckless speed, skidding from one side of the road to the other. Snow was falling heavily and it was all he could do to see the road ahead.

He sped on through Nympsfield, Frocester, Eastington and Frampton until he reached the canal at Saul. Having worked the waterways, he knew there would be coasters and barges plying the waterway to Gloucester, Birmingham and beyond.

446

They found themselves near a wet dock Jonah was familiar with, having worked there as a shipwright.

He dragged Clara from the shelter of the Daimler to the snow-covered dockside.

'We have to get rid of the car, Clara, come tomorrow all the country will be looking for it.'

He crashed the car into gear, leaping from it at the last moment, as it lurched over the edge of the dock and plunged through the thin ice.

~

Mary Llewelyn was wide-awake despite the lateness of the hour. She'd felt the boat move and nudged her husband to wakefulness.

'What's the matter,' he groaned sleepily.

'Someone's aboard, Jack!'

'No one's aboard, it's just a boat passing by - go back to sleep.'

'I can't sleep. I've been awake for more than an hour and there's been no boats Jack, please have a look!'

'Oh for Christ sake,' he said in exasperation, struggling from their bunk in the tiny cabin of the aging coaler. He hauled up his breeches and after lighting a lamp, made his way on deck. Icy air flooded the tiny cabin, normally so warm from the engine room below.

Jack Llewelyn was annoyed with his wife, for who would want to steal coal in this weather? There was no coal to steal for they were heading west for more. It had all gone ashore in Birmingham and everyone could see she was light-ship.

Mary heard him returning, but there were other footsteps too. 'You can come in and warm yourselves, then you must be on your way,' she heard him say.

The door opened and a young man and woman entered; they were white with snow and shivering with cold; the woman was weeping. Mary made them tea and listened to their tale. They were lovers running away to marry. Mary suspected the girl was pregnant but didn't pry. Whatever their shame, she'd refuse no-one shelter on a night like this.

Reluctantly, Jack Llewelyn was persuaded to take them to Port Talbot. The young man whose name was Bill Smith, thought to seek employment in the pits and the Milly Dory's destination of Port Talbot would be as good a starting point as any.

Having gone outside, Llewelyn was alarmed at how much ice had already encircled them and decided to get up steam and be on his way. He went below to the tiny engine room and threw coal into the dull glowing gullet of the Scotch boiler, before opening the air damper that would breathe life into the Milly Dory.

He blew the gauge glasses and tapped the pressure gauge. 40lbs left over from drawing the fire the night before. He needed 80lbs to steam, but it might be just enough for the Weir's pump. He blew the condensate from the pump's valves and pistons and the Weir's clanked into action, steam and water spitting and hissing from its glands. Soon it steadied, as it picked up water from the hot well beneath. Llewelyn opened the feed valve and watched the level in the glass creep up to half way. He shut the valve once more and the pump stopped. He busied himself, draining cold steam lines, opening the boiler stop valve and lubricating his beloved engine. Above him, Mary was telling Jonah and Clara everything there was to tell about their lives.

Though they were originally from Aberystwyth, they had no home now except the boat and no family left either, but Mary showed them photos, all neatly inscribed with names and dates. There were photos of their wedding too and Jonah was amazed how much the young Llewelyn's resembled Clara and himself. By the time Jack got the Milly Dory underway, there was little Jonah Tull didn't know about Jack and Mary Llewelyn.

Llewelyn steered the heavy barge along the broad canal, the splintering of ice clear to hear about the bow. Other barges were on the move too, anxious as Jack was, to get clear of the fresh water canal where they would surely be trapped by the ice.

Jack Llewelyn tried to prise a story from "Bill Smith" as he believed him to be, but it was difficult to get a conversation from the lad. He was handy enough with the lock gates and bridges, however, and clearly knew what he was about.

Though short on answers, he'd asked many questions. Questions about the steam throttle valve, whose shaft disappeared through the wheelhouse deck and of the reversing lever that Llewelyn occasionally used to slow the boat or put it astern. He seemed a handy chap, so Llewelyn showed him how to throw coal in the furnace each time the pressure dropped below 90lbs.

'I've done a bit with steam engines' he said, 'but I ain't seen nothing like this before, not on the move anyway! How do you manage to steer and run the boilers all at the same time? When do you get any sleep?'

Llewelyn laughed and said, 'My Mary's as good a skipper as any man on the river, Bill, and the boiler only needs a few shovel-full's every once in a while when we're in the canal. It's only when we reach the river that we need to work together. So long as I know the boiler level and pressure I'm all right,' he said, tapping the wheelhouse Igema gauge to show Jonah the remote boiler water level indicator in question.

To Jonah Tull, the night seemed endless, yet it was still only 4a.m when they approached the docks at Sharpness. It was as they entered the lock that everything went wrong once more. Jonah was just emerging from the engine room when the wheelhouse was illuminated by torchlight from the docks above. The beams of two hand lamps shone from the far gates, 'Ahoy there Skipper, Your name and destination please,' called a voice.

'Jack Llewelyn of the Milly Dory!'

'And where bound?'

'Port Talbot in ballast; what's the problem?'

'Jack, this is Harry James,' said the other, more familiar voice. 'The police are here checking the boats for stowaways, have you seen anyone.'

Llewelyn recognised the harbourmaster's voice well enough from years of plying the canal.

'There's been a murder,' cut in the policeman, his helmet and uniform recognisable now, despite the snowflakes that had settled on their greatcoats. 'We're looking for a young dark haired chap; he's got a girl with him.'

The muzzle of Tull's pistol pressed into the base of Llewellyn's spine. 'Say a word and I'll kill you - them too,' whispered Jonah, 'tell them no... tell them now!'

'No... no I've seen no one,' said Llewelyn.

'Who else is aboard?' asked the policeman.

'Just the wife, she's sleeping,' he said.

'You'll need to tie up Jack; it'll be an hour or so before the tides high enough to open the gates,' said Harry James. 'Best you check the boat over when you're alongside, just to make sure.'

'Tell him okay,' whispered Tull, grinding the gun against him.

'Aye, I will, thanks Harry!'

449

James cranked the winding gear that operated the lock gates and the Milly Dory slipped silently into the holding basin beyond.

Tull forced Llewelyn through to the cabin at gunpoint. His wife gasped and her hands flew to her mouth.

'Shout and I'll shoot you both,' said Jonah, 'Get a rope Clara, quick as you can.'

Jonah pointed the gun at Llewellyn's head with a shaking hand.

'You've been good to us, Jack and that's a fact. Please don't do anything fer us to hurt you; I don't want to hurt neither of you!'

He forced them both to the engine room and there he had Clara tie Mary Llewellyn's hands and ankles to the engine bedplate. He tied Llewelyn in a similar fashion, whilst Clara held the revolver to Mary Llewellyn's head.

'All we want is a chance Jack, no more; we've got no fight with you and Mary. I shall take this boat out into the channel and you will tell me what to do. Help me and no harm will come to you, and that's a promise.' Half an hour later, Harry James opened the outer harbour gates and the basin was open to the river.

Jonah released Llewellyn's legs but kept his hand tied. Gun in hand; he steadied Llewelyn, as he climbed from engine-room to wheelhouse.

'Throttle the steam a bit and steer to starboard,' said Llewelyn, 'now midships... midships damn you! Too late; go to port... that's it, come to midships again.'

The barge passed through the harbour entrance with just the slightest graze to her stern, then the Milly Dory was out and free. Llewelyn told Tull to steer to port as the tide caught them; then at the channel buoy he turned South West for Cardiff and beyond.

Tull tried to win Llewelyn around - to get him to see their side of things. Llewelyn said nothing but his eyes spoke for him. No word would he exchange with Tull other than to guide their passage. Slowly he coaxed him nearer and nearer the Lydney sands, then with a jolt that threw them against the wheelhouse windows, the Milly Dory sank her keel deep into the cloying mud and stuck fast.

'You did that deliberately,' shouted Tull.

'It should have been okay; I don't know what happened!' lied Llewelyn. 'Take the dotty boat, you'll get ashore easily from here.'

'No, said Tull, do you think I'm bloody stupid!' He waved the gun at Llewellyn's head. 'You bloody bastard - get below,' he screamed.

As the engine slowly pushed the Milly Dory further onto the mud, Tull tied Jack Llewelyn to the engine bedplate, close to the boiler where Tull could watch him from the wheelhouse above. Jonah returned to the wheelhouse and dragged the reversing gear into astern, before opening the throttle fully.

'What are we going to do Jonah?' said Clara in alarm, 'will we sink?'

'Of course not Clara, the tides still coming in, we'll be off here before we know it.'

So it was to be, for ten minutes later, with a growl and a lurch, the Milly Dory broke free of the mud and immediately swung to port, turning broadside on to a current that pushed her back up the river. Tull somehow managed to get her about, but they'd lost all steam and the engine was starting to slow.

'Just keep her in the middle Clara,' he shouted, the desperation clear to hear in his voice as he dived below.

Tull threw shovel after shovel of coal into the boiler and the pressure began to rise once more. The engine spun at furious speed so that cranks and con rods were little less than a blur in the lamp light. For all its speed, the beautiful little triple expansion engine ran almost silently with nothing but the faintest wish,wish,wish,wish… from glands and stuffing boxes; it was then Tull realised the boiler level was too low.

'How do I feed it,' said Tull in alarm.

'Go to hell,' was Llewelyn's reply.

'There's no water in the glass!'

'Then let me free!'

Tull was no fool where engines were concerned. He knew agricultural engines as well as any man, and told himself he could surely find the feed pump. It had to be the Weirs pump; it too was moving up and down in a frenzy just like the engine, yet it seemed to be pumping nothing.

Tull opened the pump telltales but only steam came out; it should be water; why wasn't it water; it had to be water to feed the boiler. Steam was rising from the hot-well beneath the engine plates, just below the pump from where it took its suction; the whole engine room was like a Turkish bath.

Tull began to panic. Breathing was becoming difficult and the atmosphere choking; he was losing control of the situation and he didn't know what to do.

451

'Help me Jack,' he pleaded.

'Let me free,' said Llewelyn.

'No!' said Jonah.

'For God's sake,' sobbed Mary Llewelyn hysterically, 'the boiler needs water, let Jack free, or you'll kill us all.'

'No,' said Tull once more.

Ships had condensers; he knew that from his days in the shipyard. Traction engines drew water from the nearest ditch and threw their waste steam away, but ships had condensers to use the steam again and again, the saltwater in the river being far too saline for boiler use.

It must be the condenser, Tull told himself. He needed to get cooling water through the condenser to cool the waste steam to condensate or they were done for.

Jonah found it on the bulkhead above Mary Llewelyn; a huge cast iron drum with lagged pipes running to and from it. He opened every valve not knowing their purpose, but still nothing happened. The lagged pipes had to be steam, so the unlagged pipes must be seawater for cooling, but they were scalding hot and their valves were also open. One went overboard, but the other went to an engine driven pump. Tull opened the pump valves and to his delight and relief, the pipes began to cool. Slowly the scorching condenser began to cool too. Steam cleared from the hot-well beneath the Weirs pump, then the Weirs slowed to a steady, beautiful, wonderful, ga-dump! ga-dump! ga-dump! Tull raced to the boiler, watching the level as it slowly crept back up the glass once more.

'Damn you Jack!' He said to Llewelyn, shaking with the stress of his dilemma, 'damn you to hell, you bastard.'

He climbed the ladder to the bridge; his nerves shattered, his heart in his mouth; 'Are you all right?' he asked Clara.

'I'm so frightened, Jonah.'

'It's okay, it's okay, I've got it under control, don't worry.'

However, Tull too had been frightened for there had been no water in the glass when he finally found the problem. Had the level continued to drop, he might have killed them all, for when a boiler has no water to cool its furnace throat, that furnace will sag as any boiler man will know. It sags and sags as the metal gets hotter and hotter, until finally, steam pressure pushes it out of shape like red-hot putty until the drum ruptures and explodes.

There would be no warning, no noise or slow escape of steam. The doomed boiler would wrench itself from its mountings and blast its way through machinery, bulkheads, deckheads, and anything else that stood in its way, until the Milly Dory and everyone aboard her was blown to pieces. Jonah Tull felt his heart slowing down, but he was still shaking like a leaf. He considered himself a very lucky man indeed.

Tull did not have the faintest idea where they were. Clara had kept the Milly Dory somewhere near the middle of the channel as Jonah had told her, judging her distance by the shore lights, but they meant nothing at all to either of them. All he knew was that they grew increasingly far apart and increasingly difficult to see through the snowfall. Though the night was calm, the Milly Dory began to rock gently and Tull knew they must be well down the river and nearing the estuary by now.

'What are we going to do Jonah?' asked Clara.

'I don't know, but I didn't want all this business,' he replied, nodding toward the engine room. 'I just want to get some miles between us and... and what happened! We could try and get to Ireland maybe, or Portugal... I dunno.'

Every quarter hour, he would go below and shovel more coal into the boiler. Each time he did so, Llewelyn would goad him a little more.

'Why don't you give up and let me free?' he would say. 'You can't go on forever. You won't handle this boat past the estuary; she'll be too much for you. Judging by her movements she's...'

'Shut your mouth, Jack.'

'A bit of snows one thing, but what if the weather gets up? Do you have any idea where you are or what you're doing? It won't be mud out there any longer; it'll be rocks - rocks as hard and sharp as your bloody teeth!'

'Shut your mouth... why don't you shut your bloody mouth,' shouted Tull, his nerves worn to shreds. He picked up a heavy spanner to strike Llewelyn, but Llewelyn didn't flinch.

'If I'm going to die,' he said, 'at least I'll have the consolation of knowing you'll die with me cus this river's killed better men than murderous bastards like you!'

'No-one's going to die! We don't mean you no harm Jack... you nor Mary.'

'Then let me free and I'll drop you in a quiet bay somewhere. I've got no fight with you! You can be on your way - no-one the wiser!'

'No! I don't trust you. I... I need to think.'

453

Cardiff was now to the North, Weston Super Mare to the South, though Tull did not know this for he knew nothing of the Severn beyond Sharpness. He was confused by so many navigation lights, river buoys and shore lights, the latter seeming ever more distant and difficult to see. They all but struck the rocks of Flat Holm Island and steered north as a result, thinking Flat Holm to be the English coast. The snowfall grew ever thicker and visibility was little more than 50 yards. Tull heard the bassoon thrum of a ships whistle sending out its urgent warning - beware, beware!

Muted by the snowfall, the vessel was closer than Tull realised. Again, the vessel boomed out its warning and Tull turned west; back towards the coast as he thought, but directly into the path of the oncoming steamer.

Too late, Tull saw the whiteness of its bow wave and threw the wheel to starboard, trying his best to turn the Milly Dory away; but she was too sluggish to respond. The flare of the steamer's port bow smashed against the barge, crushing the bulwark planking and throwing splinters everywhere, as iron rivets and plate laps slashed the Milly Dory's bow like saw teeth. The Milly Dory lurched first to port, then to starboard and was almost dragged under by the irresistible force of the larger vessel, but she recovered and was pushed sideways along the steamers side.

Tull held his breath, his heart thumping in his chest, for he'd glanced two letters of the steamers name, as the flare of the bow tipped the Milly Dory over like a cork in a barrel. W A . . . was all he'd seen, but that was enough to strike fear into his heart, for the paddle steamer Waverley plied the channel between Lynmouth and Bristol. The dark water held them fast to the steamers side, like a child clamped to its mother's breast, and soon the massive port paddle would smash the tiny coaler to matchwood. If their bodies were not cut in two by the giant paddle, they would surely suffer hideous injuries and drown in the freezing river.

Jonah had resigned himself to his fate when the steamer's midships passed them by without event. Then the Milly Dory was thrown about again; sucked irresistibly under the steamer's stern by two huge propellers. As the Milly Dory cast about in the boiling wake, Tull saw the steamers name, high above him on the fantail stern. "SS Washington", it read - "Newcastle".

Still afloat, the Milly Dory's brave little engine spun on as though nothing had happened, but Clara and Mary Llewelyn were both screaming with shock and fear. Tull too, was shaking with fright.

Llewelyn did not need to be told what had happened. He guessed the Milly Dory was badly damaged and probably sinking, and he had to do something or they would both die there in her engine room.

He'd not spent the hours in idleness, for patient rubbing had slowly worn through the threads of his bonds. The jolt the Milly Dory had taken, had snapped the last few threads and his hands were finally free, albeit lifeless and without feeling or grip. He kept his hands behind his back as he rubbed life back into wrists and fingers. The pain was excruciating as blood began to circulate once more, but feeling slowly returned. He loosened his feet, but left the rope about his ankles so Tull would not realise he was free if he glanced through the hatch.

He whispered to Mary to take heart and then shouted to Jonah.

'You're in the wrong shipping lane you stupid bastard; for God's sake let me see where we are before you kill us all.'

'Okay...okay,' said Jonah, realising that, without Llewelyn, they would not survive the river. 'Just wait a minute,' he said, as he fumbling for his revolver. He climbed down into the engine room and placed the revolver on the checker plating beside him, then knelt to loosen Llewellyn's bonds. Too late, he realised that Llewellyn's legs were drawn up in front of him and the rope was loose.

Llewelyn boots hit Jonah full in the face, with such force that he was temporarily blinded. He could only see through a veil of red mist; the force of the blow knocking him back against the boiler front and scalding him badly. Llewelyn scrambled to his feet, but hours of forced inactivity had stiffened his joints. He grabbed a huge red fire axe with a vicious point on its back and began to lift it high above his head. Jonah reached about for the pistol, realising he was suddenly fighting for his life. As the massive axe came flashing down, Jonah fired and flame leapt from its muzzle. The bullet passed clean through Jack Llewellyn's belly.

Instead of the axe crushing Jonah's skull as Llewelyn intended, it struck a valve on the boiler front with bone jarring force.

The gunmetal sample cock fractured at its flange. Boiler water at 100lbs pressure, blasted from the boiler with so much force that it would have hit the far bulkhead, had Jack Llewelyn not been in its path. Llewelyn was drenched by the scalding water; his screams of agony filling the tiny space. The shrieking man was picked up bodily and thrown backwards into the flailing cranks and crossheads of the Milly Dory's engine, splattering con rods, entablatures and his wife Mary, with his blood and brains.

For a few seconds, the engine slowed and faltered as Llewelyn's shattered body was drawn into the sump, and pulped to bloodied meat by the thrashing crank. Then it picking up again, spewing out parts of Jack Llewelyn's body as though nothing had happened.

Within an instant of the cock fracturing, the boiling jet of water turned to steam and pushed every ounce of air from the engine room. Jonah - himself badly scalded - used what little oxygen he had in his lungs to climb the ten rungs to the wheelhouse. The blast of steam followed him through the wheelhouse hatch, even though he slammed the hatch shut behind him.

Steam was belching from the skylight, but there was no sound other than it's shrill, for screams; even Mary Llewelyn's desperate, terrified screams, could not carry through the heavy moistness. Jonah put the dotty boat over the side and thrust Clara into it. He rowed as fast and as far from the Milly Dory as he could.

It took ten full minutes for the water to escape the boiler. Slowly the furnace throat began to glow red and sparks and flame shot from the smoke stack, high into the night sky. Finally, with a deafening roar, the furnace roof sagged like pastry then ruptured inwards, blowing the after deck high into the air. So high did the pieces fly, that wood and twisted metal fell all about them, though they had rowed two hundred yards from the stricken boat. The Milly Dory was ablaze from stem to stern and would have burnt to the waterline, but the explosion had punched heavy chunks of boilerplate and machinery straight through the wooden hull. With a lurch to starboard, the brave little coaler slipped beneath the surface of the river and took its terrible secrets with it.

Thirty minutes later, eager hands hauled Jonah and Clara aboard the Barry lifeboat.

'What happened?' asked the linesman.

'We had a steam leak; I couldn't get near it; we abandoned ship and fifteen minutes later, the boiler blew.

'You can say that again boyo,' replied their rescuer, 'we thought world war two had started - we weren't expecting to find any survivors - what's your name?'

'I'm Jack Llewelyn, skipper of the Milly Dorey - this is my wife Mary.'

'Where are you from, Jack Llewelyn?'

'Aberystwyth originally, we've no home save the boat; we've lost everything we own except the clothes we're wearing - it's all gone down with her.'

Wrapped in blankets; shocked and stunned; a speechless Jonah and weeping Clara, were taken to shore and the home of Mrs Jones, a kindly lady and mother of one of the crew. They stayed with her for three days whilst they recovered their shattered nerves. The old lady encouraged them to put the past behind them and thank the good Lord for their salvation.

Jonah - or Jack Llewelyn as he now called himself - told her he could never set foot on the deck of a boat again, and would turn his hand toward his other skill as a mechanic.

A joyous Mrs Jones told her guests that, by good fortune, her brother was a mining engineer at the Alice Colliery in Pencryn and they were always on the lookout for Millwrights, and if that was not proof of God's bounteous love, then she would like to know what was!

So it was that they made the long journey to the grimy coal town of Pencryn and set up home in a colliery cottage as Jack and Mary Llewelyn. They never called themselves Jonah and Clara ever again, not even in private, and eventually they even erased the shame of what they'd done from their own memories.

Jack Llewelyn became one of the best Millwrights the Alice had ever known and they were embraced by the local community as one of their own. Mary Llewelyn or Clara as she was once known, soon gave birth to Thomas Llewelyn, a poorly child who fell victim to polio at nine. Jack died of silicosis at the age of forty-seven and of the nature of Mary's passing to the ravages of cervical cancer, you are already aware.

CHAPTER 66

Tremaine arrives

When the knock came at the door, Llewelyn stopped his tale mid sentence. He looked anxiously at the policeman.

'Wibberley are you there - it's Tremaine,' said a voice from the landing.

'Yes I'm here - just a minute,' replied the policeman, crossing the room to the door and turning the key in the lock. He opened the door the merest fraction and peeped through the gap.

'I've friends with me...' said Tremaine cryptically, glancing over his shoulder at the two white coated nurses.

'Mr. Llewelyn's a bit distressed at the moment doctor - best you leave your friends outside for now - if you don't mind!'

Tremaine entered the dark, airless room and the stench hit him like a wall. It had been unpleasant outside, but was rank, nauseous and unmistakeable within. Sunk in the shadows were two figures sat about the dying embers of a fire. Another breath of the fetid air made his gorge rise despite a lifetime in medicine and the doctor fought an overwhelming urge to vomit.

Striding to the window, he drew back the heavy velvet drapes and fought with the ancient sashes, but paint of ages had seized them to their runners. Defeated, he turned to better see the figures that were seated about the hearth.

Grey light from a grey day, penetrated the grimy windows and illuminated the motionless figures, but nothing in his career had prepared him for the macabre scene before him. Seated in an easy chair with his back to him was Llewelyn and opposite him, the rotting cadaver of his mother. Her body was arranged in an armchair, her head lolling against the wing; her mouth open in a hideous smile. Between them, was a vacant chair where Wibberley had clearly been sitting.

Time and the grave had been unkind to Mary Llewelyn's corpse, but the warmth of the fire had speeded the corruption over the previous few hours. Black blotches stained the burial shroud in many places and foul smelling fluid seeped from ears, nose and mouth. Receding lips exposed her teeth in a macabre grin, whilst sightless eyes stared unblinkingly at him. Once over his initial shock, professional interest took over and Tremaine took a closer look at the corpse. He had last seen Mary Llewelyn on her deathbed and was surprised at how quickly she had deteriorated. Llewelyn sat with his head bowed, ignoring him and not looking his way; he deeply resenting the doctors intrusion.

458

Tremaine gave the policeman a questioning glance. The policeman shrugged, casting a glance at Llewelyn and the cadaver. 'It's very complicated' he said.

'So I see... how long have you been here?'

'About two hours.'

'Good God have you really; I admire your constitution Ken, I must say!'

'I couldn't think of anywhere I was more needed,' the policeman replied.

Tremaine gave Wibberley a wry smile and elevated his respect for the man one more notch.

He slipped the catch on his bag and took out a tiny ampoule, checking its label in the thin light from the window.

'There was a disturbance... in the graveyard in the early hours.'

'All his own work?' asked Tremaine pointedly.

'I think so,' said the policeman.

'How are you feeling today, Mr Llewelyn?' said Tremaine, turning his attention to his patient.

Llewelyn did not reply.

Out of sight from Llewelyn, Tremaine pushed a syringe into the ampoule. 'It's Doctor Tremaine Mr Llewelyn; you remember me don't you?'

Llewelyn nodded.

'We're a little concerned about you, Mr Llewelyn... Your mother should be at rest now, shouldn't she... we're wondering why you've brought her home?'

'He told me to,' came the reply.

Tremaine cast a questioning glance at Wibberley; 'Who told you to?' he asked.

'Gwynfa ap Eldred,' said Llewelyn, as though no further explanation were necessary.

Tremaine seemed ever more confused as he bled the air from the syringe. 'And who is Gwynfa ap Eldred?' he asked.

'A thirteenth century knight,' provided Wibberley, 'feudal lord of Penmaenddu!'

Tremaine raised his eyes to heaven. 'Mr. Llewelyn, I'm going to give you something to help you sleep. It's been a long, long night and you need to sleep now.'

459

Are you going to re-bury her?' he asked.

'We'll see; don't worry about that right now.'

'You mustn't bury her there,' he said anxiously, 'not there! I've told Mr Wibberley about it - you won't let them put her back there will you?'

'She must be laid to rest Mr Llewelyn, she can't stay here can she; this is your home? You wouldn't deny your mother her peace surely; not after so many years of suffering?'

'Not there' he said, becoming agitated; his voice shaking; 'not there - not in that grave!' He tried to stand up, a look of terror in his eyes, Tremaine held him back with a steady hand upon his shoulder.

'He wants to go back to his grave but she can't be there with him - he must be alone!' said Llewelyn, his voice trembling and his hands shaking. If she's buried there he'll be angry; he'll possess me, you must help me - for God's sake, please help me!'

'We'll take care of her, Mr Llewelyn; there's no need to be distressed,' said Tremaine and before Llewelyn realised what was happening, he'd pumped the sedative into his arm with one swift and practiced movement.

Llewelyn continued to plead, imploring both men to listen, weeping constantly, but within moments the powerful drug took effect and Llewelyn sank into a deep sleep. Tremaine checked his pulse and pupils and made sure there was no blockage of his windpipe. Get those chaps in here Ken - there's a good fellow.

The male nurses carried Llewelyn on a stretcher to the waiting ambulance.

'I thought I'd seen it all,' said Tremaine, putting his instruments back in his bag and snapping the clasp shut. 'You've done a good job here, Ken! The poor fellow's obviously in a bit of a state and its good you were here to keep him calm. I'm really sorry I couldn't get here sooner.'

'In some ways, I wish you'd taken a few minutes longer!'

'Whatever for?' asked Tremaine in astonishment.

'He was telling me about his grandmother. You turned up just before he finished his story, so I never learnt what happened to her. I'd have quite liked to know!'

'Was he conversing sensibly then?'

'No, not really! It was all very fanciful stuff, but he told his tale very well, and telling it seemed to keep him calm so I let him talk. He told it so well, in

460

fact, I'd have liked to hear the end of it! That's the thing about a good story! No matter how daft it might be, it captures your imagination and you want to know what happens in the end.'

'Yes I know what you mean, but I'm still sorry I took so long, given your trying circumstances! Tegwyn Hughes went into early labour and had a very difficult time of it. I thought at one stage we'd lose the child, but we got it breathing in the end. Just couldn't leave them I'm afraid.'

'It wasn't a problem - will he be alright?'

'It's hard to say,' Tremain replied. 'He's been through a lot these past few years; caring for a terminally sick mother, then losing her in the most prolonged and harrowing fashion ever invented. I shouldn't say this Ken, but you wouldn't keep a dog that way, you really wouldn't! Now, after all that's gone before, he finds himself all alone in the world and there's only so much the human mind can stand before something snaps. But in answer to your question, his state of mind is so out of kilter with his usual self, that sedation and a few days' rest might well be all he needs - we'll see! Bad though this poor chap's difficulties are, mental trauma of this kind can often be easier to put back on track than a fear of spiders, let's say! Time will tell!

'Let's keep our fingers crossed then,' said PC Wibberley throwing a blanket over the corpse. 'I'll stand guard here and wait for the undertaker, and I'll be grateful if you can get him here as soon as possible!'

461

CHAPTER 67

Hospital Visit

One week later, PC Wibberley parked his car in the visitors' car park, then crunched his way up the gravel path to the imposing mansion. Several people were tending the immaculate lawns or sitting quietly on benches in the warm afternoon sun.

He stopped at the front door with its mock Doric columns and turned to study the view. The lawns fell away from the jutting promontory on which the house was built, to rolling pastureland studded with woods, copses and the occasional stretch of shimmering water. It was an imposing building with a majestic view, well worthy of a gentleman of substance, had it not been the West Country's asylum for the insane.

Wibberley entered the hall and rang the bell. Eventually a man in a white coat answered his call.

'I've come to see someone who recently came into your care, a Mr Thomas Llewelyn.'

'Are you friend or relative,' asked the nurse?

'Neither,' replied the policeman, 'I'm PC Wibberley of the South Wales Constabulary. I'm the bobby who sat with him through his difficulties; wasn't it you who took him away?'

'Yes.'

I thought I recognised you; how's he doing?'

'Not very well I'm afraid! He's got an imaginary friend... if you could call him a friend.'

'I think I know who that might be!' replied the policeman.

Together they walked through long corridors until they reached the secure wing. There they passed through a lobby where another nurse sat at a desk reading a western novel. After a few words, he unlocked a door that led to a short corridor of secure cells.

Once locked inside the corridor, his escort said, 'I'll stay outside whilst you go in, but I'll need to lock the door behind you. You'll be perfectly safe; he's not a danger to anyone except himself, but our instructions are to keep the door locked at all times. When you're finished, shout "Frank" - that's my name.'

He unlocked the door and went inside, 'I've got a visitor for you Mr Llewelyn - cheer you up a bit.'

The policeman thanked him and the nurse took his leave of them, locking the door behind him. It was an odd feeling for a policeman to be on the wrong side of the lock.

The room was padded on every surface to a height of seven feet. Out of reach on the far wall, was a sealed and barred window that let in natural light but afforded no view whatsoever. There was no furniture within the room, except a bed that was bolted to the floor; it was the dreariest room he'd ever seen, including the station cells at Merthyr.

'Hello Mr Llewelyn,' he said to the seated man, 'I thought I'd come to see you as promised, I've brought you "Micah Clarke", I hope you haven't read it?'

'Many times,' he replied, 'but I will enjoy reading it again; books are all they will allow me; they know I would never harm a book.'

Wibberley sat on the bed beside Llewelyn and they talked together about generalities. Llewelyn was particularly concerned about the library, especially the hole in the roof. He spoke as rationally and intelligently as any sane man, and Wibberley could not help but reflect upon the tragedy that had reduced him to his present situation; he could only hope that his aberration would pass.

When conversation began to wane, Wibberley said, 'Mr. Llewelyn, you don't have to tell me if it will distress you, but you didn't finish your story did you! I was just wondering...?'

'About her?'

'Yes, about your grandmother - I was wondering what happened to her - things were cut a bit short if you remember.'

'She died Mr Wibberley.'

'Yes, I thought you might say that. Are you able to tell me how?'

Wibberley was angry with himself for asking, for he knew better than to do such a thing. Asking Llewelyn to revisit the events of that day might revive his difficulties all over again and here was he - an experienced policeman - asking an insane man about his imaginary grandmother. It was a foolish, selfish, irresponsible thing to do, but Llewelyn's story had so captured his imagination that he had to know the end of his tale.

Far from being distressed, Llewelyn was clearly pleased that Wibberley wanted to know about her, and began again where he'd left off. When he finished Polly's tale, both men fell silent - the policeman deep in thought.

463

'She was my grandmother Mr Wibberley, perhaps I have her madness.'

The end of Polly's life was not the end P.C Wibberley had expected. It had left him deeply moved and unable to find any suitable words to say. Eventually he replied, 'Perhaps so, Mr Llewelyn and let us hope you are soon well again; but remember that she had kindness, gentleness and humanity too; perhaps you have those qualities also.'

'I'm tired Mr Wibberley,' said Llewelyn with a sigh; 'I would like to rest now if you don't mind. You won't know how tiring it can be - doing so little! Thank you for your gift, I will read it tomorrow.'

They shook hands and the policeman called the nurse who unlocked the door.

'Will you come again?'

The policeman hesitated in the open doorway. 'If you want me to,' he replied, 'If I can help in some way.'

Once outside the nurse locked the door but put a finger to his lips indicating that the policeman should make no noise. He closed the outer door as though they had passed through, then returned to where the policeman stood, signalling again for him to remain silent.

After a few moments, a voice within the cell broke the silence. Wibberley listened in astonishment for it was not Llewelyn's quiet voice but the deep resonant voice of a man twice his build. It was a harsh voice, cold, arrogant and sneering; the voice of a brutish man - a man used to having his own way.

'So you have visitors now - how nice!'

Silence.

'I didn't know you had friends,' continued the brutish voice.

'He's not a friend.'

'Who is he then,' snarled the voice angrily?

Wibberley had to listen carefully for the voice was speaking in an ancient Welsh dialect he found hard to understand.

'He's a policeman.'

'A policeman... what is a policeman?'

'He's like a soldier.'

There followed a bellow of laughter that echoed about the corridor and set the hairs on Wibberley's neck on end.

'A soldier that hath no sword! What kind of a soldier is he?' remarked the voice in a hollow, sneering tone.

'He's a new soldier, they carry no swords.'

The voice bellowed with laughter again; 'No sword you say, I should like to meet such a soldier on the battlefield. My horse would wear his guts for a garland. Why then did he come - your toothless soldier?'

'He wanted to know about my grandmother. How she died - what happened to her.'

'Bah,' said the voice in total indifference; 'she is of no consequence here. Bring me the man who put your whore mother back in my grave against my will - that is the charge I have given you - was it he?'

'No'

'Who then?'

'I don't know... I don't know...! I asked them - I pleaded with them - bury her elsewhere I said...! I pleaded with them but they wouldn't listen to me - you heard me pleading with them - they don't believe in you.'

There was a bellow of rage that shook the air in the corridor and an almost simultaneous cry from Llewelyn, whereupon the nurse pressed a button. Outside in the lobby a bell sounded.

'If I can't return to rest in peace through your folly,' continued the voice, 'then you must die - and die you shall!'

Llewelyn screamed hysterically, his cries filling the small space with fear and loathing.

'And when you die,' continued the voice, 'as soon you shall...! So too will I be buried with you, for they will not suspect that I possess your body and hide within your bowels. And when you are buried and I have consumed you, then blessed sleep will come once more.'

Wibberley made an instinctive move for Llewelyn's cell, but the nurse caught his arm, 'Leave this to us please sir,' he said.

Two more nurses burst through the passage door, one carrying a straitjacket, the other a medical bag.

Wibberley watched in horror through the open door, as the nurses restrained the screaming Llewelyn. He had stripped his clothing from the waist down and was crashing his head and body against the cell wall with all his might. His hands and inner thighs were smeared with blood and faeces.

Two nurses restrained him whilst the third slipped on the straitjacket and tied the traces behind his back. With practised skill, he shot sedative into Llewelyn buttocks and the three of them held him down until the drug took effect.

The nurse took P.C Wibberley's arm and led him out of the corridor and into the lobby once more.

'I'm sorry you had to witness that,' he said.

'I had no idea,' came the reply.

He's not usually so bad, but he does the voice thing each time someone leaves the room; it's always the same thing - paranoia about re-burying his mother.'

'He always wanted her buried somewhere else,' said the policeman.

'Yes something like that - goodness knows why - did they?'

'No. She was reinterred in the same plot three days ago. There was a short service, no public, just myself, Doctor Tremaine whom you met that day, the undertaker, and the vicar.'

'He's convinced there's a devil up his backside, that's why the room is bare. We gave him pen and paper when he first came here and found him an hour later, screaming at the top of his voice and covered in blood. He'd been trying to dig the demon out of his backside with the pen and it was lodged inside him.'

Wibberley was too shocked to respond.

'We do what we can Mr Wibberley, but we often don't understand the workings of the human mind. Sometimes, what little we do understand is just not enough.'

'Is there any chance he will get better?'

The nurse shrugged his shoulders, 'Who can say,'

The two men shook hands, and Wibberley made his way down the drive to the car park.

He felt exhausted and drained by what he'd seen. There was a seat well placed to capture the view, and he sat there for a few minutes gathering his thoughts.

He decided he wouldn't visit again given, the bad ending, but he wondered if it would have hurt so very much to have buried her elsewhere. Llewelyn had pleaded with them to bury her elsewhere, but no one would listen. Was that really too much to ask? Like everyone else he'd ignored what seemed so pointless and unimportant, but what would it have cost in comparison with a man's sanity.

One matter that further unnerved him was how Llewelyn could possibly have known she had been interred in the same plot. He hadn't told him, and the nurse clearly didn't know. He felt for the first time in his life that he'd let a fellow human being down, and he bitterly regretted his inertia.

Part Three

P.C Wibberley's Tale (The Grains of Sand)
The Cotswolds - 1975 - Present

CHAPTER 68

The Sexton

Llewellyn died some three years after his committal, at just thirty-two years of age. He was buried in the hospital grounds, there being no one to claim his body for private burial. The end of Llewellyn's life was marked by an entry in the hospital records stating the date of death and burial plot number.

With the news of his passing, Wibberley put aside his regrets and filed the matter in the recesses of his brain, along with other fading memories from his professional life. There it would have stayed, but for a chance encounter with a road sign some seven years later.

Wibberley was still the bobby at Pencryn at that time, but he and his wife were travelling to Stratford upon Avon, for Mrs Wibberley was very fond of the works of William Shakespeare. They were to stay in Stratford for three days in a small hotel of good repute; then a further two-day stay was planned for Symonds Yat in the Forest of Dean on their return journey to Pencryn.

It was a holiday they had looked forward to for some time, neither of them having had occasion to venture far from their native Wales.

The little Morris Minor pulled gamely over the newly built Severn Bridge, its engine enjoying the excursion almost as much as its passengers. Mrs Wibberley looking up from her knitting very briefly, to survey the broad river that stretched into the distance on either side.

'Is this Mr Brunel's bridge, dear?' she asked in passing, being vaguely aware from her school days that the great engineer had built a suspension bridge at Bristol.

'No, that one's in the Avonmouth Gorge; this one's by Wimpey or Costain, or someone like that. Anyway Brunel's been dead for over a hundred years.'

Nonplussed she turned her attention back to the bridge and remarked, 'Well it's a very nice bridge nonetheless, and I'm sure that if Mr Brunel *had* built it, he'd be very pleased with it!'

An hour later, the A38 trunk road took them to a crossroads somewhere between Bristol and Gloucester. The policeman checked their progress with a glance at a road sign. To his left was the village of Slimbridge, but it was the sign to the right of the crossing that caught his eye. Dursley, 3 miles, it announced.

469

He brought the little car to a halt and to his wife's surprise, put it into reverse, backing it to the point where he could see the sign once more. There was another name upon the signpost, even more familiar than Dursley. Coaley 2 miles it declared.

He sat staring at the sign for several moments; 'What's wrong Kenneth,' she asked.

'Nothing much,' he replied, 'but the name of that village is familiar; do you mind if we take a look?'

The little car travelled through a village that was very ordinary, straggling and a little bedraggled. Its most notable features were a derelict water mill, three pubs and a Norman church with a square tower. "The Parish Church of St Bartholomew's" declared the notice board outside.

Opposite the church was a small Post Office and General store, outside of which, two petrol pumps offered National Benzole petrol for sale. P.C Wibberley brought the car to a halt beside the pumps, whereupon a grey haired man in a white shopkeeper's apron came out to serve him.

Fill her up,' he said in response to the shopkeeper's inquiry.

The shopkeeper reset the clock and began winding the handle. 'Going far?' he asked with friendly politeness. The premium pump was electric and much faster, but he preferred the economy pump as it gave him an excuse to chat.

'To Stratford for a bit of a holiday,' Wibberley replied.

'You're wrong for Stratford,' replied the shopkeeper, 'you need to go back to the A38 then head for Gloucester.'

'Yes I know, we just thought we'd explore a bit. Is there a smithy in the village by any chance?'

Used to be a long time ago; that's it up yonder, the red brick building on the end of the stone cottage; it's not been worked since the turn of the century.'

'Do you know who the last blacksmith was?'

'I do,' said the shopkeeper confidently, 'fer I own the land and his names on the title deeds; he was a man name of John Smith.'

'Thank you,' said the policeman, handing over seven shillings and thruppence for the fuel.

They stopped opposite what had been the smithy. It had two decaying enamel signs on its gable wall. "Ovum for Poultry" declared one; "Lactifer for Cattle", entreated the other. The policeman opened the gate, its hinges stiffly protesting every push. The garden was overgrown and the house looked equally derelict. Curtains - eaten through by moths and hanging like dusty cobwebs - made it difficult to see into the room beyond; but he could just make out a rusty hearth and a door to the rooms above. A heavy chain barred his way into the smithy, but there was no glass left in the tiny window beside the weather-beaten door. Inside, Wibberley could see a hearth and bellows, an anvil leaning askew on a beaten earth floor and hammers, tongs and swages by the hundreds, all arranged on rails about the dark and dusty shelves. A pile of soot was stacked in one corner and a similar pile of dusty coke was stacked in another.

The policeman returned to the little Morris Minor; his wife noting an unusual change in his mood for he had become quiet and thoughtful. She knew he would tell her about it in his own time, so she returned to her knitting, content to let him pass the time as he pleased.

They carried on through the village, climbing all the way to a high saddle between two sloping hills. They had left all sign of habitation behind them and saw nothing but the occasional barn or hayrick. There was little to identify the narrow, winding track, but Wibberley began to feel he knew every yard of it. All doubt evaporated when they drove through an unusually deep dip in the road that looked as though it would flood easily. Even on such a bright and sunny day, it was wet with spillage from the stream.

Eventually, the road began to descend and before them were the rooftops of another village.

'Where on earth are you taking us Ken?' enquired his wife.

'It's a village called Uley,' he replied automatically.

His wife looked at him askance, 'How on earth did you know that?' He didn't reply, for at the bottom of the pitch before them was a crossroads; might it be *her* crossroads he thought to himself!

Finding the smithy and villages - just as Llewelyn described them - unsettled the eminently sensible policeman. He told himself the villages themselves might exist, but the tale Llewelyn wove about them had to be fantasy, nothing more! Llewelyn was a bookworm and it would not be difficult to unearth such geographical information, even about two nondescript Cotswold villages - their existence was hardly an official secret after all. Yes, it was remarkable that he'd stumbled across them, but that alone, didn't make Llewelyn's story true.

With great sadness, he recalled Llewelyn arguing with himself in that appalling asylum cell, his trousers soaked in urine, his fingers smeared with blood and faeces. The story he'd told just moments before, about the village and Polly and how she died - moving though that story was - must surely be just fantasy. An

471

imaginary story, told about imaginary people, but woven about real places by a lonely, inadequate bookworm in the grip of insanity.

The problem for the policeman was that now he'd stumbled across the villages so central to Llewelyn's story, he needed to prove the story to be true or false - one way or the other.

At the bottom of the pitch, beyond the crossroads was a meadow, just where a meadow should be according to the story. It looked like any other meadow, but he knew in his heart that it would be her meadow. Grazing quietly amongst the tussocks of course grass was a small herd of cows. In a far corner, a farm implement lay abandoned, its faded paint blistered with rust.

Wibberley parked the Morris Minor and told his wife he wouldn't be long. He walked across the road and climbed a rickety gate into the field. He could see the stream on the far side of the gently sloping pasture. Two cows were drinking from it, enjoying its coldness in the warmth of the afternoon.

He stood for some while, just looking about him, and every feature was just as Llewelyn described it in his story. The shallow ford, the steeply sloping banks, the willow tree with its tendrils dipping in the stream. There was even ripe corn swaying gently in the field beyond. It was as though he were visiting somewhere he'd seen in a photograph.

In his mind's eye, P.C Wibberley could see the fair in full swing and could feel the warmth of the cloudless summer's day. Ladies with parasols and gay summer hats, bought bric-a-brac at the bring and buy, tried their hand at the lucky dip, or endeavoured to look graceful as they heaved a ball they could barely lift, down a makeshift skittle alley.

Laughing children danced about the Maypole, queued for vanilla ices, or waited their turn to ride on the gaily-coloured swingboats. Gentlemen sporting Malacca canes and looking dapper in their top hats shared humorous stories with fellow fairgoers, whilst a fairground organ rocked gently on iron-rimmed wheels, as it played the popular tunes of the day. The scene could not have been more vivid, more cheery or more English.

'I'll give a penny fer um!' said a voice that broke in upon his thoughts.

Wibberley turned to see who had spoken, for he thought himself quite alone among the cow parsley and dandelion.

'I beg your Pardon?' he replied.

'A penny fer thy thoughts! Thee was bloody miles away, thee was,' said an old man who leant over the parapet of a stone bridge, beneath which a stream flowed steadily onwards.

'Sorry,' said the policeman; 'Yes miles away like you said - is this where they hold the village fair?'

'Used ter be but not no more. Ain't bin no fair here in years... Years, an' years, an' years - might even be longer!'

'Just a thought' the policeman replied, as he walked on toward the brook.

'Tha's private property, case thee didn't know!'

'No, I didn't know - is it yours?'

'Well... not so as to speak, but I d' sort of look after un!'

He was a scruffy fellow, this keeper of the cow pasture, a thin, weatherworn man of eighty years or more. He wore a threadbare coat and heavy trousers that rolled over a broad leather belt. His boots were worn and dirty from the road.

'Don't worry,' replied the policeman with a smile, 'I'll leave it just as I found it.' He walked on towards the brook and then as an afterthought asked, 'Why don't they use it anymore - for the fair?'

The old man chuckled, 'Ah... thee've asked a good un there, thee as! That's a good un that is!'

The policeman had the feeling that it would be.

'And in your capacity as trustee of the field, are you at liberty to tell me why?'

'I don't see no reason why not,' came the reply, ''tis all on account of that brook! No-one don't go near there no more - 'cepting the cows - sort of haunted, see.'

The policeman walked over to the bridge. 'No I don't see,' he replied, 'why should it be haunted?' The old man chuckled once more, for there was nothing he enjoyed more than telling a yarn!

'Right, well, seeing as thee've asked, I'll tell e'! Must be some forty odd year ago now... Some say t'wer an accident; some d' say suicide; some do even say murder, but all agree, 'tis haunted by a woman as drowned in that brook on the very same night 'er father were bludgeoned t' death. Whas' think of that un then!'

'Go on,' said the policeman.

'Well twern't just the drowning as upset folk, twer' other things besides - unnatural things...! On the night 'er died t'wer dead of winter an' snowin' hard. T'wer hours afore anyone missed 'er on account of 'er father 'aving been murdered in his own study, by his own chauffeur. Anyway, they searched high

473

an' low an' no one could find er', fer after she fell through the ice, it froze over agin', an' got covered in more'n a foot of snow. Twern't until the thaw come, some three weeks later, that 'er was found staring up from the bottom of yonder pool, just there where the cows be drinking now.'

'We pulled er out an' lay er on't bank, an' first we thought t'wer a young girl for er looked no more'n twenty, but t'wer her all right. Thee won't believe this, but 'er hair ad changed from white to gold and everyone said the same - just like gold. Some folk's reckoned t'wer the lime in the water an' some said t'wer dye from the mills, but there ain't bin no cloth dyeing done round yer in years. Then there was the look on er face... peaceful an calm like er was looking out over some beautiful view as stretched on fer miles an' miles... It were the eyes as done it fer I... wide open they were, an' they looked straight at thee no matter where thee stood. It were as though er'd' come back to life all over agin'... Give I the bloody creeps it did!'

'You were there?'

"Twas I as found 'er an' I shan't never ferget it neither! All the years 'ad fallen from er, an er looked beautiful... that was everyone's word for it... beautiful! I ain't sin' nothing like it, before nor since! Course, folk was just getting over that, when along comes Harry the Hare.'

'Who was Harry the Hare?'

'Ah well... Thee've asked us another good un' there thee ave; that's another good un' that is... 'Arry were a gentleman's poacher see, an' well in the know 'e were an all. Many's a magistrate ave' sat down to a plate of Arry's trout with never a question asked! That d' tell 'e all thee needs ter know about the gentry don't it! Anyway... One night Arry's out on business see, an about two 'o'clock e' finds himself, stood in that brook, exactly a year to the minute, an' the hour, an' the day, since her drowned. He said 'e were stood there quiet like, not making a sound, when all of a sudden 'e hears voices - lots of voices - all talking and laughing together. He thought t'wer the gamekeeper and set to leg it, but then 'e hears a child calling fer its mother... A girl 'e says it were, an her sobs were the saddest sound he'd ever erd'. He hears other voices too. There was music playing an' people talking... It went on fer a long time, an all the while 'Arry never moved a muscle, fer the voices was all about him; as near to him as I am to you.'

'If they was ghosts 'e couldn't see um, fer it were as black as a coal scuttle, but 'e erd their voices, an' felt the air move as they passed un' by. He said 'e ain't never bin so scared in all is life, 'e just stood there in the pitch dark, waitin' fer a hand ter touch 'is shoulder, but nothing never did. To the best of anyone's knowledge, 'Arry never went poachin', ever again!'

474

The old man expected the stranger to look surprised, but wasn't expecting him to look so stunned. 'You all right?' he asked.

'Yes I'm fine,' replied Wibberley, 'look... I suppose you wouldn't know where she's buried?'

'Course I do - sexton fer forty year I were. I've sin um all on their way, I ave - er included.

I've buried um all, I ave,' he continued, as they made their way to the church. 'Rich man, poor man, prince an pauper, an one thing I've learnt along the way... money don't help a bit when thee gets to where we're going!' They passed through the lych gate, the old man relentless in his nonsense.

'I don't know about thee, but I don't believe in all that standin' round the grave, bawlin' an' caterwauling an' carrying on... It d' just upset folk! I used ter try an' cheer things up a bit if they did happen to come back later when I was backfilling. I used ter say... 'Ah...! Old Jack - 'e was a bugger, 'e was... or summut like that... Then I used ter say... Ah...! I was the last t' see un dead I was! Then I used ter laugh, an' they used ter laugh, an' we was all laughing fit ter bust afore we'd finished. It were like a play on words see! Yer tis...'

He'd brought P.C Wibberley to a far corner of the graveyard, undisturbed for many years and overgrown with hawthorn, ivy and nettle. The old man pointed to a small headstone, buried beneath the undergrowth, its inscription unreadable for the moss and creeping tendrils of ivy. PC Wibberley took out a penknife and began cutting back the worst of the ivy, but it was many minutes before he could fully read the inscription.

Beloved of Elizabeth and Richard

Their Daughter Polly Durcan

Departed this life January 17th, 1932 Aged 51 years.

Hours Fly

Flowers Die

Sorrowed Days,

Men's Foolish Ways,

All Pass By.

But Love Stays.

'Course, I knew er meself when I were younger,' continued the old man. 'She were a bit flighty, fer all 'er airs an' graces. Always talking t' the boys 'er were! I could ave 'ad 'er meself if I'd a mind, but I always 'ad me mind on me job in them days. His lordship never did nothing before 'e spoke to I. Yer what's think of this then Ned, or what's think of that then Ned? Askin' us all the time 'e were. Anyway, stead of marrying among the gentry like 'er father wanted, 'er goes and gets caught by the local blacksmith! That were a good un that were, we all 'ad a laugh about that un I can tell 'e. That's where flighty d' get thee, see! I always say's...'

The policeman sat back on his haunches with a heavy heart, for now there was no doubt in his mind. The simple poem carved on her tombstone was Isaac's poem, written on the craggy beauty of Hurlstone Point the day of Becky's funeral, and kept thereafter in a locket about Polly's neck; simple words cherished above all others, by the woman whose earthly remains lay beneath him. He closed his eyes and an immense sadness flooded over him.

He had thought Llewelyn's story to be a madman's tale, just a story, nothing more. He remembered it almost word for word, partly because of the peculiar circumstances of its telling and partly because Llewelyn cherished the story and had told it so movingly. It left the policeman deeply troubled because what he'd seen with his own eyes and what the old man had told him, all confirmed Llewelyn's tale. It was a tale that had moved him very deeply, and if Llewelyn's story of their lives and their love for one another was true, might not the very end of his story be true - the final part that Llewelyn had retold so movingly in that grim asylum cell.

Llewellyn had tried to explain everything, but no one would listen for no one believed him. He too - a seasoned bobby who had learnt to expect the unexpected - hadn't believed him! Instead, he'd thought him mad, and left him to his madness in that sad and lonely place. Angry with himself, he opened his penknife once more, and scratched a jagged cross through the name "Durcan". That done he scratched the name "Smith" beneath it.

'Her name was Smith, not Durcan,' he said abruptly, turning on the old man angrily; cutting through his endless diatribe. Mrs Polly Smith, the wife of Isaac Smith! A beautiful, gentle, faithful wife and a devoted mother, not the flighty hussy you would have me believe...'

'Yer that desiccating private property that is,' said the old man, pointing to the scratches he'd made. 'Thee can't go round...'

'I know you,' said the policeman angrily! 'Your name is Meadows, isn't it - Ned Meadows...! You set the dogs on him didn't you... you nearly killed him!'

'Yer what's this,' said Ned, angrily. 'Bloody stranger's coming round yer accusing decent folk of thing's thee don't know nothing about...'

'Go away,' said the policeman angrily, 'Please go away! Look... Here's five pounds for you - take it for your troubles, but please just go away!'

The old man slipped the fiver in a waistcoat pocket and started back the way he'd come; mumbling to himself as he went. 'Bloody buggers coming round yer...! Upsetting decent folk...! Bugger off back where thee d' come from... bloody buggers...'

The policemen returned to his car some minutes later and sat silently in the driving seat, gazing at the meadow and the brook that marked its lower edge.

'Are you all right Kenneth?' asked his wife with concern; 'you look as though you've seen a ghost!'

'Perhaps I have,' he replied solemnly; 'perhaps I just have!'

CHAPTER 69

Packed Lunch

Wibberley's wife decided not to press him on his strange remark or the identity of the old man he'd been talking to. He would tell her in his own good time as usual. It was lunchtime and both she and the little Morris were glad of a rest from their journey. They were parked where they would be of no hindrance to other travellers, and the view of the meadow and the hills beyond was a very peaceful and pleasant one. She suggested they have their lunch where they were.

She took a hamper from the boot of the Morris and unwrapped the cheese sandwiches she'd prepared before setting out from Pencryn. They sat with a napkin on their laps and a flask of coffee between them.

They chatted for some minutes, comparing the Cotswold Valley before them, with their own valley back home.

'It's beautifully green,' she remarked.

'Home is where the heart lies,' he replied.

'Of course it is dear, and I'm not sure they have chapel in this part of the world either.'

'Or a male voice choir.'

'Nor a decent colliery band.'

The policeman smiled, finished the last of his sandwich, poured himself the last of the coffee and took her cup from her fingers, for her eyes had closed and she was snoring softly. It never ceased to amaze him, how casually she could nod off to sleep. In fairness, it was 1p.m. They had left their home at 7a.m that morning, and it was tiring to be a passenger for so long. He decided a nap would do her no harm before they set out on the last leg of their journey to Stratford.

He tried to follow his wife's example, but the plan didn't work. He couldn't drag his mind from Polly and Llewelyn's tale of how she had died. For all those years he'd assumed Llewelyn's story was no more than the imaginings of a deranged mind, but now the facts of Polly's life and death had been established beyond all doubt, his thoughts kept returning to the manner of her passing.

CHAPTER 70

The River

The first snow of winter came the night Richard Durcan met his end, but before the chill, the land was sodden with weeks of relentless rain. Swollen rivers rushed onwards, whilst low meadows flooded and were still. All was a quagmire of rutted paths and muddy puddles, pressed deep into the earth by aimless cattle and lumbering carts. Then Jack Frost called, and everywhere felt the touch of his hand.

High above the dark and frozen land, chill fingers fashioned snowflakes from the moisture-laden air. They fell to earth like winter leaves; gently, relentlessly, floating this way and that. They settled upon higgledy-piggledy rooftops, crooked hedgerows, huddled cattle and one another. Soon all Gloucestershire was covered in a thick eiderdown of crisp white snow.

So deep was the snow that year that work upon the land all but ceased. About the village, excited children with socks for mittens, glowing faces and dripping noses, pelted one-another with snowballs whilst shrieking with delight and alarm in equal measure. They made slides, sucked icicles, and undertook hazardous expeditions to the icebound island of the duck pond. Village pumps creaked to a halt, their pistons frozen to the barrel; housewives melted snow to brew tea and few, save tradesman like old farmer Jack - selling his frozen milk by the penny lump - bothered to venture far. Deep mid winter was upon them with all its beauty and hardship, and all anyone could do was throw an extra log on the fire and draw the windows tight.

The deep freeze lasted for three long weeks, and made the tragedy at Oxtalls all the more tragic, for Elizabeth Durcan could neither bury her husband nor find her daughter because of it. Though the men of the village searched far and wide; prodding snowdrifts along the hedgerows with long rods; it was not until the thaw that Ned Meadows discovered Polly's naked body in the river; her eyes wide open, her hair turned from grey to gold.

Had it been Ned's word alone, no one would have believed it, but others came quickly and saw for themselves. They included John Long and the doctor, neither man known for their flights of fancy or wild imagination.

~

It was late, and all the household was abed. All, that is, except Clara and Jonah, for this was the night they had chosen to enact their plan; their hearts set on greed.

They thought they were alone in the house, not knowing that other souls were abroad that night. They didn't know about the Watchers - those who came from near and far, silent and invisible. They came in single file along familiar paths to congregate outside the big house. They waited silently in the snow for the tragedy yet to unfold.

They came from places they loved in life; places they could not easily leave in death. A tattered armchair by a parlour fire, or a warm kitchen; its mantelshelf stacked with pots and pans, its smell, homely and comforting.

They came from places humble and grand, old and new, and near and far. They came from cottages where widows sat alone, and where words were seldom heard now they were gone. They came from homes where once happy children asked endlessly when their father, or mother, or favourite grandparent would be coming home.

They came from blackened, grimy factories, alive with machinery, sparks and speed, or busy ticket offices, full of bustle, rush-hour travellers, and the shrill of engine whistles.

It did not matter from whence they came, for it was just a tiny corner of endless space. It served only for those who loved them in life to mourn their passing; but many stayed on in those places where they were content in life - unable to let go. They watched over those who loved them then, and cherished them still, waiting for the "togetherness" that would come one day.

When it came and they were reunited, then perhaps, they might leave those familiar places to earth, air, and sky, having no further use for them, but until then, they watched and waited, silently, patiently, rarely seen by the human eye, but sometimes sensed by the human spirit. They have no formal name for they don't exist, but Llewelyn called them "The Watchers".

Among them, there were men and women, children and infants, and those who lost the struggle to leave the womb alive. Some had not been whole in life, their bodies broken and twisted, their mind damaged and impaired; but they were whole in this other world beyond the Silver Mountain, for they had no use for mortal flesh there.

They pressed onward through the falling snow their sad duty to be done and were all gathered at the big house when the enormous hound struggled to its feet, only to fall again among the fire irons. The clatter could not be heard in the servant's quarters for it was at the rear of the house, but Richard Durcan and Polly heard it well enough and were awake in an instant.

Dressed in his nightshirt and dressing gown, his army revolver in his hand, Richard Durcan made his way quickly and quietly along the bedroom passage toward the gallery.

'Is anything wrong Papa?' he heard Polly ask as he passed her door.

'Go back to sleep, Polly,' he whispered, 'it's just the dog moving about - go back to sleep, darling!'

Polly got out of bed despite her father's reassurances, and crossed to the window in case the noise she'd heard was Isaac. She saw the snow upon the balustrade, little more than a sprinkling at that time, but settling fast. Lights came on in the study and she saw that the lawn too was powdered in snow as far as the light would penetrate. But there was no Isaac waiting in the light from the window, beckoning her to come; there was only the chill of the night.

She made her way to the landing and the gallery beyond, in time to see her father flushing the young chauffeur from the window recess and the scullery maid they called Clara, dashing his brains out with the heavy lamp.

Polly called the girl Nancy for she knew who she was; she had always known, despite what they said. She had only to look at her daughter's eyes to see Nance Ridler staring back at her. Her face was like a cold hand upon Polly's shoulder.

Time stood entirely still and she watched her father's slaughter through a red veil of shock and grief. The murderers moved slowly, spoke silently, pointing her way with hands red with blood.

The young man took up her father's gun and began to climb the stairs pointing the gun at her, his hand shaking, a look of desperation on his face.

Halfway up the stairs he stopped, his expression changing to disbelief, then horror. He no longer looked at her but scanned the whole gallery, unable to believe what he saw. He ran from the room, dragging the girl with him; the gun loose in his hand.

Polly went to her father, cradling his head in her lap, his blood soaking her nightdress. She could see his brain pulsing through the terrible wound. His looked at her with eyes that could no longer see, lost, helpless, dying.

'Oh Papa,' she sobbed; 'Oh my darling Papa. This is my fault - all my fault.'

His eyes began to close as life slipped from him.

'I love you so much,' she whispered.

Richard Durcan died in her arms and it took just moments, but it seemed to Polly as though hours passed by. She held him close so he wouldn't be alone and she wept for him.

A voice broke through the veil of shock and desolation that engulfed her. It was a soft voice, a beautiful voice - kind and understanding.

'Polly,' said the voice; 'Polly look at me!'

Polly looked up to see who had spoken. A beautiful woman stood nearby, her slender hand outstretched, her eyes sad, for she too was weeping. She was the most beautiful woman Polly had ever seen. Others were gathered beside her, though Polly had not heard them arrive. There were men and women, both old and young, and children holding the grown-up's hands - all looking on with sadness.

The people were grey and indistinct, their clothing grey too. Polly blamed it on the tears that filled her eyes, for even the beautiful woman was grey, but she was not afraid, as the young man had been afraid, even though it must have been they who alarmed him so.

'You loved him, didn't you?' said the beautiful woman.

'Yes,' she replied.

'Don't be sad Polly, for he is with us now and we will care for him.'

'Who are you?'

'Don't you know?' replied the beautiful woman.

'I think so,' she replied, 'You are the Watchers.'

'Yes we are the Watchers,' she replied softly.

'Did you watch over Isaac and Becky?' she asked, 'He was blind - he couldn't see. She was so young - I was so afraid.'

'Yes, we watched over them and you shouldn't be afraid for they are safe now, never fear.'

Polly began to sob once more as she held her father close, her cheek upon his.

'Everyone I have ever loved,' she whispered softly.

The Watchers gathered about her and they too were sad.

'You miss them don't you?' said the woman kindly.

Polly nodded her head, 'With all my heart! I think of them every day and I will never stop loving them, I never could.'

Just then, there was a noise on the landing; the flicker of candle light reflected on panelled walls; the Watchers looked towards the light and one by one, they disappeared.

'Oh please don't go' said Polly but soon only the beautiful woman was left. 'Please don't go,' she begged.

'People are coming Polly; I cannot stay... but we know how you've suffered and you may come with us if you wish.'

'I don't know how!' she said, as the beautiful woman faded.

'Follow the cat,' she whispered softly. Before the first of the household arrived, the beautiful woman was gone.

Mrs. Jeffries was talking to her; lifting her to her feet, taking her from her father. She too was in tears. 'What shall we do - oh whatever shall we do?' she said repeatedly.

Mother was knelt above him now; Polly could hear her sobbing pitifully in her anguish, whispering his name over and over. She heard Jeffries calling the police. 'Yes I'm afraid so,' he said, 'yes, yes... the chauffeur and scullery maid we think... I don't know; they've taken the Daimler... yes... yes, thank you... yes, as soon as you can please.'

Mrs. Jeffries took Polly by the arm, leading her from the room and talking of rest, but Polly pushed her away. Somehow, she found herself alone on the lawn; flakes of snow falling through the yellow shafts of light that spilled from every window. So beautiful and yet so awful was this night. She heard Jeffries voice from the stable-yard. 'Fetch the doctor lad and be quick about it!'

Then came the unmistakable clatter of the trap crossing the cobbled yard and the soft, shush, shush, shush, shush as the pony trotted through the fresh snow of the drive. Faster and faster it went, its carriage lights bobbing. She saw the watchers in its path, but too late to shout a warning. Polly could only gasp in horror as the carriage ploughed through them without slowing.

She thought they must be dreadfully injured, but they continued on their way, heads bowed against the storm, coat tails flapping, a tiny lantern held aloft and swinging wildly. On they trudged, as though the trap had never existed. Polly ran after them, calling to them, 'Please don't go' she cried. Her bare feet sinking into the snow to her ankles, but when she reached the drive, they were gone.

She saw them ahead on the road to the village. The lantern swung back and forth, caught by the wind that fashioning deep drifts and sculpturing snow buttresses about the trees and hedgerows. No matter how fast she ran, she couldn't keep up with them and soon she lost their light completely.

The bitter cold, at first unnoticed, then ignored; gnawed at her flesh and bones until every inch of her body shivered from it. The thin cotton of her nightdress became sodden and heavy, its wet skirt dragging at her ankles, tripping her as she walked. Beneath the snow, stones and the frozen earth cut her feet and she stumbled and fell, for her legs were like frozen stumps, numb to all feeling.

The road twisted and turned on its journey to the village; a road she and her beloved Parson Pimm once knew so well. She was exhausted and wanted to rest; only the need to stay with the watchers drove her on.

On and on she went, calling to the beautiful woman, but the light had disappeared now. It was only when she reached the crossroads - with no idea which road to follow - that she sobbed in despair.

Ahead was the village, and to her left, the lonely lane that led to Coaley; the same lane she'd travelled with Ned Meadows so many years before. To her right were the Tetbury road and the stone sheep pool with its spring that trickled into the brook beyond. Its cheery waters were silent now; frozen to the wells edge like sugar icing.

Near collapse from cold and exhaustion, Polly took shelter from the wind beneath a stone wall. Gathering her legs to her chest, she put her head on her knees, closed her eyes and wept.

Miserable with failure, her senses numbed, she began to drop into that everlasting sleep, so beguiling of bitter cold and exhaustion, but then the trap passed by. The stable boy was at the reins with the doctor beside him; both were white from the driving snow. It clung to their whiskers and eyebrows and the mufflers about their necks. They didn't see her there, for she too was covered in snow, but the rattle of the trap stirred her from her stupor and by its lights, she saw the cat.

It sat on its haunches in the gateway; the tiny beads of ice that clung to its fur seeming almost luminescent. It watched her intently with its bright green eyes, as though she were expected.

She knew the gateway well, for the meadow beyond was a place of many memories. Memories of sunny days, village fete's and idle hours spent damming the stream that meandered by from somewhere near, to somewhere far.

484

It was the very stream in which Isaac had slipped and fallen and from which he would emerge to see Polly - no longer just a foolish girl with a childish infatuation - but the beautiful woman who would steal his heart forever.

The cat got up, turned, and walked away. Somehow, Polly summoned the strength to follow; "Follow the cat," the beautiful woman had said.

'Arthur wait,' she cried, 'please wait.'

If Arthur understood he showed no sign, for he carried on in the haughty manner of cats, turning from time to time to be sure she followed. She could see the faint luminescence of the ice crystals upon his fur and occasionally he would stop and turn to watch her. She could see his bright green eyes - impassive, unblinking. When she got near, he would walk on once more.

He led her between clumps of rye grass that barred their way like crystal wheat sheaves stacked for harvest. The meadow became steeper and she knew she must be near the stream.

Its banks were steep except for those places where the cattle came to drink, so she trod carefully, unsure how near the edge might be. The cat was nowhere to be seen, so she stopped and called its name, but there was no answer.

When she spotted him once more, he was not ahead as she expected, but far to her left and farther away than ever; so far she could barely make him out through the snowstorm. She called his name, but he came no nearer; he merely sat and stared.

What must I do?' she asked, but of course, he did not reply. Instead, he sat and watched, his eyes, the only light in that dark, dark place. She turned toward him and instantly her foot slipped. She felt it strike out into space and the next moment she fell onto the ice covered river with a jarring crash. She heard it splinter and crack with the impact of her fall. She crawled to what she thought was the bank, but in her confusion she had crawled ever nearer the middle of the stream where the ice was thinnest.

Suddenly, with a splintering crash, the ice gave way. She fell between the bobbing shards; the pull of the river drawing her down and under the ice, her body too weak to resist.

In shock from the numbing cold, she drifted with the flow to shallower water and became trapped between the ice above and the riverbed below. In fear and panic, she pushed upwards, but the ice was too thick - too strong. She knew then that she was going to die.

The freezing water poured into her lungs as she struggled for breath. Soon they faltered and were still. She felt her heart stopping, and she wanted so much to sleep. She lay still, waiting for whatever was to come; there was no pain - no pain at all.

Suddenly there was movement above her. Someone - something - was on the ice, and scrabbling at the snow, for she felt the tiny tremors through the water. Luminous eyes appeared above her, peering through the glass-like ice. She saw them clearly - green and burning bright.

The cat studied her for many moments, curious, yes... but untroubled. Satisfied with his work, he left her to her fate.

As she drifted to sleep in the icy water, something remarkable, something very beautiful and wonderful happened. Through the tiny window the cat made in the snow, Polly watched the blackness of winter's night turn to indigo, then charcoal, then to the grey of dawn. Slowly, the snow disappeared and the ice became as clear as glass. Very soon, it melted and cracked, with pieces large and small, turning upon their edge in the rivers flow, to bob gracefully along like crystal galleons on a Spanish Maine.

Through the chill water, Polly watched the sky turn to blue, with cotton clouds skittering by, too busy to stop and stare. Never had she seen the sky so beautiful. It was the deep, warm, powder-blue of childhood summers. It was the heat hazy blue of swarming gnats, roasted apples, wild garlic stinking in shady glades, and swallows soaring on the wing. The sun was too bright to follow as it arched higher and higher, warming the river like a tumbler of forgotten lemonade.

Then suddenly there was movement on the bank. The beautiful young woman stood watching her, but she was no longer grey. Her complexion was as smooth as alabaster, the colour of cream; her hair fell nearly to her waist and shimmered in the sunshine like a million threads of gold.

She looked down at Polly and smiled. 'Welcome Polly,' she said softly, 'welcome to this lovely place. I am sorry about Arthur; he is not very... well he is Arthur and that is just the way of cats, I'm afraid. He gave you a terrible fright I know, but you must not think poorly of him for he too has those whom he loves, and he did what he did for them.'

She was about to speak again when a sound caught her attention. She listened intently, then said excitedly, 'They are coming; they are here at last; I must go now - don't be afraid,' and with those words she was gone.

Moments later, Polly heard familiar sounds, indistinct at first, then louder and brighter by the moment. There was the toot and Oom-pah of a mechanical organ, the shrill of an engine whistle, a showman haranguing a crowd with bawdy enticements, market traders shouting their wares, people talking, others laughing, the sudden wail of a startled infant.

Suddenly, the sky shook in a kaleidoscope of silver and blue. Ripples spread across the surface as one heavy boot plunged into the water followed by another, then another. Men were wading across the shallow river; so close that their footsteps threatened to crush her. She heard women laughing and men's good-natured banter.

'Right then, ladies and gentlemen,' said the Master of Ceremonies, Tom Baldoodle, 'I'll be lookin fer penalties if there's any shenanigans like last year - on the count of three now - one, two, three!' She heard men groaning, women clapping, girls cheering, children shrieking, everyone shouting their team on to greater effort. There was chanting, singing and nonsense rhymes. "Coaley born and Coaley bred; strong in't arm and thick in't head!"

The ripples subsided and Polly could see the tug-o-war teams on either bank; some dressed in frocks like pantomime dames. A mighty cheer went up and a rope slapped the water followed by the grunts and groans of straining men.

Within moments, the image shattered like a broken mirror as a man fell in the water just inches from her. She couldn't see his face, for he lay face downward on the riverbed, but she knew instinctively who he was, and her heart leapt for joy. The man wore his hair in a sailor's cue and the long brown threads of the ponytail fanned out in the flow of the river like a horse mane. Polly knew only one man who tied his hair that way.

Isaac lay still, stunned by the huge stone that brought him to a halt, whilst wisps of blood seeped from the cut to his forehead. Polly's joy turned to alarm, as he lay unmoving in the silt, face down and unconscious. She tried to move, to reach out to him, but she'd not the strength after her terrible ordeal. After what seemed an eternity, a fist plunged into the water and dragged him to his knees by the collar of his shirt.

Polly watched anxiously, as Isaac retched and coughed the water from his lungs, gasping aloud for air the way he had that wonderful day so many years ago when their love story began. Everything was just as it was then, the fair, the tug-o-war - everything. She heard others laughing, and was angry with them for being so cruel, but in her concern, she missed the relief in their laughter.

He stood up, still coughing and retching. She tried to call out to him, but her lungs would not move. She watched in anguish as he waded away.

'Come back - oh my darling come back,' she tried to say.

Just as he reached the bank, something made him turn. Perhaps it was her hair, waving gently in the stream like the fronds of some delicate sea anemone, or perhaps it was a sixth sense that sent him back to kneel again where he'd fallen.

He stared at the river's rippled surface, his eyes trying to adjust to the shimmering image of the face in the water. He reached out a hand to touch her cheek, and there could be no doubt anymore.

'Polly,' he whispered, as a hand gripped his heart; 'Oh my darling Polly.'

He put his arms beneath her and lifted her gently from the water; he carried her along the riverbank to a cornfield where he laid her gently in a bower of corn stalks, turned golden by the sun. He whispered her name repeatedly like a mother waking her child from the deepest slumber, but her body remained limp and lifeless in his arms. Fear that he had found her - only to lose her - filled him with dread, and his voice faltered and cracked.

'Please wake up my darling,' he whispered, his eyes brimming with tears.

She had no way to tell him she could hear him, and see him, and feel his touch, nor tell him that she loved him with all her heart, for the river had taken away the force we know as life; but there were other forces in the cornfield that day; forces far more powerful than the river. Never were the sun's rays warmer, nor their love for one another stronger than at that moment. Slowly, gradually, the power of that love gave back the life the river had taken away and Polly smiled, then moved her lips in silent words.

'So cold' she whispered.

His tears spilled over and he wept for them both; overjoyed that she had survived her journey across the Misty Mountains. He held her close, afraid to let her go, for that crossing was a journey on which so many souls foundered and were lost.

She smiled once more, and he could see she too had been weeping. She wanted to hold him but didn't have the strength. Instead, she moved her lips once more; 'I love you so much,' she said.

He kissed her tenderly and told her that he loved her too.

'So cold,' she said.

They were still in their sodden clothing, so Isaac lifted the tatters of Polly's nightdress over her head, and took off his own shirt and breeches before lying down beside her, his arms about her.

'The sun will soon warm us, Polly, and dry our clothes too. We've done this before haven't we,' he said, willing her back to life, willing her to grow strong. 'Do you remember - during the storm - our roaring fire in the hospital?'

She smiled and said yes, for how could she ever forget the first time they made love.

'What if ...?' she began.

'No one will see us,' he replied, knowing she would be anxious about their nakedness. 'I can barely see over the corn, it's so high. The sun will soon dry my clothes; my shirt for you, my breeches for me - we'll look a proper pair then Polly, won't we?

She smiled for him, 'Yes, we will my darling, but I don't want anyone to see me like this,' she said.

'I want to see you,' he replied, 'I want to see you and look at you for as long as I can, because you are beautiful.'

Polly turned her head from him, her smile fading.

'What's wrong Polly,' he asked tenderly; turning her head back; concerned to see her sudden distress.

She said in a whisper, 'I'm not who I was Isaac - not anymore. You are so handsome - just as you were before Rufus and Satan, just as you were when I gave myself to you, when I could not bear to be without you another moment, but I've grown old - old and ugly. There have been too many lonely years between us; how can we be as we once were?'

'But you are beautiful Polly, you always will be beautiful to me, don't you see!' but she turned her head away from him, and it cut him like a knife to see her tears.

'Do you think there is only one reason I love you,' he said softly, but she didn't reply.

He lowered her gently to the cornstalks and got up from where he lay to walk the few feet from the corn bower to the riverbank.

He reached down and picked up a shard of ice, caught among the reeds at the water's edge, for strong though the sun was, it hadn't yet managed to penetrate the reeds and melt all the ice from the river. He took it back to her, still dripping and shining like a mirror, and held it before her so she could see her own reflection.

489

In it, Polly saw not the lonely old woman who sat with her memories by an open window, but the beautiful woman who had been the mother of his child, his wife and his lover. There were no lines etching her face - no grey in her hair, no sag in her breasts; her skin was soft and smooth and she was beautiful. She was the Polly of their youth, of Selworthy, of the smallpox hospital and of their beautiful Leathernbottle Cottage.

'You see - you are beautiful!'

'Yes I am,' she replied tearfully. 'Yes I am.'

He lay down beside her and took her in his arms and she cried for joy.

'Just look at the two of you' said a familiar voice, 'Not a stitch of clothing between you. Sometimes I wonder if that's all you think about, you young people.'

Isaac made a grab for his breeches as Amy looked down upon them from the bower edge, a basket in her hand.

'It's a bit too late for that young man,' she continued reproachfully, putting down her basket and kneeling beside Polly as Isaac struggled into his breeches. Amy knelt over her and kissed her, taking Polly's hand in hers.

'Are you all right dear,' she asked with concern... 'After your journey! I told Isaac not to send that fool cat, but you know what he's like; stubborn as a mule.' She cast a disparaging look in his direction, 'He said you'd understand what to do if the cat came for you, though goodness knows why.'

Polly put her arms about her mother-in-law and sobbed in her arms.

'There, there, Amy's here darling,' she said kindly, 'it's been hard for you, I know; but Amy's here.'

'How did you know where we were?' asked Isaac sharply, not a little put out by Amy's sudden appearance.

'I saw you take her from the water and bring her over to the cornfield. You left a path through the corn you could drive a herd of elephants through, you great lummox! I'd have been here sooner, but I stopped at the rummage to find something for Polly to wear, and just as well by the look of things. She held up a pretty floral frock of yellow and blue. 'There, isn't that pretty and just your size!'

Together they helped her stand, for she was as weak as a newborn foal. Amy helped her into the frock and ran a comb through her hair until it shone in the noonday sun, like silken thread of gold. With Isaac holding her about the waist, they made their way to the meadow and the May Day celebrations.

The tug-o-war had finished and most folk had moved to the Maypole where the children were dancing.

'Is she there,' said Polly anxiously, not needing to say more. They could not get close for the crowds, so they watched instead from higher ground near the road.

'Yes, she's there Polly; she's wearing the yellow dress with the bow in her hair, can you see her, but she doesn't know it was your journey day, today - we thought it best not to tell her.'

Polly nodded - her hand to her mouth. She'd caught sight of Rebecca that very moment and didn't trust herself to speak. It had been over twenty-five, long, lonely years since she'd lost her and she'd missed her so very, very much.

'We wanted it to be a special surprise, Polly! She talks about you every day and prays for you each bedtime, bless her. She's never forgotten you and misses you so much. She looks so lovely doesn't she?'

Polly nodded once more as tears spilled down her cheeks. Isaac held her tighter and took her hand in his.

They watched the children weaving among one another, holding their pretty ribbons, winding and unwinding them as they danced. An accordionist played a folk tune whilst Morris dancers danced, voices singing, bells ringing, and stave's clattering.

Polly's thoughts returned to the last time she'd seen her darling Becky; her tiny mouth open in one last desperate gasp for air, her beautiful face twisted with pain. She had fought so bravely but died so cruelly in her mother's arms. She had looked so frightened. A long time after all life was gone, Amy had taken Becky from her as gently as she could, for it was time to give her up. Those hours were a memory that haunted Polly every day of her life, but now she was well once more and that filled her heart with joy.

'Oh Amy, she's so beautiful' she said at last, 'I want to hold her so very much.'

Within the circle, "Jack o' the Green" cavorted about like a mad thing, prodding any child who dared come close with his stick and cotton Dolly.

'I know darling, but let her finish her dancing first,' replied the old lady, 'she was so looking forward to it.'

Just outside the circle of children stood John Smith, watching the spectacle and clapping along to the tune. He turned and waved when he caught site of

Polly, his pleasure clear to see. She waved back, and he indicated "just one minute," with his finger.

'He'll not leave Becky for one moment,' said Amy watching her husband with pride. 'He was always with her, but you knew that didn't you. I told myself that was why he went first - to be here for Becky, and I didn't mind so much then. She was never, ever alone Polly - John made sure of that. She thinks the world of him of course, and she's the apple of his eye. Only her grandpa is allowed to put her to bed at night and that's when he fills her head with so much nonsense you'd never believe. He's the same silly old fool, I'm afraid.'

But Polly did believe and it filled her heart with joy to see that lovely, gentle man again.

The dancers collected their gingerbread from "Jack o' the Green," and Becky sought out John to proudly show him her gingerbread. He took her by the hand and stooping to whisper something to her, pointed in Polly's direction.

The little girl looked their way, confused at first, then, letting her gingerbread fall to the ground, she ran across the meadow crying, 'Mummy, Oh, my mummy.'

Folk nearby smiled and wiped away a tear, for they too had known the joy of that moment.

Polly and Rebecca hugged one another and cried in one another's arms, and Amy cried too. John Smith put an arm about his wife's shoulder, pleased to see his family whole once more.

There were many, many reunions that wonderful day, not least among them her father, who walked her darling Parson Pimm by the halter. She hugged them both and told her father she loved him so and insisted Isaac and John shake his hand. They did so with good enough grace, agreeing that what was done was done for love of Polly.

She told Isaac and her father she was sure they could be friends now, for they were both obstinate, arrogant and insufferable, but for some reason she loved them dearly. As for Parson Pimm, she put her arms about his neck, stroking him gently and telling him that he too, was every bit as obstinate as every other man in her life, but that she loved him with all her heart. The Parson listened contentedly, his head upon her shoulder, nudging her with his nose the moment she took her arms away, happy to be with his beloved mistress once more.

It was the sound of the music that finally tore her from him. The strains of the mournful tune carried on the air above the hubbub of the fair, clear, moving, and unmistakable. It came from the edge of the cornfield they'd so recently left. The familiar melody, melancholy and beautiful, seemed to ripple and sway the corn, though no doubt the true master was a gentle breeze that kept the warmth of the afternoon at bay.

Polly took Isaac by the hand and together they followed the music to a willow tree, its branches dipping the water gratefully. The slender tendrils reminded Polly of barefoot children, dangling their feet in the river, contemplating the flow, and grumbling about history and the injustice of school.

If there was doubt before they reached the willow, then the sweet smell of Daniel Pretty's tobacco dispelled that doubt once and for all. Aromatic and unmistakable, its hazy blue smoke filtered through the umbrella of green. Polly parted the canopy and two men greeted her with a smile.

Pretty was crouched on his haunches, his back against the bole of the tree, the pipe he had so recently taken from his mouth, smouldering in his hand. Jacko laid the battered hurdy gurdy upon the ground and said simply and for both of them, 'Welcome to you, Miss Polly.'

Of all the wonderful reunions that day, none upset her so much as this one, for though she had known Daniel Pretty and Jacko for such a short time, she owed them so very much. She stood among the drooping tendrils; her husband's arm about her waist and tears filled her eyes.

As Daniel Pretty got to his feet, Polly took Jacko's hands in hers and with deep sincerity said simply; 'You always came, Jacko! I looked out for you each year and you always came.'

'It was nothing miss, I was just doing Dan'l's bidding.'

'That terrible night... You were so badly hurt; it was all my fault.'

'It was no one's fault Miss Polly; it just panned out that way - like things do sometimes. And if I could have come closer than the wood's edge those nights then I'd have told you it wasn't your fault. Maybe you'd have gotten better then, like we all wanted you to, but the men showed me their guns and it wasn't safe to come no closer.'

Her eyes were bright with tears as she kissed him on the cheek and said, 'I knew what you wanted to say, Jacko, for that wonderful melody and those beautiful words said it for you. I will always be grateful that you watched over me all those long and troubled years. You gave me such comfort, and I shall never, ever forget your kindness.'

'Like I said Miss Polly, it was all Dan'l's bidding. Dan'l told me to look out for you in his last letter, and that's what I did! You need to thank him, not me.'

493

She turned to Daniel Pretty, wondering where she would find the words to say what was in her heart. He was just as awesome as she remembered, and towered a full head and shoulders above her. His blond hair fell to his shoulders from beneath a wide brimmed hat, his beard and whiskers were neatly trimmed. He wore the familiar coat despite the heat of the day, and his intelligent blue eyes turned to Isaac for just a moment before returning to Polly once more.

'I'm sorry I let you down,' he said simply.

In disbelief, Polly said softly, 'Oh Daniel, how could you have let me down - how could you have let me down when you gave your life for me...!' She took his hand in hers, her eyes glistening with new tears, and reaching up on tiptoe, she kissed him tenderly.

Turning to Isaac she said, 'Isaac, my darling; Mr Pretty is a brave, dear friend who tried so hard to help me - We owe him so very much!'

The two men shook hands with genuine warmth and Isaac thanked him for what he'd done, but Pretty was adamant that he'd done nothing but fail her, and expressed deep sorrow that he'd not left her to grieve at Leathernbottle, as he should have.

'And if you had, then I would not have known you,' she said simply, 'and I would have lived in fear for the rest of my life. I would know nothing of Ballycara, or Father Riley, or your field of stones; I would know nothing of the hardship you suffered, or the bitterness that hardened your soul, and I would know nothing of the sacrifices you made to help me!'

'I needed you to identify Molly - that was all!'

'No you didn't Daniel, you didn't need me for that at all! You and your people would have found him anyway; Jacko told me so when we were in the boat and you were swimming into danger, he told me you wanted to help me, and protect me, and I won't believe you if you tell me anything different.'

Pretty turned to stare at Jacko who treated him to a toothless grin. 'He talks too much,' he said.

'But it's true isn't it?'

'It was my fault that Ridler was free to do what he did,' Pretty replied heavily. 'I could have turned him in to the law, and seen him hung for his crimes as he deserved, but I told myself I needed yet another navvy. It was my fault he ruined your life; you have nothing to thank me for!'

'But you could not have known - how could you have known?'

494

'I didn't know, but I should have guessed. When I realised what I'd done, I wanted to take you out of harm's way, that was all - you owe me nothing.'

'But Daniel even if that is true, I could not expect you to give your life for me!'

'I grew fond of you,' he said with a wry smile. 'You won me over in those long, cold hours we spent together in that room above the Rookeries - where you saved my leg if you remember! You're not like other protestants of my acquaintance.'

'Nor are you whom you seem to be, Daniel Pretty. There is a kind and gentle man within you as I know well.' She reached up and kissed his cheek again. 'Why did you hide away beneath this tree, where we could so easily have missed you?'

Pretty pointed to the leafy canopy, 'Nature's sunshade' he replied with a smile, 'besides which,' he said, pointing his hand at the revellers in the field, 'those people are your friends - you don't want them to see you hobnobbing with a pair of Irish tinkers.'

'Daniel, you are our friends too,' said Polly stopping him before he could carry on, 'You are our dear, dear friends and you are always welcome here and always will be, and you must never be ashamed to know me, for I will never be ashamed to know you.'

As she continued to talk to Daniel Pretty, John Smith took his opportunity to tug at Isaac's shirtsleeve and draw him outside the canopy of the tree.

'I think she's had enough now lad and very soon it is bound to take its toll. It's time we took her home before it all becomes too much.'

Isaac nodded his agreement and John Smith added soberly, 'She's sure to ask the question soon, so you'd best be prepared for it.'

'I don't know what to tell her John; how am I to explain.'

'You just start with the truth and the rest will follow; you'll find the words when it comes down to. I'll go get the trap from the paddock and collect Amy and Rebecca at the same time. You watch out for me on the road.'

Daniel Pretty and Jacko insisted they should also be on their way and, after a promise to visit the fair each year, Polly bid them farewell. 'You will come won't you,' she asked? 'Yes we will come,' he replied.

'I liked your Irishman.' said Isaac.

'He was so kind to me,' she replied. 'He took me away from danger and left his people to watch over Amy so Ridler couldn't hurt us again. He's like you in so many ways - I told him that.'

'He's a handsome fellow, I grant you, but you think he's clever too?'

'No, I think he's stubborn, and pig headed, and shows off if he can't get his own way.'

Isaac laughed. 'Did you tell him that?'

'Yes,' she replied, 'that and other things!'

'What other things?'

'Just other things!'

'What other things?'

Polly said sincerely, her mood suddenly changing; 'I told him how much I loved you, and missed you, and how my life had no meaning without you. I told him his life was soured by hatred, but just a day later, I let hatred consume me. He was so very brave Isaac; he let them hang him for a crime he didn't commit, just to save me, and I lived with that, and the guilt of Molly burning to death in that horrible way, for the rest of my life. I know he isn't a saint, but he is an honourable man and a good man in his own way. There's good in most people isn't there - deep down inside.'

'Yes, perhaps there is.'

Taking him by the hand, she sat them down by the bole of the tree and told him that they must put it all behind them now and not let those regrets spoil a wonderful, special day.

He nodded and said, 'And it is a special day - even this old weeping willow is special to us, do you remember?'

'Should I,' she said knowing full well what was special about this particular willow, for it was within the privacy of its leafy canopy that she had kept watch over his recovery from the bump on the head. She pretended not to remember, however, so that he would talk to her about that happy memory of so many years past.

'You must remember this tree,' he said askance, 'it is where we fell in love!'

'Oh is it,' she replied with mock indignation.

'Well wasn't it?'

'For you perhaps Mr Smith, but then you had all your other young ladies to think about. I couldn't expect you to rush into another romance just for me.'

Isaac laughed; pleased to see the Polly he loved had come back to him. 'So if it wasn't here then, Mrs Smith - in this official spot - where the devil was it?'

'Do you remember when Parson Pimm really did pick up a stone and we called at the smithy for the very first time and you were working at the forge and looking so handsome?'

'Yes I do - I was filthy with soot and fly ash.'

'You ponged a bit!'

'I'd been working!'

'It didn't matter,' she said, reaching out to him; touching his cheek with her fingertips; drawing him towards her. 'I didn't care that you were wiffy!' She kissed him tenderly; kissing his eyes, kissing the cheek that no longer bore the terrible scars, and kissed his lips too; 'Nothing could have stopped me falling in love with you.'

She put her head on his shoulder and he held her close for a very long time before sensing that a great sadness had come over her.

'What's the matter, Polly?' he asked with concern.

'I'm afraid,' she replied.

'But why?'

'Because I know this will end as it always ends - that it is nothing but a beautiful dream - that I will find myself back at Oxtalls - in that room - lonely and old.'

Isaac took her face in his hands and tilted her head gently until she was looking directly at him.

'Polly,' he said softly, 'my darling Polly. You can't go back there, not this time, not like you did in your dreams. Very soon, John will come, and we'll go to Coaley first, then on to Selworthy and...'

'But he'll be there if we go to Selworthy,' she said becoming ever more upset; her anxiety clear to hear. 'He'll be there just as he always has been - he'll destroy us all over again.'

'No he won't Polly; he won't be there - not this time. There is no Nance Ridler at Selworthy anymore - no Jack; no Molly; no flourmill, no leat nor wheel; not even a gate where the mill once stood. Leathernbottle is the first building you come to as you walk the hill; there is no flour mill or wickedness or jealousy there my darling; I promise you - I promise you with all my heart.'

'But how can that be Isaac; how can things just disappear.'

Isaac sighed; searching for the words he needed, for here was the very question John had warned him about.

'Because this place,' he began, pointing his hand beyond the willow canopy; 'this beautiful place you think you know so well is not really what you think. It's not the old world though it looks just like it I grant you, but there is no wickedness here my darling, no sorrow or sadness.'

'But how Isaac, I don't understand?'

'Because this is a world that you have made, Polly,' he continued. 'All of us here, everything you see about you; it is here because of the love that is within you. Do you remember the beautiful woman who brought you here, who told you to follow Arthur, who told you not to be afraid? She was you, my darling - she was your soul. She brought us all together in this lovely place for that was your prayer - you never asked for anything else. Ours was a love so deep and sincere that death could only part us for a short while - it could never break us apart. When John comes with the trap we will go to Coaley, then in the morning we will go on to Selworthy and all the village will be there to greet us - all except Nance Ridler, and that is my promise.'

'Will Ira...?'

'Yes, Ira will be there,' continued Isaac knowing her question before it was even asked. 'He was so pleased to hear that you would soon be with us again, but poor McNab got a bit upset. I never thought I would see that cantankerous old misery weeping, but he wept for you, for he's missed you so very much.'

Polly's eyes brimmed with tears for she knew Isaac would never lie to her, and she so much wanted to see them both again.

'It's just as you remember,' he continued, 'the mill wheel still creaks and the cockerel still makes an awful racket, and Parsley is still eating your borders; it's all just as it was.'

She was too tearful to speak, so he put his arm about her and carried on with what he needed to say.

'Do you remember the picture book we bought Becky, the one that was full of stories about the universe and stars and sky? It said the universe has billions of galaxies and trillions of stars and zillions of worlds and planets - more than you could ever imagine, more than there are grains of sand upon a beach. It said

498

there might even be universes beyond our own, just as vast and endless and beyond all human understanding. What difference would one more world or one more grain of sand make amongst so many Polly? And if God were to make a grain of sand just for you, because of the love that is in you; would it really matter to him if it was just like another? Would it really matter if it were made of the people and places you loved so dearly in that other world? Would it really matter to him?'

He took her hand in his, watching her tenderly as she struggled with her emotions.

'I love you with all my heart,' he whispered softly, 'I always have and I always will.'

He kissed her tenderly and their kiss lasted a very long time.

'Isaac, how long do we have?' she asked tearfully.

'A long time,' he replied, 'a very long time. I think this time we have forever.'

CHAPTER 71

Grains of Sand

Some years after his chance encounter with the road sign that ultimately led P.C Wibberley to Polly's grave, he took a transfer from the South Wales constabulary and ended up as the local bobby in the market town of Dursley. I assume he did so, having taken a liking to our beautiful Cotswolds, but on that matter I am not entirely clear. Whatever the reason, he soon fitted in to our little community, for he was a policeman of the old school - ear to the ground and always time for a chat and a cup of tea. That was the manner of our meeting as I recall.

When he retired from the force, he found work with the local undertaker, and so it was that he asked a chance favour of me one December day. With nothing more pressing to do, I agreed to accompany him on a journey to the Black Mountains to return a body to its village of birth. Unfortunately, it was a day that was never destined to go well.

An overheated engine delayed us quite badly, but even when we got on our way again, the engine never seemed quite the same. As darkness fell on a lonely and wind-swept mountain, its knocking became so loud, we had to stop for fear of wrecking the engine beyond repair. At first, we were confident of help passing our way, but this never came and the cold and dark soon took a grip of the mountain. Sleet and rain, blew across its naked flanks in a gusting, swirling blizzard, and none but a fool would venture into it.

For all that, I was for walking on to find a phone, for the local man must surely be wondering what had happened to us, but Wibberley would have none of it. 'These mountains have killed better men than you,' he declared, 'besides which - we cannot leave our companion!'

So it was that we were destined to spend a very long night in a freezing hearse, and I must say the cold was more to our companions liking than ours. Sleep was impossible, so we talked, and talked frankly, as men do in such situations. We discussed matters you might not consider in ordinary circumstances, and gave answers you might not give, with less time to consider them.

I recall asking him which events were most memorable from his days as a policeman and he told me many tales of the valleys - a place he clearly loved. They were stories of humour and sometimes of tragedy, but the one that stuck forever in his mind, was the hour he spent in that grim room above the Pencryn bakery, listening to Llewelyn's story.

To my surprise, it was a story he'd never told another soul - not because there was a particular secret to keep, but because he thought it too long and intricate a tale to do it justice. But we had time - lots of it - and so I sat with the collar of my overcoat drawn about my ears, listening to the soft lilt of the valleys, as he retold the story that Llewelyn had told him all those years before.

I suppose some may reflect upon it as everything that is base and evil in mankind, but perhaps because I had recently lost someone very dear to me, I saw it differently. To me it was a beautiful story, full of hope.

As his tale unfolded, he seemed to become lost within it, and I believe he forgot I was even there. He told it with a beautiful simplicity that touched my soul and though he never knew it, his words moved me to tears. As we sat cold and shivering on that bleak and lonely mountainside, I was obliged to brush them aside in the darkness.

The following morning we were rescued from the mountain, and spent the time it took to fix the hearse, eating bacon rolls and drinking tea in a cafe that was luxuriously warm after our night's ordeal.

It was over our third cuppa that I asked if he would allow me to write down the story he had told me on the mountain. I argued that it would be a shame if Polly and Isaac's story died with him, for though, in itself, it proved nothing, I believed its retelling might be a comfort to those, who like myself, had lost someone they deeply loved.

This idea was important to me, for as I grow older, so I have come to the realisation that the only way to avoid the sorrow of losing, is to love no living creature and have no living creature love you. For if you do, sooner or later, death will come like a thief in the night to steal them away. You will look around in a dark and empty hall that echo's with their laughter, and their smile, and their love for you; and there will be a space where once they stood, of such loneliness, emptiness and sorrow, that it will break your heart in two. All that is true, and if you are of any age, you know it to be true, and thus, in truth; I saw the policeman's story as a story for us all.

To my immense pleasure, he agreed and we made plans to visit the places that would bring his story to life in my mind's eye. This we did soon after we returned to Gloucestershire.

We visited the river, of course, but it all looks so different now - not at all, how Llewelyn described it. The once energetic flow has withered to a trickle, for there are no mill wheels to harness its energy, no bolts of cloth to wash, or

501

dye to steep. There are no council workers to keep it clear of silt and undergrowth, or befriend the woodland creatures that call it home. Instead, the run-off from the land drains through huge concrete drainage pipes that are convenient, unseen, and forgotten. The once useful river has no purpose anymore and has disappeared in all but old folks' memories.

However, the cows still drink at the ford where the banks are low; where the men of the village fought the tug 'o' war and where Polly died beneath the ice; but for most of its course, the stream is lost beneath the overhang of trees, stinging nettles, vines and undergrowth.

Wibberley showed me the ford, and told me that it was there - at the very place she died - that he would leave a small bunch of flowers each year. He asked if I would take over that task if it ever became too much for him, and I was happy to agree. Consequently, for the last few years, it has fallen to me to leave those flowers on his behalf.

He told me it was his habit to leave his flowers on the anniversary of the night she drowned, and on one occasion he'd stood silent in the stream through the very hour she died, just as Harry the Hare had reputedly done before him. I've never dared go there after dark, for the thought of being alone in that cold, lonely place sends a shiver down my spine. I asked him why on earth he would do such a thing, to which he smiled and said, 'Just curious!'

I asked him if he'd heard or seen anything, and he replied that it was very difficult to tell. He thought he heard voices that may have been human, but he couldn't be sure, and perhaps they were nothing more than the wind in the trees, or creatures of the night going about their business. Either way, he never kept a vigil there again, and I have never had the nerve to do so either.

But what would I achieve if I did? If there were no souls abroad, no laughter and no stirring of the air! If there was only darkness, and stillness, and time passing, then I would be deeply sad, for as I grow older and life takes its course, there are so many who have journeyed on before me whom my heart aches to see again - people whom I loved and cherished so much, and who in return, loved me.

And if I did hear something - Jacko's hurdy gurdy perhaps, or John Smith's laughter, or McNab grousing - how could I hold that knowledge to myself and not rejoice and say I'd heard them.

And if I did say, who would believe me? I would join the ranks of the cranks, frauds, and charlatans who prey upon other's sadness with their Red Indian guides, and hokus pokus, and claims of hotlines to the afterlife. No one truly knows what becomes of us in death, and all in all, I think that's just as well, for in uncertainty, at least there is hope.

So if you seek assurance that there is life beyond this one, you'll not find it in the story I have chronicled for you. If you seek proof that God and heaven exist - be it your God or mine - you will not find it here within these pages. But if you are content to hope as I do, then there is hope within this book and it is to that hope that we must cling. For if there is a better life beyond this world - amongst the galaxies, or planets, or lowly grains of sand - a place where we will know, and touch, and love again, those whom we have loved in this life, then that would be a wonderful thing wouldn't it? I think that would be so wonderful!

And so I leave my flowers each year, just as the policeman did before me, and I take a little silt from the river in the palm of my hand. I wonder how many souls I hold there and how many memories too. I say a short prayer for them and lay them back where I found them - gently, lest I disturb them too much.

It only takes a few moments of my time - no time at all really!

Printed in Great Britain
by Amazon